THIS PRESENT DARKNESS

PIERCING THE DARKNESS

Two Bestselling Novels
Complete in One Volume

Frank E. Peretti

INSPIRATIONAL PRESS

NEW YORK

First Inspirational Press edition published in 1997.

Inspirational Press
A division of BBS Publishing Corporation
386 Park Avenue South
New York, NY 10016

Inspirational Press is a registered trademark of BBS Publishing Corporation.

Published by arrangement with Crossway Books.

Book design by K.L. Mulder.

Library of Congress Catalog Card Number: 97-73417

ISBN: 0-88486-178-3

Printed in the United States of America.

Contents

THIS
PRESENT
DARKNESS

To Barbara Jean,
wife and friend,
who loved me, and waited

*For we are not contending
against flesh and blood, but
against the principalities, against
the powers, against the world rulers of
this present darkness, against the
spiritual hosts of wickedness
in the heavenly places.*

Ephesians 6:12 (RSV)

Late on a full-mooned Sunday night, the two figures in work clothes appeared on Highway 27, just outside the small college town of Ashton. They were tall, at least seven feet, strongly built, perfectly proportioned. One was dark-haired and sharp-featured, the other blond and powerful. From a half mile away they looked toward the town, regarding the cacophonic sounds of gaiety from the storefronts, streets, and alleys within it. They started walking.

It was the time of the Ashton Summer Festival, the town's yearly exercise in frivolity and chaos, its way of saying thank you, come again, good luck, and nice to have you to the eight hundred or so college students at Whitmore College who would be getting their long awaited summer break from classes. Most would pack up and go home, but all would definitely stay at least long enough to take in the festivities, the street disco, the carnival rides, the nickel movies, and whatever else could be had, over or under the table, for kicks. It was a wild time, a chance to get drunk, pregnant, beat up, ripped off, and sick, all in the same night.

In the middle of town a community-conscious landowner had opened up a vacant lot and permitted a traveling troupe of enterprising migrants to set up their carnival with rides, booths, and portapotties. The rides were best viewed in the dark, an escapade in gaily lit rust, powered by unmuffled tractor engines that competed with the wavering carnival music which squawked loudly from somewhere in the middle of it all. But on this warm summer night the roaming, cotton-candied masses were out to enjoy, enjoy, enjoy. A ferris wheel slowly turned, hesitated for boarding, turned some more for unboarding, then took a few full rotations to give its passengers their money's worth; a merry-go-round spun in a brightly lit, gaudy circle, the peeling and dismembered horses still prancing to the melody of the canned calliope; carnival-goers threw baseballs at baskets, dimes at ashtrays, darts at balloons, and money to the wind along the hastily assembled, ramshackle midway where the hawkers ranted the same try-yer-luck chatter for each passerby.

The two visitors stood tall and silent in the middle of it all, wondering how a town of twelve thousand people—including college students—could produce such a vast, teeming crowd. The usually quiet population had turned out in droves, augmented by diversion-seekers from elsewhere, until the streets, taverns, stores, alleys, and parking spots were jammed, anything was allowed, and the illegal was ignored. The police did have their hands full, but each rowdy, vandal, drunk, or hooker in cuffs only meant a dozen more still loose and roaming about the town. The festival, reaching a crescendo now on its last night, was like a terrible storm that couldn't be stopped; one could only wait for it to blow over, and there would be plenty to clean up afterward.

The two visitors made their way slowly through the people-packed carnival, listening to the talk, watching the activity. They were inquisitive about this town, so they took their time observing here and there, on the right, on the left, before and behind. The milling throngs were moving around them like swirling garments in a washing machine, meandering from this side of the street to the other in an unpredictable, never-ending cycle. The two tall men kept eyeing the crowd. They were looking for someone.

"There," said the dark-haired man.

They both saw her. She was young, very pretty, but also very unsettled, looking this way and that, a camera in her hands and a stiff-lipped expression on her face.

The two men hurried through the crowd and stood beside her. She didn't notice them.

"You know," the dark-haired one said to her, "you might try looking over there."

With that simple comment, he guided her by a hand on her shoulder toward one particular booth on the midway. She stepped through the grass and candy wrappers, moving toward the booth where some teenagers were egging each other on in popping balloons with darts. None of that interested her, but then . . . some shadows moving stealthily behind the booth did. She held her camera ready, took a few more silent, careful steps, and then quickly raised the camera to her eye.

The flash of the bulb lit up the trees behind the booth as the two men hurried away to their next appointment.

They moved smoothly, unfalteringly, passing through the main part of town at a brisk pace. Their final destination was a mile past the center of town, right on Poplar Street, and up to the top of Morgan Hill about a half mile. Practically no time at all had passed before they stood before the little white church on its postage-stamp lot, with its well-groomed lawn and dainty Sunday-School-and-Service billboard. Across the top of the little billboard was the name "Ashton Community Church," and in black letters hastily painted over whatever name used to be there it said, "Henry L. Busche, Pastor."

They looked back. From this lofty hill one could look over the whole town and see it spread from city limit to city limit. To the west sparkled the caramel-colored carnival; to the east stood the dignified and matronly Whitmore College campus; along Highway 27, Main Street through town, were the storefront offices, the smalltown-sized Sears, a few gas stations at war, a True Value Hardware, the local newspaper, several small family businesses. From here the town looked so typically American—small, innocent, and harmless, like the background for every Norman Rockwell painting.

But the two visitors did not perceive with eyes only. Even from this vantage point the true substratum of Ashton weighed very heavily upon their spirits and minds. They could feel it: restless, strong, growing, very designed and purposeful . . . a very special kind of evil.

It was not unlike either of them to ask questions, to study, to probe. More often than not it came with their job. So they naturally hesitated in their business, pausing to wonder, Why here?

But only for an instant. It could have been some acute sensitivity, an instinct, a very faint but for them discernible impression, but it was enough to make them both instantly vanish around the corner of the church, melding themselves against the beveled siding, almost invisible there in the dark. They didn't speak, they didn't move, but they watched with a piercing gaze as something approached.

The night scene of the quiet street was a collage of stark blue moonlight and bottomless shadows. But one shadow did not stir with the wind as did the tree shadows, and neither did it stand still as did the building shadows. It crawled, quivered, moved along the street toward the church, while any light it crossed seemed to sink into its blackness, as if it were a breach torn in space. But this shadow had a shape, an animated, creaturelike shape, and as it neared the church sounds could be heard: the scratching of claws along the ground, the faint rustling of breeze-blown, membranous wings wafting just above the creature's shoulders.

It had arms and it had legs, but it seemed to move without them, crossing the street and mounting the front steps of the church. Its leering, bulbous eyes reflected the stark blue light of the full moon with their own jaundiced glow. The gnarled head protruded from hunched shoulders, and wisps of rancid red breath seethed in labored hisses through rows of jagged fangs.

It either laughed or it coughed—the wheezes puffing out from deep within its throat could have been either. From its crawling posture it reared up on its legs and looked about the quiet neighborhood, the black, leathery jowls pulling back into a hideous death-mask grin. It moved toward the front door. The black hand passed through the door like a spear through liquid; the body hobbled forward and penetrated the door, but only halfway.

Suddenly, as if colliding with a speeding wall, the creature was knocked backward and into a raging tumble down the steps, the glowing red breath tracing a corkscrew trail through the air.

With an eerie cry of rage and indignation, it gathered itself up off the sidewalk and stared at the strange door that would not let it pass through. Then the membranes on its back began to billow, enfolding great bodies of air, and it flew with a roar headlong at the door, through the door, into the foyer—and into a cloud of white hot light.

The creature screamed and covered its eyes, then felt itself being grabbed by a huge, powerful vise of a hand. In an instant it was hurling through space like a rag doll, outside again, forcefully ousted.

The wings hummed in a blur as it banked sharply in a flying turn and headed for the door again, red vapors chugging in dashes and streaks from its nostrils, its talons bared and poised for attack, a ghostly siren of a scream rising in its throat. Like an arrow through a target, like a bullet through a board, it streaked through the door—

And instantly felt its insides tearing loose.

There was an explosion of suffocating vapor, one final scream, and the flailing of withering arms and legs. Then there was nothing at all except the ebbing stench of sulfur and the two strangers, suddenly inside the church.

The big blond man replaced a shining sword as the white light that surrounded him faded away.

"A spirit of harassment?" he asked.

"Or doubt . . . or fear. Who knows?"

"And that was one of the *smaller* ones?"

"I've not seen one smaller."

"No indeed. And just how many would you say there are?"

"More, much more than we, and everywhere. Never idle."

"So I've seen," the big man sighed.

"But what are they doing here? We've never seen such concentration before, not here."

"Oh, the reason won't be hidden for long." He looked through the foyer doors and toward the sanctuary. "Let's see this man of God."

They turned from the door and walked through the small foyer. The bulletin board on the wall carried requests for groceries for a needy family, some baby-sitting, and prayer for a sick missionary. A large bill announced a congregational business meeting for next Friday. On the other wall, the record of weekly offerings indicated the offerings were down from last week; so was the attendance, from sixty-one to forty-two.

Down the short and narrow aisle they went, past the orderly ranks of dark-stained plank and slat pews, toward the front of the sanctuary where one small spotlight illumined a rustic two-by-four cross hanging above the baptistry. In the center of the worn-carpeted platform stood the little sacred desk, the pulpit, with a Bible laid open upon it. These were humble furnishings, functional but not at all elaborate, revealing either humility on the part of the people or neglect.

Then the first sound was added to the picture: a soft, muffled sobbing from the end of the right pew. There, kneeling in earnest prayer, his head resting on the hard wooden bench, and his hands clenched with fervency, was a young man, very young, the blond man thought at first: young and vulnerable. It all showed in his countenance, now the very picture of pain, grief, and love. His lips moved without sound as names, petitions, and praises poured forth with passion and tears.

The two couldn't help but just stand there for a moment, watching, studying, pondering.

"The little warrior," said the dark-haired one.

The big blond man formed the words himself in silence, looking down at the contrite man in prayer.

"Yes," he observed, "this is the one. Even now he's interceding, standing before the Lord for the sake of the people, for the town . . ."

"Almost every night he's here."

At that remark, the big man smiled. "He's not so insignificant."

"But he's the only one. He's alone."

"No." The big man shook his head. "There are others. There are always others. They just have to be found. For now, his single, vigilant prayer is the beginning."

"He's going to be hurt, you know that."

"And so will the newspaperman. And so will we."

"But will we win?"

The big man's eyes seemed to burn with a rekindled fire.

"We will *fight*."

"We will fight," his friend agreed.

They stood over the kneeling warrior, on either side; and at that moment, little by little, like the bloom of a flower, white light began to fill the room. It illuminated the cross on the back wall, slowly brought out the colors and grain in every plank of every pew, and rose in intensity until the once plain and humble sanctuary came alive with an unearthly beauty. The walls glimmered, the worn rugs glowed, the little pulpit stood tall and stark as a sentinel backlit by the sun.

And now the two men were brilliantly white, their former clothing transfigured by garments that seemed to burn with intensity. Their faces were bronzed and glowing, their eyes shone like fire, and each man wore a glistening golden belt from which hung a flashing sword. They placed their hands upon the shoulders of the young man and then, like a gracefully spreading canopy, silken, shimmering, nearly transparent membranes began to unfurl from their backs and shoulders and rise to meet and overlap above their heads, gently undulating in a spiritual wind.

Together they ministered peace to their young charge, and his many tears began to subside.

The *Ashton Clarion* was a small-town, grass-roots newspaper; it was little and quaint, maybe just a touch unorganized at times, unassuming. It was, in other words, the printed expression of the town of Ashton. Its offices occupied a small storefront space on Main Street in the middle of town, just a one-story affair with a large display window and a heavy, toe-scuffed door with a mail slot. The paper came out twice a week, on Tuesdays and Fridays, and didn't make a lot of money. By the appearance of the office and layout facilities, you could tell it was a low-budget operation.

In the front half of the building was the office and newsroom area. It consisted of three desks, two typewriters, two wastebaskets, two telephones, one coffeemaker without a cord, and what looked like all the scattered notes, papers, stationery and office bric-a-brac in the world. An old worn counter from a torn-down railroad station formed a divider between the functioning office and the reception area, and of course there was a small bell above the door that jingled every time someone came in.

Toward the back of this maze of small-scale activity was one luxury that looked just a little too big-town for this place: a glassed-in office for the editor. It was, in fact, a new addition. The new editor/owner was a former big city reporter and having a glassed-in editor's office had been one of his life's dreams.

This new fellow was Marshall Hogan, a strong, big-framed bustler hustler whom his staff—the typesetter, the secretary/reporter/ad girl, the paste-up man, and the reporter/columnist—lovingly referred to as "Attila the Hogan." He had bought the paper a few months ago, and the clash between his big-city polish and their small-town easy-go still roused some confrontations from time to time. Marshall wanted a quality paper, one that ran efficiently and smoothly and made its deadlines, with a place for everything and everything in its place. But the transition from the *New York Times* to the *Ashton Clarion* was like jumping off a speeding train into a wall of half-set jello. Things just didn't click as fast in this little office, and the high-powered efficiency Marshall was used to had to give way to such *Ashton Clarion* quirks as saving all the coffee grounds for the secretary's compost pile, and someone finally turning in a long-awaited human interest story, but with parakeet droppings on it.

On Monday morning the traffic patterns were hectic, with no time for any weekend hangovers. The Tuesday edition was being brought forth in a rush, and the entire staff was feeling the labor pains, dashing back and forth between their desks in front and the paste-up room in the back, squeezing past each other in the narrow passage, carrying rough copy for articles and ads to be typeset, finished typeset galleys, and assorted shapes and sizes of half-tones of photographs that would highlight the news pages.

In the back, amid bright lights, cluttered worktables, and rapidly moving bodies, Marshall and Tom the paste-up man bent over a large, benchlike easel, assembling Tuesday's *Clarion* out of bits and pieces that seemed to be scattered everywhere. This goes here, this can't—so we have to shove it somewhere else, this is too big, what will we use to fill this? Marshall was getting miffed. Every Monday and Thursday he got miffed.

"Edie!" he hollered, and his secretary answered, "Coming," and he told her for the umpteenth time, "The galleys go in the trays over the table, not on the table, not on the floor, not on the—"

"I didn't put any galleys on the floor!" Edie protested as she hurried into the paste-up room with more galleys in her hand. She was a tough little woman of forty with just the right personality to stand up to Marshall's brusqueness. She still knew where to find things around the office better than anyone, especially her new boss. "I've got them right in your cute little trays where you want them."

"So how'd these get here on the floor?"

"Wind, Marshall, and don't make me tell you where *that* came from!"

"All right, Marshall," said Tom, "that takes care of pages three, four, six, seven . . . what about one and two? What are we going to do with all these empty slots?"

"We are going to put in Bernie's coverage of the Festival, with clever writing, dramatic human-interest photos, the whole bit, as soon as she gets her rear in here and gives them to us! Edie!"

"Yo!"

"Bernie's an hour late, for crying out loud! Call her again, will you?"

"Just did. No answer."

"Nuts."

George, the small, retired typesetter who still worked for the fun of it, swiveled his chair away from the typesetting machine and offered, "How about the Ladies Auxiliary Barbecue? I'm just finishing that up, and the photo of Mrs. Marmaselle is spicy enough for a lawsuit."

"Yeah," Marshall groaned, "right on page one. That's all I need, a good impression."

"So what now?" Edie asked.

"Anybody make it to the Festival?"

"Went fishing," said George. "That Festival's too wild for me."

"My wife wouldn't let me," said Tom.

"I caught some of it," said Edie.

"Start writing," said Marshall. "The biggest townbuster of the year, and we've got to have something on it."

The phone rang.

"Saved by the bell?" Edie chirped as she picked up the back-room extension. "Good morning, the *Clarion*." Suddenly she brightened. "Hey, Bernice! Where are you?"

"Where is she?" Marshall demanded at the same time.

Edie listened and her face filled with horror. "Yes . . . well, calm down now . . . sure . . . well don't worry, we'll get you out."

Marshall spouted, "Well, where the heck is she?"

Edie gave him a scolding look and answered, "In jail!"

2

Marshall hurried into the basement of the Ashton Police Station and immediately wished he could disconnect his nose and ears. Beyond the heavily barred gate to the cell block, the crammed jail cells didn't smell or sound much different from the carnival the night before. On his way here he had noticed how quiet the streets were this morning. No wonder—all the noise had moved inside to these half-dozen peeling-painted cells set in cold, echoing concrete. Here were all the dopers, vandals, rowdies, drunks, and no-goods the police could scrape off the face of the town, collected in what amounted to an overcrowded zoo. Some were making a party of it, playing poker for cigarettes with finger-smeared cards and trying to outdo each other's tales of illicit exploits. Toward the end of the cells a gang of young bucks made obscene comments to a cageful of prostitutes with no better place to be locked up. Others just slumped in corners in a drunken stew or a depressed slump or both. The remainder glared at him from behind the bars, made snide remarks, begged for peanuts. He was glad he had left Kate upstairs.

Jimmy Dunlop, the new deputy, was stationed loyally at the guard desk, filling out forms and drinking strong coffee.

"Hey, Mr. Hogan," he said, "you got right down here."

"I couldn't wait . . . and I *won't* wait!" he snapped. He wasn't feeling well. This had been his first Festival, and that was bad enough, but he never expected, never dreamed of such a prolonging of the agony. He towered over the desk, his big frame shifting forward to accentuate his impatience. "Well?" he demanded.

"Hmmm?"

"I'm here to get my reporter out of the can."

"Sure, I know that. Have you got a release?"

"Listen. I just paid off those yo-yos upstairs. They were supposed to call you down here."

"Well . . . I haven't heard a thing, and I have to have authorization."

"Jimmy—"

"Yeah?"

"Your phone's off the hook."

"Oh . . ."

Marshall set the phone down right in front of him with a firmness that made the phone jingle in pain.

"Call 'em."

Marshall straightened up, watched Jimmy dial wrong, dial again, try to get through. He goes well with the rest of the town, Marshall thought, nervously running his fingers through his graying red hair. Aw, it was a nice town, sure. Cute, maybe a little dumb, kind of like a bumbling kid who always got himself into jams. Things weren't really better in the big city, he tried to remind himself.

"Uh, Mr. Hogan," Jimmy asked, his hand over the receiver, "who was it you talked to?"

"Kinney."

"Sergeant Kinney, please."

Marshall was impatient. "Let's have the key for the gate. I'll let her know I'm here."

Jimmy gave him the key. He'd argued with Marshall Hogan before.

A whoop of mock welcome poured out from the cells along with hurled cigarette butts and whistled march tunes as he passed by. He lost no time in finding the cell he wanted.

"All right, Krueger, I know you're in there!"

"Come and get me, Hogan," came the reply from a desperate and somewhat outraged female voice down near the end.

"Well, stick out your arm, wave at me or something!"

A hand stuck out through the bodies and bars and gave him a desperate wave. He got there, gave the palm a slap, and found himself face to face with Bernice Krueger, jailbird, his prize columnist and reporter. She was a young, attractive woman in her midtwenties, with unkempt brown hair and large, wire-rimmed glasses, now smudged. She had obviously had a hard night and was presently keeping company with at least a dozen women, some older, some shockingly younger, mostly trucked-in prostitutes. Marshall didn't know whether to laugh or spit.

"I won't mince words—you look terrible," he said.

"Only in keeping with my vocation. I'm a hooker now."

"Yeah, yeah, one of us," a chunky girl sang out.

Marshall grimaced and shook his head. "What kind of questions were you asking out there?"

"Right now no joke is funny. No anecdote of last night's events is funny. I'm not laughing, I'm seething. The assignment was an insult in the first place."

"Look, *somebody* had to cover the carnival."

"But we were quite right in our prognostication; there was certainly nothing new under the sun, nor the moon, as it were."

"You got arrested," he offered.

"For the sake of grabbing the reader with a scandalous lead. What else was there to write about?"

"So read it to me."

A Spanish girl from the back of the cell offered, "She tried to do business with the wrong trick," at which the whole cell block guffawed and hooted.

"I demand to be released!" Bernice fumed. "And have you stepped in epoxy? Do something!"

"Jimmy's on the phone with Kinney. I paid your bail. We'll get you out of here."

Bernice took a moment to simmer down and then reported, "In answer to your questions, I was carrying on spot interviews, trying to get some good pictures, good quotes, good *anything*. I assume that Nancy and Rosie here"—she looked toward two young ladies who could have been twins, and they smiled at Marshall—"wondered what I was doing, constantly circumnavigating the carnival grounds looking bewildered. They struck up a conversation that really got us nowhere news-wise, but did get us all in trouble when Nancy propositioned an undercover cop and we all got busted together."

"I think she'd be good at it," quipped Nancy as Rosie gave her a playful hit.

Marshall asked, "And you didn't show him your I.D., your press card?"

"He wouldn't give me a chance! I told him who I was."

"Well, did he hear you?" Marshall asked the girls, "Did he hear her?"

They only shrugged, but Bernice shifted her voice into high gear and cried, "Is this voice loud enough for you? I employed it last night while he slapped the cuffs on me!"

"Welcome to Ashton."

"I'll have his badge!"

"It'll only turn your chest green." Hogan held up his hand to halt another outburst. "Hey, listen, it isn't worth the trouble . . ."

"There are different schools of thought!"

"Bernie . . ."

"I have some things I would love to print, four columns wide, all about Supercop and that do-nothing cretin of a chief! Where is he, anyway?"

"Who, you mean Brummel?"

"He has a very handy way of disappearing, you know. *He* knows who I am. Where is he?"

"I don't know. I couldn't reach him this morning."

"And he turned his back last night!"

"What are you talking about?"

Suddenly she clammed up, but Marshall read her face clear as a bell: Make sure you ask me later.

Just then the big gate opened and in came Jimmy Dunlop.

"We'll discuss it later," said Marshall. "All set, Jimmy?"

Jimmy was too intimidated by the yells, demands, hoots, and jeers coming from the cages to answer right away. But he did have the key to the cell in his hand, and that said enough.

"Step away from the door, please," he ordered.

"Hey, when's your voice gonna change?" was characteristic of the answers he got. They did move away from the door. Jimmy opened it, Bernice stepped out quickly, and he slammed it shut again behind her.

"Okay," he said, "you're free to leave on bail. You'll be notified of the date for your arraignment."

"Just return my purse, my press card, my notepad, and my camera!" Bernice hissed, heading for the door.

Kate Hogan, a slender, dignified redhead, had tried to make good use of her time while waiting upstairs in the courthouse lobby. There was much to observe here after the Festival, although it certainly wasn't pleasant: some woeful souls were escorted and/or dragged in, struggling against their cuffs all the way and spouting obscenities; many others were just now being released after spending the night behind bars. It almost looked like a change of shifts at some bizarre factory, the first shift leaving, somewhat sheepishly, their scant belongings still in little paper bags, and the second shift coming in, all bound up and indignant. Most of the police officers were strangers from elsewhere, overtimers sent in to beef up the very small Ashton staff, and they weren't being paid to be kind or courteous.

The heavily jowled lady at the main desk had two cigarettes smoldering in her ashtray, but little time to take a drag between processing papers on every case coming in or going out. From Kate's viewpoint the whole operation looked very hurried and slipshod. There were a few cheap lawyers passing out their cards, but one night in jail seemed to be the extent of punishment any of these people would have to bear, and now they only wanted to get out of town in peace.

Kate unconsciously shook her head. To think of poor Bernice being herded through this place like so much rabble. She must be furious.

She felt a strong but gentle arm around her, and let herself sink into its embrace.

"Mmmmmm," she said, "now there's a pleasant change."

"After what I had to look at downstairs I need some healing up," Marshall told her.

She put her arm around him and pulled him close.

"Is it like this every year?" she asked.

"No, I hear it gets worse each time." Kate shook her head again, and Marshall added, "But the *Clarion* will have something to say about it. Ashton could use a change of direction; they should be able to see that by now."

"How is Bernice?"

"She'll be one heck of an editorialist for a while. She's okay. She'll live."

"Are you going to talk to somebody about this?"

"Alf Brummel's not around. He's smart. But I'll catch him later today and see what I can do. And I wouldn't mind getting my twenty-five dollars back."

"Well, he must be busy. I'd hate to be the police chief on a day like this."

"Oh, he'll hate it even more if I can help it."

Bernice's return from a night of incarceration was marked by an angry countenance and sharp, staccato footsteps on the linoleum. She too was carrying a paper bag, angrily rummaging through it to make sure everything was there.

Kate extended her arms to give Bernice a comforting hug.

"Bernice, how are you?"

"Brummel's name will soon be mud, the mayor's name will be dung, and I won't be able to print what that cop's name will be. I'm indignant, I could be constipated, and I desperately need a bath."

"Well," said Marshall, "take it out on your typewriter, swat some flies. I need that Festival story for Tuesday's edition."

Bernice immediately fumbled through her pockets and retrieved a wad of crinkled toilet paper, giving it to Marshall with forcefulness.

"Your loyal reporter, always on the job," she said. "What else was there to do in there besides watch the paint peel and wait in line for the toilet? I think you'll find the whole write-up very descriptive, and I threw in an on-the-spot interview with some jailed hookers for extra flavor. Who knows? Maybe it'll make this town wonder what it's coming to."

"Any pictures?" Marshall asked.

Bernice handed him a can of film. "You should find something in there you can use. I've got some film still in the camera, but that's of personal interest to me."

Marshall smiled. He was impressed. "Take the day off, on me. Things will look better tomorrow."

"Perhaps by then I will have regained my professional objectivity."

"You'll smell better."

"Marshall!" said Kate.

"It's okay," said Bernice. "He hands me that stuff all the time." By now she had recovered her purse, press card, and camera and threw the wadded paper bag spitefully into a trash can. "So what's the car situation?"

"Kate brought your car," Marshall explained. "If you could take her home, that should work things out best for me. I've got to get things salvaged at the paper and then try to track down Brummel."

Bernice's thoughts snapped into gear. "Brummel, right! I've got to talk to you."

She started pulling Marshall aside before he could say yea or nay, and he could only give Kate an apologetic glance before he and Bernice rounded a corner and stood out of sight near the restrooms.

Bernice spoke in lowered tones. "If you're going to accost Chief Brummel today, I want you to know what I know."

"Besides the obvious?"

"That he's a crumb, a coward, and a cretin? Yes, besides that. It's pieces, disjointed observations, but maybe they'll make sense someday. You always said to have an eye for details. I think I saw your pastor and him together at the carnival last night."

"Pastor Young?"

"Ashton United Christian Church, right? President of the local ministerial, endorses religious tolerance and condemns cruelty to animals."

"Yeah, okay."

"But Brummel doesn't even go to your church, does he?"

"No, he goes to that little dinky one."

"They were off behind the dart throwing booth, in the semidark with three other people, some blond woman, some short, pudgy old fellow and a ghostly-looking black-haired shrew in sunglasses. Sunglasses at *night!*"

Marshall wasn't impressed yet.

She continued as if she was trying to sell him something. "I think I committed a cardinal sin against them: I snapped their picture, and from all appearances they didn't want that. Brummel was quite unnerved and stuttered at me. Young asked me in firm tones to leave: 'This is a private meeting.' The pudgy fellow turned away, the ghostly-looking woman just stared at me with her mouth open."

"Have you considered how this might all appear to you after a good bath and a decent night's sleep?"

"Just let me finish and then we'll find out, all right? Now, right after that little incident was when Nancy and Rosie latched onto me. I mean to say, I did not approach them, they approached me, and soon afterward, I was arrested and my camera confiscated."

She could see she wasn't getting through to him. He was looking around impatiently, shifting his weight back toward the lobby.

"All right, all right, one more thing," she said, trying to hold him in place. "Brummel was there, Marshall. He saw the whole thing."

"What whole thing?"

"My arrest! I was trying to explain who I was to the cop, I was trying to show him my press card, he only took my purse and camera away from me and handcuffed me, and I looked over toward the dart throwing booth again and I saw Brummel watching. He ducked out of sight right away, but I swear I saw him watching the whole thing! Marshall, I went over this all last night, I replayed it and replayed it, and I think . . . well, I don't know what to think, but it has to mean something."

"To continue the scenario," Marshall ventured, "the film is gone from your camera."

Bernice checked. "Oh, it's still in the camera, but that means nothing."

Hogan sighed and thought the thing over. "Okay, so shoot up the rest of the roll, and try to get something we can use, right? Then develop it and we'll see. Can we go now?"

"Have I ever made any impulsive, imprudent, overassuming mistakes like this before?"

"Sure you have."

"Aw, c'mon, now! Extend me a little grace just this once."

"I'll try to close my eyes."

"Your wife's waiting."

"I know, I know."

Marshall didn't quite know what to say to Kate when they rejoined her.

"Sorry about this . . ." he muttered.

"Now then," Kate said, trying to pick up from where they left off, "we were talking about vehicles. Bernice, I had to drive your car here so you could have it to get home. If you drop me off at our house . . ."

"Yes, right, right," said Bernice.

"And, Marshall, I have a lot of things to do this afternoon. Can you pick up Sandy after her psychology class?"

Marshall didn't say a word, but his face showed a resounding no.

Kate took a set of keys from her purse and handed them to Bernice. "Your car is right around the corner, next to ours in the press space. Why don't you bring it around?"

Bernice took her cue and went out the door. Kate held Marshall with a loving arm and searched his face for a moment.

"Hey, c'mon. Try it. Just once."

"But cockfights are illegal in this state."

"If you ask me, she's just a chip off the old block."

"I don't know where I'll start," he said.

"Just being there to pick her up will mean something. Cash in on it."

As they started for the door, Marshall looked around and let his gut senses feel things out.

"Can you figure this town, Kate?" he said finally. "It's like some kind of disease. Everybody's got the same weird disease around here."

A sunny morning always helps make the previous night's problems seem less severe. That is what Hank Busche thought as he pushed open his front screen door and stepped out onto the small concrete stoop. He lived in a low-rent, one-bedroom house not far from the church, a little white box settled in one corner, with beveled siding, small hedged yard and mossy roof. It wasn't much, and often seemed far less, but it was all he could afford on his pastor's salary. Well, he wasn't complaining. He and Mary were comfortable and sheltered, and the morning was beautiful.

This was their day to sleep in, and two quarts of milk waited at the base of the steps. He snatched them up, looking forward to a bowl of milk-sodden Wheaties, a bit of distraction from his trials and tribulations.

He had known trouble before. His father had been a pastor while Hank was growing up, and the two of them had lived through a great many glories and hassles, the kind that come with pioneering churches, pastoring, itinerating. Hank knew from the time he was young that this was the life he wanted for himself, the way he wanted to serve the Lord. For him, the church had always been a very exciting place to work, exciting helping his father out in the earlier years, exciting going through Bible school and seminary and then two years of pastoral internship. It was exciting now too, but it resembled the exhilaration the Texans must have felt at the Alamo. Hank was just twenty-six, and usually full of fire; but this pastorate, his very first, seemed a difficult place to get the fire spread around. Somebody had wetted down all the kindling, and he didn't know what to make of it yet. For some reason he had been voted in as pastor, which meant somebody in the church wanted his kind of ministry, but then there were all the others, the ones who . . . made it exciting. They made it exciting whenever he preached on repentance; they made it exciting whenever he confronted sin in the fellowship; they made it exciting whenever he brought up the cross of Christ and the message of salvation. At this point, it was more Hank's faith and assurance that he was where God wanted him than any other factor that kept him by his guns, standing steadfast while getting shot at. Ah well, Hank thought to himself, at least enjoy the morning. The Lord put it here just for you.

Had he backed into the house again without turning, he would have spared himself an outrage and kept his lightened spirit. But he did turn to go back in, and immediately confronted the huge, black, dripping letters spray-painted on the front of the house: "YOU'RE

DEAD MEAT, _____." The last word was an obscenity. His eyes saw it, then did a slow pan from one side of the house to the other, taking it all in. It was one of those things that take time to register. All he could do was stand there for a moment, first wondering who could have done it, then wondering why, then wondering if it would ever come off. He looked closer, and touched it with his finger. It had to have been done during the night; it was quite dry.

"Honey," came Mary's voice from inside, "you're leaving the door open."

"Mmmmm . . ." was all he said, having no better words. He didn't really want her to know.

He went back inside, closing the door firmly, and joined young, beautiful, long-tressed Mary over a bowl of Wheaties and some hot, buttered toast.

Here was the sunny spot in a cloudy sky for Hank, this playful little wife with the melodic giggle. She was a doll and she had real grit too. Hank often regretted that she had to go through the struggles they were now having—after all, she could have married some stable, boring accountant or insurance salesman—but she was a terrific support for him, always there, always believing God for the best and always believing in Hank too.

"What's wrong?" she asked immediately.

Rats! You do what you can to hide it, you try to act normal, but she *still* picks it up, Hank thought.

"Ummmm . . ." he started to say.

"Still bothered about the board meeting?"

There's your out, Busche. "Sure, a little."

"I didn't even hear you come home. Did the meeting last real late?"

"No. Alf Brummel had to take off for some important meeting he wouldn't talk about and the others just, you know, had their say and went home, just left me to lick my wounds. I stuck around and prayed for a while. I think that worked. I felt okay after that." He brightened just a little. "As a matter of fact, I really felt the Lord comforting me last night."

"I still think they picked a funny time to call a board meeting, right during the Festival," she said.

"And on Sunday night!" he said through his flakes. "I no sooner give the altar call than I get them calling a meeting."

"About the same thing?"

"Aw, I think they're just using Lou as an excuse to make trouble."

"Well, what did you tell them?"

"The same thing, all over again. We did just what the Bible says: I went to Lou, then John and I went to Lou, and then we brought it before the rest of the church, and then we, well, we removed him from fellowship."

"Well, it did seem to be what the congregation decided. But why can't the board go along with it?"

"They can't read. Don't the Ten Commandments have something in there about adultery?"

"I know, I know."

Hank set down his spoon so he could gesture better. "And they were mad at *me* last night! They started giving me all this stuff about judging not lest I be judged—"

"*Who* did?"

"Oh, the same old Alf Brummel camp: Alf, Sam Turner, Gordon Mayer . . . you know, the Old Guard."

"Well, don't just let them push you around!"

"They won't change my mind, anyway. Don't know what kind of job security that gives me."

Now Mary was getting indignant. "Well, what on earth is wrong with Alf Brummel? Has he got something against the Bible or the truth or what? If it weren't this, it would certainly be something else!"

"Jesus loves him, Mary," Hank cautioned."It's just that he feels under heavy conviction, he's guilty, he's a sinner, he knows it, and guys like us will always bother guys like him. The last pastor preached the Word and Alf didn't like it. Now I'm preaching the Word and he still doesn't like it. He pulls a lot of weight in that church, so I guess he thinks he can dictate what comes across that pulpit."

"Well, he can't!"

"Not in my case, anyway."

"So why doesn't he just go somewhere else?"

Hank pointed his finger dramatically. "That, dear wife, is a good question! There seems to be a method in his madness, like it's his mission in life to destroy pastors."

"It's just the picture they keep painting of you. You're just not like that!"

"Hmmmm . . . yes, painting. Are you ready?"

"Ready for what?"

Hank drew a breath, sighed it out, then looked at her. "We had some visitors last night. They—they painted a slogan on the front of the house."

"What? *Our* house?"

"Well . . . our landlord's house."

She got up. "Where?" She went out the front door, her fuzzy slippers scuffing on the front walk.

"Oh, no!"

Hank joined her, and they drank in the view together. It was still there, real as ever.

"Now that makes me mad!" she declared, but now she was crying. "What'd we ever do to anybody?"

"I think we were just talking about it," Hank suggested.

Mary didn't catch what he said, but she had a theory of her own, the most obvious one. "Maybe the Festival . . . it always brings out the worst in everyone."

Hank had his own theory but said nothing. It had to be someone in the church, he thought. He'd been called a lot of things: a bigot, a heel-dragger, an overly moral troublemaker. He had even been accused of being a homosexual and of beating his wife. Some angry church member could have done this, perhaps a friend of Lou Stanley the adulterer, perhaps Lou himself. He would probably never know, but that was all right. God knew.

3

Just a few miles east of town on Highway 27, a large black limousine raced through the countryside. In the plush backseat, a plump middle-aged man talked business with his secretary, a tall and slender woman with long, jet-black hair and a pale complexion. He talked crisply and succinctly as she took fluid shorthand, laying out some big-scale business deal. Then something occurred to the man.

"That reminds me," he said, and the secretary looked up from her memo pad. "The professor claims she sent me a package some time ago, but I don't recall ever receiving it."

"What kind of package?"

"A small book. A personal item. Why not make a note to yourself to check for it back at the ranch?"

The secretary opened her portfolio and appeared to make a note of it. Actually, she wrote nothing.

It was Marshall's second visit to Courthouse Square in the same day. The first time was to get Bernice bailed out, and now it was to pay a visit to the very man Bernice wanted to string up: Alf Brummel, the chief of police. After the *Clarion* finally got to press, Marshall was about to call Brummel, but Sara, Brummel's secretary, called Marshall first and made an appointment for 2 o'clock that afternoon. That was a good move, Marshall thought. Brummel was calling for a truce before the tanks began to roll.

He pulled his Buick into his reserved parking space in front of the new courthouse complex and paused beside his car to look up and down the street, surveying the aftermath of the Festival's final Sunday night death throes. Main Street was trying to be the same old Main

Street again, but to Marshall's discerning eye the whole town seemed to be walking with a limp, sort of tired, sore, and sluggish. The usual little gaggles of half-hurried pedestrians were doing a lot of pausing, looking, headshaking, regretting. For generations Ashton had taken pride in its grass-roots warmth and dignity and had striven to be a good place for its children to grow up. But now there were inner turmoils, anxieties, fears, as if some kind of cancer was eating away at the town and invisibly destroying it. On the exterior, there were the store windows now replaced with unsightly plywood, the many parking meters broken off, the litter and broken glass up and down the street. But even as the store owners and businessmen swept up the debris, there seemed to be an unspoken sureness that the inner problems would remain, the troubles would continue. Crime was up, especially among the youth; simple, common trust in one's neighbor was diminishing; never had the town been so full of rumors, scandals, and malicious gossip. In the shadow of fear and suspicion, life here was gradually losing its joy and simplicity, and no one seemed to know why or how.

Marshall headed into Courthouse Square. The square consisted of two buildings, tastefully garnished with willows and shrubs, facing a common parking lot. On one side was the classy two-story brick courthouse, which also housed the town's police department and that somewhat decadent basement cell block; one of the town's three squad cars was parked outside. On the other side was the two-story, glass-fronted town hall, housing the mayor's office, the town council, and other decision-makers. Marshall headed for the courthouse.

He went through the unimposing, plain doorway marked "Police" and found the small reception area empty. He could hear voices from down the hall and behind some of the closed doors, but Sara, the secretary, seemed temporarily out of the room.

No—behind the receptionist's formica-topped counter a huge file was slowly rocking back and forth, and grunts and groans were coming up from below. Marshall leaned over the counter to see a comical sight. Sara, on her knees, dress or no dress, was in the middle of a blue-streak struggle with a jammed file drawer that had entangled itself with her desk. Apparently the score was File Drawers 3, Sara's Shins 0, and Sara was a poor loser. So were her pantyhose.

She let out an ill-timed curse just as her eye caught him standing there, and by then it was too late to rebuild her usual poised image.

"Oh, hi, Marshall . . ."

"Wear your Marine boots next time. They're better for kicking things in."

At least they knew each other, and Sara was glad for that. Marshall had been in this place often enough to become well-acquainted with most of the staff.

"These," she said with the tone of an articulate tour guide, "are the infamous file cabinets of Mr. Alf Brummel, Chief of Police. He just got some fancy new cabinets, so now I've inherited these! Why I have to have them in my office is beyond me, but upon his express orders, here they must stay!"

"They're too ugly to go in *his* office."

"But khaki . . . it's *him,* you know? Oh well, maybe a little decoupage would cheer them up. If they must move in here, the least they can do is smile."

Just then the intercom buzzed. She pressed the button and answered.

"Yes sir?"

Brummel's voice squawked out of the little box, "Hey, my security alarm is flashing . . ."

"Sorry, that was me. I was trying to get one of your file drawers shut."

"Yeah, right. Well, try to rearrange things, will you?"

"Marshall Hogan is here to see you."

"Oh, right. Send him in."

She looked up at Marshall and only shook her head pathetically. "Got an opening for a secretary?" she muttered. Marshall smiled. She explained, "He's got these files right next to the silent alarm button. Every time I open a drawer the building's surrounded."

With a good-bye wave, Marshall went to the nearest office door and let himself into Brummel's office. Alf Brummel stood and extended his hand, his face exploding in a wide, ivory smile.

"Hey, there's the man!"

"Hey, Alf."

They shook hands as Brummel ushered Marshall in and closed the door. Brummel was a man somewhere in his thirties, single, a one-time hotshot city cop with a big buck lifestyle that belied his policeman's salary. He always came on like a likable guy, but Marshall never really trusted him. Come to think of it, he didn't like him that much either. Too much teeth showing for no reason.

"Well," Brummel grinned, "have a seat, have a seat." He was talking again before either man's cushion could compress. "Looks like we made a laughable mistake this weekend."

Marshall recalled the sight of his reporter sharing a cell with prostitutes. "Bernice didn't laugh the whole night, and I'm out twenty-five dollars."

"Well," said Brummel, reaching into his top desk drawer, "that's why we're having this meeting, to clear this whole thing up. Here." He produced a check and handed it to Marshall. "This is your refund on that bail money, and I want you to know that Bernice will be receiving an official signed apology from myself and this office. But, Marshall, please tell me what happened. If I had just been there I could have put a stop to it."

"Bernie says you *were* there."

"I was? Where? I know I was in and out of the station all night, but . . ."

"No, she saw you there at the carnival."

Brummel forced a wider grin. "Well, I don't know who it was she saw in actuality, but I wasn't at the carnival last night. I was busy here."

Marshall had too much momentum by now to back off. "She saw you right at the time she was being arrested."

Brummel didn't seem to hear that statement. "But go on, tell me what happened. I need to get to the bottom of this."

Marshall halted his attack abruptly. He didn't know why. Maybe it was out of courtesy. Maybe it was out of intimidation. Whatever the reason, he began to rattle the story off in neat, almost news-copy form, much the way he heard it from Bernice, but he cautiously left out the implicating details she shared with him. As he talked, his eyes studied Brummel, Brummel's office, and any particular details in decor, layout, agenda. It was mostly reflex. Over the years he had developed the knack of observing and gathering information without looking like he was doing it. Maybe it was because he didn't trust this man, but even if he did, once a reporter, always a reporter. He could see that Brummel's office belonged to a fastidious man, from the highly polished, orderly desk right down to the pencils in the desk caddy, every point honed to perfect sharpness.

Along one wall, where the ugly filing cabinets used to stand, stood a very attractive set of shelves and cabinets of oil-rubbed oak, with glass door panels and brass hardware.

"Say, moving up on the world, huh, Alf?" Marshall quipped, looking toward the cabinets.

"Like them?"

"Love them. What are they?"

"A very attractive replacement for those old filing cabinets. It just goes to show what you can do if you save your pennies. I hated having those file cabinets in here. I think an office should have a little class, right?"

"Eh, yeah, sure. Boy, you have your own copier . . ."

"Yes, and bookshelves, extra storage."

"And another phone?"

"A phone?"

"What's that wire coming out of the wall?"

"Oh, that's for the coffeemaker. But where were we, anyway?"

"Yeah, yeah, what happened to Bernice . . ." and Marshall continued his story. He was well practiced in reading upside down, and while he continued to talk he scanned Brummel's desk calendar. Tuesday afternoons stuck out a little because they were consistently blank, even though they were not Brummel's day off. One Tuesday did have an appointment written down: Rev. Oliver Young, at 2 P.M.

"Oh," he said conversationally, "gonna pay my pastor a visit tomorrow?"

He could tell right away that he had overstepped his bounds; Brummel looked amazed and irritated at the same time.

Brummel forced a toothy grin and said, "Oh yes, Oliver Young is your pastor, isn't he?"

"You two know each other?"

"Well, not really. We have met on an occasional, professional basis, I suppose . . ."

"But don't you go to that other church, that little one?"

"Yes, Ashton Community. But go on, let's hear the rest of what happened."

Marshall was impressed at how easy this guy was to fluster, but he tried not to press his challenge any further. Not yet, anyway. Instead, he picked up his tale where he left off and brought it to a neat finish, including Bernice's outrage. He noticed that Brummel had found some important paperwork to look over, papers that covered up the desk calendar.

Marshall asked, "Say, just who was this turkey cop who wouldn't let Bernice identify herself?"

"An outsider, not even on our force here. If Bernice can get us the name or badge number, I can see that he is confronted with his behavior. You see, we had to bring some auxiliaries down from Windsor to beef things up for the Festival. As for our own men, they all know full well who Bernice Krueger is." Brummel said that last line with a slightly wolfish tone.

"So why isn't she sitting here hearing all this apologizing instead of me?"

Brummel leaned forward and looked rather serious. "I thought it best to talk to you, Marshall, rather than cause her to parade through this office, already somewhat stigmatized. I suppose you know what that girl's been through."

Okay, thought Marshall, I'll ask. "I'm new in town, Alf."

"She hasn't told you?"

"And you'd love to?"

It slipped out, and it stung. Brummel sank back in his chair just a little and studied Marshall's face.

Marshall was just now thinking that he didn't regret what he said. "I'm upset, in case you hadn't noticed."

Brummel started a new paragraph. "Marshall . . . I wanted to see you personally today because I wanted to . . . heal this thing up."

"So let's hear what you have to say about Bernice." Brummel, you'd better choose your words carefully, Marshall thought.

"Well—" Brummel stammered, suddenly put on the spot. "I thought you might want to know about it in case you might find the information helpful in dealing with her. You see, it was several months before you took over the paper that she herself came to Ashton. Just a few weeks before that, her sister, who had been attending the college, committed suicide. Bernice came to Ashton with a fierce vindictiveness, trying to solve the mystery surrounding her sister's death, but . . . we all knew it was just one of those things for which there will never be an answer."

Marshall was silent for a significant amount of time. "I didn't know that."

Brummel's voice was quiet and mournful as he said, "She was positive it had to be some kind of foul play. It was quite an aggressive investigation she had going."

"Well, she does have a reporter's nose."

"Oh, that she does. But you see, Marshall . . . her arrest, it was a mistake, a humiliating one, quite frankly. I really didn't think she would want to see the inside of this building for some time to come. Do you understand now?"

But Marshall wasn't sure he did. He wasn't even sure he'd heard all of it. He suddenly felt very weak, and he couldn't figure out where his anger had gone so quickly. And what about his suspicions? He knew he didn't buy everything this guy was saying—or did he? He knew Brummel had lied about not being at the carnival—or had he?

Or did I just hear him wrong? Or . . . where were we, anyway? C'mon, Hogan, didn't you get enough sleep last night?

"Marshall?"

Marshall looked into Brummel's gazing gray eyes, and he felt a little numb, like he was dreaming.

"Marshall," Brummel said, "I hope you understand. You do understand now, don't you?"

Marshall had to force himself to think, and he found it helped not to look Brummel in the eye for a moment.

"Uh . . ." It was a stupid beginning, but it was the best he could do. "Hey, yeah, Alf, I think I see your point. You did the right thing, I suppose."

"But I do want to heal this whole thing up, particularly between you and me."

"Aw, don't worry about it. It's no big deal." Even as Marshall said it, he was asking himself if he really had.

Brummel's big teeth reappeared. "I'm really glad to hear that, Marshall."

"But, say, listen, you might give her a call at least. She was hurt in a pretty personal way, you know."

"I'll do that, Marshall."

Then Brummel leaned forward with a strange smile on his face, his hands folded tightly on the desk and his gray eyes giving Marshall that same numbing, penetrating, strangely pacifying gaze.

"Marshall, let's talk about you and the rest of this town. You know, we're really glad to have you here to take over the *Clarion*. We knew your fresh approach to journalism would be good for the community. I can be straightforward in saying that the last editor was . . . rather injurious to the mood of this town, especially toward the end."

Marshall felt himself going right along with this pitch, but he could sense something coming.

Brummel continued. "We need your kind of class, Marshall. You wield a great deal of power through the press, and we all know it, but it takes the right man to keep that power guided in the right direction, for the common good. All of us in the offices of public service are here to serve the best interests of the community, of the human race when you get right down to it. But so are you, Marshall. You're here for the sake of the people, just like the rest of us." Brummel combed his hair with his fingers a bit, a nervous gesture, then asked, "Well, do you get what I'm saying?"

"No."

"Well . . ." Brummel groped for a new opener. "I guess it's like you said, you're new in town. Why don't I simply try the direct approach?"

Marshall shrugged a "why not?" and let Brummel continue.

"It's a small town, first of all, and that means that one little problem, even between a handful of people, is going to be felt and worried about by almost everyone else. And you can't hide behind anonymity because there simply is no such thing. Now, the last editor didn't realize that and really caused some problems that affected the whole population. He was a pathological soap-boxer. He destroyed the good faith of the people in their local government, their public servants, each other, and ultimately himself. That hurt. It was a wound in our side, and it's taken time for all of us to heal up from that. I'll cap it off by telling you, for your own information, that that man finally had to leave this town in disgrace. He'd molested a twelve-year-old girl. I tried to get that case settled as quietly as I could. But in this town it was really awkward, difficult. I did what I felt would cause the least amount of trouble and pain for the girl's family and the people at large. I didn't press for any legal proceedings against this man, provided he leave Ashton and never show his face around here again. He was agreeable to that. But I'll never forget the impact it made, and I doubt that the town has ever forgotten it.

"Which brings us to you, and we, the public servants, and also the citizens of this community. One of the greatest reasons I regret this mixup with Bernice is that I really desired a good relationship between this office and the *Clarion*, between myself and you personally. I'd hate to see anything ruin that. We need unity around here, comradeship, a good community spirit." He paused for effect. "Marshall, we'd like to know that you'll be standing with us in working toward that goal."

Then came the pause and the long, expectant gaze. Marshall was on. He shifted around a little in his chair, sorting his thoughts, probing his feelings, almost avoiding those gazing gray eyes. Maybe this guy was on the up and up, or maybe this whole little speech was some sly diplomatic ploy to shy him away from whatever Bernice may have stumbled upon.

But Marshall couldn't think straight, or even *feel* straight. His reporter had been arrested falsely and thrown into a sleazy jail for the night, and he didn't seem to care anymore; this toothy-smiled police chief was making a liar out of her, and Marshall was buying it. *C'mon, Hogan, remember why you came down here?*

But he just felt so tired. He kept recalling why he had moved to Ashton in the first place. It was supposed to be a change of lifestyle for him and his family, a time to quit fighting and scratching the big-city intrigues and just get down to the simpler stories, things like high school paper drives and cats up trees. Maybe it was just force of habit from all those years at the *Times* that made him think he had to take on Brummel like some kind of inquisitor. For what? More hassles? For crying out loud, how about a little peace and quiet for a change?

Suddenly, and contrary to his better instincts, he knew there was nothing at all to worry about; Bernice's film would be just fine, and the pictures would prove that Brummel was right and Bernice was wrong. And Marshall really wanted it to be that way.

But Brummel was still waiting for an answer, still giving him that numbing gaze.

"I . . ." Marshall began, and now he felt stupidly awkward in trying to get started. "Listen, I really am tired of fighting, Alf. Maybe I was raised that way, maybe that's what made me good at my job with the *Times,* but I did decide to move here, and that's got to say something. I'm tired, Alf, and not any younger. I need to heal up. I need to learn what being human and living in a town with other humans is really like."

"Yes," said Brummel, "that's it. That's exactly it."

"So . . . don't worry. I'm here after some peace and quiet just like everybody else. I don't want any fights, I don't want any trouble. You've got nothing to fear from me."

Brummel was ecstatic, and shot out his hand to shake on it. As Marshall took the hand and they shook, he almost felt he had sold part of his soul. Did Marshall Hogan really say all that? *I must* be tired, he thought.

Before he knew it, he was standing outside Brummel's door. Apparently their meeting was over.

After Marshall was gone and the door was safely closed, Alf Brummel sank into his chair with a relieved sigh and just sat there for a while, staring into space, recuperating, building up the nerve for his next difficult assignment. Marshall Hogan was just the warm-up as far as he was concerned. The real test was coming up. He reached for his telephone, pulled it a little closer, stared at it for a moment, and then dialed the number.

Hank was touching up his paint job on the front of the house when the phone rang and Mary called, "Hank, it's Alf Brummel!"

Wow, Hank thought. And here I am with a loaded paintbrush in my hand. I wish he was standing here.

He confessed his sin to the Lord on his way in to answer the phone.

"Hi there," he said.

In his office, Brummel turned his back to the door to make it a private conversation even though he was alone, and spoke in a lowered voice. "Hi, Hank. This is Alf. I thought I should call you this morning and see how you are . . . since last night."

"Oh . . ." said Hank, feeling like a mouse in a cat's mouth. "I'm okay, I guess. Better, maybe."

"So you've given it some thought?"

"Oh, sure. I've thought about it a lot. I've prayed about it, re-checked the Word regarding some questions—"

"Hmmm. Sounds like you haven't changed your mind."

"Well, if the Word of God would change then I'd change, but I guess the Lord won't back down from what He says, and you know where that leaves me."

"Hank, you know the congregational meeting is this Friday."

"I know that."

"Hank, I'd really like to help you. I don't want to see you destroy yourself. You've been good for the church, I think, but—what can I say? The division, the bickering . . . it's all about to tear that church apart."

"Who's bickering?"

"Oh, come on . . ."

"And for that matter, who called that congregational meeting in the first place? You. Sam. Gordon. I have no doubt that Lou is still at work out there, as well as whoever it was that painted on the front of my house."

"We're just concerned, that's all. You're, well, you're fighting against what's best for the church."

"That's funny. I thought I was fighting against *you*. But did you hear me? I said someone painted on the front of my house."

"What? Painted what?"

Hank let him have it all.

Brummel let out a groan. "Aw, Hank, that's sick!"

"And so is Mary, and so am I. Put yourself in our position."

"Hank, if I were in your position, I'd reconsider. Can't you see what's happening? Word's getting around now, and you're setting the whole town against you. That also means the whole town's going to be set against our church before long, and we have to survive in this town, Hank! We're here to help people, to reach out to them, not drive a wedge between ourselves and the community."

"I preach the gospel of Jesus Christ, and there are plenty who appreciate it. Just where is this wedge you're talking about?"

Brummel was getting impatient. "Hank, learn from the last pastor. He made the same mistake. Look what happened to him."

"I did learn from him. I learned that all I have to do is give up, bag it, bury the truth in a drawer somewhere so it won't offend anybody. Then I'll be fine, everybody will like me, and we'll all be one happy family again. Apparently Jesus was misguided. He could have kept a lot of friends by wilting and just playing politics."

"But you want to be crucified!"

"I want to save souls, I want to convict sinners, I want to help newborn believers grow up in the truth. If I don't do that, I'll have a lot more to fear than you and the rest of the board."

"I don't call that love, Hank."

"I love you all, Alf. That's why I give you your medicine, and that goes especially for Lou."

Brummel pulled a big gun. "Hank, have you considered that he could sue you?"

There was a pause at the other end.

Finally Hank answered, "No."

"He could sue you for damages, slander, defamation of character, mental anguish, who knows what else?"

Hank drew a deep breath and called on the Lord for patience and wisdom.

"You see the problem?" he said finally. "Too many people don't know—or don't want to know—what the truth is anymore. We don't stand for something, so we fall for anything, and now guys like Lou get themselves into a fog where they can hurt their own families, start their own gossip, ruin their own reputations, make themselves miserable in their sin . . . and then look for someone else to blame! Just who's doing what to whom?"

Brummel only sighed. "We'll talk it all out Friday night. You *will* be there?"

"Yes, I will. I'll be counseling somebody and then I'll go in for the meeting. Ever done any counseling?"

"No."

"It gives you a real respect for the truth when you have to help clean up lives that have been based on a lie. Think about it."

"Hank, I have other people's wishes to think about."

Brummel hung up loudly and wiped the sweat from his palms.

4

Could anyone have seen him, the initial impression would not have been so much his reptilian, warted appearance as the way his figure seemed to asborb light and not return it, as if he were more a shadow than an object, a strange, animated hole in space. But this little spirit was invisible to the eyes of men, unseen and immaterial, drifting over the town, banking one way and then the other, guided by will and not wind, his swirling wings quivering in a greyish blur as they propelled him.

He was like a high-strung little gargoyle, his hide a slimy, bottomless black, his body thin and spiderlike: half humanoid, half animal, totally demon. Two huge yellow cat-eyes bulged out of his face, darting to and fro, peering, searching. His breath came in short, sulfurous gasps, visible as glowing yellow vapor.

He was carefully watching and following his charge, the driver of a brown Buick moving through the streets of Ashton far below.

Marshall got out of the *Clarion* office just a little early that day. After all the morning's confusion it was a surprise to find Tuesday's *Clarion* already off to the printer and the staff gearing up for Friday. A small-town paper was just about the right pace . . . perhaps he *could* get to know his daughter again.

Sandy. Yes sir, a beautiful redhead, their only child. She had nothing but potential, but had spent most of her childhood with an overtime mother and a hardly-there father. Marshall was successful in New York, all right, at just about everything except being the kind of father Sandy needed. She had always let him know about it, too, but as Kate said, the two of them were too much alike; her cries for love and attention always came out like stabs, and Marshall gave her attention all right, like dogs give to cats.

No more fights, he kept telling himself, no more picking and scratching and hurting. Let her talk, let her spill how she feels, and don't be harsh with her. Love her for who she is, let her be herself, don't try to corral her.

It was crazy how his love for her kept coming out like spite, with anger and cutting words. He knew he was only reaching for her, trying to bring her back. It just never worked. Ah well, Hogan, try, try again, and don't blow it this time.

He made a left turn and could see the college ahead. The Whitmore College campus looked like most American campuses—beautiful, with stately old buildings that made you feel learned just to look at them, wide, neatly-lawned plazas with walkways in carefully laid patterns of brick and stone, landscaping with rocks, greenery, statuary. It was everything a good college should be, right down to the fifteen-minute parking spaces. Marshall parked the Buick and set out in search of Stewart Hall, home of the Psychology Department and Sandy's last class for the day.

Whitmore was a privately-endowed college, founded by some landholder as a memorial to himself back in the early twenties. From old photos of the place one could discover that some of the red-brick and white-pillared lecture halls were as old as the college itself: monuments of the past and supposedly guardians of the future.

The summertime campus was relatively quiet.

Marshall got directions from a frisbee-throwing sophomore and turned left down an elm-lined street. At the end of the street he found Stewart Hall, an imposing structure patterned after some European cathedral with towers and archways. He pulled open one of the big double doors and found himself in a spacious, echoing hallway. The close of the big door made such a reverberating thunder off the vaulted ceiling and smooth walls that Marshall thought he had disturbed every class on the floor.

But now he was lost. This place had three floors and some thirty classrooms, and he had no idea which one was Sandy's. He started walking down the hall, trying to keep his heels from tapping too loudly. You couldn't even get away with a burp in this place.

Sandy was a freshman this year. Their move to Ashton had been just a little late, so she was enrolled in summer classes to catch up, but all in all it had been the right point of transition for her. She was an undeclared major for now, feeling her way and taking prerequisites. Where a class in "Psychology of Self" fit into all that Marshall couldn't guess, but he and Kate weren't out to rush her.

From somewhere down the cavernous hall echoed the indistinguishable but well-ordered words of a lecture in progress, a woman's voice. He decided to check it out. He moved past several classroom doors, their little black numbers steadily decreasing, then a drinking fountain, the restrooms, and a ponderously ascending stone and iron staircase. Finally he began to make out the words of the lecture as he drew near Room 101.

". . . so if we settle for a simple ontological formula, 'I think, therefore I am,' that should be the end of the question. But *being* does not presuppose *meaning* . . ."

Yeah, here was more of that college stuff, that funny conglomeration of sixty-four-dollar words which impress people with your academic prowess but can't get you a paying job. Marshall smirked to himself a little bit. Psychology. If all those shrinks could just agree for a change, it would help. First Sandy blamed her snotty attitude on a violent birth experience, and then what was it? Poor potty training? Her new thing was self-knowledge, self-esteem, identity; she already knew how to be hung up on herself—now they were teaching it to her in college.

He peeked in the door and saw a theater arrangement, with rows of seats built in steadily rising levels toward the back of the room, and the small platform in front with the professor lecturing against a massive blackboard backdrop.

". . . and meaning doesn't necessarily come from thinking, for some have said that the Self is not the Mind at all, and that the Mind actually denies the Self and inhibits Self-Knowledge. . . ."

Whoosh! For some reason Marshall had expected an older woman, skinny, her hair in a bun, wearing horn-rimmed glasses with a little beady chain looped around her neck. But this one was a startling surprise, something right out of a lipstick or fashion commercial: long blonde hair, trim figure, deep, dark eyes that twitched a bit but certainly needed no glasses, horn-rimmed or otherwise.

Then Marshall caught the glint of deep red hair, and he saw Sandy sitting toward the front of the hall, listening intently and feverishly scrawling notes. Bingo! That was easy. He decided to slip in quietly and listen to the tail end of the lecture. It might give him some idea of what Sandy was learning and then they'd have something to talk about. He stepped silently through the door, and took one of the empty seats in the back.

Then it happened. Some kind of radar in the professor's head must have clicked on. She homed in on Marshall sitting there and simply would not look away from him. He had no desire to draw any attention to himself—he was rapidly getting too much of that anyway, from the class—so he said nothing. But the professor seemed to examine him, searching his face as if it were familiar to her, as if she were trying to remember someone she had known before. The look that suddenly crossed her face gave Marshall a chill: she gave him a knifelike gaze, like the eyes of a treed cougar. He began to feel a corresponding defense instinct twisting a knot in his stomach.

"Is there something you want?" the professor demanded, and all Marshall could see were her two piercing eyes.

"I'm just waiting for my daughter," he answered and his tone was courteous.

"Would you like to wait outside?" she said, and it wasn't a question.

And he was out in the hall. He leaned against the wall, staring at the linoleum, his mind spinning, his senses scrambled, his heart pounding. He had no understanding of why he was there, but he was out in the hall. Just like that. How? What happened? Come on, Hogan, stop shaking and *think!*

He tried to replay it in his mind, but it came back slowly, stubbornly, like recalling a bad dream. That woman's eyes! The way they looked told him she somehow knew who he was, even though they had never met—and he had never seen or felt such hate. But it wasn't just the eyes; it was also the fear; the steadily rising, face-draining, heart-pounding fear that had crept into him for no reason, with no visible cause. He had been scared half to death . . . by nothing! It made no sense at all. He had never run or backed down from anything in his life. But now, for the first time in his life . . .

For the first time? The image of Alf Brummel's gazing gray eyes flashed across his mind, and the weakness returned. He blinked the image away and took a deep breath. Where was the old Hogan gut strength? Had he left it back in Brummel's office?

But he had no conclusions, no theories, no explanations, only derision for himself. He muttered, "So I gave in again, like a rotted tree," and like a rotted tree he leaned against the wall and waited.

In a few minutes the door to the lecture hall burst open and students began to fan outward like bees from a hive. They ignored him so thoroughly that Marshall felt invisible, but that was fine with him for now.

Then came Sandy. He straightened up, walked toward her, started to say hello . . . and she walked right by! She didn't pause, smile, return his greeting, anything! He stood there dumbly for a moment, watching her walk down the hall toward the exit.

Then he followed. He wasn't limping, but for some reason he felt like he was. He wasn't really dragging his feet, but they felt like lead weights. He saw his daughter go out the door without looking back. The clunk of the big door's closing echoed through the huge hall with a ponderous, condemning finality, like the crash of a huge gate dividing him forever from the one he loved. He stopped there in the broad hall, numb, helpless, even tottering a little, his big frame looking very small.

Unseen by Marshall, small wisps of sulfurous breath crept along the floor like slow water, along with an unheard scraping and scratching over the tiles.

Like a slimy black leech, the little demon clung to him, its taloned fingers entwining Marshall's legs like parasitic tendrils, holding him back, poisoning his spirit. The yellow eyes bulged out of the gnarled face, watching him, boring into him.

Marshall was feeling a deep and growing pain, and the little spirit knew it. This man was getting hard to hold down. As Marshall stood there in the big empty hall, the hurt, the love, the desperation began to build inside him; he could feel the tiniest remaining ember of *fight* still burning. He started for the door.

Move, Hogan, move! That's your daughter!

With each determined step, the demon was dragged along the floor behind him, its hands still clinging to him, a deeper rage and fury rising in its eyes and the sulfurous vapors chugging out of its nostrils.

The wings spread in search of an anchor, any way to hold Marshall back, but they found none.

Sandy, Marshall thought, give your old man a break.

By the time he reached the end of the hall he was nearly into a run. His big hands hit the crash bar on the door and the door flung open, slamming into the doorstop on the outside steps. He ran down the stairs and out onto the pedestrian walkway shaded by the elms. He looked up the street, across the lawn in front of Stewart Hall, down the other way, but she was gone.

The demon gripped him tighter and began to climb and slither upward. Marshall felt the first pangs of despair as he stood there alone.

"I'm over here, Daddy."

Immediately the demon lost its grip and fell free, snorting with indignation. Marshall spun around and saw Sandy, standing just beside the door he had just burst through, apparently trying to hide from her classmates among the camelia bushes and looking very much like she was about to take him to task. Well, anything was better than losing her, Marshall thought.

"Well," he said before he considered, "pardon me, but I get the distinct impression you disowned me in there."

Sandy tried to stand straight, to face him in her hurt and anger, but she still could not look him squarely in the eye.

"It was—it was just too painful."

"What was?"

"You know . . . that whole thing in there."

"Well, I like coming on with a real splash, you know. Something people will remember . . ."

"Daddy!"

"So who stole all the 'No Parents Allowed' signs? How was I to know she didn't want me in there? And just what's so all-fired precious and secret that she doesn't want any outsiders to hear it?"

Now Sandy's anger rose above her hurt, and she could look at him squarely. "Nothing! Nothing at all. It was just a lecture."

"So just what is her problem?"

Sandy groped for an explanation. "I don't know. I guess she must know who you are."

"No way. I've never even seen her before." And then a question automatically popped into Marshall's mind, "What do you mean, she must know who I am?"

Sandy looked cornered. "I mean . . . oh, c'mon. Maybe she knows you're the editor of the paper. Maybe she doesn't want reporters snooping around."

"Well, I hope I can tell you I wasn't snooping. I was just looking for you."

Sandy wanted to end the discussion. "All right, Daddy, all right.

She just read you wrong, okay? I don't know what her problem was. She has the right to choose her audience, I suppose."

"And I don't have the right to know what my daughter is learning?"

Sandy stopped a word halfway up her throat and inferred a few things first. "You *were* snooping!"

Even as it happened, Marshall knew good and well that they were at it again, the old cats-and-dogs, fighting roosters routine. It was crazy. Part of him didn't want it to happen, but the rest of him was too frustrated and angry to stop.

As for the demon, it only cowered nearby, shying from Marshall as if he were red hot. The demon watched, waited, fretted.

"In a pig's eye I was snooping!" Marshall roared. "I'm here because I'm your loving father and I wanted to pick you up after classes. Stewart Hall, that's all I knew. I just happened to find you, and . . ." He tried to brake himself. He deflated a little, covered his eyes with his hand, and sighed.

"And you thought you'd keep an eye on me!" Sandy suggested spitefully.

"Got some law against that?"

"Okay, I'll lay it all out for you. I'm a human being, Daddy, and every human entity—I don't care who he or she is—is ultimately subject to a universal scheme and not to the will of any specific individual. As for Professor Langstrat, if she doesn't want you present at her lecture, it's her prerogative to demand that you leave!"

"And just who's paying her salary, anyway?"

She ignored the question. "And as for me, and what I am learning, and what I am becoming, and where I am going, and what I wish, I say you have no right to infringe on my universe unless I personally grant you that right!"

Marshall's eyesight was getting blurred by visions of Sandy turned over his knee. Enraged, he had to lash out at somebody, but now he was trying to steer his attacks away from Sandy. He pointed back toward Stewart Hall and demanded, "Did—did *she* teach you that?"

"You don't need to know."

"I have a right to know!"

"You waived that right, Daddy, years ago."

That punch sent him into the ropes, and he couldn't fully recover before she took off down the street, escaping him, escaping their miserable, bullish battle. He hollered after her, some stupid-sounding question about how she'd get home, but she didn't even slow down.

The demon grabbed its chance *and* Marshall, and he felt his anger and self-righteousness give way to sinking despair. He'd blown it. The very thing he never wanted to do again, he did. Why in the world was he wired up this way? Why couldn't he just reach her, love her, win her back? She was disappearing from sight even now, becoming smaller and smaller as she hurried across the campus, and she seemed so very far away, farther than any loving arm could ever reach. He had always tried to be strong, to stand tough through life and through struggles, but right now the hurt was so bad he couldn't keep that strength from crumbling away from him in pitiful pieces. As he watched, Sandy disappeared around a distant corner without looking back, and something broke inside him. His soul felt like it would melt, and at this moment there was no person on the face of the earth he hated more than himself.

The strength of his legs seemed to surrender under the load of his sorrow, and he sank to the steps in front of the old building, despondent.

The demon's talons surrounded his heart and he muttered in a quivering voice, "What's the use?"

"YAHAAAAA!" came a thundering cry from the nearby shrubs. A bluish-white light glimmered. The demon released its grip on Marshall and bolted like a terrified fly, landing some distance away in a trembling, defensive stance, its huge yellow eyes nearly popping out of its head and a soot-black, barbed scimitar ready in its quivering hand. But then there came an unexplainable commotion behind those same bushes, some kind of struggle, and the source of the light disappeared around the corner of Stewart Hall.

The demon did not stir, but waited, listened, watched. No sound could be heard except the light breeze. The demon stalked ever so cautiously back to where Marshall still sat, went past him, and peered through the shrubbery and around the corner of the building.

Nothing.

As if held for this entire time, a long, slow breath of yellow vapor curled in lacy wisps from the demon's nostrils. Yes, it knew what it had seen; there was no mistaking it. But why had they fled?

5

A short distance across the campus, but enough distance to be safe, two giant men descended to earth like glimmering, bluish-white comets, held aloft by rushing wings that swirled in a blur and burned like lightning. One of them, a huge, burly, black-bearded bull of a man, was quite angry and indignant, bellowing and making fierce gestures with a long, gleaming sword. The other was a little smaller and kept looking about with great caution, trying to get his associate to calm down.

In a graceful, fiery spiral they drifted down behind one of the college dormitories and came to rest in the cover of some overhanging willows. The moment their feet touched down, the light from their clothes and bodies began to fade and the shimmering wings gently subsided. Save for their towering stature they appeared as two ordinary men, one trim and blond, the other built like a tank, both dressed in what looked like matching tan fatigues. Golden belts had become like dark leather, their scabbards were dull copper, and the glowing, bronze bindings on their feet had become simple leather sandals.

The big fellow was ready for a discussion.

"Triskal!" he growled, but at his friend's desperate gestures he spoke just a little softer. "What are you doing here?"

Triskal kept his hands up to keep his friend quiet.

"Shh, Guilo! The Spirit brought me here, the same as you. I arrived yesterday."

"You know what that was? A demon of complacency and despair if ever I saw one! If your arm hadn't held me I could have struck him, and only once!"

"Oh, yes, Guilo, only once," his friend agreed, "but it's a good thing I saw you and stopped you in time. You've just arrived and you don't understand—"

"What don't I understand?"

Triskal tried to say it in a convincing manner. "We . . . must not fight, Guilo. Not yet. We must not resist."

Guilo was sure his friend was mistaken. He took firm hold of Triskal's shoulder and looked him right in the eye.

"Why should I go anywhere but to fight?" he stated. "Here I was called. Here I will fight."

"Yes," said Triskal, nodding furiously. "Just not yet, that's all."

"Then you must have orders! You *do* have orders?"

Triskal paused for effect, then said, "*Tal's* orders."

Guilo's angry expression at once melted into a mixture of shock and perplexity.

Dusk was settling over Ashton, and the little white church on Morgan Hill was washed with the warm, rusty glow of the evening sun. Outside in the small churchyard, the church's young pastor hurriedly mowed the lawn, hoping to be finished before mealtime. Dogs were barking in the neighborhood, people were arriving back home from work, kids were being called in for supper.

Unseen by these mortals, Guilo and Triskal came hurriedly up the hill on foot, secretive and unglorified but moving like the wind nevertheless. As they arrived in front of the church, Hank Busche came around the corner behind the roaring lawn mower, and Guilo had to pause to look him over.

"Is he the one?" he asked Triskal. "Did the call begin with him?"

"Yes," Triskal answered, "months ago. He's praying even now, and often walks the streets of Ashton interceding for it."

"But . . . this place is so small. Why was I called? No, no, why was *Tal* called?"

Triskal only pulled at his arm. "Hurry inside."

They passed quickly through the walls of the church and into the humble little sanctuary. Inside they found a contingent of warriors already gathered, some sitting in the pews, others standing around the platform, still others acting as sentries, looking cautiously out the stained glass windows. They were all dressed much as Triskal and Guilo, in the same tan tunics and breeches, but Guilo was immediately impressed by the imposing stature of them all; these were the mighty warriors, the powerful warriors, and more than he had ever seen gathered in one place.

He was also struck by the mood of the gathering. This moment could have been a joyful reunion of old friends except that everyone was strangely somber. As he looked around the room he recognized many whom he had fought alongside in times far past:

Nathan, the towering Arabian who fought fiercely and spoke little. It was he who had taken demons by their ankles and used them as warclubs against their fellows.

Armoth, the big African whose war cry and fierce countenance had often been enough to send the enemy fleeing before he even assailed them. Guilo and Armoth had once battled the demon lords of villages in Brazil and personally guarded a family of missionaries on their many long treks through the jungles.

Chimon, the meek European with the golden hair, who bore on his forearms the marks of a fading demon's last blows before Chimon banished him forever into the abyss. Guilo had never met this one, but had heard of his exploits and his ability to take blows simply as a shield for others and then to rally himself to defeat untold numbers alone.

Then came the greeting of the oldest and most cherished friend. "Welcome, Guilo, the Strength of Many!"

Yes, it was indeed Tal, the Captain of the Host. It was so strange to see this mighty warrior standing in this humble little place. Guilo had seen him near the throne room of Heaven itself, in conference with none other than Michael. But here stood the same impressive figure with golden hair and ruddy complexion, intense golden eyes like fire and an unchallengeable air of authority.

Guilo approached his captain and the two of them clasped hands.

"And we are together again," said Guilo as a thousand memories flooded his mind. No warrior Guilo had ever seen could fight as Tal could; no demon could outmaneuver or outspeed him, no sword could parry a blow from the sword of Tal. Side by side, Guilo and his captain had vanquished demonic powers for as long as those rebels had existed, and had been companions in the Lord's service before there had been any rebellion at all. "Greetings, my dear captain!"

Tal said by way of explanation, "It's a serious business that brings us together again."

Guilo searched Tal's face. Yes, there was plenty of confidence there, and no timidity. But there was definitely a strange grimness in the eyes and mouth, and Guilo looked around the room once again. Now he could feel it, that typically silent and ominous prelude to the breaking of grim news. Yes, they all knew something he didn't but were waiting for the appointed person, most likely Tal, to speak it.

Guilo couldn't stand the silence, much less the suspense. "Twenty-three," he counted, "of the very best, the most gallant, the most undefeatable . . . gathered now as though under siege, cowering in a flimsy fortress from a dreaded enemy?" With a dramatic flair, he drew his huge sword and cradled the blade in his free hand. "Captain Tal, who is this enemy?"

Tal answered slowly and clearly, "Rafar, the Prince of Babylon."

All eyes were now on Guilo's face, and his reaction was much like that of every other warrior upon hearing the news: shock, disbelief, an awkward pause to see if anyone would laugh and verify that it was only a mistake. There was no such reprieve from the truth. Everyone in the room continued to look at Guilo with the same deadly serious expression, driving the gravity of the situation home mercilessly.

Guilo looked down at his sword. Was it now shaking in his hands? He made a point of holding it still, but he couldn't help staring for a moment at the blade, still gashed and discolored from the last time Guilo and Tal had confronted this Baal-prince from the ancient times. Guilo and Tal had struggled against him twenty-three days before finally defeating him on the eve of Babylon's fall. Guilo could still remember the darkness, the shrieking and horror, the fierce, terrible grappling while pain seared every inch of his being. The evil of this would-be pagan god seemed to envelop him and everything around him like thick smoke, and half the time the two warriors had to maneuver and strike blindly, each one not even knowing if the other was still in the fight. To this day neither of them even knew which one finally delivered the blow that sent Rafar plummeting into the abyss. All they remembered was his heaven-shaking scream as he fell through a jagged rift in space, and then seeing each other again when the great darkness that surrounded them cleared like a melting fog.

"I know you speak the truth," Guilo said at last, "but . . . . would such as Rafar come to this place? He is a prince of nations, not mere hamlets. What *is* this place? What interest could he possibly have in it?"

Tal only shook his head. "We don't know. But it *is* Rafar, there's no question, and the stirrings in the enemy's realm indicate something is in the making. The Spirit wants us here. We must confront whatever it is."

"And we are not to fight, we are not to resist!" Guilo exclaimed. "I will be most fascinated to hear your next order, Tal. We cannot fight?"

"Not yet. We're too few, and there's very little prayer cover. There are to be no skirmishes, no confrontations. We're not to show ourselves in any way as aggressors. As long as we stay out of their way, keep close to this place, and pose no threat to them, our presence here will seem like normal watchcare over a few, struggling saints." Then he added with a very direct tone, "And it will be best if it not be spread that I am here."

Guilo now felt a little out of place still holding his sword, and sheathed it with an air of disgust.

"And," he prodded, "you do have a plan? We were not called here to watch the town fall?"

The lawn mower roared by the windows, and Tal guided their attention to its operator.

"It was Chimon's task to bring him here," he said, "to blind the eyes of his enemies and slip him through ahead of the adversary's choice for the pastor of this flock. Chimon succeeded, Hank was voted in, to the surprise of many, and now he's here in Ashton, praying every hour of every day. We were called here for his sake, for the saints of God and for the Lamb."

"For the saints of God and for the Lamb!" they all echoed.

Tal looked at a tall, dark-haired warrior, the one who had taken him through the town the night of the Festival, and smiled. "And you had him win by just one vote?"

The warrior shrugged. "The Lord wanted him here. Chimon and I had to make sure he won, and not the other man who has no fear of God."

Tal introduced Guilo to this warrior. "Guilo, this is Krioni, watchcarer of our prayer warrior here and of the town of Ashton. Our call began with Hank, but Hank's presence here began with Krioni."

Guilo and Krioni nodded silent greeting to each other.

Tal watched Hank finishing up the lawn and praying out loud at the same time. "So now, as his enemies in the congregation regroup and try to find another way to oust him, he continues to pray for Ashton. He's one of the last."

"If not *the* last!" lamented Krioni.

"No," cautioned Tal, "he's not alone. There's still a Remnant of saints somewhere in this town. There is always a Remnant."

"There is always a Remnant," they all echoed.

"Our conflict begins in this place. We'll make this our location for now, hedge it in and work from here." He spoke to a tall Oriental in the back of the room. "Signa, take as your charge this building, and choose two now to stand with you. This is our rest point. Make it secure. No demon is to approach it."

Signa immediately found two volunteers to work with him. They vanished to their posts.

"Now, Triskal, I'll hear news of Marshall Hogan."

"I followed him up to my encounter with Guilo. Though Krioni has reported a rather eventless situation up to the time of the Festival, ever since then Hogan has been hounded by a demon of complacency and despair."

Tal received that news with great interest. "Hm. Could be he's beginning to stir. They're covering him, trying to hold him in check."

Krioni added, "I never thought I'd see it happen. The Lord wanted him in charge of the *Clarion,* and we took care of that too, but I've never seen a more tired individual."

"Tired, yes, but that will only make him more usable in the Lord's hands. And I perceive that he is indeed waking up, just as the Lord foreknew."

"Though he could awaken only to be destroyed," said Triskal. "They must be watching him. They fear what he could do in his influential position."

"True," replied Tal. "So while they bait our bear, we must be sure they stir him up and no more than that. It's going to be a very critical business."

Now Tal was ready to move. He addressed the whole group. "I expect Rafar to take power here by nightfall; no doubt we'll all feel it when he does. Be sure of this: he will immediately search out the greatest threat to him and try to remove it."

"Ah, Henry Busche," said Guilo.

"Krioni and Triskal, you can be sure that a troop of some kind will be sent to test Hank's spirit. Select for yourselves four warriors and watch over him." Tal touched Krioni's shoulder and added, "Krioni, up until now you've done very well in protecting Hank from any direct onslaughts. I commend you."

"Thank you, captain."

"I ask you now to do a difficult thing. Tonight you must stand by and keep watch. Do not let Hank's life be touched, but aside from that prevent nothing. It will be a test he *must* undergo."

There was a slight moment of surprise and wonderment, but each warrior was ready to trust Tal's judgment.

Tal continued, "As for Marshall Hogan . . . he's the only one I'm not sure about yet. Rafar will give his lackeys incredible license with him, and he could either collapse and retreat, or—as we all hope—rouse himself and fight back. He'll be of special interest to Rafar—and to me—tonight. Guilo, select two warriors for yourself and two for me. We'll watchcare over Marshall tonight and see how he responds. The rest of you will search out the Remnant."

Tal drew his sword and held it high. The others did the same and a forest of shining blades appeared, held aloft in strong arms.

"Rafar," Tal said in a low, musing voice, "we meet again." Then, in the voice of a Captain of the Host: "For the saints of God and for the Lamb!"

"For the saints of God and for the Lamb!" they echoed.

Complacency unfurled his wings and drifted into Stewart Hall, sinking down through the main floor and into the catacombs of the basement level, the area set aside for administration and the private offices of the Psychology Department. In this dismal nether world the ceiling was low and oppressive, and crawling with water pipes and heat ducts that seemed like so many huge snakes waiting to drop. Everything—walls, ceiling, pipes, woodwork—was painted the same dirty beige, and light was scarce, which suited Complacency and his associates just fine. They preferred the darkness, and Complacency noticed that there seemed to be a touch more than usual. The others must have arrived.

He floated down a long burrow of a hallway to a large door at the end marked "Conference Room," and passed through the door into a cauldron of living evil. The room was dark, but the darkness seemed more of a presence than a physical condition; it was a force, an atmosphere that drifted and crept about the room. Out of that darkness glared many pairs of dull yellow cat-eyes belonging to a horrible gallery of grotesque faces. The various shapes of Complacency's fellow workers were outlined and backlit by a sourceless red glow. Yellow vapor slithered in lacy wisps about the room and filled the air with its stench as the many apparitions carried on their hushed, gargling conversations there in the dark.

Complacency could sense their common disdain for him, but the feeling was mutual enough. These belligerent egotists would walk on anyone to exalt themselves, and Complacency just happened to be the smallest, hence the easiest to persecute.

He approached two hulking forms in the middle of some debate, and from their massive, spine-covered arms and poisonous words he could tell they were demons who specialized in hate—planting, aggravating, and spreading it, using their crushing arms and venomous quills to constrict and poison the love out of anyone.

Complacency asked them, "Where is Prince Lucius?"

"Find him yourself, lizard!" one of them growled.

A demon of lust, a slithery creature with darting and shifty eyes and slippery hide, overheard and joined in, snatching Complacency with his long, sharp talons.

"And where have you been sleeping today?" it asked with a sneer.

"I do not sleep!" Complacency retorted. "I cause *people* to sleep."

"To lust and steal innocence is far better."

"But someone must turn away the eyes of others."

Lust thought that over and gave a smirk of approval. He dropped Complacency rudely as those who watched laughed.

Complacency passed Deception, but didn't bother to ask him anything. Deception was the proudest, haughtiest demon of them all, very arrogant in his supposedly superior knowledge of how to control men's minds. His appearance was not even as gruesome as the other demons; he almost looked human. His weapon, he boasted, was always a compelling, persuasive argument with lies ever so subtly woven in.

Many others were there: Murder, his talons still dripping with blood; Lawlessness, his knuckles honed into spikelike protrusions and his hide thick and leathery; Jealousy, as suspicious and difficult a demon to work with as any.

But Complacency finally found Lucius, the Prince of Ashton, the demon who held the highest position of all of them. Lucius was in conference with a tight huddle of other power holders, going over the next strategies for controlling the town.

He was unquestionably the demon in charge. Huge to begin with, he always maintained an imposing posture with his wings wrapped loosely around him to widen his outline, his arms flexed, his fists clenched and ready for blows. Many demons coveted his rank, and he knew it; he had fought and banished many to get where he was, and he had every intention of staying there. He trusted no one and suspected everyone, and his black, gnarled face and hawk-sharp eyes always carried the message that even his associates were his enemies.

Complacency was desperate and enraged enough to violate Lucius's ideas of respect and decorum. He shoved his way through the group and right up to Lucius, who glared at him, surprised by the rude interruption.

"My Prince," Complacency pleaded, "I must have a word with you."

Lucius's eyes narrowed. Who was this little lizard to interrupt him in the middle of a conference, to violate decorum in front of these others?

"Why aren't you with Hogan?" he growled.

"I must speak with you!"

"Dare you speak to me without my first speaking to you?"

"It is vitally important. You're—you're making a mistake. You're bothering Hogan's daughter, and—"

Lucius immediately became a small volcano, spewing forth horrible cursings and wrath. "You accuse your prince of a mistake? You dare to question my actions?"

Complacency cowered, expecting a stinging blow any moment, but he spoke anyway.

"Hogan will do us no harm if you let him alone. But you have only lit a fire within him, and he casts me off!"

The blow came, a walloping swat from the back of Lucius's hand, and as Complacency tumbled across the room he debated whether or not to speak another word. When he came to rest and regathered himself, he looked up to see every eye upon him, and he could feel their mocking disdain.

Lucius walked slowly toward him, and towered over him like a giant tree. "Hogan casts you off? Is it not you who releases him?"

"Do not strike me! Only hear my appeal!"

Lucius's big fists clenched painfully around handfuls of Complacency's flesh and snatched him up so they were eye to eye. "He could stand in our way and I won't have that! You know your duty. Perform it!"

"Well I was, well I was!" Complacency cried. "He was nothing to fear at all, a slug, a lump of clay. I could have held him there forever."

"So do it!"

"Prince Lucius, please hear me! Give him no enemy. Let him have no need to fight."

Lucius dropped him on the floor in a humiliated heap. The prince addressed the others in the room.

"We have given Hogan an enemy?"

They all knew how to answer. "No indeed!"

"Deception," Lucius called, and Deception stepped forward, giving Lucius a formal bow. "Complacency accuses his prince of bothering Hogan's daughter. You would know about that."

"You have ordered no attack on Sandy Hogan, Prince," Deception answered.

Complacency pointed his taloned finger and screamed, "You have followed her! You and your lackeys! You have spoken words to her mind, confused her!"

Deception only raised his eyebrows in mild indignation and answered sedately, "Only upon her own invitation. We have only told her what she prefers to know. That can hardly be called an attack."

Lucius seemed to take on some of Deception's maddening haughtiness as he said, "Sandy Hogan is one case, but certainly her father is quite another. She poses no threat to us. He does. Shall we send someone else to hold him in check?"

Complacency had no answer, but added another note of concern. "I . . . I saw messengers of the living God today!"

That only brought laughter from the group.

Lucius sneered, "Are you becoming that timid, Complacency? We see messengers of the living God every day."

"But they were close! About to attack! They knew my actions, I am sure."

"You look all right to me. Though if I were one of them, I would surely pick you as an easy prey." More laughter from the group spurred Lucius on. "A limp and easy target for mere sport . . . a lame demon with which a weak angel can prove his strength!"

Complacency cowered in shame. Lucius strode about, addressing the group.

"Do we fear the host of heaven?" he asked.

"As you do not, we do not!" they all answered with great polish.

As the demons remained in their basement lair, patting each other's backs and stabbing Complacency's, they took no notice of the strange, unnatural cold front outside. It moved slowly over the town, bringing a harsh wind and chilling rain. Though the evening had promised to be bright and clear, it now grew dark under a low, oppressive shroud, half natural, half spirit.

Atop the little white church, Signa and his two companions continued to stand guard as the darkness descended over Ashton, deeper and colder with each passing moment. All over the nearby neighborhood dogs began to bark and howl. Here and there a quarrel broke out among humans.

"He's here," Signa said.

In the meantime, Lucius's preoccupation with his own glory kept him from noticing the little attention he was now getting from his troops. All the other demons in the room, large or small, were gripped by a steadily rising fear and agitation. They could all feel something horrible coming closer and closer. They began to fidget, their eyes darting about, their faces twisting with apprehension.

Lucius gave Complacency a kick in the side as he walked by and continued his boasting.

"Complacency, you can be sure that we have things very much in control here. No worker from our number has ever had to sneak about for fear of attack. We roam this town freely, doing our work unhampered, and we will succeed in every place until the town is fully ours. You listless, limp, little bungler! To fear is to fail!"

Then it happened, and so very suddenly that none of them could react with anything other than air-piercing shrieks of terror. Lucius had hardly gotten the word "fail" out of his mouth before a violent, boiling cloud crashed and thundered into the room like a tidal wave, a sudden avalanche of force that crushed like iron. The demons were swept across the room like so much debris in a raging tide, tumbling, screaming, wrapping their wings tightly around themselves in terror—all except for Lucius.

As the demons recovered from the initial shock wave of this new presence, they looked up and saw Lucius's body, contorted like a broken toy, in the grip of a huge, black hand. He struggled, choked, gagged, cried for mercy, but the hand only tightened its crushing grip, inflicting punishment without mercy, descending down out of the darkness like a cyclone from a thundercloud. Then the full figure of a spirit appeared, carrying Lucius by the throat and shaking him about like a rag doll. The thing was bigger than any they had ever seen before, a giant demon with a lion-like face, fiery eyes, incredibly muscular body, and leathery wings that filled the room.

The voice gargled up from deep within the demon's torso and sprayed out in clouds of fiery red vapor.

"You who have no fear—are you now afraid?"

The spirit angrily hurled Lucius across the room to join the others, then stood like a mountain in the center of the room, wielding a deadly, S-curved sword the size of a door. His bared fangs glistened like the jeweled chains around his neck and across his chest. Obviously this prince of princes had been greatly honored for past victories. His jet black hair hung like a mane to his shoulders, and on each wrist he wore a gold bracelet studded with sparkling stones; his fingers displayed several rings, and a ruby-red belt and scabbard adorned his waist. The expansive black wings draped down behind him now like the robe of a monarch.

For an eternity he stood there, glaring at them with sinister, smoldering eyes, studying them, and all they could do was remain motionless in their terror like a macabre tableau of frightened goblins.

Finally the big voice echoed off the walls: "Lucius, I feel I was not expected. You will announce me. On your feet!"

The sword moved across the room and the tip snagged Lucius in the hide of his neck, jolting him to his feet.

Lucius knew he was being belittled in the sight of his underlings, but he made every effort to hide his rising bitterness and anger. His fear showed well enough to adequately cover his other feelings.

"Fellow workers . . ." he said, his voice quivering despite every effort. "Ba-al Rafar, the Prince of Babylon!"

Automatically they all leaped to their feet, partly out of fearful respect, mostly out of fear of the tip of Rafar's sword, still waving slowly back and forth, ready to move against any dawdlers.

Rafar gave them all a quick looking over. Then he inflicted another personal blow against Lucius.

"Lucius, you will stand with the others. I have come, and only one prince is needed."

Friction. Everyone could feel it immediately. Lucius refused to move. His body was stiff, his fists clenched as tightly as ever, and though he was visibly trembling, he purposely returned the glaring look of Rafar and stood his ground.

"You . . . have not asked me to yield my place!" he challenged.

The others were not about to intervene or even get close. They backed off, remembering that Rafar's sword could probably sweep a very wide radius.

The sword did move, but so quickly that the very first thing anyone perceived was a scream of pain from Lucius as he coiled into a twisted knot on the floor. Lucius's sword and scabbard lay on the floor, skillfully cut away by one swift slash from Rafar. Again the sword moved, and this time the flat of the blade clamped Lucius to the floor by his hair.

Rafar leaned over him, blood-red breath spewing from his mouth and nostrils as he spoke.

"I perceive you wish to challenge for my position." Lucius said nothing. "ANSWER!"

"No!" Lucius cried. "I yield."

"Up! Get up!"

Lucius struggled to his feet, and Rafar's strong arm stood him with the others. By now Lucius was a most pitiful sight, totally humiliated. Rafar reached down with his sword and with the barbed tip picked up Lucius's sword and scabbard. The sword swung like a huge crane and deposited Lucius's weapons in the deposed demon's hands.

"Listen well, all of you," Rafar addressed them. "Lucius, who fears not the hosts of heaven, has shown fear. He is a liar and a worm and is not to be heeded. I say to you, fear the hosts of heaven. They are your enemies, and they are intent on defeating you. As they are ignored, as they are given place, so they shall overcome you."

Rafar walked with heavy, ponderous steps up and down the line of demons, giving them all a closer look. When he came to Complacency, he drew close and Complacency fell backwards. Rafar caught him around the back of the neck with one finger and pulled him up straight.

"Tell me, little lizard, what did you see today?"

Complacency was suffering from a sudden memory lapse.

Rafar prodded him. "Messengers of the living God, you said?"

Complacency nodded.

"Where?"

"Just outside this building."

"What were they doing?"

"I . . . I . . ."

"Did they attack you?"

"No."

"Was there a flash of light?"

That seemed to register with Complacency. He nodded.

"When a messenger of God attacks, there is always light." Rafar addressed all of them angrily. "And you let it slip by! You laughed! You mocked! A near attack from the enemy and you ignored it!"

Now Rafar returned to grill Lucius some more.

"Tell me, deposed prince, how stands the town of Ashton? Is it ready?"

Lucius was quick to say, "Yes, Ba-al Rafar."

"Oh, then you have taken care of this praying Busche and this sleeping troublemaker Hogan."

Lucius was silent.

"You have not! First you allow them to come into places we reserved for our own special appointments—"

"It was a mistake, Ba-al Rafar!" Lucius blurted. "The *Clarion* editor was eliminated according to our orders, but . . . no one knows where this Hogan came from. He bought the paper before anything could be done."

"And Busche? It was my understanding that he fled from your attacks."

"That . . . that was another man of God. The first one. He did flee."

"And?"

"This younger man sprung up in his place. From nowhere."

A long, foul sigh hissed out through Rafar's fangs.

"The host of heaven," he said. "While you have taken them for granted, they have moved in the Lord's chosen right under your noses! It is no secret that Henry Busche is a man who prays. Do you fear that?"

Lucius nodded. "Yes, of course, more than anything. We have been attacking him, trying to drive him out."

"And how has he responded?"

"He . . . he . . ."

"Speak up!"

"He prays."

Rafar shook his head. "Yes, yes, he is a man of God. And what about Hogan? What have you done about him?"

"We—we have attacked his daughter."

Complacency's ears perked up at that.

"His daughter?"

But Complacency couldn't contain himself. "I told them it wouldn't work! It would only make Hogan more aggressive and wake him from his lethargy!"

Lucius grabbed for Rafar's attention. "If my lord would allow me to explain . . ."

"Explain," Rafar instructed Lucius while warily eyeing Complacency.

Lucius quickly formulated a plan in his mind. "Sometimes a direct attack is not wise, so . . . we found a weakness in his daughter and felt we could divert his energies toward her, perhaps destroy him at home and disintegrate his family. It seemed to work on the former editor. It was at least a start."

"It will fail," cried Complacency. "He was harmless until they tampered with his sense of well-being and comfort. Now I fear I won't be able to hold him back. He is—"

A quick, threatening gesture from Rafar's outstretched hand stifled Complacency's wailings.

"I do not want Hogan held back," Rafar said. "I want him destroyed. Yes, take his daughter. Take anything else that can be corrupted. A risk is best removed, not tolerated."

"But—" cried Complacency, but Rafar quickly took hold of him and spoke with noxious fumings right into his face.

"Discourage him. Surely you can do that."

"Well . . ."

But Rafar was in no mood to wait for an answer. With a powerful spin of his wrist he hurled Complacency out of the room and back to work.

"We will destroy him, assault him on every side until he has no solid ground left from which to fight. As for this new man of God who has sprung up, I'm sure an adequate trap can be laid. But concerning our enemies: how strong are they?"

"Not strong at all," answered Lucius, trying to recover his competency rating.

"But cunning enough to make you think they are weak. A fatal mistake, Lucius." He addressed all of them. "You are to no longer take the enemy for granted. Watch him. Count his numbers. Know his whereabouts, his skill, his name. No mission was ever undertaken that was not challenged by the hosts of heaven, and this mission is nothing small. Our lord has very important plans for this town, he has sent me to fulfill them, and that is enough to draw the very hordes of the enemy down upon our heads. Be fearful of that, and give place nowhere! And as for these two thorns in our hoof, these two implanted barriers . . . tonight we will see what they are made of."

6

It was a dark, rainy night, and the raindrops pelting against the old single-pane windows made sleep difficult for Hank and Mary. She dropped off eventually, but Hank, already troubled in spirit, found it much harder to relax. It had been a lousy day anyway; he had worked on painting that slogan off the front of the house and tried to figure out who in the world would write such a thing against him. His ears were still ringing with the conversation he'd had with Alf Brummel, and his mind was still playing over and over the bitter comments from the board meeting. Now he could add to his apprehensions the congregational meeting on Friday, and he prayed to the Lord in desperate, hushed whispers as he lay there in the dark.

Funny how every lump in the mattress seems so much more lumpy when you're upset. Hank began to worry that he would keep Mary awake with all his tossing and turning. He lay on his back, his side, his other side, put his arms under his pillow, over his pillow; he grabbed a Kleenex and blew his nose. He looked over at the clock: 12:20. They had turned in at 10.

But sleep finally does come, usually in such an unannounced way that you don't even know you're out until you wake up. Sometime that night Hank dozed off.

But after a few hours his dreams began to go sour. They were the usual silly thing at first, like driving a car through his living room and then flying in the car as it turned into an airplane. But then the images began to rush and riot through his head, growing frantic and chaotic. He started running from dangers. He could hear screams; there was the sensation of falling and the sight and taste of blood. Images went from bright and colorful to monochromatic and dismal. He was constantly fighting, struggling for his life; innumerable dangers and enemies surrounded him, closing in. None of it made any sense, but one thing was very definite throughout: stark terror. He wanted desperately to scream but didn't have time between fighting off enemies, monsters, unseen forces.

His pulse began to pound in his ears. The whole world was reeling and throbbing. The horrible conflict rushing in his head began to push its way to the surface of the conscious, everyday Hank. He stirred in the bed, rolled over on his back, drew a deep waking-up breath. His eyes half opened, not focused on anything. He was in that strange state of stupor halfway between sleep and consciousness.

Did he really see it? It was an eerie projection in midair, a glowing painting on black velvet. Right above the bed, so close he could smell sulfurous breath, a hideous mask of a face hovered, contorting in grotesque movements as it spit out vicious words he couldn't understand.

Hank's eyes opened like a sprung trap. He thought he could still see the face, just fading away, but instantly he felt like he'd been struck by a very heavy blow to his chest; his heart began to race and pound like it would burst through his ribs. He could feel his pajamas and the bedsheets sticking to him, drenched in sweat. He lay there panting for breath, waiting for his heart to calm down, for the stark terror to go away, but nothing changed and he couldn't make it change.

You're just having a nightmare, he kept telling himself, but he couldn't seem to wake up. He purposely opened his eyes wide and looked around the darkened room, even though part of him wanted to regress back to childhood and just hide under the covers until the ghosts and monsters and burglars went away.

He saw nothing in the room out of the ordinary. A goblin in the corner was nothing but his shirt hanging on a chair, and the strange halo of light on the wall was only the streetlight reflecting off the crystal of his watch.

But he had been severely frightened, and he was still scared. He could feel himself shaking as he desperately tried to sort hallucination from reality. He watched, listened. Even the silence seemed sinister. He found no comfort in it, only the dread that something evil hid behind it, an intruder or a demon, waiting, watching for the right moment.

What was that? A creak in the house? Footsteps? No, he told himself, just the wind against the windows. The rain had stopped.

Another noise, this time a rustling in the living room. He had never heard that noise at night before. I gotta wake up, I gotta wake up. Come on, heart, quiet down so I can hear.

He forced himself to sit up in bed, even though it made him feel more vulnerable, and he remained there for several minutes, trying to stifle his heart's pounding with his hand over his chest. The pounding finally settled back a little, but the rate remained rapid. Hank could feel the sweat turning cold against his skin. To get up or go back to sleep? Sleep was definitely out. He decided to get up, look around, walk it off.

A clatter this time, in the kitchen. Now Hank started praying.

Marshall had had the same kind of dreams and felt the same heart-pounding fear. Voices. It sure sounded like voices somewhere. Sandy? Maybe a radio.

But who knows? he thought to himself. This town is going crazy anyway, and now the sickies are in my house. He slid stealthily out of bed, put on his slippers, and moved over to the closet to procure a baseball bat. Just like back home, he thought. Now somebody's gonna have mush for brains.

He looked out his bedroom door, up and down the hallway. No lights were on anywhere, no flashlight beams played about. But his guts were doing a square dance under his ribs, and there had to be some reason for it. He reached for the hallway light and flipped the switch. Nuts! The bulb was burnt out. Since when he didn't know, but he stood in the dark and felt his courage deflated just that much more. He gripped the bat more tightly and moved down the hall, staying close to the wall, looking ahead, looking behind, listening. He thought he could hear a quiet rustling somewhere, something moving.

At the archway that led into the living room his eyes caught something, and he pressed himself against the wall for concealment. The front door was open. Now his heart really started pounding, thudding rudely in his ears. In a strange, jungle way he felt better; at least there was indication of a real enemy. It was this lousy fear without any reason that was spooking him. He had already been through that sort of thing once today.

With that thought came a strange idea: That professor lady must be in the house.

He moved down the hall to check Sandy's room and make sure she was all right. He wanted to stay between Kate and Sandy and whatever was out there in the rest of the house. Sandy's bedroom door was open, and that was unusual; it made him all the more cautious. He inched along the wall toward the doorway and then, bat ready in his hands, he peered into the room.

Something was up. Sandy was, at least—her bed was empty and she was gone. He flicked on her bedroom light. The bed had been slept in, but now the covers were thrown back hastily and the room was in disarray.

As Marshall moved cautiously down the darkened hallway, it did occur to him that Sandy might just be up getting a drink, using the bathroom, reading. But such simple logic weakened against the horrible feeling that something was dreadfully wrong. He took deep breaths, trying with his greatest effort to hold himself steady while all the time he felt an insidious, unearthly terror as if he were inches from the crushing teeth of some monster he couldn't see.

The bathroom was cold and dark. He turned on the light, dreading what he thought he might see. He saw nothing out of the ordinary. He left that light on and headed back toward the living room.

He peered like some kind of stalking fugitive through the archway. There was that rustling sound again. He flipped on the lights. Ah. The cold night air was coming in through the front door, rustling the drapes. No, Sandy was nowhere to be seen, not in the living room, not anywhere in or near the kitchen. Perhaps she was right outside.

But he had undeniable qualms about crossing the living room to the front door, walking past all the furniture that could hide an assailant. He gripped the bat tightly, keeping it up and ready. He kept his back to the wall as he made his way around the perimeter of the room, stepping around the sofa after checking behind it, hurriedly maneuvering around the stereo, and finally reaching the door.

He went out onto the porch, into the cool night air, and for some reason suddenly felt safer. The town was still quiet this time of night. Everyone else was certainly asleep right now, not sneaking around their houses with baseball bats. He took a moment to regather himself and then went back inside.

Locking the door behind him was just like shutting himself in a dark closet with a couple of hundred vipers. The fear returned and he tightened his grip on the bat. With his back against the door, he looked around the room again. Why was it so dark? The lights were on, but every bulb seemed so dim, as if there were some kind of brown-out. Hogan, he thought to himself, either you've really lost a screw or you're in big, big trouble. He remained frozen there by the door, motionless, looking and listening. There had to be somebody or something in the house. He couldn't hear them or see them, but he could certainly feel them.

Outside the house, lying low in the evergreens and hedges, Tal and his company watched as demons—at least forty according to Tal's count—played havoc with Marshall's mind and spirit. They swooped like deadly black swallows in and out of the house, through the rooms, around and around Marshall, screaming taunts and blasphemies, and playing with and ever increasing his fears. Tal kept careful watch for the dreaded Rafar, but the Ba-al wasn't among this wild group. There could be no doubt, however, that Rafar had sent them.

Tal and the others agonized, feeling Marshall's pain. One demon, an ugly little imp with bristling, needle-sharp quills all over his body, leaped upon Marshall's shoulders and beat upon his head, screaming, "You're going to die, Hogan! You're going to die! Your daughter is dead and you are going to die!"

Guilo could hardly control himself. His big sword slipped with a metallic ring from its sheath, but Tal's strong arm held him back.

"Please, captain!" Guilo pleaded. "Never before have I only watched this happen!"

"Bridle yourself, dear warrior," Tal cautioned.

"I will strike them only once!"

Guilo could see that even Tal was severely pained by his own order: "Forbear. Forbear. He must go through it."

Hank had the lights on in the house, but he thought his eyes must have been playing tricks on him because the rooms still looked very dark, the shadows deep. Sometimes he couldn't tell if it was himself moving or the shadows in the room; a strange, undulating motion in the light and shadows made the depths in the house shift back and forth like the slow, steady motion of breathing.

Hank stood in the doorway between kitchen and living room,

watching and listening. He thought he could feel a wind moving through the house, but not a cold one from outside. It was like hot, sticky breath laden with repulsive odors, close and oppressive.

He had discovered that the clatter in the kitchen was due to a spatula sliding off the drainboard and onto the floor. That should have calmed his nerves right down, but he still felt terrified.

He knew he would sooner or later have to move into the living room to have a look. He took his first step out of the doorway and into the room.

It was like falling into a bottomless well of blackness and terror. The hairs on his neck bristled as if with static electricity. His lips started spilling out a frantic prayer.

He went down. Before he even knew what was happening, his body pitched forward and slammed into the floor. He became a trapped animal, instinctively struggling, trying to get loose from the unseen crushing weight that held him. His arms and legs were smacking into furniture and knocking things over, but in his terror and shock he felt no pain. He squirmed, twisted, gasped for breath, and lashed out at whatever it was, feeling resistance against the motion of his arms like stroking through water. The room seemed filled with smoke.

Blackness like blindness, a loss of hearing, a loss of contact with the real world, time standing still. He could feel himself dying. An image, a hallucination, a vision or a real sight broke through for an instant: two ghastly yellow eyes full of hate. His throat began to compress, squeezing shut.

"Jesus!" he heard his mind cry out, "help me!"

His next thought, a tiny, instant flash, must have come from the Lord: "Rebuke it! You have the authority."

Hank spoke the words though he couldn't hear the sound of them: "I rebuke you in Jesus' name!"

The crushing weight upon him lifted so quickly Hank felt he would sail upward from the floor. He filled his lungs with air and noticed he was now struggling against nothing. But the terror was still there, the black, sinister presence.

He sat up halfway, drew another breath, and spoke it clearly and loudly. "In the Name of Jesus I command you to get out of this house!"

Mary awoke with a jerk, startled and then terrified by the sound of a multitude screaming in anguish and pain. The cries were deafening at first, but they faded as if moving off into the unseen distance.

"Hank!" she screamed.

Marshall roared like a savage and raised the bat high to strike down his attacker. The attacker screamed also, out of stark terror.

It was Kate. They had unknowingly backed into each other in the dark hallway.

"Marshall!" she exclaimed, and her voice quivered. She was close to tears and angry at the same time. "What on earth are you doing out here!"

"Kate. . . ." Marshall sighed, feeling himself shrink like a punctured inner tube. "What are you trying to do, get yourself killed?"

"What's wrong?" She was looking at the baseball bat and knew something was up. She clung to him in fear. "Is there someone in the house?"

"No . . ." he muttered in a combination of relief and disgust. "Nobody. I looked."

"What happened? Who was it?"

"Nobody, I said."

"But I thought you were talking to someone."

He looked at her with the utmost impatience and said with steadily building volume, "Do I look like I've been having a friendly chat with someone?"

Kate shook her head. "I must have been dreaming. But it was the voices that woke me up."

"What voices?"

"Marshall, it sounded like a New Year's Eve party in there. Come on, who was it?"

"Nobody. There wasn't anybody here. I looked."

Kate was very flustered. "I know I was awake."

"You heard ghosts."

He could feel her hand squeezing the blood out of his arm. "Don't talk like that!"

"Sandy's gone."

"What do you mean, gone? Gone where?"

"She's gone. Her room's empty, she's not in the house. She's poof! Gone!"

Kate hurried down the hall and looked in Sandy's room. Marshall followed her and observed from the doorway as Kate checked the room over, looking through the closet and some of the drawers.

She reported with alarm, "Some of her clothes are gone. Her schoolbooks are missing." She looked at him helplessly. "Marshall— she's left home!"

He looked back at her for a long moment, then around the room, then rested his head against the doorjamb with a quiet thud.

"Nuts," he said.

"I knew she wasn't herself tonight. I should have found out what was wrong."

"We didn't hit it off too well today . . ."

"Well, that was obvious. You came home without her."

"How'd she get home, anyway?"

"Her girlfriend Terry brought her."

"Maybe she went over to Terry's for the night."

"Should we call and find out?"

"I dunno . . ."

"You don't know!?"

Marshall closed his eyes and tried to think. "Naw. It's late. Either she's there or she isn't. If she isn't, we'll be getting them out of bed for nothing, and if she is, well, she's okay anyway."

Kate seemed a little panicked. "I'm going to call."

Marshall held up his hand and leaned his head against the doorjamb again as he said, "Hey, don't get all spooked now, all right? Gimme a minute."

"I just want to see if she's there—"

"All right, all right . . ."

But Kate could see something was very wrong with Marshall. He was pale, weak, shaken.

"What's the matter, Marshall?

"Gimme a minute . . ."

She put her arm around him, concerned. "What is it?"

He had quite a struggle getting it out. "I'm scared." Trembling a bit, his eyes closed, his head resting against the doorjamb, he said again, "I'm really scared and I don't know why."

That scared Kate. "Marshall . . ."

"Don't get upset, will you? Keep it level."

"Can I do anything?"

"Just be tough, that's all."

Kate thought for a moment. "Well, why don't you get your robe on? I'll warm you some milk, okay?"

"Yeah, great."

It was the first time any demons had ever been actually confronted and rebuked by Hank Busche. They had certainly come with an arrogant brashness at first, descending on the house in the dead of night to raid and ravage, screaming and swooping through the rooms and leaping on Hank, trying to terrify him. But as Krioni, Triskal, and the others watched from their hiding place, confused and scattered flocks of demons suddenly came thundering and fluttering out of the house like bats, screaming, indignant, stopping their ears. There must have been close to a hundred, all the usual demonic pranksters and troublemakers Krioni had seen at work all over the town. No doubt the great Ba-al had sent them, and now that they had been routed there was no telling what Rafar's reaction or his next plan would be. But Hank had proven himself very well.

In a moment the coast was clear, the trouble was over, and the warriors came out of hiding, breathing easier. Krioni and Triskal were impressed.

Krioni commented, "Tal was right. He's not so insignificant."

Triskal agreed, "Stern stuff, this Henry Busche."

But as Hank and Mary sat trembling at their kitchen table, she preparing an icepack and he sporting a welt on his forehead and a great many bruises and scrapings on his arms and shins, neither one of them felt entirely stern, powerful, or victorious. Hank was thankful to have escaped with his life, and Mary was still in a mild state of shock and disbelief.

It was awkward, with neither of them wanting to relate his or her experience first for fear that the whole thing was nothing but an excess of pickles and pastrami before bedtime. But Hank's welt kept growing, and he could only tell what he knew. Mary bought every word of it, scared as she was by the screams that had awakened her. As they shared their not-so-pleasant experiences, they were able to accept the fact that the whole night of madness had been very frighteningly real and not some nightmare.

"Demons," Hank concluded.

Mary could only nod.

"But why?" Hank pleaded to know. "What was it for?"

Mary wasn't ready to come up with any answers. She kept waiting for Hank to do that.

He muttered, "Like Lesson Number One in Frontlines Combat. I wasn't a bit ready for it. I think I flunked."

Mary gave him the icepack and he placed it against the welt, wincing at the pressure.

"What makes you think you flunked?" she asked.

"I don't know. I just walked into it, I guess. I let them clobber me." Then he prayed, "Lord God, help me to be ready next time. Give me the wisdom, the sensitivity to know what they're up to."

Mary squeezed his hand, said amen, and then commented, "You know, I might be wrong, but hasn't the Lord already done that? I mean, how are you going to know how to fight Satan's direct attacks unless you just . . . do it?"

That was what Hank needed to hear.

"Wow," he mused. "I'm a veteran!"

"And I don't think you flunked, either. They're gone, aren't they? And you're still here, and you should have heard those screams."

"Are you sure it wasn't me?"

"Quite sure."

Then came a long, troubled silence.

"So what now?" Mary finally asked.

"Uh . . . let's pray." said Hank. For him, that option was always easy to jump to.

And pray they did, clasping hands at the little kitchen table, having a conference with the Lord. They thanked Him for the experience of that night, for protecting them from danger, for showing them a very close glimpse of their enemy. Over an hour passed, and during that time the field of concern continued to grow outward; their own problems began to take a small place in a vastly wider perspective as Hank and Mary prayed for their church, the people in it, the town, the people that ran it, the state, the nation, the world. Through it all came the beautiful assurance that they had indeed connected with the throne of God and had conducted serious business with the Lord. Hank grew more determined to stay in the battle and give Satan a real run for his money. He was sure that was what God wanted.

The warm milk and Kate's company had a soothing effect on Marshall's nerves. With each swallow and each additional minute of normalcy, he gained more and more assurance that the world would still go on, he would live, the sun would rise in the morning. He was amazed at how bleak things had looked just a little while ago.

"Feeling better?" Kate asked, buttering some fresh toast.

"Yeah," he answered, noticing that his heart had retreated back into his chest and returned to its normal, everyday pace. "Boy, I don't know what got into me."

Kate placed the two slices of toast on a plate and set them on the table.

Marshall crunched off a bite of toast and asked, "So she's not at Terry's?"

Kate shook her head. "Do you *want* to talk about Sandy?"

Marshall was ready. "We probably need to talk about a lot of things."

"I don't know how to start—"

"You think it's my fault?"

"Oh, Marshall . . ."

"C'mon, be honest now. I've been getting my behind whipped all day. I'll listen."

Her eyes met his and remained in place, denoting a sincerity and firm love.

"Categorically, no," she said.

"I botched it today."

"I think we've all botched it, and that includes Sandy. She's made some choices too, remember."

"Yeah, but maybe it was because we didn't have anything better to give her."

"What do you think of talking to Pastor Young?"

"Case in point."

"Hmmmm?"

Hogan shook his head despondently. "Maybe . . . maybe Young's just a little too cush, you know? He's into all this family of man stuff, discovering yourself, saving the whales . . ."

Kate was a little surprised. "I thought you liked Pastor Young."

"Well . . . I guess I do. But sometimes—no, a lot of the time, I don't even feel like I'm going to church. I may as well be sitting at a lodge meeting or in one of Sandy's weird classes."

He checked her eyes. They were still steady. She was listening. "Kate, don't you ever get the feeling that God's got to be, you know, a little . . . bigger? Tougher? The God we get at that church, I feel like He isn't even a real person, and if He is, He's dumber than we are. I can't expect Sandy to buy that stuff. I don't even go for it myself."

"I never knew you felt this way, Marshall."

"Well, maybe I never did either. It's just that this thing tonight . . . I've really got to think about it; there's been so much of it going on lately."

"What do you mean? What's been going on?"

I can't tell her, Marshall thought to himself. How could he explain the strange, hypnotic persuasion he was sure he got from Brummel, the spooky feelings he'd gotten from Sandy's professor, the stark terror he'd felt that night? None of it made sense, and now, to top it off, Sandy was gone. All through these situations he had been horrified by his own inability to fight back. He had felt controlled. But he couldn't tell Kate anything like that.

"Aw . . . it's a long story," he said finally. "All I know is, this whole thing—our lifestyle, our schedule, our family, our religion, whatever it is—just isn't working. Something's got to change."

"But you don't think you want to talk to Pastor Young?"

"Aw, he's a turkey . . ."

Just then, 1 A.M. or not, the phone rang.

"Sandy!" Kate exclaimed.

Marshall snatched up the receiver.

"Hello?"

"Hello?" said a female voice. "You're up!"

Marshall recognized the voice, with disappointment. It was Bernice.

"Oh, hi, Bernie," he said, looking at Kate, whose face sank now with frustration.

"Don't hang up! I'm sorry for calling at this late hour, but I had a date and I didn't get home until late, but I wanted to develop that film . . . are you mad?"

"I'll be mad tomorrow. Right now I'm too tired. What have you got?"

"Get this. I know the film in the camera had twelve pictures of the carnival, including the ones of Brummel, Young, and those three unknowns. Today I went home and shot the rest of the roll, twelve more frames—my cat, the neighbor lady with the big mole, the evening news, et cetera. Today's pictures came out."

There was a pause, and Marshall knew he would have to ask. "What about the other ones?"

"The emulsion was blacked out, totally exposed, the film scratched and fingerprinted in a few places. There's nothing wrong with the camera." Marshall said nothing for a long moment. "Marshall . . . hello?"

"That's interesting," he said.

"They're up to something! It's got me all excited. I'm wondering if I can trace those prints." There was another long pause. "Hello?"

"What did the other woman look like, the blonde one?"

"Not too old, long blonde hair . . . kind of mean looking."

"Heavy? Thin? In between?"

"She looked good."

Marshall's forehead crinkled a bit, and his eyes shifted about as he followed his ideas. "I'll see you in the morning."

"Good-bye, and thanks for answering."

Marshall hung up the phone. He stared at the tabletop, drumming his fingers.

"What was that all about?" Kate asked.

"Mmmmmm," he said, still thinking. Then he answered, "Uh, newspaper stuff. No biggie. What was it we were talking about, anyway?"

"Well, if it still matters, we were just talking about whether or not you should talk to Pastor Young about our problem—"

"Young," he said, and almost sounded angry.

"But if you don't want to . . ." Marshall stared at the table while his warm milk got cold. Kate waited, then roused him with, "Would you rather talk about this in the morning?"

"I'll talk to him," Marshall said flatly. "I . . . I want to talk to him. You *bet* I'll talk to him!"

"It couldn't hurt."

"No, it sure couldn't."

"I don't know when he'd be able to see you, but—"

"One o'clock would be nice." He scowled a bit. "One o'clock would be perfect."

"Marshall . . ." Kate started, but she kept it back. There was something happening to her husband, and she picked it up in his voice, in his expression.

She had never really missed that fire in his eyes; perhaps she'd never known it was gone until this moment when, for the first time since they left New York, she saw it again. Some old, unpleasant feelings rose up within her, feelings she had no desire to cope with late at night with her daughter mysteriously missing.

"Marshall," she said, sliding her chair out and picking up the plate of half-eaten toast, "let's get some sleep."

"I may not be able to sleep."

"I know," she said quietly.

All this time, Tal, Guilo, Nathan, and Armoth had stood in the room, carefully observing, and now Guilo began to chuckle in his gruff, quaking way.

Tal said with a smile, "No, Marshall Hogan. You never were much of a sleeper . . . and now Rafar has helped to awaken you again!"

7

On Tuesday morning the sun was shining through the windows and Mary was busy beating the daylights out of some bread dough. Hank found the name and number in the church records: the Reverend James Farrel. He had never met Farrel, and all he knew was the tasteless and malicious gossip going around about the man who had been his predecessor and had since moved far away from Ashton.

It was a whim, a stab in the dark, Hank knew that. But he sat down on the couch, picked up the phone, and dialed the number.

"Hello?" a tired older man's voice answered.

"Hello," said Hank, trying to sound pleasant despite his tight nerves. "James Farrel?"

"Yes. Who is this?"

"This is Hank Busche, pastor of the—" he heard Farrel give a drawn-out, knowledgeable sigh, "—Ashton Community Church. I guess you must know who I am."

"Yes, Pastor Busche. So how are you?"

How do I answer that, Hank wondered. "Uhh . . . okay in some respects."

"And not okay in other respects," Farrel offered, completing Hank's thought.

"Boy, you've really been keeping up on things."

"Well, not actively. I do hear from some of the members from time to time." Then he added quickly, "I'm glad you called. What can I do for you?"

"Uh . . . talk to me, I guess."

Farrel answered, "I'm sure there's a lot I could say to you. I do hear there's a congregational meeting this Friday. Is that true?"

"Yes, it is."

"A vote of confidence, I understand."

"That's right."

"Yes, I went through the same thing, you know. Brummel, Turner, Mayer, and Stanley were in charge of that one, too."

"You gotta be kidding."

"Oh, it's strictly history repeating itself, Hank. Take it from me."

"They drummed you out?"

"They decided they didn't like what I was preaching and the direction of my ministry, so they stirred up the congregation against me and then managed to take it to a vote. I didn't lose by much, but I did lose."

"The same four guys!"

"The same four . . . but now, did I hear right? Did you really put Lou Stanley out of fellowship?"

"Well, yeah."

"Now that is something. I can't imagine Lou letting anyone do that to him."

"Well, the other three made that a pivotal issue; they haven't left me alone about it."

"And how is the congregation leaning?"

"I don't know. They could be pretty evenly divided."

"So how are you standing up under all this?"

Hank could think of no better way to phrase it. He said, "I think I'm under attack—direct, spiritual attack." Silence at the other end. "Hello?"

"Oh, I'm here." Farrel talked slowly, falteringly, as if thinking hard while trying to converse. "What kind of spiritual attack?"

Hank stammered a bit. He could imagine how last night's experience would sound to a stranger. "Well . . . I just think Satan is really involved here . . ."

Farrel was almost demanding, "Hank, what kind of spiritual attack?"

Hank began his account carefully, trying very hard to sound like a sane and responsible individual as he related the major points: the mania Brummel seemed to have for getting rid of him, the church division, the gossip, the angry church board, the slogan painted on his house, and then the spiritual wrestling match he had gone through last night. Farrel interrupted only to ask clarifying questions.

"I know it all sounds crazy. . ." Hank concluded.

All Farrel could do was let out a deep sigh and mutter, "Oh, blast it all!"

"Well, like you say, it's just history repeating itself. No doubt you've encountered things like this, right? Or am I the one who has the real problem here?"

Farrel struggled with the words. "I am glad you called. I always struggled with whether or not I should call *you*. I don't know if you're going to like hearing this, but . . ." Farrel paused for new strength, then said, "Hank, are you sure you belong there?"

Uh-oh. Hank felt a defensiveness rising in him. "I do believe firmly in my heart that God called me here, yes."

"Do you know you were chosen as pastor by accident?"

"Well, some are saying that, but—"

"It is true, Hank. You really should consider that. You see, the church ousted me; they had some other minister all picked out and ready to move in, some guy who had a wide and liberal enough religious philosophy to suit them. Hank, I really don't know how you ended up with the job, but it was definitely some kind of organizational fluke. The one thing they did not want in there was another fundamentalist minister, not after they went to such great lengths to get rid of the one they had."

"But they voted me in."

"It was an *accident*. Brummel and the others were definitely not planning on it."

"Well, that's obvious now."

"Okay, good, you can see that. So let me just get right down to some direct advice. Now, after Friday this may all be moot anyway, but if I were you, I'd get packing and start looking for a position elsewhere, no matter how the vote comes out."

Hank deflated a little. This conversation was turning sour; he just couldn't buy it. All he could do was sigh into the phone.

Farrel was forceful. "Hank, I've been there, I've been through it, I know what you're going through, and I know what you have yet to go through. Believe me, it isn't worth it. Let them have that church, let them have the whole town; just don't sacrifice yourself."

"But I can't leave . . ."

"Yeah, right, you have a calling from God. Hank, so did I. I was ready to go into battle, to make a real stand in that town for God. You know, it cost me my home, my reputation, my health, it almost cost me my marriage. I left Ashton literally planning on changing my name. You have no idea of who you're really dealing with. There are forces at work in that town—"

"What kind of forces?"

"Well, political, social . . . spiritual too, of course."

"Oh yeah, you never did answer my question: what about what happened to me last night? What do you think about that?"

Farrel hesitated, then said, "Hank . . . I don't know why, but it's very difficult for me to talk about such things. All I can say to you is get out of that place while you can. Just drop it. The church doesn't want you there, the town doesn't want you there."

"I can't leave, I told you that."

Farrel paused for a long time. Hank was almost afraid he had hung up. But then he said, "All right, Hank. I'll tell you, and you listen. What you went through last night, well, I think I may have had similar experiences, but I can assure you, whatever it was, it was only the beginning."

"Pastor Farrel—"

"I'm not a pastor. Call me Jim."

"That's what the gospel is all about, fighting Satan, shining the light of the gospel into the darkness . . ."

"Hank, all the nice homilies you can dig up won't help you there. Now I don't know how equipped or ready you are, but to be perfectly honest, if you come through it all with even your life I'll be surprised. I'm serious!"

Hank had no other answer he could give. "Jim . . . I'll let you know how it turns out. Maybe I'll win, maybe I won't come out alive. But God didn't tell me I'd come out alive; He just told me to stay and fight. You've made one thing clear to me: Satan does want this town. I can't let him have it."

Hank replaced the receiver and felt he would cry.

"Lord God," he prayed, "Lord God, what shall I do?"

The Lord gave no immediate answer, and Hank sat there on the couch for several minutes trying to regather his strength and confidence. Mary was still busy in the kitchen. That was good. He couldn't talk to her right now; there were too many thoughts and feelings to be sorted out.

Then a verse came to his mind: "Arise, walk through the land in the length of it and in the breadth of it; for I will give it unto thee."

Well, it sure beat sitting home just fussing and fuming and not really doing anything. So on went his sneakers and out the door he went.

Krioni and Triskal were outside waiting for their charge. Invisibly they joined Hank, one on each side, and walked with him down Morgan Hill toward the center of town. Hank was not a man of great stature anyway, but between these two giants he looked even smaller. He did, however, appear very, very safe.

Triskal kept a wary eye open, saying, "What's he up to, anyway?"

Krioni knew Hank pretty well by now. "I don't think he even knows. The Spirit is driving him. He's giving action to a burden in his heart."

"Oh, we'll have action, all right!"

"Just don't be a threat. So far it's the best way to survive in this town."

"So tell that to the little pastor here."

As Hank neared the main business district he paused on a corner to look up and down the street, watching old cars, new cars, vans and four-by-fours, shoppers, walkers, joggers, and bicyclers stream in four and more directions, regarding the orders of the traffic light as mere suggestions.

So where was the evil? How could it be so vivid last night and a distant, dubious memory today? No demons or devils lurked in the office windows or reached out of the storm drains; the people were the same, simple, ordinary folks he had always seen, still ignoring him and passing by.

Yes, this was the town he prayed for night and day with deep groanings of the heart because of a burden he couldn't explain, and now it was taxing his patience, unsettling him.

"Well, are you in trouble or aren't you, or don't you even care?" he said aloud.

Nobody listened. No deep, sinister voices answered back with a threat.

But the Spirit of the Lord inside him wouldn't leave him alone. *Pray, Hank. Pray for these people. Don't let them escape your heart. The pain is there, the fear is there, the danger is there.*

So when do we win, Hank answered the Lord. Do You know how long I've been sweating and praying over this place? Just once I'd like to hear my little pebble make a splash; I'd like to see this dead dog twitch when I poke it.

It was amazing how well the demons could hide, even behind the doubts he sometimes felt about their very existence.

"I know you're out there," he said quietly, gazing carefully over the blankly staring faces of the buildings, the concrete, the brick, the glass, the trash. The spirits were teasing him. They could descend on him in a moment, terrorize and choke him, and then vanish, slipping back into the hiding places behind the facade of the town, snickering, hide-and-seeking, watching him grope about like a blind fool.

He sat down on a sidewalk bench feeling miffed.

"I'm here, Satan," he said. "I can't see you, and maybe you can move faster than I can, but I'm still here, and by the grace of God and the power of the Holy Spirit I intend to be a thorn in your side until one of us has had enough!"

Hank looked across the street at the impressive structure of the Ashton United Christian Church. Hank had known some terrific Christians who belonged to that denomination, but this particular bunch in Ashton were different, liberal, even bizarre. He had met Pastor Oliver Young a few times and could never get very close to him; Young seemed rather cold and aloof, and Hank could never figure out why.

As Hank sat there, watching a brown Buick pull into the church parking lot, Triskal and Krioni stood beside the bench, also watching the car come to a stop. Only the two of them could see the car's special passengers: sitting on the roof were two big warriors, the Arabian and the African, Nathan and Armoth. No swords were visible. They were taking a passive, noncombatant posture according to Tal's orders, just like all the rest.

Marshall had seen Bernice's film. He had seen the minute scratches from some kind of mishandling: he had seen the clumsy fingerprints at regular intervals that could very well have been placed there by a hand pulling the film out of the camera, unrolling it in the light.

Marshall had gotten his appointment with Young for 1 o'clock. He pulled into the vast, blacktop parking lot at 12:45, still downing a deluxe cheeseburger and large coffee.

Ashton United Christian was one of the large, stately-looking edifices around town, constructed in the traditional style with heavy stone, stained glass, towering lines, majestic steeple. The front door fit the motif: large, solid, even a little intimidating, especially when you tried to heave it open all by yourself. The church was located near the center of town, and the carillon in the tower chimed each hour and gave a short concert of hymns at noon. It was a respected establishment, Young was a respected minister, the people who attended the church were respected members of the community. Marshall had often thought that respect and status just might be a prerequisite for membership.

He engaged the big front door in a short Indian arm wrestle and finally got inside. No, this congregation had never spared the expense, that was for sure. The floors of the foyer, stairs, and sanctuary were covered with thick red carpeting, the woodwork was all deep finished oak and walnut. On top of that was all the brass: brass door handles, coat hooks, stairway railing, window latches. The windows, of course, were stained glass; and all the ceilings were lofty, with great hanging chandeliers and delicate scrollwork.

Marshall entered the sanctuary through another ponderous door and walked down the long center aisle toward the front. This room was a cross between an opera house and a cavern: the platform was big, the pulpit was big, the choir loft was big. Of course the choir was big, too.

Pastor Young's big office, just to the side of the sanctuary, afforded a very visible access to the platform and pulpit, and Pastor Young's entrance through the big oak door each Sunday morning was a traditional part of the ceremonies.

Marshall pushed that big door open and stepped into the reception office. The pretty secretary greeted him, but didn't know who he was. He told her, she checked the appointment book and verified it.

Marshall checked the book too, reading upside down again. The 2 o'clock hour was marked A. Brummel.

"Well, Marshall," Young said with a cordial, businesslike smile and handshake, "come in, come in."

Marshall followed Young into his plush office. Young, a large-framed man in his sixties with a roundish face, wire-rimmed glasses, and thin, well-oiled hair, seemed to enjoy his position both in the church and in the community. His dark-paneled walls sported many plaques from community and charitable organizations. Along with those were several framed photographs of him posing with the governor, a few popular evangelists, some authors, and a senator.

Behind his impressive desk Young created a perfect picture of the successful professional. The high-backed leather chair became a throne, and his own reflection in the desk top made him all the more scenic and impressive, like a mountain reflected in an alpine lake.

He motioned Marshall to a chair, and Marshall sat down, noticing that he sank to an eye level quite below Young's. He began to feel a familiar tinge of intimidation; this whole office seemed designed for it.

"Nice office," he commented.

"Thank you very much," said Young with a smile that shoved his cheeks into piles against his ears. He leaned back in his chair, his fingers interlaced and wiggling on the edge of his desk. "I enjoy it, am thankful for it, and I rather appreciate the warmth, the atmosphere of the place. It sets one at ease."

Sets *you* at ease, thought Marshall. "Yeah . . . yeah."

"So how is the *Clarion* these days?"

"Oh, pulling itself together. Did you get today's?"

"Yes, it was very good. Very neat, stylish. You've brought some of that big-city class here with you, I see."

"Mm-hmmm." Marshall suddenly didn't feel too talkative.

"I'm glad you're with us, Marshall. We're looking forward to a very good relationship."

"Well yeah, thanks."

"So what's on your mind?"

Marshall fidgeted just a little, then jumped to his feet; that chair made him feel too much like a microbe under a microscope. Next time I'll bring my own big desk, he thought. He walked around the office, trying to look casual.

"We've got a lot to cover in an hour," he began.

"We can always have more meetings."

"Yeah, sure. Well, first of all, Sandy—that's my daughter—ran off last night. We haven't heard anything, we don't know where she is . . ." He gave Young a quick synopsis of the problem and its history, and Young listened intently with no interruptions.

"So," Young finally asked, "you think she has turned her back on your traditional values and that disturbs you?"

"Hey, I'm not a deeply religious person, you know what I mean? But some things have to be right, and some things have to be wrong, and I have trouble with Sandy just—just jumping over the fence from one to the other like she does."

Young rose majestically from his desk and walked toward Marshall with the air of an understanding father. He put his hand on Marshall's shoulder and said, "Do you think she's happy, Marshall?"

"I never see her happy, but that's probably because she's around me every time I see her."

"And that could be because you find it hard to understand the direction she's now choosing for her life. Obviously you project a definite displeasure toward her philosophies . . ."

"Yeah, and toward that professor lady who dumps all those philosophies on her. You ever met that, what's her name, Professor Langstrat, out at the college?"

Young thought, then shook his head.

"I think Sandy's taken a couple of courses from her now, and every quarter I find my daughter more out of touch with reality."

Young chuckled a bit. "Marshall, it sounds like she's just exploring, just trying to find out about the world, about the universe she lives in. Don't you remember growing up? So many things just weren't true until you could prove them yourself. That's probably the way it is right now with Sandy. She's a very bright girl. I'm sure she just needs to explore, to find herself."

"Well, whenever she finds out where she is I hope she calls."

"Marshall, I'm sure she would feel much more free to call if she could find understanding hearts at home. It's not for us to determine what another person must do with himself, or think about his place in the cosmos. Each person must find his own way, his own truth. If we're ever going to get along like any kind of civilized family on this earth, we're going to have to learn to respect the other man's right to his own views."

Marshall felt a flash of *déjà vu,* as if a recording from Sandy's brain had been plugged into Young's. He couldn't help but ask, "You *sure* you never met Professor Langstrat?"

"Quite sure," Young answered with a smile.

"How about Alf Brummel?"

"Who?"

"Alf Brummel, the police chief."

Marshall watched his face. Was he struggling for an answer?

Young finally said, "I *may* have met him on occasion . . . I was just trying to match the name with the face."

"Well, he thinks the way you do. Talks a lot about getting along and being peaceful. How he got to be a cop, I'll never know."

"But weren't we talking about Sandy?"

"Yeah, okay. Speak on."

Young spoke on. "All the questions you're struggling with, the matters of right and wrong, or what truth is, or our different views of these issues . . . so many of these things are unknowable, save in the heart. We all feel the truth, like a common heartbeat in each of us. Every human has the natural capacity for good, for love, for expecting and striving for the best interests of himself and his neighbor."

"I guess you weren't here for the Festival."

Young chuckled. "I'll admit we humans can certainly misdirect our better inclinations."

"Say, *did* you make the Festival, by the way?"

"Yes, some parts of it. Most of it was of little interest to me, I'm afraid."

"So you didn't drop by the carnival, eh?"

"Certainly not. It's a waste of money. But about Sandy . . ."

"Yeah, we were talking about what's true, and everyone's view . . . like the whole subject of God, for example. She can't seem to find Him, I'm just trying to pin Him down, we can't agree on our religion, and so far you haven't helped much."

Young smiled thoughtfully. Marshall could feel a very lofty homily coming.

"Your God," said Young, "is where you find Him, and to find Him, we need only to open our eyes and realize that He is truly within all of us. We've never been without Him at all, Marshall; it's just that we've been blinded by our ignorance, and that has kept us from the love, security, and meaning that we all desire. Jesus revealed our problem on the cross, remember? He said, 'Father, forgive them, for they know not . . .' So His example to us is to search for knowledge, wherever we may find it. That's what you are doing, and I'm convinced that's what Sandy is doing. The source of your problem is a narrow perspective, Marshall. You must be open-minded. You must search, and Sandy must search."

"So," Marshall said thoughtfully, "you're saying it's all a matter of how we look at things?"

"That would be part of it, yes."

"And if I might perceive something a certain way, that doesn't mean everybody's going to see it that way, right?"

"Yes, that's right!" Young seemed very pleased with his student.

"So . . . let me see if I've got this right. If my reporter, Bernice Krueger, perceived that you, Brummel, and three other people were having some kind of little meeting behind the dart throwing booth at the carnival . . . well, that was just *her* perception of reality?"

Young smiled with an odd what-are-you-trying-to-pull grin, and answered, "I suppose so, Marshall. I guess that would be a case in point. I was nowhere near the carnival, and I told you that. I abhor that kind of event."

"You weren't there with Alf Brummel?"

"No, not at all. So you see, Ms. Krueger had quite an incorrect perception of someone else."

"Of *both* of you, I suppose."

Young smiled and shrugged.

Marshall pressed a little. "What do you suppose the odds are of that happening?"

Young kept smiling, but his face got a little red. "Marshall, what do you wish me to do? Argue with you? Certainly you didn't come here for that sort of thing."

Marshall took a real stab at whatever it might catch. "She even took some pictures of you."

Young sighed and looked for a moment at the floor. Then he said coolly, "Then why don't you bring those photographs next time, and then we can discuss it?"

The little smile on Young's face hit Marshall like spittle.

"Okay," Marshall muttered, not dropping his eyes.

"Marge will set another appointment for you."

"Thanks a lot."

Marshall checked his watch, went to the door, and opened it. "Come on in, Alf."

Alf Brummel had been sitting in the reception area. At the sight of Marshall he jumped awkwardly to his feet. He looked the way one might a split second before being hit by a train.

Marshall grabbed Alf by the hand and shook that hand excitedly. "Hey, buddy! Say, seeing as how the two of you don't seem to know each other very well, let me introduce you. Alf Brummel, this is Reverend Oliver Young. Reverend Young, Alf Brummel, chief of police!"

Brummel didn't seem to appreciate Marshall's cordiality at all, but Young did. He stepped forward, grabbed Brummel's hand, shook it, and then pulled Brummel quickly into his office saying over his shoulder, "Marge, make another appointment for Mr. Hogan."

But Mr. Hogan had left.

8

Sandy Hogan sat dismally at a small lunch table in a campus plaza shaded by an expansive grape arbor. She was staring at a slowly cooling, microwaved, packaged hamburger and a slowly warming half-pint carton of milk. She had made her classes that morning, but they had all slipped by her, mostly unabsorbed. Her mind was too much on herself, her family, and her belligerent father. Besides, it had been a horrible way to spend the night, walking clear across town and sitting all night in the Ashton bus depot reading from her psychology textbook. After her last class of the day she tried to take a nap out on the lawn in the sculpture garden and had managed to doze for a short time. When she awoke, her world was no better and she had only two impressions: hunger and loneliness.

Now, sitting at this little table with a machine-vended lunch, her loneliness was stealing away her hunger and she was on the brink of tears.

"Why, Daddy?" she whispered in very soft tones, dabbling her straw in her carton of milk. "Why can't you just love me for what I am?"

How could he have so much against her when he hardly even knew her? How could he be so adamant against her thoughts and philosophies when he couldn't even understand them? They were living in two different worlds, and each disdained the other's.

Last night she and her father had not said a word to each other the whole evening, and Sandy had gone to bed depressed and angry. Even as she lay there listening to her folks turning out the lights, brushing their teeth, and turning in for the night, they seemed half a world away. She wanted to call them into her room and reach out to them, but she knew it wouldn't work; Daddy would make demands and place conditions on their relationship instead of loving her, just loving her.

She still didn't know what had terrified her in the pit of the night. All she could remember was waking up plagued by every fear she had ever known—fear of dying, fear of failure, fear of loneliness. She had to get out of the house. She knew, even as she hastily dressed and ran out the door, that it was foolish and pointless, but the feelings were greater than any common sense she could muster.

Now she felt very much like some poor animal shot into space with no means of returning, floating listlessly, waiting for nothing in particular and with nothing to look forward to.

"Oh, Daddy," she whimpered, and then she began to cry.

She let her red hair fall down like soft blinds on either side of her face and the tears dropped one by one to the tabletop. She could hear people passing , but they chose to live in their own world and left her alone in hers. She tried to cry softly, which was hard to do when her emotions wanted to rush out of her like the cascade from a broken dam.

"Uh . . ." came a soft and hesitant voice, "Excuse me—"

Sandy looked up and saw a young man, blond, slightly thin, with big brown eyes full of compassion.

The young man said, "Please forgive me for intruding . . . but . . . is there anything I can do to help?"

It was dark in the living room of Professor Juleen Langstrat's apartment, and very, very quiet. One candle on the coffee table cast a dull yellow light on the ceiling-high bookcases, the strange oriental masks, the neatly arranged furniture, and the faces of two people who sat opposite each other, the candle between them. One of the people was the professor, her head resting against the back of her chair, her eyes closed, her arms outstretched in front of her, her hands making gentle sweeping motions as if she were treading water.

The man sitting opposite her was Brummel, also with eyes closed, but not mirroring Langstrat's expression and actions very well. He looked stiff and uncomfortable. At short intervals, and for a split second, he would crack his eyes open just enough to see what Langstrat was doing.

Then she began to moan and her face registered pain and displeasure. She opened her eyes and sat upright. Brummel looked back at her.

"You don't feel well today, do you?" she asked.

He shrugged and looked at the floor. "Ehhh, I'm okay. Just tired."

She shook her head, not satisfied with his answer. "No, no, it's the energy I feel from you. You're very disturbed."

Brummel had no answer.

"Did you talk to Oliver today?" she probed.

He hesitated, and finally said, "Yeah, sure."

"And you went to talk to him about our relationship."

That got a reaction. "No! That's—"

"Don't lie to me."

He wilted a little and let out a frustrated sigh. "Yeah, sure, we talked about it. We talked about other things too, though."

Langstrat probed him with her eyes as if doing some kind of X-ray scan. Her hands opened and began to wave in the air just slightly. Brummel tried to sink out of sight into his chair.

"Hey, listen," he said shakily, "it's no big deal—"

She began to speak as if reading off a note pinned on his chest. "You're . . . frightened, you feel cornered, you went to tell Oliver . . . you also feel controlled . . ." She looked at his face. "Controlled? By whom?"

"I don't feel controlled!"

She laughed a little to put him at ease. "Well, of course you do. I just read it."

Brummel looked for a split second toward the telephone on the end table. "Did Young call you?"

She smiled with amusement. "There was no need to. Oliver is very close to the Universal Mind. I'm beginning to meld with his thoughts now." Her expression hardened. "Alf, I really wish you were doing as well."

Brummel sighed again, hid his face behind his hands, then finally blurted, "Hey, listen, I can't tackle everything at once! There's just too much to learn!"

She put her hand on his comfortingly. "Well then, let's deal with these things one at a time. Alf?" He looked up at her. "You're frightened, aren't you? What are you frightened of?"

"You tell me," and it was almost a dare.

"I'm giving you a chance to speak first."

"Well then, I'm not frightened."

At least not until this very second, when Langstrat's eyes narrowed and began to bore into him.

"You are indeed frightened," she said sternly. "You are frightened because we were photographed the other night by that reporter from the *Clarion*. Isn't that right?"

Brummel pointed his finger at her angrily. "See, now that's exactly one of the things Young and I talked about! He called you! He had to have called you!"

She nodded, unabashed. "Yes, of course he called me. He withholds nothing from me. None of us withholds truth from all the others, you know that."

Brummel knew he might as well open up. "I'm concerned about the Plan. We're getting too big, too big to hide anymore; we're risking exposure in too many places. I think we were careless to meet out in public like that."

"But it's all been taken care of. There's nothing to worry about."

"Oh no? Hogan's on our scent! I suppose you know he was asking Oliver some very delicate questions?"

"Oliver can handle himself."

"So how do we handle Hogan?"

"The same way we handle anyone else. Are you aware that he talked to Oliver about problems he's having with his daughter? You should find that interesting."

"What kind of problems?"

"She's run away from home . . . and yet she still had the desire to be in my class today. I like the sound of that."

"So how do we use it?"

She smiled her cunning smile. "All in good time, Alf. We can't rush things."

Brummel got up and began to pace. "With Hogan I'm not so sure. He may not be the pushover that Harmel was. Maybe having Krueger arrested was the wrong thing to do."

"But you got access to the film; you had it destroyed."

He turned to face her. "And what did that get us? Before that they weren't asking any questions, and now they are! Come on, I know what I'd think if I got my camera back and the film was ruined. Hogan and Krueger just aren't that gullible."

Langstrat spoke soothingly, putting her arms around him like the tendrils of a vine. "Ah, but they are vulnerable, first to you, and ultimately to me."

"Just like everybody," he muttered.

He should have expected her reaction. She grew very cold and frightening and looked right into his eyes.

"And that," she said, "is another topic you discussed with Oliver today."

"He tells you everything!"

"The Masters would tell me even if he didn't."

Brummel tried to turn his eyes away from her. He couldn't stand whatever it was that made such beauty so immensely hideous.

"Look at me!" she insisted, and Brummel obeyed. "If you are not happy with our relationship, I can always have it terminated."

He looked down, stuttered a bit. "It's—it's okay . . ."

"What?"

"I mean I'm happy with our relationship."

"Truly happy?"

He felt desperate to appease her, to get her to let go of him. "I . . . I just don't want things to get out of control . . ."

She gave him a slow, vampirish kiss. "You are the one who needs more control. Haven't I always taught you that?"

She was cutting him to pieces and he knew it, but she had him. He belonged to her.

He still had a concern he couldn't shake. "But how many adversaries can we continue to remove? It seems like every time we get rid of one, bingo, another pops up in his place. Harmel went out, in came Hogan . . ."

She completed the thought for him. "You took care of Farrel, and in came Henry Busche."

"It can't go on. The odds are against us."

"Busche is as good as gone. Isn't there a confidence vote this Friday?"

"The congregation is getting good and upset. But . . ."

"Yes?"

"You know he removed Lou Stanley from the church for adultery?"

"Ah, yes. That should help the congregation decide."

"A lot of them agreed with that move!"

She backed away in order to gaze at him better, freezing his blood with her eyes. "Are you afraid of Henry Busche?"

"Listen, he still has a lot of support in the church, more than I thought he did."

"You *are* afraid of him!"

"Somebody's on his side, I don't know who. And what if he finds out about the Plan?"

"He will never find out anything!" If she had fangs, they would have been showing. "He will be destroyed as a minister long before then. You will see to that, won't you?"

"I'm working on it."

"Do not bow to this Henry Busche! He bows to you, and you bow to me!"

"I'm working on it, I said!"

She relaxed and smiled. "Next Tuesday, then?"

"Ehh . . ."

"We'll celebrate Busche's Friday demise. You can tell me all about it."

"What about Hogan?"

"Hogan is a limp and weakened fool. Don't worry about him. He's not your responsibility."

Before Brummel knew it, he was standing outside her back door. Langstrat watched him through her window until he drove off, taking the usual alley route where he would not be seen. She opened the drapes to let some light in, extinguished the candle on the coffee table, then took a folder from her desk drawer.

Soon she had arranged in neat piles the life histories, personality profiles, and current photographs of Marshall, Kate, and Sandy Hogan. When her eyes fell on the photograph of Sandy, they glinted maliciously.

Hovering invisibly over Langstrat's shoulder was a huge black hand adorned with jeweled rings and bracelets of gold. A deep and seductive voice spoke thoughts to her mind.

Tuesday afternoon at the *Clarion* resembled a battlefield after everyone is either dead or retreated. The place was deathly quiet. George, the typesetter, usually took the day after publishing off to recover from the wild deadline race. Tom, the paste-up man, was out covering a local story.

As for Edie, the secretary/reporter/ad girl, she had resigned and walked off the job last night. Marshall had not known that she once was happily married, but gradually became unhappily married, and finally got a little thing going with a trucker that resulted in a very recent blow-up at home, with pieces of marriage flying everywhere and spouses fleeing abruptly in opposite directions. Now she was gone, and Marshall could feel the sudden void.

Bernice and he sat alone in the glass-enclosed office at the back of the little newsroom/ad room/front office. From his secondhand, ten-dollar desk Marshall could look through the glass and survey the three desks, two typewriters, two wastebaskets, two telephones, and one coffeemaker. Everything looked cluttered and busy, with papers and copy lying everywhere, but absolutely nothing was happening.

"I don't suppose you know where everything is?" he asked Bernice.

Bernice was sitting up on the worktable adjacent to Marshall's desk, her back against the wall, stirring a personalized mug of hot chocolate.

"Aw, we'll find it all," she answered. "I know where she kept the books, and I'm sure her Rolodex has all the addresses and phone numbers."

"What about the cord to the coffeemaker?"

"Why do you think I'm drinking hot chocolate?"

"Nuts. I wish somebody would've told me."

"I don't think anybody really knew."

"We'd better get an ad in for a new secretary this week. Edie carried more than her weight around here."

"I guess it was a bad blow-up. She's leaving town for good, before her husband's black eyes heal up and he can see to find her."

"Affairs. Nothing good ever comes of 'em."

"So have you heard the latest about Alf Brummel?"

Marshall looked up at her. She perched on the worktable like some coy bird, trying to look more interested in her hot chocolate than in the spicy news.

"Under the circumstances," he said, "I'm dying to hear it."

"I had lunch with Sara, his secretary, today. Guess he's gone for several hours every Tuesday afternoon and never says where, but Sara knows. Guess our friend Alf has a special girlfriend."

"Yeah, Juleen Langstrat, psychology prof out at the college."

That ruined it for Bernice. "How did you know?"

"The blonde woman you saw that night, remember? The day after one of my reporters gets busted for taking the wrong pictures at the carnival, Langstrat kicks me out of her class. Add to that Oliver Young's ears getting all red when he told me he didn't know her."

"You're brilliant, Hogan."

"Just a good guesser."

"She and Brummel do have *something* going. He calls it therapy, but I think he enjoys it, if you get my drift."

"So what's Young's connection to either of them?"

Bernice didn't hear his question. "Too bad Brummel isn't already married. I could have done more with it."

"Hey, reset your frequency, will you? We've got a little club here, and all *three* of these people are members."

"Sorry."

"What we're really after is whatever it is they don't want us to know, especially if—and I mean IF— it's worth trumping up a false arrest to cover up."

"*And* destroying my film."

"I wonder if any of those fingerprints on the film would tell us something?"

"Not much. They're not on file."

Marshall twisted in his chair to face her more directly. "All right, who do you know?"

Bernice was smug. "I have an uncle who's very close to Justin Parker's office."

"The county prosecutor?"

"Sure. He does just about anything for me."

"Hey, don't bring them into this, not yet . . ."

Bernice raised her hands as if he were pointing a gun at her and assured him, "Not yet, not yet."

"But I'm not saying they won't come in handy."

"Don't think I haven't thought of that."

"So tell me this: did Brummel ever apologize?"

"After you bowed to him the way you did, are you kidding?"

"No official, signed apology from him and his office?"

"Is that what he told you?"

Marshall had to sneer. "Aw, both Brummel and Young told me all kinds of things—how they hardly knew each other, how they were never anywhere near the carnival . . . boy, I just wish we had those pictures."

Bernice was offended. "Hey, you *can* believe me, Hogan. You really can!"

Marshall looked into space for a second or two, musing. "Brummel and Langstrat. Therapy. I guess that makes sense now . . ."

"C'mon, let's get all the pieces out on the table."

What pieces? Marshall thought. How do you lay out vague feelings, strange experiences, vibes?

He finally said, "Uh . . . this Brummel and Langstrat . . . they're both into the same kind of thing. I can tell."

"*What* kind of thing?"

Marshall felt cornered. "How about . . . whammies?"

Bernice looked puzzled. Oh c'mon, Krueger, don't make me have to explain it.

She said, "You'll have to explain that to me."

Oh boy, here we go, Marshall thought. "Well . . . now it's gonna sound crazy, but when I talked to each of them—and you ought to try it sometime—each of them had this weird, gooney-eyed thing they did . . . kind of like they were hypnotizing me or something . . ."

Bernice started to crack up.

"Ehhh, go ahead, laugh."

"What are you saying? That they're all into some kind of Svengali trip?"

"I don't know how to label it yet, but yeah. Brummel's not nearly as good at it as Langstrat. He smiles too much. Young might be into it too, but he uses words. Lots of words."

Bernice studied his face for just the slightest moment and then said, "I think you need a good, stiff drink. Would a hot chocolate do?"

"Sure, get me one. Please."

Bernice returned with another personalized mug—Edie's—full of hot chocolate. "Hope it's strong enough," she said, and hopped back onto the table.

"So why do those three try to look unconnected . . ." Marshall mused. "And what about the other two unknowns, Pudgy and the Ghost? You've never seen them before?"

"Never. They could have been out-of-towners."

Marshall sighed. "It's a dead end."

"Maybe not yet. Brummel does go to that little white church, Ashton Community, and I heard somebody just got kicked out of there for shacking up or something . . ."

"Bernice, that's gossip!"

"What would you say, then, to my talking to a friend on the Whitmore faculty who might be able to tell me something about this mysterious professor lady?"

Marshall looked doubtful. "Please don't make any more problems for me. I have enough as it is."

"Sandy?"

Back to the really tough subjects. "We haven't heard a thing yet, but we're still calling around, checking with relatives and friends. We're sure she'll come home sooner or later."

"Isn't she in Langstrat's class?"

Marshall answered with some bitterness, "She's been in *several* of Langstrat's classes—" Then he paused. "Don't you think we might be blurring the line between unbiased journalism and . . . personal vengeance?"

Bernice shrugged. "I'll only find what's really there, and it'll be news or it won't be. In the meantime, I thought perhaps you'd appreciate a little background."

Marshall couldn't shake off the memory of his encounter with the fiery Juleen Langstrat, and he hurt more deeply every time he recalled the professor's ideas coming at him through the mouth of his own daughter.

"If it's a stone, turn it over," he said finally.

"On my time or the *Clarion's?*"

"Just turn it over," he said, and started pounding his typewriter.

9

That evening Marshall and Kate set three places at the dinner table. It was an act of faith, trusting that Sandy would be there just as she always had been. They had called everyone they knew, but no one had seen Sandy anywhere. The police hadn't turned up anything. They had called the college to check whether or not Sandy had been to her classes that day, but so far none of her professors or teaching assistants could be reached for a definite answer.

Marshall sat at the table, staring at Sandy's empty chair. Kate sat across from him, silent, waiting for the rice to steam.

"Marshall," she said, "don't torture yourself."

"I blew it. I'm a wash-out!"

"Oh, stop it!"

"And the problem is, now that I know I blew it, there isn't much chance of a retake."

Kate reached across the table and took his hand. "There certainly is. She'll come back. She's old enough to be reasonable and take care of herself. I mean, just look at how much she took with her. She can't be planning on being gone indefinitely."

Just then the doorbell rang. They both jumped a little.

"Yeah," said Marshall, "go ahead, be the mailman, or a Girl Scout selling cookies, or a Jehovah's Witness. . . !"

"Well, Sandy wouldn't ring the doorbell anyway."

Kate got up to answer the door, but Marshall hurried ahead of her. They both reached the door at about the same time and Marshall opened it.

Neither of them expected a young man, blond and neat, college material. He carried no leaflets or religious propaganda and seemed shy.

"Mr. Hogan?" he asked.

"Yeah," said Marshall. "Who are you?"

The young man was quiet but assertive enough to do business. "My name is Shawn Ormsby. I'm a junior at Whitmore and a friend of your daughter Sandy."

Kate started to say, "Well, please come in," but Marshall interrupted with, "Do you know where she is?"

Shawn paused, then answered carefully, "Yes. Yes, I do."

"Well?" said Marshall.

"May I come in?" he asked politely.

Kate nodded graciously, stepping aside and almost pushing Marshall aside. "Yes, please do."

They showed him into the living room and let him have a seat. Kate held Marshall's hand just long enough to get him into a chair and silently remind him to control himself.

"Thank you very much for coming," Kate said. "We've been very concerned."

Marshall's voice was controlled as he said, "What've you got?"

Shawn was visibly uncomfortable.

"I . . . I met her on campus yesterday."

"She went to *school* yesterday?" Marshall blurted, startled.

"Let him talk, Marshall," Kate reminded him.

"Well," said Shawn, "yes. Yes, she did. But I met her in Jones Plaza, an outdoor eating area. She was by herself and so visibly upset that, well, I just felt I had to get involved."

Marshall was sitting on pins and needles. "What do you mean, visibly upset? Is she okay?"

"Oh, yes! She's perfectly all right. That is, she hasn't come to any harm. But . . . I'm here on her behalf." This time both parents were listening without interrupting, so Shawn continued. "We talked for quite a while and she told me her side of the story. She really does want to come home; I should tell you that first."

"But?" Marshall prompted.

"Well, Mr. Hogan, that's the first thing I tried to persuade her to do, but . . . if you can accept this, she feels afraid to come back, and I think a little ashamed."

"Because of me?"

Shawn was walking on some very thin ice. "Can you . . . are you able to accept that?"

Marshall was ready to be tough on himself. "Yeah, I can accept that, all right. I've been asking for it for years. I had it coming."

Shawn looked relieved. "Well, that's what I'm trying, in my own weak, limited way, to accomplish. I'm no professional—my major's geology—but I'd just like to see this family together again."

Kate said humbly, "We would too."

"Yeah," said Marshall, "we really want to work on it. Listen, Shawn, you get to know me and you'll realize I came out of a pretty bent mold and I'm really tough to straighten out . . ."

"No, you didn't!" Kate protested.

"Yeah, yeah, I did. But I'm learning all the time. I want to keep on learning." He leaned forward in his chair. "Say . . . I take it Sandy sent you here to see us?"

Shawn looked out the window. "She's out in the car right now."

Kate was on her feet immediately. Marshall grabbed her hand and settled her back into her seat.

"Hey," he said, "who's being overanxious now?" He turned to Shawn. "How is she? Is she still afraid? Does she think I'm going to jump on her?"

Shawn nodded meekly.

"Well," said Marshall, feeling emotions he really didn't want anyone to see, "listen, tell her I won't jump on her. I won't yell, I won't accuse, I won't get sly or nasty. I just . . . well, I . . ."

"He loves her," Kate said for him. "He really does."

"Do you, sir?" Shawn asked.

Marshall nodded.

"Tell me." said Shawn. "Say it."

Marshall looked right in his eyes. "I love her, Shawn. She's my kid, my daughter. I love her and I want her back."

Shawn smiled and rose from his seat. "I'll bring her in."

That evening there were four place settings at the table.

The Friday edition of the *Clarion* was on the streets, and the usual postpublication lull around the office gave Bernice the chance she needed to do some hoofing. She had been waiting eagerly for a chance to get over to Whitmore College to talk to some people. A few phone calls had landed her an important lunch appointment.

The North Campus Cafeteria was a new addition, a modern red-brick structure with floor-to-ceiling blue-tinted windows and carefully kept flower gardens. One could eat inside at a small two- or-four-person table, or sit on the patio in the sunshine. The format was buffet, and the food wasn't bad.

Bernice stepped onto the patio carrying a tray with coffee and a light salad. Alongside her was Ruth Williams, a cheerful middle-aged professor in economics, carrying a taco salad.

They chose a secluded table in the semishade. For the first half of their meal they indulged in small talk and general catching up.

But Williams knew Bernice pretty well by now.

"Bernice," she said at last, "I can tell you have something on your mind."

Bernice was able to be honest with her friend. "Ruth, it's something unprofessional and distasteful."

"Do you mean to say you've uncovered something new?"

"Oh, no, not about Pat. No, that subject's been dormant for quite some time. You can be sure it will reawaken if anything new comes up, though." Bernice looked at Williams for a long moment. "You don't think I'll ever find anything, do you?"

"Bernice, you know that I support you in your efforts one hundred percent, but with that support I must add my sincere doubts that your efforts will ever uncover anything. It was just so . . . futile. So tragic."

Bernice shrugged. "Well, that's why I'm trying to focus my efforts only where they'll do some good. Which brings me to the uncomfortable subject for the day. Did you know I was arrested and jailed Sunday night?"

Williams was, of course, incredulous. "Jailed? Whatever for?"

"Soliciting an undercover cop for an act of prostitution."

That brought the right response from Williams. Bernice went on to tell her as much of the indignities as she could remember.

"I can't believe it!" Williams kept saying. "That is disgusting! I can't believe it!"

"Well, anyway," Bernice said, bringing in the punch line, "I feel I have good cause to question Mr. Brummel's motives. Mind you, I only have theory and speculation, but I want to chase these things to their end to see if anything really lies behind them."

"Well, I can understand that. And what could I possibly know that would help you?"

"Have you ever met Professor Juleen Langstrat, over in the Psychology Department?"

"Oh . . . once or twice. We shared a table at a faculty luncheon."

Bernice caught a glint of distaste in Williams's expression. "Hmmmm. Something wrong with her?"

"Well, to each his own," said Williams, stirring her salad absent-mindedly with her fork. "But I found her very difficult to relate to. It was next to impossible to start any coherent conversation."

"How does she carry herself? Is she forceful, retiring, assertive, obnoxious . . . ?"

"Aloof, for one thing, and I guess mysterious, although I use that word for lack of one better. I get the impression that people are nothing but a bore to her. Her academic interests are very esoteric and metaphysical, and she seems to prefer them to bland reality."

"What kind of company does she keep?"

"I wouldn't know. I'd almost be surprised to find her consorting with anyone at all."

"So you've never seen her in the company of Alf Brummel?"

"Oh, and this must be the ultimate goal of your questions. No, never at all."

"But I guess you don't see her much anyway."

"She's not very social, so no. But listen, I really try to mind my own business, if you catch my meaning. I would definitely like to help you in any way I can to satisfy yourself concerning Pat's death, but what you're after this time is—"

"Unprofessional and distasteful."

"Yes, you were certainly right on that score. But, accompanied with my own advice to disengage yourself from this thing, let me, as a friend, refer you to someone who might know more. Have your pencil ready? His name is Albert Darr, and he's in the Psychology Department. From what I've heard, mostly from him, he rubs shoulders with Langstrat every day, doesn't like her at all, and loves to gossip. I'll even go so far as to call him for you."

Albert Darr, a baby-faced young professor with stylish clothes and a certain penchant for ladies, just happened to be in his office grading papers. He had time to talk, especially to the lovely reporter from the *Clarion*.

"Well, hello, hello," he said as Bernice came in the door.

"Well, hello hello yourself," she responded. "Bernice Krueger, the friend of Ruth Williams."

"Uh . . ." He looked to and fro for an empty chair, and finally moved a pile of reference books. "Have a seat. Pardon the mess." He sat down on another pile of books and papers that might have had a chair under it. "What can I do for you?"

"Well, this isn't really an official visit, Professor Darr—"

"Albert."

"Thank you. Albert. I'm actually here on a personal matter, but if my theories are right, it could be important in a newsworthy sense." She paused to indicate a new paragraph and a difficult question. "Now, Ruth tells me you know Juleen Langstrat—"

Darr suddenly smiled broadly, leaned back in his piled-up chair, and rested his hands behind his neck. This was going to be an enjoyable subject for him, it seemed.

"Ahhhh," he said gleefully, "so you dare to infringe on sacred ground!" Darr looked around the room in mock suspicion, searching for imaginary eavesdroppers, then leaned forward and said in a lowered voice, "Listen, there are certain things no one is supposed to know, not even myself." Then he brightened up again and said, "But our dear professor has had many an occasion to hurt and slight me and therefore I feel indebted to her not in the least. I'm dying to answer your questions."

Evidently Bernice could just dive right in; this guy didn't seem to need formalities.

"Okay, to begin with," she said, readying her pen and pad, "I'm really trying to find out about Alf Brummel, the chief of police. I've been informed that he and Langstrat see a lot of each other. Can you verify that?"

"Oh, definitely."

"So . . . they do have something going?"

"What do you mean, 'something'?"

"You fill in the blank."

"If you mean a romantic fling . . ." He smiled and shook his head. "Oh dear. I don't know if you'll like this answer, but no, I don't think anything like that is going on."

"But he does see her quite regularly."

"Oh yes, but a lot of people do. She gives consultations in her off hours. Tell me now, doesn't Brummel see her on a weekly basis?"

With ebbing spirit Bernice answered, "Yes, every Tuesday. On the dot."

"Well, there, you see? He goes to her for regular weekly sessions."

"But why won't he tell anybody? He's very secretive about it."

He leaned forward and lowered his voice. "Everything Langstrat does is a deep, dark secret! The Inner Circle, Bernice. No one is even supposed to know about these so-called consultations, no one but the privileged, the elite, the powerful, the many special patrons that go to her. That's the way she is."

"But what's she up to?"

"Mind you now," he said with a mischievous glint in his eye, "this is privileged information, and I might also caution you that it is not entirely reliable. I know very little of this from direct observation; most of it I've just managed to pick up around the department here. Fortunately, Professor Langstrat has made enough enemies that few of the staff feel any commitment or loyalty to her." He repositioned himself into an eye-to-eye posture. "Bernice, Professor Langstrat is, how should I say it? Not a . . . ground level person. Her areas of study go beyond anything the rest of us have had any desire to tamper with: the Source, the Universal Mind, the Ascended Planes . . ."

"I'm afraid I don't know what you're talking about."

"Oh, none of us know what she's talking about either. Some of us are very concerned; we don't know if she's very brilliant and making some real breakthroughs, or if she's somewhat deranged."

"Well, what is all this stuff, this Source, and this Mind?"

"All right. Uh . . . as nearly as we can tell, she derives it from the Eastern religions, the old mystic cults and writings, things I know nothing about and don't want to know anything about. As far as I'm concerned, her studies in these areas have caused her to lose all contact with reality. As a matter of fact, I may even be mocked and maligned among my peers for saying this, but I don't see Langstrat's advances in these areas as anything other than foolish, neo-pagan witchcraft. I think she's desperately confused!"

Bernice now recalled to mind Marshall's strange descriptions of Langstrat. "I've heard she does strange things to people—"

"Foolishness. Sheer foolishness. I think she believes she can read my mind, control me, put spells on me, whatever. I simply dismiss it and try very hard to be elsewhere."

"But does any of it have credence?"

"Absolutely not. The only people she can control or affect are the poor dupes in the Inner Circle who are stupid and gullible enough to—"

"The Inner Circle . . . you used that term before . . ."

He held up his hand to caution her. "No facts, no facts. I coined that title myself. All I have is a two here and a two there, which make a very persuasive four. I've heard her admit that she counsels these people who come to her, and I've noticed that some of them are quite important. But how could a counselor with such warped ideas possibly straighten out anyone else? Then again . . ."

"Yes?"

"I would expect her to . . . claim a special advantage in such a situation. Who knows, maybe she holds seances and mind-reading sessions. Maybe she cooks slug tails and newt's eyes and serves them with breaded spider legs to evoke some answer from the supernatural . . . but now I'm getting facetious."

"But you do see this as a possibility?"

"Well not nearly as bizarre as I've described, but yes, something along those lines, in keeping with her occult interests."

"And these people in the Inner Circle see her regularly?"

"As far as I know. I really have no idea how it's set up or why people even go. What on earth could they be getting out of it?"

"Can you give me some for-instances?"

"Well . . ." He thought for a moment. "Of course, we've already mentioned and verified your Mr. Brummel. Oh, and you might know of Ted Harmel?"

Bernice just about dropped her pen. "*Ted?*"

"Yes, the former editor of the *Clarion.*"

"I worked for him, before he left and Hogan bought the paper."

"Uh, the way I understand it, Mr. Harmel didn't just 'leave.' "

"No, he fled. But who else?"

"Mrs. Pinckston, a trustee on the board of regents."

"Ah, so it's not just men."

"Oh, certainly not."

Bernice kept writing. "Go on, go on."

"Oh dear, who else? Uh, I think Dwight Brandon . . ."

"Who's Dwight Brandon?"

Darr looked at her condescendingly. "He only owns the property the college is built on."

"Ohhhh . . ." She wrote the name down with a bold lettered explanation.

"Oh, and then there's Eugene Baylor. He's general treasurer, a very influential man on the board of regents, I understand. It seems he's been needled just a little about whatever it is he and the professor do in their sessions together, but he remains self-righteous and steadfast in his convictions."

"Hmm."

"Ah, and there's also that reverend fellow, that . . . uh . . ."

"Oliver Young."

"How did *you* know?"

Bernice only smiled. "A lucky guess. Carry on."

10

On Friday evening Hank couldn't get the upcoming business meeting off his mind, which was probably to his advantage considering the young lady sitting across from him in his little office corner of the house. He had asked Mary to stick closely around and act very loving and wifely. This young lady—Carmen was the only name she gave—was quite a case load. The way she dressed and carried herself, Hank made sure that it was Mary who answered her knock at the door and let her in. But as far as Hank could tell, Carmen wasn't trying to put on a facade; she seemed real enough, just sincerely overdone. And as for her reasons for wanting counseling . . .

"I think," she began, "I think I'm just very lonely, and that's why I keep hearing voices . . ."

Immediately she examined their faces for their reaction. But after their recent experiences nothing sounded too far out to Hank and Mary.

Hank asked, "What kind of voices? What kind of things do they say?"

She thought for a moment, searching the ceiling with big, overly innocent blue eyes.

"What I'm experiencing is legitimate," she said. "I'm not crazy."

"No problem there," Hank said. "But tell us about these voices. When do they talk to you?"

"When I'm alone, especially. Like last night, I was lying in bed and . . ." she related the words the voice spoke to her, and it could have been a perfect script for an obscene phone call.

Mary didn't know what to say; this was becoming heavy. To Hank it sounded kind of familiar, and though he felt very cautious about Carmen and her motives, he still remained open to the possibility that she was encountering some of the same demonic forces he'd been dealing with.

"Carmen," he asked, "do these voices ever say who they are?"

She thought for a moment. "I think one of them was Spanish or Italian. He had an accent, and his name was Amano, or Amanzo, or something like that. He always spoke very soothingly and always said he wanted to make love to me . . ."

Just then the phone rang. Mary quickly got up to answer it.

"Hurry back," said Hank.

She hurried away, that was for sure. Hank was watching her go when he felt Carmen touching his hand.

"You don't think I'm crazy, do you?" she asked with pleading eyes.

"Uh . . ." Hank withdrew his hand to scratch a nonexistent itch. "No, Carmen, I'm not—I mean I don't. But I do want to know where these voices came from. When did you first start hearing them?"

"When I came to Ashton. My husband left me and I came here to start over, but . . . I get so lonely."

"You first started hearing them when you came to Ashton?"

"I think it was because I was lonely. And I still am lonely."

"What was it they said at first? How did they introduce themselves?"

"I was alone, and lonely, I'd just moved here, and I thought I heard Jim's voice. You know, my husband . . ."

"Go on."

"I really thought it was him. I didn't even think about how he could talk to me without being there, but I talked back and he told me how much he missed me, and how he thought it would be better this way, and he spent the rest of the night with me." She began to shed some tears. "It was beautiful."

Hank didn't know what to make of this. "Incredible," was all he could say.

She looked at him with those big pleading eyes again and said through her tears, "I knew you'd believe me. I've heard about you. They say you're a very compassionate man, and very understanding . . ."

Depends on who you listen to, Hank thought, but then her hand was touching his again. Time to call a recess, Hank thought.

"Uh," he said, trying to be comforting, sincere, and nonjudgmental. "Listen, I think it's been a fruitful hour . . ."

"Oh, yes!"

"Would you like to come again, next week sometime?"

"Oh, I'd love to!" she exclaimed, as if Hank had asked her for a date. "I've so much more to tell you!"

"Well, okay, I think next Friday will be fine for me if it's fine for you."

Oh, it was, it was, and Hank stood up to give her the hint that the session was over for now. They hadn't covered much ground, but as far as Hank was concerned, boy, was it enough.

"Now let's both take some time to think about these things. After a week they may be a little clearer to us. They might make more sense." Where, oh where was Mary?

Ah, she came back into the room. "Oh, leaving so soon?"

"It was wonderful!" Carmen sighed, but at least she had let go of Hank's hand.

Getting Carmen out the door was easier than Hank had expected. Good old Mary. What a lifesaver.

Hank closed the door and leaned against it.

"Whew!" was all he could say.

"Hank," Mary said in a very hushed voice, "I don't think I like this!"

"She's . . . she's a real hot one, she is."

"What do you think of what she said?"

"Ehhhhh, I'll wait and see. Who was that on the phone?"

"Just wait until you hear this! It was some lady from the *Clarion* wanting to know if it was Alf Brummel we disfellowshipped from the church!"

Hank suddenly looked like an inflatable toy that had sprung a leak.

A little disappointed, Bernice walked into Marshall's office.

Marshall was at his desk, going over some new advertising copy for Tuesday's edition.

"So what'd they say?" he asked her without looking up.

"Nope, it isn't Brummel, and I guess it wasn't a very tactful question. I talked to the pastor's wife, and by her tone of voice I can infer that the whole subject is very touchy."

"Yeah, I've heard talk at the barbershop. Some guy was saying they're going to vote the pastor out tonight."

"Ah, so they do have troubles."

"But totally unrelated to ours, and I'm glad. It's gone far enough." Marshall looked again at the list of names Bernice had gotten from Albert Darr. "How am I supposed to get any work done around here with this kind of stuff hanging around unresolved? Bernie, you're getting to be a lot of trouble, you know that?"

She took it as a compliment. "And have you looked over that flyer of elective courses Langstrat is teaching?"

Marshall picked it up from his desk and could only shake his head incredulously. "What in blazes is all this stuff? 'Introduction to God and Goddess Consciousness and the Craft: the divinity of man, witch, warlock, the Sacred Medicine Wheel, how do spells and rituals work?' You gotta be kidding!"

"Read on, boss!"

" 'Pathways to Your Inner Light: meet your own spiritual guides, discover the light within . . . harmonize your mental, physical, emotional, and spiritual levels of being through hypnosis and meditation.' " Marshall read a little further and then exclaimed, "What? 'How to Enjoy the Present by Experiencing Past and Future Lives.' "

"I like that one near the bottom there: 'In the Beginning Was the Goddess'. Langstrat, perhaps?"

"Why hasn't anyone heard about all this before?"

"For some reason it was never advertised in the school paper or in the public list of classes. Albert Darr gave me the flyer himself and said it was a somewhat exclusive pass-around item among the interested students."

"And my little Sandy is sitting in this woman's class . . ."

"And in a way so are all those people on the list."

Marshall set down the flyer and picked up the list. He shook his head again; it was all he could think of to do.

Bernice added, "I guess I don't mind it too much if a bunch of dupes want to be taken in by this Langstrat, but they're all too important! Just look at that: Two of the college regents, the owner of the college land, the county comptroller, the district judge!"

"And Young! Respected, revered, influential, community-involved Oliver Young!" Marshall let some memory tapes play in his head. "Yeah, it fits, it makes sense now, all that vague, noncommittal stuff he was handing me in his office. Young's got a religion all his own. He's no hard-shell Baptist, I'll tell you that!"

"Religion I don't care about. Lies and cover-ups I do!"

"Well, he most certainly denied knowing Langstrat. I asked him directly, right to his face, and he told me he didn't know her."

"Somebody's lying," Bernice sing-songed.

"But I just wish we had some more corroboration."

"Yeah, we've only just met Darr."

"What about Ted Harmel? How well did you know him?"

"Well enough, I suppose. You heard why he left?"

Marshall sneered just a bit. "Brummel said there was some kind of scandal, but who can you believe these days?"

"Ted denied it."

"Aw, everybody's saying everything and everybody's denying everything."

"Well, call him anyway. I have the number. He's living up near Windsor now. I think he's trying to be a hermit."

Marshall looked at all the advertising copy still on his desk, awaiting his time and attention. "How am I going to get any of this stuff done around here?"

"Hey, it's no biggie. If I could do some independent hoofing, the least you can do is give Ted a call. Do it tomorrow . . . Saturday, your day off. Reporter to reporter, newsman to newsman. You might hit it off with him."

Marshall sighed. "Let's have the number."

Mary finished the dinner dishes, put up the towel, and made her way through the little house to the back bedroom. There, in the dark, Hank knelt beside the bed in prayer. She knelt down beside him, took his hand, and together they placed themselves in the hands of the Lord. God's will would be done this night, and they would accept it, whatever it was.

Alf Brummel had a key to the church and was already there, switching on the lights and turning up the thermostat. He wasn't feeling well at all. They'd just better vote right this time, he kept thinking.

Outside, even though it was still a half hour before the meeting, cars began to arrive, more than were usually there on Sundays. Sam Turner, Brummel's chief cohort, drove up in his big Cadillac and helped his wife Helen from the car. He was a rancher of sorts, not a land baron, but he acted like one. Tonight he was grim and determined, as was his wife. In another car came John Coleman and his wife Patricia, a quiet couple who came to Ashton Community after leaving a large church elsewhere in town. They really liked Hank and made no effort to hide it. They knew well that Alf Brummel would not be happy to see them there.

Others arrived and quickly coagulated into little clusters of similar sentiment, speaking in quick syllables and hushed tones and keeping their eyes to themselves, except for a few rubbernecking nose-counters trying to foresee the final tally.

Several dark shadows kept a wary eye on everything from their perch atop the church roof, their stations around the building, or their appointed posts in the sanctuary.

Lucius, more nervous than ever, paced and hovered about. Ba-al Rafar, still wanting a very low profile, had entrusted this task to him, and for this night at least Lucius was back in his old glory.

What worried Lucius the most were the other spirits standing around, the enemies of the cause, the host of heaven. They were held at bay by Lucius's forces, to be sure, but there were some new ones he had never seen before.

Nearby, but not too near, Signa and his two warriors kept watch. Upon Tal's orders they allowed demons access to the building, but monitored the demons' activities and kept an eye out for Rafar. So far their very presence, as well as the presence of so many other warriors, had had a taming effect on the demonic hosts. There had been no incidents, and for now that was all Tal wanted.

When Lucius saw the Colemans come in the front door, he was agitated. In the past, they had never been very strong against the defeats and discouragements Lucius had ordered, and their marriage had just about dissolved. Then they aligned themselves with Praying Busche, hearing his words and becoming stronger all the time. Before long they and others like them would be a real threat.

But their arrival didn't cause Lucius as much agitation as the huge, blond-haired messenger of God who accompanied them. Lucius knew for sure he'd never seen this one before. As the Colemans found a seat, Lucius swooped down and accosted this new intruder.

"I've not seen you before!" he said gruffly, and all the other spirits focused their attention on him and the stranger. "From where do you come?"

The stranger, Chimon of Europe, said nothing. He only riveted his eyes on those of Lucius and stood firm.

"I'll have your name!" Lucius demanded.

The stranger said not a word.

Lucius smiled slyly and nodded. "You are deaf, yes? And dumb? And as mindless as you are silent?" The other demons guffawed. They loved this kind of game. "Tell me, are you a good fighter?"

Silence.

Lucius drew a scimitar that flashed blood-red and droned metallically. On cue, all the other demons did the same. The clatter and ring of burnished blades filled the room as crimson crescents of reflected light danced about the walls. The other messengers of God were barred from intervening by an armed ring of demons as Lucius continued to toy with this one single newcomer.

Lucius peered at his solid, unmoving opponent with a burning hatred that made his yellow eyes bulge and his sulfurous breath chug out through widely flared nostrils. He toyed with his sword, waved it in small circles in the stranger's face, watched for the stranger to make the slightest move.

The stranger only watched him, not moving at all.

With an intense cry Lucius swept his sword across the front of the stranger, slashing his garment. Cheers and laughter came from the crowd of demons. Lucius poised for a fight, held his sword with both hands, crouched, his wings flared.

Before him stood a statue with a slashed tunic.

"Fight, you listless spirit!" Lucius challenged.

The stranger did not respond, and Lucius cut his face. Another cheer from the demons.

"Shall I remove an ear? Or two? Shall I cut out your tongue if you have one?" Lucius taunted.

"I think it's time we got started," said Alf Brummel from the pulpit. The people in the room stopped their hushed conversations, and the place began to quiet down.

Lucius leered at the stranger, and motioned with his sword. "Go stand with the other cowards."

The newcomer stepped back, then took his place with the other messengers of God behind the demonic barricade.

Eleven angels had managed to get into the church without raising too much ire from the demons: Triskal and Krioni had already entered with Hank and Mary. They had often been seen with the pastor and his wife, so they were not paid much attention other than the usual threatening expressions and postures. Guilo was there, as big and threatening as ever, but apparently no demons were the slightest bit interested in asking him any questions.

A newcomer, a burly Polynesian, made his way over to Chimon and tended the wound in Chimon's face while Chimon repaired the slash in his tunic.

"Mota, called here from Polynesia," came the introduction.

"Chimon of Europe. Welcome to our numbers."

"Can you continue?" Mota asked.

"I will continue," Chimon answered, skillfully reweaving his tunic with his fingers. "Where is Tal?"

"Not here yet."

"A demon of fever tried to stop the Colemans. No doubt Tal has encountered an attack on Duster."

"I don't know how he'll ward it off without making himself visible."

"He'll do it." Chimon looked about. "I don't see the Ba-al Prince anywhere."

"We may never."

"And may he never see Tal."

Brummel brought the meeting to order, standing behind the pulpit and looking out over the nearly fifty people who had gathered. From this vantage point even he couldn't help but try to guess the final tally. Some of the people were definitely going to give Hank the ax, some were definitely not going to, and then there was that frustrating and unpredictable group he couldn't be sure about.

"I want to thank you all for coming tonight," he said. "This is a painful matter for us to decide. I'd always hoped that this night would never come, but we all want God's will to be done and we want what will be best for His people. So, let us open with a word of prayer and commit the rest of the evening to His care and guidance."

With that Brummel began a very pious prayer, appealing to the Lord for grace and mercy in words to bring a tear to the driest eye.

In the front corner of the sanctuary, Guilo sulked, wishing an angel could spit on a human.

Triskal asked Chimon, "Getting any strength?"

Chimon answered, "Why? Is somebody else going to pray?"

Brummel finished his prayer, the roomful muttered a few Amens, and then he went on with his introduction to the proceedings.

"The purpose of this meeting is to openly discuss our feelings regarding Pastor Hank, to put an end once and for all to all the backbiting and murmuring that's been going on, and to end our meeting with a final vote of confidence. I would hope that we would all have the mind of the Lord in these matters.

"If you have something you wish to say to the group, we would ask that you limit your time to three minutes. I'll be letting you know when your time is up, so keep that in mind." Brummel looked at Hank and Mary. "I think it would be good to let the pastor have the first say. Afterwards he'll leave us alone so we can talk freely."

Mary squeezed Hank's hand as he got up. He went to the pulpit and stood behind it, gripping its sides. For the longest time he couldn't say a word, but only looked into every eye of every face. He suddenly realized how much he truly loved these people, all of them. He could see the hardness in some of the faces, but he couldn't help seeing past that to the pain and bondage these people were under, deluded, led astray by sin, by greed, by bitterness and rebellion. In many other faces he could read the pain they were feeling for him; he could tell that some were silently praying for God's mercy and intervention.

Hank let a quick prayer course through his thoughts as he began. "I have always counted it a privilege to stand behind this sacred desk, to preach the Word and speak the truth." He surveyed their faces again for just a moment and then continued, "And even tonight I feel I cannot stray from God's commission to me and the purpose for which I have ever stood before you. I am not here to defend myself or my ministry. Jesus is my advocate, and I rest the course of my life on His grace, guidance, and mercy. So tonight, since I am standing behind this pulpit once again, let me share with you what I have received from God."

Hank opened his Bible and read from Second Timothy, chapter 4. " 'I solemnly charge you in the presence of God and of Christ Jesus, who is to judge the living and the dead, and by His appearing and His kingdom: preach the Word, be ready in season and out of season, reprove, rebuke, exhort, with great patience and instruction. For the time will come when they will not endure sound doctrine, but wanting to have their ears tickled, they will accumulate for themselves teachers in accordance to their own desires; and will turn away their ears from the truth, and will turn aside to myths.

" 'But you, be sober in all things, endure hardship, do the work of an evangelist, fulfill your ministry.' " Hank closed his Bible, looked about the room, and spoke firmly. "Let each one of us apply God's Word where it may apply. Tonight I will speak only for myself. I have my call from God; I just read it. Some of you, I know, have really gotten the impression that Hank Busche is obsessed with the gospel, that it's all he ever thinks about. Well, that's true. Sometimes I even wonder why I remain in such a difficult position, such an uphill effort . . . but for me, God's call on my life is an inescapable commission, and as Paul said, 'Woe is me if I do not preach the gospel.' I understand that sometimes the truth of God's Word can become a divider, an irritation, a stone of stumbling. But that's only because it remains unchanged, uncompromising, and steadfast. And what better reason could there be to build our lives on such an immovable foundation? To violate the Word of God is only to destroy ourselves, our joy, our peace, our happiness.

"I want to be fair with you, and so I'll be truthful in letting you know exactly what you may expect from me. I intend to love all of you, no matter what. I intend to shepherd and feed you for as long as you'll have me. I will not discredit, compromise, or turn my back on what I believe the Word of God teaches, and that means that there may be times when you'll feel my shepherd's crook around your neck, not to judge or malign you, but to help you move in the right direction, to protect you, to heal you. I intend to preach the gospel of Jesus Christ, for that is my calling. I have a burden for this town; sometimes I feel that burden so strongly I have to ask myself why, but it's still there and I can't turn my back on it or try to deny it. Until the Lord tells me otherwise, I intend to remain in Ashton to answer that burden.

"If that is the kind of pastor you want, then you can let me know tonight. If you do not want that kind of pastor . . . well, I really need to know that too.

"I love all of you. I want the very best God has to give you. And I guess that's all I have to say."

Hank stepped down from the platform, took Mary's hand, and the two of them walked down the aisle to the door. Hank tried to catch the eyes of as many people as he could. Some gave looks of love and encouragement; some looked away.

Krioni and Triskal left with Hank and Mary. Lucius watched with mocking disdain.

Guilo muttered to his fellows, "While the cat's away the mice will play."

"Where is Tal?" Chimon asked again.

Brummel stood before the group. "We'll now hear statements from the congregation. Just raise your hand to be recognized. Yeah, Sam, why don't you go first."

Sam Turner stood, and walked to the front of the sanctuary.

"Thanks, Alf," he said. "Well, I've no doubt you all know me and my wife Helen. We've been citizens of this community for over thirty years, and we've supported this church through thick and through thin. Now I don't have a lot to say tonight. You all know what kind of man I am, how I believe in loving one's neighbor and living a good life. I've tried to do right and be a good example of what a Christian should be.

"And I'm angry tonight. I'm angry for my friend, Lou Stanley. You may have noticed Lou isn't here tonight, and I'm sure I know why. It used to be he could show his face in this church and be a part of it, and we all loved him and he loved us, and I think we all still do. But this Busche fellow, who thinks he's God's gift to this earth, thought he had a right to judge Lou and kick him out of the church. Now, friends, let me tell you one thing: nobody kicks Lou Stanley out of anything if Lou doesn't feel like it, and the very fact that Lou went along with this whole smear on his character only shows the goodness of his heart. He could have sued Busche by now, or he could have settled the matter like I've seen him settle other matters. He's not afraid of anything. But I just think Lou's so ashamed of the horrible things that have been said about him and so hurt by what he thinks we must think of him that he decided he'd better just stay away.

"Now we have this self-righteous, Bible-pounding gossip-monger to blame for these troubles. Forgive me if I sound a bit harsh, but listen, I can remember when this church was like a family. How long now since it's been that way? Look what's happened: here we are, having a big bicker meeting, and why? Because we let Hank Busche come in here and stir us all up. Ashton used to be a peaceful town, this church used to be a peaceful church, and I say we do what's necessary to get it that way again."

Turner took his seat as a few nearby nodded their silent encouragement and approval.

John Coleman was recognized next. A shy person, he was very nervous about speaking in front of everyone, but concerned enough to do it anyway.

"Well," he said, nervously handling his Bible and looking at the floor a lot, "I don't usually say much, and I'm scared to death to be standing up here, but . . . I think Hank Busche is a real man of God, a good pastor, and I'd really hate to see him go. The church Pat and I came from, well, it just wasn't meeting our needs, and we were getting hungry: hungry for the Word, for the presence of God. We thought we'd found those things here, and we were really looking forward to being involved and growing in the Lord under Hank's ministry, and I know a lot of other folks feel that way too. As far as this stuff about Lou is concerned, that was not just Hank's doing. *All* of us were involved in that decision, including me, and I know Hank's not trying to hurt anybody."

As John sat down, Patricia patted his arm and said, "You did fine." John was not sure.

Brummel addressed the group. "I think it might be a good idea for us to hear what the church secretary, Gordon Mayer, has to say."

Gordon Mayer went to the front with some of the church records and minutes in his hand. He was a tense man with a tight expression and gruff voice.

"I have two items I'd like to address before this group," he said. "First of all, from the business side, you all need to be aware that the offerings have been decreasing over the past several months, but our bills have been staying steady if not going up. In other words, we're running out of money, and I personally have no doubts why. There are differences among us we really need to get resolved, and withholding your giving is not the way to do it. If you have a gripe against the pastor, then do whatever you have to tonight, but let's not bring the whole church down over this one man."

"Secondly, for whatever it's worth, let me tell you that the original pulpit committee was considering *another* man for the job. I was on that committee, and I can assure you that they had no intention of recommending Busche for the office. I'm convinced the whole thing was a fluke, a grave mistake. We voted in the wrong man, and now we're paying for it.

"So let me close with this: Sure, we've made a mistake, but I have faith in the group here, and I think we can turn the whole thing around and start doing things right for a change. I say let's do it."

And so the evening went for the better part of two hours, as both sides took turns in crucifying and praising Hank Busche. Nerves got raw, bottoms got numb, backs got sticky, and the opposing views became more and more vehement in their convictions. After two hours, a common sentiment began to mutter its way around the room: "C'mon, let's have the vote . . ."

Brummel had taken his jacket off, loosened his tie, and rolled up his sleeves. He was gathering a pile of small squares of paper, the ballots.

"Okay, this will be by secret ballot," he said, handing the slips of paper to two quickly appointed ushers who passed them out. "Let's just keep it simple. If you want to keep the pastor, say yes, and if you want to find someone else, say no."

Mota nudged Chimon. "Will Hank have enough votes?"

Chimon only shook his head. "We're not sure."

"You mean he could lose?"

"Let us hope someone is praying."

"Where, oh where is Tal?"

Writing a simple yes or no didn't take long, so almost immediately the ushers were passing the offering plates among the people.

Guilo stood still in his corner, glaring at as many demons as would look at him. Some of the smaller, harassing spirits flitted about the sanctuary trying to see what people were marking on their ballots, and grinning, scowling, cheering, or cursing accordingly. Guilo could envision three or four of their wiry little necks in his fists. Someday soon, little demons, someday soon.

Brummel took charge again. "All right, in the interest of fairness, let's have representatives from the two different . . . uh . . . viewpoints come up and do the counting."

After a bit of nervous chuckling John Coleman was selected by the yeas and Gordon Mayer by the nays to count the ballots. The two men took the offering plates full of ballots to a back pew. A flock of flapping, hissing demons converged on the scene, wanting to see the outcome.

Guilo stepped out too. It was only fair, he thought. Lucius swooped down from the ceiling in an instant and hissed, "Get back in your corner!"

"I wish to see the outcome."

"Oh, don't you now?" Lucius sneered. "And what if I decide to cut you open as I did your friend?"

Something about the way Guilo answered, "Try it," may have caused Lucius to reconsider.

Guilo's approach sent the little demons fluttering away like a flock of chickens. He bent over the two men to have a look. Gordon Mayer was counting first, silently, then handing the ballots to John Coleman. But he stealthily hid a few yea ballots in his palm. Guilo checked to see how closely the demons were watching, then made a stealthy move himself, touching the back of Mayer's hand.

A demon saw it and struck Guilo's hand with bared talons. Guilo jerked his hand away and came infinitely close to tearing the demon to shreds, but he caught himself and honored Tal's orders.

"What is your name?" Guilo wanted to know.

"Cheating," the demon answered.

"Cheating," Guilo rehearsed as he went back to his corner. "Cheating."

But Guilo's move had succeeded in foiling Mayer's effort. The ballots dropped out of Mayer's hand and John Coleman saw them.

"You dropped something there," he said very sweetly.

Mayer couldn't say anything. He just handed the ballots over.

The count was finished, but Mayer wanted to count again. They counted the ballots again. The count came out the same: a tie.

The two reported the result to Brummel, who told the congregation, which moaned quietly.

Alf Brummel could feel his hands getting very damp; he tried drying them on his handkerchief.

"Well, listen," he said, "there may not be much chance that any of you will reconsider, but I'm sure none of us wants to prolong this thing past tonight. I tell you what, why don't we take a short break and give some of you a chance to get up, stretch, use the restroom. Then we'll regather and vote again."

As Brummel spoke, the two demons posted around the church saw something very unsettling. Just about a block up the street were two old women, hobbling toward the church. One walked with the assistance of a cane and a helping hand from her friend. She did not look well at all, but her jaw was set and her eyes bright and determined. Her cane clacked out a syncopated rhythm with her footsteps. Her friend, in better health and stronger, kept up with her, holding her arm to support her and talking gently to her.

"The one with the cane is Duster," said one demon.

"What went wrong?" the other wondered. "I thought she'd been taken care of."

"Oh, she's ill, all right, but she's come anyway."

"And who is the old woman with her?"

"Edith Duster has many friends. We should have known."

The two ladies made their way up the church steps, each step a major task in itself, first one foot, then the other, then the cane placed on the next step, until they were finally up to the front door.

"There, look at that now!" cackled the stronger one. "I knew you could do it. The Lord's gotten you this far, He'll take care of you the rest of the way."

"What Edith Duster needs is a stroke," murmured a sickness demon, drawing his sword.

Perhaps it was simply luck, or incredible coincidence, but just as the demon lunged forward with great speed to slash at the arteries in Edith Duster's brain, the other woman moved to open the door and stepped right in the way. The tip of the demon's sword struck the woman in the shoulder, which could have been concrete; the sword stopped short. Sickness did not, but catapulted over the two women and fluttered like a fractured kite into the church yard as Edith Duster moved inside.

Sickness gathered himself up off the ground and screamed, "The host of heaven!"

The other demon guard stared at him blankly.

Brummel saw Edith Duster come in, alone. He cursed silently. This would be the vote to break the tie, but she would most certainly vote for Busche. The people were gathering again.

The messengers of God were elated. "Looks like Tal succeeded," said Mota.

Chimon was concerned, however. "With such a heavy cover of the enemy, he most certainly had to show himself."

Guilo chuckled. "Oh, I'm sure our captain was very discreet."

A few of the demons were in fact wondering what had happened to Edith Duster's companion between the front door and the sanctuary. Sickness continued insisting it had been a heavenly warrior, but where was she now?

Tal, Captain of the Host, joined Signa and the other sentries at their concealed position.

"You had *me* fooled, captain," said Signa.

"You just might attempt it yourself sometime," Tal replied.

On the platform, Brummel mentally groped for a trump card. He could just see the burning eyes of Langstrat if this vote went the wrong way.

"Well," he said, "why don't we come to order now and get ready for another vote?" The people settled in and quieted down. The yea side was more than ready.

"Now that we've prayed and talked about it, maybe some of us will feel differently about the future of the church here. I . . . umm . . ." Come on, Alf, say something, but don't make a fool of yourself. "I guess I could say a few words; I haven't really shared my feelings. You know, Hank Busche *is* a little young . . ."

A middle-aged plumber on the yea side piped up, "Hey now, if you're going to put in some negative input we've got to have equal time for some positive!"

The yeas all murmured in agreement while the nays sat in cold silence.

"No, listen," Brummel stammered, his face bright red, "I had no intention of trying to sway the vote. I was just—"

"Let's have the vote!" someone said.

"Yes, vote, and quick!" Mota whispered.

Just then the door opened. Oh no, thought Brummel, who's coming in this time?

The silence fell like a shroud of death over the whole group. Lou Stanley had just come in. He grimly nodded greeting to them all and took a seat in a back pew. He looked old.

Gordon Mayer piped up, "Let's have the vote!"

The ushers passed out the ballots while Brummel tried to plan a good escape route in case he had to throw up—his nerves were just about shot. He caught Lou Stanley's attention. Lou looked at him and seemed to laugh nervously.

"Make sure Lou back there gets a ballot," Brummel told one of the ushers. The usher made sure.

Chimon whispered to Guilo, "I think we're ready for any tricks Lucius might have."

"Any tie breakers, you mean," Guilo answered.

"We may be in for a long night," said Mota.

The ballots were collected, and Lucius kept his demons tightly around each offering plate and his eyes on every heavenly warrior.

Mayer and Coleman counted again as the tension in the air tightened. The demons watched. The angels watched. The people watched.

Mayer and Coleman kept a close eye on each other, silently mouthing as they counted. Mayer finished counting, waited for Coleman to finish. Coleman finished, looked at Mayer and asked him if he wanted to count again. They counted again.

Then Mayer took his pen, wrote the result on a slip of paper, and carried it up to Brummel. Mayer and Coleman took their seats as Brummel unfolded the paper.

Visibly shaken, Brummel took a few moments to put on his relaxed, businesslike, public image.

"Well . . ." he began, trying to control the tone of his voice, "all right, then. The . . . pastor has been retained."

One side of the room loosened up, tittered, and smiled. The other side gathered up coats and belongings to leave.

"Alf, what was the vote?" someone wanted to know.

"Uh . . . it doesn't say."

"Twenty-eight to twenty-six!" Gordon Mayer said accusingly, looking back toward Lou Stanley.

But Lou Stanley had left.

11

Tal, Signa, and the other sentries could see the explosion from where they stood. With cries and wails of rage, demons scattered everywhere, erupting through the roof and sides of the church like shrapnel and fanning out in all directions over the town. Their cries became a loud, echoing drone of savage fury that rang over the whole town like a thousand melancholy factory whistles, sirens, and horns.

"They will wreak havoc tonight," said Tal.

Mota, Chimon, and Guilo were there to report.

"By two votes," said Mota.

Tal smiled and said, "Very well, then."

"But Lou Stanley!" Chimon exclaimed. "Was that really Lou Stanley?"

Tal caught the implication. "Yes, that was Mr. Stanley. I've been standing right here ever since I delivered Edith Duster."

"I see the Spirit has been working!" Guilo chuckled.

"Let's get Edith home safely and get a guard around her. Everyone to your posts. There will be angry spirits over the town tonight."

That night the police were busy. Fights broke out in the local taverns, slogans were spray-painted on the courthouse, some cars were stolen and joy-ridden through the lawn and flowers in the park.

Late into the night, Juleen Langstrat hovered in an inescapable trance, halfway between a tormented life on earth and the licking, searing flames of hell. She lay on her bed, tumbled to the floor, clawed her way up the wall to stand on her feet, staggered about the room, and fell to the floor again. Threatening voices, monsters, flames, and blood exploded and pounded with unimaginable force in her head; she thought her skull would burst. She could feel claws tearing at her throat, creatures squirming and biting inside her, chains around her arms and legs. She could hear the voices of spirits, see their eyes and fangs, smell their sulfurous breath.

The Masters were angry! "Failed, failed, failed, failed" pounded in her brain and paraded before her eyes. "Brummel has failed, you have failed, he will die, you will die . . ."

Did she really hold a knife in her hand, or was this too a vision from the higher planes? She could feel a yearning, a terribly strong impulse to be free of the torment, to break loose from the bodily shell, the prison of flesh that bound her.

"Join us, join us, join us," said the voices. She felt the edge of the blade, and blood trickled down her finger.

The telephone rang. Time froze. The bedroom registered on her retinas. The telephone rang. She was in her bedroom. There was blood on the floor. The telephone rang. The knife fell from her hands. She could hear voices, angry voices. The telephone rang.

She was on her knees on the floor of her bedroom. She had cut her finger. The phone was still ringing. She called out hello, but it still rang.

"I won't fail you," she said to her visitors. "Leave me. I won't fail you."

The telephone rang.

Alf Brummel sat in his home, listening to the phone ringing on the other end. Juleen must not be home. He hung up, relieved, if only for the moment. She would not be happy about the vote. Another delay, still another delay in the Plan. He knew he could not avoid her, that she would find out, that he would be confronted and berated by the others.

He flopped down on his bed and contemplated resigning, escape, suicide.

Saturday morning. The sun was out, and lawn mowers called to each other across fences, hedges, and cul-de-sacs; kids were playing, hoses were spraying dirty cars.

Marshall sat in the kitchen, at the table filled with advertising copy and a list of new and old accounts; the *Clarion* still lacked a secretary.

The front door opened and in came Kate. "I need a hand!"

Yes, the inevitable unloading of groceries.

"Sandy," Marshall hollered out the back door, "let's get going!" Over the years the family had developed a pretty good system of grocery separating, handling, and stashing.

"Marshall," said Kate, passing vegetables from a sack to him at the refrigerator, "are you still working on that copy? It's Saturday!"

"Almost finished. I hate to have stuff stack up on me. How's Joe and the gang?"

Kate stopped a bunch of celery in midtransfer and said, "You know what? Joe's gone. He sold the store and moved away, and I didn't even hear about it."

"Brother. Things happen fast around here. So where'd he move?"

"I don't know. Nobody would tell me. As a matter of fact, I don't think I like that new owner."

"What's this cleaner here?"

"Oh, put that under the sink." It went under the sink. "I asked that guy about Joe and Angelina and why they sold the store and why they moved and where they moved and he wouldn't tell me anything, just said he didn't know."

"That's the owner of the store? What's his name?"

"I don't know. He wouldn't tell me that either."

"Well, does he talk? Does he know English?"

"Enough to ring up your groceries and take your money, and that's about it. Now could we get all this stuff off the table?"

Marshall started gathering up all his papers before the oncoming invasion of cans and produce.

Kate continued, "I guess I'll get used to it, but for a while I thought I'd gone into the wrong store. I didn't recognize anybody. They might even have all new people working there."

Sandy spoke for the first time. "Something weird's going on in this town."

Marshall asked, "Oh yeah?"

Sandy didn't elaborate.

Marshall tried to draw it out of her. "Well, what do you think it is?"

"Aw, nothing, really. It's just a feeling I get. People around here are starting to act weird. I think we're being invaded by aliens."

Marshall let it go.

The groceries were all put away, Sandy went back to her studies, and Kate got ready to work in the garden. Marshall had a phone call to make. Talk about weird aliens invading the town jarred his memory and also his reporter's nose. Maybe Langstrat wasn't an alien, but she was certainly weird.

He sat on the couch in the living room and took the slip of paper with Ted Harmel's phone number from his wallet. A sunny Saturday morning would be a strange time to find someone home and indoors, but Marshall figured he'd try.

The phone on the other end rang several times and then a man's voice answered. "Hello?"

"Hello, Ted Harmel?"

"Yes, who's this?"

"This is Marshall Hogan, the new *Clarion* editor."

"Oh, uh-huh . . ." Harmel waited for Marshall to go on.

"Well, anyway, you know Bernice Krueger, right? I have her working for me."

"Oh, she's still there, eh? Has she found out anything about her sister?"

"Mm, I don't know much about that, she's never told me."

"Oh. So how's the paper doing?"

They talked for a few minutes about the *Clarion,* the office, circulation, whatever may have happened to the cord to the coffee-maker. Harmel seemed particularly concerned to hear that Edie had left.

"Her marriage broke up," Marshall told him. "Hey, it was a complete surprise to me. I came in too late to know what was going on."

"Hmmm . . . yeah . . ." Harmel was doing some thinking on the other end.

Keep it flowing, Hogan. "Yeah, well, I've got a daughter who's a freshman at the college."

"Is that right."

"Yeah, doing her prerequisites, jumping through the hoop. She likes it."

"Well, more power to her."

Harmel was certainly being patient.

"You know, Sandy has a psychology professor I thought was an interesting gal."

"Langstrat."

Bingo. "Yeah, yeah. A lot of unusual ideas."

"I bet."

"Do you know anything about her?"

Harmel paused, sighed, and then asked, "Well, what is it you want to know?"

"Where's she coming from, anyway? Sandy's bringing home some weird ideas . . ."

Harmel had trouble coming up with an answer. "It's . . . uh . . . Eastern mysticism, ancient religious craft. She's just into, you know, meditation, higher consciousness . . . uh . . . the oneness of the universe. I don't know if any of that makes sense to you."

"Not much. But she seems to spread it around a lot, doesn't she?"

"What do you mean?"

"You know, she meets with people on a regular basis; Alf Brummel, and, uh, who else? Pinckston . . ."

"Delores Pinckston?"

"Right, on the board of regents. Dwight Brandon, Eugene Baylor—"

Harmel cut in abruptly. "What is it you want to know?"

"Well, I understand you were pretty close to the situation—"

"No, that's wrong."

"Didn't you have sessions with her yourself?"

There was a long pause. "Who told you that?"

"Oh, we . . . just found out."

Another long pause. Harmel sighed through his nose. "Listen," he asked, "what else do you know?"

"Not much. It just smells like there might be a story in it. You know what that's like."

Harmel was struggling, fuming, groping for words. "Yes, I know what it's like. But you're wrong this time, you're really wrong!" Another pause, another struggle. "Oh, brother, I wish you hadn't called me."

"Hey, listen, we're both newspapermen—"

"No! You're the newspaperman! I'm out. I'm sure you know all about me."

"I know your name, your number, and that you used to own the *Clarion.*"

"All right, let's leave it at that. I still have respect for the vocation. I don't want to see you ruined."

Marshall tried not to lose a big fish. "Say, don't leave me in the dark!"

"I'm not trying to leave you in the dark. There are some things I just can't talk about."

"Sure, I understand. No problem."

"No, you *don't* understand. Now listen to me! I don't know what you've found out, but whatever it is, bury it. Do something else. Cover the Kiwanis tree planting, anything innocuous, but just keep your nose clean."

"What are you talking about?"

"And quit pumping me for information! What I'm giving you is all you're going to get, and you'd better make good use of it. I'm telling you, forget Langstrat, forget anything you may have heard about her. Now I know you're a reporter, and so I know you're going to go out and do just the opposite of what I'm telling you, but let me give you fair warning: Don't." Hogan didn't answer. "Hogan, you hear me?"

"How can I possibly leave it alone now?"

"You have a wife, a daughter? Think of them. Think of yourself. Otherwise you'll be out on your ear like everybody else."

"What do you mean, everybody else?"

"I don't know anything, I don't know Langstrat, I don't know you, I don't live there anymore. Period."

"Ted, are you in trouble?"

"Leave it alone!"

He hung up. Marshall slammed the receiver down and let his mind race as he sat there. Leave it alone, Harmel said. Leave it alone.

In a pig's eye.

Edith Duster—wise old matron of the church, former missionary to China, a widow of some thirty years—lived in the Willow Terrace Apartments, a small retirement complex not far from the church. She was in her eighties, subsisted meagerly on Social Security and a minister's pension from her denomination, and loved to have company, especially since it was difficult for her to get out and around these days.

Hank and Mary sat at her little dinette near the large window overlooking the building's courtyard. Grandma Duster poured tea from a very old, very charming teapot into equally charming teacups. She was dressed nicely, almost formally, as always when she received guests.

"No," she said as she sat down at last, the morning tea table properly set, the pastries in place. "I don't believe God's purposes are ever thwarted for long. He has His own ways of working His people through difficulties."

Hank agreed, but weakly, "I imagine so . . ." Mary held his hand.

Grandma was firm. "I *know* so, Henry Busche. Your being here is *not* a mistake; I strongly disagree with that notion. If you were not supposed to be here, the Lord would not have accomplished the things He has through your ministry."

Mary volunteered some information. "He feels a bit down about the vote."

Grandma smiled lovingly and looked into Hank's eyes. "I think the Lord is forcing a revival upon that church, but its like the turning of the tide: before the tide can come back in, it first has to stop all its going out. Give the church time to turn around. Expect opposition, even expect to lose a few people, but the direction will change after the lull. Just give it time.

"But I do know one thing: there was nothing that could keep me away from that meeting last night. I was dreadfully sick, Satan's attack, I suppose, but it was the Lord who got me out. Right about the time of the meeting I could just feel His arms bearing me up and I got my coat on and got down there, and just in time, too. I don't know if I'd even go that far to get groceries. It was the Lord, I know it. I'm just sorry I only had one vote."

"So who do you suppose the other vote came from?" Hank asked.

Mary quickly added, "It couldn't have been Lou Stanley."

Grandma smiled, "Oh, now don't say that. You never know what the Lord might do. But you are curious, aren't you?"

"I'm *really* curious," said Hank, and now he smiled too.

"Well, you might find out, and maybe you never will. But it's all in the Lord's hands, and so are you. Let me warm up your tea."

"That church can't possibly survive if half the congregation removes its support, and I can't imagine them supporting a pastor they don't want."

"Oh, but I've had dreams of angels lately." Grandma was always very matter-of-fact about such things. "I don't usually, but I've seen angels before, and always when there was great headway to be made for the kingdom of God. I just have a feeling in my spirit that something is really stirring here. Haven't you felt that way?"

Hank and Mary looked at each other to see which of them should speak first. Then Hank told Grandma all about the battle of the other night and the burden he had felt lately for the town. Mary slipped in her remembrances whenever they came to her. Grandma listened with great fascination, responding at key moments with "Oh dear," "Well, praise the Lord," and "Well . . . !"

"Yes," she said finally, "yes, that makes a lot of sense to me. You know, I had an experience just the other night, standing right by that window." She pointed to the front window overlooking the courtyard. "I was getting the place straightened up, getting ready for bed, and I walked by that window and looked out at the rooftops and the streetlight and all of a sudden I got really dizzy. I had to sit down or I'd fall down. And I never get dizzy. The only time that ever happened before was in China. My husband and I were visiting a woman's home there, and she was a medium, a spiritist, and I knew she hated us and I think she was trying to put a curse on us. But just outside her door I had the same dizzy sensation, and I'll never forget it. What I felt the other night was just like that time in China."

"What did you do?" Mary asked.

"Oh, I prayed. I just said, 'Demon, be gone in the name of Jesus!' and it went away, just like that."

Hank asked, "So you think it was a demon?"

"Oh yes. God is moving and Satan doesn't like it. I do think there are evil spirits out there."

"But don't you feel like there are more than usual? I mean, I've been a Christian all my life and I've never come up against anything that felt like this."

Her face grew pensive. " 'This kind goeth not out but by prayer and fasting.' We need to pray, and we need to get other people praying. That's just what the angels keep telling me."

Mary was intrigued. "The angels in your dreams?" Grandma nodded. "What did they look like?"

"Oh, people, but different from anybody else. They're big, very handsome, bright clothes, big swords at their sides, very large, bright wings. One of them last night reminded me of my son; he was tall, blond, he looked Scandinavian." She looked at Hank. "He was telling me to pray for you, and you were in the dream too. I could see you up behind that pulpit preaching, and he was standing there behind you with his wings stretched out over you like a big canopy, and he looked back at me and said, 'Pray for this man.' "

"I never knew you were praying for me," said Hank.

"Well, it's time somebody else was praying too. I believe the tide is turning, Hank, and now you need true believers, true visionaries who can stand with you to pray for this town. We need to pray that the Lord will gather them in."

It was so natural then to join hands in praise to the Lord and thanksgiving for the first real encouragement to come along in quite some time. Hank prayed a prayer of thanks and could hardly get through it as his emotions welled up inside him. Mary was grateful, not only for the encouragement but for Hank's revived spirits.

Then Edith Duster, who'd fought in spiritual wars before, who'd won victories on foreign soils, tightly grasped the hands of this young ministering couple and prayed.

"Lord God," she said, and the warmth of the Holy Spirit flowed through them, "I build now a hedge around this young couple, and I bind the spirits in Jesus' name. Satan, whatever your plans for this town, I rebuke you in Jesus' name, and I bind you, and I cast you out!"

CLUNK!

Rafar's eyes darted toward the sound that had interrupted his talking and saw two swords fallen from their owners' hands. The two demons, formidable warriors, were nonplussed. They both stooped hurriedly to gather up their weapons, bowing, apologizing, begging for pardon.

Slam! Rafar's foot fell on one sword, his own huge sword clamped the other down. The two warriors, startled and terrified, backed away.

"Please pardon, my prince!" said one.

"Yes, please pardon!" said the other. "This has never happened before . . ."

"Silence, you two!" Rafar bellowed.

The two warriors braced themselves for a terrible punishment; their frightened yellow eyes peered out from behind black wings unfurled for protection, as if there was any protection from Ba-al Rafar's wrath.

But Rafar did not lash out at them. Not yet. He seemed more interested in the fallen swords; he stared at them, his brow furrowed and his big yellow eyes narrowing. He walked slowly around the swords, strangely bothered in a way the warriors had never seen before.

"Uhnnnnnnnnhhh . . ." A low, gurgling growl came from deep in his throat as his nostrils belched forth yellow vapor.

He slowly went down on one knee and picked up one sword in his hand. In his huge fist it looked like a toy. He looked at the sword, looked at the demon who had dropped it, then off into space, his gnarled face registering a burning hatred that slowly rose from deep within.

"Tal," he whispered.

Then, like a slowly swelling volcano, he rose to his feet, the anger building until suddenly, with a roar that shook the room and terrified all those present, he exploded and hurled the sword through the basement wall, through the earth around Stewart Hall, through the air, through several other buildings on the college campus, and up into the sky where it tumbled end over end in a long arc of several miles.

His initial explosion released, he grabbed the sword's owner and with the order, "Go after it!" flung the demon like a spear along the same trajectory.

He grabbed up the other sword and flung it at the other demon, who sidestepped just in time to save himself. Then that demon too went sailing after his sword.

To some in the room the word "Tal" meant nothing, but they could see by the faces and deflating postures of others that it had to mean something dreadful.

Rafar began to storm about the room, growling indiscernible phrases and waving his sword at invisible enemies. The others gave him time to vent himself before daring to ask any question. Lucius finally stepped forward and bowed low, much as he hated to do so.

"We are at your service, Ba-al Rafar. Can you tell us, who is this Tal?"

Rafar spun around in fury, his wings unfurling like a clap of thunder and his eyes like hot coals.

"Who is this Tal?" he screamed, and every demon present fell on his face. "Who is this Tal, this warrior, this Captain of the Hosts of Heaven, this sneaking, conniving rival of rivals? Who is this Tal?"

Complacency happened to be within grabbing distance. With a huge fist around Complacency's scrawny neck, Rafar plucked him up like a frail weed and held him high.

"You," Rafar growled with a cloud of sulfur and steam, "have failed because of this Tal!" Complacency could only tremble, speechless with terror. "Hogan has become a hound, sniffing and barking after our scent, and I have had my fill of you and your whining excuses!"

The huge sword flashed in a wide, crimson arc, cutting a gash in space which became a bottomless abyss into which all light seemed to drain like water.

Complacency's eyes swelled in stark terror, and he screamed his last scream upon the earth. "No, Ba-al, noooooo!"

With a mighty thrust of his arm, Rafar cast Complacency headlong into the abyss. The small demon tumbled, fell, and kept falling, his screams becoming fainter until they vanished altogether. Rafar wiped the rift in space shut with the flat of his blade, and the room was just as it was before.

Just then the two warriors returned with their swords. He grabbed both of them by their wings and jerked them together in front of him.

"On your feet, all of you!" he hollered at the others. They complied instantly. Now he held the two demons aloft as an exhibit. "Who is this Tal? He is a strategist who can make warriors drop their swords!" With that, he hurled the two into the group, causing several to go sprawling. They picked themselves up as quickly as they could. "Who is this Tal? He is a subtle warrior who knows his limitations, who never enters a battle he cannot win, who knows all too well the power of the saints of God, a lesson you could all stand to learn!"

Rafar held his sword in a fist that trembled with rage, waving it about to give extra force to his words. "I knew all too well to expect him. Michael would never have sent anyone less to pit against me. Now Hogan is revived, and it is clear why he was even brought to Ashton to begin with; now Henry Busche is still retained and the Ashton Community Church has not fallen, but stands as a bastion against us; now the warriors are dropping their swords like clumsy fools!

"And all because of this . . . Tal! This is Tal's manner. His strength is not in his own sword, but in the saints of God. Somewhere somebody is praying!"

Those words brought a chill over the group.

Rafar kept pacing and thinking and growling. "Yes, yes, Busche and Hogan were handpicked; Tal's plan must revolve around them. If they fall, Tal's plan falls. There isn't much time."

Rafar selected a slimy-looking demon and asked, "Have you laid a trap for Busche?"

"Oh, yes, Ba-al Rafar," said the demon, and he couldn't help laughing with delight at his own cleverness.

"Be sure it is subtle. Remember, no frontal assault will work."

"Leave it to me."

"And what has been done to destroy Marshall Hogan?"

Strife stepped forward. "We seek to destroy his family. He derives a great amount of strength from his wife. If that support were ripped away . . ."

"Do it, any way you can."

"Yes, my prince."

"And let us not neglect some other avenues. Hogan could be lethal, and Krueger the same, but they could be manipulated to compromise each other . . ." Rafar appointed some demons to look into that possibility. "And what about Hogan's daughter?"

Deception stepped forward. "She is already within our hands."

12

The leaves were green, that fresh, new-growth kind of green they wear in the early months of summer. From their small table on the red brick plaza below, Sandy and Shawn could look up and see the glowing leaves, backlit by the sun, and watch the birds flit about in the branches between their regular scavengings for bread crumbs and french fries. This spot on campus was Sandy's favorite. It was so peaceful here, almost a world away from the strife, questions, and disputes at home.

Shawn enjoyed watching the brown sparrows cheeping and scrambling for every bread crumb he tossed onto the bricks.

"I love the way the universe all fits together," he said. "The tree grew here to give us shade, we sit here and eat and give food to the birds that live in the tree. It all works together."

Sandy was fascinated by the concept. On the surface it seemed very simple, almost storybookish, but part of her was so thirsty for this kind of peace.

"What happens when the universe doesn't fit together?" she asked.

Shawn smiled. "The universe always fits together. The problem is only when people don't realize it."

"So how do you explain the problems I'm having with my folks?"

"None of your minds are tuned in right. It's just like an FM station on your radio. If the signal is fuzzy and the voices hiss and sputter, don't blame the broadcasting station—adjust your radio. Sandy, the universe is perfect. It is unified, harmonious. The peace, the unity, the wholeness are really there, and all of us are a part of the universe; we're made of the same stuff, so there's no reason why we shouldn't just fit into the whole scheme of things. If we don't, we just took a wrong turn somewhere. We're out of touch with true reality."

"Boy, I guess so," Sandy muttered. "But that's what gets me! My folks and I are supposed to be Christians and loving each other and close to God and everything, but all we ever do is argue about who's right and who's wrong."

Shawn laughed and nodded his head. "Yeah, yeah, I know all about that. I've been there too."

"Okay, so how did you solve it?"

"I could only solve it for myself. I can't change other people's minds, only my own. It's a little hard to explain, but if you're in tune with the universe, a few little quirks in it that aren't in tune won't bother you much. That kind of thing is only an illusion of the mind anyway. Once you stop listening to the lies your mind's been telling you, you'll see very clearly that God is big enough for everybody and *in* everybody. Nobody can put Him in a jar and keep Him all to themselves, according to their own whims and ideas."

"I just wish I could find Him, for real."

Shawn looked at her comfortingly and touched her hand. "Hey, He's no trouble to find. We're all a part of Him."

"What do you mean?"

"Well, it's like I said, the whole universe all fits together; it's made of the same essence, the same spirit, the same . . . energy. Right?" Sandy shrugged and nodded. "Well, whatever our individual concept of God might be, we all know that there is something there: a force, a principle, an energy, that holds everything together. If that force is part of the universe, then it must be a part of us."

Sandy wasn't grasping this. "This is pretty foreign to me. I'm from the old Judeo-Christian school of thought, you know."

"So all you've ever learned is religion, right?"

She thought for a moment, then conceded. "Right."

"Well, you see, the problem with religion—any religion—is that it's basically a limited perspective, only a partial view of the whole truth."

"Now you sound like Langstrat."

"Oh, she's right on, I think. When you think about it long enough, it makes a lot of sense. It's just like that classic old story about the blind men who encountered the elephant."

"Yeah, yeah, I heard her tell that story too."

"Well, see? Each man's perspective of the elephant was limited to the part that he touched, so since they all touched different parts, they couldn't agree on what an elephant was really like. They got in a fight over it, just like religionists throughout history have done, and all they needed to realize was that the elephant was only one elephant. It wasn't the elephant's fault that they couldn't agree with each other. They weren't tuned in to each other and to the whole elephant."

"So we're all just like blind men . . ."

Shawn gave a strong, affirmative nod. "We're just like a bunch of bugs crawling around on the ground, never looking up. If an ant could talk, you could ask him if he knew what a tree was, and if he'd never come out of the grass and actually climbed a tree, he'd probably argue with you that the tree didn't exist. But who's wrong? Who's really blind? We're just like that. We've allowed ourselves to be fooled by our own limited perceptions. Are you into Plato at all?"

Sandy laughed a little and shook her head. "I studied that last quarter, and I don't think I got that either."

"Hey, he was into the same enlightenment. He figured there had to be a higher reality, an ideal, a perfect existence of which all we see is a copy. It's kind of like what we see with our limited senses *is* so limited, so imperfect, so broken up into pieces, we can't perceive the way the universe really is, all perfect, running smoothly, everything fitting together, all the same essence. You could even say that reality as we know it is just an illusion, a trick of our ego, our mind, our selfish desires."

"This all sounds very far-out to me."

"Oh, but it's great once you really get into it. It answers a lot of questions and solves a lot of problems."

"Yeah, if you can ever get into it."

Shawn leaned forward. "*You* don't get into *it,* Sandy. *It's* already in *you.* Think about that for a minute."

"I don't feel anything in me . . ."

"And why not? Guess!"

She twisted an invisible radio dial with her fingers. "I'm not tuned in?"

Shawn laughed with delight. "Right! Right! Listen. The universe doesn't change, but we can; if we're not lined up with it, not tuned in, we're the ones who are blind, who are living in an illusion. Say, if your life is messed up, it's really a matter of how you look at things."

Sandy scoffed, "Come on, now. You're not going to tell me that it's all in my head!"

Shawn put up hands of caution. "Hey, don't knock it until you try it." He looked again at the sunshine, the green trees, the busy birds. "Just listen for a moment."

"Listen to what?"

"The breeze. The birds. Watch those leaves waving in the wind up there."

For a moment they were silent.

Shawn spoke quietly, almost in a whisper. "Now be honest. Haven't you ever felt a sort of . . . kinship with the trees, and with the birds, with just about everything? Wouldn't you miss them if they weren't there? Have you ever talked to a houseplant?"

Sandy nodded. Shawn had a point there.

"Now don't resist that, because what you're experiencing there is just a glimpse of the real universe; you're feeling the oneness of everything. Everything is fitted together, interwoven, interlocked. Now you've felt that before, haven't you?"

She nodded.

"So that's what I'm trying to show you; the truth is already within you. You're a part of it. You're a part of God. You just never knew it. You wouldn't *let* yourself know it."

Sandy could hear the birds clearly now, and the wind seemed almost melodic as it shifted in pitch and intensity through the branches of the trees. The sun was warm, benevolent. Suddenly she felt so strongly that she had been in this place before, had known these trees and these birds before. They were trying to reach out to her, to talk to her.

Then she noticed that, for the first time in many months, she felt peace inside. Her heart was at rest. It wasn't an all-pervading peace, and she didn't know if it would last, but she could feel it and she knew she wanted more.

"I think maybe I'm tuning in a little bit," she said.

Shawn smiled and squeezed her hand encouragingly.

Meanwhile, with very gentle, very subtle combing motions of his talons, Deception stood behind Sandy, stroking her red hair and speaking sweet words of comfort to her mind.

Tal and his troops gathered once again in the little church, and the mood was better this time. They had tasted the first promises of battle; a victory, even though a small one, had been won the night before. Most of all, there were more of them. The original twenty-three had grown to forty-seven as more mighty warriors had gathered, called in by the prayers of . . .

"The Remnant!" said Tal with a note of anticipation as he looked over a preliminary list presented to him.

Scion, a red-haired, freckled fighter from the British Isles, explained the progress of the search. "They're out there, Cap, and there's plenty o' them, but these are the ones we'll be bringin' in for sure."

Tal read the names. "John and Patricia Coleman—"

Scion explained, "They were here last night and spoke up for the preacher. Now they're all the more for him, and they drop to their knees easy as droppin' a hat. We've got them workin'."

"Andy and June Forsythe."

"Lost sheep, you could say. Left the United Christian here in Ashton out of sheer hunger. We'll bring them to church tomorrow. They have a son, Ron, who's searchin' for the Lord. A bit wayward now, but reachin' his fill o' his ways."

"And plenty more, I see," said Tal with a smile. He handed the list to Guilo. "Assign some of our newcomers to this list. Gather these people in. I want them praying."

Guilo took the list and conferred with several new warriors.

"And what about relatives, friends elsewhere?" Tal asked Scion.

"Plenty o' them are redeemed and ready for prayer. Shall I send emissaries to burden them?"

Tal shook his head. "I can't let any warriors be gone for long. Instead, have messengers carry word to the watchcarers over these people's towns and cities, and let the watchcarers see that these people are burdened with prayer for their loved ones here."

"Done."

Scion set right to work, assigning messengers who immediately vanished to their missions.

Guilo had sent his warriors also and was excited to see the campaign in motion. "I like the feel of this, captain."

"It is a good beginning," Tal said.

"And what of Rafar? Do you suppose he knows of your presence here?"

"The two of us know each other all too well."

"Then he will be expecting a fight, and soon."

"Which is why we won't fight, not yet. Not until the prayer cover is sufficient and we know why Rafar is here. He's not a prince of small towns but of empires, and he would never be here for any task below his pride. What we've seen is far less than the enemy has planned. How's Mr. Hogan?"

"I hear little Complacency has been banished for failure and the Ba-al is in a rage."

Tal chuckled. "Hogan has come to life like a dormant seed. Nathan! Armoth!" They were there immediately. "You have more warriors now. Take as many as you need to surround Marshall Hogan. Greater numbers may intimidate where swords cannot."

Guilo was visibly indignant and looked longingly at his sheathed sword.

Tal cautioned, "Not yet, brave Guilo. Not yet."

Right after Marshall's call to Harmel, Bernice's phone nearly jumped off the wall. Marshall didn't ask her, he told her, "Be at the office tonight at 7, we've got work to do."

Now, at 7:10, the rest of the *Clarion* office was deserted and dark. Marshall and Bernice were in the back room, digging old issues of the *Clarion* out of the archives. Ted Harmel had been quite fastidious; most of the past issues were neatly kept in huge binders.

"So when did Harmel get run out of town?" Marshall asked as he flipped through several old pages of a back issue.

"About a year ago," Bernice answered, bringing more binders up to the big worktable. "The paper operated on a skeleton crew for several months before you bought it. Edie, Tom, myself and some of the college journalism majors kept it going. Some of the issues were okay, some of them were a lot like a college paper."

"Like this one here?"

Bernice looked at the old issue from the previous August. "I'd appreciate it if you wouldn't look too closely."

Marshall flipped the pages backward. "I want to see the issues up to the time Harmel left."

"Okay. Ted left in late July. Here's June . . . May . . . April. Just what are you looking for?"

"The reason why he got run out."

"You know the story, of course."

"Brummel says he molested some girl."

"Yes, Brummel says a lot of things."

"Well, did he or didn't he?"

"The girl said he did. She was about twelve, I guess, a daughter of one of the college regents."

"*Which* one?"

Bernice probed her brain, finally forcing the memory out. "Jarred. Adam Jarred. I think he's still there."

"Is he on that list you got from Darr?"

"No. But perhaps he should be. Ted knew Jarred pretty well. The two of them used to go fishing together. He did know the daughter, had frequent access to her, and that helped the case against him."

"So why wasn't he prosecuted?"

"I don't think it ever went that far. He was arraigned before the district judge—"

"Baker?"

"Yes, the one on the list. The case went into the judge's chambers and apparently they struck some kind of deal. Ted was gone just a few days after that."

Marshall gave the worktable an angry slap. "Boy, I wish I hadn't let that guy get away. You didn't tell me I'd be putting my fist through a beehive."

"I didn't know that much about it."

Marshall kept scanning the pages in front of him; Bernice was going through the previous month.

"You say this all blew up in July?"

"Mid to late July."

"The paper's pretty quiet about it."

"Oh sure. Ted wasn't going to print anything against himself, obviously. Besides, he didn't have to; his reputation was shot to pieces anyway. Our circulation dropped critically. Several weeks went by without any paychecks."

"Oh-oh. What's this?"

The two of them zeroed in on a letter to the editor in a Friday issue from early July.

Marshall scanned, muttered as he read, " 'I must express my indignation at the unfair treatment this board of regents has received from the local press. . . . The recent articles published in the *Ashton Clarion* amount to nothing less than blatant malfeasance of journalism, and we hope our local editor will be professional enough to check his facts from now on before printing any more groundless innuendoes . . .' "

"Yes!" Bernice brightened with recollection. "This was a letter from Eugene Baylor." And then she slapped her hands to either side of her face and exclaimed, "Oh. . . ! *Those* articles!" Bernice started flipping hurriedly through the June binder. "Yes, here's one."

The headline read, "STRACHAN CALLS FOR AUDIT." Marshall read the lead: " 'Despite continuing opposition from the Whitmore College board of regents, College Dean Eldon Strachan today called for an audit of all Whitmore College accounts and investments, still voicing his concern over recent allegations of mishandling of funds.' "

Bernice's eyes rolled up and scanned the heavens as she said, "Hoo-boy, this may be more than just a beehive!"

Marshall read a little further: " 'Strachan has asserted that there is "more than adequate evidence" to justify such an audit even though it would be costly and premature, as the board of regents still maintains.' "

Bernice explained, "You see, I never paid that much attention when all this was going on. Ted was an aggressive sort, he'd gotten on the bad side of people before, and this just sounded like another mundane political thing. I was just a reporter on the innocuous human interest staff . . . what did I care about all this?"

"So," said Marshall, "the college dean got himself in hot water with the regents. Sounds like a real feud."

"Ted was a good friend of Eldon Strachan. He took sides and the regents didn't like it. Here's another one, just the week after."

Marshall read, " 'REGENT MAULS STRACHAN. Whitmore College Regent Eugene Baylor, the college general treasurer, today accused Dean Eldon Strachan of "malicious political hatcheting," asserting that Strachan is using "deplorable and unethical methods" to further his own dynasty within the college administration.' Heh. Not exactly a harmless little tiff between friends."

"Oh, I understand it got bitter, really bitter. And Ted probably stuck his nose out a little too far. He started catching the crossfire."

"Hence Eugene Baylor's angry letter."

"Along with political pressure, I'm sure. Strachan and Ted had many meetings and Ted was finding out a lot, maybe too much."

"But you have no details . . ."

Bernice only threw up her hands and shook her head. "We have these articles and Ted's phone number, and the list."

"Yeah," Marshall mused, "the list. A lot of college regents on it."

"Plus the chief of police and the district judge who cooked Ted's goose."

"So what became of Strachan?"

"Fired."

Bernice flipped through some more old *Clarions*. A loose page fluttered out and dropped to the floor. Marshall picked it up. Something on the page caught his eye and he perused it until Bernice found what she was looking for, an article from late June.

"Yes, here's the write-up," she said. " 'STRACHAN FIRED. Citing conflicts of interest and professional incompetency as their reasons, the Whitmore College board of regents today unanimously called for Dean Eldon Strachan's resignation.' "

"Not a very long article," Marshall commented.

"Ted put it in because he had to, but it's obvious he held back any damaging details. He firmly believed Strachan's cause was just."

Marshall kept flipping through the pages. "Ehhh, what's this one here? 'WHITMORE COULD BE MILLIONS IN ARREARS, SAYS STRACHAN'." Marshall read that one carefully. "Wait a minute here, he's saying the college could be in big trouble, but he isn't saying how he knows."

"It kept coming out in bits and pieces. We just never got all of them before Strachan and Ted were silenced."

"But millions . . . you're talking real money here."

"But you see all the connections?"

"Yeah. The regents, the judge, the police chief, Young, the comptroller, and who knows who else, all connected to Langstrat and very quiet about it."

"And don't forget Ted Harmel."

"Yeah, he's quiet about it too. I mean, *real* quiet. The guy's scared out of his socks. But he wasn't a very loyal member of the group if he sided with Strachan against the regents."

"So they rubbed him out, so to speak, along with Strachan."

"Maybe. So far we have just a theory, and it's foggy."

"But we do have a theory, and my being in jail fits the pattern."

"Too nicely just yet," Marshall thought aloud. "We need to realize what we're saying here. We're talking political corruption, abuse of process, racketeering, who knows what else? We'd better be really sure of ourselves."

"What was that page there that dropped?"

"Huh?"

"The one you picked up."

"Mm. It was out of order. It's dated clear back in January."

Bernice reached for the proper binder on the archive shelf. "I don't want the archives all mixed up after—hey, what'd you fold it all up for?"

Marshall shrugged a little, gave her a very gentle look, and unfolded the page.

"There's an article about your sister," he said.

She took the page from him and looked at the news story. The headline read "KRUEGER DEATH RULED SUICIDE." She put the page down quickly.

"I figured you wouldn't want to be reminded," he said.

"I've seen it before," she said abruptly. "I have a copy at home."

"I read the article just now."

"I know."

She pulled out another binder, opening it on the worktable.

"Marshall," she said, "you may as well know everything about it. It might come up again. The case is not resolved in my mind, and it's been a very difficult battle for me."

Marshall only sighed and said, "You started this, remember that now."

Bernice kept her lips tight and her body straight. She was trying to be a detached machine.

She pointed to the first story, dated mid-January: "BRUTAL DEATH ON CAMPUS."

Marshall read silently. He wasn't prepared for the horrible details.

"The story isn't entirely accurate," Bernice commented in a very guarded tone of voice. "They didn't find Pat in her own dorm room; she was down the hall in an unoccupied room. I guess some of the girls used that room to study by themselves if it got too noisy on the floor. No one knew where she was until someone spotted the blood running out under the door . . ." Her voice cracked, and she shut her mouth tightly.

Patricia Elizabeth Krueger, age nineteen, had been found in a dorm room, naked and very dead, her throat slashed. There was no sign of a struggle, the entire college was in a state of shock, there were no witnesses.

Bernice flipped to another page and another headline, "NO CLUES TO KRUEGER DEATH." Marshall read it quickly, feeling more and more like he was invading a very sensitive area where he had no business to be. The article stated that no witnesses had come forth, no one had heard or seen anything, there was no clue to who the assailant might be.

"And you read the last one," Bernice said. "They finally ruled it was a suicide. They decided that my sister had stripped herself and cut her own throat."

Marshall was incredulous. "And that was that?"

"That was that."

Marshall closed the binder quietly. He had never seen Bernice looking so vulnerable. The feisty little reporter who could hold her own in a jail cell full of hookers had one part of her still laid bare and wounded beyond healing. He put his hands gently on her shoulders.

"I'm sorry," he said.

"It's why I came here, you know." She wiped her eyes with her fingers, reached for a nearby tissue to wipe her nose. "I . . . I just couldn't leave it at that. I knew Pat. I knew her better than anyone. She just wasn't the type to do such a thing. She was happy, well-adjusted, she liked college. She sounded just fine in her letters."

"Why . . . why don't we just pack it up for the night?"

Bernice didn't acknowledge his suggestion. "I checked the dorm layout, the room where she died, the roster for the names of every girl living in that building; I talked to all of them. I checked the police reports, the coroner's report, I went through all of Pat's personal effects. I tried to track down Pat's roommate, but she'd left. I still can't remember her name. I only met her once when I was here for a visit.

"I finally decided just to stick around, get a job, wait and see. I had some newspaper background, the job here was easy enough to land."

Marshall put his arm around her shoulders. "Well, listen. I'll help you out, any way I can. You don't have to carry this whole thing by yourself."

She relaxed a bit, leaning into him just enough to acknowledge his embracing arm. "I don't want to bother you."

"You're not bothering me. Listen, as soon as you're ready, we can go over it, recheck everything. There might still be some leads somewhere."

Bernice shook her two fists and whimpered, "If I could just be more objective about it!"

Marshall gave her a gentle, comforting chuckle and a friendly squeeze. "Well, maybe I can handle that end of it. You're doing a good job, Bernie. Just hang in there."

She was a nice kid, Marshall thought, and as far as he could remember this was the first time he'd ever touched her.

13

For obvious reasons the congregation of Ashton Community Church was much smaller and fragmented this Sunday morning, but Hank had to admit that the whole atmosphere was more peaceful. As he stood behind the old pulpit to open the service, he could see the smiling faces of his supporters peppered throughout the small crowd: yes, there were the Colemans sitting in their usual spot. Grandma Duster was there too, in much better health, praise the Lord, and there were the Coopers, the Harrises, and Ben Squires, the mailman. Alf Brummel hadn't made it, but Gordon Mayer and his wife were there, and so were Sam and Helen Turner. Some of the not-so-actives were there for their usual once-a-month drop-in, and Hank gave them special glances and smiles to let them know they were noticed.

As Mary banged out "All Hail the Power of Jesus' Name" on the piano and Hank led the singing, another couple came in the back door and took a seat near the rear, as new folks usually did. Hank didn't recognize them at all.

Scion remained near the back door, watching Andy and June Forsythe take their seats. Then he looked up toward the platform and gave Krioni and Triskal a friendly salute. They smiled and saluted back. A few demons had come in with the humans, and they were not happy to see this new heavenly stranger even lurking about, let alone bringing new people into the church. But Scion backed nonthreateningly out the door.

Hank couldn't explain why he felt as joyful as he did this morning. Maybe it was having Grandma Duster there, and the Colemans, and the new couple. And then there was that other new fellow, the big blond guy sitting in the back. He had to be a football lineman or something.

Hank kept remembering what Grandma had said to him, "We need to pray that the Lord will gather them in . . ."

He got to the sermon and opened his Bible to Isaiah 55.

" 'Seek the Lord while He may be found; call upon Him while He is near. Let the wicked forsake his way, and the unrighteous man his thoughts; and let him return to the Lord, and He will have compassion on him; and to our God, for He will abundantly pardon . . . For my thoughts are not your thoughts, neither are your ways My ways, declares the Lord. For as the heavens are higher than the earth, so are my ways higher than your ways, and my thoughts than your thoughts. For as the rain and the snow come down from heaven, and do not return there without watering the earth, and making it bear and sprout, and furnishing seed to the sower and bread to the eater; so shall my word be which goes forth from my mouth; it shall not return to Me empty, without accomplishing what I desire, and without succeeding in the matter for which I sent it. For you will go out with joy, and be led forth with peace; the mountains and the hills will break forth into shouts of joy before you, and all the trees of the field will clap their hands.' "

Hank loved that passage, and he couldn't help smiling as he began to explain it. Some people simply stared at him, listening out of obligation. But others even leaned forward in their seats, hanging on every word. The new couple sitting in the back kept nodding their heads with very intent expressions. The big blond man smiled, nodded his head, even shouted out an "Amen!"

The words kept coming to Hank's heart and mind. It had to be the Lord's anointing. He stopped by the pulpit from time to time to look at his notes, but most of the time he was all over the platform, feeling like he was somewhere between heaven and earth, speaking forth the Word of God.

The few little demons lurking about could only cower and sneer. Some did manage to stop the ears of the people they owned, but the onslaught this morning was particularly severe and painful. To them, Hank's preaching had all the soothing effect of a buzz saw.

On top of the church, Signa and his warriors refused to bend or back down. Lucius dropped by with a sizeable flock of demons just in time for the service, but Signa would not step aside.

"You know better than to tamper with me!" Lucius threatened.

Signa was sickeningly polite. "I'm sorry, we cannot allow any more demons into the church this morning."

Lucius must have had more important things for his demons to do that morning than try to hack their way through a wall of obstinate angels. He delivered a few choice insults and then the whole bunch roared off into the air, bound for some other mischief.

When the service ended, some people made a beeline for the door. Others made a beeline for Hank.

"Pastor, my name is Andy Forsythe, and this is my wife June."

"Hello, hello," Hank said, and he could feel a wide smile stretching his face.

"That was great," Andy said, shaking his head in amazement and still shaking Hank's hand. "It was . . . boy, it was really great!"

They made small talk for a few minutes, finding out about each other. Andy owned and ran the lumberyard just on the outskirts of town; June was a legal secretary. They had a son, Ron, who was in trouble with drugs and needed the Lord.

"Well," said Andy, "We haven't been saved too long ourselves. We used to go to the Ashton United Christian . . ." His voice trailed off.

June was less inhibited. "We were starving there. We couldn't wait to get out."

Andy cut back in, "Yeah, that's right. We heard about this church; well, actually we heard about you; we heard you were in a bit of trouble for being such a stickler with the Word of God, and we just thought to ourselves, 'We ought to check that guy out.' Now I'm glad we did.

"Pastor," he continued, "I want you to know there are a lot of hungry people out there. We have some friends who love the Lord and have no place to go. It's been really strange the last few years. One by one the churches around here have kind of died. Oh, they're still there, all right, and they have the people and the bucks, but . . . you know what I mean."

Hank wasn't sure that he did. "What *do* you mean?"

Andy shook his head. "Satan's really playing games with this town, I guess. Ashton never used to be this way, with so much weird stuff going on. Hey, you may have trouble believing this, but we have friends who have dropped out of three, no, *four* of the local churches."

June exchanged glances with Andy as she went through a mental list of names. "Greg and Eva Smith, the Bartons, the Jennings, Clint Neal . . ."

"Yeah, right, right," said Andy. "Like I said, there are a lot of hungry people out there, sheep without a shepherd. The churches around here just don't cut it. They don't preach the gospel."

Just then Mary walked up, all smiles. Hank happily introduced her.

Then Mary said, "Hank, I'd like you to meet—" and she turned toward the empty room. Whoever was supposed to be there wasn't. "Well . . . he's gone!"

"Who was it?" Hank asked.

"Oh, you remember that big guy sitting in the back?"

"The big blond guy?"

"Yes. I got a chance to talk to him. He told me to tell you that," Mary deepened her voice to mimic him, " 'the Lord is with you, keep praying and keep listening.' "

"Well, that was nice. Did you get his name?"

"Uh . . . no, I don't think he ever told me."

Andy asked, "Who was this?"

"Oh," said Hank, "you know, that big guy in the back. He was sitting right next to you."

Andy looked at June, and her eyes got wide. Andy started smiling, then he started laughing, and then he started clapping his hands and practically dancing.

"Praise the Lord!" he exclaimed, and Hank hadn't seen such enthusiasm in a long time. "Praise the Lord, there was nobody there. Pastor, we didn't see a soul!"

Mary's mouth dropped open, and she covered it with her fingers.

Oliver Young was a real showman; he could work an audience right down to each tear or titter and time it so well that they became just so many puppets on a string. He would stand behind the pulpit with incredible dignity and poise, and his words were so well-chosen that whatever he was saying had to be right. The vast congregation certainly seemed to think so; they had packed the place out. Many of them were professionals: doctors, teachers, lawyers, self-proclaimed philosophers and poets; a very large segment was from or connected in some way with the college. They took fastidious notes on Young's message, as if it were a lecture.

Marshall had heard a lot of this little song and dance before, so on this particular Sunday he mulled over the questions he couldn't wait to spring on Young after the service was over.

Young continued. "Did not God say, 'Let us make man in our image, according to our likeness'? What had remained in the darkness of tradition and ignorance, we find now revealed within ourselves. We discover—no, rather, we *re*discover the knowledge we have always had as a race: we are inherently divine in our very essence, and have within ourselves the capacity for good, the potential to become, as it were, gods, made in the exact likeness of Father God, the ultimate source of all that is . . ."

Marshall took a quick and furtive glance sideways. There was Kate, and there was Sandy taking notes like mad, and next to her sat Shawn Ormsby. Sandy and Shawn had hit it off pretty well, and he had a definite positive influence on her life. Today, for example, he had made a deal with Sandy: he would go to church with her if she would go with her folks. Well, it worked.

Marshall had to admit, even though a little reluctantly, that Shawn could communicate with Sandy in ways Marshall never could. There had been several occasions when Shawn had served quite well as a liaison or interpreter between Sandy and Marshall and opened lines of communication neither of them thought could ever materialize. Things were getting peaceful around the house at last. Shawn seemed a gentle sort with a real gift for refereeing.

So what do I do now? Marshall wondered. For the first time in who knows how long, my whole family is sitting together in church, and that's nothing but a miracle, a real miracle. But we sure picked one heck of a church to be sitting together in, and as for that preacher up there . . .

It would be so comfortable and so nice to let everything be, but he was a reporter, and this Young had something to hide. Nuts. Talk about conflict of interests!

So while Pastor Oliver Young was up there trying to get across his ideas on the "infinite divine potential within seemingly finite man," Marshall had his own nagging issues to think about.

The service ended punctually at noon, and the carillon in the tower automatically clicked on and began to play a very traditional, very Christian-sounding accompaniment to all the hand shaking, visiting, and filing out.

Marshall and his family entered the flow of traffic that oozed toward the foyer. Oliver Young was standing by the front door in his usual spot, greeting all his parishioners, shaking hands, cootchy-cooing the babies, being pastorly. Soon Marshall, Kate, Sandy, and Shawn had their turn with him.

"Well, Marshall, good to see you," Young gushed, shaking Marshall's hand.

"Have you met Sandy?" Marshall asked, and formally introduced Young to his daughter.

Young was very warm. "Sandy, I'm very glad to see you."

Sandy at least acted glad to be there.

"And Shawn!" Young exclaimed. "Shawn Ormsby!" The two of them shook hands.

"Oh, so you two know each other?" Marshall asked.

"Oh, I've known Shawn since he was just a little shaver. Shawn, don't make yourself so scarce, all right?"

"All right," Shawn answered with a shy smile.

The others moved on, but Marshall lagged behind and came up close on the other side to speak to Young some more.

He waited until Young had finished greeting one little group of people, and then interjected into the pause, "Hey, I just thought you'd like to know that things are going better now with Sandy and me."

Young smiled, shook a few hands, then said sideways to Marshall, "Wonderful! That's really wonderful, Marshall." He offered his hand to someone else: "Nice seeing you here today."

In another space between exiting greetees, Marshall interjected, "Yeah, she really enjoyed your sermon this morning. She said it was very challenging."

"Well, thank you for saying so. Yes, Mr. Beaumont, how are you?"

"You know, it even seemed to be along the same lines as what Sandy's getting in school, in Juleen Langstrat's classes."

Young didn't answer that, but directed all his attention to a young couple with a baby. "Oh my, she's getting so big."

Marshall continued, "You're going to have to meet Professor Langstrat sometime. There's a very interesting parallel between what she teaches and what you preach." There was no response from Young. "I understand, as a matter of fact, that Langstrat's pretty deeply involved in occultism and Eastern mysticism . . ."

"Well," Young finally responded, "I wouldn't know anything about that, Marshall."

"And you definitely don't know this Professor Langstrat?"

"No, I told you that."

"Haven't you attended several private sessions with her on a regular basis, and not only you, but also Alf Brummel, Ted Harmel, Delores Pinckston, Eugene Baylor, and even Judge Baker?"

Young turned just a little red, paused, then grimaced with embarrassed recollection.

"Oh, for goodness sake!" he laughed. "Where in the world has my mind been? You know, all this time I've been thinking of someone else!"

"So you do know her?"

"Well, yes, of course. Many of us do."

Young turned aside to greet some more people. When those people had gone, Marshall was still standing there.

Marshall pressed, "So what about these private sessions? Does she really have a clientele including community leaders, elected officials, regents at the college . . ."

Young looked directly at Marshall, and his eyes were a little cold. "Marshall, just what is your specific concern here?"

"Just doing my job. Whatever this is, it seems to be something the people of Ashton should know about, especially because it involves so many of the influential people who are shaping this town."

"Well, if you are concerned about it, I'm not the person to talk to. You should go and ask Professor Langstrat herself."

"Oh, I intend to. I just wanted to give you the chance to give me some honest answers, something I feel you're not quite doing."

Young's voice got a bit strained. "Marshall, if I seem to be elusive it is because what you are trying to pry into is protected by professional ethics. It is privileged information. I was simply hoping you would figure that out without my having to tell you."

Kate was calling from the sidewalk. "Marshall, we're all waiting for you."

Marshall stepped away from the conversation, and it was just as well. It could only have gotten hotter from that point, and it was getting him nowhere anyway. Young was cool, very tough, and very slippery.

A few states away, in a deep, secluded, and steep-sided valley rimmed by high mountains and carpeted with thick green ground cover and moss-tufted rock, a small but well-constructed cluster of buildings nestled like a lonely outpost in the center of the valley floor, accessible only by one rough and meandering gravel road.

That little cluster of buildings, once a dismal and dilapidated old ranch, had been expanded into a complex of stone and brick buildings which now housed a small dormitory, an office complex, a dining hall, a maintenance building, a clinic, and several private dwellings. There were no signs, however, no labels anywhere, nothing to indicate where or what anything was.

Drawing a charcoal streak across the sky, a sinister black object flew over the mountaintops and began to drop into the valley, piercing through the paper-thin layers of mist that hung in the air. Cloaked by oppressive spiritual darkness and silent as a black cloud, Ba-al Rafar, the Prince of Babylon, floated along. He stayed close to the contour of the mountainside, maneuvering on a course that weaved this way and that among the dead snags and rocky crags. The canopy of darkness followed him like a cast shadow, like a tiny circle of night upon the landscape; a faint streak of red and yellow vapor trailed from his nostrils and hung in the air behind him like a long, slowly settling ribbon.

Below, the ranch looked like a huge hive of hideous black insects. Several layers of ruthless warriors hovered almost stationary in a vast dome of defense over the complex, swords drawn, yellow eyes peering across the valley. Deep within this shell, demons of all shapes, sizes, and strengths darted about in a boiling mass of activity. As Rafar dropped closer, he noted a concentration of black spirits around a large multistoried stone house on the fringe of the cluster. The Strongman is there, he thought, so he banked gently to one side, changing his course for that building.

The outer sentinels saw him approaching and gave an eerie, siren-like wail. Immediately the defenders radiated outward from Rafar's flight path, opening a channel through the defense layers. Rafar swooped skillfully through the channel as demons on all sides saluted him with upheld swords, their glowing eyes like thousands of paired yellow stars on black velvet. He ignored them and passed quickly through. The channel closed again behind him like a living gate.

He floated slowly down through the roof of the house, through the attic, past rafters, walls, plaster, through an upstairs bedroom, through a thick, beam-supported floor and down into a spacious living room below.

The evil in the room was thick and confining, the darkness like black liquid that swirled about with any motion of the limbs. The room was crowded.

"Ba-al Rafar, the Prince of Babylon!" a demon announced from somewhere, and monstrous demons all around the perimeter of the room bowed in respect.

Rafar folded his wings in regal, capelike fashion and stood with an intimidating air of royalty and might, his jewels flashing impressively. His big yellow eyes studied carefully the orderly ranks of demons lined up all around him. A horrible gathering. These were spirits from the principality levels, princes themselves of their own nations, peoples, tribes. Some were from Africa, some were from the Orient, several were from Europe. All were invincible. Rafar noted their tremendous size and formidable appearance; they all matched him for size and ferocity, and he doubted he would ever venture to challenge any of them. To receive a bow from them was a great honor, a compliment indeed.

"Hail, Rafar," said a gargling voice from the end of the room.

The Strongman. It was forbidden to speak his name. He was one of the few majesties intimate with Lucifer himself—a vicious global tyrant responsible over the centuries for resisting the plans of the living God and establishing Lucifer's kingdom on the earth. Rafar and his kind controlled nations; those such as the Strongman controlled Rafar and his kind.

The Strongman rose from his place, and his huge form filled that part of the room. The evil that emanated from him could be felt everywhere, almost like an extension of his body. He was grotesque, hulking, his black hide hanging like sacks and curtains from his limbs and torso, his face a macabre landscape of bony prominences and deep, folded furrows. His jewels flashed brilliantly from his neck, chest, arms; his big black wings draped his body like a royal robe and trailed along the floor.

Rafar bowed low in homage, feeling the Strongman's presence from clear across the room. "Hail, my lord."

The Strongman never wasted words. "Shall we be detained again?"

"The errors of Prince Lucius are being corrected. The new resistance is failing, my lord. Soon the town will be ready."

"And what of the host of heaven?"

"Limited."

The Strongman did not like Rafar's answer—Rafar could feel that distinctly. He spoke slowly. "We have received reports of a strong Captain of the Host being sent to Ashton. I believe you know him."

"I have reason to believe Tal has been sent, but I have anticipated him."

The big, velvet-draped eyes burned with fury. "Is it not this Tal who vanquished you at the fall of Babylon?"

Rafar knew he must answer, and quickly. "It is this Tal."

"Then the delays have cost us our advantage. You have now been matched strength for strength."

"My lord, you will see what your servant can do."

"Bold words, Rafar, but your strengths can only succeed with immediacy; the strengths of our enemies grow with time."

"All will be ready."

"And what of the man of God and the newspaper man?"

"Does my lord even give them his attention?"

"Your lord wishes you to give them yours!"

"They are powerless, my lord, and will soon be removed."

"But only if Tal is removed," the Strongman said derisively. "Let me see it happen before you bother me in boasting about it. Until then, we remain confined here. Rafar, I will not wait long!"

"Nor shall you need to."

The Strongman only smirked. "You have your orders. Begone!"

Rafar bowed low, and with an unfurling of his wings he quietly rose through the house until he was outside.

Then, with a furious burst of rage, he swooped upward, sending unexpecting demons tumbling out of the way. He picked up speed, his wings rushing in a blinding blur, and the defenders could barely get a channel opened before he burst through it trailing a hot stream of sulfurous breath. They closed up the channel again, giving each other curious looks as they watched him soar away.

Rafar roared like a rocket up the side of the mountains and then out over the craggy peaks and back toward the little town of Ashton. In his rage he cared not who saw him, he cared not about stealth or even decorum. Let the whole world see him, and let it tremble! He was Rafar, the Prince of Babylon! Let all the world bow before him or be decimated under the edge of his sword!

Tal! The very name was bitterness itself on his tongue. The lords of

Lucifer would never let him forget that defeat so long ago. Never—until the day when Rafar redeemed his honor.

And indeed he would. Rafar could see his sword gutting Tal and scattering him in shreds and pieces across the sky; he could feel the impact in his arms, he could hear the ripping sound of it. It was only a matter of time.

Among the jagged rocks on one mountain's summit, a silver-haired man came out of hiding to watch Rafar quickly shrink into the distance, etching a long black trail across the sky until he vanished over the horizon. The man took one more look at the demon-swarmed cluster of buildings in the valley, looked again toward the horizon, then vanished down the other side of the mountain in a flash of light and a flurry of wings.

14

Well, thought Marshall, sooner or later I have to get around to it. On Thursday afternoon, when things were quiet, he closed himself in his office and made some phone calls trying to track down Professor Juleen Langstrat. He called the college, got the number of the Psychology Department, and went through two receptionists in two different offices before he finally found out that Langstrat was not in today and had an unlisted home number. Then Marshall thought of the very cooperative Albert Darr, and gave his office a ring. Professor Darr was teaching, but would return his call if he would leave a message. Marshall left a message. Two hours later, Albert Darr returned Marshall's call, and he did have the unlisted number for Juleen Langstrat's apartment.

Marshall called the number.

It was busy.

The living room of Juleen Langstrat's apartment was dimly lit by one small lamp on the mantel. The room was quiet, warm, and comfortable. The shades were drawn to block out distractions, bright light, and any other disturbances. The phone was off the hook.

Juleen Langstrat sat in her chair, speaking quietly to her counselee who sat opposite her.

"You hear only the sound of my voice . . ." she said, then repeated the sentence several times quietly and clearly. "You hear only the sound of my voice . . ."

This went on for several minutes until her subject was in a deep, hypnotic trance.

"You are descending . . . descending deep within yourself . . ."

Langstrat watched the face of her subject carefully. She then extended her hands palms out, fingers spread, and began to move her hands up and down just inches away from the subject's body, as if feeling for something. "Release your true self . . . let it go . . . it is infinite . . . at unity with all existence . . . Yes! I can feel it! Can you read my energy returning to you?"

The subject murmured, "Yes . . ."

"You are free from your body now . . . your body is an illusion . . . you feel the bounds of your body dissolving away . . ."

Langstrat leaned in close, still using her hands.

"You are free now . . ."

"Yes . . . yes, I am free . . ."

"I can feel your life force expanding."

"Yes, I can feel it."

"That's enough. You may stop there." Langstrat was intent, closely observing everything. "Go back . . . go back . . . Yes, I can feel you receding. In a moment you will feel me slipping from you; don't be alarmed, I'm still here."

In the next several minutes, she brought her subject slowly back out of the trance, step by step, suggestion by suggestion.

Finally she said, "All right, when I count to three, you will awake. One, two, three."

Sandy Hogan opened her eyes, rolled them about dizzily, then took a deep breath, coming fully around.

"Wow!" she responded.

The three of them laughed together.

"Wasn't that something?" asked Shawn, sitting next to Langstrat.

"Wow," was all Sandy could say.

This was a real first for Sandy. It had been Shawn's idea and, though she hesitated at first, now she was very glad that she had gone along with it.

The apartment shades were opened, and Sandy and Shawn prepared to go back to their afternoon classes.

"Well, thank you for coming," said the professor at the door.

" Thank *you,*" Sandy piped.

"And thank you for bringing her," Langstrat told Shawn. Then she said to the two of them, "Now remember, I wouldn't advise speaking to anyone about this. It's a very personal and intimate experience that we should all respect."

"Yeah, right, right," said Sandy.

Shawn drove her back to campus.

It was Friday again, and Hank sat at home in his little corner office looking anxiously at the clock. Mary was usually very reliable. She had said she would be back before Carmen got there for her afternoon counseling appointment. Hank had no idea if there were any spies watching the house, but he could never be sure. All he needed was for someone to figure out that Carmen was dropping in to see him while Mary went grocery shopping. Hank's fearful side could envision all kinds of plots his enemies might be forming against him, such as sending some strange and seductive woman to compromise and ruin him.

Well, he knew one thing: If Carmen didn't show a genuine responsiveness to the counseling and begin to apply real solutions to a real problem, that would be the end of it as far as he was concerned.

Oh-oh. There was the doorbell. He sneaked a look out the window. Carmen's red Fiat was parked out front. Yes, she was standing at the door, in broad daylight, in full view of ten or fifteen houses. The way she was dressed today made Hank figure he'd better let her in quickly, if only to get her out of sight.

Where, oh where, was Mary?

Mary was not sure she liked the new owners of what used to be Joe's Market. Oh, it wasn't their service or the way they ran the store, or whether or not they were friendly; they were okay in most of those departments, and Mary also figured it would take time for them to know everyone and vice versa. What bothered Mary was how obviously secretive they became any time she asked them whatever became of Joe Carlucci and his family. As far as Mary could find out, Joe, Angelina, and their children left Ashton abruptly and didn't tell anyone, and so far no one could be found who even knew where they went.

Oh well. She hurried out of the store and toward her car, a young box boy pushing a cart of groceries along behind her. She opened the trunk and watched the boy load the groceries in.

And then she felt it, suddenly, without any apparent reason: an unexplainable tinge of emotion, an odd mixture of fear and depression. She felt cold, nervous, a little shaky, and could think of nothing but getting out of that place and hurrying home.

Triskal had been accompanying her, guarding her, and he felt it too. With a metallic ring and a flash of light, his sword was instantly in his hand.

Too late! From somewhere behind him came a stunning blow on the back of his neck. He toppled forward. His wings shot out to steady him, but an incredible weight came down on his back like a pile driver and pinned him down.

He could see their feet, like the clawed feet of hideous reptiles, and the red flicker of their blades; he could hear their sulfurous hissing. He looked up. At least a dozen demonic warriors surrounded him. They were towering, fierce, with glowing yellow eyes and dripping fangs, and they were sneering and gargling with laughter.

Triskal looked to see if Mary was all right. He knew her safety would soon be threatened if he didn't act. But what could he do?

What was that? He suddenly felt an intense wave of evil rolling over him.

"Pick him up," said a voice like thunder.

A viselike hand curled around his neck and jerked him up as if he were a toy. Now he was looking at all these spirits eye to eye. They were newcomers to Ashton. He had never seen such size, strength, and brazenness. Their bodies were covered with thick, ironlike scales, their arms rippled with power, their faces were mocking, their sulfurous breath choked him.

They turned him around and held him tightly, and he found himself face to face with a vision of sheer horror.

Flanked by no less than ten more huge demonic warriors, a gargantuan spirit stood with an S-curved sword in his monstrous black hand.

Rafar! The thought coursed through Triskal's mind like a death sentence; every inch of his being tightened with the anticipation of blows, defeat, unbearable pain.

The big, fanged mouth broke into a mocking and hideous grin; amber saliva dripped from the fangs, and sulfur chugged forth in rancid clouds as the giant warlord chuckled mockingly.

"Are you so surprised?" Rafar asked. "You should feel privileged. You, little angel, are the first to look upon me."

"And how are you today?" Hank asked as he showed Carmen to a comfortable chair in his office area.

She sank into the chair with a coo and a sigh, and Hank began to wonder where he left his tape recorder. He knew he was innocent of wrongdoing here, but some proof would be nice.

"I'm much better," she answered, and her voice was pleasant and even. "You know, maybe you can tell me why, but I haven't heard any voices talking to me all week."

"Oh . . . um . . . yeah," said Hank, finally getting his counselor's thoughts in gear. "That was what we were talking about, wasn't it?"

Triskal looked toward Mary. She was thanking the box boy and closing her trunk.

Rafar watched Triskal, amused. "Oh, I see. You are here to protect her. From what? Did you expect to swat mere flies?" Triskal had no answer. Rafar's tone became cruel and cutting. "No, you are mistaken, little angel. It is a much greater power with whom you have to do."

Rafar tapped the ground with his sword, and Triskal immediately felt the iron hands of two demons clamping his arms from behind. He looked toward Mary. She was looking for the key to the car door. She was getting into the car. Another demon stretched out his sword and pierced the hood of the car. Mary tried to start the engine. Nothing happened.

Rafar looked toward the nearby laundromat that faced the parking lot. A young, greasy-looking character stood in front of it, leaning against a post. Triskal could tell the man was possessed by one of Rafar's henchmen—as a matter of fact, several of them. At Rafar's nod, the demons went into action and the man started walking toward Mary's car.

Mary checked her lights. No, she had not left them on. She turned the key on and turned on the radio. It played. The horn honked. What on earth was the matter? She saw the young character coming her way from the direction of the laundromat. Oh, great.

As Triskal watched helplessly, the demons guided the man up to the car window.

"Hey, cutie," he said, "having some trouble here?"

Mary looked out at him. He was skinny, dirty, and dressed in black leather and chrome chains.

She called through the window, "Uh . . . no thanks. I'm all right."

He only smirked, eyeing her up and down as he said, "Why don't you open up and let me see what I can do?"

Hank didn't feel right about any of this. Where was Mary? At least Carmen was making a little more sense this time. She seemed to be dealing with her problems intelligently and with a genuine desire to change things. Maybe it would be different this time, but Hank wasn't counting on it.

"So," he asked, "what do you suppose became of those amorous voices in the night?"

"I don't listen to them anymore," she answered. "There's one thing you helped me to realize, just by talking about it: Those voices aren't real. I've only been fooling myself."

Hank was very gentle when he agreed, "Yes, I think you're right."

She heaved a deep sigh and looked at him with those big blue eyes. "I was trying to cope with my loneliness, that's all. I think that was it. Pastor, you're just so strong. I wish I could be that way."

"Well, the Bible says, 'I can do all things through Christ who strengthens me.'"

"Uh-huh. Where's your wife?"

"Getting groceries. She should be back any minute."

"Well . . ." Carmen leaned forward and smiled ever so sweetly. "I'm really drawing strength from your company. I want you to know that."

Mary could feel her heart pounding. What would this guy do next?

The man leaned against the window and his breath fogged the glass as he said, "Say, sweetheart, why don't you tell me your name?"

Rafar grabbed Triskal by the hair and jerked his head around. Triskal thought his head would snap off.

Rafar breathed sulfur right into Triskal's face as he said, "And now, little angel, I will have words with you." The tip of the long sword came up to Triskal's throat. "Where is your captain?"

Triskal did not answer.

Rafar yanked his head around and let him look toward Mary.

The man tried the latch on Mary's door. She was terrified. She groped for every lock button in the car, pushing each one down only seconds before the man could grab the outside latch. He tried all the doors, a leering smile on his face. Mary tried the horn again. A demon had already taken care of that—it didn't work. Rafar twisted Triskal's head back again, and the cold blade pressed against Triskal's face.

"I will ask you again: Where is your captain?"

Carmen was still telling Hank how much good this counseling was doing her, how he reminded her of her former husband, and how she was looking for a man with his qualities. Hank had to put a lid on this stuff.

"Well," he finally cut in, "do you have any other people in your life that you feel are significant as far as strength, support, friendship, those kinds of things?"

She looked at him just a little mournfully. "Sort of. I have friends who hang out at the tavern. But nothing ever lasts." She let her thoughts brew for a moment, then asked, "Do you think I'm attractive?"

The man in black leather leaned close to Mary's window, threatened her with horrible obscenities, then started banging on the glass with a large metal buckle.

Rafar nodded to a warrior whose hand passed through Mary's window and grasped the lock button, ready to pull it up at Rafar's order. The demons in the young man were drooling and ready. His hand was on the latch.

Rafar made sure Triskal could see it all, and then said, "Your answer?"

Triskal finally spoke, moaning, "The brake . . ."

Rafar held him tighter, leaning closer. "I didn't hear you."

Triskal repeated it. "The brake."

Mary had a flash. The car was parked on an incline. It wasn't much, but it might be enough to get the car moving. She released the parking brake and the car started to roll. The creep wasn't expecting that; he banged on the window, tried to get around in front of the car to stop it, but it began to roll at a steady clip and he soon realized that his efforts to stop it were becoming a little too obvious to other shoppers.

A husky contractor standing by his big four-wheeler finally saw what was going on and hollered, "Hey, creep, whaddaya doin'?"

Rafar watched it happen, his rising anger coursing through his big iron fist, making it tighten more and more around Triskal. Triskal thought his neck would crack any moment.

But then Rafar seemed to give in.

"Desist!" he ordered the demons. They backed off; the man gave up the chase and tried to saunter nonchalantly away. The big contractor started after him, and he fled.

The car kept rolling. There was an exit from the parking lot that emptied onto a backstreet with a fairly good grade. Mary steered for it, hoping no other cars or pedestrians would get in her way.

Triskal saw that she would make it.

So did Rafar. The cold steel of his blade pressed against Triskal's throat. "Well done, little angel. You have spared your charge until a more opportune time. I will leave you with only a message for today. Pay careful attention."

With that, Rafar released Triskal into the hands of his henchmen. One huge, warty demon pounded his iron fist into Triskal's torso and sent him spinning into the air where another demon intercepted him with a swat of his sword, carving a deep gash in his back. Triskal fluttered and tumbled down in a daze, into the clutches of two more demons who pummeled his limp body with iron fists and tore at him with taloned feet. For several horrible minutes the demons made violent sport with him as Rafar coldly watched. Finally the great Ba-al gave a growled command, and the warriors let Triskal go. He flopped to the ground, and Rafar's big taloned foot stomped down on his neck. The huge sword swung down and waved in small circles before Triskal's eyes as the demon master spoke.

"You will tell your captain that Rafar, the Prince of Babylon, is looking for him." The big foot pressed harder. "You will *tell* him!"

Suddenly Triskal was alone, a limp, ragged wreck. He struggled to his feet again. All he could think of now was Mary.

Hank gently took hold of Carmen's hand, lifted it off his own, and placed it courteously in her lap. He held it there for just a moment and looked into her eyes with compassion and yet firmness. He let go of it and then leaned back in his chair to a safe distance.

"Carmen," he said with a soft and understanding voice. "I'm very flattered that you're so impressed with my masculine qualities . . . and really, I have no doubts that a woman of your particular qualities will have no trouble finding a good man with whom to build a lasting and meaningful relationship. But listen—I don't mean to sound abrupt, but I have to emphasize one thing right here and now: I am not that man. I'm here as a minister and counselor, and we have to keep this relationship strictly limited to that of a counselor and his client."

Carmen seemed very disturbed, and very offended. "What are you saying to me?"

"I'm saying that we really can't continue these appointments. They're causing emotional conflicts for you. I think you'll be better off going to someone else."

Hank couldn't explain why, but even as he said that, he felt like he had just won some kind of battle. From the icy look in Carmen's eyes, he figured she had lost.

Mary was crying, wiping the tears from her face with her sleeve and praying a mile a minute. "Father God, dear Jesus, save me, save me, save me!" The hill was beginning to flatten out; the car slowed down, fifteen, ten, five miles an hour. She looked behind and saw no one following, but she was too scared by now to be comforted. She just wanted to get home.

Then, up the street behind her and about ten feet above the ground, Triskal flew, his clothes flashing with white-hot light and his wings rushing. His flight path was wobbly and the rhythm of his wings out of sync, but he was determined nevertheless. His face was etched with deep concern for her welfare. He spread his tattered, fluttering wings like a large canopy and let them brake him to a stop as he settled down onto the roof of the car. By now it was barely rolling and Mary just kept crying and wailing, jerking her body in futile attempts to urge the car onward.

Triskal reached down through the roof and gently placed his hand on Mary's shoulder. "Shhh . . . be calm, it's all right now. You're safe."

She looked behind her again and began to quiet down a little.

Triskal spoke to her heart. "The Lord has saved you. He won't let you go. You're all right."

The car was almost to a complete stop now. Mary pulled it over to the side of the street and parked it while she still had the momentum to do so. She pulled on the parking brake and sat there for several minutes just to compose herself.

"That's it," said Triskal, comforting her in her spirit. "Rest in the Lord. He's here."

Triskal slid off the roof of the car and reached his arm down through the hood, probing around. He found whatever it was he was looking for.

"Mary," he said, "why don't you try again?"

Mary sat in the car thinking to herself that the stupid thing would never start and what horrible timing it had, to die and leave her in such a fix.

"C'mon," Triskal prodded. "Take a step of faith. Trust God. You never know what He might do."

Mary decided to take one more stab at starting the car, even though she had little faith that anything would happen. She twisted the key. The engine cranked over, then sputtered, then started. She gave it several powerful revs just to make sure it stayed awake. Then, still in a very great hurry to get home to Hank's protecting arms, she pulled out into the street and hot-rodded for home with Triskal riding on the roof.

Hank was very relieved to hear the slam of the car door outside. "Oh, that must be Mary!"

Carmen got up. "I guess I'd better go."

Now that Mary was here, Hank added, "Oh, listen, you don't have to. You can stay for a while."

"No, no, I'll just leave. Maybe I ought to go out the back, even."

"No, don't be silly. Here. I'll see you to the door. I need to help Mary with those groceries anyway."

But Mary had forgotten about the groceries and only wanted to get inside the house. Triskal ran beside her. He was battered and limping, his clothing was torn, and he could still feel the fiery wound in his back.

Hank opened the door. "Hi, hon. Boy, I was getting worried about you." Then he saw her tear-filled eyes. "Hey, what—"

Carmen screamed. It was a sudden, heart-piercing scream that halted every thought and stifled any words. Hank spun around, not knowing what to expect.

"NOOOO!" Carmen shrieked, her arms guarding her face. "Are you mad? Get away from me, you hear? Get away!"

As Hank and Mary both looked on in horror, Carmen backed into the room, waving her arms as if trying to shield herself from some invisible attacker; she stumbled around the room, she tumbled over the furniture, she cursed and spewed horrible obscenities. She was terrified and enraged at the same time, her eyes wide and glassy, her face contorted.

Krioni tried to grab Triskal and hold him back. Triskal had glorified and was a shimmering white; his tattered wings filled the room and glimmered like a thousand rainbows. He held a gleaming sword in his hand, and the sword flashed and sang in blinding arcs as he engaged in a frenzied battle with Lust, a hideous demon with a black-scaled, slippery body like a lizard and a red tongue that lashed about his face like the tail of a snake. Lust was first defending himself, then lashing back with his glowing red sword, the crescent blade cutting crimson arcs through the air. The swords clashed with explosions of fire and light.

"Let me be, I tell you!" Lust screamed, his wings propelling him like a trapped hornet about the room.

"Let him be!" shouted Krioni, trying to hold Triskal back while staying out of the path of that infinitely sharp blade. "Do you hear my order? Let him be!"

At last Triskal withdrew, but held his sword steady and kept it raised in front of him, the light from the blade illuminating his raging face, his burning eyes.

Carmen calmed down, rubbed her eyes, and looked about the room with a frightened expression. Hank and Mary went to her immediately and tried to comfort her.

"What's wrong, Carmen?" Mary asked, wide-eyed and concerned. "It's just me, Mary. Did I do something? I didn't mean to scare you."

"No . . . no . . ." moaned Carmen. "It wasn't you. It was somebody else . . ."

"Who? What?"

Lust backed off, his sword still held high.

Krioni told him, "We will give place to you no longer today. Begone, and don't come here again!"

Lust folded his wings and circled carefully around the two heavenly warriors and over to the door.

"I was leaving anyway," the demon hissed.

"I was leaving anyway," said Carmen, composing herself. "There's . . . there's bad energy in this place. Good-bye."

She bolted out the door. Mary tried to call after her, but Hank touched Mary's arm and let her know that silence would be best for now.

Krioni held Triskal until the light around him faded and he replaced his sword. Triskal was shaking.

"Triskal," Krioni scolded, "you know Tal's orders! I was with Hank the whole time; he did just fine. There was no need—" Then Krioni saw Triskal's many injuries and the deep wound in his back. "Triskal, what happened?"

"I . . . I could not let myself be assailed by still another," Triskal gasped. "Krioni, we are more than matched."

Mary finally remembered that she was about to cry. She picked up where she had left off.

"Mary, what in the world is going on here?" Hank asked, putting his arms around her.

"Just close the door, honey!" she cried. "Just close the door and hold me. Please!"

15

Kate grabbed a kitchen towel and hurriedly wiped her hands so she could pick up the phone.

"Hello?"

"Hi there." It was Marshall.

Kate knew what was coming; it had been happening a lot the last two weeks. "Marshall, I am cooking dinner and I am cooking enough for all four of us . . ."

"Yeah, well . . ." Marshall had the tone of voice he always used when he was about to weasel out of something.

"Marshall!" Then Kate turned her back toward the living room where Sandy and Shawn were studying and talking, but mostly talking; she didn't want them to see the distress in her face. She lowered her voice. "I want you home for dinner. You've been out late all this week, you've been so busy and so preoccupied I hardly have a husband anymore—"

"Kate!" Marshall broke in. "It won't be as bad as you thought: I'm just calling to say I'll be a little late, not that I won't be there."

"How late?"

"Oh brother . . ." Marshall wasn't sure at all. "How about an hour?"

Kate couldn't think of what to say. She only sighed in disgust and anger.

Marshall tried to appease her. "Listen, I'll get there as soon as I can."

Kate decided to say it over the phone; she might never get the chance any other time. "Marshall, I'm concerned about Sandy."

"What's wrong with her now?"

Oh, she could just punch him for that tone of voice! "Marshall, if you'd just be around here once in a while you'd know! She's . . . I don't know. She just isn't the same old Sandy anymore. I'm afraid of what Shawn is doing to her."

"What *Shawn* is doing to her?"

"I can't talk about it over the phone."

Now Marshall sighed. "All right, all right. We'll talk about it."

"When, Marshall?"

"Oh, tonight, when I get home."

"We can't talk right in front of them—"

"I mean . . . oh, you know what I mean!" Marshall was tiring of this conversation.

"Well, just get home, Marshall, *please!*"

"All right, all right!"

Marshall hung up the phone with hardly a loving gentleness. For a split second he regretted the act and thought about how it must have made Kate feel, but he forced his thoughts onward to the next, very pressing project: interviewing Professor Juleen Langstrat.

Friday evening. She should be home now. He dialed the number, and this time it rang. And rang. And rang one more time.

Click. "Hello?"

"Hello, this is Marshall Hogan, editor of the *Ashton Clarion.* Am I speaking with Professor Juleen Langstrat?"

"Yes, you are. What can I do for you, Mr. Hogan?"

"My daughter Sandy has been in some of your classes."

She seemed pleased to hear that. "Oh, very good!"

"At any rate, I was wondering if we might set up a date for an interview."

"Well, you'd have to speak with one of my teacher assistants. They are the ones responsible for checking the progress and problems of the students. The classes are large, you understand."

"Oh, well, no, that's not exactly what I had in mind. I was thinking I would like to interview *you.*"

"Pertaining to your daughter? I'm afraid I don't know her. I wouldn't be able to tell you much . . ."

"Well, we could talk a little about the class, of course, but I was also curious about the other interests you're pursuing there on the campus, the elective classes you've been teaching at night . . ."

"Oohh," she said, with a down note at the end that didn't sound promising. "Well, that was part of an experimental college idea we were trying. If you wish to check that out, the registrar might have some old flyers available. But I should inform you that I am very uncomfortable with the idea of granting any interview to the press, and I really cannot do so."

"So you're not willing to discuss the very influential people you have among your circle of friends?"

"I don't understand the question," and it sounded like she didn't appreciate it either.

"Alf Brummel, chief of police, Reverend Oliver Young, Delores Pinckston, Dwight Brandon, Eugene Baylor, Judge John Baker . . ."

"I have no comment," she said sharply, "and I really have some other things that are very pressing. Is there anything else I can help you with?"

"Well . . ." Marshall thought he'd go ahead and try for it. "I guess the only other thing I could ask you about is why you ejected me from your class."

Now she was getting indignant. "I don't know what you're talking about."

"Your class on Monday afternoon two weeks ago. 'The Psychology of Self,' I think it was. I'm the big guy you told to leave."

She began to laugh incredulously. "I haven't the slightest idea what you're talking about! You must have the wrong person."

"You don't remember telling me to wait outside?"

"I am convinced you have me mixed up with someone else."

"Well, do you have long blonde hair?"

She said simply, "Good night, Mr. Hogan," and hung up.

Marshall stood there a moment, then asked himself, "C'mon, Hogan, what did you expect?"

He dropped the receiver into the cradle and went out into the front office where a question from Bernice grabbed his attention.

"So I'd like to know how you're finally going to corner Langstrat," she quipped, flipping through some papers at her desk.

Marshall felt like his face must be awfully red.

"Boy, your face is sure red," Bernice confirmed.

"Talking to too many temperamental women in one night," he explained. "Langstrat was one of them. Boy, I thought Harmel was bad!"

Bernice turned around, excited. "You got Langstrat on the phone?"

"For all of thirty-two seconds. She had absolutely nothing to say to me, and she didn't remember kicking me out of her class."

Bernice made a screwy face. "Isn't it funny how no one seems to remember having any encounters with us? Marshall, we must be invisible!"

"How about very undesirable and very inconvenient?"

"Well," Bernice said, going back to her paperwork, "Professor Langstrat probably has been very busy, too busy to talk to nosy reporters . . ."

A wad of paper bounced off her head. She turned around and saw Marshall looking over some lists. He looked like he couldn't possibly have tossed that little projectile.

He said, "Boy, I wonder if I could contact Harmel again? But *he* won't talk either."

The same wad of paper bounced off his ear. He looked at Bernice and she was dead serious, all business.

"Well, it's obvious he knew too much. It's my guess that both he and former Dean Strachan are running good and scared."

"Yeah." Marshall had a memory come to the surface. "Harmel talked that way, warning *me*. He said something like, I'd be out on my ear like everybody else."

"So who's everybody else?"

"Yeah, who else do we know who could have been removed?"

Bernice looked over some of her notes. "Well, you know, now that I look over this list, none of these people have really been in their position for a very long time."

The wad of paper ricocheted off her head and skittered across her desk.

"So who did they replace?" Marshall asked.

Bernice solemnly picked up the wad of paper as she said, "We can check that out. In the meantime, the most obvious thing to do is call Strachan and see what—" she hurled the wad at Marshall "—he has to say!"

Marshall grabbed the wad in midflight and quickly crumpled another one to add to his arsenal, sending them both back in Bernice's direction. Bernice began to prepare an adequate counterattack.

"All right," Marshall said, starting to crack up with laughter, "I'll give him a ring." He was suddenly in the middle of a blizzard of paper wads. "But I think we'd better get out of here, my wife's waiting."

Bernice was not finished with the war yet, so they finished it and then had to clean up before they could leave.

Rafar paced up and down the dark basement room, chugging out hot breath that became a layer of cloud obscuring him from the shoulders up. He pounded his fists together, he tore invisible enemies in his outstretched talons, he cursed and fumed.

Lucius stood with the other warriors, waiting for Rafar to calm down and give the reason for calling this meeting. Lucius rather enjoyed the little scene before him. Obviously Rafar, the great braggart, had been cut down to size in his meeting with the Strongman! Lucius could hardly keep a hideous smirk off his face.

"Wouldn't the little angel tell you where you could find this . . . what was that name again?" Lucius asked, knowing full well Tal's name.

"TAL!" Rafar roared, and Lucius could detect Rafar's humiliation at the very sound of the name.

"The little angel, the helpless little angel, told you nothing?"

Rafar's immediate response was a monstrous black fist clamped instantly around Lucius's throat. "Do you mock me, little imp?"

Lucius had learned the right tone of groveling to please this tyrant. "Oh, be not offended, great one. I only seek your pleasure."

"Then seek this Tal!" Rafar growled. He released Lucius and turned to all the other demons present. "All of you, seek this Tal! I want him in my hands to shred him at my pleasure. This battle could be settled easily between the two of us. Find him! Bring me word!"

Lucius tried to hide his words behind a whimpering tone, but they were specially selected for another purpose. "Indeed we shall, great one! But surely this Tal must be a formidable foe to have routed you at the fall of Babylon! Whatever will you do, should we find him? Will you dare to assail him again?"

Rafar grinned, his fangs shining. "You will see what your Ba-al can do!"

"And may we not see what this *Tal* can do!"

Rafar drew close to Lucius and stared him down with fiery yellow orbs. "When I have vanquished this Tal and hurled his little pieces across the skies as my victory banner, I will most certainly give you your chance to better me. I will relish every moment of it."

Rafar turned away, and for an instant the whole room was filled with his black wings before he shot upward through the building and into the sky.

For hours afterwards as angels all over Ashton watched from their hiding places, the Ba-al flew slowly over the town like a sinister vulture, his sword visible and challenging. Up, down, back and forth he flew, weaving in among the downtown buildings, then soaring high above the town in graceful arcs.

Down below, through the window of an obscure store basement, Scion watched as Rafar passed overhead again. He turned to his captain, who sat nearby on some appliance crates with Guilo, Triskal, and Mota. Triskal, with the help of others, was getting himself patched up and back together again.

"I don't understand," said Scion. "What's he think he's doin'?"

Tal looked up from Triskal's wounds and said matter-of-factly, "He's trying to draw me out."

Mota added, "He wants the captain. Apparently he has offered great honors to whatever demon can find Captain Tal and report his whereabouts."

Guilo said gruffly, "The devils are crawling all over the church with no other aim. It was the first place they looked."

Tal anticipated Scion's next question and answered it. "Signa and the others are still there at the church. We've tried to keep our guard there looking as it usually does."

Scion watched Rafar circle over the far side of the town and come back for another pass. "I'd have trouble bein' taunted by such as *him!*"

Tal spoke the truth, without shame. "If I were to meet him now I would most certainly lose, and he knows it. Our prayer cover is insufficient—while he has all the backing he needs."

They could all hear the rushing of Rafar's huge, leathery wings and see his shadow fall over the building for an instant as he passed overhead.

"We will all have to be very, very careful."

Hank was walking through the town again, up and down the streets and storefronts, driven by the Lord and praying with every step he took. He had a feeling that God had some particular purpose for this little jaunt, but he couldn't begin to guess what it was.

Krioni and Triskal walked on either side of him; they had gotten some extra reserves to stay at the house and watch over Mary. They were wary and alert, and Triskal, still recovering from his recent encounter with Rafar, felt especially edgy when he considered where they were leading Hank.

Hank took a turn he had never taken before, down a street he had never looked at before, and finally stopped outside a business establishment he had only heard bad stories about but could never find. He stood outside the door, staring, amazed at the number of kids going in and out like bees. Finally he stepped inside.

Krioni and Triskal tried their very best to look meek and nonthreatening as they followed him.

The Cave was aptly named: the power it took to run the rows upon rows of flickering, beeping video games was made up for by the total absence of any other lights, except a little blue globe here and there in the black ceiling with an occasional watt meandering through it. There was more sound than light; heavy metal rock music pounded from speakers all around the room and clashed painfully with the myriads of electronic sounds tumbling out of the machines. One lone proprietor sat behind his little cash register in the corner, reading a girlie magazine whenever he wasn't making change for the game players. Hank had never seen so many quarters in one place.

Here were kids of all ages, with few other places to go, congregating after school and all through the weekends to hang out, hang on, play games, pair up, wander off, do drugs, do sex, do whatever. Hank knew this place was a hell hole; it wasn't the machines, or the decor, or the dimness—it was just the pungent spiritual stench of demons having their heyday. He felt sick to his stomach.

Krioni and Triskal could see hundreds of narrowing yellow eyes peering at them from the corners and dark hiding places of the room. Already they had heard several metallic rings as blades were drawn and made ready.

"Do I look harmless enough?" Triskal quietly asked.

"They do not think you are harmless anymore," Krioni said dryly.

The two looked around at all the eyes looking back at them. They smiled in a trucelike way, raising their empty hands to show no intent of hostility. The demons made no reply, but several blades could be seen glowing in the dark.

"So where is Seth?" Triskal asked.

"On his way, I'm sure."

Triskal tensed. Krioni followed his look to see a surly demon approaching them. The demon's hand was on his sword; he hadn't drawn it, but plenty of other swords were drawn behind him.

The black spirit looked the two angels up and down and hissed, "You are not welcome here! What is your business?"

Krioni answered quickly and politely, "We are watching over the man of God."

The demon took one look at Hank and lost the better portion of his cockiness. "Busche!" he exclaimed nervously while those behind him backed away. "What is he doing here?"

"That's nothing we wish to discuss," said Triskal.

The demon only sneered. "Are you Triskal?"

"I am."

The demon laughed, coughing up puffs of red and yellow. "You enjoy a fight, don't you?" Several demons joined him in laughter.

Triskal had no intention of answering. The demon had no time to demand an answer. Suddenly all the mocking spirits grew tense and agitated. Their eyes darted about, and then like a flock of timid birds they backed away and huddled in the dark corners. At the same time Krioni and Triskal could feel a new strength coursing through them. They looked down at Hank.

He was praying.

"Dear Lord," he said silently, "help us to reach these kids; help us to touch their lives."

Hank was praying at a very good time, considering the commotion just coming in the backdoor. As demons slinked away from the entrance, three of their comrades came into the building wailing, hissing, and drooling, their arms and wings over their heads. They were chased and prodded along by a very tall and quite unshakable angelic warrior.

"Well," said Triskal, "Seth has brought us Ron Forsythe and then some!"

"I was afraid of that," said Krioni.

Triskal was referring to a young man barely visible under the three demons, a very confused and disoriented victim of their destructive influence. They clung to him like leeches, causing him to stagger to and fro as they fought to avoid the goading tip of the big warrior's sword. Seth had them under very tight control, however, and he herded them right toward Hank Busche.

"Hey, Ron," said some guys at a bombardier game.

"Hey. . ." was all Ron answered, giving them a slow, heavy wave of his hand. He did not seem very happy.

Hank heard the name and saw Ron Forsythe coming, and for a moment he didn't know whether to remain where he was or get out of harm's way. Ron was a tall, spindly youth with long, unkempt hair, dirty tee shirt and jeans, and eyes that seemed to be looking into some other universe. He staggered toward Hank, looking over his shoulder as if a flock of birds was chasing him and then forward as if he were one step from a cliff. Hank, watching him approach, decided to remain right where he was. If the Lord wanted the two of them to meet, well, it was about to happen.

Then Ron stopped short and leaned against a road-racing game. This man standing in front of him looked familiar.

The demons clinging to Ron were shaking and whimpering, shooting glances toward Seth behind them and Krioni and Triskal in front of them. As for the other demons in the room, they were itching for a fight. Their yellow eyes shifted about and their red blades clattered, but something held them back—that praying man.

"Hi there," Hank said to the young man. "I'm Hank Busche."

Ron's glassy eyes widened. He stared at Hank and said with slurred speech, "I've seen you around. You're that preacher my folks keep talking about."

Hank was sure enough now to guess. "Ron? Ron Forsythe?"

Ron looked around and fidgeted as if he'd been caught doing something illegal. "Yeah . . ."

Hank stretched out his hand. "Well, God bless you, Ron, I'm glad to meet you."

The three demons snarled at that, but the three warriors shifted their weight forward just a little and kept them under control.

"Divination," said Triskal, identifying one of the demons.

Divination clung to Ron with needle-sharp talons and hissed, "And what is your business with us?"

"The lad," said Krioni.

"You can't tell us what to do!" another demon squawked, its fists stubbornly clenched.

"Rebellion?" Krioni asked.

The demon did not deny it. "He belongs to us."

The spirits in the room were getting braver, moving in closer.

"Let's get him out of here," said Krioni.

Hank touched Ron on the shoulder and said, "Can we step outside where we can visit for a minute?"

Divination and Rebellion spoke together, "What for?"

Ron protested, "What for?"

Hank just led him gently, "Come on," and they went out the backdoor. Triskal remained in the doorway, his hand on his sword.

Only the demons attached to Ron were allowed outside, constantly corralled by Seth and Krioni.

Ron sank onto a nearby bench like a rag doll in slow motion. Hank put his hand on Ron's shoulder and kept looking into those dazed eyes, wondering where to start.

"How are you feeling?" Hank finally asked.

The third demon enclosed Ron's head in his bulky, slimy arms.

The boy's head drooped toward his chest and he almost nodded off, oblivious to Hank's words.

The tip of Seth's sword got the demon's attention.

"What?" it screeched.

"Sorcery?"

The spirit laughed drunkenly. "All the time, more and more. He'll never give it up!"

Ron started to chuckle, feeling drugged and silly.

But Hank could feel something in his spirit, the same horrible presence he had felt that one very frightening night. Evil spirits? In such a young boy? *Lord, what can I do? What can I say?*

The Lord answered, and Hank knew what he had to do. "Ron," he said, whether Ron heard him or not, "can I pray for you?"

Only Ron's eyes turned to look at Hank, and Ron actually pleaded, "Yeah. Pray for me, preacher."

But the demons wanted no part of that. They all cried into Ron's brain with one voice, "No, no, no! You don't need that!"

Ron suddenly stirred, his head rocked back and forth, and he mumbled, "No, no . . . don't pray . . . I don't like that."

Now Hank wondered what Ron really wanted. Or was it even Ron who was speaking?

"I *would* like to pray for you, okay?" Hank asked, just to check.

"No, don't," Ron said, and then pleaded, "Please pray, c'mon . . ."

"Do it," Krioni prompted. "Pray!"

"No!" the demons cried. "You can't make us leave him!"

"Pray," said Krioni.

Hank knew he had better take charge of the situation and pray for this boy. He already had his hand on Ron, so he started praying very gently. "Lord Jesus, I pray for Ron; please touch him, Lord, and get through to his mind, and set him free from these spirits that are hanging on to him."

The spirits clung to Ron like spoiled brats and whined at Hank's prayer. Ron moaned and shook his head some more. He tried to get up, then he sat down again and held Hank's arm.

The Lord spoke to Hank again, and Hank had a name. "Sorcery, let go of him in the name of Jesus."

Ron squirmed on the bench and cried out as if stuck with a knife. Hank thought Ron would squeeze his arm off.

But Sorcery obeyed. He whined and hollered and spit, but he obeyed, fluttering away into the nearby trees.

Ron gave an anguished sigh and looked at Hank with eyes full of pain and desperation. "C'mon, c'mon, you're doing it!"

Hank was amazed. He took hold of Ron's hand just to assure him and kept looking into those eyes. They were clearer now. Hank could see an earnest, pleading soul looking back at him. *What next?* he asked the Lord.

The Lord answered, and Hank had another name. "Divination—"

Ron looked right at Hank, his eyes wild and his voice hoarse. "No, not me, never!"

But Hank didn't stop; he looked right into Ron's eyes and said, "Divination, in Jesus' name, let go."

"No!" Ron protested, but then said just as quickly, "Go on, Divination, get out! I don't want you with me anymore!"

Divination grudgingly obeyed. Thanks to this praying man, oppressing Ron Forsythe wasn't fun anymore.

Ron relaxed again, sniffing back some tears.

Seth poked the last little demon. "How about you, Rebellion?"

Rebellion was having trouble making up his mind.

Ron could feel it. "Spirit, please go. I've had it with you!"

Hank prayed the same thing. "Spirit, go. In the name of Jesus leave Ron alone."

Rebellion considered Ron's words, looked at Seth's sword, looked at the praying man, and finally let go.

Ron twitched as if having a terrible cramp, but then he said, "Yeah, yeah, he's out."

Seth shooed the three demons away, and they fluttered back into The Cave where they would be welcome and unhampered.

Hank hung on to Ron's hand and waited, watching and praying until he knew what else to do. This was all so incredible, so fascinating, so frightening, but so necessary. This must be the Lord's Lesson Number Two in Spiritual Combat; Hank knew he was learning something he would have to know to win this battle.

Ron was changing before Hank's very eyes, relaxing, breathing easier, his eyes returning to a normal, down-to-earth gaze.

Hank finally said a very soft "Amen," and asked, "Are you okay, Ron?"

Ron answered right away, "Yeah, I feel better. Thanks." He looked at Hank and smiled a weak, almost apologetic smile. "It's funny. No, it's neat. It was just today I was thinking I needed somebody to pray for me. I just couldn't go on with all the stuff I've been into."

Hank knew what had happened. "It was the Lord, I think, who set it up."

"Nobody's prayed for me before."

"I know your folks do all the time."

"Well, yeah, *they* do."

"And the rest of us at the church, too. We're all pulling for you."

Ron took his first clear-eyed look at Hank. "So you're my folks' pastor, huh? I thought you were older than that."

"Not too much older," Hank quipped.

"Are the other people at the church like you?"

Hank chuckled. "We're all just people; we have our good points and our bad points, but we all have Jesus, and He gives us a special love for each other."

They talked. They talked about school, the town, Ron's folks, drugs in general and particular, Hank's church, the Christians who were around, and Jesus. Ron began to notice that no matter what the subject or the issue, Hank had a way of bringing Jesus into it. Ron didn't mind. This wasn't like a phony sales pitch; Hank Busche really believed that Jesus was the answer to everything.

So, after talking about everything else with Jesus brought into it, Ron let Hank talk about Jesus, just Jesus. It wasn't dull. Hank could really get excited about Him.

16

Nathan and Armoth flew high above the beautiful summer countryside, following the speeding Buick. Things were definitely quieter out here, away from strife-torn Ashton. Still, neither one felt entirely comfortable about the two passengers in the car below; although the heavenly escorts weren't yet certain, they had a feeling that a covert plot on the part of Rafar and his guerrillas might be underway. Marshall and his good-looking young reporter were too critical a combination for those devils to pass up.

Former college dean Eldon Strachan lived on a quaint and unpretentious ten-acre farm an hour away from Ashton. He was not farming the place, just living there, and as Marshall and Bernice drove up the long gravel driveway they could tell his interests extended no further than the immediate yard of the white farmhouse. The lawn was small and manicured, the fruit trees pruned and bearing, the flower beds soft with freshly turned and weeded soil. Some chickens meandered about, pecking and scratching. A collie greeted their approach with furious barking.

"Wow, a normal human being to interview for once," said Marshall.

"That's why he moved out of Ashton," said Bernice.

Strachan stepped onto his porch as the collie ran and barked beside him.

"Hi there!" he called to Marshall and Bernice as they got out of the car. "Quiet down now, Lady," he added to the collie. Lady never obeyed such commands.

Strachan was a healthy, white-haired fellow who got plenty of exercise on this place, and showed it. He wore work clothes and still carried a pair of garden gloves in his hand.

Marshall extended his hand for a good firm handshake. So did Bernice. They exchanged introductions, and then Strachan invited them around the barking Lady and into the house.

"Doris," Strachan called, "Mr. Hogan and Miss Krueger are here."

Within minutes Doris, a sweet and rotund little grandma type, had set the coffee table with tea, coffee, rolls, and goodies, and they were having a pleasant conversation about the farm, the countryside, the weather, the neighbor's wandering cow. They all knew it was obligatory and besides, the Strachans were very pleasant people to talk and visit with.

Finally Eldon Strachan introduced the transitional sentence: "Yes, I suppose things in Ashton aren't quite this nice."

Bernice got out her notepad as Marshall said, "Yeah, and I kind of hate to drag it all out here with us."

Strachan smiled and said philosophically, "You can run but you can't hide." He looked out the window at the trees backed by endless blue sky and said, "I always have wondered if just leaving it all was the right thing. But what else could I do?"

Marshall doubled-checked his notes. "Let's see now. You told me on the telephone when you left—"

"In late June, about a year ago."

"And Ralph Kuklinski took your place."

"And he's still there, I understand."

"Yes, still there. Was he in on any of this—this 'Inner Circle' stuff? I don't know what else to call it."

Strachan thought for a moment. "I don't know for sure, but I wouldn't be surprised if he was. He really had to be one of the group to be put in as dean."

"So there really is some kind of 'in group,' so to speak?"

"Absolutely. That became pretty obvious after a while. All the regents were becoming like peas in a pod, like clones of each other. They all acted the same, talked the same . . ."

"Except for you?"

Strachan laughed a little. "I guess I just didn't fit into the club very well. As a matter of fact I became a definite outsider, even an enemy, and I think that's why they fired me."

"I suppose you're talking about that fracas over the college funds?"

"Exactly." Strachan had to resift his memory. "I never suspected anything until we started having some unexplained disbursement delays. Our bills were being paid late, our payrolls were behind. It wasn't even my job to be hounding after that sort of thing, but when I started getting some indirect complaints—you know, hearing others talking about it—I asked Baylor what the problem was. He never directly answered my questions, or at least I didn't like the sound of his answers. That's when I asked an independent accountant, a friend of a friend, to look into it and maybe do some quick scanning of what the accounting office was doing. I don't know how he ever got access to the information, but he was a clever character and he found a way."

Bernice was ready with a question. "Can we have his name?"

Strachan answered with a shrug. "Johnson. Ernie Johnson."

"How do we reach him?"

"I'm afraid he's dead."

That was a letdown. Marshall grabbed at a hope. "Did he leave you any records, anything written down?"

Strachan only shook his head. "If he did, those records were lost. Why do you think I've been sitting out here so silently? Listen, I even know Norm Mattily, the state attorney general, pretty well, and I thought of going to him and telling him what was going on. But let's face it, those big folks at the top don't give you the time of day unless you have some really substantial proof. It's tough to get the authorities to stick their necks out. They just won't do it."

"All right . . . so what was it that Ernie Johnson found?"

"He came back horrified. According to his findings, monies from grants and tuitions were being reinvested at an alarming rate, but apparently there were no dividends or returns of any kind from whatever the investments were, as if the money had been poured down a bottomless well somewhere. The figures had been juggled to cover it up, accounts payable had been staggered so that other accounts could be dipped into to pay those due . . . it was just one colossal mess."

"A mess worth millions?"

"At least. The college money had been leaking out in large amounts for years, with no clues as to where it was going. Somewhere out there was a money-hungry monster gobbling up all the college's assets."

"And that's when you called for the audit."

"And Eugene Baylor hit the ceiling. The whole thing went from professional to personal in an instant and we became intense enemies. And that convinced me all the more that the college was in big trouble and that Baylor had a lot to do with it. But of course there's nothing Baylor does that all the others don't know about. I'm sure they're all aware of the problem, and it's my feeling that their unanimous vote for my resignation was a common conspiracy."

"But to what end?" asked Bernice. "Why would they want to undermine the college's financial base?"

Strachan could only shake his head. "I don't know *what* they're trying to do, but unless there's something else hidden somewhere to explain where these funds are going and how the losses are going to be made up, that college is most certainly headed for bankruptcy. Kuklinski must know that. As far as I know, he was in total agreement with the financial policies and with my resignation."

Marshall flipped to some other notes. "So just how does our kind Professor Langstrat figure into all this?"

Strachan had to chuckle. "Ah, the dear professor . . ." He considered the question for a moment. "She was always a definite influence and mentor, to be sure, but . . . I don't think she's the ultimate center of things. It seemed to me that she had a lot to do with controlling the group while someone higher up had a lot to do with controlling her. I think—I think she's answering to someone, some unseen authority."

"But you've no idea who?"

Strachan shook his head.

"So what else do you know about her?"

Strachan searched his memory. "A graduate of UCLA . . . she taught at other universities before she came to Whitmore. She's been on the faculty for at least six years. I do recall that she always had a strong interest in Eastern philosophy and occultism. She was once involved in some kind of neo-pagan religious group in California. But you know, I never realized until maybe three years ago that she was openly declaring her beliefs to her classes, and I was rather surprised to find that her teachings had aroused a lot of interest. Her beliefs and practices were not only spreading among the students, but also among the faculty."

"Who on the faculty?" Marshall asked.

Strachan shook his head in disgust. "It started years before I was aware of it, in the Psychology Department, among Langstrat's associates. Margaret Islander—you may know of her—"

"I believe my friend Ruth Williams does," said Bernice.

"I think she was the first to be initiated into Langstrat's group, but she'd always had an interest in psychics like Edgar Cayce, so she was a natural."

"Anyone else?" Marshall prodded.

Strachan pulled out a hastily scrawled list and let Marshall have a look at it. "I've gone over and over this in the months since I left. Here. Here's a list of most of the Psychology Department . . ." He pointed out a few names. "Trevor Corcoran is new on the staff this year. He even studied in India before he came here to teach. Juanita Janke replaced Kevin Ford . . . well, as a matter of fact, a lot of people were replaced over the past few years. We had a lot of turnover."

Marshall noted another portion of the list. "So who are these people?"

"The Humanities Department, and then the Philosophy Department, and these down here are in the biology and pre-med programs. A lot of them are new as well. We had a lot of turnover."

"That's the second time you've said that," Bernice observed.

Strachan stared at her. "What are you thinking?"

Bernice took the list from Marshall and placed it in front of Strachan again. "Well, tell us now. How many of these people have come on staff during the last six years, during the time Langstrat's been there?"

Strachan took a second, more critical look at the list. "Jones . . . Conrad . . . Witherspoon . . . Epps . . ." An overwhelming percentage of the names were those of new faculty members, who had replaced former members who had resigned or whose contracts had simply not been renewed. "Well, isn't that odd?"

"I would say that's odd," Bernice agreed.

Strachan was visibly shaken. "All the turnover . . . I was getting very concerned about it, but I never even considered . . . This would explain a lot of things. I knew there was some kind of common interest spreading among all these people; they all seemed to have a very unique and undefinable rapport with each other—their own lingo, their own inside secrets, their own ideas of reality—and it seemed no one person could do anything without everyone else knowing about it. I thought it was a fad, a sociological phase—" He looked up from the list with a new awareness in his eyes. "So it was more than that. Our campus was invaded and our faculty displaced by a—a madness!"

For just a moment Marshall had a flashback, a quick, fleeting memory of his daughter Sandy saying, "People around here are starting to act weird. I think we're being invaded by aliens." That memory was immediately followed by Kate's voice over the phone: "I'm concerned about Sandy . . . she just isn't the same old Sandy anymore . . ."

Marshall snapped out of it and began leafing through his materials. He finally found the old list Bernice had gotten from Albert Darr. "All right, what about these classes Langstrat was teaching: 'Introduction to God and Goddess Consciousness and the Craft . . . The Sacred Medicine Wheel . . . Spells and Rituals . . . Pathways to Your Inner Light, Meet Your Own Spiritual Guides'?"

Strachan nodded with recognition. "It all began as part of an alternative education program, purely a voluntary thing for any interested students, paid for by special tuitions. I just thought it was a study of folklore, myths, traditions—"

"But I guess they were taking this stuff pretty seriously."

"Ehh, so it seems, and now we have a great percentage of the staff and the student body . . . bewitched."

"Including the regents?"

Strachan did some fresh thinking. "Get ready for this. I think the same kind of upheaval happened on the board of regents as well. There are twelve regent positions altogether, and five, I think, have been suddenly and abruptly replaced in the last year and a half. How else could the vote for my resignation be unanimous? I used to have some very loyal friends on that board."

"What are their names, and where have they gone?"

Bernice started writing the names down as Strachan recalled them, along with any other information he could provide about each person. Jake Abernathy had died, Morris James had gone bankrupt in a business and moved to another job, Fred Ainsworth, George Olson, and Rita Jacobson had all left Ashton with no word as to where they had gone.

"And that," said Strachan, "takes care of just about everyone. There are none left but initiates into this strange mystical group."

"Including Kuklinski, the new dean," Bernice added.

"And Dwight Brandon, the owner of the land."

"And what about Ted Harmel?" Marshall asked.

Strachan tightened his lips, looked at the floor, and sighed. "Yes. He did try to back out, but by then they'd already entrusted too much information to him. When they found they couldn't control him any-more—he has myself and our friendship to blame for that—they arranged to defame him and chase him out of town with that ridiculous scandal."

"Hmmmm," said Bernice. "A conflict of interest."

"Of course. He kept telling me it was a fascinating new science of the human mind, and he claimed he was only after a story, but he just kept getting more and more wrapped up in it, and they wooed him, I'm sure. I heard him say that they had promised him great success with his newspaper because he had aligned himself with them . . ."

Marshall had another flashback: he saw Brummel looking at him with those numbing gray eyes, saying sweetly, "Marshall, we'd like to know that you'll be standing with us . . ."

Strachan was still talking.

Marshall woke up and said, "Uh, excuse me, what was that again?"

"Oh," said Strachan, "I was just saying that Ted became torn between two loyalties: first and foremost he was loyal to the truth and to his friends, and that included me. His other loyalty was to the Langstrat group and their philosophies and practices. I guess he thought that the truth was inviolable and the press would always be free, but, whatever the reason, he began to print stories about the financial problems. And that was definitely stepping over the line as far as the regents were concerned."

"Yes," Bernice recalled. "Now I remember him saying they were trying to control him and dictate what he printed. He was really mad about it."

"Well of course," said Strachan, "when it came down to principles, regardless of what so-called science or metaphysical philosophies he may have been interested in, Ted was still a newspaperman and would not be intimidated." Strachan sighed and looked at the floor. "So, I'm afraid he got caught in the crossfire of my battle with the college regents. Consequently we both lost our positions, our good standing in the community, everything. I guess you could say I was well content to leave it all behind. It was impossible to fight it."

Marshall disliked that kind of talk. "Are they—is this thing—really that strong?"

Strachan was deadly serious. "I don't think I ever realized how vast and strong it really was, and I guess I'm still finding out. Mr. Hogan, I have no idea what the final goal of these people is, but I'm beginning to see that nothing standing in their way can escape being stamped out, eliminated. Even as we sit here I can look back over the years, and, not even considering our faculty turnover, I'm frightened to think of how many other people around Ashton have just dropped out of sight."

Joe, the supermarket owner, Marshall thought. And what about Edie?

Strachan was looking a little pale now, and asked with obvious worry in his voice, "Just what do you people intend to do with this information?"

Marshall had to be honest. "I don't know yet. There are too many missing pieces, too many assumptions. I don't have anything I can print."

"You do remember what happened to Ted? You are keeping that in mind?"

Marshall didn't want to think about that. He wanted to find out something else. "Ted wouldn't talk to me."

"He's scared."

"Scared of what?"

"Of *them,* of the system that destroyed him. He knows more about their weird goings-on than I do; he knows enough to be a lot more afraid than I am, and I believe his fears are justified. I do believe there's a genuine danger here."

"Well, does he ever talk to you?"

"Sure, about anything besides what you're after."

"But the two of you are in touch?"

"Yes. We fish, we hunt, we meet for lunch. He isn't far from here."

"Could you call him?"

"You mean, call him and put in a plug for you?"

"That's exactly what I mean."

Strachan answered cautiously, "Hey, he may not want to talk, and I can't push him."

"But will you just call him, see if he'll talk to me one more time?"

"I'll . . . I'll think about it, but that's all I can promise you."

"I'd appreciate even that."

"But, Mr. Hogan. . . ." Strachan reached over and grabbed Marshall's arm. He looked at both Marshall and Bernice and said very quietly, "You people watch out for yourselves. You're not invincible. None of the rest of us were, and I believe it's possible to lose everything if you make just one wrong move or take just one wrong step. Please, *please* be sure at every moment you know exactly what you're doing."

At the *Clarion*, Tom, the paste-up man, was getting the usual ads, fillers, and completed galleys into the Tuesday edition when the bell over the front door jingled. He had better things to do than deal with callers, but with Hogan and Bernice out on their mysterious mission of intrigue, he was the only remaining fort-holder-downer. Boy, he wished Edie had stuck around. The paper got to be more of a shambles every day and, whatever wild goose chase Hogan and Bernice were on, it took their attention away from the many tasks piling up around the place.

"Hello?" called a woman's sweet voice.

Tom grabbed a shop cloth to wipe his hands and hollered back, "Hold on, I'm coming."

He scurried up the narrow passage to the front office and saw a very attractive and neatly dressed young woman standing at the counter. She smiled when she saw him. Ah yes, thought Tom, if I were only young again.

"Hello there," he said, still wiping his hands on the shop cloth. "What can I do for you?"

The young lady said, "I read your ad for a secretary and general office manager. I've come to apply."

It had to be an angel, Tom thought. "Boy, if you can cut it, let me tell you, there's sure a job to be had around here!"

"Well, I'm ready to start," she said with a bright smile.

Tom made sure his hand was clean enough and then extended it. "Tom McBride, paste-up man and general worrier."

She shook his hand firmly and said her name, "Carmen."

"Pleased to meet you, Carmen. Uh . . . Carmen who?"

She laughed at her lapse of mind and said, "Oh, Carmen Fraser. I get so used to just going by my first name."

Tom swung the little gate open at the end of the counter and Carmen followed him into the office area.

"Let me show you what the devil's going on here," he said.

17

In the faraway secluded valley, in the little cluster of unlabeled buildings hidden by rocky crags, a hurried transition was in full swing.

In the office complex, sitting at desks and worktables, scurrying up and down the aisles, dashing in and out the doors, running up and down the stairways, over two hundred people of all ages, descriptions, and nationalities were typing letters, going through files, checking records, balancing accounts, chattering on telephones in different languages. Maintenance people in blue coveralls brought in large stacks of boxes and crates on handtrucks, and the office workers meticulously began to fill the boxes with the contents of the file cabinets, with any office paraphernalia not immediately needed, with other books and records.

Outside, trucks were being loaded with the crates as more maintenance people driving little grounds tractors went about the complex, shutting down various hookups and utilities and boarding up any buildings no longer occupied.

Nearby, on the porch of the big stone house at the edge of the grounds, a woman stood watching. She was tall and slender, with long, jet-black hair; she wore black, loose-fitting clothes, and she clutched her shoulder bag close to her side with pale, trembling hands. She looked this way and that, evidently trying to relax herself. She took a few deep breaths. She reached into her bag and brought out a pair of dark sunglasses with which she covered her eyes. Then she stepped down from the porch and started across the plaza toward the office building.

Her steps were firm and deliberate, her eyes remained straight ahead. A few office personnel passed and saluted her, pressing their palms together in front of their chins and bowing slightly. She nodded at them and kept walking.

The office staff saluted her in the same way as she entered and she smiled at them, not speaking a word. Upon receiving her smile, they returned to their feverish work. The office manager, a well-dressed woman with tightly pinned hair, stepped up, gave a slight bow and said, "Good morning. What does the Maidservant require?"

The Maidservant smiled and said, "I'd like to run off some copies."

"I can do it immediately."

"Thank you. I'd like to run them off myself."

"Certainly. I'll warm up the machine for you."

The woman scurried toward a small room off to the side, and the Maidservant followed. Several accountants and filing clerks, some oriental, some East Indian, some European, bowed as she passed and then went back to their consultations with each other.

The office manager had the copier ready in less than a minute.

"Thank you, you may go now," said the Maidservant.

"Certainly," answered the woman. "I am at your disposal if you have any problems or questions."

"Thank you."

The manager left and the Maidservant closed the door behind her, shutting out the rest of the office and any intrusions. Then, quickly, the Maidservant reached into her bag and brought out a small book. She leafed through it, skimming over the handwritten pages until she found what she was looking for. Then, laying the book open and face down on the copier, she started pressing the buttons and copying page after page.

Forty pages later she turned off the machine, folded the copies neatly, and placed them in a compartment of her bag, along with the little book. She left the office directly and went back to the big stone house.

The house was majestic in its size and decor, with a large stone hearth and soaring, rough-beamed ceilings. The Maidservant hurried up the thickly-carpeted staircase to her bedroom and closed the door behind her.

Placing the little book on her stately antique vanity, she opened a drawer and pulled out some brown wrapping paper and twine. The paper already had a name written on it, the addressee: Alexander M. Kaseph. The return address included the name J. Langstrat. She quickly rewrapped the book as if it had never been opened, then bound the package with string.

Elsewhere in the house, in a very large office, a middle-aged, roundly built man dressed in loose trousers and tunic sat Indian fashion on a large cushion. His eyes were closed, his breathing deep. The fine furnishings of a man of great prestige and power surrounded him: souvenirs from around the world, such as swords, war clubs, African artifacts, religious relics, and several rather grotesque idols of the East; a battleship of a desk with built-in computer console, multilined telephone, and an intercom; a long, deep-cushioned couch with matching hand-carved oak chairs and coffee table; hunting trophies of bear, elk, moose, and lion.

Without hearing a knock, the man spoke loftily. "Come in, Susan."

The big oak door opened silently and the Maidservant entered, carrying the brown paper package.

Without opening his eyes, the man said, "Put it on my desk."

The Maidservant did so, and the man began to stir from his motionless position, opening his eyes and stretching his arms as if awakening from sleep.

"So you finally found it," he said with a teasing smile.

"It was there all the time. With all the packing and rearranging it got shoved over in a corner."

The man rose from his cushion, stretched his legs, and walked a few laps around the office. "I really don't know what it is," he said as if answering a question.

"I didn't wonder—" said the Maidservant.

He smiled condescendingly and said, "Oh, maybe not, but it felt like you did." He went up behind her and placed his hands on her shoulders, speaking in her ear. "Sometimes I can read you so very well, and sometimes you drift away. You've been feeling so troubled lately. Why?"

"Oh, all the moving, I guess, the upheaval."

He put his arms around her waist and held her close as he said, "Don't let it bother you. We're going to a far better place. I have a house all picked out. You'll love it."

"I grew up in that town, you know."

"No. No, not really. It won't be the same town at all, not as you remember it. It will be better. But you don't believe that, do you?"

"As I said, I grew up in Ashton—"

"And all you wanted was to get out of there!"

"So you can understand why my feelings are confused."

He twirled her around and laughed playfully as he looked into her eyes. "Yes, I know! On the one hand, you have no desire at all for the town, and on the other hand, you sneak off to attend the carnival."

She blushed a little and looked at the floor. "I was searching for something from my past, something from which to envision my future."

He held her hand and said, "There is no past. You should have stayed with me. I hold the answers for you now."

"Yes, I can see that. I couldn't before."

He laughed and went behind his desk. "Well, good, good. We don't need any more meetings held in hiding places behind a noisy carnival. You should have seen how embarrassed our friends were to have to meet there."

"But why did you even have to come looking for me? Why did you have to drag them along?"

He sat at the desk and began handling a wicked-looking ceremonial knife with a golden handle and razor-sharp blade.

Looking over the edge of the blade at her, he said, "Because, dear Maidservant, I do not trust you. I love you, I am one in essence with you, but . . ." He held the knife up to the level of his eye and peered down the edge of the blade at her, his eyes as sharply cutting as the knife. "I do not trust you. You are a woman given to many conflicting passions."

"I cannot harm the Plan. I am only one person among myriads."

He rose and came around to the side of the desk where other knives were stuck into the carved head of some pagan idol.

"You, dear Susan, share my life, my secrets, my purposes. I have to protect my interests."

With that, he dropped the knife, point first, and it thudded into the idol's head.

She smiled in acquiescence and sidled up to him, giving him an alluring kiss. "I am, and will always be, yours," she said.

He gave her a sly smile, and the cutting look never left his eyes as he answered, "Yes. Of course you are."

High above the valley, amid the rocks and crevices of the mountaintops, two figures concealed themselves. One, the silver-haired man who had been here before, continually watched the activity below. He was stately and mighty, his piercing eyes full of wisdom.

The other was Tal, the Captain of the Host.

"This is what you're looking for," said the silver-haired man. "Rafar had business there only days ago."

Tal peered down into the valley. The swarms of black demons were too numerous to even estimate.

"The Strongman?" he asked.

"Undoubtedly, with a cloud of guards and warriors all around him. We've been unable to penetrate it yet."

"And she's right in the middle of it!"

"The Spirit has been steadily opening her eyes and calling her. She is close to the Strongman—dangerously close. The prayers of the Remnant have placed a blindness and stupor on the demonic hosts all around her. At present it will buy you time, but little more."

Tal grimaced. "My general, it will take more than a stupor for us to break through to her. We can barely hold the town of Ashton, much less take on the Strongman directly."

"And you can only expect this buildup to worsen. Their numbers increase tenfold each day."

"Yes, they are preparing, that's for certain."

"But, at the same time, her conflicts continue to grow. Soon she won't be able to conceal her true feelings and intentions from her lord down there. Tal, she has learned of the suicide."

Tal looked directly at the general. "I understand she and Patricia were very close."

The general nodded. "It jolted her, which made her more receptive. But her time of safety is limited. Here's your next step. The Universal Consciousness Society is holding a special fund-raising and promotional dinner in New York for its many cohorts and members in the United Nations. Kaseph can't attend because of his present activities here. He will send Susan, however, to represent him. She'll be closely escorted, but this will be the one time she'll be out from under the Strongman's demonic cover. The Spirit knows she plans to get away and make contact with one remaining friend on the outside, who can in turn contact your newspaperman. She'll take that chance, Tal. You must arrange for her to succeed."

Tal's first response was, "Is there prayer cover in New York?"

"You will have it."

Tal looked at the swarms below. "And they must not find out . . ."

"No. They must not suspect anything has happened until you can get Susan out for good. They would destroy her if they knew."

"And who is the friend?"

"His name is Kevin Weed, a former classmate and boyfriend."

"To work, then. I have some more prayer to gather in."

"Godspeed, dear captain!"

Tal climbed behind some large rocks for concealment before he unfurled his wings. Then, with the silence and grace of a drifting cloud, he floated up over the mountaintop. Once he had cleared the summit and could no longer be seen by any of the swarms in the valley, his wings snapped into a rushing pattern and he shot forward like a bullet, trailing a brilliant arc of light across the sky and over the horizon.

Marshall and Bernice drove through the forested countryside in the big brown Buick, talking about themselves, their pasts, their families, and anything else that came to mind. They were getting tired of only talking about business anyway, and finding it enjoyable to share each other's company.

"I grew up Presbyterian," said Marshall. "Now I don't know what I am."

"My folks were Episcopalian," said Bernice. "I don't think I was ever anything. They dragged me along to church every Sunday, and I couldn't wait to get out of there."

"I didn't mind it that much. I had a good Sunday school teacher."

"Yeah, maybe that's where I missed out. I never went to Sunday school."

"Aw, I think a kid needs to know something about God."

"What if God doesn't exist?"

"See what I mean? You never went to Sunday school!"

The Buick came to a crossroads, and a sign indicated the way back to Ashton was to the left. Marshall turned left.

Bernice answered one of Hogan's questions. "Nope, no parents alive anymore. Dad died in '76 and Mom died . . . let's see, two years ago."

"That's too bad."

"And then I lost my only sibling, Patricia."

"Is that right! Boy, I'm sorry."

"It's a lonely world out there sometimes . . ."

"Yeah, I suppose . . . and I wonder who there is to meet in Ashton?"

She only looked at him and said, "I'm not hunting, Marshall."

About a mile ahead of them was a wide spot in the road referred to as Baker, a little town indicated by the smallest possible dot on the map. It was one of those typical roadsides where truckers and four-wheeling hunters drop in for black coffee and cold eggs. Blink just once and you'd miss it.

Above the Buick, whisking just over the tops of the trees, Nathan and Armoth kept a careful eye on the vehicle, their wings rushing in an even pattern and their bodies trailing two streaks of diamond-studded light.

"So this is where it all begins," said Nathan with a playful tone.

"And you have been chosen to strike the blow," responded Armoth.

Nathan smiled. "Child's play."

Armoth teased him a little. "I'm sure Tal could pick someone else who would like the honor—"

Nathan drew his sword, and it flashed like a lightning bolt. "Oh no, dear Armoth! I've waited long enough. I'll take it."

Nathan banked away from Armoth, dropped down over the roadway as it wound through the tall trees, and began to keep pace with the car, flying lazily about thirty feet above it. He kept his eye on the little town of Baker now approaching, made a quick judgment as to the coasting distance the car could travel, and then, at the right moment, he hurled his sword like a fiery spear downward. The sword traveled a perfect trajectory and shot through the hood of the car.

The engine died.

"Nuts!" said Marshall, shifting quickly into neutral.

"What's wrong?" Bernice asked.

"Something's broke."

Marshall tried to restart the engine as the car continued to coast along. No response.

"Probably electrical . . ." he muttered.

"Better pull over at that station."

"Yeah, I know, I know."

The Buick limped into the little filling station in Baker and rolled to a stop right at the front door. Marshall opened the hood.

"I'm going to excuse myself," said Bernice.

"Go for me too, will you?" Marshall said crossly, looking here and there around the engine compartment.

Bernice went to the next little building, The Evergreen Tavern. Age and settling were slowly swallowing it from the bottom up, and one end was badly sunken, the paint on the front door was peeling. The neon beer logo in the window still worked, though, and the juke box inside was twanging some country hit.

Bernice pushed the door open—the bottom scraped a worn arc across the linoleum—and went inside, twisting her nose a little at the blue cigarette smoke that had replaced the air. Just a few men sat in the establishment, probably the first of the logging crews getting off work. They were talking loudly, swapping stories, cussing it up. Bernice looked directly toward the back of the room, trying to find the little Men and Women signs. Yes, there was Restrooms.

One of the men at a nearby table said, "Hey, baby, how's it goin'?"

Bernice wasn't going to even look in his direction, but did just happen to give him a glance and an appropriately dirty look. A little too *much* local color in this place, she thought.

She slowed her walk. Her eyes locked on him. He looked back at her with a boozy, lazy-eyed smile on his bearded face.

Another man said, "Looks like you got her attention, buddy."

Bernice kept looking at him. She approached the table and took an even closer look. The hair was long and tangled, bound into a ponytail with a rubber band. The eyes were glassy and now heavily lined. But she knew this man.

The man's friend said, "Good evening, ma'am. Don't let him bother you, he's just having a good time, right, Weed?"

"Weed?" Bernice asked. "Kevin Weed?"

Kevin Weed just looked up at her, enjoying the view and saying little. Finally he said, "Can I buy you a beer?"

Bernice came closer to him, made sure he could clearly see her face. "Do you remember me? Bernice Krueger?" Weed only looked puzzled. "Do you remember Pat Krueger?"

A light slowly began to dawn in Weed's face. "Pat Krueger. . . ? Who are you?"

"I'm Bernice, Pat's sister. Do you remember me? We met a couple of times. You and Pat's roommate were going together."

Weed brightened and smiled, and then he cursed and excused himself. "Bernice Krueger! Pat's sister!" He cursed again, and excused himself again. "What're you doin' in this place?"

"Just passing through. And I will take a small Coke, thank you."

Weed smiled and looked at his friends. Their eyes and mouths were getting wide, and they were starting to laugh.

Weed said with a leer, "I think it's time you boys found another table . . ."

They gathered up their hard hats and lunch boxes and laughed. "Yeah, you got it, Weed."

"Dan," Weed hollered, "a small Coke for the lady here."

Dan had to stare for a moment at the nice girl who had come into a place like his. He got the Coke and brought it to her.

"So what have you been doing?" Weed asked her.

Bernice had her pen and notebook out. She told him a little about what she had been doing and what she was doing now. Then she said, "I haven't seen you since before Pat's death."

"Hey, I'm really sorry about that."

"Kevin, can you tell me anything about it? What do you know?"

"Nothing much . . . no more than what I read in the papers."

"What about Pat's roommate? Do you hear from her anymore?" Bernice noticed Weed's eyes widen and his mouth drop open the moment she mentioned the girl.

"Man, this world is getting smaller all the time!" he said.

"You saw her?" Bernice couldn't believe her good fortune.

"Well, yeah, sort of."

"When?" Bernice insisted.

"But just for a little while."

"Where? When?" Bernice was having a very difficult time holding herself back.

"I saw her at the carnival."

"In Ashton?"

"Yeah, yeah, in Ashton. I just ran into her. She called my name, and I turned around and there she was."

"What did she say? Did she say where she's living now?"

Weed fidgeted a little. "Man, I don't know. I don't really care. She dumped me, you know, ran off with that other goon. She was even with him that night."

"What was her name again?"

"Susan. Susan Jacobson. She's a real heartbreaker, she is."

"Do you have any idea—did she give you any idea of where I might find her? I have to talk to her about Pat. She might know something."

"Man, I don't know. She didn't talk to me for very long at all. She was in a hurry, had to meet her new boyfriend or something. She wanted my phone number, that was about it."

Bernice couldn't let go of her hope. Not yet. "Are you sure she didn't give you some idea of where she's living now, or any way to get in touch with her?" Weed shrugged drunkenly. "Kevin, I've been trying to find her for ages! I've got to talk to her!"

Weed was bitter. "Talk to her boyfriend, that fat little geezer with all the bucks!"

No, no, that wasn't really a legitimate hunch that ran through Bernice's mind. Or was it?

"Kevin," she said, "what did Susan look like that night?"

He was staring off into space, like a drunken and jilted lover. "Foxy," he said. "Long, black hair, black dress, sexy shades."

Bernice felt her stomach tighten into a knot as she said, "And what about her boyfriend? Did you see him?"

"Yeah, later. Susan acted like she didn't even know me when he came into the picture."

"Well, what did he look like?"

"Like some wimp from Fat City. It had to have been his money, that's why Susan latched on to him."

Bernice picked up her pen in a shaking hand. "What's your phone number?"

He gave it to her.

"Address?"

He mumbled that off too.

"Now, you say she asked you for your phone number?"

"Yeah, I don't know why. Maybe things aren't working out with loverboy."

"Did you give it to her?"

"Yeah. Maybe I'm a sucker, but yeah, I did."

"So she just might be calling you."

He shrugged.

"Kevin . . ." Bernice gave him one of her cards. "Listen carefully to me. Are you listening?"

He looked at her and said yes.

"If she calls, if you hear anything from her at all, please give her my name and number and tell her I want to talk to her. Get *her* number so I can call *her*. Will you do that?"

He took the card and nodded. "Yeah, sure."

She finished her Coke and prepared to leave. He looked at her with his dull, glassy eyes.

"Hey, you doin' anything tonight?"

"If you hear from Susan, call me. We'll have plenty to talk about then."

He looked at her card again. "Yeah, sure."

A few moments later Bernice was back at the filling station just in time to see Marshall start the car up. The old and bent station owner was looking at the engine and shaking his head.

"Hey, that did it!" Marshall shouted from behind the wheel.

"Heck, I didn't do a thing," said the old man.

High above the filling station, Nathan soared skyward to join Armoth, his sword retrieved. "Done," he said.

"And now we'll see how the captain and Guilo succeed in New York."

The Buick started out again, and Nathan and Armoth followed behind and above it like two kites on strings.

18

Hank started the Sunday morning service with a good rousing song, one Mary performed on the piano particularly well. Both were in good spirits and feeling encouraged; in spite of the approaching sounds of battle, they sensed that God in His infinite wisdom was indeed working out a very mighty and effective plan for reestablishing his kingdom in the town of Ashton. Victories large and small were in the making, and Hank knew it had to be the hand of God.

For one thing, this morning he would be ministering to an almost entirely new congregation; at least it sure felt that way. Many of the old dissenters had dropped out of the church and taken their embittering presence with them, and the whole mood and spirit of the place had risen several notches because of their absence. Sure, Alf Brummel, Gordon Mayer, and Sam Turner still hovered around, brooding together like some kind of hit squad, but none of them were in the service this morning and a lot of new, fresh faces were. The Forsythes' example had been followed by their numerous friends and acquaintances, some married couples, some singles, and some students. Grandma Duster was there, as strong and healthy as ever and ready for a spiritual fight; John and Patty Coleman were back, and John couldn't keep from grinning in his joy and excitement.

Of the rest, Hank had only met one. Next to Andy and June, looking a little sheepish, sat Ron Forsythe, along with his girlfriend, a short, very made-up sophomore. Hank had to choke down some very strong emotion when he saw the Forsythes enter accompanied by their son: it was a miracle, a genuine act of grace by the living God. He would have shouted hallelujah right there, but he didn't want to scare the young fellow away; this could be one of those kid-gloves cases.

After the first song, Hank figured he might as well address the situation before him.

"Well," he said informally, "I don't know whether to call all you people visitors or refugees or what."

They all laughed and exchanged glances.

Hank continued, "Why don't we just take a moment here to introduce ourselves? I guess you probably know who I am; I'm Hank Busche, the pastor, and this flower sitting at the piano is my wife, Mary." Mary stood quickly, smiled meekly, then sat down again. "Why don't we go around the room here and tell everybody who we are . . ."

And the first roll call of the Remnant took place as the angels and demons watched: Krioni and Triskal stood at their posts right beside Hank and Mary while Signa and his squad, now numbering ten, kept a hedge about the building.

Again Lucius had carried on a bitter argument with Signa, trying to gain admittance. But he knew better than to push the matter too far—Hank Busche was bad enough, but now he had a whole church full of praying saints. The heavenly warriors were enjoying their first real advantage. Lucius finally ordered his demons to remain outside and hear what they could.

The only demons that had managed to enter had come in with their human hosts, and now they sat here and there in the congregation, brooding over this horrible development. Scion stood near the back like a hen watching over her brood, and Seth stayed near the Forsythes and the group with them.

There was power in this place today, and everyone could feel it grow as each new person stood and introduced himself. To Hank it seemed just like the gathering of a special army.

"Ralph Metzer, sophomore at Whitmore . . ."

"Judy Kemp, sophomore at Whitmore . . ."

"Greg and Eva Smith, friends of the Forsythes."

"Bill and Betty Jones. We run the Whatnot Shop over on Eighth Street . . ."

"Mike Stewart. I live with the Joneses, and I work out at the mill."

"Cal and Ginger Barton. We're still new in town."

"Cecil and Miriam Cooper, and we're sure glad to see you all here . . ."

"Ben Squires. I'm the guy who brings you your mail if you live on the west side . . ."

"Tom Harris, and this is my wife Mabel. Welcome to all of you and praise the Lord!"

"Clint Neal—I work at the filling station."

"Greg and Nancy Jenning. I teach and she's a writer."

"Andy Forsythe, and praise the Lord!"

"June Forsythe, and amen to that."

Ron stood to his feet, put his hands in his pockets, and looked at the floor a lot as he said, "I'm—I'm Ron Forsythe, and this here is Cynthia, and . . . I met the pastor at The Cave, and . . ." His voice cracked with emotion. "I just want to thank you people for praying for me and for caring." He stood there for a moment, looking at the floor while tears welled up in his eyes.

June stood beside him and addressed the group on his behalf. "Ron wants you all to know that he and Cynthia gave their hearts to Jesus last night."

Everyone smiled with delight and murmured encouragement, and that loosened Ron up enough to say, "Yeah, and we flushed all our drugs down the toilet!"

That brought down the house.

With increased joy and fervor, the roll call continued.

Outside, the demons listened with great alarm and hissed exclamations of forboding.

"Rafar must know of this!" one said.

Lucius, his wings half unfurled just to keep his fussing ranks from pestering him, stood still and brooded.

One little demon hovered about his head and cried out, "What shall we do, Master Lucius? Shall we find Rafar?"

"Back to whatever you were doing!" he hissed back. "Let *me* see to informing Ba-al Rafar myself!"

They gathered around him, wanting to hear his next order. Lately it seemed he had spoken so very little.

"What are you all staring at?" he shrieked. "Go, do mischief! Let me worry about these petty little saints!"

They flurried away in all directions, and Lucius stood in his place outside the church window.

Tell Rafar indeed! Let Rafar humble himself enough to *ask*. Lucius would not be his lackey.

In this part of New York City, things were tailored for the elite and discerning; the shops, boutiques, and restaurants were the exclusive kind, the hotels quite lavish. Carefully groomed flowering trees grew in round stucco planters along the sidewalks, and maintenance workers kept the streets and walks spotless.

Among the hurried shoppers and browsers crowding the district were two very large men in tan tunics, strolling the sidewalk and looking here and there.

"The Gibson Hotel," Tal read on the front of an old, distinguished stone building that towered thirty stories above them.

"I see no activity," said Guilo.

"It's early yet. They'll be along. Let's be quick about this."

The two of them slipped through the big front doors and into the hotel lobby. People passed on all sides of them, and sometimes right through them, but that, of course, was of no consequence. Within moments they had checked the schedule at the desk for the hotel's banquet facilities and verified that the Grand Ballroom was reserved that night for the Universal Consciousness Society.

"The general's information was right," Tal commented with pleasure.

They hurried down a long, thickly-carpeted hallway past a barbershop, a beauty salon, a shoeshine nook, and a gift shop, and at length came to two huge oak doors with lavishly wrought brass handles. They passed through and found themselves in the Grand Ballroom, now filled with dining tables adorned with crystal place settings and white linen tablecloths. One lone, long-stemmed rose in a bud vase stood on every table. The hotel caterers were hurriedly making final preparations, setting out the artfully folded napkins and wine glasses. Tal checked the place cards at the head table. One, towards the end, said "Kaseph, Omni Corporation."

They went through a nearby exit door and looked right and left. Down the hall, to the left and toward the back of the hotel, was the ladies' lounge. They went in, passed a few women primping at the mirrors and found what they were after: the very last stall, designated for use by the handicapped. It was built against the rear wall of the hotel, just below a window large enough for a limber human to crawl through. Tal reached up, broke the lock, and tested the window to make sure it would open and close easily. Guilo passed quickly through the wall into the alley where he found a large dumpster and, with incredible ease, moved it several feet so that it was situated below the window. He then arranged some crates and garbage cans in a very handy stair-stepped fashion against the dumpster.

Tal joined him and the two went up the alley to the street. Down one block was a phone booth. Tal picked up the receiver and made sure everything was functioning.

"Here they come!" Guilo warned, and they leaped through the wall of a department store and peered out a window just as a long, black limousine and then another and then another began an ominous parade down the street toward the hotel. Inside the limousines sat dignitaries and other VIPs from many different nations and races, and within and on top were demons, large, black, warty, and fierce, their yellow eyes darting warily in every direction.

Tal and Guilo watched with fascination. In the sky overhead, other demons began flocking to the hotel like swallows, their black winged outlines silhouetted against the reddening sky.

"A significant gathering, captain," said Guilo.

Tal nodded and continued watching. Amid the limousines were many taxis, also carrying a vast cross section of humanity: Orientals, Africans, Europeans, Westerners, Arabians—people of great power, esteem, and dignity from all over the world.

"As written in the Scriptures, the kings of the earth," Tal observed, "being made drunk with the wine of the great harlot's immorality."

"Babylon the Great," said Guilo. "The Great Harlot arising at last."

"Yes, Universal Consciousness. The world religion, the doctrine of demons spreading among all the nations. Babylon revived right before the end of the age."

"Hence the return of the Prince of Babylon, Rafar."

"Of course. And that explains why *we* were called. We were the last to confront him."

Guilo only winced at that. "My captain, our last battle with Rafar is not a pleasant memory."

"Nor a pleasant expectation."

"Do you expect him here?"

"No. This gathering is only a party before the real battle, and the real battle is slated for the town of Ashton."

Tal and Guilo remained where they were, watching the gathering forces of mankind and of Satanic evil converge on the Gibson Hotel. They kept looking for the one key person: Susan Jacobson, Alexander Kaseph's Maidservant.

They finally spotted her in a very fancy Lincoln Continental, probably Kaseph's private vehicle, driven by a hired chauffeur. She was accompanied by two escorts sitting on either side of her.

"She'll be closely watched," said Tal. "Come on, we need a better look."

They stalked quickly through the department store, through walls, displays, and people, then ducked under the street and came up inside the restaurant right across from the hotel's main door. All around them well-dressed people sat at quiet, candlelit tables eating expensive French cuisine. They hurried to a front window right next to an older couple enjoying seafood and wine and watched as the Lincoln carrying Susan pulled up in front of the hotel.

Susan's door was opened by the red-coated doorman. One escort got out and extended his hand to help her disembark; she stepped out and was immediately joined by the other escort. The two tuxedo-clad escorts were very handsome, but also very intimidating. They kept very close to her. Susan wore a very loose-fitting evening gown that draped her body stunningly and cascaded to her feet.

Guilo had to ask, "Are her plans the same as ours?"

Tal answered assuredly, "The general has yet to err."

Guilo only shook his head in apprehension.

"To the alley," said Tal.

They moved along under the cracked cobbled alley and surfaced to a hiding place behind a fire escape. Night had fallen, and it was very dark in the alley. From their vantage point they could count twenty pairs of shifting yellow eyes, evenly spaced along the alley and against the hotel.

"About a hundred sentries are around the place," said Tal.

"Under better circumstances, a mere handful," Guilo muttered.

"You need only concern yourself with these twenty."

Guilo took his sword in his hand. He could feel the prayers of the local saints.

"It will be difficult," he said. "The prayer cover is limited."

"You don't have to defeat them," answered Tal. "Just get them to chase after you. We need the alley clear for just a few moments."

They waited. The air in the alley was still and dank. The demons moved very little, remaining at their posts, mumbling back and forth in different languages, their sulfurous breath forming a strange, meandering ribbon of yellow vapor that hung along the alley like a putrid river floating in midair. Tal and Guilo could feel themselves getting more and more tense, like ever-tightening springs, with each passing second. The banquet must be in progress by now. At any time Susan could excuse herself from the table.

More time passed. Suddenly both Tal and Guilo felt the prompting of the Spirit. Tal looked at Guilo, and Guilo nodded. She was on her way. They watched the window. The light from the ladies' lounge shone brightly through it; they could just barely hear the sound of the door opening and closing as patrons came and went.

The door opened. High heels clicked on the tile floor, moving toward the window. The demons began to stir a little, muttering among themselves. The door to the last stall swung open. Guilo's hand gripped his sword. He began to breathe deeply, his big torso heaving in and out, the power of God coursing through him. Their eyes were riveted on the window. The demons became more alert, their yellow eyes wide open and darting back and forth. They were talking louder.

The shadow of a woman's head suddenly appeared on the window. A woman's hand reached for the latch.

Tal touched Guilo on the shoulder, and Guilo instantly dropped into the ground. Only a fraction of a second passed.

"YAHAAAAA!" came the sudden, deafening war cry from Guilo's powerful lungs, and the whole alley instantly exploded in a blinding flash of white light as Guilo shot up out of the ground, his sword flashing and shimmering, tracing brilliant arcs in the air. The demons jumped, hooting and shrieking in terror, but recovered immediately and drew their swords. The alley echoed with the metallic ringing, and the red glow of their blades danced like comets on the high brick walls.

Guilo stood tall and strong, and he bellowed out a laugh that shook the ground. "Now, you black lizards, I'll test your mettle!"

A big spirit on the end shrieked out an order, and all twenty demons converged on Guilo like starving predators, their swords flashing and their fangs bared. Guilo shot straight up out of their midst like a slippery bar of soap and added an agile spin as he went, throwing light everywhere in colorful spirals. The demons unfurled their wings and shot up after him. As Tal watched, Guilo looped and corkscrewed all over the sky like a loose balloon, laughing, taunting and teasing, staying just out of their reach. The demons were in a blind rage by now.

The alley was empty. The window was opening. Tal was beneath the window in an instant, unglorified and concealed in the darkness. He grabbed Susan the moment her hand came through the window and pulled so hard she practically shot through the window on his strength alone. She was dressed in a simple blouse and jeans, and had small slippers on her feet. From the neck up she was still gorgeous; from the neck down she was ready for running down dark alleys.

Tal helped her find her way down from the dumpster and then prodded her up the alley and out to the street where she hesitated, looked this way and that, and then spotted the phone booth. She ran like the wind, in a terrible and desperate hurry. Tal followed her, trying to stay as concealed as possible. He looked back over his shoulder; Guilo's diversion had worked. For now, Guilo was the main problem for the demons, and their attention was far from this one frantically running woman.

Susan leaped into the booth and slammed the door behind her. She took a pile of coins from her jeans pocket, dialed the operator, and put through a long-distance call.

Somewhere between Ashton and the little roadside of Baker, in a rundown warehouse refashioned into low-rent apartments, Kevin Weed was awakened from an exhausted sleep by the ringing of his phone. He rolled over on his mattress and lifted the receiver.

"Yeah, who's this?" he asked.

"Is this Kevin?" came the desperate voice on the other end.

Kevin perked up a little. It was a woman's voice. "Yeah, that's me. Who's this?"

In the phone booth, Susan looked up and down the street fearfully as she said, "Kevin, this is Susan. Susan Jacobson."

Kevin was beginning to wonder about all this. "Hey, what do you want with me anyway?"

"I need your help, Kevin. I don't have much time. There *isn't* much time."

"Time for what?" he asked very dully.

"Please listen. Write it down if you have to."

"I don't got a pencil."

"Then just listen. Now you know about the *Ashton Clarion?* The newspaper in Ashton?"

"Yeah, yeah, I know about it."

"Bernice Krueger works there. She's the sister of my old roommate, Pat, the one who committed suicide."

"Oh, man . . . what's going on around here?"

"Kevin, will you do something for me? Will you get ahold of Bernice Krueger at the *Clarion* and . . . Kevin?"

"Yeah, I'm listening."

"Kevin, I'm in trouble. I need your help."

"So where's your boyfriend?"

"He's the one I'm afraid of. You know about him. Tell Bernice all about Alexander Kaseph, everything you know."

Kevin was nonplussed. "So what do I know?"

"Tell her what happened, you know, between us, with Kaseph, the whole thing. Tell her what Kaseph's up to."

"I don't get this."

"I don't have time to explain. Just tell her—tell her that Kaseph is taking over the whole town . . . and let her know I have some very important information about her sister Pat. I'll try to reach her, but I'm afraid the *Clarion* phone might be bugged. Kevin, I need you to be there to answer the phone, to . . ." Susan was frustrated, full of emotion, unable to select the right words. She had too much to say and too little time.

"You're not making a whole lot of sense," Kevin muttered. "You *on* something?"

"Just do it, Kevin, please! I'll call you again as soon as I can, or I'll write, or do something, but please call Bernice Krueger and tell her everything you know about Kaseph and about me. Tell her it was me she saw at the carnival."

"How'm I supposed to remember all this stuff?"

"Please do it. Tell me you'll do it!"

"Yeah, okay, I'll do it."

"I've got to go! Good-bye!"

Susan hung up the phone and dashed out of the booth. Tal followed her, ducking inside the buildings as much as he could.

He reached the alley a few moments ahead of her to check it out. Trouble! Four more sentries had moved in to take the place of the original twenty, and they were fully alert. There was no way of knowing where Guilo and the twenty might be. Tal looked behind him. Susan was running full speed for the alley.

Tal dove headfirst through the pavement and penetrated deep under the city, gaining speed, bringing forth his big silver sword. The power of God was increasing now; the saints must be praying somewhere. He could feel it. He only had seconds and he knew it. He checked his bearings, made a wide subterranean sweep away from the hotel and then, over a mile away, he circled back, gaining speed, gaining speed, gaining speed, shining light, building power, faster, faster, faster, his sword a blinding lightning bolt, his eyes like fire, the earth a blur around him, the roar of passing clay, boulders, pipe, and stone like a freight train. He held the sword crossways, the glimmering tip ready for that one infinitesimal moment.

Quicker than a thought, like the explosion of a missile, a brilliant streak of light burst from the ground across the street and seemed to cut space in half as it pierced through the alley and right across the eyes of all four demons. The demons, stunned and blinded, fell to the ground, stumbled about, tried to find each other. The streak of light vanished back into the ground as quickly as it came.

Susan came around the corner and into the alley, heading for the window.

Tal cupped his wings and braked himself. He had to get back to help her through that window before any demons could recover and sound an alarm. He snapped his wings into a violent forward rush and doubled back.

Susan clambered up the crates and cans and onto the dumpster. The demons started to regain their vision and were rubbing their eyes. Tal emerged behind the fire escape, trying to judge the remaining time.

Good! Guilo made it back and dropped like a hawk into the alley, grabbing Susan and thrusting her through the window in an instant, holding her up so she would not tumble to the floor inside. Guilo closed the window himself.

Tal flew out to meet Guilo. "One more time," he shouted.

Nothing more needed to be said. The four sentries had recovered and were pouncing on them, and the other twenty had returned, hot on Guilo's trail. Tal and Guilo shot into the air and streaked away, chased by a flock of frothing demons. The angels flew a course high over the city and kept their speed just slow enough to encourage the demons. They headed west, off into the dark night sky, trailing brilliant white streaks behind them. The demons were tenacious in their pursuit for hundreds of miles, but eventually Tal looked back and found that they had given up the chase and returned to the city. Tal and Guilo picked up speed and headed for Ashton.

In the ladies' room, Susan hurriedly rolled up the legs of her jeans, took her evening gown from its hook in the stall, and quickly resumed her proper appearance for the banquet. She removed the slippers and put them in her handbag, slipped on her dress shoes, then opened the stall door and came out.

A man's voice outside the lounge door called, "Susan, they're waiting for you!"

She checked her appearance in the mirror, combed her hair, and tried to calm her breathing. "Hasty, hasty," she called teasingly.

With ladylike dignity she finally emerged into the hallway and took the arm of the escort. He led her back to the Grand Ballroom, now filled with people, and showed her to her seat at the head table, giving the other escort a reassuring nod.

19

The *Clarion* office was finally recovering the nice, healthy efficiency Marshall liked to see, and the new girl, Carmen, had a lot to do with it. In less than a week she had taken the old bull by the horns and had more than filled Edie's shoes, reestablishing a tight office routine.

It was only Wednesday, and already the paper was in full swing, heading for the Friday edition. Marshall stopped by Carmen's desk on his way to the coffee machine.

She handed him some fresh copy and said, "This is part of Tom's article."

Marshall nodded. "Yeah, the thing on the fire department . . ."

"I've broken it down into three headings—staff, history, and goals—and figured we could run it in three parts. Tom already has it slotted for the next two paste-ups and thinks he can bump something for the third."

Marshall was pleased. "Yeah, go with it, I like it. I'm glad you can read Tom's writing."

Carmen had already proofread the bulk of the material for Friday and was halfway through preparing the copy for George, the typesetter. She had gone through the books and balanced all the accounts. She planned on helping Tom with the paste-up tomorrow. The negatives for the Sportsman's Club layout were ready.

Marshall shook his head with happy amazement. "Glad to have you aboard."

Carmen smiled. "Thank you, sir."

Marshall went to the coffeemaker and poured two cups of coffee. Then it dawned on him: Carmen had found the cord to this fool machine!

He took the two cups back toward his office and gave her a smile of approval as he passed her desk. The location of her desk had been her only request on the job. She had asked if it could be moved to a location right outside Marshall's office door, and Marshall was happy to comply. Now all he had to do was turn and holler, and she would spring into action to do his bidding.

Marshall went into his office, set his cup of coffee on his desk, and offered the other cup to the long-haired, slightly dazed man sitting in the corner. Bernice sat in a chair she had brought in with her own cup of coffee.

"Now where were we?" Marshall asked, sitting at his desk.

Kevin Weed rubbed his face, took a sip of the coffee, and tried to pick up his thoughts again, looking around the floor as if he had dropped them down there somewhere.

Marshall prompted, "Okay, let me at least make sure I've got this straight: Now you used to be the . . . male acquaintance of this Susan, and she used to be the roommate of Pat Krueger, Bernice's sister. Have I got that right?"

Weed nodded. "Yeah, yeah, that's right."

"So what was Susan doing at the carnival?"

"Beats me. Like I said, she just came up behind me and said hi, and I wasn't even looking for her. I couldn't believe it was her, you know?"

"But she got your phone number and then she called you last night . . ."

"Yeah, all tripped out, shook up. It was wild. She didn't make a lot of sense."

Marshall looked at both Weed and Bernice and asked Bernice, "And this is the same ghostly-looking woman you photographed that night?"

Bernice was convinced. "The descriptions Kevin gave me match perfectly the woman I saw, and also that one older man who was with her."

"Yeah, Kaseph." Kevin said the name as if it tasted bad.

"All right," and Marshall made a list in his mind. "So let's talk about this Kaseph first, then we'll talk about Susan, and then we'll talk about Pat."

Bernice had her notepad ready. "What's Kaseph's full name, any idea?"

Weed strained his brain. "Alex—Alan—Alexander . . . something like that."

"But it starts with A."

"Yeah, right."

Marshall asked, "What is he?"

Weed answered, "Susan's new boyfriend, the guy she dumped me for."

"So what does he do? Where does he work?"

Weed shook his head. "I don't know. He's got bucks, though. He's a real wheeler-dealer. When I first heard about him, he was hanging around Ashton and the college and talking about buying property and stuff. Man, the guy was loaded and he liked everybody to know it too." Then he remembered, "Oh, and Susan said he's trying to take over the town . . ."

"What town? *This* one?"

"I guess."

Bernice asked, "So where is he from?"

"Back east, maybe New York. I think he's the big-city type."

Marshall told Bernice, "Make a note for me to call Al Lemley at the *Times*. He might be able to track this guy down if he's in New York." Bernice made the note. Marshall asked Weed, "What else do you know about him?"

"He's weird, man. He's into weird stuff."

Marshall was getting impatient. "C'mon, try harder."

Weed stirred and fidgeted in his chair, trying to get comfortable about talking. "Well, you know, he was like a guru, or a witch doctor, or some kind of far-out ooga-booga man, and he got Susan into all that stuff."

Bernice prodded, "Are you talking about Eastern mysticism?"

"Yeah."

"Pagan religions, meditation?"

"Yeah, yeah, all that stuff. He was into all that stuff, he and that professor lady at the college, what's-her-name—"

Marshall was sick of the name. "Langstrat."

Weed's face brightened with recollection. "Yeah, that was it."

"Were Kaseph and Langstrat associated? Were they friends?"

"Yeah, sure. They were teaching some night classes together, I think, the ones that Susan was going to. Kaseph was a special guest star or something. He really had everybody wowed. I thought he was spooky."

"All right, so Susan was attending these classes—"

"And she got crazy, and I mean *crazy*. Man, she couldn't have been on a higher trip with mescaline. I couldn't even talk to her anymore. She was always way out in space somewhere."

Weed kept talking, starting to roll a little on his own. "That's what really started to get me, how she and the rest of that bunch started keeping secrets and talking in codes and not letting me in on what they were talking about. Susan just kept telling me I wasn't enlightened and wouldn't understand. Man, she just gave it all to that Kaseph guy and he took her, I mean he really took her. He owns her now. She's gone. She's had it."

"And was Langstrat mixed up in all this?"

"Oh yeah, but Kaseph was the real heavy. He was the guru, you know. Langstrat was his puppy dog."

Bernice said, "And now Susan gets your phone number and calls you after all this time."

"And she was scared," said Weed. "She's in trouble. She said I was supposed to get in touch with you guys and tell you what I knew, and she said she had some information on Pat."

Bernice was longing to know. "Did she say what kind of information?"

"No, nothing. But she wants to get ahold of you."

"Well, why doesn't she just call?"

That question helped Weed to remember something. "Oh, yeah, she thinks your phone might be bugged."

Marshall and Bernice were silent for a moment. That was a comment they didn't know how seriously to take.

Weed added, "I guess she called me to be a go-between, to tip you guys off."

Marshall ventured, "Like you're the only one she has left to trust?"
Weed only shrugged.

Bernice asked, "Well, what do you know about Pat? Did Susan ever tell you anything while you were still going together?"

One of Weed's most painful undertakings was trying to remember things. "Uh . . . she and Pat were good friends, for a while anyway. But you know, Susan left us all out in the cold when she started following after that Kaseph bunch. She kinda pushed me off, and Pat too. They didn't get along very well after that, and Susan kept saying how Pat was . . . heh . . . just like me, trying to get in the way, not enlightened, dragging her feet."

Marshall thought of the question and didn't wait for Bernice to ask it. "So, would you say that this Kaseph bunch may have regarded Pat as an enemy?"

"Man . . ." Weed remembered some more. "She did stick her neck out, I mean, she got in the way. Her and Susan had a real fight once about the stuff Susan was getting into. Pat didn't trust Kaseph and kept telling Susan she was brainwashed."

Weed's eyes brightened. "Yeah, I talked to Pat once. We were sitting at a game, and we talked about what Susan was getting into and how Kaseph was controlling her, and Pat was really shook up about it, just like I was. I guess Pat and Susan really had some fights about it until Susan finally moved out of the dorm and ran off with Kaseph. Boy, she dropped out of her classes and everything."

"So did Pat make any enemies, I mean *real* enemies?"

Weed kept digging up new things that had been buried under the years and the alcohol. "Uh, yeah, maybe she did. It was after Susan ran off with this Kaseph guy. Pat told me she was going to check the whole thing out once and for all, and I think she may have gone to see that Professor Langstrat a few times. A while later I ran into her again. She was sitting in a cafeteria on campus, and she looked like she hadn't slept in days, and I asked her how she was, and she would hardly even talk to me. I asked how her investigation was going, you know, her checking out Kaseph and Langstrat and stuff, and she said she'd quit doing anything about that, said it was really no big deal. I thought that was a little weird, she'd been so torn up about it before. I asked her, 'Hey, are they coming after you now?' and she wouldn't talk about it, she said I wouldn't understand. Then she said something about some instructor, some guy that was helping her out and that she was doing okay, and I got the message that she didn't want me butting in, so I just sort of left her there."

"Did her behavior seem strange to you?" Bernice asked. "Did she seem like herself?"

"No way. Hey, if she hadn't been so against that whole Kaseph and Langstrat bunch, I woulda thought she was one of them; she had the same kind of dopey, lost-in-space look all over her."

"When? Just when was it that you saw her like that?"

Weed knew, but hated to say it. "Just a little while before they found her dead."

"Did she seem afraid? Did she give you any indication of any enemies, anything like that?"

Weed grimaced, trying to remember. "She wouldn't talk to me. But I saw her once after that and tried to ask her about Susan, and she acted like I was some kind of mugger or something . . . she hollered, 'Leave me alone, leave me alone!' and tried to pull away and then she saw it was me, and she looked all around like somebody was following her . . ."

"Who? Did she say who?"

Weed looked at the ceiling. "Oh . . . what was that guy's name?"

Bernice was leaning forward, hanging on his words. "There *was* somebody?"

"Thomas, some guy named Thomas."

"Thomas! Did she ever say his last name?"

"Don't remember any last name. I never met the guy, never saw him, but he sure must have owned her. She acted like he was following her all around, talking to her, maybe threatening her, I don't know. She seemed pretty afraid of him."

"Thomas," Bernice whispered. She said to Weed, "Is there anything else about this Thomas? Anything at all?"

"I never saw him . . . she didn't say who he was or where she would meet him. But it was kinda strange. One minute she'd be talking like he was the greatest thing that ever happened to her, and then the next minute she'd be hiding out and saying he was following her."

Bernice got up and headed for the door. "I think we might have a college roster somewhere." She began rummaging around in the desks and shelves of the front office.

Weed fell silent. He looked tired.

Marshall reassured him, "You're doing fine, Kevin. Hey, it's been a while."

"Uh . . . I don't know if this is important—"

"Consider everything important."

"Well, this stuff about Pat having some new instructor . . . I think some of the Kaseph bunch, maybe it was Susan, they had instructors."

"But I thought Pat didn't want anything to do with that group."

"Yeah. Yeah, that's right."

Marshall shifted directions. "So where did you fit into all these goings-on, besides your relationship with Susan?"

"Hey, nowhere! I didn't want anything to do with it, man."

"Were you going to the school?"

"Yeah, taking accounting. Man, when all this started coming down and then Pat killed herself, hey, I got out of there fast. I didn't want to be next, you know?" He looked at the floor. "My life's been nothing but hell ever since."

"You working?"

"Yeah, logging crew for Gorst Brothers up above Baker." He shook his head. "I didn't think I'd ever see Susan again."

Marshall turned to his desk and searched for some paper. "Well, we'll have to keep in touch. Let me have your number and address, at work and at home."

Weed gave Marshall the information. "And if I'm not there, you can probably find me at The Evergreen Tavern in Baker."

"Okay, listen, if you hear anything else from Susan you let us know, day or night." He gave Weed his card with his home phone number added.

Bernice came back in with the roster.

"Marshall, you have a call. I think it's urgent," she said. Then she turned to Weed. "Kevin, let's you and I step outside and go through this roster. Maybe we'll find that guy's full name."

Weed stepped outside with Bernice as Marshall picked up the phone.

"Hogan," he said.

"Hogan, this is Ted Harmel."

Marshall scrambled for a pencil. "Hi, Ted. Thank you for calling."

"So you talked to Eldon—"

"And Eldon talked to you?"

Harmel sighed and said, "You're in trouble, Hogan. I'll give you one interview. Got a pencil handy?"

"I'm ready. Shoot."

Bernice had just said good-bye to Weed and seen him to the door when Marshall emerged from his office with a scribbled-on piece of paper in his hand.

"Any luck?" he asked.

"Zilch. There are no Thomases of any kind, first or last name."

"It's still a lead though."

"Who was that on the phone?"

Marshall produced the scrap of paper. "Thank God for small favors. That was Ted Harmel." Bernice brightened considerably as Marshall explained, "He wants to see me tomorrow, and here are the directions. It must be way back in the sticks. The guy is still paranoid as all get-out; I'm surprised he didn't make me wear a disguise or something."

"He wouldn't say anything about all this?"

"No, not over the phone. It has to be just the two of us, in private."

Marshall leaned over just a little and said, "He's another one who thinks our phone might be bugged."

"So how do we make sure it isn't?"

"Make that one of your assignments. Now here's the rest of them." Bernice grabbed her notepad off her desk and made her list as Marshall spoke. "Check the New York phone book—"

"I did. No A. Kaseph listed."

"Scratch that one. Next: Check around with the local real estate offices. If Weed's right about Kaseph looking for property around here, some of those people might know something. And I'd look around in the commercial listings as well."

"Mm-hmm."

"And while you're at it, find out what you can about whoever owns Joe's Market."

"It's not Joe?"

"No. The place used to belong to Joe and Angelina Carlucci, c-a-r-l-u-c-c-i. I want to know where they went and who owns the store now. See if you can get some straight answers."

"And you were going to check with your friend at the *Times* . . ."

"Yeah, Lemley." Marshall added a note to his piece of paper.

"That it?"

"That's it for now. In the meantime, let's get back to running this paper."

All the time, all through their meeting with Weed and their following conversation, Carmen sat at her desk busily working and acting like she hadn't heard a word.

The morning had been tight, with the next issue's deadline galloping up on them, but by noon the paste-up was ready to go to the printer and the office had a chance to resume its normal pace.

Marshall put in a call to Lemley, his old comrade-in-arms at the *New York Times*. Lemley got all the information Marshall had on this strange character Kaseph, saying he'd get right on it. Marshall hung up the phone with one hand and grabbed his suit jacket with the other; his next stop was his afternoon appointment with the reclusive Ted Harmel.

Bernice drove off for her appointed stops. She parked her red Toyota in the parking lot of what used to be Joe's Market and was now called the Ashton Mercantile, and went into the store. About a half hour later, she returned to her car and drove away. It had been a wasted trip: no one knew anything, they only worked there, the manager wasn't in, and they had no idea when he would be back. Some had never heard of Joe Carlucci, some had but didn't know whatever happened to him. The assistant manager finally asked her to quit bothering all the employees on company time. So much for getting any straight answers.

Now it was off to the realty offices.

Johnson-Smythe Realty occupied an old house remodeled into an office on the edge of the business part of town; the house still had a very charming front yard, with a redwood tree standing tall in the middle of it and a quaint, log cabin mailbox out front. It was warm and welcoming inside, and quiet. Two desks occupied what used to be the living room; both were empty at the time. On the walls hung bulletin boards with snapshots of house after house, with cards below each photograph describing the building, the property, the view, nearness to shopping and so forth, and—last but not least—the price. Boy, what people would pay these days for a house!

At a third desk in what used to be the dining room a young lady stood and smiled at Bernice.

"Hi, can I help you?" she asked.

Bernice smiled back, introduced herself, and asked, "I need to ask a question that might seem a little odd, but here goes. Are you ready?"

"Ready."

"Have you done any business with anyone by the name of A. Kaseph in the last year or so?"

"How do you spell that?"

Bernice spelled it for her, then explained. "You see, I'm trying to get in touch with him. It's just a personal matter. I was wondering if you might have a phone number or address or anything."

The young lady looked at the name she had just written on a piece of paper and said, "Well, I'm new here, so I sure don't know, but let me ask Rosemary."

"In the meantime, might I have a look through your microfiche?"

"Sure. You know how to run it?"

"Yes."

The lady went toward the back of the house where Rosemary— apparently the boss lady—had her office in a back bedroom. Bernice could hear Rosemary talking on the phone. Getting an answer from her might take a while.

Bernice went to the microfiche reader. Where to start? She looked at a map of Ashton and vicinity on the wall and found the location of Joe's Market. The hundreds of little celluloid plates were arranged by Section, Township, Quarters, and the street numbers. Bernice had to do a lot of looking back and forth to get all the numbers off the map. Finally she thought she might have found the right microfiche to put into the viewer.

"Excuse me," came a voice. It was Rosemary, marching down the hall toward her with a grim expression on her face. "Ms. Krueger, I'm afraid the microfiche is only for the use of our staff. If there's something you'd like me to find for you . . ."

Bernice kept cool and tried to keep things flowing. "Sure, I'm sorry. I was trying to find out the new owner of Joe's Market."

"I wouldn't know."

"Well, I thought it might be on the machine here somewhere."

"No, I don't think so. It's been a while since the files have been updated."

"Well, could we look anyway?"

Rosemary totally ignored the question. "Is there anything else you'd like to know?"

Bernice stood firm and unshaken. "Well, there was my original question. Have you done any business with anyone named Kaseph in the last year or so?"

"No, I've never heard the name."

"Well, perhaps someone else on your staff—"

"They've never heard it either." Bernice was about to question that, but Rosemary interrupted with, "I would know. I know all their accounts."

Bernice thought of one other thing. "You wouldn't have a—a cross-reference file, would you—"

"No, we don't," Rosemary answered very abruptly. "Now is there anything else?"

Bernice was tired of being nice. "Well, Rosemary, even if there was, I'm sure you would not be able or willing to supply it. I'm leaving now, so breathe easy."

She left hurriedly, feeling very lied to.

20

Marshall was beginning to worry about his shock absorbers. This old logging road had more potholes than surface; apparently it wasn't used that much anymore by the logging companies, but was left to hunters and hikers who knew the area well enough to keep from getting lost. Marshall did not. He looked again at the scribbled directions and then at the odometer. Boy, the miles go by slowly on roads like this one!

Marshall bumped his way around a gravelly corner and finally saw a vehicle ahead, parked alongside the road. Yes, an old Valiant. It was Harmel. Marshall pulled up behind the Valiant and got out. Ted Harmel got out of his car, dressed in clothing for the outdoors: wool shirt, faded jeans, work boots, a wool cap. He looked the way he had sounded: exhausted and very scared.

"Hogan?" he asked.

"Yeah," said Marshall, extending his hand.

Harmel shook it and then turned away abruptly. "C'mon with me."

Marshall followed Harmel to a trail off the road and they hiked up among the tall timber, picking their way through logs, rocks, and underbrush. Marshall was wearing a suit and his shoes were definitely the wrong kind for this sort of terrain, but he wasn't about to complain—he'd recaptured the big fish that got away.

At last Harmel seemed satisfied with their seclusion. He went to a huge fallen log, weathered and bleached by years of changing seasons, and sat down on it. Marshall joined him.

"I want to thank you for calling me," Marshall said for an opener.

"We never had this meeting," Harmel said bluntly. "Is that an agreement?"

"You've got it."

"Now what do you know about me?"

"Not much. You used to be the editor of the *Clarion,* Eugene Baylor and the other college regents were on your case, you and Eldon Strachan are friends . . ." Marshall reviewed quickly all he had learned, which was mostly what he and Bernice had gleaned from the old *Clarion* articles.

Harmel nodded. "Yeah, that's all true. Eldon and I are still friends. We went through basically the same thing, so that gives us a sort of comradeship. As far as the molesting of Marla Jarred, Adam Jarred's girl—that was a bizarre set-up. I don't know who coached her, or how, but somebody got that girl to say all the right words to the police. I do find it significant that the whole matter was settled so quietly. What I was supposed to have done is a felony; you don't just settle a thing like that quietly."

"Why did it happen, Ted? What did you do to bring it on yourself?"

"I got too involved. You're right about Juleen and all the others. It's a secret society, a club, a whole network of people. Nobody has any secrets from anybody else. The eyes of the group are everywhere; they watch what you do, what you say, what you think, how you feel. They're working toward what they call a Universal Mind, the concept that sooner or later all the inhabitants of the world will make a giant evolutionary leap and meld into one global brain, one transcending consciousness." Harmel stopped, looked at Marshall. "I'm spilling it as it comes to me. Is it making sense?"

Marshall had to compare Harmel's "spillings" with what he already knew. "Every person affiliated with this exclusive network subscribes to these ideas?"

"Yeah. The whole thing is built around occult ideas, Eastern mysticism, cosmic consciousness. That's why they meditate and do psychic readings and try to meld their minds together . . ."

"Is this what they do in Langstrat's therapy sessions?"

"Yes, exactly. Every person who joins the network goes through a certain initiation process. They meet with Juleen and learn to achieve altered states of consciousness, psychic powers, out-of-body experiences. The sessions could involve just one person, or several, but

Juleen is at the core of it all, like some kind of guru, and we were all her disciples. We all became like one, growing, interdependent organism, trying to become one with the Universal Mind."

"You said something about . . . melding your minds together?"

"ESP, telepathy, whatever. Your thoughts are not your own, and neither is your life. You're only one segment of the whole. Juleen's highly skilled in such things. She—she knew my every thought. She owned me . . ." This part became difficult for Harmel to speak about. He grew tense, and his voice faltered and dropped in volume. "Maybe she still does. Sometimes I still hear her calling to me . . . moving through my brain."

"Does she own all the others as well?"

Harmel nodded. "Yeah, everybody owns everybody, and they won't stop until they own that whole town. I could see it coming. Anybody who gets in their way suddenly drops out of sight. That's why I'm still wondering about Edie. Ever since this whole thing started happening, I've been leery about anyone just dropping out of the picture suddenly . . ."

"What danger would Edie be to them?"

"Maybe she's just one more step toward taking you out. I wouldn't be surprised. They took out Eldon, they took out me, they took out Jefferson . . ."

"Who's Jefferson?"

"The district judge. I don't know how they did it, but suddenly he decided he wouldn't run for reelection. He sold his home, left town, no one's heard from him since."

"And now Baker's in—"

"He's part of the network. He's owned."

"So did you know this at the time you had your little crime settled so quietly?"

Harmel nodded. "He told me he could make it really rough for me, turn me over to the county prosecutor and then it would be out of his hands. He knew good and well it was a frame-up! He had me checkmated, so I took him up on it. I got out of town."

Marshall took out a pad and pen. "Who else do you know that belongs to this bunch?"

Harmel looked away. "If I tell you too much, they'll trace it back to me. You'll have to find out for yourself. All I can do is point you in the right direction. Check the mayor's office and the town council; see who's new there and who they replaced. They've had a lot of turnover lately." Marshall made a note of it. "You've got Brummel?"

"Yeah, Brummel, Young, Baker."

"Check the county land commissioner, and the president at the Independent Bank, and . . ." Harmel kept probing his memory. "The county comptroller."

"I've got him on the list."

"The board of regents at the college?"

"Yeah. Say, wasn't it the tiff with them that got you run out of town?"

"That was only part of it. I wasn't controllable anymore. I got in the way. The network took care of me before I could hurt them. But there's no way I can prove it. It doesn't matter anyway. The whole thing's too big; it's like a huge organism, a cancer that just keeps spreading. You can't go after just one part of it like the regents and expect to kill the whole thing. It's everywhere, at every level. Are you religious?"

"In a limited sense, I suppose."

"Well you're going to need *something* to fight it. It's spiritual, Hogan. It doesn't listen to reason, or to the law, or to any set of morals but its own. They don't believe in any God—*they* are God." Harmel paused to calm down and then took off on a different note. "I first got involved with Juleen when I wanted to do a story on some of the so-called research she was doing. I was intrigued by it all—the parapsychology, the strange phenomena she was documenting. I started having these *counseling* sessions with her myself. I let her read and photograph my aura and my energy field. I let her probe my mind and meld our thoughts. I went into it after a novelty story, actually, but I got hooked. I couldn't tear myself away from it. After a while I started picking up on some of the same things she was heavily involved in: I'd leave my body, go out into space, talk to my instructors—" Harmel caught himself. "Oh man, that's right: you're never going to believe any of this stuff!"

Marshall was firm—and maybe he did believe it. "Tell me anyway."

Harmel gritted his teeth and looked skyward. He fumbled, he stammered, his face went pale. "I don't know. I don't think I can tell you. They'll find out."

"Who'll find out?"

"The network."

"We're out in the middle of nowhere, Ted!"

"It doesn't matter . . ."

"You used the word *instructors*. Who are they?"

Harmel only sat there, trembling, terror etched in his face. "Hogan," he said finally, "you just can't cross them. I can't tell you! They'll know about it!"

"But who are they? Can you at least tell me that?"

"I don't even know if they're real," Harmel muttered. "They're just . . . there, that's all. Inner teachers, spirit guides, ascended masters . . . they're called all kinds of things. But anyone who follows Juleen's teachings for very long invariably gets mixed up with them. They come from nowhere, they speak to you, sometimes they appear to you when you're meditating. Sometimes you visualize them yourself, but then they take on a life and personality of their own . . . it's not just your imagination anymore."

"But what are they?"

"Beings . . . entities. Sometimes they're just like real people, sometimes you only hear a voice, sometimes you only feel them—like spirits, I suppose. Juleen works for them, or maybe they work for her, I don't know which way it goes. But you can't hide from them, you can't run, you can't get away with anything. They're part of the network, and the network knows everything, controls everything. Juleen controlled me. She even came between me and Gail. I lost my wife over this whole thing. I started to do everything Juleen told me . . . she'd call me in the middle of the night and tell me to come over, and I'd come over. She'd tell me not to print a certain story, I wouldn't print it. She'd tell me what kind of news to cover and I'd print it, just like she said.

"She owned me, Hogan. She could have told me to take a gun and shoot myself, and maybe I would have done it. You gotta know her to understand what I'm saying."

Marshall remembered standing in the hallway outside Langstrat's class wondering how he got there. "I think I understand."

"But Eldon found out about the college finances, and we both checked into it, and he was right. The college was headed for the rocks, and I'm sure it still is. Eldon tried to stop it, to get the whole mess straightened out. I tried to help him. Juleen came after me right away and made all kinds of threats. I ended up going in two directions, following two different loyalties. It was like being torn apart inside. Maybe that's what snapped me out of it; I made up my mind I wasn't going to be controlled anymore, not by the network, not by anyone. I was a newspaperman; I had to print it the way I saw it."

"And they took care of you."

"And it came as a total surprise. Well, maybe not total. When the police came to the paper and arrested me, I almost knew what it was about. It was something I could have predicted from the way Juleen and the others were threatening me. They've done that sort of thing before."

"For instance?"

"I can't help thinking the real estate offices, the tax rolls, any information you can get on the properties around the town, might show something. I couldn't follow it up when I was still there, but all the recent real estate deals didn't feel quite right to me."

The real estate business wasn't feeling quite right to Bernice either. Just as she pulled up in front of Tyler and Sons Realty, she saw the owner, Albert Tyler, locking up the place and getting ready to leave.

She rolled down her car window and asked him, "Say, aren't you supposed to be open until 5?"

Tyler only smiled and shrugged. "Not on Thursdays."

Bernice could read the hours on the front door. "But your hours say Monday through Friday, 10-5."

Tyler got just a little cross. "Not on Thursdays, I said!"

Bernice noticed Tyler's son Calvin driving his Volkswagen out from behind the building. She got out of her car and waved him down. Unwillingly, he paused and rolled down his window.

"Yeah?" he said.

"Aren't you people usually open on Thursday until 5?"

Calvin only shrugged and made a face. "What do I know? The old man says go home, we all go home."

He drove off. "Old man" Tyler was getting into his Plymouth. Bernice ran up to the car and waved to get his attention.

He was really miffed by now. He rolled down his window and said gruffly, "Lady, we're closed and I have to get home!"

"I just wanted to look through your microfiche. I need some information on some property."

He shook his head. "Hey, I can't help you anyway. Our microfiche is broken down."

"Wha. . . ?"

But Tyler rolled up his window and pulled away, screeching his tires a little.

Bernice shouted angrily after him, "Did Rosemary tip you off?"

She hurried to her car. There was still the Top of the Town Realty. She knew the owner regularly helped out with youth baseball on Thursday afternoons. Maybe the other gal who worked there wouldn't know who she was.

Harmel looked grim and haggard as he said, "They'll do you in, Hogan. They have the clout and the connections to do it. Look at me: I lost all I owned, lost my wife and family . . . they cleaned me out. They'll do the same to you."

Marshall wanted answers, not doomsaying. "What do you know about some guy named Kaseph?"

Harmel grimaced with fresh disgust. "Go after that. He might be the source of all the trouble. Juleen worshiped that guy. Everybody did Juleen's bidding, but she did his."

"Do you know whether or not he was looking for any real estate around Ashton?"

"He was drooling over the college, I know that."

Marshall was taken aback. "The college? Keep going."

"I never got the chance to dig after it, but there might be something there. Talk around the Network said that the college would be taken over entirely by some Network higher-ups, and Eugene Baylor seemed to be spending a lot of time talking money with Kaseph or his reps."

"Kaseph was trying to buy the college?"

"He hasn't *yet*. But he did end up buying everything else around town."

"Like what?"

"A lot of homes, I know, but I couldn't find out very much. Like I said, check the tax rolls or the real estate offices to see if he's been buying up anything else. I know he had the bucks to do it." Harmel pulled a ragged manila envelope from under his jacket. "And take this off my hands, will you?"

Marshall took the envelope. "What is it?"

"A curse, that's what. Something happens to everyone who has it. Eldon's accountant friend, Ernie Johnson, gave it to me, and I hope Eldon told you what happened to *him!*"

"He told me."

"It's Johnson's findings from the college accounting office."

Marshall couldn't believe his luck. "You gotta be kidding! Did Eldon know about this?"

"No, I just came across them myself, but don't start dancing yet. You'd better get some accountant friend of your own to try to decipher it for you. It doesn't make much sense to me . . . I think there's still a whole other half of it missing."

"It's a start. Thanks."

"If you want to play with theories, try this out: Kaseph comes to Ashton and wants to buy everything he can get his hands on. The college is not even thinking of selling. Next thing you know, thanks to Baylor, the college gets itself in such deep financial trouble that selling may be the only way to get out of it. Suddenly Kaseph's offer isn't so far-fetched, and by now the board of regents is stacked with yea-sayers."

Marshall opened the envelope and leafed through the pages and pages of photocopied columns and figures. "And you couldn't find any leads in all this?"

"More leads you don't need, not as much as proof. What you really need to see is who's on the other end of all those transactions."

"Kaseph's books, perhaps?"

"With all the friends and confederates he has at that college, I wouldn't be surprised if Kaseph was coming back to buy the college with its own money!"

"That's some theory. But what would a man like that even want with a little town, or with a whole college?"

"Hogan, a guy with the power and bucks that guy seems to have could take a town like Ashton and do anything he wanted with it. I think he already has to a great extent."

"How do you know?"

"Just check it out."

21

Bernice was in a hurry. She was in the back room of the Top of the Town Realty, going through their microfiche files. Carla, the girl out in front, was new enough to the job and the town that she bought Bernice's little talk about being a historian from the college looking for background on Ashton. It didn't take long for Carla to give Bernice a tour of the files and a short course on how to run the viewer. When Carla left her alone, Bernice went straight for the criss-cross file. This was certainly a wonderful stroke of luck: the other real estate offices had files that told you what land was owned by whom if you knew where the property was; the criss-cross file told you what various people owned if you knew the names of the people.

Kaseph. Bernice flipped through the microfiche holder to the *Ks*. She slipped the celluloid into the viewer and began scanning up and down, across, zigzag, the myriads of microscopic letters and figures streaking in a blur across the viewscreen as she looked for the right column. There. Kw . . . Kh . . . Ke . . . Ka . . . across to the next column. Hurry it up, Bernice!

She found no listing under Kaseph.

"How're you doing?" asked Carla from up front.

"Oh, just fine," Bernice answered. "I'm not finding much yet, but I know where to look."

Well, there was still Joe's Market. She went back to the regular file and pulled out the microfiche for the Section, Township, and Quarter for that address. Into the viewer the celluloid went, and again Bernice raced the myriads of listings up and down, looking for the listing. There! The legal description of what used to be Joe's Market, now the Ashton Mercantile. It was tax assessed at $105,900, and owned by Omni Corporation. That was all it said.

Bernice went back to the crisscross file. Into the viewer went the Ok–Om celluloid. Up, down, across. Olson . . . Omer . . . Omni. Omni. Omni. Omni. Omni. Omni. The listings under Omni Corporation went down, down, down the column; there could have been over a hundred. Bernice got her pen and pad and started writing furiously. The many addresses and legal descriptions meant little to her; many of them weren't even decipherable, but she kept scribbling as fast as she could, hoping she would be able to read her own writing when she looked at it later. She abbreviated, filling page after page in her notepad.

Out front, the telephone rang, as it had been doing; but this time Carla's conversation didn't sound too happy. Her voice was hushed and serious, and she sounded very apologetic. The jig might be up, kid, keep writing!

In a moment Carla appeared. "Are you Bernice Krueger, from the *Clarion?*" she asked directly.

"Who's asking?" Bernice said. That was dumb, but she didn't want to come right out with the truth either.

Carla looked very disturbed. "Listen, you're going to have to leave right away," she said.

"That was your boss on the phone, right?"

"Yes it was, and I'd appreciate it if you wouldn't tell him I let you back here. I don't know what this is all about, and I don't know why you lied to me, but would you please just leave? He's coming over here to lock the place up, and I told him you hadn't come by . . ."

"You're a doll!"

"Well, I lied for you, now you please lie for me."

Bernice scrambled to gather up all her notes and replace the celluloids. "I was never here."

"I appreciate it," said Carla as Bernice raced out the door. "Wow, you just about got me fired."

Andy and June Forsythe had a very nice home, a modern log house on the outskirts of town, not far from Forsythe Lumber. Tonight Hank and Mary had gathered there for a dinner fellowship along with many others of the Remnant, as Krioni, Triskal, Seth, Chimon, and Mota sat up in the lofty rafters looking on. The angels could feel the growing power of this little cluster of praying people. The Joneses were there, as were the Colemans, the Coopers, the Harrises, some of the college students; Ron Forsythe was there along with his girlfriend Cynthia. A few more brand-new Christians were with him, just now getting introduced to the rest of the group. Other latecomers were continually trickling in.

After dinner the people gathered and settled around the big stone hearth in the living room, while Hank took his place on the hearth with Mary beside him. Each person began to share his background.

Bill and Betty Jones had been churchgoers all their lives, but only made a serious commitment to Jesus Christ a year ago. The Lord had spoken to their hearts, and they searched Him out.

John and Patty Coleman had been to another church in town, but never knew much about the Bible or about Christ until coming to this church.

Cecil and Miriam Cooper had always known the Lord, and they were glad to see a new flock gathering to replace the old one. "It feels a lot like replacing a flat tire," Cecil quipped.

As others shared, their various backgrounds were brought out; there were different traditions and different doctrinal backgrounds, but any differences were not very important right now. All of them had one main concern: the town of Ashton.

"Oh, it's a war, all right," said Andy Forsythe. "You can't go out on those streets and not feel it. Sometimes I feel like I'm running through a shower of spears, you know?"

A new couple, friends of the Coopers, Dan and Jean Corsi, spoke up.

Jean said, "I really think it's Satan out there, just like the Bible says, just like a roaring lion trying to devour everyone."

Dan commented, "The problem is that we've all just sat to the side and let it happen. It's time we got concerned and scared and on our knees to see that the Lord does something about it."

Jean added, "Some of you know our son is having some real problems right now. We really wish you'd pray for him."

"What's his name?" someone asked.

"Bobby," Jean answered. She swallowed and went on to say, "He enrolled at the college this year and something's really happened to him . . ." She had to stop, choked with emotion.

Dan picked it up, and his tone was bitter. "Seems like something happens to any kid who goes off to that college. I never knew what kind of weird stuff they were really teaching over there. The rest of you should find out about it and make sure you don't let your kids get involved."

Ron Forsythe, silent up to this time, piped up, "I know what you're talking about, man. It's in the high school, too. The kids are messing around with Satanic stuff like you wouldn't believe. We used to trip out on drugs; now it's demons."

Jean ventured through her tears, "I know this sounds awful, but I really wonder if Bobby isn't possessed."

"I was," said Ron. "I know I was. Man, I heard voices talking to me, telling me to get some drugs, or steal something, all kinds of horrible things. I never let my folks know where I was, I never came home, I'd end up sleeping in the weirdest places . . . and with the weirdest people."

Dan muttered, "Yeah, that's Bobby. We haven't seen him in about a week."

Jean wanted to know, "But how did you get started in such things?"

Ron shrugged. "Hey, I was already going the wrong way. I'm not sure I'm even all the way straightened out yet. But I'll tell you when I think I got into the Satanic Stuff: it's when I had my fortune told. Hey, that's when I caught it, no doubt." Someone asked if the fortune-teller was a certain woman. "No, it was somebody else. It was at the carnival three years ago."

"Aw, they're all over the place," someone else moaned.

"Well that just goes to show how far off-base this town has gotten!" Cecil Cooper protested. "There are more witches and fortune-tellers around here than Sunday school teachers!"

"Well, we'll just see what we can do about that!" said John Coleman.

Ron picked it up again. "It's all heavy duty, man. I mean, I saw some pretty weird things when I was into that stuff: I've seen things just float around by themselves, I've read people's minds, I even left my body once and floated around town. You'd just better all be good and prayed up!"

Jean Corsi began to cry. "Bobby's possessed . . . I just know it!"

Hank could see it was time to take control. "Okay, people, now I have a real burden to pray for this town, and I know you do too, so I think that's where the answer lies. That's the first thing we need to do."

They were all ready. Many felt awkward praying out loud for the first time; some knew how to pray loudly and confidently; some prayed in phrases they'd learned from certain liturgies; all meant every word, however they managed to express it. The fervency slowly began to rise; the prayers became more and more earnest. Someone started a simple song of worship and those who knew it sang, while those who didn't know it learned it.

In the rafters the angels sang along, their voices smooth and flowing like cellos and basses in a symphony. Triskal looked at Krioni, smiled broadly, and flexed his arms. Krioni smiled and flexed back. Chimon took his sword and made it dance from the pivot of his wrist, tracing streaks and curls of shimmering light in the air as the blade sang with a beautiful resonance. Mota just looked toward heaven, his silken wings spreading, his arms upraised, caught up in the rapture of the song.

Kate quietly set her kitchen table with one plate, one cup, and a saucer. That evening she ate by herself, hardly able to get anything down because of the emotions tightening her throat and twisting her stomach. Oh well, it was leftovers anyway—leftovers from those many other meals Marshall never showed up for. It was happening again.

Maybe the place had nothing to do with how busy a newsman could be. Perhaps, even though Marshall had moved to a small, supposedly dull town, he still had that cursed nose for news that led him on his wild hunts into all hours of the night, making a story where one didn't even exist before. Perhaps this was, after all, his first love, more than his wife, more than his daughter.

Sandy. Where was she tonight? Hadn't they made this move for her sake? Now she was further away from them than ever, even though she still lived in the same house. Shawn had grown into her life like a cancer, not a friend, and Kate and Marshall never did talk about it like he had promised. His mind had been totally preoccupied. He was married to that newspaper, maybe enamored by that young, attractive reporter.

Kate shoved her plate away and tried to keep from crying. She couldn't start fussing and shedding tears now, not when she had to think clearly. Undoubtedly there would be decisions to make, and she would have to make them alone.

On the outskirts of Ashton, next to the railroad yard, Tal conferred with his warriors inside an old, unused water tower.

Nathan was pacing back and forth, his voice echoing off the walls of the huge tank. "I could feel it coming, captain! The enemy is luring Hogan into a trap. There has been a dangerous shift in affection toward Krueger. His family is in grave danger."

Tal nodded his head and remained deep in thought. "Exactly as one might expect. Rafar knows no frontal attack will work; he's trying his evil hand at subtlety, at moral compromise."

"And succeeding, I say!"

"Yes, I agree."

"But what can we do? If Hogan loses his family, he'll be destroyed!"

"No. Not destroyed. Knocked down, perhaps. Decimated, perhaps. But it's all because of the dross in his own soul, which the Spirit of God has yet to convict him of. We can do nothing but wait and let all things take their course."

Nathan could only shake his head in frustration. Guilo stood nearby, pondering Tal's words. Of course what Tal said was true. Men will sin if men will.

"Captain," Guilo said, "what if Hogan falls?"

Tal leaned back against the dank metal wall and said, "We can't be concerned with the question of 'if.' The question we must deal with is 'when.' Both Hogan and Busche are now laying the foundation we need for this battle. Once that's done, Hogan as well as Busche *must* fall. Only their clear defeat will coax the Strongman out of hiding."

Guilo and Nathan both looked at Tal with consternation.

"You—you would *sacrifice* these men?" Nathan asked.

"Only for a season," Tal answered.

Marshall brought out Ernie Johnson's large packet of pirated records from the Whitmore College accounting office and handed them across the *Clarion*'s reception counter to Harvey Cole. Cole was a CPA Marshall knew well enough to trust.

"I don't know what you'll be able to make of all this," said Marshall, "but see if you can find whatever Johnson found, and see if it looks crooked."

"Wow!" said Harvey. "This is going to cost you!"

"I'll swap you some free advertising. How about that?"

Harvey smiled. "Sounds fine. Okay, I'll get to it and get back to you."

"A.S.A.P."

Harvey went out the door and Marshall returned to his office, rejoining Bernice in their evening, after-hours project.

They were working amid a flurry of notes, papers, phone books, and any other public records they could get their hands on. In the middle of it all, a consolidated list of names, addresses, jobs, and tax records was forming piece by piece.

Marshall looked over his notes from his interview with Harmel. "Okay, what about that judge, what's-his-name, Jefferson?"

"Anthony C.," Bernice replied, flipping through last year's phone book. "Yeah, Anthony C. Jefferson, 221 Alder Street." She immediately went to her scrawled notes from the Top of the Town Realty. "221 Alder . . ." Her eyes scanned one sheet in her notebook, then another, until finally, "Bingo!"

"Another one!"

"So check me out on this: Jefferson was bumped by the Network and Omni came in and bought his house?"

Marshall scribbled some reminder notes to himself on a yellow legal pad. "I'd like to know why Jefferson moved and how much he sold that house for. I'd also like to know who's living there now."

Bernice shrugged. "We'll just have to go down the list and check all these Network people's addresses. I'll lay you odds it's one of them."

"What about Baker, the judge who replaced Jefferson?"

Bernice looked at another list. "No, Baker's over in the house that used to belong to the high school principal, uh, Waller, George Waller."

"Oh yeah, he's the one who lost his house in the sheriff sale."

"Oh, there are a lot of those, and I'll bet we might find more if we knew where to look."

"We'll have to snoop around the County Finance Office. Somehow, some way, those people's property taxes never got to where they were supposed to go. I can't believe this many people would be delinquent on their taxes."

"Someone diverted the money so the taxes were never paid. It's dirty, Hogan, just plain dirty."

"It wasn't Lew Gregory, the old comptroller. Look at this. He had to resign because of some conflict of interest rap. Now Irving Pierce is in, and he's Omni-owned, right?"

"You got it."

"And what was that you had on Mayor Steen?"

Bernice consulted her notes, but shook her head. "He just recently bought his house; the deal looks legitimate except for the previous owner being the former police chief who left town for no apparent reason. It might mean something, it might not. It's what happened to all those other people that has me wondering."

"Yeah, and why none of them ever squawked or made a fuss about it. Hey, I wouldn't let the county just come in and auction off my house right out from under me, not without asking at least a few questions. There's something else about this that we don't know."

"Well, think about the Carluccis. Did you know their house sold to Omni for $5,000? That's ridiculous!"

"And the Carluccis went poof! Gone, just like that!"

"So I wonder who's living in their house now?"

"Maybe the new high school principal, or the new fire marshal, or a new city councilman, or a *new* this or a *new* that!"

"Or one of the *new* college regents."

Marshall scrambled for some more papers. "Boy, what a mess!" He finally found the list he was looking for. "Let's go through those regents and see what we come up with."

Bernice flipped through a few pages in her notebook. "I know for sure that Pinckston's place is owned by Omni. Some kind of trust arrangement."

"What about Eugene Baylor?"

"Don't you have that somewhere?"

"One of us does, but now I can't remember who."

They both fumbled through their notes, papers, lists. Marshall finally found it among his scattered leaves.

"Here it is. Eugene Baylor, 1024 SW 147th."

"Oh, I think I saw that here somewhere." Bernice perused her notes. "Yes, Omni owns that too."

"Sheesh! Deeding everything over to Omni Corporation must be a requirement for membership."

"Well, that makes Young and Brummel card-carrying members. It makes sense, though. If they all want to meld into one Universal Mind, they have to do away with individuality, and that means no private ownership."

One by one, Marshall read off the names of the college regents, and Bernice researched their addresses. Of the twelve regents, eight were living in homes owned by Omni Corporation. The others rented apartments; one of the apartment buildings was owned by Omni. Bernice had no information on the other apartment buildings.

"I think we've ruled out coincidence," said Marshall.

"And now I can't wait to hear what your friend Lemley has to say."

"Sure, that Kaseph and Omni Corporation are linked. That's obvious." Marshall took just a moment to ponder. "But you know what really scares me? So far, everything we see here is legal. I'm sure they've been crooked somewhere to get where they are, but you can see they're working within the system, or at least doing a very good job of looking like it."

"But come on, Marshall! He's taking over a whole town, for crying out loud!"

"*And* he's doing it legally. Don't forget that."

"But he must leave some tracks somewhere. We've been able to sniff him out at least this far."

Marshall took a deep breath and then sighed it out. "Well, we can try to track down every person who sold out and left town, try to find out why it happened. We can check into what positions they held before they left and who holds that position now. Whoever holds the position now can be asked what connection he or she has with Omni Corporation or with this Universal Consciousness mind-tripping group. We can ask each and every one of them what they might know about the elusive Mr. Kaseph. We can do some more research on the Omni Corporation itself, find out where it's based, what it deals in, what else it owns. We have our work cut out for us. And then I guess it'll be time to go directly to our friends with what we know and get a response from them."

Bernice could feel something coming across in Marshall's manner. "What's bothering you, Marshall?"

Marshall tossed his notes on the desk and leaned back in his chair to ponder. "Bernie, we'd be fools to think we're immune to any of this."

Bernice gave a resigned nod. "Yeah, I've been wondering about it, wondering what they might try."

"I think they already have my daughter." It was a blunt statement. Marshall himself was shocked at the sound of it.

"You don't know that for sure."

"If I don't know that, I don't know *anything*."

"But what kind of real power could they wield except economic and political? I don't buy all this cosmic, spiritual stuff; it's nothing but a mind trip."

"That's easy for you to say, you're not religious."

"You'll find it's a lot easier."

"So what if we end up like—like Harmel, no family left, just hiding in the bushes and talking about . . . spooks?"

"I wouldn't mind ending up like Strachan. He seems comfortable enough just being out of this whole thing."

"Well, Bernie, even so, we'd better see it coming before it gets here." He grabbed her hand in earnest and said to her, "I hope we both know what we're getting ourselves into. We may be in too deep already. We could quit, I suppose . . ."

"You know we can't do that."

"I know *I* can't. I'm not putting any expectations on you. You can get out now, go somewhere else, work for some ladies' journal or something. I won't mind."

She smiled at him and held his hand tightly. "Die all, die merrily."

Marshall only shook his head and smiled in return.

22

In another state, in a low-income section of another town, a little panel truck weaved its way down a kid-cluttered street through a housing project. All the little duplexes, except for different color schemes, came from the same mold. As the truck pulled to a stop at the end of an aging asphalt cul-de-sac, "Princess Cleaners" could be seen printed on its side.

The driver, a young lady in blue overalls, her hair in a red scarf, got out. She opened the side door and pulled out a large laundry bundle and some bag-draped dresses on hangers. Rechecking the address, she made her way up one walk to one particular door and rang the bell.

First the curtain of the front window pulled to the side for a moment, and then there were footsteps toward the door. The door opened.

"Hi, got some cleaning here," said the young lady.

Oh, yes . . ." said the man who answered the door. "Just bring it in."

He opened the door wider so she could make her way into the house as three children tried to keep out of her path despite their great curiosity.

The man called to his wife, "Honey, the cleaning lady is here."

She came in from the small kitchen, looking tense and nervous. "You children go outside and play," she ordered.

They whined a bit, but she herded them out the door, closed it, then drew shut the one window that still remained open.

"Where'd you get all this laundry?" the man asked.

"It was in the truck. I don't know who it belongs to."

The man, a heavyset Italian with graying curly hair, offered his hand. "Joe Carlucci."

The young lady set down the laundry and shook his hand. "Bernice Krueger from the *Clarion*."

He showed her to a chair and then said, "They told me I was never to talk to you or Mr. Hogan . . ."

"For the sake of our children, they said," Mrs. Carlucci added.

"This is Angelina. It was for her sake, for the children's sake, that we—we moved away, we left it all, we said nothing."

"Can you help us?" asked Angelina.

Bernice got her pad ready. "Okay, just take your time. We'll start at the beginning."

At what Al Lemley called "the halfway point" between Ashton and New York, Marshall pulled the Buick into the parking lot of a little insurance office in Taylor, a small town at the crossing of two major highways with no other real reason for being there. He stepped into the little office and was immediately recognized by the lady at the desk.

"Mr. Hogan?" she asked.

"Yes, good morning."

"Mr. Lemley is already here. He's waiting for you."

She showed him to another door which led to a back office that no one was using at the time. "Now there's coffee out here on the counter, and the bathroom is right through this door and to the right."

"Thank you."

"You're welcome."

Marshall closed the door, and only then did Al Lemley stand up and give him a warm handshake.

"Marshall," he said, "it's great to see you. Just great!"

He was a smaller man, bald, with a hooked nose and sharp blue eyes. He had spunk and sparkle, and Marshall had always known him as a priceless associate, a friend who could come through with almost any much-needed favor.

Al sat behind the desk, and Marshall pulled a chair up beside him so they could both look over the materials Al had brought. For a little while they talked old times. Al was pretty much filling the vacancy that

Marshall had left in the City Room at the *Times,* and he was beginning to have a real appreciation for Marshall's ability to handle the job.

"But I don't think I want to trade places with you now, buddy!" he said. "I thought you moved to Ashton to get away from it all!"

"I guess it followed me there," he said.

"Eh . . . in a few weeks New York may be a lot safer."

"What've you got?"

Al pulled an 8 x 10 glossy photo from a file folder and let it slide across the desk under Marshall's nose. "Is this your boy?"

Marshall looked at the picture. He'd never seen Alexander M. Kaseph before, but from all the descriptions he knew, "This has to be him."

"Oh, it's him, all right. He's known and then he's not known, if you catch my drift. The general public never heard of the guy, but start asking investors on Wall Street, or government people, or foreign diplomats, or anyone else in any way connected with international wheeling and dealing and politics and you'll get a response. He is the president of Omni Corporation, yes; they are definitely connected."

"Surprise, surprise. So what do you know about Omni Corporation?"

Al shoved a stack of materials toward Marshall, a stack several inches thick. "Thank goodness for computers. Omni was just a little nontypical in tracking down. They have no central headquarters, no main address; they're scattered into local offices all over the world and keep a very low profile. From what I understand, Kaseph keeps his own immediate staff with him and likes to be as invisible as possible, running the whole operation from no one knows where. It's weirdly subterranean. They're not on the New York or American Stock Exchanges, not by their name, at least. The stocks are all diversified among, oh, maybe a hundred different front corporations. Omni is the owner and controller of retail chain stores, banks, mortgage companies, fast food chains, soft drink bottlers, you name it."

Al continued talking as he thumbed through the stack of materials. "I had some of my staff digging into this stuff. Omni doesn't come right out and print anything about itself. First you have to find out what the front corporation is, then you sort of sneak in the back door and find out what interest the Big Mother Company has in it. Take this one here . . ." Al produced a stockholder's annual report from an Idaho mining company. "You don't know what you're really reading about until you get down here to the end . . . see? 'A subsidiary of Omni International.' "

"International—"

"*Very* international. You wouldn't believe how influential they are in Arab oil, the Common Market, the World Bank, international terrorism—"

"*What?*"

"Don't expect to find any stockholder's reports on the latest car bombing or mass murder, but for every documented aboveboard item here there are a couple hundred pieces of under-the-table scuttlebutt that no one can prove but everyone seems to know."

"And such is life."

"And such is your man Kaseph. I want to tell you, Marshall, he knows how to spill blood if he has to and sometimes when he doesn't have to. I'd say this guy is a perfect cross between the ultimate guru and Adolf Hitler, and he makes Al Capone look like a Boy Scout. Word has it that even the Mafia is afraid of him!"

Angelina Carlucci tended to spill words more from emotions than from objective recall, which made her story travel in agonizing circles. Bernice had to keep asking questions to get things clear.

"Getting back to your son Carl—"

"They broke his hands!" she wept.

"*Who* broke his hands?"

Joe intervened to help his wife. "It was after we said we would not sell the store. They had asked us . . . well, they didn't ask, they told us we'd better . . . but they talked to us about it a few times and we wouldn't sell . . ."

"And that's when they started threatening you?"

"They *never* threaten!" Angelina said angrily. "They say they *never* threatened us!"

Joe tried to explain. "They—they threaten you without sounding like they are. It's hard to explain. But they talk the deal over with you, and they let you know how very wise you will be to go along with the deal, and you know, you just know that you should go along with it if you don't want anything evil to befall you."

"So just who was it that you talked to?"

"Two gentlemen who were—well, they said they were friends of the new people who own the store now. I just thought at first that they were realtors or something. I had no idea . . ."

Bernice looked over her notes again. "All right, so it was after you turned them down the third time that Carl had his hands broken?"

"Yes, at school."

"Well, who did it?"

Angelina and Joe looked at each other. Angelina answered, "No one saw it. It was during recess at school, and no one saw it!"

"Carl must have seen it."

Joe only shook his head and waved his hand at Bernice to stop short. "You cannot ask Carl about it. He is still tormented, he has bad dreams."

Angelina leaned forward and whispered, "Evil spirits, Miss Krueger! Carl thinks it was evil spirits!"

Bernice kept waiting for these two responsible adults to explain the strange perceptions of their young son. She had trouble phrasing a question. "Well, what does—why—what do you . . . Well, surely you must know what really happened, or at least have some idea." The two of them only stared at each other blankly, at a loss for words. "There were no teachers on the grounds who assisted him after it happened?"

Joe tried to explain. "He was playing baseball with some other boys. The ball rolled into the woods and he went after it. When he came back, he was—he was crazy, screaming, he'd wet himself . . . his hands were broken."

"And he never said who did it?"

Joe Carlucci's eyes were glazed with terror. He whispered, "Big black things . . ."

"Men?"

"*Things*. Carl says they were spirits, monsters."

Don't knock it, Bernice told herself. It was clear these poor deluded people really believed something of this nature was attacking them. They were very devout Catholics, but also very superstitious. Perhaps that explained the many crucifixes on every door, the pictures of Jesus and the figurines of the Virgin Mary everywhere, on every table, over every doorway, in every window.

Marshall had perused the materials on the Omni Corporation. He still hadn't read about one thing.

"What about any kind of religious affiliation?"

"Yeah," said Al, reaching for another folder. "You were right on that. Omni is just one of several underwriters for the Universal Consciousness Society, and that's a whole other ball of financial and political wax, and perhaps the main motivation behind the company, even more than money. Omni owns or backs—oh brother, there must be hundreds of them—Society-owned businesses, from cottage-level enterprises clear up to banks, retail stores, schools, colleges—"

"Colleges?"

"Yeah, and law firms too, according to this news clipping. They have a major lobbying task force in Washington, they've been regularly pushing their own special interest legislation . . . it's usually anti-Jewish and anti-Christian, if that's of any interest to you."

"How about towns? Does this Society like to buy towns?"

"I know Kaseph's done it, or other things similar to that. Listen, I got in touch with Chuck Anderson, one of our foreign correspondents, and he's heard all kinds of interesting things besides seeing a lot of it himself. It seems these Universal Consciousness people are a worldwide club. We've located Society chapters in ninety-three different countries. They just seem to pop up everywhere, no matter what part of the world, and yes, they have acquired full control of towns, villages, hospitals, some ships, some corporations. Sometimes they buy their way in, sometimes they vote their way in, sometimes they just crowd their way in."

"Like an invasion without guns."

"Yes, usually quite legally, but that's probably out of sheer cleverness, not any integrity, and remember you're also looking at a lot of power and pull here. You're standing right in the path of Big Daddy himself, and from what I gather, he doesn't slow, stop, or even go around."

"Nuts . . ."

"I'd . . . well, I'd cool it, buddy. Call the feds, let somebody bigger handle it if they want. You still have a job back at the *Times* if you ever want it. At least cover the story from a distance. You're a class-A reporter, but you're too close, you have too much to lose."

All Marshall could think was, Why me?

Bernice had stumbled too far into a touchy situation. The Carluccis were getting more unsettled and terrified the more she questioned them.

"Maybe this wasn't a good idea," Joe finally said. "If they ever find out we talked to you . . ."

Bernice was about to scream if she heard that word again. "Joe, who do you mean by 'they'? You keep saying *they* and *them,* but you never say who."

"I—I can't tell you," he said with great difficulty.

"Well, let me at least clear this much up: Are they people, I mean real people?"

He and Angelina thought for a moment, then he answered, "Yes, they are real people."

"So they are real, flesh-and-blood people?"

"And maybe spirits too."

"I'm talking about the real people now," Bernice insisted. "Was it real people who audited your taxes?"

Reluctantly, they nodded.

"And it was a real, flesh-and-blood man who posted the auction notice on your door?"

"We didn't see him," Angelina said.

"But it was a real piece of paper, right?"

"But nobody told us it would happen!" Joe protested. "We always paid our taxes, I have the canceled checks to prove it! The people at the County Office wouldn't listen to us!"

Angelina was angry now. "We had no money to pay the taxes they wanted. We already paid them, we couldn't pay them again."

"They said they would take our store, take all our inventory, and business was bad, very bad. Half our customers left and wouldn't come in anymore."

"And I know what kept them away!" said Angelina defiantly. "We could all feel it. I tell you, windows don't break by themselves, and groceries don't fly off the shelves by themselves. It was the Devil himself in our store!"

Bernice had to reassure them. "All right, I'm not arguing with that. You saw what you saw, I don't doubt you—"

"But don't you see, Miss Krueger?" Joe asked with tears in his eyes. "We knew we could not stay. What would they do next? Our store was failing, our home was sold out from under us, our children were being tormented by evil people, spirits, whatever. We knew it would be best not to fight. It was God's will. We sold the store. They gave us a good price . . ."

Bernice knew that wasn't so. "You didn't get half of what that store was worth."

Joe broke down and cried as he said, "But we are free . . . We are free!"

Bernice had to wonder.

Then came the blitz, a die-all-die-merrily push for information accompanied by mixed feelings of determination and foreboding, by conflicts between initial impulses and second thoughts. Every Tuesday and Friday for two weeks the *Ashton Clarion* still appeared on the newsstands and in all the mailboxes of subscribers, but its editor and chief reporter were very hard to contact or even catch a glimpse of. Marshall's phone messages stacked up unreturned, Bernice was simply never home; there were several nights when Marshall never went home at all, but slept here and there, now and then in the office, waiting for special calls, making other calls, working at keeping the paper afloat with one hand while going over lists of contacts, tax records, business reports, interviews, and leads with the other.

The people who had left their positions, and usually Ashton, and the people who replaced them were definitely two separate groups of widely different persuasions; after a while, Marshall and Bernice could just about predict what their responses were going to be.

Bernice called Adam Jarred, the college regent whose daughter was allegedly molested by Ted Harmel.

"No," said Jarred, "I really don't know anything about any special . . . what did you call it?"

"A society. The Universal Consciousness Society."

"No, afraid not."

Marshall spoke with Eugene Baylor.

"No," Baylor replied somewhat impatiently, "I've never even heard the name Kaseph, and I really don't understand what you're driving at."

"I'm trying to chase down some claims that the college might be negotiating a sale of its property with Alexander Kaseph of the Omni Corporation."

Baylor laughed and said, "You must have heard about another college. There's nothing like that happening here."

"And what about the information we've received that the college is in heavy financial trouble?"

Baylor didn't like that question at all. "Listen, the last editor of the *Clarion* tried that one too, and it was the dumbest move he ever made. Why don't you just run your paper and leave the running of the college to us?"

The former regents had a different tune.

Morris James, now a business consultant in Chicago, had nothing but bad memories of his last year with the college.

"They really taught me what it must be like to be a leper," he told Bernice. "I felt I could be a good voice on the board, you know, a stabilizing factor, but they simply would tolerate no dissent. I thought it was highly unprofessional."

Bernice asked him, "And what about Eugene Baylor's handling of the college finances?"

"Well, I left before any of this really serious trouble arose, this trouble you've described to me, but I could foresee it. I did try to block some decisions the board made regarding the granting of special powers and privileges to Baylor. I thought it was giving too much unauthorized control to one man without the oversight of the other regents. Needless to say, my opinion was very unpopular."

Bernice asked a very pointed question. "Mr. James, what finally precipitated your resigning from the board and leaving Ashton?"

"Well . . . that's a tough one to answer," he began reluctantly. His answer took about fifteen minutes, but the bottom line came down to, "My wholesale business was so harassed and so sabotaged by . . . unseen mobsters, I guess I would call it . . . that I became too great an insurance risk. I couldn't fill my orders, clientele dropped way off, and I just couldn't stay above water anymore. The business folded, I took the hint, and I got out of there. I've been doing fine ever since. You can't keep a good man down, you know."

Marshall managed to track down Rita Jacobson, now living in New Orleans. She was not happy to hear from someone in Ashton.

"Let the Devil have that town!" she said bitterly. "If he wants it so bad, let him have it."

Marshall asked her about Juleen Langstrat.

"She's a witch. I mean a real, live witch!"

He asked her about Alexander Kaseph.

"A warlock and a gangster rolled into one. Stay out of his way. He'll bury you before you even feel it."

He tried to ask her some other questions, but she finally said, "Please don't ever call this number again," and hung up.

Marshall tracked down as many former members of the city council as he could by telephone and found out that one had simply retired, but all the others stepped down because of some form of hardship: Allan Bates fell ill of cancer, Shirley Davidson went through a divorce and ran off with a new lover, Carl Frohm was "set up," as he called it, with a phony tax scam, Jules Bennington's business was "strongarmed" out of town by a bunch of mobsters whom he knew better than to identify. By cross-checking Marshall found that, in every case, the deposed city councilman or councilwoman was replaced by a new person connected in some way with either the Universal Consciousness Society or Omni Corporation or both; and in every case the deposed person thought that he or she was the only one who had left. Now, out of fear, out of self-interest, out of that typical reluctance to get involved, all of them remained far away, out of touch, out of the picture, saying nothing. Some were cooperative in answering Marshall's questions, and some felt very threatened. All in all, though, Marshall got what he was after.

As for those who used to own businesses now run by this mysterious incognito corporation, very few of them had planned on selling out, moving out, or giving up their peaceful lives in Ashton or their successful businesses. But the reasons for leaving were consistently along the same lines: tax bunglings, harassments, boycotts, personal problems, marriage dissolutions, perhaps a disease or a nervous breakdown here and there, with an occasional macabre tale of strange, maybe-supernatural occurrences.

Former Ashton District Judge Anthony C. Jefferson's story was ominously typical. "Word started circulating around the courthouse and the legal community that I was on the take, receiving bribes for fixing sentences and letting people off. Some false witnesses even confronted me and made accusations, but it never happened—I swear it with all that I have in me!"

"Then can you tell me the truth about why you left Ashton?" Marshall asked, almost knowing what kind of answer to expect.

"Personal reasons as well as professional. Some of these reasons remain with me even now and are still viable enough to restrict what I can share with you. I can say, however, that my wife and I were needing a change. We were both feeling the pressure, she more than I. My health was failing. We at length thought it best to get out of Ashton altogether."

"May I ask, sir, if there were any . . . unfavorable outside influences . . . that brought about your decision to step down from the bench?"

He thought for a moment, and then, with some bitterness in his voice, said, "I cannot tell you who they were—I have my reasons—but I can say yes, some very highly unfavorable influences."

Marshall's last question was, "And you really can't tell me anything about who they might be?"

Jefferson gave a sardonic chuckle and said, "Just keep going the way you are, and you'll find out soon enough yourself."

Jefferson's words were beginning to haunt both Marshall and Bernice; they had heard many similar warnings as they went along, and both of them were growing more aware of something out there around them, building, coming closer, growing more and more malevolent. Bernice tried to shrug it off, Marshall found himself resorting more and more to quickly blurted prayers; but the feeling was still there, that disturbing sense that you are nothing but a sand castle on the beach and a twenty-foot wave is about to crash down on you.

On top of all this, Marshall had to wonder how Kate was holding up through all of this, and how he would ever patch things up between them when this was finally over. She was talking about being a widow again, a newspaper widow, and had even made some very embarrassing suggestions about Bernice. Man, this thing just had to get over with; much more of it and he wouldn't have much of a marriage to come home to.

And then of course there was Sandy, whom Marshall hadn't seen in weeks. But when this was all over, when it was really finally over, things would be different.

For now, the investigation he and Bernice were doing was incredibly urgent, a top priority, something that grew more ominous with every new stone they turned.

23

When things around the office were in their usual quiet, post-Tuesday state, Marshall had Carmen search out a good-sized cardboard box and some file folders and he began to organize the piles of papers, records, documents, scattered notes, and other information he and Bernice had compiled in their investigation into an orderly file. As he went through it all, he also compiled a list of questions on a legal pad on his desk—questions he intended to use in his interview with the first of the real principals in this plot: Alf Brummel.

That afternoon, after Carmen had left for a dentist appointment, Marshall made a call to Alf Brummel's office.

"Police Department," said Sara's voice.

"Hi, Sara, this is Marshall Hogan. Can I have a word with Alf?"

"He's out of the office right now . . ." Sara let out a long sigh and then added in a very strange, very quiet tone of voice, "Marshall—Alf Brummel does not want to talk to you."

Marshall had to think for a moment before he said, "Sara, are you caught in the middle?"

Sara sounded miffed. "Maybe I am, I don't know, but Alf told me in no uncertain terms that I was not to put through any calls from you and that I was to let him know whatever your intentions were."

"Huh . . ."

"Look, I don't know where friendships end and professional ethics begin, but I sure wish I knew what was going on around here."

"What *is* going on around there?"

"What'll you trade me for it?"

Marshall knew he was taking a chance. "I think I can find something of equal value if I look hard enough."

Sara hesitated for just a moment. "From all appearances, you've become his worst enemy. Every once in a while I hear your name coming through that office door of his, and he never says it nicely."

"Who's he talking to when he says it?"

"Uh-uh. It's your turn."

"All right. Well, we talk about him too. We talk about him a lot, and if everything we've uncovered checks out, yeah, I just might be his worst enemy. Now who's he talking to?"

"Some of them I've seen before, some of them I haven't. He's put several calls through to Juleen Langstrat, his whatever-she-is."

"Anyone else?"

"Judge Baker was one, and several members of the city council . . ."

"Malone?"

"Yes."

"Everett?"

"Yes."

"Uh—Preston?"

"No."

"Goldtree?"

"Yes, plus some other VIPs from out of town, and then Spence Nelson from the Windsor Police Department, the same department that supplied our extra manpower for the Festival. I mean, he's been talking to a lot of people, far more than usual. Something's up. What is it?"

Marshall had to be careful. "It might involve me and the *Clarion*, it might not."

"I don't know if I'll accept that or not."

"I don't know if I can trust you or not. Whose side are you on?"

"That depends on who the bad guy is. I know Alf is shady. Are you?"

Marshall had to smile at her spunk. "I'll have to let you be the judge of that. I do try to run an honest paper, and we have been carrying on a very intensive investigation of not only your boss, but just about every other bigwig in this town—"

"He knows it. They all do."

"Well, I've talked to just about all of them. Alf was next on my list."

"I think he knew that too. He told me just this morning that he did not want to talk to you. But he's sure talking up a storm with everybody else, and he just left here with a pile of papers under his arm, heading for another hush-hush meeting with someone."

"Any idea of what they're going to do about me?"

"Oh, you can be sure they *will* do something, and I get the feeling they're loading for bear. Consider yourself warned."

"And I'd advise you to be the sweet, ignorant angel who knows nothing and says nothing. Things could get messy."

"If they do, Marshall, can I come to you for answers, or at least a ticket out of town?"

"We'll be able to deal."

"I'll give you anything I can find if you'll keep me safe."

Marshall caught it in her voice: this gal was scared. "Hey now, remember, I didn't ask you to get involved."

"I didn't ask to be involved. I just am. I know Alf Brummel. I'd better pick you for my friend."

"I'll keep you posted. Now hang up and act normal."

She did.

Alf Brummel was in Juleen Langstrat's office, and the two of them were looking over a very thick portfolio of information Brummel had brought.

"Hogan now has enough to fill a front page!" Brummel said quite unhappily. "You've berated me for being slow in taking care of Busche, but as far as I can see, you've given Hogan nothing but a clear freeway since the beginning."

"Calm down, Alf," Langstrat said soothingly. "Just calm down."

"He's going to be coming after me for an interview any day now, just like he's gone after all the others. What do you suggest I say to him?"

Langstrat was a little shocked at his stupidity. "Don't say anything, of course!"

Brummel paced the room, exasperated. "I don't have to, Juleen! By this point, nothing I say or don't say will make any difference anyway. He already has everything he needs: he knows about the property sales, he has very good leads on all the sheriff sales of the tax delinquent homes, he knows all about the Corporation and the Society, he has good information on the college embezzlements . . . he even has more than enough evidence to accuse me of false arrest!"

Langstrat smiled with pleasure. "Your spy has done very well."

"She brought me a lot of this material today. He's getting it all organized in a file now. He's about to make his move, I'd say."

Langstrat gathered all the material neatly, placed it back in its portfolio, and leaned back in her chair. "I love it."

Brummel only looked at her in amazement and shook his head. "You could lose at this game someday, you know. We could *all* lose!"

"I love a challenge," she exulted. "I love taking on a strong opponent. The stronger the opponent, the more exhilarating the victory! Most of all, I love winning." She smiled at him, truly pleased. "Alf, I've had my doubts about you, but I think you've come through bountifully. I think you should be there to see Mr. Hogan step into the snare."

"I'll believe it when I see it."

"Oh, you will. You will."

There was a short lull, and it got strangely quiet around the town of Ashton. People weren't in touch. Nothing much was said.

During the day Marshall and Bernice organized their materials and stuck close to the office. Marshall took Kate out to dinner one night. Bernice sat at home and tried to read a novel.

Alf Brummel kept regular hours, but he didn't have much to say to Sara or anyone else about anything. Langstrat fell ill, or so the word was from her office, and her classes were canceled for a few days.

Hank and Mary thought that maybe their phone was out of order, the thing had been so silent. The Colemans visited relatives out of town. The Forsythes took the chance to do some inventory at the lumberyard. The rest of the Remnant all went about their normal business.

There was an odd stillness everywhere. The skies were hazy, the sun a blurred ball of light, the air warm and sticky. It was quiet.

But no one could relax.

High on a hill above the town, in the top of a graying, long-dead snag of an old tree, like an enormous black vulture, Rafar, the Prince of Babylon, sat. Other demons attended him, waiting to hear his next command, but Rafar was silent. Hour upon hour, a tense scowl on his face, he sat and gazed down at the town with his slowly shifting yellow eyes.

On another hill, directly across the town from Rafar's big dead tree, Tal and his warriors concealed themselves in the woods. They also were looking out over the town, and they could feel the lull, the silence, the ominous deadness of the air.

Guilo stood at his captain's side, and he knew this feeling. It had always been the same throughout the centuries.

"It could be any time now. Are we ready?" he asked Tal.

"No," Tal said flatly, looking intensely over the town. "Not all the Remnant are gathered. Those who have gathered are not praying, not enough. We haven't the numbers or the strength."

"And the black cloud of spirits over the Strongman grows a hundredfold each day."

Tal looked up into the sky over Ashton. "They will fill the sky from horizon to horizon."

From their hiding place they could look across the valley, over several miles, and see their hideous opponent sitting in the big dead tree.

"His strength has not waned," said Guilo.

"He is more than ready to do battle," said Tal, "and he can pick his own time, his own place, and the best of his warriors. He could attack on a hundred different fronts at once."

Guilo only shook his head. "You know we can't defend that many."

Just then a messenger rushed toward them, on the wing.

"Captain," he said, alighting next to Tal, "I've brought word from the Strongman's Lair. There is a stirring there. The demons are growing restless."

"It's beginning," said Tal, and this word was passed back through the ranks. "Guilo!"

Guilo stepped up. "Captain!"

Tal took Guilo aside. "I have a plan. I want you to take a small contingent with you and set up watch over that valley—"

Guilo was not one to argue with the captain, but "A *small* contingent? To watch the *Strongman?*"

The two of them continued in conference, Tal mapping out his instructions, Guilo shaking his head dubiously. At length Guilo came back to the group, picked out his warriors, and said, "Let's be off!"

With a rush of wings the two dozen weaved and zigzagged through the forest until they were far enough away to take to the open sky.

Tal summoned a strong warrior. "Replace Signa in guarding the church, and tell him to come to me."

Then he summoned another messenger. "Tell Krioni and Triskal to rouse Hank and get him praying, and all the Remnant."

In a short moment Signa arrived.

"Come with me," said Tal. "Let's talk."

It had been a quiet afternoon for Hank and Mary. Mary spent most of it in the little garden behind the house, while Hank worked to repair a corner of the backyard fence that kids had broken a hole through. As Mary hunted for weeds among her vegetables, she noticed Hank's hammering getting more and more sporadic until finally it stopped altogether. She looked his way and saw him sitting there, the hammer still in his hand, praying.

He seemed very disturbed, so she asked, "Are you all right?"

Hank opened his eyes, and without looking up he shook his head. "I don't feel good at all."

She went over to him. "What is it?"

Hank knew where the feeling came from. "The Lord, I guess. I just feel something's really wrong. Something terrible is about to happen. I'm going to call the Forsythes."

Just then the phone in the house rang. Hank went in and answered it. It was Andy Forsythe.

"Sorry to bother you, Pastor, but I was just wondering if you feel a real burden of prayer right now. I know I sure do."

"Come on over," said Hank.

The fence would have to wait.

On into the evening the angelic host waited, while Hank, the Forsythes, and several others prayed. Rafar continued to sit up in the dead tree, his eyes beginning to glow in the steadily thickening darkness. His taloned fingers continued to drum his knee; his brow stayed crinkled with his intense scowl. Behind him a host of demons began to gather, primed with anticipation and rapt with attention, waiting to hear Rafar's order.

The sun dipped behind the hills on the west side; the sky was washed with red fire.

Rafar sat and waited. The demonic host waited.

In her bedroom Juleen Langstrat sat on her bed, her legs crossed in the lotus position of Eastern meditation, her eyes closed, her head erect, her body perfectly still. Except for one single candle, the room was dark. There, under the shroud of the darkness, she convened her meeting with the Ascended Masters, the Spirit Guides from the higher planes. Deep within her consciousness, far within the depths of her inner being, she spoke with a messenger.

To the eyes of Langstrat's entranced mind the messenger appeared as a young lady, all dressed in white, with flowing blonde hair that reached nearly to the ground and was constantly in motion, wafted by the breeze.

"Where is my master?" Langstrat asked the messenger.

"He waits above the town, watching over it," came the girl's answer. "His armies are ready for your word."

"All is ready. He may await my signal."

"Yes, my lady."

The messenger departed like a beautiful gazelle, leaping gracefully away.

The messenger departed, a filthy black nightmare of a creature borne on membranous wings; he departed to take word to Rafar, who still waited.

Darkness deepened over Ashton; the candle in Langstrat's room dwindled to one round, ebbing flame in a pool of wax, the inky blackness overtaking its weak, orange light. Langstrat stirred, opened her glazed eyes, and arose from the bed. With a very small puff of breath she extinguished the candle and moved in a half daze into the living room where another candle was burning on the coffee table, the wax flowing and hardening into macabre fingers across the photograph of Ted Harmel on which the candle sat.

Langstrat sank to her knees beside the coffee table, her head held high, her eyes half shut, her movements slow and liquid. As if floating in space, her arms rose upward over the candle, stretching out an invisible canopy over the flame, and then, so very quietly, the name of an ancient god began to form itself on her lips again and again. The name, a guttural, harsh sound, spilled forth from her like the spitting of hundreds of invisible pebbles, and with each mention of the name, her trance deepened. Steadily, steadily the name tumbled forth, louder and faster, and Langstrat's eyes widened and remained unblinking and glaring. Her body began to quiver and tremble; her voice became an eerie wailing sound.

Rafar could hear it all from where he sat and waited. His own breathing began to deepen and chug out of his nostrils like putrid yellow steam. His eyes narrowed, his talons flexed.

Langstrat swayed and quivered, calling out the name, calling out the name, her eyes fixed on the candle's flame, calling out the name.

And then she froze.

Rafar looked up, very still, very attentive, listening.

Time stood still. Langstrat remained motionless, her arms extended over the candle.

Rafar listened.

Air began to slowly flow into Langstrat's mouth and nostrils, her lungs began to fill, and then, with one sudden cry from deep within, she brought her hands down like a trap, clapping them on the candle's wick, snuffing out the flame.

"Go!" shouted Rafar, and hundreds of demons shot into the sky like a thunderous flock of bats, rushing along a straight and level trajectory northward.

"Look," said an angelic warrior, and Tal and his host all saw what looked like a black swarm silhouetted against the night sky, an elongated puff of smoke.

"Going north," observed Tal. "Away from Ashton."

Rafar watched the squadron disappear at great speed and let a mocking grin bare his fangs. "I'll keep you guessing, Captain of the Host!"

Tal shouted out his orders. "Cover Hogan and Busche! Awaken the Remnant!"

A hundred angels soared downward into the town.

Tal could still see Rafar sitting in the big dead tree.

"Just what are your plans, Prince of Babylon?" he murmured.

The phone startled Marshall out of a restless sleep. The clock said 3:48 A.M. Kate moaned at being awakened. He grabbed up the receiver and mumbled hello.

For a moment he didn't have the slightest idea who was on the other end or what they were saying. The voice was wild, hysterical, high-pitched.

"Hey, simmer down and slow down or I'll hang up!" Marshall snapped hoarsely. Suddenly he recognized the voice. "Ted? Is this Ted?"

"Hogan . . ." came Ted Harmel's voice, "they're coming for me! They're all over the place!"

Marshall was awake now. He pressed the receiver to his ear, trying to understand what Ted was blubbering about. "I can't hear you! What'd you say?"

"They found out I talked! They're all over the place!"

"Who is?"

Ted started crying and screaming unintelligibly, and the sound of it was enough to make Marshall's insides curl up. He groped around the bedside stand for his pen and pad.

"Ted!" he shouted into the phone, and Kate jerked with a start and turned over to look at him. "Where are you? Are you home?"

Kate could hear the cries and wailings squawking out of the receiver, and it unnerved her. "Marshall, who is it?" she demanded.

Marshall couldn't answer her; he was too occupied trying to get a clear answer from Ted Harmel. "Ted, listen, tell me where you are." Pause. Some more cries. "How do I get there? I said, how do I get there?" Marshall began scribbling hurriedly. "Try getting out of there if you can . . ."

Kate listened, but couldn't make out what the party on the other end was saying.

Marshall told whoever it was, "Listen, it's going to take me at least half an hour to get there, and that's if I can find a station open to get some gas. No, I'll get over there, just hang tight. All right? Ted? All right?"

"Who's Ted?"

"All right," said Marshall into the phone. "Give me time, I'll get out there. Just take it easy. Good-bye."

He hung up the phone and bolted out of bed.

"Who in the world was that?" Kate needed to know.

Marshall grabbed his clothes and began to dress hurriedly. "Ted Harmel, remember, I told you about him . . ."

"You're not going over there tonight, are you?"

"The guy's going crazy or something, I don't know."

"You get back in bed!"

"Kate, I have to go! I can't afford to lose this contact."

"No! I don't believe this! You can't be serious!"

Marshall *was* serious. He kissed Kate good-bye before she could even bring herself to believe he was really going, and then he was gone. She sat there in the bed for a few moments, stunned, then flopped down angrily on her back, staring at the ceiling as she heard the car back down the driveway and speed off into the night.

24

Marshall drove about thirty miles north, through the town of Windsor and a little beyond. He was surprised to find out how close to Ashton Ted Harmel still lived, especially after they both met in the mountains over a hundred miles further up Highway 27. This guy has to be crazy, Marshall thought, and maybe I'm just as crazy to be going along with this whole routine. The guy's paranoid, a real space case.

But he sure sounded convincing over the phone. Besides, it was a chance to reopen communications with him after that one-time-only interview.

Marshall had to do some backtracking and groping around the maze of winding, unmarked backroads in his efforts to make sense of Harmel's directions. When he finally located the little shake-sided house at the end of a long gravel road, a ribbon of pink light was growing on the horizon. He'd taken an hour and a half to get there. Yes, there was the old Valiant, parked in the driveway. Marshall pulled in behind it and got out of the car.

The front door of the house was open. The front window was broken. Marshall crouched just a little behind his car, taking a moment to check out the situation. He didn't like the feelings he was getting at all; his insides had gone through this kind of a dance before, that night when Sandy had run off, and again there seemed no obvious, up-front reason for it. He hated to admit it, but he was afraid to take another step.

"Ted?" he called, not too loudly.

There was no answer.

It didn't look good at all. Marshall forced himself to make his way around his car, up the walk, and onto the front porch very slowly, very carefully. He kept listening, looking, feeling. There was no sound except his own pounding heart. His shoes crunched just a little on the shards of broken glass from the window. The sound seemed deafening.

C'mon, Hogan, get with it. "Ted?" he called through the open door. "Ted Harmel? It's Marshall Hogan."

No answer, but this had to be Ted's place. There was his coat hanging on the rack; on the wall above the dining room table was a framed front page from the *Clarion*.

He ventured inside.

The place was a mess. The dishes that had been in the corner hutch were now shattered all over the floor. In the living room a chair lay broken on the floor just below a large hole in the plaster wall. The bulbs were shattered out of the ceiling light fixture. Books from the shelves were thrown everywhere. The side window was also broken out.

And Marshall could feel it, just as strongly as before: that fierce, gut-wrenching terror he had felt that other night. He tried to shake it off, tried to ignore it, but it was there. His palms were slick with sweat; he felt weak. He looked around for a weapon and grabbed a fireplace poker. Keep your back to the wall, Hogan, keep quiet, look out for blind corners. It was dark in here, the shadows were very black. He tried to take his time, tried to let his eyes get used to the dark. He felt for a light switch somewhere, anywhere.

Behind and above him, a black, leathery wing quietly repositioned. Leering yellow eyes watched his every move. Here, there, over there, all over the room, in the corners of the ceiling, upon the furniture, clinging like insects to the walls, were the demons, some of them letting out little snickers, some of them drooling blood.

Marshall made his way stealthily to the desk in the corner and, using a handkerchief to prevent fingerprints, slid the drawers open. They had not been disturbed. Keeping the poker at the ready, he continued to move through the house.

The bathroom was a mess. The mirror was shattered; the shards were in the sink and all over the floor.

He moved down the hall, staying close to the wall.

Hundreds of pairs of yellow eyes watched his every move. There was an occasional hacking from the throat of a demon, a short burst of vapor from its dripping mouth.

In the bedroom the most loathsome spirits of all awaited him. They watched the bedroom doorway from their positions on the ceiling, on the walls, in every corner, and their breathing sounded like the dragging of chains through gravel-filled mud.

From where he stood, Marshall could see just the corner of the bed through the bedroom door. He approached cautiously, making frequent checks behind and even above him.

When he reached the bedroom door a single image, like a photograph, was instantly engraved on his mind. One second seemed like an eternity as his eyes darted from the blood-spattered bedspread to the bullet-blasted skull of Ted Harmel to the large revolver still dangling from Harmel's limp hand.

Shrieks! Thunder! Fangs bared to bite! The demons exploded from the walls, corners, every nook of the room and like arrows went for Marshall's heart.

A blinding flash! Then another, then another! The whitest hot light traced brilliant fiery arcs, a searing edge that cut through the flock of evil spirits like a scythe. Parts of demons tumbled into nothingness; other demons imploded and vanished in instantaneous billows of red smoke. Waves of spirits still poured down upon the one lone man who stood there in reasonless terror, but suddenly this man was surrounded by four heavenly warriors robed in glorious light, their crystalline wings unfurled like a canopy over their charge, their swords blurring into waving, swirling sheets of brilliance.

The air was filled with the deafening cries of hideous spirits as blades met flanks, necks, torsos, and demon after demon was flung aside in pieces that instantly disintegrated and vanished like vapor. Nathan, Armoth, and two other angels, Senter and Cree, darted, feinted, spun, batted away one spirit and sliced another, thrusting their blades in a myriad of directions. The lightning from their swords flashed against the walls, bright enough to bleach out all colors.

Nathan gutted one demon and sent it spiraling through the roof, leaving a red trail of vapor until it vanished. With his sword he slashed; with his free hand he collected demons by their heels.

Armoth and Senter whirled in a high-powered blur, mowing through demons as through grass. Cree threw himself against Marshall and kept his wings spread to protect the stunned man.

"Push them back!" shouted Nathan, and he began to spin his fistful of demons about his head, feeling the shock of their bodies striking other demons with the rhythm of a stick on a picket fence.

The demons began to shy back; half their numbers were now gone, as was half their zeal. Nathan, Armoth, and Senter started flying a tight spiral around Marshall, their swords knifing through the fading demonic ranks.

One demon shot straight into the sky with a wail of terror. Senter got right after it and quickly dispatched it like a slaughtered gamebird. He remained above the house for a time, containing any fleeing spirits very neatly and abruptly, swatting them out of existence as if they were fast-served tennis balls.

And then, almost as suddenly as it had begun, it was over. No demon remained; none had escaped.

Nathan alighted back in the hallway as his wings folded and the light around him faded. "How's our man?"

Cree was relieved to say, "He's still very shaken, but he's all right. He still has the will to fight."

Armoth came in for a landing and immediately checked Ted Harmel's pitiful frame. Senter dropped through the ceiling and joined him.

Armoth shook his head and sighed. "As Captain Tal said, Rafar can choose any front he wants, at any time."

"They have owned and tormented Ted Harmel for a long time," Senter conceded.

"Is Kevin Weed covered?" Nathan asked.

Armoth answered with a little curiosity, "Tal sent Signa to watchcare Weed."

"Signa? Was he not assigned to guard the church?"

"Tal must have a change in plans."

Nathan got back to the immediate business. "We'd best see to Marshall Hogan."

Marshall got a grip on himself. For a moment he thought he would really panic, and that would have been the very first time in his life. Nuts, I don't need to get involved in this stuff, not now, he thought. He took a few more moments to ease up and think the thing through. Harmel was history. But what about the others?

He went into the dining room and found the phone. Using his handkerchief again and a pen to dial, he called the operator, who put him through to the police department in Windsor, a town closer than Ashton, fortunately. Something told Marshall that Brummel and his cops were definitely not the ones to call on this.

"This is an anonymous call," he said. "There's been a fatal shooting, a suicide . . ." He told the sergeant who answered how to get there and then hung up.

Then he got out of there.

Several miles further north, he pulled the Buick into a filling station and went into a phone booth. He first called Eldon Strachan's number. There was no answer.

He had the operator ring the *Clarion*. Bernice should be there by now. C'mon, girl, answer the phone!

"*Ashton Clarion*." It was Carmen.

"Carmen, this is Marshall. Put Bernice on, will you?"

"Sure thing."

Bernice picked up her extension immediately. "Hogan, are you calling in sick?"

"Act normal, Bernie," Marshall said. "I've got some heavy developments."

"Well, take an aspirin or something."

"Good girl. Brace yourself for this one. I just came from Ted Harmel's place. He just blew his brains out. I got a call from him early this morning and he was talking crazy, talking about somebody coming after him, so I drove to his place and just now found him. It looked like he'd had an all-out fight with *something*. The place was a mess."

"So how are you feeling really?" Bernice said, and Marshall could tell this was the acting job of her career.

"I'm shook up but all right. I called the Windsor police but chose to get out of there. Right now I'm up near Windsor on Highway 38. I'm going to head north and drop by Strachan's place to check up on him. I want you to check on Weed right away. I don't want any more sources dying on me."

"Do you—do you think it's catching?"

"I don't know yet. Harmel was a little crazy; it may be an isolated incident. I do know I've got to talk to Strachan about it, and I don't want you to wait to check on Weed."

"Okay, I'll do that today."

"I should be back this afternoon. Be careful."

"You take care of yourself."

Marshall got back in his car and checked his map for the best way to get to Eldon Strachan's place. It took him another hour to make the drive, but soon he was pulling up the same old driveway to the quaint little farmhouse.

He slammed on the brakes and the Buick lurched to a halt, skidding on the gravel. He opened the car door and had another look from outside his car windows. There was no mistake.

The windows were broken in this house too. Come to think of it, by now that collie would be barking, but the place was dead silent.

Marshall left the car where it was and quietly made his way toward the house. No sounds. The windows on the side of the house were also broken. He noted that the glass was broken inward this time, unlike the Harmel house where the glass was broken out. He passed along the side of the house and checked the parking area in the back. No cars. He began praying that Eldon and Doris were gone and nowhere near whatever was happening.

He went around the other side of the house, completely encircling it, then stepped onto the front porch and tried the front door. It was locked. He looked through the front window—the glass was mostly gone—and saw total chaos inside: the house had been ransacked.

He carefully stepped through the window into the once quaint living room, now a pitiful shambles. The furniture was thrown everywhere, the cushions on the sofa were slashed open, the coffee table had been chopped in several pieces, some floor lamps had been thrown down and broken, everything was out of its place and thrown about.

"Eldon!" Marshall called. "Doris! Anybody home?"

As if I really expected an answer, he thought. But what was that on the mirror over the fireplace? He went for a closer look. Someone had taken red paint . . . or was it blood? Marshall checked closely. With great relief he smelled the unmistakable scent of paint. But someone had scrawled an obscene message of hate on the mirror, a very clear threat.

He knew he would have to check every room in the house, and right at this moment he wondered why he didn't feel the same terror he had felt at Harmel's. Maybe this day was turning him numb. Maybe he just wasn't believing any of it anymore.

He checked the whole house, upstairs and downstairs and even the cellar, but there were no terrible discoveries, and he was very glad. That didn't make him any less concerned, nervous, or perplexed, however. This was too much of a coincidence despite the basic differences. As he took a second look around the living room, he tried to think if there could be a connection. Obviously, both Harmel and Strachan had been sources for Marshall's investigation and could have become targets for intimidation. But Harmel in his terrible fear could have done the damage around his house by himself, fighting off whatever it was, while this damage to Strachan's house was clearly the act of vandals, of malicious characters out to scare him. That was one connection: fear. Both Harmel and Strachan were the brunt of fear tactics, whatever form they took. But why would . . .

"All right! Freeze! Police!"

Marshall stayed still, but he did look out through the broken window. There, on the porch, was a sheriff's officer aiming a gun at him.

"Take it easy," Marshall said very gently, without moving.

"Get both hands in the air, in plain sight!" the officer commanded.

Marshall obeyed. "The name's Marshall Hogan, editor of the *Ashton Clarion*. I'm a friend of the Strachans."

"Just hold steady. I'll have to see some I.D., Mr. Hogan."

Marshall explained everything he did as he did it. "I'm going to reach into my back pocket here, see? Here's my wallet. Now I'm going to toss it to you through the window there."

By now the officer's partner had mounted the porch and also had his gun trained on Marshall. Marshall tossed his wallet through the broken window, and the first policeman picked it up.

The officer checked Marshall's I.D. "What are you doing here, Mr. Hogan?"

"Trying to figure out what in blazes happened to Eldon's house. And I'd also like to know what happened to Eldon and Doris, his wife."

The officer seemed satisfied with Marshall's I.D. and relaxed just a little, but his partner kept a gun trained on Marshall.

The officer tried the front door and then asked, "How'd you get in there?"

"Through that window," Marshall answered.

"Okay, Mr. Hogan, I am going to ask you to step very carefully back through the window, and do it very slowly. Please keep both hands in plain sight."

Marshall obeyed. As soon as he got out on the porch the officer turned him around, his hands against the wall, and frisked him.

Marshall asked, "You guys from Windsor?"

"Windsor Precinct," came the short answer, and with that, the officer grabbed Marshall's wrists one at a time and slapped handcuffs on him. "We're placing you under arrest. You have the right to remain silent . . ."

Marshall could think of all kinds of questions to ask and it was all he could do to keep from disassembling these two, but he knew better than to say a word.

25

Bernice called Kevin Weed right after she got off the phone with Marshall, but there was no answer. He was probably working with the logging crew today. She dug through her file and found the phone number for Gorst Brothers Timber.

They told her Kevin had not been in today, and if she saw him she'd better tell him to show up quick or he'd be out of a job.

"Thanks, Mr. Gorst."

She dialed The Evergreen Tavern in Baker. Dan, the proprietor, answered.

"Sure," he said, "Weed was in here this morning, just like he always is. He was in a gosh-awful mood though. He got in a fight with one of his buddies, and I had to throw them both out."

Bernice left Dan the *Clarion's* number in case he saw Weed again. Then she hung up and thought for a moment. It wasn't out of the question to drive out to Baker, and besides, orders were orders. She went over her schedule for the day and tried to rearrange her jobs to accommodate the trip.

"Carmen," she said, grabbing her jacket and handbag, "I'll be gone for the day, I think. If Marshall calls, tell him I've gone out to check on a source. He'll know what I mean."

"Righto," said Carmen.

Baker was about seventeen miles north on Highway 27; the apartments where Weed lived were about two miles closer. Bernice found them without too much trouble, a sad complex of dry-rotting cubicles honeycombed into a sun-bleached old warehouse. Bernice's nose told her the septic system was failing.

She went up the plank stairs onto the loading dock which now served as a patio and entranceway. Inside, she was appalled at how dark the building was. She looked down one long corridor and noted many closely spaced doors; these weren't apartments, they were lockers.

She had heard some footsteps on the old planks upstairs, and now they came down the stairway just behind her. She turned her head just enough to see an unpleasant-looking character stepping down, a skinny, pimple-faced apparition in black leather. She immediately decided she had a very pressing appointment at the other end of the hall and started in that direction.

"Hi there," the man called to her. "Looking for someone?"

Make it quick, Bernice. "Just visiting a friend, thank you."

"Have a nice visit," he said, and he kept looking her over as if she were a steak.

She walked quickly down the corridor, hoping it wouldn't be a dead end, and though she didn't look back she could tell he was still watching her. Hogan, I'll get you for this.

She was glad to find another stairway leading upstairs. Weed's apartment had a two hundred number, so up the stairs she went. The stairwell was old weathered planks, illumined with one bare light bulb hanging from a very high rafter. Some thirty years ago someone had tried to paint the walls. She wound her way upward, ignoring the disgusting graffiti everywhere, her shoes making hollow thuds on the worn planks.

She reached the upstairs corridor and doubled back, following the descending numbers on the doors. From behind some of the doors came sounds of soap operas, FM rock stations, marital spats.

She finally found Weed's door and knocked; there was no answer. But her knocking nudged the door, and it drifted slowly open. She helped it quietly on its way.

The place was an absolute mess. Bernice had seen the homes of messy people before, but how could Weed possibly live in a disaster area like this?

"Kevin?" she called.

No answer. She stepped inside and closed the door.

It had to be vandalism; Weed didn't own that much, but what he did own was thrown about, broken, spilled, and shattered. Papers and bric-a-brac were everywhere, the little cot in the corner was overturned, Weed's guitar was facedown on the floor, the back stomped through, the bulbs were broken out of the ceiling fixture, the few secondhand dishes were in shattered pieces all over the floor in the little kitchen cubicle. Then she saw words spray-painted across one whole wall, an incredibly obscene threat.

For the longest time she didn't move. She was afraid. The implications were clear enough—how long would it be before they struck her or Marshall? She wondered what Marshall would find at Strachan's, she wondered what her own home looked like, and she realized there were no police to call; the police were with *them*.

Finally she slipped quietly out the door, wrote Weed a quick note in case he ever came back, and shoved it in the crack just above the doorknob. She looked this way and that and then went along the corridor and back down the stairs again.

Just one flight below the second floor, a wall formed a blind corner between the two flights at the middle landing. Bernice was just thinking how she didn't like blind corners in a place like this, and how the lighting was so poor . . .

A black figure leaped at her from the flight below. Her body slammed into the old shiplap wall as her teeth clapped together.

The man in leather! A rough, dirty hand grabbing a fistful of blouse. A violent, sideways jerk. Tearing cloth, her body reeling. An impact like an explosion in her left ear. A blurred, hate-filled face.

She was falling. Her arms went out against the rough plank corner, they were limp, they buckled, she slid down the wall to the floor. A black boot blotted out her vision, her glasses were driven into her face, her skull thudded against the wall. She went numb. Her body kept jerking about—he was still hitting her.

Step step step step step step step—he was gone.

She was dreaming, her head was reeling, there was blood upon the floor and broken glasses in bent pieces. She slumped against the wall, still feeling the fist in her ear and the boot in her face, and hearing blood dripping from her mouth and her nose. The floor drew her down like a magnet until her head finally thumped on the boards.

She whimpered, a gurgling sound as blood and saliva bubbled over her tongue. She spit it all out, raised her head, and cried out in a sound that was half cry, half moan.

From somewhere up above, the boards began to pound and clatter with a sudden flow of traffic. She heard people shouting, swearing, thundering down the steps. She couldn't move; she kept half-dreaming as light and sound faded in and out, were there, were not there. Hands began to hold her, move her, cradle her. A cloth wiped across her mouth. She felt the new warmth of a blanket. A towel kept dabbing her face. She gurgled again, spit again. She heard someone swear again.

Marshall still wouldn't reply to any questions, although the detective at the Windsor Precinct kept trying.

"We're talking about murder here, bub!" the detective said. "Now we have it from reliable sources that you were there at Harmel's place early this morning, and that's right near the time of death. Do you have anything to say about that?"

This flunky was born yesterday, Marshall thought. Sure, punk, I'll tell you all about it so you can hang me! In a pig's eye it was murder.

But what really bothered Marshall was just who this "reliable source" was, and how that reliable source not only knew he'd been at Harmel's, but also knew these cops could find him at Strachan's. He was still working on the answer to that riddle.

The detective asked, "So you're still not going to say anything?"

Marshall wouldn't even nod or shake his head.

"Well," the detective said with a half shrug, "at least give me the name of your lawyer. You're going to need counsel."

Marshall had no name to give him and couldn't even think of one. It became a waiting game.

"Spence," said a deputy, "you've got a call from Ashton."

The detective picked up the phone at his desk. "Nelson. Oh, hi there, Alf. What's up?"

Alf Brummel?

"Yeah," the detective said, "he's right here. Would you like to talk to him? He sure won't talk to *us*." He offered Marshall the receiver. "Alf Brummel."

Marshall took the receiver. "Yeah, this is Hogan."

Alf Brummel was acting shocked and dismayed. "Marshall, what's going on up there?"

"I can't say."

"They tell me Ted Harmel was murdered and that they have you as a suspect. Is that true?"

"I can't say."

Alf was beginning to catch on. "Marshall . . . listen, I'm calling to see if I can help. Now, I'm sure there's been a mistake and I'm sure we can work something out. What were you doing up at Harmel's place anyway?"

"I can't say."

That flustered him. "Marshall, for crying out loud, will you just forget that I'm a cop? I'm also your friend. I want to help you!"

"Do it."

"I want to. I really want to. Now listen, let me talk to Detective Nelson again. Maybe we can work something out."

Marshall handed the receiver back to Nelson. Nelson and Brummel talked for a while, and it sounded like they knew each other pretty well.

"Well, you might be able to do more with him than I ever will," said Nelson quite pleasantly. "Sure, why not? Huh? Yeah, okay." Nelson looked at Marshall. "He's on another line. Guess he'll vouch for you, and I think he can take jurisdiction over your case, if there is one."

Marshall nodded all too knowingly. Now Brummel would have

Marshall right where he wanted him. If there was a case! If there wasn't one, Brummel would find one. What would it be now, Harmel and Hogan running a child-molesting ring with a gangland-type murder?

Nelson heard Brummel come back on the line. "Yeah, hello. Yeah sure." Nelson handed Marshall the receiver again.

Brummel was upset, or at least he sounded like it. "Marshall, that was the fire district that just called. They've just sent an aid car out toward Baker. It's Bernice; she's been assaulted."

Marshall never thought he'd hope Brummel *was* lying. "Tell me more."

"We won't know more until they get out there. It won't take long. Listen, they're going to release you on personal recognizance under my supervision. You'd better get back to Ashton right away. Can you see me in my office at, say, 3?"

Marshall thought he would have a seizure trying to contain all the cuss words he had for this whole thing. "I'll be there, Alf. Nothing could keep me away."

"Good, I'll see you then."

Marshall returned the receiver to Nelson.

Nelson smiled and said, "We'll take you back to your car."

The man in black leather was back in Ashton, running down the streets and then through the alleys like a man possessed, looking behind him, panting, crying, terrified.

Five cruel spirits rode on his back, ducked in and out of his body, clung to him like huge leeches, their talons deeply embedded in his flesh. But they were not in control. They too were terrified.

Just above the five demons and their running victim, six angelic warriors floated along with their swords drawn, moving this way and that, to the right, to the left, whatever it took to keep the demons herded in the right direction.

The demons hissed and spit and made shooing motions with their sinewy hands.

The young man ran, swatting at invisible bees.

The young man and his demons came to a corner. They tried to go left. The angels blocked their way and prodded them with their swords to the right. With a cry and a terrible wailing, the demons fled to the right.

The demons began to cry for mercy. "No! Let us alone!" they pleaded. "You have no right!"

Just up the street, Hank Busche and Andy Forsythe were walking together, taking some time to share their burdens and pray.

Right alongside them walked Triskal, Krioni, Seth, and Scion. The four warriors all saw what their comrades were herding their way, and they were more than ready.

"Time for an object lesson for the man of God," said Krioni.

Triskal only beckoned to the demons with his finger and said, "Come, come!"

Andy looked down the street and saw the man first. "Well . . .!"

"What?" asked Hank, seeing the dumfounded look on Andy's face.

"Get ready. Here comes Bobby Corsi!"

Hank looked and cringed at the sight of a wild-looking character running toward them, his eyes filled with terror, his arms beating the air as he battled unseen enemies.

Andy cautioned, "Be careful. He could be violent."

"Oh, terrific!"

They stood still and waited to see what Bobby would do.

Bobby saw them and cried out in even more terror, "No, no! Leave us alone!"

Heaven's warriors were bad enough, but the five demons wanted no part of Busche and Forsythe. They twisted Bobby around and tried to run away, but were instantly hemmed in by the angelic six.

Bobby stopped dead in his tracks. He looked at nothing ahead of him, then looked at Hank and Andy, then looked again at his unseen enemies. He screamed, standing still where he was, his hands clawlike and trembling, his eyes bulging and glazed.

Hank and Andy moved forward very slowly.

"Easy, Bobby," Andy said soothingly. "Take it easy now."

"No!" Bobby screamed. "Leave us alone! We want no business with you!"

An angel gave one of the demons a prod with the tip of his sword.

"Awww!" Bobby cried out in pain, collapsing to his knees. "Leave us alone, leave us alone!"

Hank stepped forward quickly and said firmly, "In Jesus' name, be quiet!" Bobby let out one more scream. "Be quiet!"

Bobby grew still and began to weep, kneeling there on the sidewalk.

"Bobby," said Hank, bending down and speaking gently, "Bobby, can you hear me?"

A demon clapped his hands over Bobby's ears. Bobby did not hear Hank's question.

Hank, hearing from the Spirit of God, knew what the demon was doing. "Demon, in the name of Jesus, let go of his ears."

The demon jerked his hands away, a surprised look on his face.

Hank asked again, "Bobby?"

This time Bobby answered, "Yeah, preacher, I hear you."

"Do you want to be free from these spirits?"

Immediately one demon answered, "No, you don't! He belongs to us," and Bobby spit the words in Hank's face, "No, you don't! He belongs to us!"

"Spirit, be quiet. I'm talking to Bobby."

The demon said no more, but backed off sulkingly.

Bobby muttered, "I've just done a horrible thing . . ." He began to weep. "You gotta help me . . . I can't stop from doing this stuff . . ."

Hank spoke quietly aside to Andy. "Let's get him somewhere where we can deal with him, where he can make a scene if he has to."

"The church?"

"Come on, Bobby."

They took him by his arms and helped him up, and the three, and the five, and the six, and the four headed up the street.

Marshall sped through Baker and then made a quick swing by the apartment complex where Weed lived. There seemed to be no activity there, so he drove on into Ashton. When he reached the hospital, the aid car was parked outside.

An emergency medical technician who was securing the stretcher back in the vehicle filled Marshall in. "She's in the emergency room, two doors down."

Marshall burst through the main doors and got to the right room in an instant. He heard a cry of pain from Bernice just as he reached the door.

She was lying on a table, attended by a doctor and two nurses who were washing her face and dressing her cuts. At the sight of her, Marshall could contain himself no longer; all the anger and frustration and terror of this whole day exploded from his lungs in one vehement expletive.

Bernice responded through swollen and bleeding lips, "I guess that about covers it."

He hurried to the side of the table as the doctor and two nurses gave him room. He took her hand in both of his and couldn't believe what had happened to her. Her attacker had been merciless.

"Who did this to you?" he demanded, his blood boiling.

"We went the whole fifteen rounds, boss."

"Don't clown with me, Bernie. Did you see who did it?"

The doctor cautioned him, "Easy now, let's take care of her first . . ."

Bernice whispered something. Marshall couldn't make it out. He leaned closer and she whispered it again, her swollen mouth slurring her words. "He didn't rape me."

"Thank God," Marshall said, straightening up.

She wasn't satisfied with his response. She motioned to him again to lean forward and listen. "All he did was beat me up. That's all he did."

"Aren't you satisfied?" Marshall whispered back rather loudly.

She was handed a glass of water to wash her mouth out. She swirled the water around in her mouth and spit into a bowl.

"Was Strachan's house nice and neat?" she asked.

Marshall held back his answer. He asked the doctor, "When can I talk to her in private?"

The doctor thought about it. "Well, she's going in for X-rays in just a few minutes—"

"Give me thirty seconds," Bernice requested, "just thirty seconds."

"It can't wait?"

"No. Please."

The doctor and the nurses stepped out of the room.

Marshall spoke softly. "Strachan's place was a mess; somebody really went through it. He's gone; I've no idea where he is or how he is."

Bernice reported, "Weed's place was the same way, and there was a threat spray-painted on the wall. He didn't show up for work today, and Dan at The Evergreen Tavern said he was really upset about something. He's gone, too. I didn't find him."

"And now they've got me wrapped up with Ted Harmel's death. They found out I was there this morning. They think I did it."

"Marshall, Susan Jacobson was right: our phone must be bugged. Remember? You called me at the *Clarion* and told me you'd been at Ted's and where you were going next."

"Yeah, yeah, I figured that. But that means the Windsor cops would have to be in on it too. They knew right where and when to find me at Strachan's."

"Brummel and Detective Nelson are like *that*, Marshall," Bernice said, holding two fingers together.

"They must have ears everywhere."

"They knew I'd be at Weed's alone . . . and when . . ." Bernice said, and then something else dawned on her. "Carmen knew it too."

That revelation hit Marshall almost like a death sentence. "Carmen knows a *lot* of things."

"We've been hit, Marshall. I think they're trying to get a message to us."

He straightened up. "Wait'll I find Brummel!"

She grabbed his hand. "Be careful. I mean, *really* be careful!"

He kissed her forehead. "Happy X-rays."

He stormed out of the room like a raging bull, and no one dared get in his way.

26

Marshall was seeing red, and was so angry that he parked crooked-ly across two parking places in the Courthouse Square parking lot. He thought that walking fast across the parking lot to the police department's door might air-cool him a bit, but it didn't. He jerked open the door and went into the reception area. Sara wasn't at her desk. Brummel wasn't in his office. Marshall checked his watch. It was 3 o'clock on the dot.

A woman came around the corner. He'd never seen her before.

"Hello," he said, and then added very abruptly, "Who are you?"

She was quite taken aback by the question, and timidly answered, "Well, I'm . . . I'm Barbara, the receptionist."

"The receptionist? What happened to Sara?"

She was intimidated and a little indignant. "I—I don't know of any Sara, but can *I* help you?"

"Where's Alf Brummel?"

"Are you Mr. Hogan?"

"That's right."

"Chief Brummel is waiting for you in the conference room, right down at the end of the hall."

She hadn't finished her sentence before Marshall was already on his way. If the door latch would have given the slightest resistance, it wouldn't have survived Marshall's entrance. He burst into the room ready to wring the first neck he could get his hands around.

There were many necks to choose from. The room was full of people Marshall had not been expecting, but as he looked around at all the faces, he had no trouble guessing the meeting's agenda. Brummel had friends with him. Big shots. Liars. Schemers.

Alf Brummel sat at the conference table surrounded by his many comrades and smiling that toothy grin. "Hello, Marshall. Please close the door."

Marshall kicked the door shut with his foot without looking away from all these people now gathered, no doubt to have it out with him. Oliver Young was there, as was Judge Baker, County Comptroller Irving Pierce, Fire Marshall Frank Brady, Detective Spence Nelson from Windsor, a few other men Marshall didn't recognize, and finally the mayor of Ashton, David Steen.

"Well, hello there, Mayor Steen," Marshall said coldly. "How interesting to find you here."

The mayor only smiled cordially and silently, like the dumb puppet Marshall always thought he was.

"Have a seat," said Brummel, waving his hand toward an empty chair.

Marshall didn't move. "Alf, is this the meeting you and I were going to have?"

"This is the meeting," said Brummel. "I don't think you know everyone in the room . . ." With overcooked graciousness, Brummel introduced the new or possibly new faces. "I'd like you to meet Tony Sulski, a local attorney, and I believe you've dealt with Ned Wesley, president of the Independent Bank. We understand you've had a conversation at least with Eugene Baylor, college regent. And you of course remember Jimmy Clairborne, from Commercial Printers." Brummel showed his teeth widely, obnoxiously. "Marshall, please have a seat."

Cusswords were going through Marshall's mind as he told Brummel squarely, "Not while I'm outnumbered."

Oliver Young piped up in answer to that. "Marshall, I can assure you that this will be a civil and cordial meeting."

"So which one of you beat the ever-living daylights out of my reporter?" Marshall was hardly feeling civil.

Brummel responded, "Marshall, these things happen to people who aren't careful."

Marshall smeared some descriptions on Brummel like icing from a sewer trap and then told him seethingly, "Brummel, this didn't just happen. She was set up. She was assaulted and injured and your cops haven't done a thing, and we all know why!" He glared at them. "You're all in on this whole thing, and your tricks come real cheap. You vandalize homes, you make threats, you drive people out, you act like some kind of Mafia boys' club!" He aimed an accusing finger at Brummel. "And you, buddy, are a disgrace to your profession. You've used your entrusted powers to silence and intimidate, and to cover up your own dirty work!"

Young tried to interject. "Marshall—"

"And you call yourself a man of God, a pastor, a pious example of what a good Christian should be. You lied to me all along, Young, hiding behind some excuse you call professional ethics, guzzling down all that mystical bull from that Langstrat witch and then acting like you knew nothing about it. How many people who trusted you have you sold out to a lie?"

The men in the room sat silent. Marshall kept unloading. "If you guys are public servants, Hitler was a great humanitarian! You schemed and manipulated and horned your way into this town like mobsters, and you silenced anybody who spoke up or got in your way. You will read about it in the paper, gentlemen! If you want to make any comments or denials I'll be glad to hear them, I'll even print them, but it's press time for all of you whether you like it or not!"

Young raised his hands to get just a short moment to speak. "Marshall, all I can say is, be sure of your facts."

"Don't worry about that. I have my facts, all right. I have innocent people like the Carluccis, the Wrights, the Andersons, the Dombrowskis, over a hundred of them, who were driven out of their homes and businesses by intimidation and trumped up tax delinquencies."

Young piped in, "*Intimidation?* Marshall, it's hardly within our control to prevent fear, foolish superstition, family break-ups. Just what will you print? That the Carluccis, for example, were convinced their store was haunted and that evil spirits, of all things, broke their small son's hands? Come now, Marshall."

Marshall pointed at Young straight from the shoulder. "Hey, Young, that's your specialty. I'll print that you and your bunch preyed on their fears and orchestrated their superstitions, and I'll tell all about the wild practices and philosophies you used to pull it off. I know all about Langstrat and her mind-tripping hocus-pocus, and I know that every one of you is into it.

"I'll print that you set people up with phony raps just to get them removed from their jobs and offices so your own people could move in: you framed Lew Gregory, the former comptroller, with a phony conflict of interest charge; you pushed and pressed for that big turnover on the Whitmore College Board of Regents after Dean Strachan caught Eugene Baylor"—Marshall looked right at Baylor as he said it—"juggling the books! You put Ted Harmel out of town on his ear with that phony child-molesting rap, and I find it interesting that Adam Jarred's poor little victim daughter now has a special fund set up for her college education. If I look far enough, I'll probably find the money came out of your pockets!

"I'll print that my reporter was falsely arrested by Brummel's flunkies because she took a picture she wasn't supposed to, a picture of Brummel, Young, and Langstrat with none other than Alexander M. Kaseph himself, the Big Boy behind a conspiracy to take over the town, aided and abetted by all of you, a bunch of power-hungry, pseudo-spiritualized neo-Fascists!"

Young smiled calmly. "Which means you plan to write about the Omni Corporation."

Marshall couldn't believe he was actually hearing it coming from Young's mouth. "So now it's tell-the-truth time?"

Young continued, very relaxed, very confident. "Well, you have been tracking down everything that Omni has bought and owns, isn't that right?"

"That's right."

Young laughed a little when he asked, "And how many houses would you say were turned over to Omni because of tax delinquency?"

Marshall refused to play games. "You tell me."

Young simply turned to Irving Pierce, the comptroller.

Pierce shuffled through some papers. "Mr. Hogan, I believe your records show that one hundred and twenty three homes were auctioned to Omni for failure to pay taxes . . ."

He knew. Well, so what? "I'll stand by that."

"You were in error."

Let's hear the lie, Pierce.

"The correct number is one hundred and *sixty-three*. All legally, all legitimately, over the past five years."

Marshall hated it, but he couldn't think of a comeback.

Young spoke on. "You *are* correct about Omni owning all these properties, plus many other commercial enterprises as well. But you also should note how these properties have been substantially improved under this new ownership. I would say that Ashton is certainly a better town for it."

Marshall could feel the steam rising in his pipes. "Those people paid their taxes! I've talked to over a hundred of them!"

Pierce was unmoved. "We have substantial evidence to show that they did not."

"In a pig's eye!"

"And in regard to the college . . ." Young looked at Eugene Baylor, giving him his cue.

Baylor stood to speak. "I've really had quite enough of this slander and gossip about the college being in financial arrears. The college is doing just fine, thank you, and this—this smear campaign that Eldon Strachan began must stop or we will sue! Mr. Sulski has been retained for just that eventuality."

"I have records, I have proof, Baylor, that you've embezzled Whitmore College out of millions."

Brummel piped in, "You have no proof, Marshall. You have no records."

Marshall had to smile. "Oh, you ought to just see what I have."

Young said simply, "We have seen it. All of it."

Marshall had the feeling deep inside that he had just stepped off a cliff.

Young continued with a progressively cooling tone. "We've been following your futile attempts from the very beginning. We know you talked to Ted Harmel, we know you've been interviewing Eldon Strachan, Joe Carlucci, Lew Gregory, and hundreds of other quacks, malcontents and doomsayers. We know you've been harassing our people and our businesses. We know that you've been snooping in all our personal records." Young paused for effect, and then said, "That's all going to stop now, Marshall."

"Hence this meeting!" Marshall said with sarcastic flair. "What's in store for me, Young? How about it, Brummel? Got a nice morals rap to pin on me? You gonna send someone to tear up my house too?"

Young stood up, motioning for a chance to speak. "Marshall, you may never understand our true motivations, but at least give me one opportunity to try to clear the matter up for you. There is no predatory thirst for power here among us, as you probably think. We do not seek power as an end."

"No, you just came upon it purely by accident," Marshall said cuttingly.

"Power for us, Marshall, is only necessary as one means toward our real goal for mankind, and that is nothing other than universal peace and prosperity."

"Who's 'we' and 'us'?"

"Oh, you already know that too, all too well. The Society, Marshall, the Society you've been hounding after all this time as if chasing after some mysterious burglar."

"The Universal Consciousness Society. And we have our own little chapter here in Ashton, our own little piece of the Conquer the World Club!"

Young smiled ever so tolerantly. "More than a club, Marshall. Actually, a long-awaited, newly rising force for global change, a world-wide voice that will finally unite mankind."

"Yeah, and such a wonderful, humanitarian movement that you have to sneak in with it, you have to hide it . . ."

"Only from old ideas, Marshall, from the old obstacles of religious bigotry and intolerance. We live in a changing and growing world, and mankind is still evolving, still maturing. Many still lag behind in the maturing process and cannot tolerate the very thing that will be best for them. Marshall, too many of us just don't know what's best. Someday—and we hope it will be soon—everyone will understand, there will be no more religion, and then there will be no more secrets."

"In the meantime, you do what you can to scare people and chase them from their homes and businesses—"

"Only, *only* if they are limited in their perspective and resist the truth; only if they stand in the way of what is truly right and good."

Marshall was getting as sick as he was angry. "Truly right and good? What? All of a sudden, you guys are the new authority on what right and good is? C'mon, Young, where's your theology? Where does God fit into all this?"

Young gave a resigned shrug and said, "*We* are God."

Marshall finally did sink into a chair. "Either you people are crazy or I am."

"I know it's quite beyond anything you've ever considered before. Admittedly, ours are very high and lofty ideals, but what we've come to achieve is inevitable for all men. It is nothing more than the final destination of man's evolution: enlightenment, self-realization. Some-day all men, even yourself, must realize their own infinite potential, their own divinity, and become united in one universal mind, one universal consciousness. The alternative is to perish."

Marshall had heard enough. "Young, that is pure, unadulterated horse hockey and you are out of your ever-loving mind!"

Young looked at the others and almost looked sad. "We all hoped you would understand, but in truth, we did expect you to feel this way. You have so far to go, Marshall, so very far to go . . ."

Marshall took a good long look at them all. "You plan to take over the town, don't you? Buy out the college? Make it some kind of hive for your cosmic, mind-blown Society?"

Young looked at him with a very sober face and said, "It's for the very best, Marshall. It has to be this way."

Marshall got up and headed for the door. "I'll see you in the paper."

"You have no paper, Marshall," Young said abruptly.

Marshall only turned and shook his head at Young. "Drop dead."

Ned Wesley, the president of the Independent Bank, spoke on cue from Young. "Marshall, we have to foreclose on you."

Marshall did not believe what he had heard.

Wesley opened his file to the records of Marshall's business loan on the *Clarion*. "You've been delinquent in your payments for eight months now, and we've received no response whatsoever from our many inquiries. We really have no choice but to foreclose."

Marshall was totally prepared to make Wesley eat his phony records, but didn't have time before Irving Pierce, the county comptroller, spoke up.

"As for your taxes, Marshall, I'm afraid those have become quite delinquent as well. I just don't know how you thought you could go on living in that house without meeting your obligations."

Marshall knew he could be a murderer right about now. It would be the easiest thing in the world, except that there were two cops in the room who would love to pin such a rap on him and a judge who would love to lock him away for good.

"You are all crazy," he said slowly. "You'll never get away with it."

Just then Jimmy Clairborne from Commercial Printers put in his two cents. "Marshall, I'm afraid we've been having some trouble with you as well. My records here show that we haven't been paid for the last six runs of the *Clarion*. There's no way we can continue to print the paper for you until these accounts are cleared up."

Detective Nelson added, "These are very serious matters, Marshall, and as far as our investigation of Ted Harmel's murder, these things do not put you in a very good light."

"As for the courts," said Judge Baker, "whatever decisions we ultimately render will depend, I suppose, on your behavior from now on."

"Especially in light of the complaints of sexual misconduct we've just received," added Brummel. "Your daughter must be a very frightened girl to have remained silent for so long."

He felt like bullets were ripping into him. He could feel himself dying, he was sure of it.

The five demons clung tenaciously to Bobby Corsi, hissing their sulfurous oaths and cursings as they cowered in the front of the little sanctuary of the Ashton Community Church. Triskal, Krioni, Seth, and Scion were there along with six other warriors, their swords drawn, surrounding the little prayer group. Hank had his Bible handy and had already gone through a few references in the Gospels to get some idea of how to proceed. He and Andy held Bobby firmly but gently as Bobby sat on the floor in front of the pulpit. John Coleman had come right over to help, and Ron Forsythe wouldn't have missed it.

"Yeah," Ron observed, "he's got it bad. Hey, Bobby. Remember me, Ron Forsythe?"

Bobby looked at Ron with glassy, staring eyes. "Yeah, I remember you . . ."

But the demons also remembered Ron Forsythe and the hold their comrades once had on his life. "Traitor! Traitor!"

Bobby began to scream at Ron, "Traitor! Traitor!" as he struggled to free himself from Hank and Andy. John stepped in to help hold Bobby down.

Hank commanded the demons, "Stop it! Stop it right now!"

The demons spoke through Bobby as Bobby turned and cursed at Hank. "We don't need to listen to you, praying man! You will never defeat us! You will die before you defeat us!" Bobby glared at the four men and screamed, "You will all die!"

Hank prayed aloud so everyone, including Bobby, could hear. "Lord God, we come against these spirits now in Jesus' name, and we bind them!"

The five spirits ducked their heads under their wings as if being pelted by stones, crying and whimpering.

"No . . . no . . ." said Bobby.

Hank continued, "And I pray right now that you will send your angels to help us . . ."

The ten warriors were ready and waiting.

Hank addressed the spirits. "I want to know how many are in there. Speak up!"

One demon, a smaller one, ducked inside Bobby's back and shrieked, "Nooo!"

The scream came belching out of Bobby's throat.

"Which one are you?" Hank asked.

"I won't tell you! You can't make me!"

"By the name of Jesus—"

The demon responded immediately, "Fortune-telling!"

Hank asked, "Fortune-telling, how many of you are in there?"

"Millions!" Triskal jabbed Fortune-telling lightly in the flank. "Awww! Ten! Ten!" Another jab. "Aww! No, we are five, only five!"

Bobby began to twitch and shake as the demons got into a scuffle. Fortune-telling found himself the brunt of some very harsh blows.

"No! No!" Bobby screamed for the demon. "Now see what you've made me do! The others are hitting me!"

"In Jesus' name, leave," said Hank.

Fortune-telling let go of Bobby and floated up over the group. Krioni grabbed him.

"Depart from the region!" he ordered.

Fortune-telling obeyed immediately and soared out of the church, not looking back.

A large and hairy demon shouted after the departed spirit, and Bobby stared at the ceiling shouting, "Traitor! Traitor! We'll get you for that!"

"And who are you?" Hank asked.

The demon shut its mouth, as did Bobby, and glared at the men with eyes full of fire and hatred.

"Spirit, who are you?" Andy demanded.

Bobby remained silent, his entire body strained, his lips tightly together, his eyes bulging out. He was taking frantic, short breaths through his nose. His face was crimson.

"Spirit," said Andy, "I command you to tell us who you are in Jesus' name!"

"Don't you mention that name!" the spirit hissed and then cursed.

"I will mention that name again and again," said Hank. "You know that name has defeated you."

"No . . . No!"

"Who are you?"

"Confusion, Madness, Hatred . . . Ha! I do them all!"

"In the name of Jesus I bind you and command you to come out!"

The demons all made a sudden rushing of their wings together, pulling, tearing at Bobby, trying to get away.

Bobby struggled to get free from the men who held him, and it was all they could do to hold him down. They outweighed him at least four to one, and yet he almost threw them off.

"Come out!" all four commanded.

The second spirit lost his grip on Bobby and jolted upward as Bobby suddenly relaxed. The spirit immediately found himself in the waiting hands of two warriors.

"Depart from this region!" they ordered him.

He looked down at Bobby glaringly, and at his three remaining cohorts, then shot out of the church and streaked away.

The third demon spoke right up, speaking through Bobby's voice. "You'll never get me out! I've been here most of his life!"

"Who are you?"

"Witchcraft! Lots of witchcraft!"

"It's time for you to leave," said Hank.

"Never! We're not alone, you know! There are many of us!"

"Only three by my count."

"Yes, in him, yes. But you'll never get to us all. Go ahead and cast us out of this one; there are still millions in the town. Millions!" The demon laughed uproariously.

Andy ventured a question. "And what are you all doing here?"

"This is our town! We own it! We're going to stay, forever!"

"We're going to cast you out!" said Hank.

Witchcraft only laughed and said, "Go ahead, try it!"

"Come out in Jesus' name!"

The demon held tightly, desperately, to Bobby. Bobby's whole body strained again.

Hank commanded again, "Witchcraft, in Jesus' name, come out!"

The demon spoke through Bobby as Bobby's eyes, wild and bulging, glared at Hank and Andy, and every sinew in his neck strained like piano wire. "I won't! I won't! He's mine!"

Hank, Andy, John, and Ron all began to pray together, pounding at Witchcraft with their prayers. The demon ducked inside Bobby and tried to hide his head under his wings; he drooled from pain and agony, he winced at every mention of Jesus. The praying continued. Witchcraft began to gasp for breath. He cried out.

"Rafar," Bobby cried. "Ba-al Rafar!"

"Say that again?"

The demon continued to cry out through Bobby, "Rafar . . . Rafar . . ."

"Who is Rafar?" Hank asked.

"Rafar . . . is Rafar . . . is Rafar . . . is Rafar . . ." Bobby's body twitched, and he spoke like a sickening broken record.

"And who is Rafar?" Andy asked.

"Rafar rules. He rules. Rafar is Rafar. Rafar is lord."

"Jesus is Lord," John reminded the demon.

"Satan is lord!" the demon argued.

"You said Rafar was lord," Hank said.

"Satan is lord of Rafar."

"What is Rafar lord of?"

"Rafar is lord of Ashton. Rafar rules Ashton."

Andy tried a hunch. "Is he prince over Ashton?"

"Rafar is prince. Prince of Ashton."

"Well, we rebuke him too!" said Ron.

Near the big dead tree, Rafar spun quickly around as if someone had just pricked him, and he eyed several of his demons suspiciously.

The demon continued to spout his boasts, speaking through Bobby, whose face contorted in almost a perfect representation of the demon's expressions.

"We are many, many, many!" the demon boasted.

"And Ashton is your town?" asked Hank.

"Except for you, praying man!"

"Then it's time to start praying," said Andy, and they all did.

The demon grimaced in terrible pain, desperately hiding its head under its wings and hanging onto Bobby with all its rapidly ebbing strength.

"No . . . no . . . no!" it whimpered.

"Let go, Witchcraft," said Hank, "and come out of him."

"Please let me stay. I won't hurt him, I promise!"

A sure sign. Hank and Andy glanced at each other. The thing was about to go.

Hank looked directly into Bobby's eyes and commanded, "Spirit, come out in Jesus' name! Now!"

The demon shrieked as his talons began to slip loose from Bobby. Slowly, inch by inch, they began to withdraw despite the demon's most frantic efforts to keep them driven in. He screamed and cursed, and the sounds came out through Bobby's throat as the very last talon broke loose and the demon fluttered upward. The angels were about to command him to leave the region, but he was already on his way.

"I'm going, I'm going!" he hissed, streaking away.

Bobby relaxed, as did the four men who were ministering to him.

"Okay, Bobby?" Andy asked.

Bobby—the real Bobby—answered, "Yeah . . . there are still some in there, I can feel them."

"We'll rest a minute and then get them all out," said Hank.

"Yeah," said Bobby. "Let's do that."

Ron patted Bobby's knee. "You're doing all right, man!"

Just then, Mary walked into the sanctuary to see if she could help in any way. She had heard they were ministering to someone in here and she didn't feel right staying home.

But then she saw Bobby. The man! The man in leather! She froze in her place.

Bobby looked up and saw her.

So did one of the demons inside him. Suddenly Bobby's face changed from that of an exhausted and frightened young man to that of a leering, lustful, raping spirit.

"Hey there," said the spirit through Bobby, and then the spirit referred to Mary in lascivious, obscene terms.

Hank and the others were shocked, but they knew who was doing the speaking. Hank looked toward Mary, and she was backing away, terrified.

"He's—he's the one who threatened me in the parking lot!" she cried.

The demon spouted more obscenities.

Hank intervened immediately. "Spirit, be quiet!"

The spirit cursed at him. "That's your wife, eh?"

"I bind you in Jesus' name."

Bobby curled and writhed as if in terrible pain; the demon was feeling the sting of their prayers.

"Leave me alone!" it screamed. "I want to—I want to . . ." It went on to describe rape in hideous detail.

Mary recoiled, but then regathered herself and spoke back, "How dare you! I'm a child of God, and I don't have to put up with that kind of talk. You be silent and come out of him!"

Bobby curled like a stuck worm and retched.

"Let him go, Rape!" commanded Andy.

"Let go of him!" said Hank.

Mary stepped closer and said firmly, "I rebuke you, demon! In Jesus' name I rebuke you!"

The demon fell from Bobby as if struck by a wrecking ball and fluttered about on the floor. Krioni scooped him up and flung him out of the church.

The one remaining spirit was quite intimidated but very obnoxious anyway. "I beat up a woman today!"

"We don't want to hear about it," said John. "Just get out of there!"

"I hit her and I kicked her and I beat her up—"

"Be quiet and come out!" Hank ordered.

The demon cursed loudly and left, helped on his way by Krioni.

Bobby slumped to the floor exhausted, but a gentle smile crossed his face and he started to laugh happily. "They're gone! Thank God, they're gone!"

Hank, Andy, John, and Ron moved in to comfort him. Mary stayed back, still unsure of this seedy-looking character.

Andy was clear and direct. "Bobby, you need to have the Holy Spirit in your life. You need Jesus if you want to stay free of those things."

"I'm ready, man, I'm ready!" Bobby said.

Right then and there, Bobby Corsi became a new creation. And his first words as a Christian were, "Guys, this town's in trouble! Wait'll you hear what I've been up to and who I've been working for!"

27

It always took place in Professor Juleen Langstrat's apartment, in the darkened living room, sitting on the warm, comfortable sofa, illumined by the one candle on the coffee table. Langstrat was always the teacher and guide, giving instructions in her calm, clear voice. Shawn was always there as a moral supporter and fellow-participant. Sandy was never alone.

They had been meeting like this regularly now, and each time was a whole new adventure. The quiet, restful excursions into other levels of consciousness were like opening a whole new door to a higher reality, the world of psychic powers and experiences. Sandy was totally enthralled.

The metronome on the coffee table ticked, a slow, restful, steady rhythm, breathing in, breathing out, relax, relax, relax.

Sandy was getting quite skilled at dropping below the upper levels of consciousness, those levels in which all humans normally operate, but which are the most distracted and cluttered by outside stimuli. Somewhere below that were the deeper levels where true psychic ability and experience could be found. To reach these levels took careful, methodical relaxation, meditation, concentration. Langstrat had taught her all the steps.

As Sandy sat very still on the couch and Shawn watched intently, Langstrat counted down slowly, steadily, in cadence with the metronome.

"Twenty-five, twenty-four, twenty-three . . ."

In Sandy's mind she was riding an elevator, descending into the lower levels of her being, relaxing, putting her upper levels of brain activity on hold while she moved through the lower realms.

"Three, two, one, Alpha level," said Langstrat. "Now, open the door."

Sandy visualized herself opening the elevator door and stepping into a beautiful green meadow bordered by trees covered with pink and white blossoms. The air was warm, and a playful breeze wafted across the meadow like gentle caresses. Sandy looked here and there.

"Do you see her?" Langstrat asked gently.

"I'm still looking," Sandy answered. Then her face brightened. "Oh, here she comes! She's beautiful!"

Sandy could see the girl coming toward her, a beautiful young lady with cascading blonde hair, all dressed in shimmering white linen. Her face glowed with happiness. She was extending her hands in greeting.

"Hello!" Sandy called happily.

"Hello," said the girl in the most beautiful and melodic voice Sandy had ever heard.

"Have you come to guide me?"

The blonde girl took Sandy's hands in her own and looked into her eyes with tremendous kindness and compassion. "Yes. My name is Madeline. I will teach you."

Sandy looked at Madeline with amazement. "You look so young! Have you lived before?"

"Yes. Hundreds of times. But each life was simply a step upward. I'll show you the way."

Sandy was ecstatic. "Oh, I want to learn. I want to go with you."

Madeline took Sandy by the hand and began to lead her across the green meadow toward an immaculate golden walkway.

As Sandy sat on the sofa in Langstrat's apartment, her face full of joy and rapture, gleaming talons penetrated her skull as the black and gnarled hands of a hideous demon held her head in a viselike grip. The spirit leaned over her and whispered the words to her mind, "Then come. Come with me. I will introduce you to others who have ascended even before me."

"Love to!" Sandy responded.

Langstrat and Shawn smiled at each other.

Tom McBride, the paste-up man, heard the little bell over the front door ring and could only moan. This day had been the most traumatic he'd ever been through. He scurried to the front just in time to see Marshall come in and make a beeline for his office.

Tom was distraught and full of questions. "Marshall, where have you been, and where's Bernice? The papers haven't come from the printer! I've had nothing but calls all day—I finally had to put the phone on the answering machine—and people have been coming by wondering where today's paper is."

"Where's Carmen?" Marshall asked, and Tom noticed Marshall looked very, very sick.

"Marshall," Tom asked, very worried, "what—what's wrong? What's going on around here?"

Marshall just about bit Tom's head off when he growled, "Where's Carmen?"

"She's not here. She was here, but then Bernice took off, and then she took off, and I've been here alone all day!"

Marshall flung the door to his office open and got inside. He went straight for a file drawer and yanked it out. It was empty. Tom stood at a safe distance and watched. Marshall reached under his desk and pulled out a cardboard box. The box slid out easily and lightly. He saw that it was empty too and dashed it to the floor with a loud oath.

"Is . . . is there anything I can do?" Tom asked.

Marshall flopped into his chair, his face like chalk, his hair disheveled. For a moment he just sat there, leaning his head on his hand, breathing deeply, trying to think, trying to calm down.

"Call the hospital," he finally said in a very weak voice that didn't sound much like Marshall Hogan at all.

"The—the hospital?" Tom didn't like the sound of that at all.

"Ask them how Bernice is doing."

Tom's mouth dropped open. "Bernice! Is she in the hospital? What happened?"

Marshall exploded, "Just do it, Tom!"

Tom scurried to a phone. Marshall got up and went to his door. "Tom . . ."

Tom looked up, but kept trying to dial the phone.

Marshall leaned on the doorpost. He felt so weak, so helpless. "Tom, I'm sorry. I'm really sorry. Thanks for making that call. Let me know what they say."

And with that, Marshall turned and went back into his office, flopping into his chair and sitting there motionless.

Tom came back with his report. "Uh . . . Bernice had a cracked rib, and they wrapped it . . . but no other serious injuries. Somebody brought her car back from Baker, so they released her and she drove home. That's where she is now."

"Yeah . . . *I* gotta get home . . ."

"What happened to her?"

"She was beat up. Somebody jumped her, clobbered her."

"Marshall . . ." Tom was almost too horrified for words. "That's . . . well . . . that's terrible."

Marshall worked himself out of the chair and leaned against his desk.

Tom was still concerned. "Marshall, is there going to be a Friday edition? We sent paste-ups to the printer . . . I don't understand."

"They didn't print it," Marshall answered blandly.

"What? Why not?"

Marshall let his head fall forward, and he shook it just a little. He blew out a sigh, then looked at Tom again. "Tom, just go ahead and take the day off, what's left of it. Let me get squared away here and then I'll call you, okay?"

"Well . . . okay."

Tom went into the back room for his lunchbox and his coat.

The phone rang, a different line, a number Marshall reserved for special calls. Marshall picked it up.

"*Clarion*," he said.

"Marshall?"

"Yeah . . ."

"Marshall, this is Eldon Strachan."

Oh, thank God, he's alive! Marshall felt his throat tighten. He thought he would cry. "Eldon, are you all right?"

"Well, no. We just got back from a trip. Marshall, someone just tore up my house. The place is a mess!"

"Is Doris all right?"

"Well, she's upset. *I'm* upset."

"We've all been hit, Eldon. They're on to us."

"What's happened?"

Marshall recounted it all to him. The hardest part of all was telling Eldon Strachan that his friend and fellow outcast, Ted Harmel, was dead.

Strachan had trouble speaking for quite some time. Several minutes were spent in an awkward, painful silence, interrupted only a few times by either man asking if the other was still on the line.

"Marshall," Strachan finally said, "we'd better run. We'd just better get the heck out of here and not come back."

"Run where?" Marshall asked. "You already ran once, remember? As long as you're alive, Eldon, you're going to be living with this and they're going to know it."

"But what can any of us do anyway?"

"You have friends, for crying out loud! What about the state attorney general?"

"I told you, I can't go to Norm Mattily with nothing but my word; I need more than just our friendship. I need proof, some kind of documentation."

Marshall looked down at the empty cardboard box. "I'll get you something, Eldon. One way or another, I'll get you something to show to anybody who'll listen."

Eldon sighed. "I just don't know how much longer this is going to have to go on . . ."

"As long as we let it, Eldon."

He thought for a moment, then said, "Yeah, yeah, you're right. You get me something solid, and I'll see what I can do."

"We have no choice. Our necks are on the block right now; we've got to save ourselves!"

"Well, I certainly intend to do that. Doris and I are going to disappear, and fast, and I'd advise you to do the same. We sure can't stay around here."

"So where do I reach you?"

"I won't tell you over the phone. Just wait to hear from Norm Mattily's office. It'll mean I got through to him, and that's the only way I'll be any good to you anyway."

"If I'm not here, if I've skipped town or ended up dead, have him contact Al Lemley at the *New York Times*. I'll try to leave word with him."

"I'll see you again sometime."

"Let's pray that you do."

"Oh, I'm starting to pray a lot these days."

Marshall hung up, locked all the doors, and headed for home.

Bernice lay on her couch with an ice bag over her face and an uncomfortable bandage around her rib cage, and she really did want a phone call. She had already thrown up once, her head was throbbing, and she felt miserable, but she wanted a phone call. What was happening out there? She tried calling the *Clarion,* but no one answered. She called Marshall's home, but no one answered there either.

Well, what do you know! The phone rang. She snatched it up like an owl grabbing a mouse.

"Hello?"

"Bernice Krueger?"

"Kevin?"

"Yeah, man . . ." He sounded very nervous and high-strung. "Hey, I'm dying, man, I mean I am really scared!"

"Where are you, Kevin?"

"I'm at home. Hey, somebody came in here and tore the place apart!"

"Is your door closed?"

"Yeah."

"Then why don't you lock it?"

"Yeah, I got it locked. I'm scared, man. They must have a contract out on me."

"Be very careful what you say, Kevin. What we heard about our phones being bugged is probably true. They may have bugged your phone."

Weed didn't say anything for a moment; then he cursed out of sheer fright. "Oh man, I just got a call from you know who! You think they heard us talking?"

"I don't know. We just have to be careful."

"What am I gonna do? It's all going down, man. Susan says she's got the goods, and it's all going down! She's gonna split that place—"

Bernice cut him short. "Kevin, don't say another word. You'd better tell me in person. Let's meet somewhere."

"But won't they know where we're meeting?"

"Hey, if they know they know, but at least we'll have some control over what they hear."

"Well, let's do it quick, and I mean *quick!*"

"How about that bridge a few miles north of Baker, the one over the Judd River?"

"The big green one?"

"Yeah, that one. There's a turn-off right at the north end of it. I can be there by . . ." Bernice looked at her wall clock. ". . . let's say 7."

"I'll be there."

"Okay. Good-bye."

Bernice immediately dialed the *Clarion.* No answer. She dialed Marshall at home.

The telephone in the Hogan kitchen rang and rang, but Marshall and Kate remained silent at the kitchen table, letting it ring until finally it stopped.

Kate, her hands shaking just a little, her breathing consciously controlled, looked at her husband with tear-filled eyes.

"The telephone has a way of bringing consistently bad news," she quipped, her eyes dropping for a moment.

Right now Marshall had as much intestinal fortitude as an empty garbage bag, and for one rare occasion in his life he was at a loss for words.

"When did you get that call?" he finally asked.

"This morning."

"But you don't know who it was?"

Kate took a deep breath, trying to stay on top of her emotions. "Whoever it was, he knew just about everything about you and me, and even Sandy; so he wasn't just a crank in that respect. His . . . credentials were very impressive."

"But he was lying!" Marshall said angrily.

"I know," Kate answered assertively.

"It's just another smear tactic, Kate. They're trying to take away my newspaper, they're trying to take away my home, and now they're trying to destroy my marriage. There isn't now, nor has there ever been any kind of goings-on between Bernice and me. For crying out loud, I'm old enough to be her father!"

"I know," Kate answered again. She took a moment to build up strength to continue. "Marshall, you are my man, and if I were ever to lose you I know I'd never find one better. I also know you're not a man given to just tossing around his passions. I have a prize in you, and I've never forgotten that."

He took her hand. "And you're all the woman I could ever handle."

She squeezed his hand as she said, "I do have confidence that these things will never change. I suppose it's that kind of confidence that's kept me hanging on, waiting . . ."

Her voice trailed off, and there was a moment of silence. Kate had to choke down her emotions, and Marshall couldn't think of anything to say.

"Marshall," she said finally, "there are some other things that haven't changed either, but those things were supposed to change; you and I agreed together that they would. We agreed that things would be different after we moved from New York, that you would take it easy, that you would have more time for your family, that maybe we could all get to know one another again and patch things up." The tears began to flow and it was difficult for her to speak, but she was committed now, so she kept going. "I don't know what it is, whether the ultimate scoop simply tags after you no matter where you go or if you concoct it on your own, time after time. But if I were to ever be jealous or suspicious of another lover, that's what the lover would be.

You do have another love, Marshall, and I just don't know if I can compete with it."

Marshall knew he'd never be able to fully explain everything. "Kate, you've no idea how big this whole thing is."

She shook her head. She didn't want to hear it. "That's not at issue here. As a matter of fact, I'm sure it is big, it is extremely important, it probably does warrant the amount of time and energy you've put into it. But what I am coping with now is the detriment that this whole thing has been to myself, to Sandy, and to this family. Marshall, I don't care about comparisons; no matter where Sandy and I have been placed on your list of priorities, we are still suffering, and that is the direct problem that I'm dealing with. I can't care about anything else."

"Kate . . . that's what they want!"

"They're getting it," she countered abruptly. "But don't you dare blame anyone else for your failure to live up to your promises. No one else is responsible for your promises, Marshall, and I am holding you responsible for the promises you made to your family."

"Kate, I didn't ask for this to come up, I didn't ask for this to happen. When it's all over—"

"It's over now!" That stopped him cold. "And it's not really a matter of choice for me. I have my limitations, Marshall. I know there's only so much I can take. I have to get away."

Marshall was too weak to say a word. He couldn't even think of any words. All he could do was look her in the eye and let her speak, let her do whatever she had to do.

Kate kept going. She had to get it all out before she would be unable to. "I talked to my mom this morning. She was very supportive of both of us, and she's not taking sides at all. As a matter of fact—and you might find this interesting—she's been praying for us, for you in particular. She says she even dreamt about you the other night; she dreamt that you were in trouble and that God would send His angels to help you if she prayed. She took the whole thing pretty seriously, and she's been praying ever since."

Marshall smiled weakly. He appreciated that, but what good was it doing?

Kate came to the bottom line. "I'm going to stay with her for a while. I need time to think. And *you* need time to think. We both need to know for sure just which of your promises you are truly willing to live up to. We need to get it settled once and for all, Marshall, before we go one step further.

"As for Sandy, right now I don't even know where she is. If I can find her I might ask her to come with me, although I doubt she'll want to leave Shawn and everything they're involved in." She drew a deep breath as this new pain took hold of her. "All I can say is, you don't know her anymore, Marshall. *I* don't know her. She's been slipping away and slipping away . . . and you were never here." She couldn't go on. She buried her face in her hands and wept.

Marshall found himself wondering if he should even go to her, comfort her, put his arms around her. Would she accept it? Would she even believe that he cared?

He did care. His own heart was breaking. He went to her and gently put his hand on her shoulder.

"I won't give you any pat answers," he said quietly. "You're right. Everything you've said is right. And I don't dare make any more promises now that I may not be able to keep." The words hurt even as he forced himself to say them. "I do need to think about it. I need to do some real housecleaning. Why don't you go ahead? Go ahead and stay with your mom for a while, get away from all this mess. I'll . . . I'll let you know when it's all over, when I'm settled on what's important. I won't even ask you to come back until then."

"I love you, Marshall," she said as she wept.

"I love you too, Kate."

She rose suddenly and embraced him, giving him a kiss he would remember for a long time, a kiss when she held him desperately tight, when her face was wet with tears, when her body trembled with her weeping. He held her with his strong arms as if he were hanging on to his very life, a priceless treasure he might never have again.

Then she said, "I'd better just go," and gave him one final hug.

He held her for one last moment and then said as comfortingly as he could, "It'll be okay. Good-bye."

Her bags were already packed. She didn't take much. After the front door quietly closed behind her and their little pickup truck eased out of the driveway, Marshall sat alone at the kitchen table for a very long time. He numbly stared at the woodgrain patterns in the tabletop, a thousand memories flooding through his mind. Minutes upon minutes passed without his heed; the world went on without him.

At last his stupor crumbled as all his thoughts and feelings came to rest on her name, "Kate . . ." and he cried and cried.

28

Guilo bit his lower lip and surveyed the valley below, along with his two dozen warriors. From their vantage point halfway down the mountain slopes and in among the rocks, the Strongman's Lair was a boiling, humming caldron of black spirits, their myriads forming a swarming, living haze over the cluster of buildings below. The sound of their wings was a constant, low-pitched drone that echoed back upon itself from the rocky crags all around. The demons were very disturbed right now, like an angry hive of bees.

"They're building up for something," a warrior observed.

"Even so," said Guilo, "something doesn't feel right, and I would venture to say it has to do with *her*."

All around the complex, vans and trailers were packed with everything from the office supplies right down to Alexander M. Kaseph's stuffed trophies. The personnel were now going through their dormitories, packing up their personal belongings and sweeping out the rooms. Everywhere there was a pervading excitement and anticipation, and people clustered here and there, chattering in their native languages.

In the big stone house, secluded from all the activity, Susan Jacobson worked hurriedly in her private room, consolidating a huge box of records, ledgers, documents, printed matter. She was trying to eliminate anything she didn't absolutely need, but almost every item seemed indispensable. Even so, only one suitcase—now sitting on her dresser—would have to contain it all. So far, the load was too bulky to fit in the suitcase and too heavy for Susan to carry even if it did.

With some hastily muttered prayers and some more quick perusals, she eliminated half of the items. She then took what was left and began to carefully arrange it all in the suitcase, a ledger here, some affidavits there, more documents, some photographs, another ledger, a computer printout, a thick ream of photocopies, some undeveloped film.

Footsteps in the hall! She hurriedly closed the suitcase, pressing the lid shut so she could fasten the latches, and then lugged the heavy thing over to the big bed where she quickly slid it underneath. She then threw all the other unpacked items back into the box and concealed the box on a shelf behind some linens in a small closet.

Without knocking, Kaseph came into the room. He wore casual clothes because he too had been packing and taking part in all the activity.

She went to him and threw her arms around him. "Well, hi! How are things on your end?"

He returned her embrace briefly, then dropped his arms and began to look around the room.

"We were wondering whatever became of you," he said. "We are meeting in the dining hall, and we were hoping you would attend." There was something strange and ominous in his tone.

"Well," she said, a little abashed at his demeanor, "of course I'm going to attend. I wouldn't miss it for anything."

"Good, good," he said, still looking around the room. "Susan, may I look through your suitcase?"

She looked at him curiously. "What?"

He would not change or qualify his question. "I want to look in your suitcase."

"Whatever for?"

"Bring it here," he said in a tone not to be argued with.

She went to her closet, brought out a large blue suitcase full of clothes, and laid it on the bed. He opened the latches and threw back the lid, then proceeded to very quickly and very rudely unpack it, throwing its contents here and there.

"Hey," she protested, "what are you doing? It took me hours to get all that in there!"

He thoroughly emptied it, opening every side pocket, unloading and shaking out every garment. When he had finished, she was quite angry.

"Alex, what is the meaning of this?"

He turned to her with a very grim expression, and then his face suddenly broke into a smile. "I'm sure you can pack your suitcase even more efficiently the second time." She knew she didn't dare give him any comeback for that. "But it was necessary for me to check on something. You see, dear Susan, you've been absent from the normal flow of the population and absent from my presence for a considerable time." He began to walk slowly around the room, his eyes darting over every nook and corner of it. "And it seems there are some very important records and files missing, things of a very delicate nature—things that you, my Maidservant, would have access to." He smiled that same old smile that cut like a knife. "Of course, I know that your heart is indeed in union with mine, despite your . . . second thoughts and petty fears of late."

She raised her head high and looked right at him. "Those things are strictly the weakness of my humanity, but something over which I expect to gain a victory."

"The weakness of your humanity . . ." He thought that over for a moment. "That same little weakness that has always made you so intriguing, because it could make you so very dangerous."

"You are implying, then, that I could betray you?"

He approached her and rested his hands on her shoulders. Susan imagined how his hands would not have to move far to clamp around her neck.

"It is possible," he said, "that someone is trying to betray me, even now. I can read it in the atmosphere." He looked at her very closely, his eyes burrowing into hers. "I might even be reading it in your very own eyes."

She turned her eyes away and said, "I would not betray you."

He leaned closer and said very coolly, "Nor would anyone else . . . if they knew what would be in store for them. It would be a very serious business indeed."

She felt his hands tighten their grip.

A messenger streaked across the sky and then darted, zigzagged, and weaved through the woods above Ashton looking for Tal.

"Captain!" he called, but Tal was not there among the others. "Where is the captain?"

Mota answered, "Carrying out another prayer gathering at Hank Busche's home. Be careful not to attract attention."

The messenger soared down the hillside and floated quietly into the maze of streets and alleys below.

At Hank's house, Tal remained carefully hidden within the walls while some of his warriors carried out his orders, bringing in people ready to pray.

Hank and Andy Forsythe had called a special prayer meeting, but they hadn't expected so many people to show up. More and more cars kept arriving, and more and more people kept filing through the door: the Colemans, Ron Forsythe and Cynthia, newly saved Bobby Corsi, his parents Dan and Jean, the Joneses, the Coopers, the Smiths, the Bartons, some college students and their friends. Hank brought out whatever extra chairs he had. People began to find places on the floor. The room was getting stuffy; the windows were opened.

Tal looked out front and saw an old station wagon pull up. He smiled broadly. This was one arrival Hank would be glad to see.

When the doorbell rang several people hollered, "Come in," but whoever it was didn't come in. Hank stepped over several people to get to the door and opened it.

There stood Lou Stanley, together with his wife Margie. They were holding hands.

Lou smiled timidly and asked, "Hi, Hank. Is this where you're holding the prayer meeting?"

Hank believed again in miracles. Here was the man who had been removed from the church for adultery, now standing before him re-united with his wife and wanting to pray with all the others!

"Wow," said Hank, "it sure is! Come on in!"

Lou and Margie entered the packed living room, where they were greeted with love and acceptance.

Just then there was another knock on the door. Hank was still standing there, so he opened the door and saw an older man and his wife standing outside. He had never seen either one of them before.

But Cecil Cooper knew who they were; he called to them from where he was sitting. "Well, praise the Lord! I don't believe it! James and Diane Farrel!"

Hank looked at Cecil, and then at the couple standing there, and his mouth dropped open. "Reverend Farrel?"

Reverend James Farrel, former pastor of Ashton Community Church, extended his hand. "Pastor Henry Busche?" Hank nodded, taking his hand. "We got word there was a prayer meeting here to-night."

Hank invited them in with outstretched arms.

Meanwhile, the messenger arrived and found Tal. "Captain, Guilo sends word that Susan's time is very short! She is very near discovery. You must come *now!*"

Tal took a quick survey of the prayer cover he had gathered. It had to be enough for tonight's plan to work.

Hank was starting the meeting. "The Lord has impressed on all of us that we need to pray tonight for Ashton. Now we've learned some things this afternoon, and we were sure right about Satan having a grip on this town. We need to pray that God will bind the demons that are trying to take over, and we need to pray for victory for the people of God, and for the angels of God . . ."

Good, good! Tal thought. It might be enough. But if what the messenger said was truly the situation at the Strongman's Lair, they would have to proceed with the plan whether the prayer cover was sufficient or not.

The demonic cloud over the valley continued to thicken and swirl, and from their vantage point Guilo and his warriors could see the glimmer of millions of pairs of yellow eyes.

Guilo could not relax at all, but continually watched over the mountaintops for the one streak of light that would mark Tal's arrival. "Where is Tal?" he muttered. "Where is he? They know. They *know!*"

At this very moment Kaseph's entire staff, the implementing force behind Omni Corporation, was gathered in the dining hall for a make-shift banquet and final get-together before the big move for which they had all prepared. It was an informal buffet affair; everything was casual, and the mood was light. Kaseph himself, usually aloof from his inferiors, mingled freely with them now, and hands often reached out to him as if imploring a special blessing.

Susan remained steadfastly by his side, dressed again in her customary black suit, and hands also reached out to her for a special touch, a special glance or look of blessing. These she freely bestowed on the grateful followers.

As the meal got underway, Kaseph and Susan took their places at the head table. She tried to act normal and enjoy her food, but her master still maintained that smile, that strange, cutting, wicked smile, and it unnerved her. She had to wonder how much he really knew.

Toward the end of the dinner Kaseph stood, and as if on signal everyone in the room immediately became silent.

"As we have done in other regions, in other parts of our rapidly uniting world, so we shall do here," Kaseph said, and the whole room applauded. "As a decisive and powerful tool of the Universal Consciousness Society, Omni Corporation is about to establish still another foothold for the coming New World Order and the rule of the New Age Christ. I have received word from our advance people in Ashton that the purchase of our new facility can be finalized on Sunday, and I will personally go before you to close the deal. After that, the town will be ours."

The room broke into applause and cheers.

But then, with a rather abrupt change of mood, Kaseph let a scowl come upon his face, to which all those present responded with an equal sobriety. "Of course, all through this massive effort we have often been reminded of how serious this business really is in which we are involved, to which we have vowed our lives and our allegiances. We have often pondered how dire the results would be to everything we have worked toward if any one of us should ever turn toward the wrong and answer the persistent call of greed, temporality, or even,"— he looked at Susan—"human weakness."

Suddenly the room was dead quiet. Everyone's gaze was upon Kaseph as his eyes scanned slowly across the whole group.

Susan could feel a terror starting to form deep down inside, a terror she had always tried to push down, avoid, control. She could feel the one thing she feared most of all slowly stalking up on her.

Kaseph continued, "Only a few of you are aware that in the course of transferring the files from the head office we discovered that several of our most sensitive folders were missing. Apparently someone with high privilege and inside access thought those files would be of value . . . some other way." The people began to gasp and murmur. "Oh, don't be alarmed. I have a happy ending to this story. The missing files have been found!" They were all relieved, and chuckled amongst themselves. This, they seemed to think, was another one of Kaseph's little teasers.

Kaseph signaled to some security men toward the back of the room, and one of them picked up—what was it? Susan rose from her chair just a little to see.

A cardboard box. No! *The* cardboard box? The one she had hidden behind the linens? He was bringing it toward the front, toward the head table.

She remained where she was, but she thought she would faint. Her whole body trembled with fear. The blood drained from her face; her insides were riddled with horrible pain. She had been discovered. There was no way out. It was a nightmare.

The security guard lifted the heavy box onto the table, and Kaseph flung it open. Yes, there were all the materials she had so painstakingly sorted out and hidden. He lifted them out, and held them up for all to see. The whole crowd gasped in astonishment.

Kaseph threw the materials back into the box and let the guard carry it away.

"This box," he announced, "was found hidden in the Maidservant's linen closet."

All were stunned. Some remained frozen with shock. Some shook their heads.

Susan Jacobson prayed. She prayed furiously.

The messenger arrived back in the valley, and Guilo was voracious for news.

"Yes, speak up!"

"He is gathering the prayer cover for the operation tonight. He should be here any moment."

"Any moment may be too late." Guilo looked toward the buildings below. "Any moment and Susan might be dead."

Tal watched while the gathered people prayed intently as the Holy Spirit led them and empowered them. They were praying specifically for the confounding of the demonic hosts. It just might be enough! He slipped out of the house, shrouded by the darkness. He would pass quickly through the town and then fly to the Strongman's Lair, hopefully in time to save Susan's life.

But no sooner had he stepped into the narrow and rutted alley behind the house than he felt a sharp pain in his leg. His sword flashed into view in an instant, and in one quick movement he beheaded a small spirit that had been clinging to him. It dissolved in a puff of blood-red smoke.

Another spirit clamped onto his back. He swept it away. Another on his back, another on his leg, two more slashing and nipping at his head!

"It is *Tal!*" he heard them squeak and chatter. "It is Captain Tal!"

Much more of this noise and they would bring Rafar! Tal knew he would have to vanquish them all or risk exposure. The demons around his head went quickly enough. He swept his sword up and across his back and dismembered the one clinging there.

But they seemed to multiply. Some of them were quite sizable, and all were greedy for the reward Rafar would give for whoever revealed Tal's whereabouts.

A large, laughing spirit flew in close for a look at Tal, and then shot straight into the sky. Tal followed after him in an explosion of light and power and grabbed his ankles. The spirit screamed and began to claw at him. Tal dropped back to earth like a stone, dragging the spirit down with him, the spirit's wings flapping and fluttering like a torn umbrella. Once under the cover of trees and houses, Tal's sword sent the spirit into the abyss.

But more demons were coming upon him from all directions. The word was spreading.

Two powerful and muscular guards, the same two men who had once been her tuxedoed escorts, dragged and carried Susan between them, hardly letting her use her own feet to carry herself, across the grounds, up onto the porch of the big stone house, inside, up the ornate staircase, and down the upstairs hall to her room. Kaseph followed, cool, collected, perfectly ruthless.

The guards threw Susan down in a chair and held her there with their full weight, preventing her escape. Kaseph took a long, icy look at her.

"Susan," he said, "my dear Susan, I am not really shocked at this. Such problems have happened before, with many others, many times. And every time we've had to deal with it. As you well know, such problems never remain. Never."

He moved in close, so close his words seemed to slap her like little whips. "I never trusted you, Susan, I told you that. So I've kept my eye on you, I've had the others keep their eye on you, and I see now that you have rekindled your friendship with my . . . *rival,* Mr. Weed." He laughed at that.

"I have eyes and ears everywhere, dear Susan. Since the moment your Mr. Weed went to the *Ashton Clarion,* we have made his business, every aspect of it, our business: where he goes, whom he knows, whomever he calls, and whatever he says. And as for the hurried and careless call you made to him today . . ." He laughed loudly. "Susan, did you really think we wouldn't monitor every phone call going out of here? We knew you would make your move sooner or later. All we had to do was wait and be ready. An undertaking such as ours is naturally going to have enemies. We understand that."

He leaned over her, his eyes cold and cunning. "But we most certainly do not tolerate it. No, Susan, we deal with it, harshly and abruptly. I had thought that one little harassment would silence Weed, but now I find that, thanks to you, he knows far too much. Therefore, it will be best if you *and* your Mr. Weed are taken care of."

All she could do was tremble; she could think of nothing to say. She knew it would be useless to beg for mercy.

"You have never been to one of our blood rituals, have you?" Kaseph began to explain it to her as if giving a short lecture. "The ancient worshipers of Isis, or Molech, or Ashtoreth, were not too far afield in their practices. They understood, at least, that the offering of a human life to their so-called gods seemed to bring the gods' favor upon them.

"What they performed in ignorance, we now continue with enlightenment. The life-force that intertwines itself through us and our universe is cyclical, never-ending, self-perpetuating. The birth of the new cannot occur without the death of the old. The birth of good is created by the death of evil. This is karma, dear Susan, your karma."

In other words, he was going to kill her.

A warrior asked Guilo, "What is that? What are they doing?"

They both listened. The cloud, still stirring and swirling slowly about the valley floor, was trickling and babbling now with a strange sound, an indefinable noise that gradually rose in volume and pitch. At first it sounded like the rush of faraway waves, then it grew into the roar of a numberless mob. From this it crescendoed into an eerie wailing of millions of sirens.

Guilo slowly brought his sword out, and the metal of the blade rang.

"What are you doing?" asked the warrior.

"Prepare!" Guilo ordered, and the order was spread among the group. Ring, ring, ring went their blades as each warrior took his sword in his hand.

"They're laughing," said Guilo. "There's nothing we can do but go in."

The warrior was willing, and yet the thought was unthinkable. "Go in? Go into . . . that?"

The demons were strong, brutal, savage . . . and now they were laughing with the smell of approaching death like sweet perfume in their nostrils.

Triskal and Krioni came swooping into the valley, swords blazing and sweeping in lethal arcs of light as demons disintegrated on all sides. Other warriors shot into the sky like flares from a cannon, plucking fleeing demons out of the air, silencing them.

Tal was in a real bind, wishing he could release his fighting power full force and yet needing to remain subdued lest he draw attention to himself. Thus he could not vanquish the spirits now clustering on him like angry bees in one violent attack, but rather had to pluck them off one by one, hacking and chopping with his sword.

Mota entered the scuffle and came in close to Tal, swinging his sword and plucking demons off his captain like bats off a cave wall. "There! There now! And another!"

Then came one infinitesimal moment when Tal was clean of demons. Mota quickly slipped into his place while Tal vanished into the ground.

The spirits were enraged by the fighting, and at first continued to flock and circle about the area; but then they realized that Tal had somehow slipped away and they were only placing themselves in the hands of heavenly warriors to be destroyed for no reason.

Their numbers quickly dwindled, their cries ebbed away, and soon they were gone.

Several miles outside of Ashton, Tal shot out of the ground like a bullet from a rifle, streaking across the sky, a trail of light following him like the tail of a comet, his sword held straight out in front of him. Farms, fields, forests, and highways became a blur beneath him; the clouds became rushing mountains passing by on either side.

He could feel his strength building with the prayers of the saints; his sword began to burn with power, glowing brilliantly. He almost felt it was pulling him through the sky.

Faster and faster, the wind screaming, the distance shrinking, his wings an invisible roar, he flew for the Strongman's Lair.

A very strange-looking, black-robed and beaded, long-haired little guru from some dark and pagan land stepped into Susan's room at Kaseph's bidding. He bowed in obeisance to his lord and master, Kaseph.

"Prepare the altar," said Kaseph. "There will be a special offering for the success of our endeavor."

The little pagan priest left quickly. Kaseph returned his attention to Susan.

He took one look at her and then gave her the back of his hand.

"Stop that!" he shouted "Stop that praying!"

The force of the blow nearly knocked her out of the chair, but one guard held her firmly. Her head sank and she began to sob in very short, shallow gasps of terror.

Kaseph, like a conqueror, stood above her and boasted over her limp and trembling form. "You have no God to call upon! With the nearness of your death you crumble, you fall back upon old myths and religious nonsense!"

Then he said, almost kindly, "What you don't realize is that I'm actually doing you a favor. Perhaps in your next life your understanding will be deeper, your frailties will have fallen away. Your sacrificial gift to us now will build wonderful karma for you in the lives to come. You'll see."

Then he spoke to the guards. "Bind her!"

They grabbed her wrists and held them behind her; she heard a click and felt the cold steel of the manacles. She heard herself screaming.

Kaseph went to his office, now a bare room except for a few remaining shipping crates and travel cases. He went directly to a small case covered with fine old leather and tucked it under his arm.

Then he went down the big staircase to the lower floor, through an imposing plank door and down another stairway into the deep basement below the house. He turned one corner, passed through another door, and entered a dark, candlelit room of stone. The strange little priest was already there, lighting candles and moaning some strange, unintelligible words over and over. Some of Kaseph's closest confidants were present, waiting quietly. Kaseph handed the little case to the priest, who laid it beside a large, rough-hewn bench at one end of the room. The little priest opened the case and began to set out knives—Kaseph's knives—ornate, jeweled, delicately wrought, razor-sharp.

Tal could see the mountains ahead. He would have to stay in close to their rocky sides. He must not be seen.

Guilo and his warriors remained in the darkness, unglorified, stalking step by step downward toward the complex, concealing themselves behind rocks and old snags. Just above them now, boiling and towering like a thunderhead, the cloud of leering, laughing spirits continued to swirl. Guilo was sensing some prayer cover; surely the demons would have noticed them by now, but their eyes were strangely unseeing.

Down below, parked very near the main administration building, was a large van. Guilo found a spot from which he could see the van clearly, then had his warriors fan out, keeping one warrior close by for special instructions.

"Do you see the upper window in the big stone house?" Guilo asked him.

"Yes."

"She is there. On my signal, go alone and get her out."

29

In the strange dark room below the house, Alexander M. Kaseph and his little entourage remained transfixed in deep meditation. Before them, just behind the rough wooden bench, stood the Strongman, flanked by his close guards and assistants. His sagging face was spread now with a hideous, drooling grin that bared his fangs as he chuckled with demonic delight.

"One by one the obstacles are falling," he said. "Yes, yes, your offering will bring you good fortune, and it will please me." The big yellow eyes narrowed with the command. "Bring her!"

Upstairs, sitting helplessly between the two guards, her feet and hands bound with manacles, Susan Jacobson waited and prayed. With all that was within her, she cried out to the one true God, the God whom she did not know but must be there, had to hear her, and was the only one who could help her now.

Tal reached the mountains and soared up their steep face, climbing, climbing, easing back his speed. He continued to slow as he neared the top, and then, just as he crested the summit, he stopped all motion and all sound, and let himself glide down the other side silently, invisibly. He noticed with concern that the cloud had grown even more since he'd been away. He could only hope the prayer cover would at least be sufficient to blind these foul creatures.

Guilo had been watching for the captain, and his sharp eyes saw Tal descending like a silent hawk toward them.

"Get ready," Guilo told the warrior at his side.

The warrior was poised, his eyes on that upstairs window.

Tal dropped down so low he was almost skidding along the ground. He finally came to rest right beside Guilo.

"We have the cover," he said.

"Go!" Guilo commanded the warrior, and the warrior half-flew, half-ran toward the big stone house.

The little priest, his eyes darting about with anticipation, made his way up the big staircase, humming and muttering a mantra to himself.

Kaseph and his people waited downstairs in a hushed silence, Kaseph standing right next to the knives.

Susan Jacobson tried to work the shackles loose, but they were clamped on tightly enough to cut into her even if she didn't struggle. The guards only laughed at her.

"Dear God," she prayed, "if You are truly the ruler of this universe, please have mercy on one who dared to stand for Your sake against a terrible evil . . ."

And then—as if she were no longer in that room, as if she were slowly waking up from a nightmare—the agonizing, heart-twisting fear began to ebb from her mind like a fading thought, like the slow, steady calming of a storm. Her heart was at rest. The room seemed strangely quiet. All she could do was look around with very curious eyes. What had happened? Had she died already? Was she asleep, or dreaming?

But she had felt this way before. The memory of that one night in New York came back to her; she thought of that strange, buoyed-up feeling she had had even as she clambered desperately through that window. There was someone in the room. She could sense it.

"Are you here to help me?" she asked in her heart, and the faintest little spark of hope came to life again somewhere deep inside her.

Clink! Her feet were suddenly released and could swing unbound from the chair. The shackles lay on the floor, opened. She felt something break loose from around her wrists, and she pulled her arms free. The manacles clinked to the floor, just like the shackles that had bound her feet.

She looked at the two guards, but they were just standing there looking at her, still smirking, then looking elsewhere as if nothing had happened.

Then she heard a click, and looked just in time to see the window latch twist loose and the big bedroom window swing open all by itself. The cool night air began to waft into the room.

Whether this was illusion or reality, she accepted it. She jumped up from the chair—the guards did nothing. She ran for that open window. Then she remembered.

Still keeping a wary and unbelieving eye on those guards, she hurried to the bed, reached under it, and pulled out the suitcase that Kaseph and his people had not found, even in such an obvious hiding place! It felt strangely light for all the papers she had loaded in it, but nothing at this moment made much sense anyway, so she simply accepted how easy it was to carry the suitcase to the window and set it on the rooftop outside. She looked behind her. The guards were smiling confidently at an empty chair!

Feeling as if someone was lifting her, she climbed through the window and onto the roof. A thick vine grew up one side of the house. It would make a perfect escape ladder.

Outside the administration building, some security people were talking in hushed tones about the fall of the Maidservant and her imminent fate when suddenly they heard footsteps running across the parking area.

"Hey, look there!" someone shouted.

The security men looked just in time to see a woman dressed in black scurrying for one of the trucks.

"Hey, what are you doing?"

"It's the Maidservant!"

They ran after her, but she had already reached a big moving van and climbed inside. The starter growled, the engine came to life, and with a lurch and a whine the van started rolling away.

Guilo leaped from his hiding place and bellowed, "YA-HAAA!" as
his little troop of three and twenty popped into the air like fireworks
and trailed after the van. "Cover yourselves, warriors!"

The little priest reached Susan's bedroom, and his bony hand
opened the door.

"We are ready," he declared, and suddenly realized that he was
talking to a pair of very dedicated guards making very sure an empty
chair would not get away.

The little pagan had a first-class fit; the guards had no explanation.

The van sluggishly headed up the winding and precarious road that
led out of the valley and over the mountains. Four angels swooped
down behind it and started pushing it up the grade, helping it to top
sixty. They were making good time, but looking back they could see
an oncoming legion of demons in hot pursuit, the glimmer of their
fangs and the red flicker of their blades filling the night sky.

From high above, Guilo watched the cloud. It remained where it
was, covering the Strongman. Only a small contingent of demonic
warriors had been sent after the runaway van.

Roaring up the mountain road in pursuit, four of Kaseph's armed
security men gave chase in a high-powered jeep. Even so, they had a
surprising amount of trouble catching up.

"I thought that thing had a full load!" said one.

"It does," said the other. "I loaded it myself."

"How many horses does that thing *have?*"

By now Kaseph had gotten word of Susan's escape. He ordered
eight more armed men in two more vehicles to join the chase. They
leaped into another jeep and a V-8 powered sports car and squealed
out of the parking lot.

Demons and angels converged on the van, still chugging up the
steep grade at more than sixty miles an hour, its tires growling and
often skidding sideways across the winding, reeling gravel road. The
four angels kept pushing it from behind while the other nineteen did
their best to encircle it and ward off demonic attack. Demons dove
down from above, their red swords gleaming, and engaged the heavenly warriors in fierce dogfights, the blades singing, droning, and clashing
metallically with bursts of sparks.

The van came to the summit and picked up more speed. The
pursuing vehicles topped the summit only seconds behind it. As the
van accelerated more and more, the bumps and curves in the roadway
became one death-dealing jolt or one frame-bending wrench after

another, and the van rocked, dancing on two and three wheels as it careened down the steep grade. The road went straight, then turned abruptly, then twisted back the other direction, then took a dip. The van wrestled the road as the rocks and guardrails blurred by. With each sharp curve it groaned and leaned heavily toward the outside, the big frame bottoming out the springs, the tires screeching in protest.

A very sharp left turn! The van's heavy back end fishtailed into the guardrail with a loud grinding and a fiery shower of sparks. Down the road, another dip, the springs bottoming out, the frame crunching down on the axles, groaning and creaking.

The jeeps and the sports car followed behind, doing much better at negotiating the treacherous curves but getting the ride of their lives all the same. Two men in the lead jeep had high-powered rifles ready, but it was impossible to get any clear shot. They fired a few rounds anyway, if only to scare the Maidservant.

The van was headed right for a hairpin turn, with yellow signs everywhere screaming at it to slow down and be cautious. The four angels who had been behind the van pushing were now pressed up against its sides, trying to keep it on the road. Guilo himself swooped down, his sword flashing, hacking his way through demon interceptors until he could work his way to the van. It was only a fraction of a second from the guardrail and the sheer drop beyond it when Guilo slammed forcefully into its side, jolting the front wheels to the left with a sharp jerk. The van made the turn and rolled on. The pursuers in the other vehicles had to slow down or go right through the guardrail.

But the heavenly warriors trying to encircle the van were being steadily cut away. Guilo looked just in time to see one huge spirit pounce with bared talons on top of a warrior like a hawk on a sparrow, knocking the angel senseless, making it flutter down into the deep canyon below. Another dogfight high above and to the left ended in a cry of pain from another warrior who went into a crazy spin, one wing shredded, and disappeared inside the wall of a mountain. The ringing clashes of blades echoed all around. There went a demon, disappearing in a trail of red smoke. Another angel fell toward the canyon floor, still holding his sword but listless and stunned, his demon pursuer right behind him.

The hideous warriors of hell finally began to break through and reach the van. One reached the warrior right behind Guilo and knocked him away. Guilo didn't have time to think another thought before his own sword went up to fend off the incredibly powerful blow of a spirit at least equal to himself. Guilo returned the blow, their swords locked for a moment, arm against arm, and then Guilo made good use of his foot to cave in the demon's face and sent it tumbling out over the canyon.

The van began to swerve wildly, the tires tiptoeing on the very edge of the chasm. Guilo pushed with all his might to get it back on course. The van lurched again and he realized a band of demons must be on the other side, pushing against him. He looked around for help and saw more fangs and yellow eyes than friends. A huge blade swept downward over his shoulder, and he parried it off. Another one thrust toward his midsection, and he struck that away. The van veered toward the cliff. He tried to push back, parry a blow, look for help, strike another demon, kick a face, push the van, cut a flank, parry a blow, guide the van . . .

A blow! He didn't see it coming and had no idea who had struck it, but it stunned him. He lost his grip on the van, saw the canyon floor spinning far below, saw the earth, the sky, the earth, the sky. He was falling. He spread his wings and floated downward like a torn and fallen leaf. From up above he heard a bloodcurdling howl. He looked up. This must be the one who had struck him, a very large, bulb-eyed nightmare with reptilian skin and serrated wings.

"Come, come," Guilo muttered, waiting for the thing to pounce.

It dove straight at him, its jaws gaping, its fangs glimmering, a wide, flat blade with keen edge flashing. Guilo waited. The thing raised its sword high and brought it down with a *woosh!* Guilo was suddenly three feet away from where he had been, and the blade continued on its way without their having met, the demon somersaulting wildly after it. Guilo made a blinding sweep with his own sword and dewinged the demon, then finished it.

The boiling trail of red smoke cleared away from Guilo's eyes just in time for him to see the van crash through a guardrail and sail out over the precipice. The fall was so far, so very long and extended, that the van seemed to float for an eternity before folding and crushing on the rocks below, twisting, turning, bouncing like a pop can as chairs, desks, and cabinets tumbled out the back and papers upon papers fluttered through the air like snowflakes. About thirty demons hovered high above or roosted on the remaining guardrail to watch their work come to completion. After turning and rolling over and over, the van, no longer recognizable as anything, finally came to rest in a heap of scrap and glass at the base of the mountain. The three pursuing vehicles pulled to a stop, and the twelve security men got out to take a satisfied look.

Guilo rested on a rocky crag, setting his sword down and looking skyward. High above he could make out minute streaks of light heading in several different directions, each one followed by two or three streaks of red-accented black. His warriors—what was left of them— were scattering in all directions. Guilo thought it best to remain where he was until the skies cleared. He, Tal, and their warriors would all regroup in Ashton soon enough.

Rafar still sat in his big dead tree, watching over the town of Ashton as a master at chess would sit and look over a gameboard. He enjoyed watching the many pieces and pawns make their moves against each other.

When a demon messenger brought the welcome news from the Strongman's Lair that the Maidservant, that traitorous wench, had come to a miserable end and the heavenly host had been routed, Rafar gloated and laughed. He had taken his opponent's queen!

"And so shall it be for the rest," Rafar said with diabolical glee. "The Strongman entrusted the preparation of the town to me. When he comes, he will find it unoccupied, swept, and put in order!"

He called some of his warriors. "It's time to clean house. While the heavenly host are weak and cannot stand against us, we should take care of the final obstacles. I would like Hogan and Busche put away like vanquished kings! Make use of the woman Carmen, and see to it that they are bound and helpless, a byword and a mockery! As for Kevin Weed . . ." The demon warlord's eyes narrowed with disdain. "He could never be a worthy prize for such as myself. See that he is killed, any way you wish; then bring me word." The warriors departed to carry out his orders.

Rafar heaved a deep, half-mocking sigh. "Ah, dear Captain of the Host, perhaps I will see my battle won with no more than a raised finger, a casual order, the poison of my subtlety; your sky-rending trump of battle will be displaced by a pitiful whimper, and my victory will be won without my ever having seen your face, or your sword." He looked over the town and broke into his fiendish grin, clicking his thumb talon across his other four.

"But do be sure of this: We shall meet, Tal! Do not think to hide behind your praying saints, for we can both see they have failed you. You and I shall meet!"

Bernice knew it would be difficult, even dangerous, to drive without her glasses, but Marshall never answered his phone, so the meeting with Kevin Weed was entirely up to her and certainly worth the risk. So far, as she drove up Highway 27, the daylight was sufficient to make out the center line and the oncoming blobs, so she pressed on toward the big green bridge north of Baker.

Kevin Weed also had that bridge in mind as he sat at the bar at The Evergreen Tavern with his hands around a beer and his eyes on the big Lucky Lager clock. Somehow he felt safer here than at home by himself. He had buddies around, lots of noise, the ball game on television, the shuffleboard game going on behind him. His hands still shook, though, every time he let go of his beer mug; so most of the time he hung on to it and tried to act normal. The front door kept scraping the linoleum as more people came in.

The place was warming up, which was just fine. The more the merrier. Several loggers had beers to buy and stories to tell. There were bets going around on the shuffleboard game—tonight a long-standing rivalry would be settled once and for all. Kevin took time to smile and greet his friends and exchange a little jaw time. That helped him loosen up.

Two loggers came in. They were new, he figured; he'd never seen them before. But they fit right in with the rest of the bunch and were quick to get everyone caught up on where they were working and for how long and how the weather had been good, bad, or indifferent.

They even came up and sat with him at the bar.

"Hey," said one, extending his hand, "Mark Hansen."

"Kevin Weed," he said, shaking Mark's hand.

Mark introduced Kevin to the other guy, Steve Drake. They hit it off fine, talking logging, baseball, deer hunts, and booze, and Kevin's hands quit shaking. He even finished his beer.

"Want another beer?" Mark asked.

"Yeah, sure, thanks."

Dan brought the beers, and the conversation kept rattling on.

A loud cheer went up from the shuffleboard championship-for-all-time, and the three of them spun around in their seats to see the winner shaking hands with the loser.

Mark was quick. When no one was looking, he emptied a small vial into Kevin's beer.

The shuffleboard crowd began to congregate at the bar. Kevin checked the clock. It was time to go anyway. In all the hubbub and chatter he managed to say so long to his two new acquaintances, down his beer, and head for the door. Mark and Steve gave him a friendly wave as he went.

Kevin climbed in his old pickup and drove off. He figured he would even get to the bridge a little early. Just thinking about it made him start shaking again.

Mark and Steve wasted no time. Kevin had no sooner pulled out onto the highway than they were in their own pickup truck, following some distance behind. Steve checked his watch.

"It won't be long now," he said.

"So where do we dump him?" asked Mark.

"What's wrong with the river? He's heading there anyway."

It must have been that last beer, Kevin was thinking to himself. He must have chugged it down too fast or something; his stomach was letting him know about it. On top of that, he had to go to the bathroom. On top of that, he was really getting sleepy. He spent a few miles debating what to do, but finally he figured he had better pull over before he just plain keeled over.

A garishly painted, sagging, low-overhead hamburger joint was just ahead. He pulled off the highway and managed to bring the truck to a safe stop beside the building.

He didn't notice the pickup truck that pulled off the highway and then waited some hundred yards behind him.

"Terrific!" said Mark angrily. "So what's he going to do, keel over right in front of that hamburger place? I thought that stuff was supposed to hit hard and fast!"

Steve only shook his head. "Maybe he just has to go to the bathroom. We'll have to wait and see."

It looked like Steve was right. Kevin stumbled and staggered his way into the men's restroom behind the building. For a minute or so they stared at the restroom door. Steve looked at his watch again. Time was getting short.

"If he comes out and gets back on the road, the stuff should hit him before he reaches the bridge."

"If he even comes out!" Mark muttered. "What if we have to drag him out of there?"

No. Here he came, out the restroom door, looking a little better. As the two men watched, Kevin climbed back into his truck and pulled back out onto the highway. They followed him, waiting for something to happen.

It did. The truck began to swerve, first to the left, then back to the right.

"There he goes!" said Steve.

Up ahead was the Judd River Bridge, a steel span over a very deep chasm carved out by the Judd River. The little truck kept speeding along crazily, veering clear over into the left lane, then back again into the right lane, and then over onto the shoulder.

"He's fighting it, trying to stay awake," Steve observed.

"It's probably watered down with too much beer."

The truck went over onto the shoulder, and the tires began to wobble and dig into the soft gravel. The rear wheels spun and threw rocks, and the truck fishtailed along for several feet, heading for the bridge, but by now the driver had no control and seemed to have slipped into sleep with his foot on the gas pedal. The truck roared and accelerated, then shot across the road, roared across the wide turn-off just before the bridge, leaped upon a clump of alder saplings, and finally soared off the rocky precipice and into the river canyon below.

Mark and Steve pulled to a stop on the bridge just in time to look over the side and see the truck sinking wheels-up into the river.

"Score one more for Kaseph," said Steve.

Another driver in an oncoming car screeched to a halt and jumped out of his auto. Soon another vehicle pulled up. The bridge was starting to get clogged with excited people. Mark and Steve eased away, making their way off the bridge.

"We'll call the fire department!" Mark shouted out his window.

And away they went, never to be seen or heard from again.

30

Kate. Sandy. The Network. Bernice. Langstrat. The Network. Omni. Kaseph. Kate. Sandy. Bernice.

Marshall's thoughts went around and around as he stood at the sliding glass door just off the kitchen and watched daylight ebb slowly away from the backyard, from the delicate orange wash of sunset to the sad, ever deepening gray of nightfall.

Maybe it was the longest time he had ever spent in just one spot in his whole life, but maybe this right here and now was the end of the life he had always known. Sure, he had gone through several little attempts at denial, at trying to prove to himself that these cosmic characters, these far-out conspirators, were nothing but wind, but he kept coming back to the cold, hard facts. Harmel was right. Marshall was now out on his ear, like everybody else. Believe it, Hogan. Hey, it's happened whether you believe it or not!

He was out, just like Harmel, just like Strachan, just like Edie, just like Jefferson, Gregory, the Carluccis, Waller, James, Jacobson . . .

Marshall rubbed his hand over his head and stopped the train of names and facts coursing through his brain. Such thoughts were beginning to hurt; each one of them seemed to punch him in the stomach as it passed through his brain.

But how did they do it? How could they be so powerful that they actually destroyed lives on a personal level? Was it only coincidence? Marshall couldn't settle that question. He was too close to it, having lost his own family and having the Network to blame, but also himself. It would be so easy to blame the conspiracy for tampering with his family and turning his wife and daughter against him, and undoubtedly they had tried it. But where could he draw the line between their responsibility and his?

All he knew was that his family had fallen apart and now he was out, just like all the others.

Wait! There was a noise at the front door. Could it be Kate? He stepped to the kitchen door and looked toward the front room.

Whoever it was ducked around a corner very hurriedly as soon as he showed his face.

"Sandy?" he called.

For a moment there was no answer, but then he heard Sandy reply in a very strange, cold tone of voice, "Yes, Daddy, it's me."

He almost broke into a run, but he forced himself to take it easy and walk lightly to her bedroom. He looked in and saw her going through her closet, moving rather hurriedly and nervously, and she showed a definite discomfort at his watching her.

"Where's Mom?" she asked.

"Well . . ." he said, trying to come up with an answer. "She's gone to her mother's for a while."

"She's left you, in other words," she replied quite directly.

Marshall was direct too. "Yeah, yeah, that's right." He watched her for a while; she was grabbing clothing and belongings and throwing them into a suitcase and some shopping bags. "Looks like you're leaving too."

"That's right," she said, without slowing down or even looking up. "I felt it coming. I knew what Mom was thinking, and I think she was right. You get along so well all by yourself, we may as well let you have it that way for keeps."

"Where will you go?"

Sandy looked up at him for the first time, and Marshall was chilled and even sickened by the look in her eyes, a strange, glassy, maniacal expression he had never seen before.

"I'll never tell you!" she said, and Marshall couldn't believe the way she said it. It was not Sandy at all.

"Sandy," he said gently, pleadingly, "can we talk? I won't put any pressure or demands on you. Could we just talk?"

Those very strange eyes glared at him again and this person who used to be his loving daughter responded with, "I'll see you in hell!"

Marshall immediately sensed those all too familiar sensations of fear and doom. Some *thing* had come into his house.

Hank answered the door and immediately felt a certain check in his spirit. Carmen stood there. She was dressed neatly and conservatively this time, and her demeanor was much more down to earth; yet Hank had his qualms.

"Well, hi," he said.

She smiled disarmingly and said, "Hello, Pastor Busche."

He stepped aside and motioned for her to come in. She stepped inside the door in time to see Mary coming from the kitchen.

"Hello, Mary," she said.

"Hello," said Mary. She took an extra step and gave Carmen a loving embrace. "Are you all right?"

"Much better, thank you." She looked at Hank, and her eyes were full of repentance. "Pastor, I really owe you an apology for the way I acted before. It must have been very alarming for you both."

Hank hemmed and hawed a little and finally said, "Well, we certainly were concerned for your welfare."

Mary moved toward the living room and said, "Won't you have a seat? Can I bring you anything?"

"Thank you, no," said Carmen, sitting down on the sofa. "I won't be staying long."

Hank sat in a chair opposite the sofa and looked at Carmen, praying a mile a minute. Yes, she looked different, like she'd gotten a lot of loose ends finally tied together in her life, and yet . . . Hank had seen a lot in the last few days, and he had the distinct impression that he was seeing more of the same thing this very moment. There was something about her eyes . . .

Sandy backed up a little and narrowed her eyes at Marshall like a wild bull about to charge. "You get out of my way!"

Marshall remained in the bedroom door, blocking it with his body. "I don't want a big fight, Sandy. I won't stand in your way forever. I just want you to think for a moment, okay? Can you just calm down and give me an audience just one last time? Huh?"

She stood there rigidly, breathing heavily through her nose, her lips shut tightly, her body crouched a little. It was simply unreal!

Marshall tried to calm her down with his voice as if approaching a wild horse. "I'll let you go anywhere you want. It's your life. But we don't dare part without saying what needs to be said. I love you, you know." She didn't respond to that. "I really do love you. Do you—do you believe that at all?"

"You—you don't know the meaning of the word."

"Yeah . . . yeah, I can understand that. I haven't done very well these past years. But listen, we can put it back together. Why let this thing go in the shape it's in when we could heal it?"

She looked him over again, observed how he was still standing in the doorway, and said, "Daddy, all I want right now is to get out of here."

"In a minute, in a minute." Marshall tried to speak slowly, carefully, gently. "Sandy . . . I don't know if I can explain it to you very clearly, but remember what you said yourself about the town that one Saturday, how you thought—what was it? Aliens were taking over the town? Do you remember that?"

She didn't answer, but she seemed to be listening.

"You don't know how right you were, how true that theory really was. There are people in this town, Sandy, right now, that want to take the whole town over, and they also want to destroy anyone who gets in their way. Sandy, I'm someone who got in their way."

Sandy began to shake her head incredulously. She wasn't buying it.

"Listen to me, Sandy, just listen! Now . . . I run the paper, see, and I know what they're up to, and they know that I know, so they're just doing what they can to destroy me, take away my house, the newspaper, undermine my family!" He looked at her in earnest, but had no idea if any of this was getting through. "All that's happening to us . . . it's what they want! They want this family to fall apart!"

"You're crazy!" she finally said. "You're a maniac! Get out of the way!"

"Sandy, listen to me. They've even been using you against me. Did you know those cops in town are trying to find anything they can to put me away? They're trying to pin a murder rap on me, and it even sounds like they're accusing me of abusing you! That's how terrible this whole thing is. You have to understand—"

"But you did it!" Sandy cried. "You know you did it."

Marshall was stunned. All he could do was stare at her. She *had* to be crazy. "Did *what,* Sandy?"

She actually broke down and tears came to her eyes as she said, "You raped me. You *raped* me!"

Carmen seemed to be having a very difficult time getting around to whatever she had come to tell them. "I—I just don't know how to begin . . . it's just so difficult."

Hank reassured her, "Oh, you're among friends."

Carmen looked at Mary sitting at the other end of the sofa, and then at Hank, still sitting opposite her. "Hank, I just can't live with it anymore."

Hank said, "Then why don't you just give it over to Jesus? He's the Healer, you know. He can take away your regrets and your sorrows, believe me."

She looked at him and only shook her head incredulously. "Hank, I am not here to play games. It's time we were truthful and cleared the air once and for all. We're just not being fair to Mary."

Hank didn't know what she was talking about, so he just leaned forward and nodded, his way of telling her he was listening.

She continued, "Well, I guess I'll just have to say it and get it out. I'm sorry, Hank." She turned to Mary, her eyes filling with tears, and said, "Mary, for the last several months . . . ever since our first counseling appointment . . . Hank and I have been seeing each other on a regular basis."

Mary asked, "What do you mean by that?"

Carmen turned to Hank and implored him, "Hank, don't you think you should be the one to tell her?"

"Tell her what?" Hank asked.

Carmen looked at Mary, took her hand, and said, "Mary, Hank and I have been having an affair."

Mary looked startled, but not very stunned. She did pull her hand away from Carmen's. Then she looked at Hank.

"What do you think?" she asked him.

Hank took another good look at Carmen and then nodded to Mary. Mary turned directly toward Carmen, and Hank got up out of his chair. They both looked intently at Carmen, and she began to look away from their eyes.

"It's true!" she insisted. "Tell her, Hank. Please tell her."

"Spirit," said Hank firmly, "I command you in the name of Jesus to be silent and come out of her!"

There were fifteen of them, packed into Carmen's body like crawling, superimposed maggots, boiling, writhing, a tangle of hideous arms, legs, talons, and heads. They began to squirm. Carmen began to squirm. They moaned and cried out, and so did Carmen, her eyes turning glassy and staring blankly.

Outside the room, Krioni and Triskal watched from a distance.

Triskal fumed, "Orders, orders, orders!"

Krioni reminded him, "Tal knows what he's doing."

Triskal pointed toward the living room and cried, "Hank's playing with a bomb in there. You see those demons? They'll tear him apart!"

"We have to stay out of it," Krioni said. "We can protect Hank's and Mary's lives, but we cannot keep the demons from doing whatever they might do . . ." Krioni was having trouble with it himself.

Sandy got louder and louder. Marshall felt that any moment he would lose control of her altogether.

"You . . . you let me out of here or you're going to be in big trouble!" she nearly screamed.

Marshall could only stand there in total dismay and horror. "Sandy, it's me, Marshall Hogan, your father. *Think*, Sandy! You know I never touched you, I never molested you. I only loved you and cared for you. You're my daughter, my only daughter."

"You did it to me!" she cried hysterically.

"When, Sandy?" he demanded. "When did I ever touch you wrongly?"

"It was something my mind had blocked out for years, but Professor Langstrat brought it out!"

"Langstrat!"

"She put me under hypnosis, and I saw it like it was yesterday. You did it, and I hate you!"

"You never remembered it because it never happened. *Think, Sandy!*"

"I hate you! You did it to me!"

Nathan and Armoth, from outside the house, could see the hideous deceiving spirit clinging to Sandy's back, its talons deep in her skull.

Alongside them was Tal. He had just given them their special orders.

"Captain," said Armoth, "we don't know what that thing might do."

"Preserve their lives," said Tal, "but Hogan must fall. As for Sandy, see to it that a special detachment follows her at a distance. They'll be able to move when the time is right."

Just then, with a very low, stealthy trajectory, Signa floated in for a landing.

"Captain," he reported, "Kevin Weed is dead. It worked."

Tal gave Signa a strange, knowing look and smile. "Excellent," he said.

The fifteen spirits in Carmen were foaming and frothing, wailing and hissing. Hank held Carmen down gently, one hand on her right hand, one hand on her left shoulder. Mary stood beside him, clinging to him a little out of her own timidity. Carmen moaned and twisted, her eyes glaring at Hank.

"Let us go, praying man!" Carmen's voice warned, and the sulfurous odor coming from deep inside her was strong and nauseating.

"Carmen, do you want to be delivered?" Hank asked.

"She can't hear you," said the spirits. "Let us alone! She belongs to us!"

"Be silent and come out of her!"

"No!" Carmen screamed, and Mary was almost sure she saw a puff of yellow vapor from Carmen's throat.

"Come out in the name of Jesus!" said Hank.

The bomb exploded. Hank was thrown backward. Mary leaped aside. Carmen was on top of Hank, clawing, biting, mauling. Her teeth clamped onto his right arm. He pushed and pounded with his left.

"Demon, let go!" he ordered.

The jaws opened. Hank gave all the shove he had and Carmen's body staggered backward, twitching and shrieking. Her hands found a chair. Instantly it shot upward and came down with a crash, but Hank scurried out of the way. He dove for Carmen and tackled her as she was grabbing another chair. Her leg came up like a catapult and flung him across the room where he thudded into the wall. Her fist was right behind him. He dodged it. It rammed a hole in the plaster. He was looking into the eyes of a beast; he smelled the sulfurous breath hissing through the bared teeth. He jerked himself away. Sharp fingernails snagged and tore at his shirt. Some dug into his flesh. He could hear Mary screaming, "Stop it, spirit! In Jesus' name, stop it!"

Carmen doubled over and clapped her hands over her ears. She staggered and screamed.

"Be silent, demon, and come out of her!" Hank ordered, trying to keep his distance.

"I won't! I won't!" Carmen screamed, and her body careened toward the front door. She hit it full force. The center of the door caved in with a loud crack. Hank ran to the door and pulled it open, and Carmen flew out the door and down the street. As Hank and Mary watched her go, all they could do was hope the neighbors wouldn't see.

"Sandy," said Marshall, "this isn't you. I know it isn't you."

She said nothing, but like the strike of a rattlesnake she pounced at him, trying to get through the door. He held his hands up to protect his face from her flying fists.

"Okay, okay!" he told her, stepping aside. "You can go. Just remember, I love you."

She grabbed her suitcase and a shopping bag and bolted for the front door. He followed her down the hall toward the living room.

He came around the corner. He looked to see her, but all he saw was the lamp that smacked into his skull. He heard and felt the blow in every part of his body. The lamp fell to the floor with a crash. Now he was on one knee, slumped against the couch. His hand went to his head. He looked up and saw the front door still standing open. He was bleeding.

His head was so light he was afraid to try to stand up. His strength was gone anyway. Nuts, now there's blood on the rug. What will Kate say?

"Marshall!" came a voice above him. A hand rested on his shoulder. It was a woman. Kate? Sandy? No, Bernice, squinting at him through blackened eyes. "Marshall, what happened? Are you—are you still there?"

"Help me clean up this mess," was all he could say.

She scurried into the kitchen and found some paper towels. She brought them back and pressed a wad of them against his head. He winced at the pain.

She asked him, "Can you get up?"

"I don't want to get up!" he answered crossly.

"Okay, okay. I just saw Sandy drive off. Was this her doing?"

"Yeah, she pitched that lamp at me . . ."

"It must have been something you said. Here, hold still."

"She's not herself at all, she's gone crazy."

"Where's Kate?"

"She's left me."

Bernice settled to the floor, her bruised face the picture of shock, dismay, and exhaustion. Neither of them said anything for a few moments. They just stared at each other like two shot-up soldiers in a foxhole.

"Man, you're a mess!" Marshall finally observed.

"At least the swelling's gone down. Don't I look foxy?"

"More like a raccoon. I thought you were supposed to be resting at home. What are you doing here, anyway?"

"I just got back from Baker. And I have nothing but bad news from there too."

He anticipated it. "Weed?"

"He's dead. The truck he was driving went off the Judd River Bridge and into that big canyon. We were supposed to have met each other. He'd just gotten a call from Susan Jacobson, and it sounded pretty important."

Marshall's head fell back against the couch, and he closed his eyes. "Aw, great . . . just great!" He wanted to die.

"He called me this afternoon, and we set up the appointment. I imagine either my phone or his was bugged. That accident was set up, I'm sure of it. I got out of there fast!"

Marshall took the wad from his head and looked at the blood on it. He placed it back over the gash.

"We're going down, Bernie," he said, and went on to tell her about his whole afternoon, his meeting with Brummel and Brummel's buddies, his loss of the house, his loss of the paper, his loss of Kate, of Sandy, of everything. "And did you know that I've made it a habit to molest my daughter besides having an affair with my reporter?"

"They're cutting you up into little pieces, aren't they?" she said very quietly, her throat constricted with fear. "What can we do?"

"We can get the heck out of here, that's what we can do!"

"You're going to give up?"

Marshall only let his head sink downward. He was tired. "Let somebody else fight this war. We were warned, Bernie, and we didn't listen. They got me. They got all our records, any proof we ever had. Harmel blew his brains out. Strachan's getting as far away from it as he can. They took out Weed. Right now I think I'm just barely alive and that's all I have left."

"What about Susan Jacobson?"

It took some extra effort and willpower to make himself think about it. "I wonder if she even exists, and, if so, if she's alive."

"Kevin said she had the goods and she was getting ready to get out of wherever she was. That sounds to me like a defection, and if she has the evidence we need to seal this thing up—"

"They took care of that, Bernie. Remember? Weed was our last contact with her."

"Want to toy with a theory?"

"No."

"If Kevin's phone was bugged, they know what Weed and Susan talked about. They heard it all."

"Naturally, and Susan's as good as dead too."

"We don't know that. Maybe she managed to get away. Maybe she was going to meet Kevin someplace."

"Ehhh . . ." Marshall passively listened.

"What I'm toying with is that somewhere there must be a recording in somebody's hands of that phone call."

"Yeah, I suppose there is." Marshall felt half-dead, but the half of him that was still alive was thinking. "But where would it be? This is a big country, Bernie."

"Well . . . like I said, it's a theory to toy with. It's all we have left, really."

"Which sure isn't much."

"I'm dying to know what Susan had to say—"

"Please don't use that word 'dying.'"

"Well, think for a minute, Marshall. Think of all the people who seem to have responded to the alleged bug. There were the Windsor cops who knew they could find you at Strachan's after you told me you'd be there—"

"It's not likely they'd have the recording equipment. They're too far away."

"So somebody who did have the recording equipment must have tipped them off."

Marshall got an idea, and a little bit of color returned to his face. "I'm wondering about Brummel."

Bernice's eyes brightened. "Sure! Like I said, he and the cops in Windsor are in cahoots all the time."

"He fired Sara, you know. She wasn't there today. She'd been replaced." New ideas began to form in Marshall's mind. "Yeah . . . she talked to me on the phone and ratted on Brummel a little. She said she'd help me out if I could help her out . . . we agreed to deal . . . and Brummel fired her! He must have heard that conversation too." Then it hit him. "Yeah! Sara! Those filing cabinets! Brummel's filing cabinets!"

"Yeah, you're cooking, Marshall, just keep going!"

"He had his filing cabinets moved out into Sara's reception area to make room for some new office equipment. I saw it there, sitting right in his office, and there was a wire coming out of the wall . . . he said it was for the coffeemaker. But I didn't see any coffeemaker!"

"I think you might have it there!"

"It was telephone wire, not appliance cord." Excitement made his head hurt, but he said anyway, "Bernice, it was telephone wire."

"If we could find out for sure that the recording equipment is there in his office . . . if we could find any tapes of phone conversations . . . well, that might be enough to bring some kind of charges at least: illegal wiretapping—"

"Murder."

That was a chilling thought.

"We need Sara," Marshall added. "If she's on our side, now's when she can prove it."

"Whatever you do, don't call her. I know where she lives."

"Help me up."

"*You* help *me* up!"

31

Hank and Mary were still shaking as he took a careful look at the front door.

He shook his head and whistled his astonishment. "She cracked the doorjamb. Look at this! The stop is moved out about an inch."

"Well, how about changing your shirt?" Mary asked, and Hank remembered that half his shirt was gone.

"Here's another one for the rag box," he said, slipping the shirt off. Then he winced a little. "Oooo!"

"What's wrong?"

As the shirt came off Hank raised his arm to have a look, and Mary gasped. Carmen's teeth had made some very impressive welts. The skin was broken in some places.

"We'd better put some peroxide on those," said Mary, hurrying into the bathroom. "Come here!"

Hank went into the bathroom, still carrying the torn shirt. He held his arm out over the sink, and Mary started dabbing the wounds.

She was astonished. "Goodness! Hank, she bit you in four different places. Look at this!"

"Boy, I hope she's had all her shots."

"I knew that woman was up to no good the first time I saw her."

The doorbell rang. Hank and Mary looked at each other. What now?

"Better go answer it," said Hank.

She went out into the living room while Hank finished cleaning his arm.

"Hank!" Mary called. "I think you'd better come out here!"

Hank went out into the living room, still carrying the torn shirt in his hand and sporting the bite marks on his arm.

Two policemen stood at the door, an older, taller one and a younger, new-on-the-force type. Yeah, the neighbors must have thought something terrible was happening in here. Come to think of it, they were right.

"Hi there," said Hank.

"Hank Busche?" the older one asked.

"Yeah," he answered. "This is Mary, my wife. You must have received a call from the neighbors, right?"

The big officer was looking at Hank's arm. "What happened to your arm?"

"Well . . ." Hank wasn't sure how to answer. Even the truth would sound like a pretty tall tale.

No matter. He didn't have time. The younger officer grabbed Hank's shirt right out of his hand and unfolded it, holding it up in both hands. The older one happened to have the rest of Hank's shirt discreetly hidden behind his back. Now he produced the torn piece and made a quick comparison of the materials.

The older one nodded to the younger one, and the younger one got out a pair of handcuffs and rather forcefully twisted Hank around. Mary's mouth dropped open and she squealed, "What on earth are you doing?"

The older one started rattling off the prisoner's liturgy. "Mr. Busche, we are placing you under arrest. It's my duty to advise you of your rights. You have the right to remain silent, anything you say can and will be used against you . . ."

Hank had an idea, but he asked anyway, "Uh . . . mind telling me what the charges are?"

"You oughta know," snapped the older one.

"Suspected rape," said the younger.

"What?" Mary exclaimed.

The younger one held up his hand as a warning. "Just stay out of this, lady."

"You're making a mistake!" she pleaded.

The two officers led Hank down the front walk. It happened so fast that Mary hardly knew what to do. She ran after them, pleading, trying to reason with them.

"This is crazy! I don't believe this!" she said.

The younger one just told her, "You'll have to stay out of the way or face charges of obstructing justice."

"Justice!" she cried. "You call this justice? Hank, what should I do?"

"Make some calls," Hank answered.

"I'm going with you!"

"We can't allow you in the squad car, ma'am," said the older one.

"Make some calls, Mary," Hank repeated.

They strong-armed him into the car and closed the door. The two officers got in and away they went, down the street, around the corner and out of sight, and Mary remained there on the curb all by herself, without her husband, just like that.

Tal and his warriors and couriers knew where to look and they knew what to listen for; so they heard the telephones ringing all over town, they saw the many people roused from their televisions or from their sleep by the phone calls. The entire Remnant was buzzing with the news of Hank's arrest. The praying began.

"Busche has fallen," said Tal. "Only Hogan remains." He turned to Chimon and Mota. "Does Sara have the keys?"

Chimon answered, "She had several keys copied before she left her job at the police station."

Mota looked across the town as he said, "They should be meeting with her right about now."

Sara, Bernice, and Marshall conferred in a tight, hushed little huddle in the middle of Sara's small kitchen. Except for the light from one lamp out in the dining room, there were no other lights on in the house. Sara was still up, fully dressed. She was packing to move.

"I'll take whatever I can squeeze into my car, but I'm not staying around past tomorrow, especially after tonight," she said in a near whisper.

"How are you set for money?" Marshall asked.

"I've enough gas money to get out of the state, and after that I don't know. Brummel didn't give me any severance pay."

"Just booted you right out?"

"He didn't say so, but I've no doubt he overheard that conversation I had with you. I didn't survive very long after that."

Marshall handed her a hundred dollars. "I'd give you more if I had it."

"That's all right. I'd say we have a deal." Sara passed a set of keys to him. "Now listen carefully. This one here is for the main door, but first you have to deactivate the burglar alarm. That's this little key here. The box is around the back, just above the garbage cans. You just open the cover and flip the switch off. This key here, with the round head, is to Brummel's office. I don't know if that equipment is locked up or not, but I don't have any key for it. You'll just have to take the risk. The night dispatcher is still posted at the fire station, so there shouldn't be anyone else there."

"What do you think of our theory?" Bernice asked.

"I know Brummel's very protective of that new equipment in there. Ever since he had it installed, I've not been allowed in his office and he keeps the door closed. It's the first place *I'd* look."

"We'd better go," Marshall said to Bernice.

Bernice gave Sara a hug. "Good luck."

"Good luck yourselves," Sara replied. "Be very quiet going out."

They sneaked away in the darkness.

Later that night Marshall picked up Bernice at her apartment and they rode together downtown.

Marshall found a good spot to hide the Buick just a few blocks from Courthouse Square, a nice vacant lot with lots of overgrown shrubs and trees. His slipped the big car down into the jungle and turned off the engine. For a moment he and Bernice just sat there wondering what the next move should be. They thought they were ready. They had even changed into dark clothes, and they had brought flashlights and rubber gloves.

"Sheesh!" said Marshall. "The last time I did something like this was when we kids stole the neighbor's corn."

"How did that turn out!"

"We got caught, and boy, did we get it!"

"What time does your watch say?"

Marshall checked his watch with his flashlight. "1:25."

Bernice was clearly nervous. "I wonder if real burglars work this way. I feel like I'm in some kind of hokey movie."

"How about some charcoal for your face?"

"It's black enough now, thank you."

They both sat there for a few more moments, trying to build up the nerve to proceed.

Bernice finally said, "Well, are we going to do it or aren't we?"

"Die all, die merrily," Marshall replied, opening his door.

They tiptoed up an alley and through a few yards until they reached the back of the courthouse/police station. Fortunately, the town hadn't gotten the funds together yet for any floodlights over the parking lot, so the darkness was pretty concealing.

Bernice couldn't help feeling petrified; only sheer determination kept her carrying on. Marshall was nervous, but for some reason he felt an odd exhilaration in doing something so sneaky and dirty against these enemies. As soon as they had crossed the parking lot they ducked into a nearby shadow and stood tightly against the wall. It was so nice and dark there that Bernice didn't want to leave.

About twenty feet down the wall were the garbage cans, and above them a small gray panel. Marshall got there quickly, found the right key, opened the little door, and found the switch. He signaled to Bernice, and she followed him. They walked quickly around to the front of the building, and now they were in the open, facing the large parking area between the police station and the town hall. Marshall had the key ready, and they were able to get into the building without delay. Marshall quickly closed the door behind them.

They rested just a minute and listened. The place was deserted and dead quiet. They heard no sirens or alarms going off. Marshall found the next key and went to Brummel's office door. So far Sara had predicted right on the money. Brummel's door opened too. They both ducked inside.

And there sat the cabinetry housing the mysterious equipment—if it was truly there. Marshall clicked on his flashlight and kept the beam subdued under his hand so that it would not play on the walls or shine out the window. Then he swung open the lower left cabinet door. Inside he found some shelves on roller tracks. He pulled the upper one out . . .

And there sat a recording machine with a good supply of tape. "Eureka!" Bernice whispered.

"Must be signal activated . . . switches on automatically whenever an input comes in."

Bernice clicked on her flashlight and checked the other door on the lower right. Here she found some files and folders.

"It looks like a catalog!" she said. "Look—names, dates, conversations, and what tape they're on."

"That handwriting looks familiar."

They were both astounded at how many names were on the list, how many people were being listened in on.

"Even Network people," Marshall observed. Then he pointed to a listing near the bottom of one page. "There *we* are."

He was right. The *Clarion* phone was listed, the conversation noted as being between Marshall and Ted Harmel, recorded on tape 5-A.

"Who in the world has the time to list all this stuff?" Bernice wondered.

Marshall only shook his head. Then he asked, "When was that conversation between Susan and Weed?"

Bernice thought for a moment. "We'll just have to check all of today, yesterday . . . who knows? Weed didn't say exactly."

"Maybe that call came in today. There's no record of that here."

"It must be on the tape that's on the machine now. Those calls haven't been logged yet."

Marshall wound the tape back, put the machine into play, flipped on the speaker switch, and set the volume down low.

Conversations began to unfold from the recording, a lot of everyday, innocuous stuff. Brummel's voice was in a lot of them, talking business. Marshall ran the tape ahead on Fast Forward a few times, skipping over several conversations. Suddenly he recognized a voice. His own.

"You already ran once, remember?" came his recorded voice. "As long as you're alive, Eldon, you're going to be living with this and they're going to know it . . ."

"Eldon Strachan and I," he told Bernice.

It was scary hearing his very words coming out of the machine, words that could tell the Network anything and everything.

Marshall skipped forward some more.

"Man, this whole thing is crazy," came a voice.

Bernice brightened. "That's him! That's Weed!"

Marshall wound the tape back and flipped it to Play again. There was a gap, then the abrupt start of a conversation.

"Yeah, hello?" said Weed.

"Kevin, this is Susan."

Bernice and Marshall listened intently.

Weed replied, "Yeah, I'm listening, man. What can I do?"

Susan's voice was tense and her words hurried. "Kevin, I'm getting out, one way or another, and I'm doing it tonight. Can you meet me at The Evergreen tomorrow night?"

"Yeah . . . yeah."

"See if you can bring Bernice Krueger with you. I have materials to show her, everything she needs to know."

"Man, this whole thing is crazy. You ought to see my place. Somebody came in here and tore it all up. You be careful!"

"We're *all* in great danger, Kevin. Kaseph's moving to Ashton to take over everything. But I can't talk now. Meet me at The Evergreen at 8. I'll try to get there somehow. If not I'll call you."

"Okay, okay."

"I have to go. Good-bye, and thanks."

Click. The conversation was over.

"Yeah," said Bernice, "he called to tell me about this."

"It wasn't much," said Marshall, "but it was enough. Now the only question is, did she manage to get away?"

A key rattled in the front door. Bernice and Marshall never moved so fast. She replaced all the files, and Marshall slid the machine back inside the cabinet. They closed the cabinet doors.

The front door opened. The lobby lights came on.

They ducked behind Brummel's big desk. Bernice's eyes were full of one question: What do we do now? Marshall gestured to her to keep cool, then he made fists to show her they might have to fight their way out.

Another key worked at Brummel's office door, and then it opened. Suddenly the room was flooded with light. They heard someone going to the cabinets, opening the doors, sliding out the machine. Marshall figured the person's back had to be toward them. He raised his head to take a quick peek.

It was Carmen. She was winding the tape back to the beginning and preparing to make more entries in the record.

Bernice took a look also, and both of them felt the same rage and indignation.

"Don't you ever sleep?" Marshall asked Carmen right out loud. That startled Bernice and she jumped a little. It startled Carmen and she jumped a lot, dropped her papers, and gave a short little scream. She spun around.

"What!" she gasped. "What are you doing here?"

Marshall and Bernice both stood up. From their battered and dark-clothed appearance, this looked like anything but a nonchalant, cordial visit.

"I might ask you the same thing," Marshall said. "Do you have any idea what time it is?"

Carmen looked them both over, and she was speechless.

Marshall could certainly think of some things to say. "You're a spy, aren't you? You were a spy in our office, you wiretapped our phones, and now you've run off with all our investigation materials."

"I don't know—"

"—what I'm talking about. Right! So I suppose you do this every night too, go over all the recorded phone conversations and log them, listen for anything the big boys might want to know."

"I wasn't—"

"And what about all the *Clarion's* business records? Let's take care of that first."

She suddenly broke down crying, saying, "Ohhh . . . you don't understand . . ." She went out into the reception area.

Marshall was right on her heels, not about to let her out of his sight. He took her by the arm and spun her around.

"Easy, girl! We have some real business to take care of here."

"Ooohhh!" Carmen wailed, and then she threw her arms around Marshall as if she were a frightened child and sobbed into his chest. "I thought you were some burglar . . . I'm glad it was you. I need help, Marshall!"

"And we want answers," Marshall snapped back, unaffected by her tears. He sat her down in Sara's old chair. "Have a seat and save your tears for some soap opera."

She looked up at both of them, her mascara running down her cheeks. "Don't you understand? Don't you have any heart? I came here for help! I've just had a terrible experience!" She built up the strength to say it, and then burst out in a fit of tears, "I've been raped!"

She collapsed to the floor, sobbing uncontrollably.

Marshall looked at Bernice, and Bernice looked at Marshall.

"Yeah," said Marshall unsympathetically, "there seems to be a lot of that going around these days, especially among the people your bosses want out of the way. So who was it this time?"

All she did was lie there on the floor and cry.

Bernice had something boiling inside her. "How do you like my looks tonight, Carmen? I think it's interesting that you were the only one who knew I'd be going out to visit Kevin Weed. Did you tip off the thug who beat me up?"

She still lay there on the floor crying, not saying a word.

Marshall went into Brummel's office and returned with some of the files, including the notes Carmen had written that very night.

"It's all in your handwriting, Carmen, my dear. You've been nothing but a spy from the very beginning. Am I right or am I right?"

She kept crying. Marshall took hold of her, lifting her from the floor. "C'mon, get up!"

It was just as he saw her hand come off the silent alarm button in the floor that the front door burst open and he heard a voice holler, "Freeze! Police!"

Carmen was no longer crying. As a matter of fact, she was smirking. Marshall put his hands up, and so did Bernice. Carmen ran behind the two uniformed police who had just come in. Their guns were trained right on the two burglars.

"Friends of yours?" Marshall asked Carmen.

She only smiled an evil smile.

Just then Alf Brummel himself came into the building, fresh out of bed and in his bathrobe.

"What's going on here?" he asked, and then he saw Marshall. "What . . . ? Well, well, who do we have here?" Then he actually chuckled a bit. He walked up to Marshall, shaking his head and showing those big teeth. "I don't believe this! I just can't believe it!" He looked at Bernice. "Bernice Krueger! Is that you?"

Bernice had nothing to say, and Brummel was too far away to spit on.

Oh no. Now they had a full house. Juleen Langstrat, also in a bathrobe, walked in the door! She sidled up to Brummel, and the two of them stood there looking proudly at Marshall and Bernice, as if they were trophies.

"Sorry for disturbing all of you like this," said Marshall.

Langstrat smiled lusciously and said, "I wouldn't have missed this for the world."

Brummel kept on grinning with those big teeth and told the policemen, "Read them their rights and take them into custody."

The opportunity was too good to pass up. There stood the two cops trying to do their job, and there were Brummel and Langstrat, standing just a little in front of them. The situation was perfect, and it had been building up inside Marshall for a long time. Instantly, with all his weight, he dove into Brummel's stomach and toppled Brummel and Langstrat backward into the two cops.

"Run, Bernie, run!" he shouted.

She ran. She didn't stop to consider if she had the courage or the will or even the speed. She just ran for all she was worth, down the long hallway, past all the office doors, straight for the exit at the end. The door had a crash bar. She crashed into it, it opened, and she stumbled out into the cool night air.

Marshall was in the middle of a tangle of arms, hands, bodies, and shouts, hanging on to as many of them as he could. He was almost enjoying it, and he didn't try that hard to get away. He wanted to keep them all busy.

One cop recovered and ran after Bernice, bursting out through that back door. He was close enough on her trail to pick up the sound of footsteps heading up the back alley, and away he went in hot pursuit.

Here was Bernice's chance to find out what kind of shape she was in, cracked rib and all. She chugged down the alley, taking long strides, making her way through the blurry dark; she longed for her glasses, or at least a little more light. She heard the cop hollering at her to stop. Any moment he would fire that warning shot. She made a sharp left through a yard and a dog started barking. There was a space of light between two low-hanging fruit trees. She headed for that and encountered a fence. Two garbage cans helped her over with a clatter that told the cop where she was.

Bernice stomped through a freshly tilled garden, flattening several unseen bean poles. She ran onto a lawn, turned back toward the alley, knocked over some more cans, clambered over a fence, and kept running. The cop seemed to be fading back a little.

She was getting desperately tired and could only hope that he was, too. She couldn't keep this up much longer. Every panting breath brought a sharp pain from that cracked rib. She couldn't breathe.

She whipped around one house and doubled back through a few more yards, raising a tumult of barking from tattletale dogs, then crossed a street, and dove into some woods. The branches lashed at her and entangled her, but she plowed through them until she reached another fence bordering a service station. She ran along the fence, found an old dumpster just on the other side, went just a little further—and then her eyes were attracted by a fragment of street light filtering through the leaves and illuminating a pile of rubbish some litterbug had dumped. She grabbed the first thing her hand found, an old bottle, then dropped to the ground, trying not to breathe too loudly, trying not to cry from the pain.

The cop was moving rather slowly through the woods, groping his way along in the dark, snapping twigs under his feet, huffing and puffing. She lay there silently, waiting for him to pause to listen. Finally he did stop and fall silent. He was listening. She pitched the bottle over the fence. It bounced off the top of the dumpster and shattered on the pavement behind the service station. The cop came crashing through the woods and up to the fence. He climbed over and stood still behind the station.

Bernice could not see him from where she was, but she listened very intently. So did he. Then she heard him walk slowly along the back of the station and stop. A moment passed, and then he walked away at a normal pace. He had lost her.

Bernice remained where she was, trying to calm the pounding of her heart and the rushing of blood in her ears, trying to calm her nerves and her panic, and wishing the pain would go away. All she wanted to do was gasp deep breaths of air; she couldn't seem to get enough.

Oh, Marshall, Marshall, what are they doing to you?

32

Marshall was facedown on the floor, his pockets emptied, his hands cuffed behind him. He was being very cooperative with the cop who stood over him with his gun drawn. Carmen, Brummel, and Langstrat were in Brummel's office going over the tape that Marshall and Bernice had listened to.

"Yes," said Carmen, "here's my notation of the tape counter. I thought the tape hadn't run very far for such a long period of surveillance. The recordings continue after this stopping point. They wound the tape back."

Brummel stepped out of his office and stood over Marshall. "So what did you and Bernice listen to?"

"Big band jazz, I think," Marshall answered. That response brought Brummel's heel down on Marshall's neck. "Aaauu!"

Brummel had another question. "So who gave you the keys to this place? Did Sara?"

"Ask me no questions, I'll tell you no lies."

Brummel muttered, "I'll have to put out an APB on her too!"

"Don't bother," Langstrat said from the office. "She's gone now and she's nothing. Don't bring trouble back once you're rid of it. Just concentrate on Krueger."

Brummel told the cop who was guarding Marshall, "Ed, go out and see if you can help John. Krueger's the one we really need to round up."

But just then John came back in through the door at the end of the hall, and he did not have Bernice in tow.

"Well?" Brummel demanded.

John only gave a timid shrug. "She ran like a scared rabbit, and it's dark out there!"

"Aw, terrific!" Brummel moaned.

Marshall thought it really was terrific.

Langstrat's voice came from the office. "Alf, come listen to this."

Brummel went into his office, and Marshall could hear the conversation between Weed and Susan being replayed.

Langstrat said, "So they've heard this conversation. We picked it up from Susan's end today." The dialogue between Susan and Weed came to an end. "Unless I miss my guess, Krueger could very well be headed for The Evergreen Tavern in Baker to meet Susan—" She broke into laughter.

"I'll have it staked out, then," said Brummel.

"Get a stakeout on her apartment also. She'll want to get to her car."

"Good idea."

Brummel and Langstrat came out of the office and stood over Marshall like vultures over a carcass.

"Marshall," Brummel gloated, "you're in for quite a downhill slide, I'm afraid. I've enough against you to put you away for good. You should have gotten out of this thing while you had the chance."

Marshall looked up at that silly grinning face and said, "To use a cliché, you'll never get away with this, Brummel. You don't own the whole court system. Sooner or later this thing's going to go beyond your reach; it's going to get bigger than you are."

Brummel only smiled a smile that Marshall longed to kick into oblivion and said, "Marshall, a lower court decision is all we need, and I'm sure we can manage that. Let's face it. You're nothing but a liar and a third-rate burglar, not to mention a child molester and a possible murderer. We have witnesses, Marshall: fine, upstanding citizens of this community. We'll see to it that you have the fairest of trials, so you would have no grounds for appeal. It could go very hard for you. The judge might give you a break, but . . . I don't know."

"You mean Baker, the wheeler-dealer?"

"I understand he can be a very compassionate person . . . under the right circumstances."

"So don't tell me. You're going to book Bernice on charges of prostitution? Maybe you can dig up those hookers again, that bogus cop again, set the whole thing up."

Brummel chuckled mockingly. "That all depends on the evidence at hand, I guess. We can book her for burglary, you know, and the two of you set that one up yourselves."

"So what about the laws against illegal wiretaps?"

Langstrat answered that one. "We know of no wiretaps. We don't do that sort of thing." She paused for effect, then added, "And they wouldn't find anything even if they did believe you." Then something occurred to her. "Oh, and I can sense what you're thinking. Don't put your hopes in Susan Jacobson. We've received the sad news today that she was killed in a terrible motor vehicle accident. The only people Ms. Krueger can expect to meet at The Evergreen Tavern will be the police."

Bernice felt faint. Her rib cage felt like it was shattered; her bruises throbbed without mercy. For the better part of an hour she didn't have the strength or the nerves to get up from where she lay in the brambles. She tried to think what to do next. Every wisp of wind through the trees was an approaching policeman to her; every sound brought new horror. She looked at her watch. It was going on 3 in the morning. Soon it would be day, and there would be no more sneaking around. She had to get moving, and she knew it.

She slowly struggled to her feet, then stood there, slightly crouched, under the low hanging branches of a vine-tangled madrona, waiting for enough blood to circulate through her brain for her to stay standing.

She took a step, then another. She gained confidence and started moving ahead, feeling her way through the trees and underbrush, trying to fend off the scratching branches.

Back out on the street, it was quiet and dark. The dogs were no longer barking. She began to plot her course for her apartment, about a mile across town, making the trip in quick dashes from tree to hedge to tree. Only once did a vehicle drive by, but it was not a squad car; Bernice hid behind a large maple tree until it had passed.

She could not distinguish her physical pain and sickness from her emotional exhaustion and despair. A few times she got confused and lost her bearings and couldn't make out any of the street signs, and it was then that she almost cried, slumping against a fence or a wall.

But she remembered Marshall throwing himself into the jaws of those lions for her sake, and she couldn't let him down. She had to make it. She had to get out of town, get free, meet Susan, get help, do *something*.

For nearly an hour, block by block, step by step, she worked her way along and finally approached her apartment building. She cautiously followed a circuitous route around it, wanting to check it from all sides. Finally, from behind a neighbor's station wagon, she thought she could make out the telltale rack of lights atop one car parked at the end of the block. From that position, the occupants of that car would have a perfect view of anyone trying to get into any apartment. So that was out.

The back of the building was much easier to sneak into; there were small parking stalls along a dark, narrow alley, the lighting was poor, the parking stalls could not be seen from ground level up above. It was a terrible place to park a car in terms of security, but perfect for Bernice tonight.

She darted across the street a block away and out of view of that squad car, then doubled back and slipped into the alley, staying close to the dank, concrete retaining wall as the alley dipped down below the grade. She reached her Toyota, removed the little magnetic key box from under the bumper, and used those emergency keys to open the door.

Oh, so near and yet so far! There was no way she could start her car and get away without being heard on this very still night. But there were some things she could make very good use of. She clambered in as quickly as she could and closed the door after her enough to extinguish the dome light. Then she opened the ashtray in the front console and emptied the quarters, dimes, and nickels into her pocket. Just a couple of bucks, but it would have to do. In the glovebox she found her prescription sunglasses; now she could see better and use them to conceal her black eyes.

There was nothing else to do but get out of town, maybe get some sleep somewhere, somehow, and then, one way or another, get out to Baker and The Evergreen Tavern by 8 that coming night. That was all, but it was enough. She strained to think of anyone she knew that *they* would not know, any friend who could still aid and abet a fugitive from the law, without questions.

Her mental list of names was too short and too doubtful. She started walking, making her way toward Highway 27 while searching her mind for any other ideas.

Down below the courthouse, alone in a cell at the end of the dismal cellblock, Hank lay on his cot, asleep at last.

It had not been the most enjoyable of evenings: they had stripped him, searched him, fingerprinted him, photographed him, and then stuck him in this cell with no blanket to keep warm. He had asked for a Bible, but they wouldn't allow him to have one. The drunk in the next cell had thrown up during the night, the writer of phony checks in the cell after that had a very dirty mouth, and the mugger in the next cell turned out to be a very vociferous, opinionated Marxist.

Oh well, he thought, Jesus died for them and they need His love. He tried to be kind and share some of God's love with them, but someone had told them that he was an accused rapist, which put somewhat of a damper on his testimony.

So he had lain down, identifying with Paul and Silas and Peter and James and every other Christian who had ever spent time in a forlorn prison even though innocent. He wondered how long his ministry would survive, now that his reputation had been so blasted. Would he still be able to hang on in his already shaky pastorate? Brummel and his buddies were sure going to make full use of this. For all he knew, they had been the ones who set it up. Ah well, it was in the Lord's hands; God knew what was best.

He prayed for Mary and for all his new, motley sheep, and mentally recited memorized Scripture to himself until he dropped off to sleep.

In the very early hours of the morning Hank was awakened by footsteps coming down the cellblock and the jingle of the guard's jail keys. Oh no. The guard was opening his cell door. Now Hank would have to share the cell with . . . a drunk, a mugger, a *real* rapist? He pretended he was still asleep, but he opened one eye just a little to have a look. Oh brother! This hoodlum was big and grim looking, and from the bandage and bruise on his head it looked like he had just been in a brawl. He was muttering something about having to be stuck in a cell with a rapist. Hank started praying for the Lord's protection. This big character had to weigh twice as much as he did, and he looked violent.

The new guy flopped down on the other cot and breathed that heavy kind of breath one associates with bears, dragons, and monsters. *Lord, please deliver me!*

Rafar strutted back and forth on his hilltop overlooking the town, allowing his wings to trail and wave like a regal cape behind him. Demon messengers had been bringing him regular reports of how his final preparations of the town were going. So far it had been nothing but good news.

"Lucius," Rafar called with the tone one would use in calling a child, "Lucius, come here, won't you?"

Lucius stepped forward with all the dignity he could muster, trying to get his wings to wave and undulate like Rafar's.

"Yes, Ba-al Rafar?"

Rafar looked down at him gloatingly, a wry smile on his face, and said, "I trust you have learned from this experience. As you have so clearly seen, what you could not do in years, I have accomplished in days."

"Perhaps." That was all Lucius would give him.

Rafar thought that was funny. "And you disagree?"

"One could think, Ba-al, that your work was merely the capstone on the years of my labor wrought before your coming."

"Years of labor nearly undone by your blundering, you mean!" Rafar retorted. "Which does give one pause. Having won the town for the Strongman, do I dare now leave it in the hands of one who nearly lost it before?"

Lucius did not like the sound of that at all. "Rafar, for years this town has been my principality. *I* am the rightful Prince of Ashton!"

"You *were*. But honors, Lucius, reward deeds, and in deeds I do find you lacking."

Lucius was indignant, but he controlled himself in the presence of this giant power. "You have not seen my deeds because you have not chosen to look. Your will was set against me from the beginning."

Lucius had said too much. Immediately he was snatched from the ground by Rafar's burly fist around his throat, and now Rafar held him up and looked him straight in the eye.

"I," said Rafar slowly and fiercely, "and only I, am the judge of that!"

"Let the Strongman judge!" Lucius responded very brazenly. "Where is this Tal, this adversary whom you were to vanquish, whose little pieces you were to hurl across the sky as your victory banner?"

Rafar allowed a slight smile to cross his face, even though his eyes kept their fire. "Busche, the praying man, is defeated and his name sullied. Hogan, the once tenacious hound, is now a worthless and defeated wretch. The traitorous Maidservant is destroyed, and her scum of a friend is also eliminated. All others have fled."

Rafar waved his hand over the town. "Look, Lucius! Do you see the fiery hosts of heaven descending over the town? Do you see their flashing and polished swords? Do you see their numberless guard posted around about?"

He sneered at Lucius and Tal at the same time. "This Tal, this Captain of the Host, now commands a stricken and debilitated army, and he is afraid to show his face. Again and again I have defied him to confront me, to stop me, and he has not appeared. But don't worry. As I have spoken, so shall I do. When these other pressing matters are settled, Tal and I *will* meet, and you will see it take place . . . just before I vanquish *you!*"

Rafar held Lucius high as he called to another demon, "Courier, take word to the Strongman that all is ready and that he may come at his will. The obstacles are removed, Rafar has completed his task, and the town of Ashton is ready to fall into his hands"—Rafar dropped Lucius as he said it—"like a ripe plum."

Lucius bolted up from the ground and flew away in a humiliated flurry while the demonic ranks laughed and laughed.

33

Edith Duster had felt a certain stirring in her spirit before she went to bed that night. So when she was awakened abruptly by two luminous beings in her bedroom she was not entirely surprised, even though awestruck.

"Glory to God!" she exclaimed, her eyes wide, her face enraptured.

The two tall men had very kind and compassionate faces, but their expressions were serious. One was tall and blond, the other dark-haired and youthful. Both towered as high as the ceiling, and the glow from their white tunics filled the room. Each had a magnificent golden scabbard and belt, and the handles of their swords were purest gold, with fiery jewels.

"Edith Duster," said the big blond one in a deep, resonant voice, "we are going into battle for the town of Ashton. The victory rests on the prayers of the saints of God. As you fear the Lord, pray, and call others to prayer. Pray that the enemy will be vanquished and the righteous delivered."

Then the dark-haired one spoke. "Your pastor, Henry Busche, has fallen prisoner. He will be delivered through your prayers. Call Mary, his wife. Be a comfort to her."

Suddenly they were gone, and the room was dark once again. Edith knew somehow that she had seen them before, perhaps in dreams, perhaps as unimpressive, normal people here and there. And she knew the importance of their request.

She rose and grabbed her pillow, placed it on the floor, and then knelt upon it there beside the bed. She wanted to laugh, she wanted to cry, she wanted to sing; there was a burden and a power deep within her, and she clasped her shaking hands together there upon the bed, bowed her head, and began to pray. The words flowed forth from her deepest soul, an outcry on behalf of God's people and God's righteousness, a plea for power and victory in the name of Jesus, a binding of the evil forces that were trying to take the very life, the very heart of that community. Names and faces cascaded before her mind's eye and she interceded for all of them, pleading before the throne of God for their safety and salvation. She prayed. She prayed. She prayed.

From high above, the town of Ashton was spread out like an innocent toy village on a patchwork quilt, a small and unpretentious community still sleeping, but now awash with the slowly rising flood of predawn gray and pink that grew over the mountains in the east. As yet, nothing stirred in the town. There were no lights being switched on; the milk truck was still parked.

From somewhere in the skies, beyond the pink-edged clouds, a solitary, rushing sound began. One angelic warrior, soaring like a gull, spiraled quickly and covertly downward, until his form was lost in the patterns and textures of the streets and buildings far below. Then another appeared and he too dropped quietly into the town, disappearing somewhere within it.

And Edith Duster kept praying.

Two appeared, their wings swept back, their heads sharply downward, diving like hawks into the town. Then came another, gliding along a more shallow path that would carry him to the far side of town. Then four, dropping in four different directions. Then two more, then seven . . .

Mary was awakened from fitful sleep on the couch by the telephone.

"Hello?" Her eyes brightened immediately. "Oh, Edith, I'm so glad you called! I've been trying to reach you, I haven't even gone to bed, I must have your number written down wrong, or the phones aren't working . . ." Then she started crying, and told Edith all about the events of the previous night.

"Well, you just rest and be quiet until I get there," said Edith. "I've been on my knees all night and God is moving, yes He is! We'll get Hank out of there and more besides!"

Edith grabbed her sweater and her sneakers and was off to Mary's house. She had never felt younger.

John Coleman awoke early that morning, so shaken by a dream he couldn't get back to sleep. Patricia knew the feeling—the same thing had happened to her.

"I saw angels!" John said.

"I did too," said Patricia.

"And . . . and I saw demons. Monsters, Patty! Hideous things! The angels and the demons were fighting it out. It was—"

"Terrible."

"Awesome. Really awesome."

They called Hank. Mary answered. They got the story of last night, and they went right over.

Andy and June Forsythe couldn't sleep all that night. This morning Andy was crabby, and June just tried to stay out of his way. Finally, as Andy tried to eat some breakfast, he was able to talk about it. "It must be the Lord. I don't know what else it could be."

"But why are you so crabby?" June asked as tenderly as she could.

"Because I've never felt this way before," Andy said, and then his voice started to quiver. "I . . . I just feel like I have to pray, like . . . like something's really got to be settled and I can't rest until it is."

"You know," said June, "I really know what you mean. I don't know if I can explain it, but I feel like we haven't been alone all night. Somebody's been here with us, filling us with these feelings."

Andy got wide-eyed. "Yeah! That's it! That's the feeling!" He grabbed her hand with great joy and relief. "June, honey, I thought I was going crazy!"

Just then the phone rang. It was Cecil Cooper. He had had a very disturbing dream that night, and so had many others. Something was up. They didn't wait to gather to pray. They started praying right then and there.

From north, from south, from east and west, from all directions, and so very silently, heavenly warriors continued to drop into the town like snowflakes, walk into the town like people, sneak into the town like guerrillas, glide through fields and orchards into the town like bush pilots. Then they hid themselves and waited.

Hank woke at about 7; the nightmare had not ended. He was still in the cell. His new cellmate continued snoring for another hour until the guard brought in breakfast. The big man said nothing, but took the little plate that was handed through the bars. He didn't look too excited about the burnt toast and cold eggs. Perhaps this would be the time to break the ice.

"Good morning," Hank said.

"Good morning," the big man replied very half-heartedly.

"My name is Hank Busche."

The big man slid his plate out under the door for the guard to pick up. He hadn't touched the food. He stood there, looking out through the bars like a caged animal. He did not respond to Hank's introduction, nor did he tell Hank his name. He was obviously hurting; his eyes seemed so longing, and so vacant.

All Hank could do was pray for him.

Step, step, stumble, then step again. All morning long, through fields of corn, pastures of cows, thick forests, Bernice trudged along, slowly making her way north on a meandering route that ran roughly parallel to Highway 27, somewhere off to her left. The sound of the vehicles roaring along the highway helped her get her bearings.

She was beginning to trip over her own feet, her thoughts getting sluggish. Row upon row of cornstalks marched past her, their big green leaves brushing against her with a steady, almost annoying rhythm. The dirt under her feet was softly tilled and dusty. It was working into her shoes. It absorbed the strength from her strides.

After crossing the sea of corn, she came to a very long and very narrow grove of trees, a windbreak planted between the fields. She went into the middle of it and immediately found a patch of soft, grassy ground. She checked her watch: 8:25 A.M. She had to rest. She would get to Baker somehow . . . it was the only hope . . . she hoped Marshall was okay . . . she hoped she wouldn't die . . . she was asleep.

By the time lunch was brought in, Hank and his cellmate were a little more ready to eat. The sandwiches weren't that bad and the beef vegetable soup was quite good.

Before the guard got away Hank asked him, "Say, are you sure I couldn't have a Bible somehow?"

"I told you," the guard said rudely, "I'm waiting on authorization, and until I get it, no dice!"

Suddenly the big silent cellmate burst out, "Jimmy, you've got a stack of Gideon Bibles in your desk drawer and you know it! Now give the man a Bible."

The guard only sneered at the man. "Hey, you're on that side of the bars now, Hogan. *I'll* run the show out here!"

The guard left, and the big man tried to shift his attention to his lunch. He looked up at Hank, though, and quipped, "Jimmy Dunlop. He thinks he's a real man."

"Thanks for trying, anyway."

The big man heaved a deep sigh and then said, "Sorry for being rude all morning. I needed time to heal up from yesterday, I needed time to check you out, and I guess I needed time to get used to the idea of being in jail."

"I can sure identify with that. I've never been in jail before," Hank tried again. He extended his hand and said, "Hank Busche."

This time the man took it and gave him a firm shake. "Marshall Hogan."

Then something clicked for both of them. Before they had even dropped their hands again, they looked at each other, pointed at each other, and both began to ask, "Say, aren't you . . . ?"

And then they stared for a moment and didn't say anything.

The angels were watching, of course, and brought Tal word.

"Good, good," said Tal. "Now we'll just let those two talk."

"You're the pastor of that little white church," Marshall said.

"And you're the editor of the paper, the *Clarion*," Hank exclaimed.

"So what in the wide world are you doing here?"

"I don't know if you'd be able to believe it."

"Kid, you'd be amazed—*I'm* amazed—at what I'd believe!" Marshall lowered his voice and leaned close as he said, "They told me you were in here for rape."

"That's right."

"That sounds just like you, doesn't it?"

Hank didn't quite know what to make of that statement. "Well, I didn't do it, you know."

"Doesn't Alf Brummel go to your church?"

"Yes."

"Ever cross him?"

"Uh . . . well, yes."

"So have I. And that's why I'm in here, and that's why you're in here! Tell me what happened."

"When?"

"I mean, what really happened? Do you even know this girl you supposedly raped?"

"Well . . ."

"Where'd you get those bite marks on your arm?"

Hank was getting some doubts. "Say, listen, I'd better not say anything."

"Was her name Carmen?"

Hank's face said a yes that was almost audible.

"Just thought I'd take a stab at it. She's really a treacherous gal. She used to work for me and last night she told me she'd been raped and I knew then that it was a lie."

Hank was completely flabbergasted. "This is too much! How do you know about all this?"

Marshall looked around the cell and shrugged. "Ah well, what else is there to do? Hank, have I got a story for you! It's going to take a few hours. You ready for that?"

"If you're ready to hear mine, I'm ready to hear yours."

"Hello? Ma'am?"

Bernice jolted awake. There was someone leaning over her. It was a young girl about high school age, maybe older, with big brown eyes and black, curly hair, dressed in bib overalls, a perfect farmer's daughter.

"Oh! Uh . . . hi." It was all Bernice could think of to say.

"Are you all right, ma'am?" the girl asked in a slow and easy drawl.

"Um, yes. I was just sleeping. I hope that's all right. I was out for a walk, you know, and . . ." She remembered her bruised face. Oh, great! Now this kid will think I've been mugged or something.

"You looking for your sunglasses?" the girl asked, reaching down and picking them up. She handed them to Bernice.

"I . . . uh . . . guess you're wondering what happened to my face."

The girl only smiled a disarming smile and said, "Aw, you ought to see how I look when I first wake up."

"I take it this is your property? I didn't mean to—"

"No, I'm just passing through, like you are. I saw you lying here and thought I'd check up on you. Can I give you a lift anywhere?"

Bernice was about to say an automatic no, but then she looked at her watch. Oh no! It was almost 4 o'clock in the afternoon. "Well, you wouldn't happen to be going north, would you?"

"I'm heading up toward Baker."

"Oh, that's perfect! I could catch a ride with you?"

"Right after lunch."

"What?"

The girl walked out of the trees to the next field of corn, and then Bernice noticed a shiny blue motorcycle parked in the sun. The girl reached into a side saddle and brought out a brown paper sack. She returned and set that sack in front of Bernice, along with a carton of cold milk.

"You eat lunch at 4 in the afternoon?" Bernice asked with a conversational chuckle.

"No," the young lady answered with a chuckle of her own, "but you've come a long way, and you have a long way to go, and you need something to eat."

Bernice looked into those clear and laughing brown eyes, and then at the simple little lunch bag in front of her, and she could feel her face turning red and her eyes filling up.

"Eat up, now," said the girl.

Bernice opened the paper bag and found a roast beef sandwich that was truly a work of art. The beef was still hot, the lettuce crisp and green. Below that was a carton of blueberry yogurt—her favorite flavor—still cold to the touch.

She tried to keep her emotions down, but she began to quake with weeping, and the tears ran down her cheeks. Oh, I'm making a fool of myself, she thought. But this was so altogether different.

"I'm so sorry," she said. "I'm just . . . very touched by your kindness."

The girl touched her hand. "Well, I'm glad I could be here."

"What is your name?"

"You can call me Betsy."

"I'm—well, you can call me Marie." It was Bernice's middle name.

"I'll just do that. Listen, I have some cold water too, if you want that."

There came another wave of emotion. "You're a wonderful person. What are you doing on this planet?"

"Helping you," Betsy answered, running to her motorcycle for the water.

Hank sat on the edge of his cot, enraptured by the story Marshall was relating.

"Are you serious?" he responded suddenly. "Alf Brummel is into witchcraft? A board member in my church?"

"Hey, call it what you want, bub, but I'm telling you, it is spacy! I don't know how long he and that Langstrat have been bosom buddies, but enough of her cosmic consciousness crud has rubbed off on him to make him dangerous, and I mean that!"

"So who's in this group again?"

"Who *isn't* in it? Oliver Young's in it, Judge Baker's in it, most of the cops on the local police force are in it . . ." Marshall went on to give Hank just a small segment of the list.

Hank was amazed. This had to be the Lord. So many of the questions he had had for so long were finally finding their answers.

Marshall kept going for another half an hour or so, and then he started losing momentum. He had come to the part about Kate and Sandy.

"That's the part that hurts the most," he said, and then started looking out through the bars instead of into Hank's eyes. "It's a whole other story in itself, and you don't need to hear it. But I sure went over and over it this morning. It's my fault, Hank. I let it happen."

He heaved a deep breath and wiped wetness from his eyes. "I could have lost everything; the paper, the house, the—the battle. I could have taken it if I only had them. But I lost them too . . ." Then he said the words, "And that's how I ended up here," and he stopped. Abruptly.

Hank was weeping. He was weeping and smiling, raising his hands up to God, shaking his head in wonderment. To Marshall, it looked like he was having some kind of religious experience.

"Marshall," Hank said excitedly, unable to sit still, "this is of God! Our being here is no accident. Our enemies meant it for evil, but God meant it for good. He's brought the two of us together just so we could meet, just so we could put the whole thing together. You haven't heard my story yet, but guess what? It's the same! We've both been coming up against the exact same problem from two different sides."

"Tell me, tell me, I want to cry too!"

So Hank began telling how he suddenly found himself the pastor of a church that didn't seem to want him . . .

Betsy's motorcycle flew like the wind up Highway 27, and Bernice held on tight, sitting behind her on the soft leather seat, watching all the scenery go by. The whole trip was exhilarating; it made her feel like a kid again, and the fact that both of them wore helmets with dark face shields made Bernice feel all the more safe from discovery.

But Baker was coming up rapidly, and with it the risks and dangers and the big question of whether Susan Jacobson would even be there or not. Part of Bernice wanted to stay on the motorcycle with this sweet, likable kid and just keep right on going to . . . wherever. Any life had to be better than this one.

The landmarks became familiar: the Coca-Cola sign, and that big lot full of firewood for sale. They were coming into Baker. Betsy let off the throttle and started whining down through the gears. Finally she pulled off the highway and bumped along to a stop in a gravel parking lot just in front of the aged Sunset Motel.

"Will this do for you?" Betsy shouted through her face shield.

Bernice could just make out The Evergreen up the highway. "Oh, yeah, this will do just fine."

She climbed off the motorcycle and struggled with the chin strap of her helmet.

"Leave it on a while," said Betsy.

"What for?"

Bernice's eyes immediately gave her a good reason that *she* would know of: a squad car from the Ashton precinct just happened to drive by, slowing down as it entered Baker. Bernice watched as it then signaled left and pulled into the parking area in front of The Evergreen Tavern. Two officers got out and went inside. She looked down at Betsy. Did she know?

She didn't act like it. She pointed to a little diner attached to the motel. "That's Rose Allen's little cafe. It looks like a terrible place, but she makes the best homemade soup in the world and she sells it cheap. It'd be a great place to kill some time."

Bernice removed her helmet and set it on the bike.

"Betsy," she said, "I owe you a very great debt. Thank you so very much."

"You're welcome." Even through the face shield that smile shone brightly.

Bernice looked at the little cafe. No, it didn't look very nice. "The best soup in the world, eh?"

She turned back to Betsy and stiffened. For a moment she felt she would stumble forward as if a wall had suddenly disappeared in front of her.

Besty was gone. The motorcycle was gone.

It was like awaking from a dream and needing time to adjust one's mind to what was real and what was not. But Bernice knew it had not been a dream. The tracks of the motorcycle were still plainly visible in the gravel, leading from where it had left the highway to the spot directly in front of Bernice. There they ended.

Bernice backed away, stunned and shaken. She looked up and down the highway, but knew even as she did that she would not see that girl on her motorcycle. As a matter of fact, as a few more seconds went by Bernice knew she would have been disappointed if she had. It would have been the end of a very beautiful *something* she had never felt before.

But she had to get off the highway, she kept telling herself. She was sticking out like a sore thumb. She tore herself away from that spot and hurried into Rose Allen's little cafe.

Dinner came through the bars at 6. Marshall was ready to eat the fried chicken and cooked carrots, but Hank was so much into his story that Marshall had to prompt him to eat.

"I'm really getting to the good part!" Hank protested, and then he asked, "How are you keeping up with this?"

"A lot of it is new," Marshall admitted.

"What were you again? Presbyterian?"

"Hey, don't blame them. I'm just me, that's all, and I always thought that spooks only come out on Halloween."

"Well, you always wanted an explanation for Langstrat's strange pull, and how the Network could have all that powerful influence on people, and what may have really been tormenting Ted Harmel, and especially who these spirit guides might be."

"You're—you're asking me to believe in evil spirits."

"Do you believe in God?"

"Yes, I believe there's a God."

"Do you believe in a devil?"

Marshall had to think for a moment. He noticed that he'd gone through a change of opinion somewhere along the line. "I . . . well, yeah, I guess I do."

"Believing in angels and demons is simply the next step after that. It's only logical."

Marshall shrugged and picked up a drumstick. "Just keep going. Let me hear the whole thing."

34

Bernice killed another hour and a half in Rose Allen's cafe, buying a bowl of Rose's soup—Betsy was right, it was good—and eating it very slowly. She kept her eye on Rose the whole time. Boy, if that woman made one move toward that telephone, Bernice was going to be *out* of there! But Rose didn't appear to think a beat-up woman in her cafe was all that unusual, and nothing happened.

When 7:30 rolled around, Bernice knew she would have to try for that meeting one way or another. She paid Rose for the soup out of the change in her pocket and stepped outside.

It looked like that police car that had stopped at The Evergreen was gone now, but the light was getting poor and it was too far away for Bernice to tell for sure. She would just have to take it one step at a time.

She walked along carefully, her eyes looking in all directions for police, stakeouts, suspicious vehicles, anything. The parking lot of The Evergreen was overflowing, and that was probably typical for a Saturday night. She kept her sunglasses on, but apart from that she looked every bit like the Bernice Krueger the police were searching for. What else could she do?

As she approached the tavern, she looked here and there for any escape routes. She did notice a trail going back into the woods, but had no idea how far it went or where it eventually led. All in all, there didn't seem to be too many places to run or hide.

The back of The Evergreen Tavern was the one part of the building nobody seemed to care about at all; the three old cars, the forgotten refrigerators, the dented beer kegs, and the piles of delaminating tables and rusting, broken-through chairs were parted just enough to allow a narrow pathway to the back door.

This door also scraped an arc in the linoleum. The music from the jukebox hit Bernice like a wave, as did the smoke from cigarettes and the sickeningly sweet smell of beer. She closed the door after her, and found herself in a dark cavern full of silhouettes. She cautiously looked over, under, and around her sunglasses, trying to see where she was and where everyone else was without taking the sunglasses off.

There had to be someplace to sit in here. Most of the booths were full of loggers and their girlfriends. There was one chair in the corner. She took it and settled in to survey the room.

From this spot she could make out the front door and could see people coming in, but she could not distinguish their faces. She did recognize Dan behind the bar; he was pouring beers while trying to keep a bridle on things. Her ears verified that the shuffleboard game was in full swing, and two video games against a far wall were bleeping and burpling through the quarters.

It was 7:50. Well, just sitting here wasn't going to work; she felt too obvious, and she simply couldn't see. She got up from her chair and tried to mingle with the crowd, staying close to the walls.

She looked at Dan again. He was a little closer and he could have been looking back at her, but she didn't know. He didn't act like he recognized her, or cared if he did. Bernice tried to find an unobtrusive spot from which to look at the people at the front tables. She joined a small group around one of the video games. These people in the front were still silhouettes, but none of them could have been Susan.

There was Dan again, leaning over one table and pulling the front windowshade half down. Some of the people nearby didn't like it, but he gave them some explanation, and left it that way.

She decided to go back to her chair and wait. She worked her way back to the shuffleboard game, then went slowly behind the crowd toward the back of the room.

Then a thought hit her. She had seen that pulling-down-the-windowshade trick in some movie. A signal? She turned her head toward the front, and at that exact moment the front door opened. Two men in uniforms came in. Police! One pointed right at her. She moved as quickly as she could for the back door. It was nothing but dark in front of her. How in the world was she even going to *find* that door?

She could hear a shout over the noise of the crowd. "Hey! Stop that woman! Police! You! Hold it!"

The people around her began muttering, "Who? What woman? *That* woman?" One other voice out of the blackness said, "Hey, lady, I think he's talking to you!"

She didn't look back, but she could hear the shuffling of chairs and feet. They were coming after her.

Then she saw the green exit sign over the back door. Forget about keeping cool! She broke into a run toward that light.

People were hollering everywhere, coming to help her, wanting to see what was going on. They got in the policemen's way, and the police started hollering, "One side, please! Get out of the way! Stop her!"

She couldn't see the latch or knob or whatever that door had. Hoping it had a crash bar, she slammed her body against it. It didn't have a crash bar, but she could hear something break and the door opened anyway.

It was lighter out here than inside. She could make out the path through all the junk and raced through it, running for all she was worth just as she heard the backdoor crash open again. Then came the sound of their footsteps. Could she get out of sight before they got clear of all that junk?

She tore off her sunglasses just in time to spot the trail through the woods, on the other side of the fence.

It was amazing what a person could do when scared enough. Planting her hands on the top of the fence, she swung her body up and vaulted over it, tumbling down into the brush on the other side. Without stopping to congratulate herself, she scrambled up that trail into the woods like a scared rabbit, ducking to avoid the low-hanging branches she could see and being whipped in the face by the ones she couldn't.

The trail was soft and clear, and kept her footsteps quiet and muffled. It was darker in the woods, and at times she had to stop abruptly just to see where the trail led next. During those times she would also listen for her pursuers; she could hear some kind of yelling going on far behind her, but it seemed no one had thought of this trail.

There was light up ahead. She came to a gravel back road, but hesitated in the trees long enough to look up and down that road for cars, cops, anyone. The road was quiet and deserted. She stepped out quickly, trying to decide which way to go.

Suddenly, at an intersection a little way down the road, a car appeared, pulling onto this road and heading her way. They had to have seen her! There was nothing to do but keep running!

Her lungs were laboring, her heart was aching and felt like it would pound itself apart, her legs felt like lead. She couldn't help crying out in anguish and fear with each exhalation as she ran across a field toward a cluster of buildings in the distance. She looked back. A figure was after her, running swiftly in hot pursuit. No! No! Please don't chase me, just let me go! I can't go on like this!

The buildings were getting closer. It looked like an old farm. She was no longer thinking, only running. She couldn't see; her eyes were doubly blurred now with tears. She was gasping for breath, her mouth was dry, the pain from her rib cage shot up and down her whole side. The grass whipped against her legs, almost tripping her with every step. She could hear the footsteps of her pursuer swishing through the grass not far behind her. Oh, God, help me!

Ahead was a large, dark building, a barn. She would go for it and try to hide. If they found her, they found her. She could run no further.

She stumbled, trudged, dragged one foot after the other around one end, and found the big sliding door half open. She practically fell through it.

Inside, she found herself in inky blackness. Now her eyes were useless to her. She stumbled ahead, her arms out in front of her. Her feet were shuffling through straw. Her arms bumped into boards. A stall. She went further. Another stall. She could hear the footsteps coming around the corner and through the door. She ducked into one of the stalls and tried to quell her gasping. She was on the verge of fainting.

The steps slowed. The pursuer was encountering the same darkness and trying to feel his way along. But he was coming closer.

Bernice backed further into the stall, wondering if there might be some way to hide herself. Her hand encountered some kind of handle. She felt downward. A pitchfork. She took it in her hands. Could she really use this thing in cold blood?

The footsteps moved ahead methodically; the pursuer was checking each stall, working his way through the barn. Now Bernice could see a small beam of light sweeping here and there.

She held the pitchfork high as her cracked rib punished her in protest. You're going to be very sorry you ever chased me, she thought. She was playing by jungle rules now.

The footsteps were very close now. The little beam of light was just outside the opening. She was ready. The light shined in her eyes. There was a slight gasp. Come on, Bernice! Throw the pitchfork! Her arms would not move.

"Bernice Krueger?" asked a muffled, female voice.

Bernice still didn't move. She held the pitchfork high, still panting for air, the little shaft of light illuminating her crazed, blackened eyes and her terrified face.

Whoever it was stepped back abruptly at the sight of her and whispered, "Bernice, no! Don't throw it!"

That made Bernice want all the more to throw that thing. She was whimpering and gasping, trying to get her arms to move. They would not.

"Bernice," came the voice, "it's Susan Jacobson! I'm alone!"

Bernice still did not put down the pitchfork. For the moment she was beyond rationality, and words meant nothing.

"Do you hear me?" came the voice. "Please, put the fork down. I won't hurt you. I'm not the police, I promise you."

"Who are you?" Bernice asked finally, her voice gasping and quivering.

"Susan Jacobson, Bernice." She said it again slowly. "Susan Jacobson, your sister Pat's old roommate. We had an appointment."

It was as if Bernice suddenly recovered from a hallucination or a sleepwalking nightmare. The name sank into her mind at last and awoke her.

"You . . ." she panted. "You gotta be kidding!"

"I'm not. It's me."

Susan shone her little penlight on her own face. The black hair and pale complexion were unmistakable, even though the black clothes were replaced now with jeans and a blue jacket.

Bernice lowered the pitchfork. Then she dropped it and let out a muffled wail, putting her hand over her mouth. She suddenly realized she was in terrible pain. She sank to her knees in the straw, her arms around her rib cage.

"Are you all right?" Susan asked.

"Turn out that light before they see you," was all Bernice would say.

The light clicked off. Bernice could feel Susan's hand touching her.

"You're hurt!" Susan said.

"I . . . I try to keep everything in perspective," Bernice gasped. "I'm still alive, I've found the real live Susan Jacobson, I haven't had to kill anybody, the police haven't found me . . . and I have a cracked rib! Ooooooohhh . . ."

Susan put her arms around Bernice to comfort her.

"Gently, gently!" Bernice cautioned. "Where in the world did you come from? How did you find me?"

"I was watching the tavern from across the street, waiting to see if you or Kevin would show up. I saw the police go in, and you running out the back, and I knew it was you right away. We college kids used to hang around here a lot, so I knew about that trail you took, and I knew how it emptied out onto that road out there. I drove around, thinking I could head you off and let you jump into my car, but you were too far ahead of me and you took off running."

Bernice let her head drop a bit. She could feel herself getting emotional again. "I used to think I'd never seen a miracle, but now I don't know."

Hank finished his whole story and, with Marshall's prodding, had also put away most of his dinner. Marshall began to ask questions, which Hank answered from his knowledge of the Scriptures.

"So," Marshall asked and mused at the same time, "when the Gospels talk about Jesus and His disciples casting out unclean spirits, that's what they were really doing?"

"That's what they were doing," Hank answered.

Marshall leaned back against the bars and kept right on thinking. "That would sure explain a lot of things. But what about Sandy? Do you suppose that she—she's . . . ?"

"I don't know for sure, but it could be."

"What I talked to yesterday. . . that wasn't her. She was just crazy; you wouldn't have believed it." He caught himself. "Aw, then again, you probably would."

Hank was excited. "But don't you see what's happened? It's a miracle of God, Marshall. All along, you were looking into all this racketeering and intrigue, and wondering how these things could be happening so smoothly and so forcefully, especially in the individual lives of so many people. Well, now you have your 'how.' And now that you've told me what you've found out and all that you've been through, I have my 'why.' All this time I've been encountering demonic powers in this town, but I never really knew just what they were up to. Now I know. It has to be the Lord who brought us together."

Marshall gave Hank a wry smile. "So where do we go from here, Preacher? They've locked us in, they haven't allowed us any communication with our families, friends, lawyers, or anyone. I have a feeling that our constitutional rights aren't going to have much to do with it at this juncture."

Now Hank leaned back against the cold concrete wall and thought about it. "That part only God knows. But I have a very strong feeling that He got us into this, and that He also has a plan for getting us out."

"If we must talk about strong feelings," Marshall countered, "I have some pretty strong feelings that they just want us out of the way while they finish once and for all what they've started. It's going to be interesting to see what's left of the town, our jobs, our homes, our families, and everything else we treasured once we get out of here. *If* we get out of here."

"Well, have faith. God's in control here."

"Yehhh, I just hope He hasn't dropped the ball."

As the two women sat there in the straw, in the dark, Bernice tried to explain everything to Susan: her battered face, her cracked rib, what she and Marshall had been through, and the death of Kevin Weed.

Susan digested it all for a moment, and then said, "It's Kaseph's way. It's the Society's way. I should have known better than to have brought Kevin into it."

"Don't—don't blame yourself. All of us are in this thing whether we really want to be or not."

Susan forced herself to be unemotional and calculating. "You're right . . . at least for now. Someday soon I'll sit down and really think about it, and I'll weep over that man." She stood up. "But right now there's too much to do and too little time. Do you think you can walk?"

"No, but that hasn't stopped me so far."

"My car is rented, and I have too many important materials in it to leave it sitting out there. Come on."

With careful and very quiet, well-picked steps, Susan and Bernice made their way to the big barn door. It was very quiet out there.

"Want to go for it?" Susan asked.

"Sure," said Bernice, "let's do it."

They started back across the expansive field toward the road where Susan had left her car, using one tree that jutted up against the starry sky as their heading. As they crossed the field again, Bernice noted how much shorter the trip seemed now that she was not fleeing for her life.

Susan led the way to where her car was parked. She had pulled it off the road a little way and nestled it in among some trees. She began fumbling in her pocket for the keys.

"Susan!" said a voice from the woods.

The two of them froze.

"Susan Jacobson?" came the voice again.

Susan whispered excitedly. "I don't believe it!"

Bernice answered, "I don't believe it either!"

"Kevin?"

Some bushes began to move and swish, and then a man stepped out of the woods. There was no mistaking that lanky frame and that lazy walk.

"Kevin Weed?" Bernice had to ask again.

"Bernice Krueger!" said Kevin. "You made it. Aw, that's great!"

After a short moment of speechless amazement and surprise, the embraces came automatically.

"Let's get out of here," said Susan.

They piled into her car and put some miles between themselves and Baker.

"I got a motel room in Orting, up north of Windsor," said Susan. "We can go there."

It was okay with Bernice and Kevin.

Bernice said very happily, "Kevin, you've just made a liar out of me! I thought for sure you were dead."

"I'm alive for now," Kevin said, not sounding too sure about anything.

"But your truck went into the river!"

"Yeah, I know. Some jerk stole it and crashed it. Somebody was trying to kill me."

He realized he didn't make much sense, so he started over. "Hey, I was on my way to meet you at the bridge like you said. I stopped at The Evergreen to have a few, and I bet some guy slipped me a mickey—you know, put something in my beer. I mean, I got *stoned*.

"I was driving down the road to meet up with you, and I was really spacing out, so I pulled over at Tucker's Burgers to throw up or get a drink of water or go to the bathroom or something. I fell asleep in the men's room, man, and I must have slept there all night. I woke up this morning and went outside and my truck was gone. I didn't know what happened to it until I read about it in the paper. They must still be searching the river for my body."

"It's obvious Kaseph and his Network have us all marked," said Susan, "but . . . I think somebody's looking out for us. Kevin, something very similar happened to me: I ran away from Kaseph's ranch on foot, and the only reason I got away was because all the security personnel went chasing somebody else who was trying to get away in one of the big moving vans. Now who in their right mind would try that, and at just that precise moment?"

Bernice added, "And I still haven't figured out who in the world that Betsy was."

Susan had been formulating her theory for days. "I think we'd better start thinking about God."

"*God?*"

"And angels," Susan added. She quickly recounted the details of her escape, and concluded, "Listen, somebody came into that room. I know it."

Kevin piped up, "Hey, like maybe it was an angel that stole my truck."

And then Bernice recalled, "You know, there was something about Betsy. It made me just cry. I've never run into anything like that before."

Susan touched her hand. "Well, it looks like we're all running into *something*, so whatever we do we'd better pay attention."

The car continued to speed along back roads, taking a slightly roundabout route toward the little resort town of Orting.

Like two comrades-in-arms, Marshall and Hank were beginning to feel they had known each other all their lives.

"I like your kind of faith," Marshall said. "It's no wonder they've tried so hard to get you out of that church." He chuckled a little. "Boy, you must feel like the Alamo! You're the only thing standing between the Devil and the rest of the town."

Hank smiled weakly. "I'm not much, believe me. But I'm not the only one. There are saints out there, Marshall, people praying for us. Sooner or later something's going to break. God won't let Satan have this town that easy!"

Marshall pointed his finger at Hank, even shook it a little. "See there? I like that kind of faith. Good and straight, laid right on the line." He shook his head. "Sheesh! How long has it been since I've heard it come across like that?"

Hank seasoned his words with salt, but he knew the time had come to say it. "Well, Marshall, since we're talking so straight here, right on the line, what do you say we talk about you? You know, there could be some more reasons God put us in this cell together."

Marshall was not defensive at all, but smiling and ready to listen.

"What are we going to do, talk about the fate of my eternal soul?"

Hank smiled back. "That's exactly what we're going to talk about."

They talked about sin, that aggravating and destructive tendency of man to stray from God and choose his own way, always to his own hurt. That brought them around to Marshall's family again, and how so many attitudes and actions were the direct result of that basic, human self-will and rebellion against God.

Marshall shook his head as he saw things in this light. "Hey, our family never did know God. We only went through the motions. No wonder Sandy wouldn't buy it!"

Then Hank talked about Jesus, and showed Marshall that this Man whose name was so casually thrown around and even trampled upon in the world was far more than just a religious symbol, a lofty untouchable personality in a stained-glass window. He was the very real, very alive, very personal Son of God, and He could be the personal Lord and Savior of anyone who asked Him to be.

"I never thought I'd be lying here listening to this," Marshall said suddenly. "You're really hitting me where it hurts, you know that?"

"Well," said Hank, "why do you suppose that is? Where's the pain coming from?"

Marshall took a deep breath as he took the time to think. "I guess from knowing that you're right, which means I've been wrong a long, long time."

"Jesus loves you anyway. He knows that's your problem, and that's what He died for."

"Yeah . . . right!"

35

The motel in Orting was nice, quaint, homey, just like the rest of this town situated along the Judd River on the border of the national forest. It was a stopping place for sportsmen, built and decorated in a pleasing hunt-and-fish, hike-in-the-woods motif.

Susan wanted no trouble or attention, so she paid for two more occupants for the room that night. They went into the room and pulled the shades.

They all made a stop in the bathroom, but Bernice remained just a little longer, carefully rewrapping her ribs and then washing her face. She looked herself over in the mirror and touched her bruises very gingerly, whistling at the sight. It could only get better from here.

In the meantime, Susan had flopped her big suitcase on the bed and opened it up. When Bernice finally came out, Susan took a small book from the suitcase and handed it to her.

"This is where it started," she said. "It's your sister's diary."

Bernice didn't know what to say. A diamond would not have been a greater treasure. She could only look down at the little blue diary in her hands, a last surviving link with her dead sister, and struggle to believe it was really there. "Where . . . how did you get this?"

"Juleen Langstrat made sure no one ever saw it. She had it stolen from Pat's room and she gave it to Kaseph, from whom I stole it. I became Kaseph's girl, you know; his Maidservant, he called it. I had regular access to him all the time, and he trusted me. I came across the diary one day while I was straightening up his office, and I recognized it right away because I used to watch Pat write in it almost every night in our dorm room. I sneaked it out, read it, and it woke me up. I used to think Alexander Kaseph was . . . well, the Messiah, the answer for all mankind, a true prophet of peace and universal brotherhood . . ."

Susan made a face like she was getting sick. "Oh, he filled my mind with all that kind of talk, but somewhere deep inside I always had my doubts. That little book right there told me to listen to the doubts and not to him."

Bernice thumbed through the pages of the diary. It went back a few years, and seemed very detailed.

Susan continued, "You may not want to read it just now. When I read that diary . . . well, it made me sick for days."

Bernice wanted the end of the story. "Susan, do you know how my sister really died?"

Susan said angrily, "Your sister Pat was methodically and viciously done away with by the Universal Consciousness Society, or I should say, the forces behind it. She made the same fatal mistake I've seen so many others make: she found out too much about the Society, she showed herself to be an enemy of Alexander Kaseph. Listen, what Kaseph wants, he gets, and he doesn't care who has to be destroyed, murdered, or mutilated to make sure of it." She shook her head. "I had to be blind not to have seen it happening to Pat. It was right out of the textbook!"

"So what about some man named Thomas?"

Susan answered directly, "Yes, it was Thomas. He was responsible for her death." Then she added rather cryptically, "But he wasn't a man."

Bernice was slowly catching on to this new game with its very weird rules. "And now you're going to tell me it wasn't a woman either."

"Pat was taking a psychology class, and one of her requirements was that she be in a subject pool for psychology experiments—it's in the diary, you'll read it all. A friend persuaded her to volunteer for an experiment involving relaxation techniques, and it was during that experiment that she had what she called a psychic experience, some kind of insight into a higher world, she called it.

"I'll make it short; you can read it for yourself later. She became extremely enamored by the experience and saw no connection between this 'scientific' exploration and the 'mystical' practices I was into. She kept going back, kept taking part in the experiments, and finally contacted what she called a 'highly evolved, disembodied human' from another dimension, a very wise and intelligent being named Thomas."

Bernice struggled with what she was hearing, but knew she held the documentation for Susan's account, her sister's diary. "So who was this Thomas really? Just a figment of her imagination?"

"Some things you're just going to have to accept for now," Susan replied with a sigh. "We've talked about God, we've toyed with the idea of angels; now let's try evil angels, evil spirit entities. To the atheistic scientists, they might appear as extraterrestrials, often with their own spaceships; to evolutionists they might claim to be highly evolved beings; to the lonely, they might appear as long-lost relatives speaking from the other side of the grave; Jungian psychologists consider them 'archetypal images' dredged from the collective consciousness of the human race."

"*What?*"

"Hey, listen, whatever description or definition fits, whatever shape, whatever form it takes to win a person's confidence and appeal to his vanity, that's the form they take. And they tell the deluded seeker of truth whatever he or she wants to hear until they finally have that person in their complete control."

"Like a con game, in other words."

"It's all a con game: Eastern meditation, witchcraft, divination, Science of Mind, psychic healing, holistic education—oh, the list goes on and on—it's all the same thing, nothing but a ruse to take over people's minds and spirits, even their bodies."

Bernice reviewed memory after memory of their investigation, and Susan's claims fell right into place.

Susan continued, "Bernice, we are dealing with a conspiracy of spirit entities. I know. Kaseph is crawling with them and takes his orders from them. They do his dirty work. If anyone gets in his way, he has numberless resources in the spiritual realm to clear away the problem in whatever manner is most convenient."

Ted Harmel, Bernice thought. The Carluccis. How many others? "You're not the first person to try to tell me all this."

"I hope I'm the last person who will have to."

Kevin piped in. "Yeah, I remember how Pat talked about Thomas. He never sounded like he was human. She acted like he was more of a god. She had to ask him before she'd even decide what to eat for breakfast. I—I thought she'd found some guy, you know, some male chauvinist type."

Susan eased into the bottom line of the story. "Pat had given her will over to Thomas. It didn't take long; it usually doesn't once a person really submits to a spirit's influence. No doubt he took control of her, then terrified her, then convinced her that—well, the Hindus call it karma; it's the delusion that your next life will be better than this one because you've earned enough brownie points. In Pat's case, a self-inflicted death would be nothing more than a way to escape the evil of this lower world and join Thomas in a higher state of existence."

Susan gently flipped the pages of the diary still in Bernice's hands, and found the last entry. "There. The last thing in Pat's diary is a love letter to Thomas. She planned to join him soon, and she even mentions how she'll do it."

Bernice could feel revulsion at the thought of reading such a letter, but she began to work her way through the last few pages of her sister's diary. Pat wrote in a style of someone under a very strange, lofty-sounding delusion, but it was clear she was also disoriented by an irrational fear of life itself. Terrible pain and spiritual anguish had taken over her soul, changing her from the happy-go-lucky Patricia Krueger that Bernice had grown up with to a terrified, aimless psychotic completely out of touch with reality.

Bernice tried to read on, but she began to feel old wounds reopening; emotions that had waited for this very moment of final revelation burst from their hiding places like a river through an opened floodgate. The scrawled and ambling words on the pages blurred behind a sudden cascade of tears, and her whole body began to quake with sobs. All she wanted to do was shut out the world, disregard this gallant woman and this poor, disheveled logger, lie down on the bed, and cry. And she did.

Hank slept peacefully on his cot in the cell. Marshall was not sleeping at all. He sat up in the dark, his back against the cold, hard bars of the cell, his head drooping, his hand making nervous little trips around his face.

He had been shot through the guts. That's what it felt like. Somewhere he had lost his armor plating, his strength, his strong and tough facade. He had always been Marshall Hogan, the hunter, the hound, the stay-out-my-way getter of whatever he wanted, a foe to be reckoned with, a guy who could take care of himself.

A lump, that's what he was, and nothing but a fool. This Hank Busche was right. Just look at yourself, Hogan. Don't worry about

God dropping the ball; you dropped it a long time ago. You blew it, man. You thought you had everything under control, and now where's your family and where are you?

Maybe you've been tricked by these demons Hank's been talking about, and then maybe you've even fooled yourself. Come on, Marshall, you know why you shortchanged your family. You were copping out, singing the same old tune again. And you enjoyed working with that good-looking reporter, didn't you? Teasing her, tossing paper wads at her, for crying out loud! How old are you, sixteen?

Marshall let his own mind and heart tell him the truth, and much of it felt as if he had known it somewhere but had never listened. How long, he began to wonder, had he been lying to himself?

"Kate," he whispered there in the dark, his eyes glistening with tears. "Kate, what have I done?"

A big hand reached across the cell and nudged Hank's shoulder. Hank stirred, opened his eyes, and said quietly, "Yeah, what's up?"

Marshall was weeping and he said very quietly, "Hank, I'm just no good. I need God. I need Jesus."

How many times in his life had Hank said the words? "Let's pray."

After several minutes had passed, Bernice began to feel the flood subsiding. She sat up, still sniffling, but trying to get back to the business at hand.

"That's what woke me up," Susan reiterated. "I thought these beings were benevolent; I thought Kaseph had all the answers. But I saw them all in their true form when I read what they did to my best friend, your sister."

Kevin asked, "So is that why you came up to me at the carnival and got my number?"

"Kaseph had a special meeting in town with Langstrat and some other vital conspirators, Oliver Young and Alf Brummel. I came to Ashton with Kaseph, tagging right along as I always did, but when I got the opportunity I sneaked away. I had to take the chance that maybe I'd see you somewhere. Maybe it was God again; it was nothing short of a miracle that I spotted you at the carnival. I needed a friend on the outside I could confide in, someone obscure."

Kevin smiled. "Yeah, that describes me pretty well."

Susan continued, "Kaseph never liked to feel that he didn't have complete control of me. When I slipped away to the carnival, he probably told the others that he'd already sent me there and that they would meet me. When he found me and dragged me behind that silly booth, he talked to them like I had gone ahead and picked out that spot."

Bernice said, "And that's when I came across you and snapped your picture!"

"And then Brummel slipped some bills to those two hookers and some instructions to a few of his Windsor friends, and you know the rest."

Susan went to her suitcase. "But now for the really big news. Kaseph is making his move tomorrow. There's a special meeting scheduled with the Whitmore College regents at 2 in the afternoon. Omni Corporation—as a front for the Universal Consciousness Society—plans to buy Whitmore College, and Kaseph is closing the deal."

Bernice's eyes widened with horror. "Then we were right! He *is* going for the college!"

"It's good strategy. The whole town of Ashton is practically built around that college. Once the Society and Kaseph get established there at Whitmore, they'll have overwhelming influence over the rest of the town. Society people will come in like a swarm and Ashton will become another 'Sacred City of the Universal Mind.' It's happened enough before, in other towns, in other countries."

Bernice pounded the bed in frustration. "Susan, we have records of Eugene Baylor's financial transactions, evidence that might show how the college was undermined. But we haven't been able to make any sense of it all!"

Susan pulled a little canister out of her suitcase. "Actually, you only have half the picture. Baylor's no fool; he knew how to cover his tracks so his embezzlements on behalf of Omni wouldn't be noticed. What you need is the other side of those transactions: Kaseph's own records." She held the canister out for them to see. "I didn't have room for all that material. I did photograph it, though, and if we could get this film developed—"

"We have a darkroom at the *Clarion*. We could print that film right away."

"Let's check out of here."

They scrambled.

The Remnant continued to pray. None had been able to see or even hear from Hank since his arrest. The police station was manned at all times by strange police no one had ever seen in Ashton before, and none of these officers knew anything about how to visit anyone in jail, or how to bail them out, nor would they let anyone in to find out. It seemed Ashton had become a police state.

Fear, anger, and prayer increased. Something terrible was happening to the town, and they all knew it vividly, but what could be done in a town with deaf authorities, in a county whose offices were closed for the weekend?

The phone lines continued to hum, both in the town and going out across the country to relatives and friends, all of whom dropped to their knees to intercede and called their own authorities and legislators.

Alf Brummel stayed away from his office, avoiding any distraught Christians with sermons to deliver about their pastor's constitutional rights, or an official's duty to the will of the people, or anything else. He remained in Langstrat's apartment, pacing the floor, worrying, sweating, waiting for 2 o'clock on Sunday afternoon.

Grandma Duster kept praying and reassuring everyone that God had everything under control. She reminded them of what the angels had told her, and then many recalled what they had dreamed, or heard in their mind while praying, or seen in a vision, or felt in their spirits. And they continued to pray for the town.

And everywhere, from every direction, new visitors continued to arrive in the town of Ashton, riding in on passing hay trucks, hitchhiking in like summer backpackers, gliding in through the cornfields and then through the back streets, roaring in like wild bikers, bussing in like high schoolers, hiding in the trunks and under the bellies of every vehicle that traveled through on Highway 27.

And steadily the nooks, crannies, unused rooms, and countless other hiding places all over the town became alive with still, silent figures, their burly hands upon their swords, their golden eyes piercing and alert, their ears tuned to one particular sound from one particular trumpet.

Above the town, concealed in the trees, Tal could still look out across the wide valley and see Rafar in the big dead tree, overseeing the activities of his demons.

Captain Tal continued to watch and wait.

In the remote valley, a rapidly growing cloud of demon spirits churned for a radius of two miles all around the ranch, towering as high as the mountaintops. Their numbers were beyond counting, their density such that the cloud totally obscured anything within it. The spirits danced and wailed like drunken brawlers, waving their swords, raving and drooling, their eyes wild with madness. Myriads of them paired off, jousting, sparring, testing one another's skills.

In the darkened center of the cloud, in the big stone house, the Strongman sat with narrowed eyes and a crooked smirk that deepened the folds of his sagging face. In the company of his generals, he took time to gloat over the news he had just received from Ashton.

"Prince Rafar has satisfied my wishes, he has fulfilled his mission," the Strongman said, and then bared his ivory fangs with a drooling smile. "I will like that little town. In my hands, it will grow like a tree and fill the countryside."

He savored the next thought: "I may never have to stir myself from that place. What do you think? Shall we have our home at last?"

The tall and loathsome generals all muttered affirmatively. The Strongman rose from his seat, and the others snapped to a stiff and upright stance of attention.

"Our Mr. Kaseph has been calling me for some time now. Prepare the ranks. We will leave immediately."

The generals shot out through the roof of the house into the cloud, shrieking their orders, assembling their troops.

The Strongman unfolded his wings in a regal manner, then floated like a monstrous, overweight vulture into the basement room where Alexander Kaseph, sitting cross-legged on a large cushion, chanted the Strongman's name again and again. The Strongman alighted right in front of Kaseph and observed him for a moment, drinking in Kaseph's worship and spiritual groveling. Then, with a swift movement, the Strongman stepped forward and let his huge frame dissolve into Kaseph's body as Kaseph twitched and writhed grotesquely. In a moment the possession was complete, and Alexander Kaseph awakened from his meditation.

"The time has come!" he said, with the Strongman's look in his eyes.

36

Susan turned the rented car into the little gravel parking area behind the *Ashton Clarion*. It was 5 in the morning, and just beginning to get light outside. Somehow, as far as they knew, they had not been seen by any of the police. The town seemed quiet, and the day promised to be pleasant and sunny.

Bernice went to a special hiding place behind a pair of dented garbage cans and found the key to the back door. In a quick and silent moment, all three were inside.

"Don't turn any lights on, make any noise, or go near any windows," Bernice cautioned them. "The darkroom's in here. Everybody come in before I turn on the light."

All three squeezed into the little darkroom. Bernice closed the door and then found the light switch.

She prepared her chemicals, double-checked the film, then got the little developing tank ready. She switched off the light, and they stood in total blackness.

"Freaky," Kevin said.

"This will only take a few minutes. Boy, I haven't the slightest idea of what's happening to Marshall, but I don't dare try to find out."

"What about your answering machine? There might be some messages on it."

"That's a thought. I can check that as soon as I get this film all loaded in here. I'm almost finished." Then Bernice had another thought. "I wonder about Sandy Hogan, too. She pitched a lamp at her father and ran out of the house."

"Yes, you were telling me about that."

"I don't know where she'd go, unless she's decided to run off with that Shawn character."

"With who?" Susan asked abruptly. "Who did you say?"

"Some guy named Shawn."

"Shawn Ormsby?" Susan asked.

"Oh-oh, it sounds like you know him."

"I'm afraid Sandy Hogan could be in real trouble! Shawn Ormsby appears quite a few times in your sister's diary. He's the one who got Pat involved in those parapsychology experiments. He encouraged her to continue them, and he's the one who eventually introduced her to Thomas!"

The darkroom light clicked on. The developing tank was loaded and ready, but all Bernice could do was stare white-faced at Susan.

Madeline was not a beautiful, golden-haired, highly evolved, superhuman from a higher dimension. Madeline was a demon, a hideous, leather-skinned monster with sharp talons and a subtle, deceiving nature. For Madeline, Sandy Hogan had been a very easy and vulnerable prey. Sandy's deep wounds concerning her father made her an ideal subject for the candy of illusionary love Madeline was able to dangle before her, and now it seemed that Sandy would follow whatever course Madeline said was right for her life, believing whatever Madeline said. Madeline loved it when she got people to that point.

Patricia Krueger, though, had been a challenge. Then, disguised as handsome, benevolent Thomas, this demon had quite a struggle getting Patricia to believe he was really there; it had taken some very heavy-handed hallucinations and well-timed coincidences, not to mention the very best of his psychic signs and wonders. It wasn't enough to just bend keys and spoons; he had to carry out some very impressive materializations as well. Finally he had succeeded, though, and fulfilled Ba-al Lucius's bidding. Pat had ceremonially done away with herself, and she would never know the love of God again.

But what of Sandy Hogan? What would the new Ba-al, Rafar, want done with her? The demon, now calling himself—or herself—Madeline, approached the great prince on his big dead tree.

"My lord," said Madeline, bowing low with respect, "do I understand that Marshall Hogan is defeated and powerless?"

"He is," said Rafar.

"And what would you wish for Sandy Hogan, his daughter?"

Rafar was about to answer, but then hesitated, giving the matter a little more thought. At length he said, "Do not destroy her, not yet. Our foe is as subtle as I, and I would like one more assurance against any success of this Marshall Hogan. The Strongman comes today. Hold her against that time."

Rafar dispatched a messenger along with Madeline to visit Professor Langstrat.

Shawn was awakened by an early morning phone call from the professor.

"Shawn," said Langstrat, "I've heard from the masters. They want some extra assurances that Hogan will not be an obstacle to today's business. Is Sandy still there with you?"

Shawn could look out from his bedroom into the living room of his small apartment. Sandy was still on the couch, still asleep.

"I still have her."

"The meeting with the regents will take place in the Administration Building, the third-floor conference room. A room across the hall, 326, has been reserved for us and the other psychics. Bring Sandy with you. The masters want her there."

"We'll be there."

As Langstrat hung up the phone, she could hear Alf Brummel clattering about in the kitchen.

"Juleen," he called, "where's the coffee?"

"Don't you think you're nervous enough?" she asked him, leaving her bedroom and going into the kitchen.

"I'm just trying to wake up," he muttered, shakily putting a pot of water on the stove.

"Wake up! You haven't even slept, Alf!"

"Have you?" he retorted.

"Quite well," she said very mildly.

Langstrat, primly dressed, looked ready to leave for the college. Brummel was a wreck, his eyes sunken, his hair disheveled, still in a bathrobe.

He said, "I'll just be glad when this day is over and everything quiets down. As chief of police, I think I've broken about every law in the books."

She put her hand on his shoulder and said reassuringly, "All this new world growing around you will be your friend, Alf. *We* are the law now. You've helped to bring in the New Order, an ultimately good deed that deserves reward."

"Well . . . we'd better make good and sure of that, that's all I have to say."

"You can help, Alf. Several of the prime leaders will be meeting just across the hall the same time as the closure meeting this afternoon. With our combined psychic energies, we can assure that nothing will stand in the way of complete success."

"I don't know if I even dare go out in public. I guess the arrests of Busche and Hogan have a lot of people riled—*church* people, I might add! This rape charge hasn't hurt Busche nearly as much as it was supposed to. Most of the people in the church are coming at *me*, wondering what *I'm* trying to pull!"

"You will be there," she said plainly. "Oliver will be there, as will the others. And Sandy Hogan will be there."

He spun and looked at her in horror. "What? Why is Sandy Hogan going to be there?"

"Insurance."

Brummel's eyes widened, and his voice trembled. "Another one? You're going to kill another one?"

Her eyes grew very cold. "I do not kill anyone! I only let the masters decide!"

"So what have they decided?"

"You are to let Hogan know that his daughter is in our hands and that he would be very wise not to interfere with anything that happens from this day forward."

"You want *me* to tell him?"

"Mr. Brummel!" Her voice was chilling. She stepped toward him intimidatingly, and he backed up a few steps. "Marshall Hogan happens to be in your jail. You are in charge of him. You will tell him."

With that, she stepped out the front door and went off to the college.

Brummel stood there for a moment, nonplussed, frustrated, afraid. His thoughts swam about like a school of frightened fish. He forgot why he was even in the kitchen.

Brummel, you've had it. What makes you think you're not just as dispensable as anyone else the Society considers a commodity, a tool, a pawn? And, let's face it, Brummel. You are a pawn! Juleen's using you to do her dirty work, and now she's setting you up as nothing less than an accessory to murder. If I were you, I'd start looking out for Number One. This whole plan will be found out sooner or later, and guess who'll be caught holding the bag?

Brummel kept thinking about it, and his thoughts ceased to swim about. They all began to run the same direction. This was madness, utter madness. The masters say this and the masters say that, but what's it to them? They don't have wrists that can be handcuffed, they don't have jobs to lose, they don't have faces they could be afraid to show around town someday.

Brummel, why don't you stop Juleen before she totally ruins your life? Why don't you stop all this madness and be a real, genuine lawman for once?

Yeah, thought Brummel. Why don't I? If I don't, we're all going to sink on this crazy ship.

Lucius, the deposed Prince of Ashton, stood in the kitchen with Alf Brummel, the chief of police, having a little discussion with him. This Alf Brummel always was rather flimsy; perhaps Lucius could make use of this commodity.

Jimmy Dunlop arrived at the courthouse at 7:30 Sunday morning, ready to begin his shift. To his surprise the parking lot was full of people: young couples, old couples, little old ladies; it looked like a misplaced church picnic. Even as he pulled in, he could see every eye focusing on his policeman's uniform. Oh, no! Now they were coming his way!

Mary Busche and Edith Duster recognized Jimmy right away; he was the young and very rude officer who turned them away from visiting Hank last night. Now they were right up at the head of this crowd, and although none of these people had any intention of doing anything rash or improper, they were not about to be trodden on.

Jimmy had to get out of his car whether he wanted to or not. He did have to report to work today.

"Officer Dunlop," said Mary, quite brazenly, "I believe you told me last night that you would arrange for me to visit my husband today."

"If you'll excuse me," he said, trying to push his way past.

"Officer," said John Coleman respectfully, "we're here to ask that you honor her request to see her husband."

Jimmy was a police officer. He did represent the law. He had a lot of authority. The only problem was, he didn't have any guts.

"Uh . . ." he said. "Listen, you'll have to break up this gathering or face possible arrest!"

Abe Sterling stepped forward. He was an attorney who was a friend of a friend of an uncle of Andy Forsythe and he had been gotten out of bed last night and invited for just this occasion.

"This is a legal, peaceful gathering," he reminded Jimmy, "according to the definition of RCS 14.021.217 and the decision rendered in Stratford County Superior Court in *Ames versus the County of Stratford.*"

"Yeah," said several, "that's right. Listen to the man."

Jimmy was flustered. He looked toward the front door of the courthouse. Two officers from the Windsor precinct were guarding the fort. Jimmy walked toward them, wondering why they were letting this continue.

"Hey," he asked them with a subdued voice, "what's all this about? Why didn't you get rid of these people?"

"Hey, Jimmy," said one, "this is your town and your ball game. We figured you had the answers, so we told them to wait until you got here."

Jimmy looked at all the faces looking back at him. No, ignoring this problem would not make it go away. He asked the officer, "How long have all these people been here?"

"Since about 6. You should have been here then. They were having a regular church service."

"And they can *do* that?"

"Talk to that lawyer of theirs. They have the right to peaceful demonstration as long as they don't impede the regular conduct of business. They've been behaving themselves."

"So what do I do now?"

The two officers only looked at each other somewhat blankly.

Abe Sterling was right behind Jimmy. "Officer Dunlop, you are within the law to hold a suspect for up to seventy-two hours without charges, but seeing as the suspect's wife does have the right to contact her husband, we are ready to file suit in Stratford County Superior Court requiring you to appear and show just cause why she has been denied that right."

"You hear that?" someone piped up.

"I'll . . . uh . . . I'll have to talk to the police chief . . ." Under his breath he was cursing Alf Brummel for getting him into this mess.

"Where is Alf Brummel, anyway? This is his *pastor* he's thrown in jail," Edith Duster declared.

"I—I don't know anything about it."

John Coleman said, "Then we as citizens are asking you to find out. And we would like to talk to Chief Brummel. Can you please arrange that?"

"I'll—I'll see what I can do," Jimmy said, turning for the door.

"I wish to see my husband!" Mary said quite loudly, stepping forward with her jaw set firmly.

"I'll see what I can do," Jimmy said again, and ducked inside.

Edith Duster turned to the others and said, "Just remember, brothers and sisters, we are not contending against flesh and blood, but against the principalities, against the powers, against the world rulers of this present darkness, against the spiritual hosts of wickedness in the heavenly places." She got several Amens to that, followed by someone starting a worship song. Immediately the whole Remnant took up the song and sang it loudly, worshiping God and making His praise heard in that parking lot.

Rafar could hear the praise from where he stood on the hill above the town, and he glowered at these saints of God. Let them whine over their fallen pastor. Their singing would be curtailed soon enough when the Strongman and his hordes arrived.

Countless spirits were arriving in the town of Ashton—but they were not the kind Rafar desired. They rushed in under the ground, they filtered in under the cover of occasional clouds, they sneaked in by riding invisibly in cars, trucks, vans, buses. In hiding places all over the town one warrior would be joined by another, those two would be joined by two more, those four would be joined by four. They too could hear the singing. They could feel the strength coursing through them with every note. Their swords droned with the resonance of the worship. It was the worship and the prayers of these saints that had called them here in the first place.

The remote valley was now a huge bowl of boiling, swirling ink accented by myriads of glowing, yellow eyes. The cloud of demons had multiplied so that it filled the valley like a boiling sea.

Alexander Kaseph, possessed by the Strongman, stepped out of his big stone house and got into his waiting limousine. All the papers were ready for signing; his attorneys would meet him at the Administration Building on the Whitmore College campus. This was the day he had waited and prepared for.

As the limousine carrying Kaseph—and the Strongman—made its way up the winding road, the sea of demons began to shift in that direction like the turn of the tide. The drone of countless billions of wings rose in pitch and intensity. Streams of demons began to trickle over the sides of the big bowl, flowing out between the mountain peaks like hot, sulfurous tar.

In the darkroom at the *Ashton Clarion*, Bernice and Susan stood at the enlarger, looking down at the projected image of the negatives Bernice had just developed.

"Yes!" said Susan. "This is the first page of the college embezzlement records. You'll notice the name of the college doesn't appear anywhere. However, the amounts received should match exactly the amounts dispersed from the college records."

"Yes, the records we have, or our accountant has."

"See here? It's been a pretty steady flow of funds. Eugene Baylor has been skimming and channeling college investments just a little at a time into various accounts elsewhere, every one of which is actually a front organization for Omni and the Society."

"So the so-called investments have all been going into Kaseph's pocket!"

"And I am sure they will comprise a substantial part of the monies Kaseph will use to buy the college out."

Bernice moved the film forward again. Several frames of financial records rolled by in a blur.

"Wait!" said Susan. "There! Go back a few frames." Bernice rolled the film back. "Yes! There! I got this from some of Kaseph's personal notes. It's hard to make out the handwriting, but look at this list of names."

Bernice did have trouble making out the handwriting, but she had written those names herself quite a few times.

"Harmel . . . Jefferson . . ." she read.

"You haven't seen these yet," Susan said, pointing to the bottom of a very lengthy list.

There, in Kaseph's own writing, were the names Hogan, Krueger, and Strachan.

"I take it this is some kind of hit list?" Bernice asked.

"Exactly. It goes on for hundreds of names. Notice the red *Xs* after many of them."

"They were disposed of?"

"Bought out, driven out, maybe murdered, maybe ruined reputations or finances or both."

"And I thought *our* list was long!"

"This is the tip of the iceberg. I have other documents that we need to get photocopied and stored somewhere safe. It could all work into a very good case against not only Kaseph but the Omni Corporation—evidence that could prove a long history of wiretapping, extortion, racketeering, terrorism, murder. Kaseph's creativity in these areas knows no bounds."

"The ultimate gangster."

"With an international mob, don't forget, unnaturally unified by their common allegiance to the Universal Consciousness Society."

Just then Kevin, who had been running off photocopies of Susan's stolen documents, hissed at them, "Hey, there's a cop out there!"

Susan and Bernice froze.

"Where?" asked Bernice. "What's he doing?"

"He's across the street. It's a stakeout, I'll bet!"

Susan and Bernice went carefully toward the front to look. They found Kevin crouched in the doorway of the copier room. It was broad daylight now, and light was streaming in the front office windows.

Kevin pointed to a plain old Ford parked across the street, just visible through the front windows. A plainly dressed man sat behind the wheel, doing nothing in particular.

"Kelsey," said Weed. "I've had some run-ins with him. Dressed in his civies and driving an old Ford, but I'd know that face a mile away."

"More of Brummel's doing, no doubt," said Bernice.

"So what do we do now?" Susan asked.

"Get down!" Kevin hissed.

They ducked into doorways just as another man came up to the front window and looked inside.

"Michaelson," said Kevin. "Kelsey's partner."

Michaelson tried the door. It was locked. He looked through the other front window, and then he walked out of sight.

"Time for another miracle, huh?" Bernice said, a little sarcastically.

Hank awoke early that morning and thought for sure that some great miraculous intervention of God had occurred, or that he was about to ascend into heaven, or that the angels had come to rescue him, or . . . or . . . or he just didn't know what. But as he lay there on his cot, half asleep, still in that semiconscious state where you're not too sure of what is real and what isn't, he heard worship songs and hymns floating around his head. He even thought he could hear Mary's voice singing among all those other voices. For a long time he just lay there enjoying it, not wanting to wake up for fear that it might go away.

But Marshall exclaimed, "What the heck is that?"

He heard it too? Hank woke up at last. He jolted up from his cot and went to the bars. The sound was coming in through the window at the end of the cellblock. Marshall joined him and they listened together. They could hear the name "Jesus" being sung and praised.

"We've made it, Hank," said Marshall. "We're in heaven!"

Hank was crying. If those people out there only knew what a blessing this was! Suddenly he knew he was not in prison any longer, not really. The gospel of Jesus Christ was not imprisoned, and he and Marshall were now two of the freest men in the world.

The two of them listened for a while, and then, startling Marshall a little, Hank started singing too. It was a song painting Jesus Christ as a victorious warrior and the church as His army. Hank knew all the words, of course, and belted them right out.

A little embarrassed, Marshall looked around. The two car thieves in the next cell were still too dumbfounded to complain yet. The phony check writer only shook his head and went back to his paperback novel. Some other guy in the last cell, offense unknown, cursed a little, but not too loudly.

"C'mon, Marshall," prodded Hank. "Jump in! We just might sing ourselves out of this place."

Marshall only smiled and shook his head.

Just then the big door at the end of the cellblock burst open and in strode Jimmy Dunlop, his face red and his hands shaking.

"What's going on in here?" he demanded. "Do you know you're causing a disturbance?"

"Oh, we're just enjoying the music," Hank said, all smiles.

Jimmy shook his finger at Hank and said, "Well, you cut that religious stuff out right now! It has no place in a public jail. If you want to sing, you do it in church somewhere, not here."

Yeah, thought Marshall, I think I know the words well enough by now. He started singing as loudly as he could, singing right at Jimmy Dunlop.

It brought a very satisfying response from Jimmy. He turned on his heels and got out of there, slamming the door after him.

Another song began, and Marshall thought that maybe he'd heard this one somewhere before, maybe at Sunday school. "Thank you, Lord, for saving my soul." He sang it loudly, standing next to that young man of God, the two of them holding on to those cell bars.

"Paul and Silas!" Marshall suddenly exclaimed. "Yeah, now I remember!"

From that point, Marshall wasn't singing for Jimmy Dunlop's sake.

Tal could hear the music from where he stood in hiding. His face was still a little grim, but he nodded his head with satisfaction.

A messenger arrived with the news. "The Strongman is on his way."

Another messenger informed him, "We have prayer cover now from thirty-two cities. There are fourteen more being raised up."

Tal brought out his sword. He could feel the blade resonating with the worship of the saints, and he could sense the power of God's presence. He smiled a slight smile and put the sword back. "Gather in the sources: Lemley, Strachan, Mattily, Cole, and Parker. Do it abruptly. The timing will be important."

Several warriors disappeared to their missions.

37

Sandy Hogan continued to primp in front of the mirror in Shawn's bathroom, nervously brushing her hair, checking her makeup. Oh, I hope I look okay . . . whatever will I say, what will I do? I've never been to a meeting like this before.

Shawn had given her some explosively good news: Professor Langstrat had decided that Sandy was an excellent subject with exceptional psychic abilities, so much so that Sandy was now being considered as a prime candidate for a special initiation into some kind of exclusive fellowship of psychics, an *international* fellowship! Sandy now recalled hearing just a fleeting mention here and there of some kind of Universal Consciousness group, and it had always sounded like something very lofty, very secret, even sacred. She had never dreamed that she would be granted such an extraordinary opportunity, to actually meet other psychics and become a part of their circle of confidence! She could imagine the new experiences and the higher insights that could be achieved in the company of so many gifted people, all combining their psychic skills and energies in the continuing search for enlightenment!

Madeline, did you have something to do with this? Just wait until we meet again! I have a hug and a load of thanks to give you!

Bernice, Susan, and Kevin could do nothing but try to preserve the evidence Susan had gathered at so great a risk. Bernice made prints of all the pictures Susan had taken, then Kevin ran photocopies of the prints, along with copies of all the other material. Bernice looked about the building for a good hiding place to stash all the material. Susan looked over a map and pondered different escape routes out of town, different means of getting out, different people they could call once they did get out.

Then the telepone rang. They had ignored it before and let the answering machine squawk out its usual message. But this time, after the little beep tone, a voice said, "Hello, this is Harvey Cole, and I've completed working on those accounts you gave me . . ."

"Wait!" said Bernice. "Turn it up!"

Susan crawled over to the desk in the front office where the answering machine was sitting and turned up the volume.

Harvey Cole's voice continued, "I really need to get in touch with you as soon as possible."

Bernice snatched up the telephone in Marshall's office. "Hello? Harvey? This is Bernice!"

Susan and Kevin were horrified.

"What are you doing?"

"The cops are going to hear this, man!"

Harvey said through the telephone and also through the turned-up answering machine, "Oh, you're *there!* I heard you were arrested last night. The police won't tell me anything. I didn't know where to call . . ."

"Harvey, just listen. Got a pen or a pencil?"

"Yeah, now I do."

"Call my uncle. His name is Jerry Dallas; his number is 240-9946. Tell him you know me, tell him it's an emergency, and tell him you have materials to show Justin Parker, the county prosecutor."

"What? Not so fast."

Bernice labored through the information again, more slowly. "Now, this conversation is probably being listened to by Alf Brummel or one of his lackeys on the Ashton Police Force, so I want you to make sure that if anything happens to me that information will still go to the prosecutor so he'll wonder what's going on in this town."

"Am I supposed to write that down too?"

"No. Just make sure you get in touch with Justin Parker. If you possibly can, get him to call us here."

"But, Bernice, I was going to say, it's pretty clear that the funds have been going out, but the records don't show where—"

"We have the records that show where. We have everything. Tell my uncle that."

"Okay, Bernice. You really are in trouble, then?"

"The police are after me. They'll probably find out I'm here because I'm talking to you and our phone has been bugged. You'd better hurry!"

"Yeah, yeah, okay!"

Harvey hung up quickly.

Susan and Kevin looked at each other and then at Bernice.

She looked back at them and could only say, "Call it a gamble."

Susan shrugged. "Well, we didn't have any better ideas."

The phone rang again. Bernice hesitated, waiting for the answering machine to go through its little recitation.

Then came the voice. "Marshall, this is Al Lemley. Listen, I've got some pretty stirred-up feds here in New York that want to talk to you about your man Kaseph. They've been tracking him for quite some time, and if you can supply them with any good evidence, they'd be interested . . ."

Bernice picked up the phone again. "Al Lemley? This is Bernice Krueger. I work for Marshall. Can you bring those men to Ashton today?"

"What? Hello?" Lemley was taken aback. "Are you real or a recording?"

"Very real, and very much in need of your help. Marshall's in jail and—"

"In jail?"

"A bum rap. It's Kaseph's doing. He's taking over the Whitmore College today at 2, he has Marshall in the slammer to keep him out of the way, and I'm a fugitive at large. It's a long story, but your friends will love it and we've secured the documents to prove every word of it."

"What was the name again?"

Bernice labored through her name again and had to spell it twice. "Listen, they've bugged this phone, so they probably know where I am now, so would you please hurry up and get here and bring all the good guys you can find? There are none left in this town."

Al Lemley knew enough. "Okay, Bernice, I'll do anything and everything I can. And those eight-balls who've bugged your phone had better be warned that if things aren't downright peachy by the time we get there, there will most certainly be trouble!"

"Make it the Administration Building on the Whitmore College campus at or before 2."

"See you then."

Now Kevin and Susan were beginning to lighten up a bit.

"What was that you wanted?" asked Susan. "Another miracle?"

The phone rang again. Bernice didn't wait this time, but snatched it right up.

A voice said, "Hello, this is State Attorney General Norm Mattily, calling for Marshall Hogan."

Susan couldn't hold down a little squeal. Kevin said, "All right, all right!"

Bernice spoke to Mattily. "Mr. Mattily, this is Bernice Krueger, a reporter for the *Clarion*. I work for Mr. Hogan."

"Oh . . . uh, yes . . ." Mattily seemed to be conferring with someone else. "Yes, uh, Eldon Strachan is standing right here with me, and he tells me there's some kind of trouble there in Ashton—"

"The worst kind. It's all coming together today. We've gained some substantial evidence to show you. How soon can you get here?"

"Well, I wasn't planning on doing *that* . . ."

"The town of Ashton is going to be taken over by an international terrorist organization at 2 o'clock today."

"What?"

Bernice could hear the muffled voice of Eldon Strachan, probably pounding away at Mattily's other ear. "Uh . . . well, where is Mr. Hogan? Eldon is concerned for his safety."

"I am sure that Mr. Hogan is not at all safe. He and I were ambushed by the local mobsters last night during a routine investigation. Marshall fought them off while I fled. I've been in hiding ever since and I have no idea what's happened to Mr. Hogan."

"What on earth! Are you . . ." Eldon kept on talking in Mattily's other ear. "Well, I'm going to need some kind of concrete evidence, something that will wash legally. . ."

"We have it, but we'll need your direct and immediate intervention. Can you come, and bring some *real* police with you? It's a matter of life and death."

"This had better be on the up and up!"

"Get here, please, before 2. I would advise meeting us at the Administration Building on the Whitmore College campus."

"All right," said Mattily, his voice still sounding a bit hesitant, "I'll get down there and see whatever it is you have to show me."

Bernice hung up and the phone immediately rang again.

"Clarion."

"Hello, this is County Prosecutor Justin Parker. With whom am I speaking?"

Bernice clapped her hand over the receiver and whispered to Susan, "There *is* a God!"

Alf Brummel could not stand it anymore. Things were getting out of his control, things that had a lot to do with his own future and security. He could not stay away from the police station any longer. He had to be there to be sure of what was going on, to keep things from becoming irreversibly messed up, to . . . oh, where were those car keys?

He got into his car and raced through town to the station.

The Remnant was still singing in the parking lot when he arrived, and by the time he knew who they were and why they were there, it was too late to sneak away. He had to pull in and park.

They converged on his car like a voracious swarm of mosquitoes.

"Where have you been, chief?"

"When's Hank going to get out?"

"Mary would like to see him."

"What in blazes do you think you're doing to that man? He hasn't raped anyone!"

"You'd better be ready to kiss your job good-bye!"

Best foot forward, Alf, if you intend to save the rest of you. "Uh, where is Mary?"

Mary waved to him from the front steps of the courthouse. He tried to make a beeline for her, and once the people saw the direction he was heading, they were more willing to make way for him.

Mary started asking him questions as soon as he was within ear-shot of her shouts. "Mr. Brummel, I would like to see my husband, and how dare you allow this travesty!"

Brummel had never in his life seen sweet, seemingly vulnerable Mary Busche so feisty.

He tried to think of what to say. "It's been a real madhouse around here. I'm sorry I've been away . . ."

"My husband is innocent and you know it!" she said quite firmly. "We don't know how you intend to get away with this, but we are here to see that you don't."

With that comment, a flurry of shouts in agreement thundered up from the crowd.

Brummel tried the intimidation approach. "Now listen to me, all of you! No one is above the law, regardless of who they are. Pastor Busche has been accused as a sexual offender, and I have no choice but to carry out my duties as an officer of the law. I can't help it if we are friends or fellow church members, this is a matter of law—"

"Bunk!" came a deep-throated shout near Brummel.

Brummel turned toward the voice to correct it, but then turned pale as he saw the face of Lou Stanley, his old comrade-in-arms.

Lou stood his ground firmly, one hand on his belt, the other pointing right into Brummel's face as he said, "You've talked about pulling a stunt like this many times, Alf! I've heard you say that all you needed was the right opportunity. Well, now I'm saying that you've done it. I'm accusing you, Alf! If anybody wants my testimony in any court of law against you, they've got it!"

A cheer and some jeers went up.

Then Brummel got another shock. Gordon Mayer, the church treasurer, stepped to the front of the crowd, and he too pointed his finger right in Brummel's face.

"Alf, simple dissent is one thing, but flat-out conspiracy is quite another. You'd better be really sure of what you're doing."

Brummel was backed against the wall. "Gordon . . . Gordon, we have to do what's best . . . we . . ."

"Well, count me out!" Mayer said. "I've done enough for you!"

Brummel turned away from his two former comrades, only to come face to face with the suddenly cleaned-up Bobby Corsi!

"Hey, Chief Brummel," said Bobby. "Remember me? Guess who I'm working for *now*."

Brummel was speechless. He began to walk toward the police department door, as if there would be some shelter in there from all this disaster.

Andy Forsythe did not block his way, but walked close enough to him to cause him to stop.

"Mr. Brummel," said Andy, "there's a young wife back there who would still like her requests considered."

Brummel walked more briskly. "I'll see what I can do, all right? Let me check the status of things. Just wait. I'll be with you in a moment."

As quickly as he could, he ducked through the door and locked it behind him just in time. The crowd followed him like a wave and pressed up against the door, blockading him inside.

His new receptionist sat wide-eyed at the reception desk, looking out the window at all the angry faces.

"Should . . . should I call the police?" she asked.

"No," said Brummel. "They're just some friends here to see me."

With that, he disappeared into his office and closed the door.

Juleen, Juleen! This was her fault! He was sick of her, sick of this whole thing!

He saw a note on his desk. Sam Turner had left a message to call. He rang the number, and Sam answered.

"How's it looking, Sam?" Brummel asked.

"No good, Alf. Listen, I've been on the phone all morning, and no one wants to call any emergency congregational meeting. They have no intentions of voting Hank out, and few of them buy this rape business. Let's face it, Alf, you blew it."

"*I* blew it?" Brummel exploded. "*I* blew it? Wasn't this your idea too?"

"Don't you say that!" came Turner's reply very threateningly, "Don't you ever say that!"

"So now you're not going to stand by me either."

"There's nothing to stand by, Alf. The plan just didn't fly. Busche is a boy scout and everybody knows it, and you just won't get this rape charge to stick."

"Sam, we were in this together! It was going to work!"

"It didn't, buddy. Hank's in to stay, that's the way I see it, and I'm withdrawing from this whole thing. You do what you have to, but you'd better do something, or your name won't be worth a dung heap by the time this is over."

"Well thanks a lot, *buddy!*" Brummel angrily hung up.

He looked at the clock. It was just about noon. The meeting would take place in two hours.

Hogan. He still had to get a message to Hogan about Sandy. Oh brother, here was another of Juleen's fine messes. Sure, Juleen, you bet! I'm already pegged with this bum rap against Busche, and now you want me to go on record as an accessory to whatever you have planned for Sandy Hogan.

And what about Krueger? Who had she been able to snitch to about this whole thing? He bolted from his office and went down the hall to the dispatch room.

"Anything yet on that fugitive?" he asked the lone dispatcher.

The dispatcher stuffed a bite of peanut butter sandwich into his cheek and said, "No, it's been pretty quiet."

"Nothing even at the *Clarion?*"

"There's a strange car parked out back, but it's out of state and they haven't traced the plates yet."

"They haven't . . . ! Get those plates traced! Check that building! Somebody could be in there!"

"They haven't seen anybody—"

"Check the building!" Brummel exploded.

The receptionist called from up the hall, "Captain Brummel, Bernice Krueger is on the telephone. Should I take a message?"

"Nooo!" he screamed, running up the hall to his office. "I'll take it in here!"

He slammed his office door behind him and grabbed his telephone. "Hello?" He hit the second button on his phone. "Hello?"

"Mr. Alfred Brummel!" came a very condescending voice.

"Bernice!"

"It's time we had a talk."

"All right. Where are you?"

"Don't be an absolute idiot. Listen, I'm calling to give you an ultimatum. I've been talking to the state attorney general, the county prosecutor, and the feds. I have evidence—and I mean some really hard stuff—that will blow your little plot wide open, and they're all on their way here to see it."

"You're bluffing!"

"You have the conversations on tape, no doubt. Just play them back."

Brummel smiled a bit. She had given away where she was. "And just what is your ultimatum?"

"Spring Hogan. Now. And call off your manhunt for me. In two hours I intend to show my face in this town, and I want no harassment, especially since I'll be accompanied by many very special guests!"

"You're at the *Clarion* right now, aren't you?"

"Yes, of course I am. And I can see . . . what's his name? Kelsey, sitting out there in that old heap, he and his partner Michaelson. I want you to call those guys off. If you don't, all the big boys in the world will know what happened to me. If you do, it can only help you."

"You're . . . I still say you're bluffing!"

"Play your little bugging machine, Alf. See if I'm telling you the truth. I'll wait to see that car pull away."

Click. She hung up.

Brummel dashed to the cabinet and opened the doors. He pulled out the recorder. He hesitated, thought furiously, froze for a moment. He shoved the recorder back into the cabinet, slammed the doors shut, and dashed down the hall to the dispatch room.

The dispatcher was still munching on his sandwich. Brummel reached right across his lap and grabbed the microphone, throwing the talk switch.

"Units two and three, Kelsey, Michaelson, 10-19. Repeat: 10-19 immediately."

The dispatcher looked up with delight. "Hey! What happened? Did Krueger turn herself in?"

Alf Brummel never was good at comebacks for stupid or ill-timed questions. He dashed up the hall to the front desk and dialed the courthouse.

"Get me Dunlop."

Dunlop picked up the other end.

"Jimmy, Hogan and Busche are being released on personal recognizance. Turn them loose."

Jimmy gave him some more dumb questions.

"Just do what you're told and leave the paperwork to me! Now go!"

He slammed down the phone and disappeared into his office. The receptionist continued looking out the window at all those people. They were starting to sing again. It sounded kind of nice.

Bernice, Susan, and Kevin waited nervously for either a very good or a very bad thing to happen. Either Brummel would play ball, or they would be getting high on tear gas within minutes. But then they heard an engine starting up across the street.

"Hey!" said Kevin.

Susan still wrung her hands a little. Bernice just watched, unwilling to believe anything good too quickly.

The old Ford pulled away, with both Kelsey and Michaelson in it.

Bernice didn't want to wait around. "Let's pack all this stuff in that suitcase again and get over to the courthouse. Marshall's going to need a catching up."

"You don't have to tell me twice!" said Kevin.

All Susan could say was, "Thank you, God. Thank you, God!"

Alf Brummel heard only one short segment of one telephone conversation, the one between Bernice and State Attorney General Norm Mattily. He knew Mattily's voice, and, yes, it made perfectly good sense that Eldon Strachan would go to Mattily, *if* Strachan had some genuinely reliable information.

Brummel cursed aloud. Reliable information! All Mattily had to do was find this blankety-blank recorder sitting here, tapped illegally into all those phones!

The receptionist buzzed him. He reached over to his desk and hit the intercom switch.

"Yeah?" he said very crossly.

"Juleen Langstrat on line two," she said.

"Take a message!" he said, and flipped off his switch.

He knew why she was calling. She was going to nag him, remind him to be there at the afternoon meeting involving Sandy Hogan.

He opened the other cabinet door and pulled out the records and stored tape recordings. Where in the world could he stash all this stuff? How could he destroy it?

The receptionist buzzed him again.

"What?"

"She insists that you talk to her."

He picked up the telephone, and Langstrat's oily voice came over the line.

"Alf, are you ready for today?"

"Yes," he answered impatiently.

"Then please come as soon as you can. We must prepare the energies of the rooms before the meeting begins, and I want to have all things in unison before Shawn arrives with Sandy."

"So you're really going to bring her into this?"

"Only as a safeguard, naturally. Marshall Hogan is out of the way, but we must be sure we keep him there, at least until all our efforts and visions have been fulfilled and the town of Ashton has been afforded its victorious leap into Universal Consciousness." She paused to relish the thought for a moment, and then asked rather nonchalantly, "And have you heard any news of our runaway burglar?"

Before he even knew why he was doing it, he lied. "No, nothing yet. She's out of the way."

"Certainly. I'm sure she'll be found soon enough, and after today she will have no hope at all."

He said nothing to that. He was suddenly distracted by a thought that poured over him like a ten-foot wave: *Alf, she believed you. She really doesn't know!*

"You will be here immediately, Alf?" she asked and ordered at the same time.

She doesn't know what's been happening, was all Brummel could think. She's vulnerable! *I* know something *she* doesn't!

"I'll be right over," he said mechanically.

"See you soon," she said with an authoritarian finality, and hung up.

She doesn't know! She thinks everything is going fine and there will be no trouble! She thinks she'll get away with it all!

Brummel let his thoughts race as he considered his options, his newly acquired exclusive knowledge, and the strange sense of power it gave him. Yes, it was all as good as over, and he was probably going to go down . . . but he had the power to bring that woman, that spider, that witch, down with him!

Suddenly he had no desire to destroy the tapes and the records. Let the authorities find them. Let them find everything! Maybe he'd even show them.

As for the Plan, if Kaseph and his Society are so all-knowing and so invincible, why should you tell them anything? Let them find out for themselves!

"Wouldn't it be nice to see your dear Juleen sweating for once?" asked Lucius.

"It would be nice to see Juleen sweating for once," Brummel muttered.

38

Hank and Marshall stepped out the basement door of the court-house and found themselves all alone. Their friends were still congregated at the police department door, singing, talking, praying, demonstrating.

"Praise the Lord," was all Hank could say.

"Oh, I believe it, I believe it," Marshall answered.

It was John Coleman who first spotted them and let out a whoop. The others all turned their heads and were shocked and ecstatic. They came running up to Hank and Marshall like chickens to feed.

But they all made room for Mary, even gave her loving pushes forward as she ran by. The Lord was so good! Here was Hank's dear Mary, weeping and hugging and kissing and whispering her love to him, and he could hardly believe it was really happening. He had never felt so separated from her before.

"Are you all right?" she kept asking him, and he kept telling her, "I'm just fine, just fine."

"It's a miracle," said the others. "The Lord has answered our prayers. He got you out of prison just like Peter."

Marshall understood when they virtually ignored him. This was Hank's moment.

But what was going on over there? Through the heads, shoulders, and bodies Marshall noted Alf Brummel ducking quickly out the front door and into his car. He sped away. The creep. If I were him, I'd duck out too.

And here came . . . No! No, it couldn't be! Marshall started easing his way through the crowd, craning his neck to see for sure if the passengers in this just arriving car were who they seemed to be. Yes! Bernice was even waving to him! And there was Weed, alive! That other gal, the one driving . . . she couldn't be! But she had to be! Susan Jacobson, back from the dead, no less!

Marshall made his way through Hank's admirers and broke into a very brisk, wide-grinned walk to where Susan was just parking the car. Wow! When these people pray, God listens!

Bernice burst from the car and threw her arms around him.

"Marshall, are you all right?" she said, almost crying.

"Are you all right?" he asked her back.

A voice behind them said, "Oh, Mrs. Hogan, I've really wanted to meet you."

It was Hank. Marshall looked at the man of God, standing there all smiles, with his little wife by his side and God's people all behind him, and he felt the hug go out of his arms.

Bernice slipped limply out of the embrace.

"Hank," said Marshall with a broken kind of tone Bernice had never heard from him before, "this is not my wife. This is Bernice Krueger, my reporter." Then Marshall looked at Bernice and said with great love and respect, "And a good one, too!"

Bernice knew immediately that something had happened to Marshall. It didn't surprise her; something had been happening to her too, and she could see in Marshall's face and detect in his voice that same inner brokenness she had been feeling in herself. Somehow she knew that this young man standing next to Marshall had something to do with it all.

"And who is your fellow jailbird here?" she asked.

"Bernice Krueger, meet Hank Busche, pastor of Ashton Community Church and a very recent, very good friend of mine."

She shook his hand, shoving all her thoughts and emotions aside. Time was running out.

"Marshall, listen carefully. We have a sixty-second crash course to give you!"

Hank excused himself and returned to his excited flock.

When Bernice introduced Susan to Marshall, he thought he was extending his hand to nothing less than a miracle.

"I'd heard that you'd been killed, and Kevin too."

"I'm looking forward to sharing the whole story with you," Susan replied pleasantly, "but right now our time is very short and there's a lot you need to know."

Susan opened the trunk of her car and showed Marshall the contents of her battle-weary suitcase. Marshall loved every minute of it. It was all there, everything he thought he'd lost to sticky-fingered Carmen and these creeps, this "Society."

"Kaseph is coming to Ashton today to close the deal with the college board of regents. At 2 o'clock, the papers will be signed and the Whitmore College campus will be quietly sold to Omni Corporation."

"The Society, you mean," said Marshall.

"Of course. It's a key move. When the college goes, the town will ultimately go with it."

Bernice burst in with her news about Mattily, Parker, and Lemley, not to mention Harvey Cole's untangling of Baylor's records.

"So when do they get here?" Marshall asked.

"Hopefully in time for that board meeting. I told them to meet us there."

"I just might invite myself to the meeting. I know they'll all be very happy to see me."

Susan touched Marshall's arm and said, "But you need to be warned that they've been working on your daughter Sandy."

"Don't I know that!"

"They might have her under their influence right now; it's Kaseph's style, believe me. If you try to make a move against him, it could endanger her."

Bernice told Marshall about Pat, about the diary, about the mysterious friend named Thomas, and about that deceiving devil's advocate, Shawn Ormsby.

Marshall looked at them for a moment, then called, "Hank, this is where you and your people come in!"

A summer Sunday in Ashton is usually one of the happiest, carefree days of the week. The farmers jaw with each other; the storeclerks enjoy a leisurely pace; other business owners close up shop; moms, dads, and kids think of fun things to do and neat places to go. Many lawnchairs are occupied, the streets are a lot quieter, and families are usually together.

But this sunny, summer Sunday did not feel right to anyone: one farmer had a cow bloating on him while another had a tractor with a burned out magneto that no one seemed to have in stock; and though neither farmer was in any way responsible for the other's problems, they still got into a fight about it. The storeclerks working today were having trouble counting change, and were getting into very uncomfortable discussions with the customers whose change they were trying to count. Every business owner had no desire but to get out of his or her business, because no matter what it was, it was doomed to fail sooner or later. Many wives were nervous and wanted to go somewhere, anywhere, they didn't know where; their husbands would load the kids into all the station wagons, then the wives wouldn't want to go anymore, then the kids would get into fights in the cars, then their parents would get into fights, and then the families would go nowhere while the station wagons remained parked in all those driveways with screams coming through their windows and their horns honking. The lawnchairs either ripped through under their owners' bottoms or just plain couldn't be found; the streets were hectic with frantic drivers driving with no destination in mind; the dogs, those ever vigilant dogs of Ashton, were barking and howling and whining again, this time with their fur bristling, their tails up and their faces toward the east.

Faces toward the east? There were many. Here a college adminstrator, there a Post Office employee, over here a family of potters and weavers, over there an insurance salesman. All over the town, certain people who knew a certain destiny and a certain sympathetic spiritual vibration stood silently, as if worshiping, their faces toward the east.

And there was no small stir around the big dead tree. Rafar rose from his big branch, his gamemaster's seat of power, and stood on the hill, looking out over the little town of Ashton with his leering yellow eyes as his hordes of attending spirits gathered around him. His muscular arms rippled, his expansive black wings rising behind him like a royal train, his jewels gleaming and glittering in the sun.

He too looked toward the east.

He waited until he saw it. Then his breath sucked in through his fangs like a gasp of surprise, but this was no surprise. It was the highest kind of thrill, a demonic exhilaration such as he felt only rarely, a precious and very ripe fruit to be enjoyed only after much labor and preparation.

His black-haired hand grabbed the golden handle of his sword and he pulled the blade from its sheath, making it sing and drone and shimmer with blood-red light. The attending demons all gasped and cheered as Rafar held the sword high, bathing the whole gathering in its sinister red light. The huge wings suddenly disappeared into a blur and with a rush of wind and a blast of power they carried him into the air, out over the wide valley, out over the little town, out into the open where he could be seen from any part of the town or any hiding place near it.

He climbed to a lofty height, then hovered, his sword still in his hand. His head turned this way and that, his body slowly rotating, his eyes shifting about.

"Captain of the Hosts of Heaven!" he bellowed, and the echoes of his booming voice traveled back and forth across the valley like thunder. "Captain Tal, hear me!"

Tal could hear Rafar perfectly. He knew Rafar was about to make a speech, and he knew what the demon warlord was about to say. He too was watching the eastern horizon as he stood hidden in the forest, his chief warriors beside him.

Rafar continued to look everywhere for any sign of his adversary. "I who have never yet seen your face in this, our adventure, now show you mine! Behold it, you and your warriors! For today I place this face forever in your memory as the face of him who vanquished you!"

Tal, Guilo, Triskal, Krioni, Mota, Chimon, Nathan, Armoth, Signa—all were there together, gathered for this moment, gathered to listen to this long-awaited oration.

Rafar continued, "Today I place the name of Rafar, Prince of Babylon, forever in your memory as the name of him who remains bold and stands undefeated!" Rafar took a few more quick turns, looking all around him for any sign of his archenemy. "Tal, Captain of the Hosts of Heaven, will you dare to show your face to me? I think not! Will you even dare to assail me! I think not! Will you and your motley little band of highwaymen dare to stand in the path of the powers of the air?" Rafar threw in a derisive chuckle. "I think not!"

He paused for effect, and allowed himself a mocking grin. "I give you leave, dear Captain Tal, to withdraw yourself, to spare yourself the anguish awaiting you at my hand! I grant to you and to your warriors now the occasion to turn away, for I do pronounce that the battle's decision is made already!" Rafar then pointed his sword toward the eastern horizon and said, "Look to the east, captain! There is the outcome clearly written!"

Tal and his chiefs were already looking toward the eastern horizon, their attention rapt and unswerving, even when a young messenger came soaring in with the news—"Hogan and Busche are free! They've—" He stopped in midsentence. His eyes followed every other gaze to the east, and he saw what so held their interest.

"Oh, no!" he said in a whisper. "No, no!"

At first the cloud had been only a distant fingertip of blackness poking up over the horizon; it could have been a raincloud, or factory smoke, or a distant, haze-darkened mountain appearing suddenly. But then, as it drew nearer, its borders expanded outward like the slowly emerging edge of a blunt arrowhead stretching slowly and surely across the horizon like a dark shroud, like a steadily rising tide of blackness blocking out the sky. At first, one direct glance could contain it all; in just a few minutes, the eyes had to sweep back and forth, from one end of the horizon to the other.

"Not since Babylon," Guilo said quietly to Tal.

"They were there," said Tal, "every one of them, and now they're back. Look at the front ranks, flying multiple layers over, under, and within."

"Yes," said Guilo, observing. "Still the same style of assault."

A new voice said, "Well, so far, Tal, your plan is working very well. They've all come out of hiding, and in countless numbers."

It was the General. He was expected.

Tal answered, "And hopefully they are planning on a rout."

"At least your old rival is, to hear him boast."

Tal only smiled and said, "My General, Rafar boasts with or without reason."

"What of the Strongman?"

"By the shape of the cloud, I would say he precedes it by just a few miles."

"Having possessed Kaseph?"

"That would be my guess, sir."

The General looked carefully at the approaching cloud, now a deep, inky black and spread like a canopy across the sky. The deep, rumbling drone of the wings was just becoming audible.

"How do we stand?" the General asked.

Tal answered, "Prepared."

Then, as the sound of the wings grew louder and the shadow of the cloud began to fall across the fields and farmlands beyond Ashton, a reddish tint began to spread through the cloud as if it were burning from within.

"They've drawn their swords," said Guilo.

Why am I so afraid? Sandy wondered.

Here she was, holding Shawn's hand, going up the front steps of the Administration Building on campus, about to meet some people who had to be the real keys to her destiny, her stepping-stone to real spiritual fulfillment, to higher consciousness, maybe even to self-realization, and yet . . . all the talk could not remove a nagging fear she felt deep within her. Something just wasn't right. Maybe it was just a normal nervousness such as one would feel before a wedding or any other very significant event, or maybe it was that last remaining shred of her old, discarded Christian heritage still holding her, pulling her back as if with a leash. Whatever it was, she tried to ignore it, overcome it with reason, even use relaxation techniques she had learned in her college yoga class.

Come on, Sandy . . . steady breaths now . . . focus, focus . . . realign your energies.

There, that's better. I don't want Shawn or Professor Langstrat or anyone to think I'm not ready to be initiated.

All the way up the elevator she talked and prattled and tried to laugh, and Shawn laughed along, and by the time they reached the third floor and the door numbered 326, she thought she was ready.

Shawn opened the door, saying, "You'll love this," and they went in.

She didn't see them. To Sandy, this was only the staff lounge, a very pleasant room with soft carpet, leather-upholstered couches, and massive burl coffee tables.

But the room was occupied, very densely and hideously, and the yellow eyes glared and stared at her from all around, from every corner and chair and wall. They were waiting for her.

One hissed out asthmatically, "Hello there, child."

Sandy extended her hand to Oliver Young. "Pastor Young, what a pleasant surprise," she said.

Another let out a long, drooling snicker and said, "I'm very glad you could make it."

Sandy gave Professor Juleen Langstrat an embrace.

She looked around the room and recognized many of the college faculty, some of her own professors, even some business people and blue-collar workers from around town. There, in the corner, stood the new owner of what used to be Joe's Market. These thirty people looked like a cross section of Ashton's best.

The spirits were all ready and waiting. Deception showed her off like a trophy. Madeline was there, smiling wickedly, and beside her, or it, was another demon accomplice, with loop after loop of heavy glistening chains draped over his bony hands.

In the cloud, the myriads of demons were haughty, wild, drunk with the anticipation of victory, of slaughter, of unprecedented power and glory. Below them, the town of Ashton was a mere toy, such a very small little hamlet in such a vast countryside. Layer upon layer of spirits droned steadily forward, and myriads of yellow eyes peered down at the prize. The town was quiet and unguarded. Ba-al Rafar had done his work well.

A series of harsh screeches came from the front ranks of the cloud—the generals were calling out orders. Immediately the demon commanders on the fringes of the cloud relayed the orders to the swarms behind each of them, and as the commanders flew out from the cloud and began to drop downward, followed by their countless squadrons, the edges of the cloud began to wilt and stretch toward the ground.

In the large, formally furnished third-floor conference room, the regents began to gather. Eugene Baylor was there with a pile of financial records and reports, smoking a cigar and feeling chipper. Dwight Brandon looked just a little somber, but he was conversational enough. Delores Pinckston was not feeling well at all, and only wanted to get the whole thing over with. Kaseph's four lawyers, very professional, sharp-as-a-whip types, came in smirking. Adam Jarred strolled in and seemed more concerned with going fishing afterward than with the business they would be conducting. Every once in a while, someone would look at his watch or at the fancy clock on the wall. It would soon be 2 o'clock. Some were feeling just a little nervous.

The evil spirits that had come into the room with them were feeling nervous also—they realized they would soon be in the presence of the Strongman. This would be their very first time.

Alexander M. Kaseph's long, black, chauffeur-driven limousine entered the city limits and turned onto College Way. Kaseph sat in regal splendor in the back, cradling his briefcase in his lap and taking a lustful look out the tinted windows at the beautiful town passing by. He was making plans, envisioning changes, deciding what he would keep and what he would remove.

So was the Strongman, sitting inside him. The Strongman laughed his deep, gargling laugh, and Kaseph laughed the same way. The Strongman couldn't remember when he had been so pleased and so proud.

The cloud was drooping down at the edges as it continued to move forward, and Tal and his company kept watching from their hiding place.

"They're lowering their perimeter," said Guilo.

"Yes," said Tal with fascination. "As usual, they intend to contain the town on all sides before actually descending into it."

As they watched, the edges of the cloud dropped like black curtains that gradually wrapped around the town; demons were slipping into place like bricks in a wall. Every sword was drawn, every eye was wary.

"Hogan and Busche?" Tal asked a messenger.

"They are moving into place, along with the Remnant," the messenger answered.

Kaseph's limousine cruised toward the college, and Kaseph could see the stately, red brick buildings reaching up through the maples and oaks all around the campus. He looked at his watch. He would be right on time.

As the limousine passed through an intersection, a green, unmarked squad car pulled out onto College Way and began to follow. Its driver was Chief of Police Alf Brummel. He looked grim and very nervous. He knew whom he was following.

As the limousine and then the squad car passed through another intersection, the light changed and a stream of cars all turned right onto College Way and followed behind. The first car making the turn was the big brown Buick.

"Well, well!" said Marshall as he, Hank, Bernice, Susan, and Kevin all noticed the two cars they were following.

"Did you recognize Kaseph?" Susan asked Bernice.

"Yes, good old Pudgy himself."

Marshall had to wonder, "So what's up here? It looks like the meeting is still on, regardless."

Bernice said, "Maybe Brummel didn't believe me after all."

"Oh, he believed you, all right. He did everything you told him to do."

"So why hasn't Kaseph called this whole thing off? He's walking right into it."

"Either Kaseph thinks he's untouchable, or Brummel hasn't told him anything."

Hank looked behind them. "Looks like they all made it through the light."

The others looked back. Yes, there was Andy, driving his Volkswagen bus crammed with praying believers, and there came Cecil Cooper's pickup with the cab and the bed full. The ranch wagon of John and Patty Coleman followed behind that, and somewhere back there was the former pastor, James Farrel, driving a good-sized van carrying Mary and Grandma Duster and several others.

Marshall looked ahead, and then behind, and then concluded, "This is going to be one heck of a meeting."

39

At Juleen Langstrat's direction, all the smiling psychics, along with Sandy and Shawn, made themselves comfortable in the plush chairs and couches, arranged in a rough circle around the room.

"This is a significant day," said Langstrat warmly.

"Yes, indeed!" said Young.

The others also agreed. Sandy smiled back at them all. She was very impressed with the reverence they all seemed to have for this great woman, this great pioneer.

Langstrat assumed a lotus position in her big chair at the head of the group. Several others who had the desire and the flexibility did likewise. Sandy just relaxed where she was, settling into the couch and resting her head back.

"Our purpose here is to combine our psychic energies to assure the success of today's venture. Our long awaited goal will soon be realized: the Whitmore College campus, and afterward the whole town of Ashton, are going to become a part of the New World Order."

Everyone in the room started applauding. Sandy applauded as well, even though she didn't really know what Langstrat was talking about. It did sound vaguely familiar, though. Was it her own father who had said something about people wanting to take over the town? Oh, but he couldn't have been talking about the same thing!

"I have a wonderful new Ascended Master to introduce to you," said Langstrat, and faces all around the room immediately lit up with excitement and expectation. "He has lived long and traveled far, and has learned the wisdom of countless ages. He has come to Ashton to oversee this project."

"We welcome him," said Young. "What is his name?"

"His name is Rafar. He is a prince from long ago, and once ruled in ancient Babylon. He has lived many lives, and now returns to let us benefit from his wisdom." Langstrat closed her eyes and breathed deeply. "Let us call him, and he will speak to us."

Sandy could feel a queasiness in the pit of her stomach. She thought she felt chilled. The gooseflesh on her arms was real enough. But she brought these feelings under discipline, closed her eyes, and began her own relaxation, listening intently for the sound of Langstrat's voice.

The others also relaxed and went into a trance. For a moment the room was silent except for the deep breaths being drawn and expelled by everyone present.

Then the name formed on Langstrat's lips. "Rafar . . ."

They all echoed, "Rafar . . ."

Langstrat called the name again, and continued to call, and the others let all their thoughts narrow down to that one name as they spoke it softly.

Rafar was standing by the big dead tree, gleefully watching as the cloud spread over the town. At the sound of the call, his eyes narrowed with a very crafty expression and his mouth stretched slowly into a fang-baring grin.

"The pieces now fall into place," he said. He turned to an aide. "Any word from Prince Lucius?"

The aide was happy to report, "Prince Lucius says he has surveyed all fronts and finds no trouble or resistance."

Rafar roused ten demon monsters with a sweep of his wing, and they gathered at his side in an instant.

"Come," he said, "let us finish this business."

Rafar's wings clapped downward, and he shot into the air, his ten rogues following him like a regal honor guard. High above, the cloud stretched across the sky like an oppressive, light-blocking shroud, its shadow of evil and spiritual darkness falling over the town. As Rafar sailed over Ashton in a high arc, he could look up and see the myriads of yellow eyes and the red swords waving in salute. He waved his own sword back, and they cried out jubilantly, their numberless swords bristling downward like a wind-stirred, inverted field of crimson wheat. They filled the air with sulfur.

Ahead and far below was the Whitmore campus, the ripest of

ready plums. Rafar eased the whirring of his wings and began to drop toward the Administration Building.

As he descended, he saw the big limousine carrying the Strongman come up the circular drive and stop right at the building's front door. The sight filled him with exhilaration. This was it: *the* moment! He and his demon escorts disappeared through the roof of the building just as the Strongman and his human host emerged from the car . . . and just a little too soon to see a stream of cars not far behind that limousine, now finding parking spots here, there, and everywhere.

Alf Brummel got out of his car in one hurried jolt. He stood there for just a moment, building up courage, and then started for the main door of the building with stiff, jittery strides.

Marshall parked the Buick, and the five of them got out. All around, they could hear car doors slamming as the Remnant found parking spaces and then each other.

"Brummel doesn't look too happy," Marshall observed.

The other four looked just in time to see Brummel go through the front door.

"Maybe he's going to warn Kaseph," said Bernice.

"So where are all our powerful friends?" Marshall asked.

"Don't worry . . . at least not too much. They said they'd be here."

Susan said, "I'm quite sure the meeting is to take place in the third-floor conference room. It's where the board of regents usually meets."

"So where do I find Sandy?" Marshall asked.

Susan could only shake her head. "That I don't know."

They hurried toward the building, and from every direction the Remnant converged on the front steps.

Lucius could sense the tension in the air, like one huge rubber band pulled to its limit and about to snap. As he dropped quietly out of the sky and alighted on the roof of Ames Hall, right across the commons from the Administration Building, he could see the cloud still lowering its perimeter, spreading a thick drapery all around the town. The atmosphere became thick and choking with the presence of so many foul spirits.

Suddenly he heard a frantic flapping behind him and turned to see a little sentry demon, a petty creature, a busybody, flitting up to speak to him.

"Prince Lucius, people are gathering below! They are not *ours!* They are saints of God!" the little thing gasped.

Lucius was irritated. "I have eyes, little insect!" he hissed. "Pay them no mind."

"But what if they start praying?"

Lucius grabbed the little demon by one wing, and it fluttered about in pitiful little circles at the end of his arm. "Silence, you!"

"Rafar must know!"

"Silence!"

The little creature settled down, and Lucius brought him to the edge of the roof for a brief lesson.

"So what if they do pray?" Lucius said with a fatherly tone. "Has it helped them to this point? Has it slowed our progress one iota? And you have seen the power and might of Ba-al Rafar, have you not?" Lucius couldn't help the sarcastic tone with which he added, "You know that Rafar is all-powerful, and undefeatable, and does not need our help!" The little demon listened with wide eyes. "Let us not bother the great Ba-al Rafar with our petty worries! He can handle this endeavor . . . all by himself!"

Tal remained steady and kept watching. Guilo grew more and more restless, pacing about, looking from one end of the town to the other.

"Soon the perimeter will be entirely enclosed," he said. "They will have enveloped the entire town, and there will be no escape."

"Escape?" said Tal, his eyebrows raised.

"Purely a tactical consideration," Guilo replied with a shrug.

"The moment is approaching very quickly now," said Tal, looking toward the college. "In just a few minutes, all the players will be in their places."

The demons in the conference room could feel *him* coming, and they braced themselves. The hair bristled on their arms, necks, and backs. A darkness, a crawling cloud of evil was coming down the hall. Quickly each one looked himself over to make sure nothing was out of place, that his appearance was impeccable.

The door opened. They froze in respect and homage.

And there he stood, the Strongman, nothing less than the most horrible nightmare.

"Good day to you," he said.

"Good day to you, sir," the regents and lawyers answered Alexander Kaseph as he entered the room and started shaking their hands.

Alf Brummel had no desire to meet up with Alexander Kaseph. He even waited to take a different elevator. When the elevator opened on the third floor, he peeked to see if the coast was clear before he stepped out. Only after he heard the big door to the conference room down the hall click shut did he make his way down the hall himself, going very quietly to Room 326.

He stood for a moment outside the door, listening intently. It was pretty quiet in there. The session must be underway. He turned the knob very slowly and cracked the door just enough to see in. Yes, there was Langstrat in meditation, her eyes closed. She was the only one Brummel was worried about, and for now she wasn't looking.

He stepped into the room quietly and found a chair halfway around the circle from Langstrat. He looked around, sizing up the situation. Yes, they were calling for a certain spirit guide. He had never heard this particular name before. This entity must be some new personage brought in for the project today.

Oh no. There was Sandy Hogan, also meditating. She was calling the name as well. Well, Brummel, what do you do now?

Outside, the Remnant was ready for orders. Hank and Marshall gave them a very brief rundown on the present situation, and then Hank concluded, "We really don't know what we're going to encounter in there, but we know we have to go in, at least to see if we can locate Sandy. There's no question that this is a spiritual battle, so you know what you all have to do."

They all knew, and they were ready.

Hank continued, "Andy, I'd like you and Edith and Mary to take charge out here and lead in the prayer and worship. I'll be going inside with Marshall and the others."

Marshall conferred with Bernice. "Stay here and keep an eye out for our visitors. The rest of us will go in and see if we can find where this meeting is taking place."

Marshall, Hank, Kevin, and Susan went into the building. Bernice went to a vacant spot on the steps and sat down there to watch and wait. She could not help but observe the Remnant. There was something about them that felt all too familiar, and very . . . well, very wonderful.

Rafar and his ten escorts had been in the lounge for quite some time now, just listening and watching. Finally Rafar stepped up behind Langstrat and sank his talons deep into her skull. She twitched and gagged for a moment and then slowly, hideously, her countenance took on the unmistakable expressions of the Prince of Babylon himself.

"Indeeeeeeeed!" said Rafar's deep, guttural voice from Langstrat's throat.

Everyone in the room shuddered. Several eyes popped open with a start, and then widened at the sight of Langstrat, her eyes bulging, her teeth bared, her back arched like a crouching lion. Brummel could only cringe and wish he could disappear into his chair before that thing spotted him. But it was looking at Sandy, drooling.

"Indeeeed!" the voice said again. "Have you come together to see your vision truly fulfilled? So it shall be!" The creature sitting in the chair pointed a crooked finger at Sandy. "And who is this newcomer, this searcher for the hidden wisdom?"

"S—Sandy Hogan," she answered, her eyes still closed. She was afraid to open them.

"I understand that you have walked many pathways with your instructor, Madeline."

"Yes, Rafar, I have."

"Descend within yourself again, Sandy Hogan, and Madeline will meet you there. We will wait."

Sandy had only a fraction of a second to wonder how she would ever be able to relax herself into an altered state. Then a slimy, death-like spirit behind her clapped his bony hand down on her head, and she went under immediately. Her eyes rolled upward, she wilted in her chair, and she felt her body dissolving away, along with her rational thoughts and nagging fears. All outside sensations began to vanish, and she was floating in pure, ecstatic nothingness. She heard a voice, a very familiar voice.

"Sandy," the voice called.

"Madeline," she answered. "I'm coming!"

Madeline appeared deep within some endless tunnel, floating forward, her arms outstretched. Sandy moved toward the tunnel to meet her. Madeline came into sharp focus, her eyes sparkling, her smile like warming sunshine. Their hands met and grasped each other tightly.

"Welcome!" said Madeline.

Alf Brummel watched it all happen. He could see the dopey, ecstatic look on Sandy's face. They were going to take her! All he could do was sit there and fidget and shake and sweat.

Lucius floated silently down through the roof of the Administration Building and landed on the third floor, folding his wings behind him. He could hear Rafar bellowing and boasting in the lounge; he could hear the Strongman going through his preliminaries in the conference room. So far they had no fears or suspicions.

He heard the elevator opening down the hall and then the footsteps of several people. Yes, this would be Hogan the hound and the praying man, Busche, and the one person the Strongman would be the most loath to see alive: the Maidservant.

Suddenly there was a flutter of wings and a frantic gasping. A demon shot down the hall toward him, wings rushing, his face filled with terror.

"Prince Lucius!" it cried. "Treachery! We've been tricked! Hogan and Busche are free! The Maidservant is alive! Weed is alive!"

"Silence!" Lucius cautioned.

But the demon just kept spouting. "The saints are gathered and are praying! You must warn the Ba-al—"

The demon's ranting ended abruptly in a choked gargle, and he looked at Lucius with his eyes full of horror and questions. He began to shrivel. He clawed at Lucius in an effort to remain upright. Lucius pulled his sword out of the demon's belly and swung it in a fiery arc through the ebbing body. The demon disintegrated, dissolved in a puff of red smoke.

Outside on the front steps, even as passersby stared and gawked, the Remnant was in prayer.

Sandy could see other beautiful beings emerging from the tunnel behind Madeline.

"Oh . . ." she asked, "who are these?"

"New friends," said Madeline. "New spirit guides to take you higher and higher."

Alexander Kaseph began to exchange important documents and contracts with the regents and the attorneys. They were discussing all the little loose ends that needed sewing up. Most of it was minor. It would not take long.

The cloud finally formed a complete enclosure around the town of Ashton. Tal and his company found themselves trapped under a thick, impenetrable tent of demons. The spiritual darkness became deep and oppressive. It was difficult to breathe. The steady drone of the wings seemed to permeate everything.

Suddenly Guilo whispered, "They're descending!"

They all looked up and could see the ceiling of demons, that boiling red and yellow tinted blanket of black, starting to settle downward, coming closer and closer to the town. Soon Ashton would be buried.

Several cars were just turning onto College Way. The first carried County Prosecutor Justin Parker, the second Eldon Strachan and State Attorney General Norm Mattily, the third Al Lemley and three federal agents. As they passed through an intersection, a fourth car turned right and joined the procession. This car just happened to carry that true-blue accountant Harvey Cole, with a sizable stack of papers beside him on the seat.

Tal now held a golden trumpet in his hand, gripping it very tightly, every muscle and every tendon tensed.

"Get ready!" he ordered.

40

Marshall, Hank, Susan, and Kevin walked quietly down the hall, listening for any sounds and checking the numbers on all the doors. Susan gestured toward the conference room, and they paused just outside. Susan recognized Kaseph's voice. She nodded to the others.

Marshall put his hand on the doorknob. He gestured to the others to wait. Then he opened the door and stepped inside. Kaseph sat at the head of the big conference table, and the regents and the four attorneys were seated around it. The demons in the room immediately drew their swords and backed up against the walls. Not only was this the very unexpected newspaperman, but he was accompanied by two very mean-looking heavenly warriors, a huge Arabian and a fierce African who looked more than ready for a fight!

The Strongman knew this meant trouble, but . . . not that much trouble. He looked at the intruders defiantly, even grinning just a little, and said, "And just who are you?"

"The name is Marshall Hogan," Marshall told Kaseph. "I'm the editor of the *Ashton Clarion*—that is, as soon as I prove to the right people that I still rightfully own it. But I understand you and I have had a lot to do with each other, and I think it's time we met."

Eugene Baylor did not like the looks of this at all, and neither did any of the others. They were speechless, and some looked like frightened mice with nowhere to run. They all knew where Hogan was supposed to be, but now, suddenly, shockingly, he was in the worst possible place: Here!

The Strongman's eyes took on an icy stare, and the demons attending him drew strength from the thought that the Strongman was invincible and diabolically clever. He would know what to do!

"How did you get *here?*" Kaseph asked for them all.

"I took the elevator!" Marshall snapped. "But now I have a question for you. I want my daughter, and I want her unharmed. Let's deal, Kaseph. Where is she?"

Kaseph and the Strongman only laughed derisively. "Deal, you say? You, a mere man, wish to deal with me?" Kaseph took a few side glances at his team of lawyers and added, "Hogan, you have no idea what kind of power you're dealing with."

The demons snickered along. Yes, Hogan, the Strongman cannot be tampered with!

Nathan and Armoth were not laughing.

"Oh, no," said Marshall. "That's where you're wrong. I do know what kind of power I'm dealing with. I've had some really good lessons all through this thing, and some good lectures from my friend here."

Marshall opened the door and in came Hank—and Krioni, and Triskal, this time under no orders of peace.

The Strongman jumped up, his jagged jaws gaping. The demons in the room started trembling and tried to hide behind their swords.

"Relax, relax!" said a lawyer. "They're nothing!"

But the Strongman could feel the presence of the Lord God enter the room with this man. The demon monarch knew who this was. "Busche! The praying man!"

And Hank knew whom he faced. The Spirit was crying it out very loudly within Hank's heart, and that face . . .

"The Strongman, I presume!" said Hank.

Sandy asked Madeline again, "Madeline, where are we going? Why are you hanging on to me so?"

Madeline would not answer but kept pulling Sandy deeper and deeper into the tunnel. Madeline's friends were all around Sandy, and they did not seem kind or gentle at all. They kept pushing her, grabbing her, forcing her along. Their fingernails were sharp.

The people around the conference table were shocked and nonplussed, suddenly finding themselves in the presence of a hideous creature; they had never seen such an expression on Kaseph's face before, and they had never heard such a vicious voice. Kaseph rose from his chair, his breath hissing through his teeth, his eyes bulging, his back arched, his fists clenched.

"You cannot defeat me, praying man!" the Strongman bellowed, and the demons around him clung with desperate hope to those words. "You have no power! *I* have defeated *you!*"

Marshall and Hank stood their ground unflinchingly. They had tackled demons before. This was nothing new or surprising.

Kaseph's attorneys could not think of anything to say.

Marshall reached over and opened the door. With her head held high and her face full of determination, Susan Jacobson, the Maidservant, stepped into the room, followed by the very angry Kevin Weed, and four more towering guards with them. The room was getting crowded, and tense.

"Hello, Alex," said Susan.

Kaseph's eyes were full of shock and fear, but still he gasped and sputtered, "Who are you? I don't know you. I've never seen you before."

"Don't say anything, Alex," an attorney advised him.

Hank stepped forward. It was time for battle.

"Strongman," Hank said in a firm and steady voice, "in the name of Jesus, I rebuke you! I rebuke you and I bind you!"

Madeline would not let go! Her hands felt like icy steel as she pulled Sandy along. The tunnel was getting dark and cold.

"Madeline!" Sandy cried. "Madeline, what are you doing? Please let go of me!"

Madeline kept her face forward and would not look back at Sandy. All Sandy could see was that long, flowing, blonde hair. Madeline's hands were hard and cold. They were hurting Sandy's wrists, cutting into them.

Sandy cried in desperation, "Madeline! Madeline, please stop!" Suddenly the other spirit guides pressed in all around her. They were clamping onto her, and their steely hands hurt. "Please, don't you hear me? Make them stop!"

Madeline turned her head at last. Her hide was soot-black and leathery. Her eyes were huge yellow orbs. Her jaws were the jaws of a lion, and saliva dribbled off her fangs. A low guttural growl rumbled out of her throat.

Sandy screamed. From somewhere in this blackness, this tunnel, this nothingness, this altered state, this pit of death and deception, she screamed from the depths of her tortured and dying soul.

Tal leaped from the earth. He exploded in a burst of wings and light. The ground dropped away and the town became a map below him as he shot over Ashton like a comet, piercing the spiritual darkness like a fiery arrow, illuminating the whole valley like a prolonged lightning bolt. He climbed, he circled; his wings were a blurred flurry of jewels.

The trumpet went to his lips, and the call went forth like a shock wave to shake the heavens. It echoed across the valley and back again, and back again, and back again. With wave after wave it washed over the ground, it deafened the demons it soared down the streets and rumbled through the alleys, it rang in every ear with volley after volley of notes, building higher and sounding longer, and the still, thick air was shattered with the sound. Tal blew and blew as he soared over the town, his wings flashing, his garments glowing.

The moment had come.

The Strongman was suddenly silent. His big eyes rolled back and forth.

"What was that?" he hissed.

The demons all around him were shaken and looking at him for answers, but he had none.

The eight heavenly warriors drew their swords. That was answer enough.

Rafar screamed through Langstrat, "*I* am speaking here! Let nothing else draw your attention!"

The demons in the room tried to pay attention again, as did the psychics they controlled.

For a fraction of a moment, Madeline's grip weakened. But only for a moment.

But they all knew they had heard something.

The evil warriors in the cloud steadily settled downward upon the town; but now their eyes were dazzled by the sudden appearance of one lone angel tracing brilliant streaks of light across the sky below them. And what was this horribly loud trumpet all about? Were not the heavenly forces already defeated? Did they dare to think they could possibly defend this town?

Suddenly tiny bursts of light appeared all over the town far below, flashes that did not dissipate but remained and grew brighter. They thickened and grew in numbers and density. The town was on fire; it was disappearing under myriads of tiny lights, as numerous as grains of sand. It was blinding!

The eerie screams began at the center of the cloud and rippled outward across the layers upon layers of demons: "The Host of Heaven!"

Thunderous shouts began the moment Tal touched down on his hill and raised his blazing sword high above his head.

"For the saints of God and for the Lamb!"

Tal shouted it, Guilo shouted it, myriads of heavenly warriors shouted it, and the entire landscape from one end of the valley to the other, the entire town, and even the forested hills surrounding Ashton erupted in brilliant stars.

From the buildings, streets, alleys, sewers, lakes, ponds, vehicles, rooms, closets, nooks, crannies, trees, thickets, and every other imaginable hiding place, flaming stars shot into the air.

The Host of Heaven!

Sandy was tumbling, struggling. The thing called Madeline had both her arms; the other spirits held her legs, her neck, her torso. They were biting her. From somewhere the mocking voice of the Ascended Master, Rafar, said, "Take her, Madeline! We have her! We cannot fail now."

Sandy tried to get out of the trance, out of the altered state, out of the nightmare, but she couldn't remember how. She heard the metallic clinking of chains. No! NOOOOO. . . .

"You cannot defeat me!" the Strongman screamed, and his demons hoped, or rather wished it were true.

"Be quiet and come out of him!" Hank ordered.

His words threw the demons against the walls and hit the Strongman like a left hook.

Kaseph hissed and spat curses and obscenities at the young minister. The regents around the table were all speechless; some ducked under the table. The lawyers were trying to calm Kaseph down.

"I want my daughter!" Marshall said. "Where is she?"

"It's all over," said Susan. "I've given them all the right documents! The feds are coming to hang you, and I'm going to tell them everything!"

From behind the other three Kevin shouted, "Kaseph, you think you're so tough, let's step outside and settle this man to man!"

The descending cloud of demons and the rising fireball of angels began to collide in the skies over Ashton. Thunder began to rip the sky in response to the terrific clash of the spiritual forces. Swords flashed, and a hail of screams and shouts echoed across the sky. The heavenly warriors mowed through the ranks of demons like blurring scythes. Demons began to fall out of the sky like meteors, spinning, smoking, dissolving.

Tal, Guilo and the General streaked toward the college, swords ready, the town a blur beneath them. A very strong regiment of angelic hosts had pushed its way through the demonic offensive and began cordoning off the college campus. Soon there would be an angelic canopy over the college within the demonic canopy over the town. The breaking of the enemy's strength would begin there.

"They have nearly contained the Strongman!" Guilo shouted over the roar of the wind and their wings.

"Find Sandy!" Tal ordered. "There is no time to spare!"

"I'll take the Strongman," said the General.

"And Rafar will soon get his wish," Tal said.

They fanned out, shot forward with a new burst of speed, and began cutting their way through the demons who were still trying to blockade the college. The demon warriors fell upon them like an avalanche, but for Guilo this was good sport. Tal and the General could hear his uproarious laughter through the thudding sounds of his blade going through demon after demon.

Tal was busy himself, being such a valuable prize for the demon lucky enough to vanquish him. The most horrible warriors were singling him out, and they didn't fall easily. He skidded through the air sideways, slammed one spirit with his sword, went into a blurred spin and split the next warrior with the force of a saw-blade. Two more dove down at him; he shot toward them, impaled the first as he passed it, grabbed its wingtip and whipped around in a tight circle, coming up behind the other, his blade like a bullet. They vanished in a cloud of red smoke. He slipped through the clutches of several more, then dove and zigzagged toward the college, cutting demons down as he went. He could hear Guilo still roaring and laughing somewhere over his left shoulder.

The conference room was quickly losing its calm atmosphere.

Delores Pinckston was distraught. "I knew it! I knew it! I knew we were all getting in too deep!"

"Hogan," fumed Eugene Baylor, "you're only bluffing. You have nothing."

"I have *everything*, and you know it."

Kaseph was beginning to look very ill. "Get out! Get out of here! I'll kill you if you don't leave!"

Was this the real Kaseph that Marshall had been tracking down all this time? Was this the ruthless occult mobster who controlled such a vast international empire? Was he actually *afraid*?

"You're sunk, Kaseph!" said Marshall.

"You're defeated, Strongman!" said Hank.

The Strongman began to shake. The demons in the room could only cower.

"So let's deal," Marshall offered again. "Where's my daughter?"

Brummel was about to have a heart attack, and he wished he really could. It was horrible! The others were sitting around the room listening raptly to this beast speaking through Langstrat, and actually relishing what was happening to Sandy. She trembled and shook in her chair, moaning, screaming, struggling against some unseen assailant.

"Let me go!" she screamed. "Let me go!"

Her eyes were wide open, but she was seeing unspeakable horrors from another world. She gasped for air, pale with terror.

She's going to die, Brummel! They are going to kill her!

The hulking, bug-eyed creature sitting in Langstrat's chair was bellowing in a voice that made Brummel's insides quiver. "You are lost, Sandy Hogan! We have you now! You belong to us, and we are the only reality you know!"

"Please, God," she screamed. "Get me out of here, please!"

"Join us! Your mother has fled, your father is dead! He is gone! Think of him no longer! You belong to us!"

Sandy went limp in her chair as if she had been shot. Her face suddenly numbed with despair.

Brummel could take no more. Before he had time to realize what he was doing, he jumped out of his chair and ran to her. He shook her gently and tried to speak to her.

"Sandy!" he pleaded. "Sandy, don't listen to them! It's all a lie! Do you hear me?"

Sandy could not hear him.

But Rafar could. Langstrat jumped up from her chair and screamed at Brummel in that same, deep, devilish voice, "Be silent, you little imp, and step aside! She belongs to *me!*"

Brummel ignored her. "Sandy, don't listen to this lying monster. This is Alf Brummel talking to you. Your father is all right."

Rafar's rage grew so that Langstrat's body nearly burst from the intensity of it. "Hogan is defeated! He is imprisoned!"

Brummel looked right into Langstrat's—and Rafar's—crazed eyes and shouted, "Marshall Hogan is free! Hank Busche is free! I released them myself! They are free, and they are coming to destroy you!"

Rafar was stymied for a moment. He simply could not believe the ravings of this weak little man, this insignificant little puppet who had never before acted in this brazen fashion. But then Rafar heard a very inappropriate snicker coming from behind Brummel, and he saw a familiar face laughing him to scorn.

Lucius!

Tal and Guilo swooped down into the Administration Building, but Tal suddenly stopped short.

"Wait now! What is this?"

Lucius drew his sword and said, "You are not so mighty, Rafar! Your plan has failed, and I am the only true Prince of Ashton!"

Rafar's sword rang from its sheath. "Do you dare to oppose *me*?"

Rafar's sword cut through the air with a rush of wind, but Lucius stopped the big blade with his own; the force of the blow almost knocked him over.

The many demons in the room were startled and confused. They let go of their hosts. What was *this*?

Kaseph was indignant with his lawyers and even threw some punches at them. "Stop it! You will not tell me what to do! This is *my* world! *I* am in charge here! *I* say what is and what is not! These people are fools and liars, every one of them!"

Susan spoke directly to Kaseph. "You, Alexander Kaseph, are responsible for the murder of Patricia Krueger *and* the attempted murder of myself and Mr. Weed here. I have the many lists I helped you write up, lists of people who ended up dead by your order."

"Murder!" exclaimed one regent. "Mr. Kaseph, is this true?"

"Don't answer that," said a lawyer.

"No!" Kaseph screamed.

Several other regents looked at each other. They knew Kaseph pretty well by now. They didn't believe him.

"How about it, Kaseph?" Marshall said grimly.

The Strongman wanted with all his evil heart to lunge at this brazen hound and maul him, and he would have, guards or no guards—if not for that horrible praying man who stood in the way.

Langstrat stalked like a lion toward Brummel, as many of the psychics, having lost their spirit guides, came out of their trances to see what in the world had happened.

"I will vanquish you for this treachery!" she hissed at him.

"What is this?" Oliver Young demanded. "Have you both gone mad?"

Brummel stood his ground and pointed a shaking finger at Langstrat. "You will no longer rule over me. This plan will not succeed for your glory. I will not let it!"

"Be quiet, you little fool!" Langstrat ordered.

"No!" Brummel shouted, driven on by the crazed and brazen Lucius. "The Plan is doomed. It has failed, just as I knew it would."

"And *you* are doomed, Rafar!" Lucius screamed, dodging the lethal thrusts of Rafar's sword. "Do you hear the battle outside? The Hosts of Heaven are everywhere!"

"Treachery!" Rafar hissed. "You will pay for your treachery!"

"Treachery!" some of the demons cried.

"No, Lucius speaks the truth!" others shouted back.

Sandy forced herself to look into those evil yellow eyes and plead, "What's—what's happened to you, Madeline? Why have you changed?"

Madeline only cackled and answered, "Do not believe what you see. What is evil? It is but an illusion. What is pain? It is but an illusion. What is fear? It is but an illusion."

"But you lied to me! You deceived me!"

"I have never been other than I am. It is you who have deceived yourself."

"What are you going to do?"

"I am going to set you free."

Just as Madeline spoke those words, Sandy's arms suddenly dropped with such a ponderous weight that she almost fell to the ground.

Chains! Links upon links of glistening, heavy chains hung around her wrists and her arms. Crooked hands were whipping them around her. The cold and bruising links slapped against her legs, her body, her neck. She could no longer struggle against them. She tried to scream, but her breath was gone.

"Now you are free!" Madeline said gleefully.

Brummel started speaking for himself. "The authorities . . . the state attorney general . . . Justin Parker . . . the feds! They know everything!"

"What?" some of the psychics cried, jumping out of their seats. They started to ask questions, to panic.

Young tried to keep order, but he was failing.

Rafar dropped his hold on Langstrat so he could better handle this traitorous upstart.

Langstrat snapped out of her trance and could feel the psychic energy in the room collapsing.

"Get back in your seats, everyone!" she shouted. "We have not accomplished our purpose here!" She closed her eyes and called out, "Rafar, please return! Bring order!"

But Rafar was busy. Lucius was smaller, but he was very quick and very determined. The two swords flashed about the room like fireworks, burning and clanging. Lucius flitted about Rafar's head like a pesky hornet, jabbing, swinging, and slashing. The whole room was filled with Rafar's swirling wings and his chugging breath, and his big sword traced fiery red sheets through the air.

"Traitor!" Rafar screamed. "I'll cut you to pieces!"

Langstrat moved toward Brummel with wild eyes. "Traitor! I'll tear you apart!"

"No," Brummel muttered with widened eyes, his hand going to his side. "Not this time . . . no more!"

Young shouted at them both, "Stop it! You don't know what you're doing!"

The demons in the room were dividing into camps.

"Prince Lucius speaks the truth!" said some. "Rafar has led us to our doom!"

"No, it is *Lucius* who is the enemy's fool!"

"You are the fools, but we will save ourselves!"

More swords flashed into view.

Rafar knew he was losing control.

"Fools!" he roared. "This is a trick of the Enemy! He is trying to divide us!"

It only took that one brief moment when Rafar's eyes were on his quarreling demons and not on Lucius's sword.

It only took that one moment of terror to push Brummel over the edge. He pointed his police revolver at the wild-eyed Langstrat.

Lucius's blade sang through the air and slipped just under Rafar's parrying sword. The tip ripped deeply through Rafar's hide and opened his flank with a deep, gushing wound.

Langstrat made just one wrong move and the bullet thudded into her chest.

In the conference room they all heard the shot. Marshall was out in the hall in an instant.

41

Bernice leaped from her spot on the front steps. It was Eldon Strachan with Norm Mattily himself, and Justin Parker, and that had to be Al Lemley—and those three guys in their nice three-piece suits had to be FBI! Oh, and there was Harvey Cole with a stack of papers under his arm.

She ran up to them, her black eyes wild with excitement. "Hello! You made it!"

Norm Mattily's eyes got big. "What's happened? Are you all right?"

Bernice had paid a lot for these bruises; she was going to use them. "No, no, I've been attacked! Please hurry inside! Something terrible is happening!"

The VIPs ran into the building with serious business in their eyes and guns in their hands.

Tal had seen enough. He shouted the order to Guilo, "Go in!" and then soared out of the building to signal for more troops.

Smoke and red tar were pouring from Rafar's side, but his rage spelled certain doom for the rebellious Lucius. The light of a thousand angels beamed in through the windows. They would be in the room in an instant, but that was all the time Rafar needed. He whipped his plank-sized sword in vicious circles over his head. He brought it down in blow after blow upon Lucius as the defiant demon's little sword parried every blow with a loud clang and a shower of sparks.

The roar of angels' wings outside grew louder, louder. The floors and walls rumbled with the sound.

Rafar let out a roar and brought the blade straight down. Lucius blocked the blow, but collapsed under the power of it. The blade ripped through the air in a flat circle and caught Lucius under the arm. The arm went spinning into space, and Lucius cried out. The blade came down again, passed straight through Lucius's head, shoulders, torso. The air filled with boiling red smoke.

Lucius was gone.

"Kill the girl!" Rafar shouted to Madeline.

Madeline drew out a horrible, crooked knife. She placed it gently in Sandy's hand. "These chains are the chains of life; they are a prison of evil, of the lying mind, of illusion! Free your true self! Join me!"

Shawn had a knife ready. He placed it in the entranced Sandy's hand.

Rafar staggered through a wall just as the light of a million suns exploded into the room with a deafening thunder of wings and the warcries of the Heavenly Host.

Many demons tried to flee, but were instantly disintegrated by slashing swords. The whole room was one huge, bombastic, brilliant blur. The roar of the wings drowned out every sound except the screams of falling spirits.

Kaseph leaped from his chair and fell across the table. The regents and lawyers shied away and pressed against the wall. Some headed for the room's other door.

Hank, Susan, and Kevin watched from a safe distance. They knew what was happening.

Kaseph's face seemed numb with death and his mouth hung open as the most hideous scream came out of him.

The Strongman was face to face with the General. His demons

were gone, washed away by an overwhelming tide of angels that were still roaring through the room like an avalanche. The General's sword moved faster than the ponderous Strongman could even anticipate. The Strongman fought back, screaming, slashing, swinging. The General just kept coming at him.

Marshall was out in the hall, listening for any disturbance. He thought he heard a commotion from down the hall.

Sandy still held that knife, but now Madeline was hesitating and looking around frantically. The chains still held Sandy tightly, an iron cocoon.

Guilo could see the chains wrapped tightly around her, the horrible demonic bondage they had used to enslave her.

"No more!" he shouted.

He raised his sword high above his head and brought it down, trailing a wide ribbon of light. The tip passed through the many windings of those chains like a series of small explosions. The chains burst outward and away from her, writhing like severed snakes.

Guilo's big fist clamped onto the fleeing Madeline's grisly neck. He jerked her backward, spun her around, and hacked her into vanishing particles.

Sandy felt herself spinning, then rushing upward as if she were a rocket in an elevator shaft. Sounds began to register on her ears. She could feel her physical body again. Light registered on her retinas. She opened her eyes. A knife fell from her hands.

The room was in chaos. People were screaming, running back and forth, trying to calm each other down, fighting, arguing, trying to escape from the room; several men were wrestling Alf Brummel to the floor. There was a haze of blue smoke and a strong smell like fireworks.

Professor Langstrat was lying on the floor, with several people huddled over her. There was blood!

Someone grabbed her. Not again! She looked to see Shawn holding her arm. He was trying to comfort her, trying to keep her in her chair.

The monster! The deceiver! The liar!

"Let me go!" she screamed at him, but he wouldn't let go.

She hit him in the face, then pulled away from him; she leaped to her feet and ran for the door, bumping into several people and stepping on some others. He went after her, calling her name.

She burst through the door and stumbled out into the hall. From somewhere down the hall she heard a familiar voice shouting her name. She screamed and ran for that voice.

Shawn went after Sandy. He had to contain this woman before all control was lost.

What! Before him, filling the entire hallway with fiery wings, stood the most frightening being he had ever seen, holding a terrible flaming sword right at his heart. Shawn braked to a stop, his shoes skidding on the floor.

Marshall Hogan appeared suddenly, running right through that being. A huge fist slammed into Shawn's jaw, and the whole matter was settled.

"C'mon, Sandy," Marshall said, "we'll take the stairs!"

Rafar, somewhere inside that shaking, besieged building, knew he had to get out. He tried to get his wings to stir. They only quivered. He had to build up the strength. He could not be defeated in the presence of these petty warriors; he would not go to the abyss!

He sank to one knee, his hand holding his oozing side, and let his rage grow inside him. Tal! This was all Tal's doing! No, clever captain, you'll not gain your victory this way!

The yellow eyes burned with new fire. He tried again. This time his wings roused themselves and went into a blurred rushing. Rafar gripped his sword tightly and turned his eyes skyward. The wings surged with power and began to lift him up through the building, faster and faster, until he soared up through the roof and into the open air . . . and found himself face to face with the very captain he had taunted and challenged time and again.

All around them the battle raged; demons—and Rafar's great victory—fell like smoking, burning rain from the sky. But for one very short moment of awe and mutual horror, Tal and Rafar remained frozen.

They had met at last! And each could not help but be numbed by the memories he had of the other. Neither remembered the other looking so fierce.

And neither could be entirely sure of winning this contest.

Rafar shot sideways, and Tal braced himself for a blow, but—Rafar was fleeing! He dashed away across the sky like a bleeding bird, trailing a stream of ooze and vapor.

Tal went after him, wings rushing, dashing this way and that through falling demons and charging angels, looking far ahead through the wild flurry of the battle clashing and thundering all around. There! He spotted the demon warlord dipping down toward the town. He would be hard to find in that maze of buildings, streets, and alleys. Tal quickened his speed and closed the distance. Rafar must have seen him coming up from behind; the evil prince shot ahead with a surprising burst of speed and then dropped suddenly and sharply toward an office building.

Tal saw him disappear through the roof of that building and dove after him. The black tar roof came at him, growing in an instant from the size of a postage stamp to more than the eye could see. Tal plunged through it.

Roof, room, floor, room, then pull up, then down a hall, through a wall, up again, turn back, follow that smoke, through an office, follow up a wall, dip through a floor, rush along, the passing walls slap, slap, slapping the eyes and rushing past like speeding freight cars.

A smoking black missile followed by a flaming comet roared down the hall, down through several floors, back up again, right through the office and over all the desks, up through the ceiling panels, up through the roof and out into the open sky again.

Rafar was soaring, dashing, looping, zigzagging through falling demons, doubling back, ducking down side streets, but Tal stayed right on his tail and retraced his every turn perfectly.

How much longer could that bleeding demon keep this up?

The other door of the conference room burst open, and the body of Alexander Kaseph rolled across the hallway floor. He was retching and screaming.

The General swung his sword at the Strongman again and again, weakening him, cutting him more and more frequently as the Strongman continued to lose his power.

"You will not defeat me!" the Strongman still boasted, as did Kaseph, but the boast was empty and futile. The Strongman was gushing red vapor and tar like a wretched and broken sieve. His eyes were full of evil and hate and he slashed with his big sword, but the prayers . . . ! The prayers could be felt everywhere, and the General could not be defeated.

Bernice had her group of vindicators gathered in the lobby downstairs, and she was trying to figure out where to start explaining everything when Marshall and Sandy burst out of the stairway door.

"Get yourselves upstairs!" Marshall hollered, holding his weeping daughter. "Someone's been shot!"

Lemley's feds went right into action. "Call the police! We'll cordon off the building!"

Bernice remarked, "I see some cops outside there . . ."

The police had come purely in response to a call about all these religious fanatics assembled on the campus. They were trying to break up the gathering when Norm Mattily and one federal agent ran out to them, identified themselves, and ordered them to close off the building.

Brummel's men were no fools. They obeyed.

Rafar darted and weaved all over the sky, still trailing a stream of red smoke from his wound. With that telltale marker it was easy to follow him, and Tal kept up the chase unrelentingly. Rafar sped toward a very large warehouse several blocks away.

He shot through the outside wall at about the third floor, and Tal dove into the building after him. This floor was open, with no places to hide; Rafar dove immediately to a lower floor, and Tal followed that trail of smoke. The gray, concrete floors came up at them.

Tal came out on the first floor and could see the smoke trail veering off sideways and corkscrewing through the distant wall. He shot after it. The wall slapped around him as he passed through.

Impaled!

A burning edge cut through his side! He spun and spun from the impact and the sword went flying from his hand. He tumbled to the floor, doubled up with pain.

There stood Rafar, bent and wounded, his back against the wall Tal had just come through. He had been waiting in ambush. The tip of his ugly sword was still draped with part of Tal's tunic.

No time to think! No time to feel pain! Tal dove for his fallen sword.

Crash! Rafar's sword came down with a shower of sparks. Tal rolled and fluttered out of the way. The big red sword ripped through the air again, and the keen edge whistled just over Tal's head. Tal clapped his wings and jerked sideways several feet.

Whoosh! That horrible sword sliced the air with brilliant red streaks. Rafar's eyes turned from yellow to red, his mouth frothed with putrid foam.

The huge wings roared, and Rafar came at Tal like a pouncing cat. His powerful arm raised that blade to strike again.

Tal lurched forward and ducked under Rafar's raised arm, his head butting into Rafar's chest. The sulfur exploded from those huge lungs as Tal spun around Rafar's body and beyond the tip of that red blade as it slashed through the air.

This was what Tal needed: he was now between Rafar and his fallen sword. He dove at it, grabbed it, and turned.

Clang! The blade of hell came down upon Tal's sword with a flash of fire. They faced each other, swords held ready. Rafar was grinning.

"So now, Captain of the Host, we are alone together, and evenly matched. I am opened, and you are opened. Shall we assail each other for *another* twenty-three days? We will be finished long before that, eh?"

Tal said nothing. This was Rafar's way; cutting words were part of his strategy.

The swords met again, and again. An envelope of darkness began to fill the room: Rafar's creeping, growing evil.

"Is the light fading?" Rafar sneered. "Perhaps it is your *strength* we now see ebbing away!"

Saints of God, where are your prayers?

Another blow! Tal's shoulder. He returned with a swipe that caught Rafar under the ribs. The air was filling with darkness, with red vapor and smoke.

Several more clashes of the fiery blades . . . ripping hides, tearing garments, more darkness.

Saints! Pray! PRAY!

When the police reached the third floor, they thought at first that Kaseph was the gunshot victim. They found out differently when this wild animal threw them off as if they weighed nothing.

"You cannot defeat me!" he screamed.

The General slashed at the Strongman again, and the Strongman screamed again. The swords clashed and sang and flashed with fire.

"You cannot defeat me!"

The police aimed their guns. What was this nut going to do next?

Hank shouted, "No, take it easy! It's not him!"

They did not understand that statement at all.

Hank stepped forward and gave it one more try: "Strongman, I know you can hear me. You *are* defeated. The shed blood of Jesus has defeated you. Be silent and come out of him and depart from this region!"

Now the police were aiming at *Hank!*

But the Strongman could take no more of this praying man's rebukes. He wilted. His sword dropped. The General took one swipe with his flashing blade, and the Strongman was gone.

Kaseph collapsed to the floor and lay there as if dead. The lawyers and regents shouted from the conference room, "Don't shoot!" and came out with their hands raised whether ordered to or not. The police still did not know who to arrest.

"In here!" someone shouted from the lounge. The police ran in and found the pitiful wreck that Alf Brummel had become, and the very deceased Juleen Langstrat.

42

Rip! Rafar's sword took off a corner of Tal's wing. Tal kept darting and flitting, dodging and swinging, and he clipped Rafar's shoulder and thigh. The air was filled with the stench of sulfur; the evil darkness was thick like smoke.

"The Lord rebuke you!" Tal shouted.

Clang! Rip!

"Where is the Lord?" Rafar mocked. "I see Him not!"

Whoosh!

Tal screamed in pain. His left hand hung useless.

"Lord God," Tal cried, "His name is Rafar! Tell them!"

The Remnant were not praying so much now; instead they watched all the excitement and the police dashing in and out of the Administration Building.

"Wow!" said John Coleman. "The Lord's really answering our prayers!"

"Praise the Lord!" Andy replied. "That just goes to show . . . Edith! Edith, what's wrong?"

Edith Duster had sunk to her knees. She was pale. The saints gathered around.

"Should we call an aid car?" someone asked.

"No! No!" Edith cried. "I know this feeling. I've felt it before. The Lord is trying to speak to me!"

"What?" asked Andy. "What is it?"

"Well, quit your gabbing and let me pray and I'll tell you!"

Edith started to weep. "There's still an evil spirit out there," she cried. "He's doing great mischief. His name is . . . Raphael . . . Raving . . ."

Bobby Corsi spoke up. "Rafar!"

Edith looked up at him with wide eyes. "Yes! Yes! That's the name the Lord's impressing upon me!"

"Rafar!" Bobby said again. "He's the big wheel!"

Tal could only back away from the fearsome onslaught of the demon prince, his one good hand still holding his sword up for defense. Rafar kept swinging and slashing, the sparks flying from the blades as they met. Tal's arm sank lower with each blow.

"The Lord . . . rebuke you!" Tal found the breath to say again.

Edith Duster was on her feet and ready to shout it to the heavens. "Rafar, you wicked prince of evil, in the name of Jesus we rebuke you!"

Rafar's blade zinged over Tal's head. It missed.

"We bind you!" shouted the Remnant.

The big yellow eyes winced.

"We cast you out!" Andy said.

There was a puff of sulfur, and Rafar bent over. Tal leaped to his feet.

"We rebuke you, Rafar!" Edith shouted again.

Rafar screamed. Tal's blade had torn him open.

The big red blade came down with a clang against Tal's, but that angelic sword was singing with a new resonance. It cut through the air in fiery arcs. With his one good hand, Tal kept swinging, slashing, cutting, pushing Rafar back. The fiery eyes were oozing, the foam was bubbling out the mouth and fizzing down the chest, the yellow breath had turned deep crimson.

Then in one horrible, rage-empowered swipe, the huge red sword came sizzling through the air. Tal went tumbling backward like a tossed rag toy. He fell to the floor stunned, his head spinning, his body drenched in fiery pain. He could not move. His strength was gone.

Where was Rafar? Where was that blade? Tal tried to turn his head. He strained to see. Was that his enemy? Was that Rafar?

Through the vapor and darkness he could see Rafar's battered frame swaying like a big tree in the wind. The demon did not move, he did not charge. As for the sword, the huge hand still held it, but the blade now hung limply, the tip resting on the floor. The breaths were coming in long, slow wheezes. The nostrils spewed deep red clouds. Those eyes—those hate-filled eyes—were like huge, glowing rubies.

The dripping, foaming jaws trembled open, and the words gargled through the tar and the froth. "But . . . for . . . your . . . praying saints! But for your saints . . . !"

The big beast swayed forward. He let out one last hissing sigh, and rumbled to the floor in a cloud of red.

And it was quiet.

Tal could not breathe. He could not move. All he could see was red vapor spreading along the floor like thin fog and darkness all around that huge body.

But . . . yes. Somewhere the saints were praying. He could feel it. He was healing.

What was that? From somewhere the sweet music found its way to him. It soothed him. Worship. The name of Jesus.

He lifted his head up from the floor and let his eyes explore the cold, concrete room. Rafar, the mighty, loathsome Prince of Babylon, was gone. Nothing remained but a shrinking cloud of darkness. Above the cloud of darkness light was coming through, almost like a sunrise.

He could still hear the music. It echoed throughout the heavenlies, washing them clean, clearing away the darkness with God's holy light.

And his heart was the first to tell him: You've won . . . for the saints of God and for the Lamb.

You've won!

The light grew and grew, blossoming, filling the room, and the darkness continued to shrink and ebb and fade away. Now Tal could see light coming in through the windows. Sunlight? Yes.

The Heavenly Host? Yes!

Tal struggled to his feet and waited for more strength. It came. He stepped forward. His gait became firm and steady. Then, like unfurling silk spun from sparkling diamonds, he spread his wings, fold by fold, inch by inch. They blossomed outward from his shoulders and back, and he let them grow strong.

He drew a deep breath, took the handle of his sword in both hands, held it out in front of him, and the wings took over. He was into the air, climbing into the fresh, light-washed sky, looking straight up and seeing no darkness, no oppression, no clouds.

What he did see was light: light from the Heavenly Host as they swept the sky clean from one end to the other. The air was so fresh, the smells were so clean.

He sailed over the little town and back to the college just in time to see the many flashing lights of squad cars and aid cars and official cars parked everywhere.

Where was Guilo? Oh, where was that blustery Guilo?

"Captain Tal!" came the shout, and Tal dropped toward Ames Hall where his burly friend awaited him with an almost crushing bear hug.

"Surely the battle is over?" Guilo roared happily.

"*Is* it?" Tal wanted to know.

He looked all around to make sure. Yes, in the very great distance he could see the last fleeing fragments of the cloud scattering in all directions, swept away by the heavenly forces. The sky was a very lovely blue. Below them he could see the faithful Remnant still singing and cheering. It looked like the police were going through some kind of final clean-up.

Norm Mattily, Justin Parker, and Al Lemley huddled around Bernice and her new friend.

"Well, everybody," said Bernice, "I'd like you to meet Susan Jacobson. She has a lot to show you!"

Norm Mattily took Susan's hand and said, "You are a very brave woman."

Susan could only point at Bernice through tears of relief and say, "Mr. Mattily, look right there. You're looking at bravery personified."

Bernice looked at the stretcher being carried out of the building by two medics. Juleen Langstrat was completely covered with a white sheet. Behind the stretcher came Alf Brummel, handcuffed and escorted by two of his own officers.

Behind Brummel came the number-one man himself, Alexander M. Kaseph. Susan stared at him long and hard, but he never raised his eyes. He got into the squad car with a federal agent without saying a word.

Hank and Mary were embracing and crying because it was over . . . and yet it was just beginning. Look at all these fired-up saints! Hallelujah—what God could do with a bunch like them!

Marshall held Sandy as if he had never held her before. Both of them had lost count of how many times they had each said they were sorry. All they wanted to do now was get caught up on some badly missed love.

And then . . . what was this, some kind of fairy tale? Forget the doubts and the questions, Hogan, that's *Kate* coming your way! Her face was shining, and boy, did she look good!

All three of them held on to each other, and the tears dripped all over everybody.

"Marshall," Kate said with tearful giddiness, "I couldn't possibly stay away. I heard you were *arrested!*"

"Aw," Marshall said, giving her a loving squeeze, "how else was God ever going to get my attention!"

Kate cuddled close to him and said, "Wow, this does sound promising!"

"Just wait'll I tell you about it."

Kate looked around at all the people and the activity. "Is this the end of your . . . big project?"

He smiled, held his two favorite girls, and said, "Yeah, it is. You *bet* it is!"

The General touched Tal on the shoulder. Tal looked and saw that big, golden trumpet in the General's hand.

"Well, captain," said the silver-haired angel, "how about doing the honors? Sound the victory!"

Tal took the trumpet in his hand and found he could not see through a sudden flow of tears. He looked down at all those praying saints and that little praying pastor.

"They . . . they will never know what they have done," he said. Then he took a breath to sober up and turned to his old buddy-in-arms. "Guilo, how about you?" He pushed the trumpet toward the big angel.

Guilo was reluctant. "Captain Tal, you are always the one who sounds the victory."

Tal smiled, gave Guilo the trumpet, and sat down right there on the roof. "Dear friend . . . I am just too tired."

Guilo thought about that for one short moment, then started guffawing, then slapped Tal on the back and sailed into the air.

The victory signal went forth loud and clear, and Guilo even did a tight corkscrew climb for effect.

"He loves to do that!" said Tal.

The General laughed.

So Hank had Mary and his little newborn church; Marshall had his family back together again, ready to patch things up; Susan and Kevin would be busy for a while as state witnesses; Bernice figured Marshall would let her cover the story to its final end.

But as Bernice stood there, bruised and exhausted, she felt very separate, far away from this happy crowd. She was glad for them, and her professional, public-minded side acted the part very well. But the rest of her, the real Bernice, couldn't smile away that same old burden of deep sorrow that had been her closest companion for so long.

And now she missed Pat. Perhaps it was the mystery of her death and the obsession with finding the answers that kept Pat alive in her heart for so long. Now there was nothing left to delay the final step Bernice had never been able to take: saying good-bye.

And there was that strange yearning deep in her heart, something she had never felt before she met that strange girl, Betsy; had she really been touched by God somehow? If she had been, what was she to do about it?

She started walking. The skies were bright again, the air was warm, the campus was quiet. Maybe a walk along the red brick pathways would calm her and help her to think, help her to make sense of all that was happening around her and inside her.

She paused under a big oak tree, thought of Pat, thought of her own life and what she would ever do with it, and then let herself cry. She thought maybe she should pray. "Dear God," she whispered, but then she couldn't think of what to say.

Tal and the General were assessing the situation below them.

"I would say this whole thing has left the town in quite a mess," said the General.

Tal nodded. "The college won't be the same for a long time, what with the investigation by the state and federal authorities, not to mention all that money to be tracked down."

"So do we have a good contingent to set the town back in order?"

"They're assembling for that now. In the meantime Krioni and Triskal will remain with Busche; Nathan and Armoth will remain with Hogan. Hogan's family will have a good church where they can heal, and—" Tal suddenly noticed one downcast figure standing alone across the campus. "Hold on." He got the attention of one particular angel. "There she is. Let's not let her get away."

Bernice finally thought of one little sentence to pray. "Dear God, I don't know what to do."

Hank Busche. The name just came to her. She looked back toward the Administration Building. That pastor and his people were still there.

You know, said a voice inside her, *it wouldn't hurt to talk to that man.*

She looked at Hank Busche, and then at all those people who seemed so happy, so at peace.

You've been calling out to God. Well, maybe that preacher can introduce the two of you once and for all.

He sure did something for Marshall, Bernice thought.

There's something back there that you need, girl, and if I were you I'd find out about it.

The General was eager to be gone. "We're needed in Brazil. The revival is going well, but the enemy is concocting some plan against it. You should like that kind of a challenge."

Tal rose to his feet again and drew his sword. Just then, Guilo returned with the trumpet. Tal told him, "Brazil."

Guilo laughed excitedly and drew his sword also.

"Wait," said Tal, looking below.

It was Bernice, timidly making her way toward the young pastor and his new flock. By the quiet surrender in her eyes, Tal could see she was ready. Soon the angels would be rejoicing.

He waved his approval to the little curly-haired angel sitting in the crook of the big oak, and she smiled and waved back, her big brown eyes sparkling. Her glowing white gown and golden slippers suited her much better than bib overalls and a motorcycle.

The General asked with pleasure in his voice, "Shall we be going?"

Tal was looking at Hank when he said, "Just a moment. I want to hear it one more time."

As they watched, Bernice found her way to Hank and Mary. She began to weep openly, and spoke some quiet but impassioned words to them. Hank and Mary listened, as did the others nearby, and as they listened, they began to smile. They put their arms around her, they told her about Jesus, and then they began to weep as well. Finally, as the saints were gathered and Bernice was surrounded with loving arms, Hank said the words, "Let's pray . . ."

And Tal smiled a long smile.

"Let's be off," he said.

With a burst of brilliant wings and three trails of sparkling fire, the warriors shot into the sky, heading southward, becoming smaller and smaller until finally they were gone, leaving the now peaceful town of Ashton in very capable hands.

PIERCING
THE
DARKNESS

To Gene and Joyce,
my dad and mom,
who gave me my heritage,
and always encouraged me

"The light shines in the darkness,
and the darkness has not overcome it."

John 1:5 (RSV)

1

It could have begun in any town. Bacon's Corner was nothing special, just one of those little farming towns far from the interstate, nothing more than a small hollow dot on the AAA road map, with exit signs that offered gas, no lodging, maybe a little food if the place was open, and little more.

But it began in Bacon's Corner.

It was a normal Tuesday evening. The workday was over, supper was on in most of the homes, the stores were locking up, the tavern was filling up. All the employees at the Bergen Door Company had clocked out, and the security guard was checking the locks. Mr. Myers's son was bringing all the lawn mowers and tillers in for the night at the Myers Feed and Farm Store. The lights were winking out in the local mercantile. Two retirees sat in their chairs in front of the barbershop, putting in their idle hours.

The fields and farms right across the Toe Springs–Claytonville Road were getting warmer and greener with each day, and now the evening breeze was carrying a lot of mid-April smells—apple and cherry blossoms, plowed dirt, a little mud, some cattle, some manure.

It was a normal Tuesday evening. No one expected anything unusual. No one saw or heard a thing. No one could have.

But the commotion started behind a dismal little rented farmhouse just south of Fred Potter's place—a flapping, a fluttering, a free-for-all, and then a cry, a long, eerie shriek, an echoing, slobbering wail that raced into the forest like a train whistle through a town, loud, muffled, loud, muffled, moving this way and that through the trees like a hunted animal; then a flash of light, a fireball, blinking and burning through the forest, moving with blinding speed, right behind that siren, almost on top of it.

More cries and screams, more flashing lights! Suddenly the forest was filled with them.

The trees ended abruptly where the Amhurst Dairy began. The chase broke into the open.

First out of the forest came a bug, a bat, a black, bulb-eyed thing, its dark wings whirring, its breath pouring out like a long yellow ribbon. It just couldn't fly fast enough, but clawed the air with its spidery arms, desperate for speed and shrieking in total panic.

Right behind it, so close, so dangerously close, the sun itself exploded out of the forest, a brilliant comet with wings of fire tracing a glimmering trail and a sword of lightning outstretched in burly bronze hands.

The black thing and the comet shot into the sky over Bacon's Corner, zigzagging, shooting this way and that like wild fireworks.

Then the forest, like a row of cannons, spewed out more hideous creatures, at least twenty, each one fleeing in utter panic with a dazzling, flaming figure tenaciously on its tail, scattering in all directions like a crazy meteor shower in reverse.

The first demon was running out of tricks and maneuvers; he could feel the heat of the warrior's blade right at his heels.

He spit over his shoulder, "No, turn away, I am going!"

The fiery blade cut an arc through the air. The demon met it with his own and the blow sent him spinning. He corrected with his wings, turned and faced his assailant, shrieking, cursing, parrying blow after blow, looking into the fiery eyes of more power, more glory, more holiness than he'd ever feared before. And he could see it in those eyes—the warrior would never turn away. Never.

The demon withered even before the blade struck its final blow; it slipped from the earth, from the world of mankind, into outer darkness, gone in a tumbling puff of red smoke.

The warrior turned and soared higher, spinning his long sword above his head, tracing a circle of light. He burned with the heat of battle, the fervor of righteousness.

His fellows were consumed with it, striking demons from the sky like foul insects, vanquishing them with strong swords, relentlessly pursuing them and hearing no pleas.

On the right, a long, slithering spirit took one more swipe at his heavenly assailant before curling tightly in anguish and vanishing.

On the left, a loud-mouthed, boasting imp cursed and taunted his opponent, filling the air with blasphemies. He was quick and confident, and just beginning to think he might prevail. His head went spinning from his body while the proud sneer still twisted the face, and then he was gone.

There was one left. It was spinning, tumbling on one good wing.

"I'll go, I'll go," it pleaded.

"Your name?" ordered the angel.

"Despair."

The warrior swatted the demon away with the flat of his blade, and it fled, gone, yet still able to work evil.

And then it was over. The demons were gone. But not soon enough.

"Is she all right?" asked Nathan the Arabian, sheathing his sword.

Armoth the African had made sure. "She's alive, if that's what you mean."

The mighty Polynesian, Mota, added, "Injured and frightened. She wants to get away. She won't wait."

"And now Despair is free to harass her," said Signa the Oriental.

Armoth replied, "Then it's begun, and there will be no stopping it."

Sally Roe lay in the grass, clutching her throat and gasping for air, taking long, deliberate breaths, trying to clear her head, trying to think. A raw welt was rising on her neck; her plaid shirt was reddened from a wound in her shoulder. She kept looking toward the goat pen, but nothing stirred there. There was no life, nothing left to harm her.

I have to get moving, I have to get moving. I can't stay here—no, not one more minute.

She struggled to her feet and immediately rested against the farmhouse, her world spinning. She was still nauseous, even though she'd already lost everything twice.

Don't wait. Go. Get moving.

She staggered up the back porch steps, stumbled once, but kept going. She wouldn't take much with her. She couldn't. There wasn't time.

Ed and Mose were quite comfortable, thank you, just sitting there in front of Max's Barber Shop right on Front Street, which is what they called the Toe Springs–Claytonville Road where it passed through town. Ed was sixty-eight, and Mose wouldn't tell anyone his age, so nobody asked him anymore. Both their wives were gone now—God bless 'em, both men had pretty good retirements and Social Security, and life for them had slowed to a comfortable crawl.

"Ain't bitin', Ed."

"You shoulda moved downriver, Mose. Downriver. They get cranky swimmin' clear up to your place. You gotta catch 'em in a good mood."

Mose listened to the first part, but not the second. He was staring at a green Plymouth hurrying through town with two upset children in the backseat.

"Ed, now don't we know those kids there?"

"Where?"

"Well, why don't you look where I'm pointing?"

Ed looked, but all he could see was the back end of the Plymouth and just the tops of two blond heads in the backseat.

"Well," he said, shading his eyes, "you got me there."

"Oh, you never look when I tell you. I know who they were. They were that schoolteacher's kids, that . . . uh . . . what's his name . . ."

Irene Bledsoe sped along the Toe Springs–Claytonville Road, wearing a scowl that added at least a decade to her already crinkled face. She kept her fists tightly around the wheel and her foot on the gas pedal, spurring the green Plymouth onward whether Ruth and Josiah Harris liked it or not.

"You two be quiet now!" she yelled over her shoulder. "Believe me, we're doing this for your own good!"

Bledsoe's words brought no comfort to Ruth, six, and Josiah, nine.

Ruth kept crying, "I want my Daddy!"

Josiah could only sit there silently, numb with shock and disbelief.

Bledsoe hit the throttle hard. She just wanted to get out of town before there was any more trouble, any more attention.

She was not enjoying this assignment. "The things I do for those people!"

Sally stepped out onto the back porch, still trembling, looking warily about. She'd changed her shirt and donned a blue jacket. She gripped her wadded-up, bloodstained plaid shirt in one hand, and a paper towel dipped in cooking oil in the other.

It was quiet all around, as if nothing had happened. Her old blue pickup was waiting. But there was still one more thing to do.

She looked toward the goat pen, its gate swung wide open and the goats long gone. She took some deep breaths to keep the nausea from coming back. She had to go into that little shed once more. She just had to.

It didn't take long. With her heart racing, her hands now empty, and her pockets stuffed, she got out of there and ran for the truck, clambering inside. It cranked and groaned and started up, and with a surge of power and a spraying of gravel it rumbled down the long driveway toward the road.

Irene Bledsoe was speeding, but there were no cops around. The speed limits were inappropriate anyway, just really impractical.

She was coming to a four-way stop, another stupid idea clear out here in the middle of nowhere. She eased back on the throttle and figured she could just sneak through.

What! Where did—?

She hit the brakes, the wheels locked, the tires screamed, the car fishtailed. Some idiot in a blue pickup swerved wildly through the intersection trying to avoid her.

Little Ruth wasn't belted in; she smacked her head and started screaming.

The Plymouth skidded to a stop almost facing the way it had come.

"Be quiet!" Bledsoe shouted at the little girl. "You be quiet now—you're all right!"

Now Josiah was crying too, scared to death. He wasn't belted in either, and had had quite a tumbling back there.

"You two kids shut up!" Bledsoe screamed. "Just shut up now!"

Josiah could see a lady get out of the pickup. She had red hair and a checkered scarf on her head; she looked like she was about to cry, and she was holding her shoulder. Bledsoe stuck her head out the window and screamed a string of profanity at her. The lady didn't say a thing, but Bledsoe must have scared her. The other driver got back in her truck and drove off without saying a word.

"The idiot!" said Bledsoe. "Didn't she see me?"

"But you didn't stop," said Josiah.

"Don't you tell me how to drive, young man! And why isn't your seat belt fastened?"

Ruth was still screaming, holding her head. When she saw blood on her hand, she went hysterical.

When Bledsoe saw that, she said, "Oh, great! Oh, that's just terrific!"

Cecilia Potter, Fred's wife, was glad that one of those fool goats wore a bell. At least she was able to hear something and run out into the yard before they ate up all her flowers.

The two kids bolted and ran back toward the rental home. As for the doe, she thought she owned anything that grew, and she wasn't timid about it.

"You, GIT!" Cecilia shouted, waving her strong arms. "Get out of those flowers!"

The doe backed off just a little, but then lowered her head, giving Cecilia a good look at her horns.

"Oooh, you're really scary!" said Cecilia. She ran right up, clamped an angry fist around the doe's collar, and lifted the doe's front legs off the ground in turning her around.

"You're going back where you came from, and right now, and don't you think you can scare me!" *WAP!* "And you lower those horns right now!"

The doe went with Cecilia, mostly on four legs, but on two if she even dared to hesitate, and got more than two earfuls of sermonizing on the way.

"I don't know how you got out, but if you think you're going to run rampant around here, you've got another think coming! Sally's going to hear about this! She knows better! I'm really surprised . . ."

She crossed the field between the two houses and then saw the goat pen, its gate wide open.

"Sally!" she called.

There was no answer. Hmm. The truck was gone. Maybe Sally wasn't home yet. Well, she was late then. She always came home from work before this. But how did that gate get open?

She dragged the doe alongside her and through the gate.

"Back where you belong, old girl. No more of this free and easy stuff—"

Well . . . who was that in the shed?

"Sally?"

The doe, suddenly free, walked out through the still-open gate. Cecilia didn't follow it.

She was looking at the body of a woman, thrown down in the straw like a discarded doll, limp and white.

She was dead.

Nathan, Armoth, and the other warriors made a low, slow pass over the farmhouse and saw a distraught Cecilia running from the goat pen. Nathan gave the others a signal, and with an explosive surge of their wings they shot forward, etching the evening sky with streaks of light.

The fields below them passed by with the swiftness of a thought, and then the green canopy of the forest swallowed them up, the leaves and branches whipping by, over, around, and through them. They rushed through shadows and shafts of fading light, through tall trunks and thick, entangling limbs, and finally reached the clearing where the captain was waiting.

With wings snapping full like opening parachutes, they came to a halt and settled to the forest floor with the silence of snowflakes. The moment their feet touched down, the lightning glimmer of their tunics faded to a dull white, their fiery swords cooled to copper, and their wings folded and vanished.

Tal, the mighty, golden-haired Captain of the Host, was waiting, his fiery eyes burning with expectation, his face tight with the tension of the moment. Beside him stood Guilo, the Strength of Many, a dark, bearded, massive spirit with thick, powerful arms and a heart yearning for a fight. They were dressed in dull white as well, and wore formidable swords at their sides.

Nathan called his report even as Tal and Guilo were stepping forward to greet them. "All the demons were routed except for Despair."

"Good enough," said Tal. "Let him carry word back to his comrades and then continue his work. Any other spirits from Broken Birch involved in this?"

"Several. Formidable, but defeated for now. We didn't see Destroyer anywhere. He sent his lackeys and stayed out of it himself."

"Of course. Now what of Sally?"

"Sally Roe is fleeing. Her truck is several miles down the road, heading south toward Claytonville. We sent Chimon and Scion to follow her."

"The assassin?" asked Tal.

"Slain, by our hand. We had no choice. Sally was close to death."

Guilo rumbled his approval of the action.

"How is Sally now?" Tal asked.

Armoth reported, "A minor throat injury, a welt on her neck, a shallow knife wound in the shoulder. No immediate physical danger."

Tal sighed just a little. "No, not immediate anyway. What about the near-collision with Irene Bledsoe?"

Nathan and Armoth looked toward Signa, and the lithe Oriental smiled. "Successful, but by a hair. Ruth Harris suffered a small injury on her forehead, but Sally was clearly seen by everyone in the car, and she saw them just as clearly."

Armoth picked up from there. "And now Mrs. Potter has found the assassin, and she is calling the police."

Tal had to take a moment just to shake his head at the immensity of it all. "Just that is news enough."

Guilo expressed his anxiety with a gravelly chuckle. "Captain, we have never before hoped for so many things to go right . . . that can go so wrong!"

Tal looked toward Heaven and smiled a cautious smile. "We can hope for them all to go right as long as the saints are praying, and they are."

There was a mutter of agreement from all of them. They could feel it.

"So," Tal continued, "if all goes well, this time *we* advance, *we* conquer, *we* set the enemy back . . . *We* purchase just one more season of restraint."

"One more season," they all echoed.

"Sally should arrive in Claytonville safely enough with Chimon and Scion as escorts. The demon Terga has much to answer for now; I expect he'll send some spirits after her to tear her down. Even so, Chimon and Scion have orders not to intervene unless absolutely necessary."

"*More* pain, captain? *More* destruction?" Guilo blurted in anger. "One would think these wretched spirits can never inflict enough suffering!"

Tal looked into those dark eyes, so full of the fire of battle, and yet so tender toward God's elect. "Good friend, we all hurt for her. But her suffering will bring about God's purpose, and you will see it."

"May it come soon," Guilo said, gripping the handle of his sword. He looked at Nathan and prompted sarcastically, "I'm sure you have more joyful news?"

"Yes," said Nathan. "Of Tom Harris. He is at the police station now, trying to do something to get his children back, trying to reason with Sergeant Mulligan."

At the mention of Mulligan's name, Guilo laughed a roaring, spiteful laugh, and the others made a distasteful face. Nathan only nodded with resignation. They were right.

"So now comes the testing of Tom's faith, a real trying of his commitment," said Tal.

"*I'll* be watching the saints," said Guilo. "I'll see how they handle this one."

Tal touched Guilo's shoulder. "This will be one of those things we hope will go right."

"Oh, may it go right, may it go right."

"For Tom's sake," said Nathan.

"For *everyone's* sake," said Armoth.

"Which brings us to Ben Cole," Tal prompted.

Nathan responded, "He's about to walk into it right now."

2

O fficer Ben Cole pulled the squad car into the lot behind the precinct and sat behind the wheel for a moment after the engine was still. It had been a long day, and he was tired. Bacon's Corner didn't have that much heavy action, but today was a little more trying. The trucker he'd stopped for speeding was twice his size and didn't like being one-upped by such a young officer, much less one who was black; Bill Schultz still hadn't contained that dog of his, and now someone else had been bitten; he'd caught the Krantz boy with some pot again, and his parents still wouldn't believe it.

That was the rub with police work—you always had to see the bad side of people, when they were angry, defensive, self-righteous, drunk, drugged . . . *Oh, let it go, Ben. The day's over. There are some good people in the world, really. You just need to get home, have some supper, see Bev. Yeah, that'll make it all right.*

He got out of the car; he was going to write up some quick reports and get home so . . . *Now whose cars are these?* Two strange cars were sitting in the reserved parking spaces, and wasn't that Tom Harris's little station wagon? The office was closed by now; it was too late for visitors. He'd better check it out once he got inside.

He went in the back door and started down the long hallway that connected the rear offices and cell block to the front office area.

Oh brother, now who's Mulligan hollering at?

He could hear Sergeant Mulligan's voice from clear down the hall, booming through the open door of his office. "So all right, you don't have to tell me anything! Go ahead and lie! You guys always lie, and I'll be happy to listen to that so I can use it against you!"

"Sir, I'm not lying . . ."

Ben stopped in the hall to listen. That other voice sounded familiar.

"So let's have the truth, huh?" said Mulligan. "You've been having yourself a real party with those little kids, haven't you?"

"Sir, *again*, there is nothing going on at the school, or at my home, or anywhere! This whole thing is a terrible mistake!"

Yeah, that *was* Tom Harris's car out there, and this was Tom getting outtalked by the sergeant.

Ben had to look. This conversation was sounding worse all the time. *Lord, please don't let it be what it sounds like. I was just feeling better thinking about the good people in the world.*

He went down the bare hallway to Mulligan's door, and stuck his head in.

"I'm back, Harold." *No big deal, I'm just reporting in, nice and businesslike, just finding out what's going on.*

Ben stood there frozen, looking at the shaken, upset man sitting across the dented, green, metal desk from big Sergeant Mulligan.

Mulligan was in his overweight, ugly glory, and really enjoying this. He always got his kicks from all the wrong things. "Hey, Cole, look what I caught today! Another Christian! I'll bet you two know each other!"

Ben looked confused "Hey, Tom. What gives?"

"Child abuse!" interrupted Mulligan, proud of the fact, proud of his catch. "Got a real case brewing here."

"Then you know far more about this than *I* do!" Tom said. He looked up at Ben with tear-reddened eyes. "The sergeant here just . . . just *stood* there while some welfare lady came and took away Ruth and Josiah, just dragged them from the house, and . . ." Tom's voice rose in fear and anger. "I want to know where they are."

Mulligan remained as hard as nails and sneered at Ben. "Wait'll you hear what this creep's been doing with some kids at the Christian school."

Tom rose from his seat. "I haven't been doing *anything*! Can't you get that straight?"

"You sit down, buddy!" Mulligan easily outweighed Tom and made every effort to show it.

Ben's heart twisted in his chest. The Christian school? Bacon's Corner only had one—the Good Shepherd Academy, a little first-through-sixth-grade ministry run by—

"I'd say your church is in big trouble!" Mulligan told Ben.

Ben looked down at Tom Harris, one of the gentlest, most godly men he'd ever met. Tom was in his thirties, with dark curly hair and a young face. Ben knew the guy was more than just honest—he was downright vulnerable. *No way, man. Tom Harris didn't do anything.*

"Tom," Ben said gently, "are you aware of your rights?"

"He's not under arrest!" Mulligan snapped. "He came here himself!"

"And I'm not leaving until I get some cooperation!" said Tom.

"Hey, don't come after me," said Mulligan. "The state people have to check this all out."

"So let's call them!" said Ben.

"You get out of this, Cole! You two are friends and everybody knows it. You're not coming anywhere near this case!"

Tom demanded in slow, enunciated words, "I want to see my children!"

"You're talking to the wrong man."

Tom pointed his finger. "You were right there! You abused your authority and let this . . . this Bledsoe woman march right into my house like some kind of . . . gestapo raid! She terrorized my children and invaded my privacy right under your nose!"

Mulligan remained straight and tall in his chair and said firmly and simply, "You watch it, Harris. Ms. Bledsoe had a bona fide court order to pick up your kids in response to a complaint filed against you!"

Tom was flabbergasted. "*What* complaint?"

"I don't know. Ask Bledsoe. That's her department."

"Then you must know how to contact her."

"I'll find out," said Ben.

"Isn't your shift over?" Mulligan roared.

"Yes, sir."

"Then get out of here!"

Ben had to obey. He told Tom, "Give me a call," and turned to leave.

Just then the police radio came to life. The sound of it always froze time in the station as everyone stopped to hear the message. "Bacon's Corner, Bacon's Corner, possible DOA at Fred Potter farm, 12947 197th SW. Aid crew is en route."

Mulligan jumped from his chair, making it rumble backward and smack against the wall. "Where's Leonard—is he here yet?" Then the phone rang. "Nuts! When it rains it pours. Get that!"

Ben hurried to the front desk.

A man and a woman were sitting in the reception area. Ben recognized the man: John Ziegler, reporter for the *Hampton County Star*; he worked the local police beat and hung around the station a lot. The lady was obviously a photographer. Ziegler had a notepad handy, and was apparently scribbling down everything he heard!

The phone rang again.

Ben kept staring at the news-hounds while he grabbed the phone. "Police Department." The voice on the other end was frantic. "Slow down, ma'am, please. I can't understand you." It was Cecilia Potter. She'd already called 911; now she wanted to make sure the police were coming.

Ben knew where their farm was. "We just got the call on the radio. We'll be right there." So much for going home.

The back door opened.

"Here's Leonard now," Ben reported.

Officer Leonard Jackson was reporting in for the night shift. He was a calm, thin, easy-paced sort of guy in his forties, almost a permanent fixture around the place. Mulligan nearly ran over him bursting out of his office.

"Let's move it, Leonard! There's a suicide down at the Potter place!"

"The Potter place?" Leonard had trouble imagining either of the Potters doing such a thing.

Ben was quite unsettled about an additional matter. "What about John Ziegler out there?"

Mulligan looked at the reporters and started cursing, looking this way and that. "Harris! Get out here!"

Tom stepped out of the office, trying to be cooperative.

Mulligan shoved him forward toward the front office. "Have a seat with those nice people—they want to talk to you! Leonard, we'll take your squad car."

Tom looked at Ben for help. "They were at my house today when that lady took the kids. They took pictures of it!"

Ben could feel his temper rising. "Tom, you don't have to say anything to them. Just go right on by them and go home!"

Mulligan must have seen something he didn't like. "Cole, you're coming too!"

Leonard was ready to roll. Mulligan grabbed his hat and jacket. The reporters were on their feet and coming toward Tom.

Ben asked, "Is Tom free to leave?"

Mulligan rolled his eyes at such a question. "Cole, he came in here on his own two feet—he can go out the same way. Hear that, Harris?"

Ben said quietly, "Tom, just get out of here. You don't have to talk to anyone."

Mulligan growled at him, "Are you about ready, Cole? C'mon, let's move!"

Ben didn't like this one bit, but orders were orders. He headed for the back door again.

Mulligan tipped his hat to John Ziegler and the camera lady. "Just make yourselves comfortable. We'll be back in about an hour, and I'll have a statement for you."

Ben told Tom, "I'll call you," then followed Mulligan and Leonard.

Mulligan muttered over his shoulder as they went out to the cars, "I'm not leaving you in there with that Christian buddy of yours, no way. If you're gonna be on duty, you're gonna work, and you're gonna do what I tell you and no static. We don't need you two fanatics having some powwow in there, no sir!"

Tom went back into Mulligan's office for his jacket and then stepped into the hall again.

John Ziegler was standing right in front of him, blocking his path.

"Excuse me," Tom said, trying to get around.

John was insistent on having a conversation.

"John Ziegler, with the *Hampton County Star*—"

"Yes, I saw you at my house," said Tom curtly.

Ziegler asked, "Mr. Harris, what is your response to these allegations?"

"*What* allegations? I don't even know why this is happening to me!"

"Do you think this will hurt the Christian school?"

"I don't know."

"Do you deny any abuse of children in the Christian school?"

That question stopped Tom cold. He was troubled by it.

Ziegler picked up on that. "You do deny the allegations?"

Tom found his voice for that one. "I don't know of any allegations."

Ziegler scribbled it down.

"Has there been any reaction from your family?"

"Besides the fact that my children were terrified?"

The woman began clicking a camera at him.

"Hey, come on, now . . ."

The camera kept clicking.

Ziegler raised an eyebrow. "I understand you're a widower. So you live at home alone with your children?"

Tom was indignant. "That's it! I'm leaving. Good night."

Ziegler threw questions at Tom's back as they followed right behind him toward the front door. "Is the state considering your children as possible victims as well?"

Tom jerked the door open and glared at them for a moment.

The camera caught his angry expression.

Ziegler was satisfied. "Thank you very much, Mr. Harris."

Just across the street, Despair sat on the roof of the Bacon's Corner Library and Gift Shop, a forlorn beanbag of melancholy filth, whimpering over his wounds and watching the two squad cars speed away.

"Oh, there they go, there they go. What now?"

Several other dark spirits were with him, staying low, muttering, hissing, slobbering in agitation. They were a motley band of tempters, harassers, and deceivers, suddenly half as strong, half as numerous, and full of anguish over the recent, terrible defeat of their comrades.

Despair was living up to his name. "Lost, lost, lost, all is lost! Our best are gone, all vanquished but for me!"

A sharp slap bounced his round head against his shoulder. "Stop that whimpering! You make me ill!"

"Terga, my prince, you were not there!"

Terga, the Prince of Bacon's Corner, resembled a slimy toad with a fright wig of black wire and two rolling, yellow eyes. He was indignant, and kept scratching his gnarled head purely from an itch of frustration. "Failure, that's what it was. An abominable display of ineptitude!"

Murder was quick to object. "Had the mission succeeded, no doubt you would have been the first to praise it!"

"It did not, and I do not!"

Deception tried to objectively assess the debacle. "Our forces were strong, and I'm sure they fought valiantly, but . . . the prayers of the saints are stronger. The Host of Heaven are stronger. They were waiting for our warriors, and they were ready. We severely underestimated their numbers and their power. It's quite simple."

Terga spun around and glared at Deception, hating his words, but knowing the astute demon was quite correct. He paced, he fidgeted, he struggled to comprehend what was happening. "We have moved against Tom Harris and the school! The Plan of the Strongman is unfolding at this very moment. It is underway, right now! But here you are, lamenting a rout and telling me that the Plan could be marching headlong toward destruction, and all because of this . . . this . . . *woman?*"

Deception thought about the question, and then nodded. "That would be a fair assessment."

Terga rolled his eyes toward the sky and wailed his fear and frustration. "Destroyer will have all our hides for this! Those who did not fall in this rout will certainly fall under *his* sword!" He counted the demons around him and came up shorter than he wanted. "Where is Hatred?"

"Gone," they all answered. "One of the first to fall."

"And Violence?"

"In chains in the Abyss, I imagine," said Deception.

"Greed? Lust? Rape?"

He only got forlorn stares. He looked out over the town, and his head just kept twitching from side to side. He could not fathom what had happened. "Such an easy task . . . a simple little murder . . . We've all done it before . . ."

Despair moaned, "When the Strongman finds out . . ."

WAP! Terga bounced Despair's head off his other shoulder.

"He must know!" said Divination.

"Then tell him!" said Terga. "Go yourself!"

Divination fell silent, hoping some other demon would speak up.

Terga snatched a fistful of Despair's baggy hide and held him up like a trophy. "Our envoy!"

They began to cheer, their talons clicking their applause.

"No . . . not the Strongman!" Despair whined. "Is not one thrashing enough?"

"Go now," said Terga, "or the Strongman's will be your *third* today!"

Despair fluttered crazily into the air. One wing was still battered and bent.

"Go!" said Terga. "And be quick about it!" Despair hurried away, whining and wailing as he went. "And when you're through with that, go back to the woman and continue your duty as you should!"

Some snickers caused Terga to spin around. A few small spirits cowered, looking up at him—they'd been caught.

"Ah," said Terga, and they could see the slime on the roof of his mouth. "Fear, Death, and Insanity, three of the woman's favorite pets! You look rather idle at the moment."

The three demons looked at each other stupidly.

"Back to your posts! Follow the woman!"

They fluttered into the air like frightened pigeons, clawing after altitude.

Terga wasn't satisfied. He slapped several more demons with his wings. "You too! All of you! Find her! Torture her! Terrorize her! Do you want Destroyer to think you are the worthless lumps you are? Correct your blunder! Destroy the woman!"

The air was filled with roaring, fluttering wings. Terga covered his head to keep from getting clouted with a wild wingtip. In only moments, they were gone. Terga looked down the street, down the road that would take the squad cars to Potter's farm.

"Our sergeant isn't going to find what he expected," he muttered.

3

It was getting dark when the two squad cars rumbled down the gravel driveway to the Potters' house. The aid car was already there, its doors flung open, its lights flashing. Fred and Cecilia were out on the wide front porch waiting for the police, holding each other close. They were strong, rugged people, but tonight they were obviously shaken.

Mulligan locked the wheels and slid to an impressive, slightly side-skidding halt in the loose gravel, then bolted from the car in time to emerge like a god from the cloud of dust he'd stirred up.

Leonard waited for the dust to blow by before getting out—he didn't want it all over the seat when he got back in the car.

Ben pulled to a careful stop behind the first car and got out in calm, businesslike fashion. He was being overcautious, aware that his emotions were on a thin edge.

Mulligan was already talking with one of the paramedics, getting the lowdown. The paramedic had just come from a little farmhouse across the field. Ben could see two more flashlights sweeping about in the darkness over there. Apart from that, there were no lights.

"Deceased," said the paramedic. "Dead at least an hour."

"Okay," said Mulligan, clicking on his big silver flashlight, "let's go."

He headed into the field, swishing through the wild grass with long, powerful strides, his nightstick swinging from his hip, his belly bouncing on his buckle. Leonard and Ben followed close behind.

"It's that Roe woman," said Mulligan. "Sally Roe. You know anything about her?"

Leonard assumed the question was directed to him. "Very little, Harold."

"I think she's one of those weird types, some kind of leftover hippie, a loser. Guess she decided to end it all."

Ben was probing his brain as they continued toward the dark farmhouse. Sally Roe. The name didn't register.

"All right," said Mulligan. "There's the goat pen. Spread out a bit, you guys. No hiding behind me."

They came out of the field, crossed an unused, heavily weeded roadway, and came to the goat pen. The fence was crude and aged, made of rusted wire nailed to split rail posts, with a creaking gate hanging crookedly on one good hinge and one loose one. The gate was still open; all the goats were now corraled over at the Potters'. Two emergency medical technicians were standing outside the pen, putting away their gear.

"She's all yours," said one.

Ben glanced around the pen, shining his light here and there, just checking for anything unusual, not wanting to disturb it. His eye caught a spilled pail of goat feed near the door of the goat shed.

"Hey, check that out," he said, pointing with his light.

Mulligan ignored him and charged right across the goat pen and into the weathered, tin-roofed shed, leaving a big manured footprint in the middle of the spilled feed. Then he stopped short. He'd found something. Leonard and Ben came up behind him and looked in through the doorway.

There she was. The dead woman. Ben couldn't see her face; Mulligan was in the way. But she was dressed all in black, and lay on her back in the straw, her body and limbs twisted and limp as if someone had wadded her up and thrown her there.

Ben shined his light around the inside of the shed. The beam fell on a plaid shirt next to the body. Apparently Mulligan hadn't seen it. He reached in and picked it up. It was stained with blood.

"Hey, Harold, look at this."

Mulligan spun around as if rudely surprised. "Cole! Get back to the Potters and get a statement from them!"

"Yes, sir. But take a look at this."

Mulligan didn't take it—he grabbed it. "Go on, get over there. We can handle things at this end."

Leonard was shining his light at the woman's face and Ben caught his first glimpse of it. She was young and beautiful, but dead—violently dead. The expression on the face was blank, the eyes dry and staring, the shoulder-length black hair a tangled shadow upon the straw.

Ben didn't know he was staring until Mulligan hollered at him.

"Cole! Have you seen enough? Get moving!"

Ben got out of there, and hurried back across the field to the Potters' house. His mind was racing. This was going to be a bigger case than they'd thought. The appearance of that body, the bloodied shirt, the spilled feed, the obvious violence . . .

This was no suicide.

The aid crew drove away in the aid car, their work completed. Ben put on a calm demeanor as he went up the porch steps. The Potters heard him coming and immediately came to the door.

"Hi. I'm Officer Ben Cole."

Ben extended his hand, and Fred took it.

Fred stared at Ben just a little. "Have we met before?"

"No, sir. I'm new in Bacon's Corner. I've been here about four months."

"Oh . . . well, welcome to the neighborhood. Things aren't usually this exciting around here."

"Of course, sir. Uh, with your permission, I'd like to get a statement."

Cecilia opened the door. "Please come in . . . Ben, was it?"

"Yes, ma'am. Thank you."

Fred and Cecilia took their place on the couch and offered Ben a chair facing them. He took out his notepad.

"How are you doing?" he asked.

"Oh . . . fair," said Fred.

Cecilia just shook her head. "Poor Sally." Tears returned to her eyes. "This is just awful. It's terrifying."

Ben spoke gently. "I . . . understand it was you who first found her?"

She nodded.

"Did you touch her or move her in any way?"

Cecilia was repelled by the very thought. "No. I didn't go near her. I didn't even look at her face."

"About what time was this?"

"About 6."

Ben jotted these items down. "Now, why don't you just tell me everything that happened?"

She started telling him about the goats being out, and about the nanny goat trying to butt her, and then tried to remember what she did to get that goat back to the pen, and then a strong opinion took precedent over her narrative and she blurted, "I think somebody killed her!"

Fred was shocked at that, of course. "What? What gives you that idea?"

Ben had to get control of this. "Uh . . . we'll work on that when the time comes. But for now you need to tell me what you saw . . . just what you saw."

She told him, and it wasn't much different from what he himself had seen. "I didn't want to see her that way. I just didn't stay there."

"Okay. Can you tell me the victim's full name?"

"Sally Roe. She was such a quiet sort," Cecilia said, her face full of grief and puzzlement. "She never said much, just kept to herself. We enjoyed having her for a renter. She was clean, responsible, we never had any trouble from her. Why would anyone want to hurt her?"

"So you can't think of anyone who might . . . have some kind of grievance or grudge against her?"

"No. She was a very private sort. I don't remember ever seeing her having company or visitors."

"Can you think of anything else that may have seemed out of the ordinary?"

"Did you see the feed spilled on the ground?"

"Yes, ma'am."

"Someone may have jumped out and grabbed her."

"Uh-huh. Anything else?"

"I saw a long piece of rope in her hand. Maybe it was to tie the goats, I don't know."

Ben noted it.

There were loud footsteps on the porch. It was Sergeant Mulligan. He let himself in, and removed his hat.

"Well, folks, it's been quite an evening. We've seen a real tragedy here. Got their statement, Cole?"

Ben rose and looked over his notes. "Just what Mrs. Potter saw initially. I suppose—"

Mulligan took the notes from Ben's hand and looked them over.

Ben finished his thought. "I suppose once we check the house and comb the area we'll have more to go on."

Mulligan didn't seem to hear him. "Umm. Okay, I'll get these typed into the report." He pocketed Ben's notes and told the Potters, "Guess she hung herself from the rafters of the shed, who knows why."

"Hung herself?" said Cecilia in surprise.

"How about any suicide notes? Did you find anything like that around?"

Cecilia was still taken aback. "No . . . no, I—"

"Well, we'll be checking the scene over tonight and maybe we'll find something." He headed out the door again. "Cole, go ahead and call it a day. Leonard and I will check the area over and wait for the coroner."

"You say it was a *suicide*?" Ben asked, following him out the door.

"Cut and dried," said Mulligan.

"Well . . . maybe."

Mulligan got impatient with that kind of response. "What do you mean, 'maybe'?"

"Well, you saw what it looked like in there . . ."

"Yeah, I saw it all, and you didn't."

"But Mrs. Potter did. The body wasn't hanging when she found it. It was lying in the straw just like when we first saw it."

Mulligan turned back toward the rental. "Go on home, Cole. Don't worry about things that aren't your responsibility."

Mulligan headed across the field, cutting the conversation short. Ben went back to his car and sat in it with the door open, flipping through his notepad. He clicked his pen and started scribbling some notes to himself, things he wanted to remember: "plaid shirt with blood . . . position of body suggests violence . . . spilled feed . . . rope in hand, not around neck . . . victim not hung . . ."

Just outside Claytonville, Sally turned off the highway onto an obscure, overgrown and rutted road that meandered deep into the forest, winding around trees and stumps, passing under low limbs, dipping into black mudholes, and making the old pickup buck and rock with every new pothole, rut, bump, and turn. This road—or maybe it was a trail—had probably been used by surveyors and developers, but now was kept in existence only by kids on dirt bikes and perhaps an equestrian or two. Maybe somewhere back in here she could find a good spot to abandon the truck.

She finally found what looked like a turnaround or dead end, a short section of once-cleared area the dirt bikers hadn't found yet, quickly being reclaimed by the thick brush. She cranked the wheel hard and let the pickup push its way forward, plowing through the brush and flattening the weeds that rose in front of the headlights.

Far enough. She turned off the lights and shut down the engine.

And then she sat there, her elbows on the wheel and her head in her hands. She had to hold still for just a minute. She had to think, to assess the situation, to sort out thought from feeling. She didn't move for a minute, and then another, and then another. The only sound was her own breathing—she was conscious of every breath—and the steadily slowing *tink*, *tink*, *tink* of the engine cooling. It occurred to her how still it was out in these woods, and how dark it was, and especially how lonely it was. She was alone in the darkness, and no one knew.

How poetic, she thought. *How appropriate.*

But to the business at hand: *How about it, Sally? Do you keep going or do you give up? You can always call them, or send them a letter, and just let them know where you are so they can come and finish the job. At least then it will all be over and you won't have to wait so long to die.*

She drew a long, tired breath and leaned back from the steering wheel. *Such thoughts, Sally, such thoughts!*

No, she finally admitted to herself, *no—I want to live. I don't know why, but I do. I don't know how much longer, but I will. And that's all I know for now.*

That's all I know. But I wish I knew more. I wish I knew how they found me . . . and why they want to kill me.

She clicked on the dome light—it would only be for a second—and reached into her jacket pocket for a small object. It was a ring, ornate, probably pure gold. She took a close and careful look at it, turning it over and over in her fingers, trying to make out the strange design on its face. It made no sense to her, try as she might to understand what it could mean. For now, she only knew one thing for sure about this ring—she'd seen it before, and the memories were her worst.

She clicked off the dome light. Enough sitting. She put the ring back in her pocket, took the keys from the ignition, and opened the door. In this deep, surrounding quiet, the dry, dirty hinges seemed to scream instead of groan. The sound frightened her.

The dome light came on again, but then winked out as she closed the door as quietly as possible, which still amounted to a pretty loud slam. Now the only light in the middle of that thick, forlorn forest was gone. She could hardly see, but she was determined to get out of these woods even if she had to feel her way out. She had to get moving, get someplace safe. She pressed on, fighting the brush as it pulled at her legs, scratched her with its thorns, jabbed at her out of the dark. Somewhere ahead was that old roadway where the ground was still bare and walkable. She only had to find it.

Underneath a fallen log, deep down in a dark and rotted pocket, two yellow eyes were watching her, two taloned hands curled in hate. The thing let out a little snicker as she stumbled past.

In the low, overhanging branch of a tree, another spirit crouched like a grotesque owl, its black wings hanging at its sides like long, drooping curtains, its head not more than a knob above its shoulders. The yellow eyes were following her every move.

They were out to do Terga's wishes; they hoped to appease Destroyer.

She made it to the old roadway; she could feel firm, bare ground under her feet and discern just a little more light ahead of her. She quickened her pace. She was starting to feel like a little girl again, afraid of the dark, afraid of unseen horrors, longing for some light to drive all the spooks away.

Two black shapes hovering just above the roadway waited for her to pass beneath them. They drifted in little back-and-forth patterns, floating on unfurled, shadowy wings, their long, spindly legs and arms hanging down like spiders' legs, each tipped with long, clawed talons that flexed and curled with anticipation.

Sally stopped. Did the roadway turn here? *Come on, girl, don't get lost. That's all you need.*

Three more spirits, some of Terga's worst, sailed down through the trees like vultures gathering for a feast. They came in behind her, slobbering and cackling, jostling each other to get closer.

Sally thought she saw the roadway again, heading off to her left. She tried that direction. Yes, she'd found it. But her legs were getting weak. Her heart was beating against her ribs like it wanted out. *No, please, not again, no more . . .*

But it was fear, all right, the old-fashioned kind—the kind she'd lived with for years. Just when she thought she'd gotten rid of it, escaped from it, forgotten it, here it was, back again, as fierce as ever, digging into her, scrambling her thoughts, making her tremble, sweat, stumble.

Her old friends were back.

She passed under the two hovering demons.

"YAAAK!" they screamed, enveloping her with sulfur.

The spirits following behind slapped through her soul with their black wings.

OOF! She pitched forward into the dirt, a muffled cry in her throat. She struggled to get her legs under her again, to get moving again. Where was that road?

The spirits alighted on her back and dug their talons in deep.

She covered her mouth tightly with her hands, trying to keep a cry inside, trying to keep quiet. She couldn't get her balance. Something was after her. She had to get away. She was still trying to get up.

The demons gave her a stab and a kick, cackling and shrieking with delight, and then they let her go.

She was on her feet again. She could see the roadway and she ran, her arms in front of her face to block the forest limbs that slapped and grabbed her. She could hear some traffic out on the highway. How much further?

The dark spirits fluttered and flapped after her, chattering and spitting. It was a wonderful, cruel game.

But warriors were watching. Deep within the texture of the forest, here and there within the trees, the logs, the thick brush, there were deep golden eyes watching it all, and strong arms upon ready swords.

The Good Shepherd Community Church had a prayer chain, a simple system for spreading prayer requests throughout the church via the telephone. Every participant had a list of all the other participants and their phone numbers. When you needed prayer for something, you called the next person on the list after yourself, who then called the next person on the list, who then called the next person, and so on. The whole church could be praying for a request in just a matter of hours any day of the week.

Tom's request for prayer set the lines buzzing with the news about Ruth and Josiah, and with each phone call, more saints started praying. At the top of the list was Donna Hemphile, a supervisor at the Bergen Door Company; next on the list was the Waring family, then the Jessups, followed by Lester Sutter and his wife Dolly, then the Farmers, then the Ryans, then the widow Alice Buckmeier, then the elders on the church board—Jack Parmenter and his son Doug, Bob Heely, and Vic Savan. On down the list it went until all the numbers were called.

That started a flurry of prayer, of course, but also a flurry of phone calls back to Tom to find out more. To his great sorrow, he had nothing more he could tell them; and to his frustration, a lot of the information being passed through the chain was wrong.

He tried to call the Child Protection Department, but they were closed.

He tried to find Irene Bledsoe's home phone number; it was unlisted.

He tried the office of the State Ombudsman. The lady there

told him to call the CPD or try the Department of Social and Health Services.

He called the DSHS and they told him to contact the CPD in the morning. They had no number for Irene Bledsoe, but weren't free to give out numbers anyway.

Pastor Mark Howard and his wife Cathy were out of town, but would be back sometime tomorrow.

Ben Cole made good on his promise and called, but by now there was nothing that could be done until morning.

After one last call to a state representative who didn't answer, Tom dropped the receiver into its cradle and hid his face in his hands. He had to stop, to breathe, to calm himself. It couldn't be as horrible as it seemed. Somehow, sometime, somewhere he had to find Ruth and Josiah. It just couldn't be this difficult.

The silence, the emptiness of his little house was so odd, almost taunting. Right now he should have been tucking Ruth and Josiah in for the night. But he was alone, and so tired.

"Lord God," he prayed, "Lord God, please protect my children. Bring them back to me. Please end this nightmare!"

Wednesday morning.

The Bacon's Corner Elementary School reeked of demons. As Nathan and Armoth flew high above, they could feel them, sense them, often see them, buzzing and swirling in and out of that brand-new brick and concrete structure the community was so proud of. The playground was full of kids, about two hundred, running, playing, and squealing before the first bell signaled the start of classes. Then they would gather in all those classrooms where the spirits would be busy, more than ever before.

The two warriors passed over the school, continued on for another mile, then banked sharply and sideslipped toward the earth, dropping like stones, twisting slowly about until they were facing the way they had come. Then, easing back their speed, they skimmed across the fields of hay and young corn, across some gravel access roads, right through some sprinklers, and finally came to an old chicken house on a farm next to the school.

Their wings snapped like parachutes, and they went through the old clapboard walls of the chicken house feet first. Inside, a cackling chorus of eight hundred leghorns carried on, pecking at feed, rolling out eggs, oblivious to their presence.

They hurried toward one end of the long house, moving through floating white feathers, fine brown dust, and chickens, chickens everywhere.

Tal stood at a window, looking toward the school.

Armoth quipped, "One might ask why you chose this place."

"For the view," said Tal. Then he looked toward the school again. "They have quite a project going over there, well established."

"The saints are buzzing with the news about Tom's children. They are praying," said Nathan.

"And the Lord is responding, so we're well covered so far. But the real attack is still coming this morning. Place a guard around Tom. It's going to be hard enough for him; I don't want any extra harassments against him while he's down."

"Done."

"Where is Sally now?"

"She made it to Claytonville, and she has a motel room. Chimon and Scion are watching, but Terga's spirits are tormenting her, hoping to regain Destroyer's favor."

Tal bristled at that. "What spirits?"

Armoth had a mental list. "Fear, Death, Insanity. They and some others tormented her last night, and they've followed her today as well, trying to break her spirit."

"What about Despair?"

"Terga sent him to inform the Strongman."

Tal was amused. "How bold of him." He looked toward the school again. "I want Signa and Mota to clear a path into that school, do some screening, some diversions. We'll need to get in and out of there without the whole demonic network finding out about it. As for Cree and Si, they'll need to do the same thing at Omega, which means they'll need twice the warriors just to get Sally in and out of there with her life."

Armoth drew a deep, long breath. "A touchy business, captain."

"And getting touchier with each move we make. What about the room at the Schrader Motor Inn in Fairwood?"

Nathan reported, "We have warriors there now, keeping it open. And the old hiding-place for the ring is still intact."

Tal took a moment to think. "So those fronts are covered. Now all we can do is play the game, one careful move at a time." He smiled with amusement. "So I suppose the Strongman should be hearing from Despair any moment now."

"And who is stationed there?"

"Guilo."

Nathan and Armoth nodded. That was no surprise.

4

Guilo had often noted how the darkest, most horrible evil seemed to choose the most beautiful places to build a nest, and so it was again. The mountains around him were towering, jagged, snowcapped, picturesque. The early morning air was clear, the visibility unlimited, the wind steady and gentle, the sky deep blue. Tall armies of evergreens stood at attention on every hillside, and crystal-clear streams trickled, splashed, and cascaded down from the pure white glaciers. Below him, the little town of Summit nestled peacefully in the green, wild-flowered valley, surrounded by a restful, noticeable quiet.

He whistled at the thought: all those little people down there, surrounded by all this beauty, could not see the horror all around them, the impending storm about to swallow them up, the cancerous darkness that first blinds, then consumes.

He and some dozen warriors were staying out of sight, sticking close to the pines, not showing any light of glory. He didn't want to be spotted by the evil powers that only spirits could see—a cloud of demons that swarmed and swirled like a smoke-black whirlwind on the mountainside only a mile away from the town. Below the guarding whirlwind, almost invisible in the trees, was a quaint, alpine village, a picturesque campus of ornate buildings, fastidious walkways, fascinating trails, stunning gardens. The whole place shouted invitation, exuding a welcoming, embracing sense of peace, beauty, and brotherhood.

It was the home of the Strongman, his outpost, the hub of an ever-widening evil. The sooty spirits were bold and riotous, reveling in a constantly growing tally of victories over human souls.

Guilo stood still, watching their moves, sizing them up, getting an idea of their numbers. Yes, it was nice to see them so cocky; demons in that state of mind were always easier to catch unawares. But they wouldn't be so cocky for long—he and his warriors had seen the recent arrival of one little whimpering demon, one little envoy from one little insignificant farming town, and the news that spirit was bringing was sure to change things throughout that supposedly charming village. An assault would have been difficult enough beforehand. Now it was going to be nothing short of a real nightmare.

A cry! A wail, a shaking rippled through the whirlwind. The

ranks of demons began to compress, shrinking tighter, packing closer, growing even darker, thicker.

"Oh . . ." said Guilo. "Looks like the Strongman's gotten the news."

"*ROOOOOOAARRRRR!!*"

Despair's shapeless little blob of a body stretched, warped, and bulged this way and that, like a big black bubble fresh from the wand, as he sailed across the chalet and then dropped to the floor, whimpering loudly, his black body limp and flat like a sobbing, shuddering bear rug. All around him, the demon princes and generals were in a chugging, slobbering, sulfurous dither, hollering and shouting out curses and yellow vapor as thick as cigar smoke. The chalet was filling with a heavy, putrid fog that almost obscured their shadowy forms.

They didn't like his news either.

At the end of the living room, the Strongman was glaring at the pitiful little demon, his huge yellow cat eyes almost popping from his head, his nostrils flared, the sulfur chugging out of them in swirling clouds. The immense, hulking spirit was trying to decide if he felt better now, or needed to hurl Despair across the chalet again.

The princes and generals—almost a hundred of them—were beginning to turn on each other, waving their arms, throwing their black wings in each other's faces, shouting and hissing; some were demanding explanations, some were beginning to pass blame, some wanted to know what to do next, and some just stood there cursing.

The Strongman filled his end of the room with his wings and held out his arms. "Silence!"

He got it.

He took one huge step toward the center of the room, and all the demons backed one step away, bowing, folding their wings. He took a few more steps, and the room echoed with the sound of them.

Then he addressed the little rug on the floor. "Have you anything else to report to me?"

"No, my Ba-al."

"No further casualties?"

"No, my Ba-al."

"No further blunders?"

"No, my Ba-al."

The demon lord considered that for just a moment.

Then the order exploded from his gaping mouth as from a cannon: "Then get out of here!"

The force of the Strongman's breath was more than enough to get Despair started. He was out of the chalet and into the sky before he even opened his wings.

The Strongman paced back to his end of the room and sank onto his throne—the fireplace hearth—with a deep scowl. The demonic ranks on either side of him trimmed their lines, standing straight and tall against the walls. The room came back to order, filled with darkness, shadows, yellow fog, and a deathlike stench.

"She is alive," he mused bitterly. "We were rid of her, we thought for good, but then she popped up again. We sought to kill her, but now she is still alive and . . . under *their* protection."

The princes stood like statues, silently waiting for his next word.

"RRROOOOOOWWWLLLLLL!"

The demonic ranks had to trim their lines again.

"Broken Birch . . ." he continued to muse. "Such a delightful group of people, so unabashed and forthright. So ready to kill. So . . . so CLUMSY!" He fumed, he drummed his huge fingers, he glared at nothing in particular. "These humans . . . these worshipers of our lord are marvelously evil, but sometimes . . . sometimes they stumble ahead of *us*! No subtlety, no caution.

"So now we have a blunder, and a slippery little soul has escaped from our fist, a worse threat to us now than ever she was!"

A prince stepped forward and bowed. "Will my lord consider aborting the Plan?"

The Strongman straightened, and his fists thundered down on the hearthstones. "NO!"

The prince stepped back into the ranks under the condemning stares of his fellows.

"No," growled the Strongman, "not this Plan. Too much is at stake, too much has already been established and prepared. There is too much to be gained to let one little woman, one little pitiful soul, ruin it all!"

The loathsome spirit tried to relax, leaning his head back and letting his amber tongue roll across his lips.

"The town was so perfect," he mused. "The saints of God so few, so penniless . . . and *our* people, oh, so strong, so numerous, so . . . so pioneering! We worked so hard to establish the foothold we have in that town. Ah . . . who knows how long it took . . . ?"

"Twenty-three years, Ba-al," said a well-meaning aide.

The Strongman glared at him. "Thank you. I know."

The aide bowed and retreated.

The Strongman continued his mental review. "And the petty little saints in the town were . . . obscure, don't you see, far from help, far from the mainstream, alone amid the rolling farm-lands . . . unknown. It was a perfect place to begin the process." His beastly face grew tight and bitter. "Until they started praying. Until they ceased being so comfortable and started weeping before God! Until they began to reclaim the power of the . . ." The Strongman sealed his lips.

"The Cross?" the aide volunteered.

"YAAAAA!!" The Strongman's sword sizzled through the air and missed the aide by inches. No matter. Several princes grabbed this foul-mouthed vassal and ousted him.

The Strongman settled onto the hearth with a thud. "Destroyer!"

The princes looked toward the other end of the room. A mutter moved through their ranks. Some stepped back.

A shadow stepped forward, a silhouette. It was tall, shrouded in billowing wings. It moved so smoothly, so silently, that it seemed to float. The other demons dared not touch it. Some bowed slightly.

It moved across the room and then stood before the Strongman, its head lowered in obeisance. It remained absolutely still.

The Strongman studied this dark, silent shape for a moment. "You have been noticeably silent during these discussions."

The thing raised its head and looked at its lord with narrow, calculating eyes. The face was not entirely hideous; it was almost human. But it was evil; it was cold and filled with hate.

"Speak, my Ba-al," he said, "and I will answer."

The Strongman's eyes narrowed. "Your minions failed, Destroyer. She is alive and free. What do you say to that?"

Destroyer's face was rock-hard, his spine straight. "Is she still mine?"

There was a strange, cutting tone in the Strongman's voice. "Do you still deserve her, Destroyer?"

Destroyer didn't seem to appreciate the question.

The Strongman spoke clearly, threateningly. "I want you to remove her, so that she will never reappear again." There was a slight tinge of doubt in the Strongman's voice as he asked, "*Can* you do that?"

The thing didn't move for a moment.

SLASH! Red flash! A sizzling sword cut through the air and divided space into burning segments. Black wings filled the room like smoke and rolled like thunder. The princes fell back against the walls; the Strongman actually flinched.

The thing stood there motionless again, the eyes burning with anger, the black wings slowly settling, the glowing red sword steady in his hand.

His low, sinister voice was seething with resentment. "Give me some real warriors, not Terga and his bungling, whining little imps of Bacon's Corner! Turn over your best to my command and let them empower Broken Birch, and you will see what your servant can do!"

The Strongman studied Destroyer's face and without the slightest smile asked, "What about the rumors I hear?"

Destroyer puffed a derisive laugh through his flaring nostrils. "They are rumors spread in fear by cowering spirits! *If* our opponent be this Tal, so much more the thrill of the challenge."

"He is mighty."

Destroyer countered, "He is *clever*. His strength is not in his own sword, but in the saints of God. The ranks have made a legend of his victory over us in Ashton, but they pay him too much respect. It was the prayers of the saints that defeated us, not this wily Captain of the Host." Destroyer waved his sword slowly through the air, admiring the burning after-image that trailed behind its razor-sharp edge. "And so it was in this recent, minor setback. But I now have an advantage, Ba-al: I have tasted the enemy's wiles, I have tested his strength, and I know the source of his power."

The Strongman was dubious. "And just how do you expect to thwart him where once you could not?"

"I will go to the saints first. Already there is plenty in Bacon's Corner for them to be upset about, plenty to divide them. I will keep them busy censuring and smiting each other, and then their hearts will be far from praying." He held the sword high; its red glow lit up the room and his yellow eyes reflected the glow in bloodshot crimson. "I will pull Tal's strength right out from under him!"

The Strongman was impressed, at least for the moment. "I will commission my best to accompany you. Broken Birch is clumsy at times, but totally devoted to us. Use them at your pleasure. Now go!"

Ben sat at his small desk in the front office of the police station and tried to get some paperwork cleared up before going out on patrol. It was a nice little office, with two small desks, a copy machine, some colorful traffic safety posters, and a low wood railing partition. Right now the morning sun was streaming in through the big windows, warming the place up. Under different circumstances he'd always enjoyed working here.

But Ben was far from cheery this morning, and his mind was far from his paperwork. He'd seen Mulligan's final report on the so-called suicide, and found it unbelievable. He couldn't be sure, but the photographs of the body and of the surrounding conditions simply did not match what he remembered seeing. Suddenly there was a rope around the woman's neck—last night Ben saw no rope around her neck, and even Mrs. Potter said the woman had the rope in her hand. The spilled goat feed had mysteriously vanished, and the straw around the body seemed undisturbed, not at all in the trampled, kicked-around mess it was in last night.

Ben didn't like the thought of it, but it was obvious that the scene—and the photographs of it—had been sanitized, as if Mulligan and Leonard had done away with all the evidence before taking the photographs and writing up the report.

As if that wasn't enough to stew about, there was also Mulligan's deriding and accusing of Tom Harris, and in front of reporters. And what in the world was the press doing in the station anyway? A lot of things were looking suspicious to Ben right now.

The *Hampton County Star* was lying on the corner of his desk. He had to go all through the paper before he could find even the slightest mention—and that's all it was—of the death at the Potter farm. The article was more a space filler than any real news, as if the reporter dropped all the facts on the floor somewhere and forgot about them . . . or purposely ditched them there. The whole thing felt wrong, so wrong it turned Ben's stomach.

I've got to get out of here, get out on patrol. I don't want to talk to Mulligan, don't even want to look at him.

But Mulligan was hard to ignore—he liked it that way. He came up to the front, belched loudly, and sat behind the desk across the room like a load of grain landing on a wharf. He had the investigation report in his hand, and started flipping through it for one last look.

"Well," he said, his booming voice shattering the nerves, "that does it."

"Any next of kin we can notify?" Ben asked.

Mulligan pulled a manila envelope out of a drawer. "There aren't any. Roe was a nobody, a loner." He slid the report, along with its accompanying sketches and photographs, into the envelope and folded it shut. "She pulled her own plug, and now it's our job to plant her quietly and get on with business."

"I don't suppose there will be a coroner's report?"

Ben knew he'd overstepped. Mulligan was getting steamed. "Of course there will. What about it?"

Ben wanted to back off, but now he had to answer Mulligan's question. "Well . . . with all due respect . . . the coroner might find some evidence to suggest another cause of death."

Mulligan didn't have time for this. "Listen, Cole, if just being a plain, hard-working, clean-nosed cop isn't enough for you . . . if you just don't feel you have enough responsibility . . . I'm sure I can find you some more important jobs, something you can really take pride in. The place could use some sweeping, and I know you'd be thorough; you'd get that broom into every corner, you'd catch every cobweb, huh?"

Ben knew he was glaring at Mulligan, but he made no effort to soften his expression. "I could be very thorough in checking the accuracy of last night's investigation."

Mulligan yanked a file drawer open and tossed the envelope in. "You just concentrate on doing your job, Cole. I'm not paying you to be my conscience."

5

Postmaster Lucy Brandon couldn't keep her mind on her work. Debbie, the postal clerk, had already asked her three questions —one about the Route 2 driver, one about the cracked mailing trays, and one about . . . now she couldn't remember the third question. She couldn't answer any of them; she couldn't recall the information; she just couldn't think.

"Hey," Debbie said finally, "are you feeling okay?"

Lucy removed her glasses and rubbed her eyes. She was usually a strong person, tough enough. A tall brunette in her late thirties, she'd been through plenty of life's little trials by this time: poverty, the early death of her parents, a wild and rebellious youth, a shaky marriage, picking up the pieces after a bitter divorce, and raising a young daughter alone—all in all, a well-rounded package of scrapes. So she'd learned to cope, usually; most troubles never really got her upset—as long as they didn't touch her family.

She looked around the small Post Office, and fortunately it was quiet right now. The midday rush was still a few hours away, the drivers had all left for their routes, the stack of work on her desk was growing, but she could catch up.

She was determined to answer at least one question. "Well, no, not really."

Debbie was young, pretty, and compassionate. Maybe she hadn't lived long enough to develop a tough exterior. She touched Lucy's shoulder tenderly. "Anything I can do?"

"Well . . ." Lucy checked the clock on the wall. "I have an appointment coming up in just a few minutes. Think you and Tim can hold down the fort until I get back?"

"Oh, sure."

A flash of reflected sunlight danced along the wall. A deep-blue fastback pulled up outside.

"Oh, there's my ride."

"You go ahead. Don't worry about us."

The driver of the car was Claire, a wonderful friend and counselor for not only Lucy, but many people of all walks of life around the town. She was a beautiful woman with blonde hair arranged neatly around her head and adorned with combs and pins that twinkled and shined. Her blouse and long skirt, both of beautifully woven natural fibers, draped about her like regal robes, and in Lucy's eyes Claire *was* a real queen. She and her architect male friend Jon were the perfect couple, constantly growing together in self-realization and harmony and becoming an enduring example to all their friends.

As Lucy climbed in, Claire leaned over and gave her a hug. "And how are you, Lucy?"

"Oh . . . coping," she answered, finding her seat belt.

Claire pulled out of the Post Office parking lot and headed down Front Street.

"And how is Amber?" she asked.

"She's doing all right. I didn't tell her we'd be coming by today. I didn't want to cause any alarm before we had to."

"Fine, fine."

"I'm going to take her back to the elementary school on Monday and see if I can get her worked into her classes there again. Miss Brewer doesn't think she'll have too much trouble catching up and just finishing out the year."

"Oh, no, not Amber, and it's so close to the end of the year anyway."

They drove through town and then turned onto 187th, commonly called Pond Road because it passed by a large and popular cattailed pond some two miles west. Along with the street sign naming the road was another sign pointing the direction to the Good Shepherd Community Church and the Good Shepherd Academy.

"I think John and Paula will be there today," said Claire. "I hope you don't mind."

"I guess not. I haven't even met them yet."

"Well, you'll find they're wonderful people. I'm glad we'll be working with them on this thing. Reporters aren't always as courteous as they are."

Lucy was quiet for a moment, just watching the farmlands and small forests go by.

Finally she said, "Why did we have to bring in the press?"

"Oh, it's very simple. In a case like this, public opinion is important. It's the public mind that eventually creates the laws we all have to live by. You see, we fight our battles at two levels: in the courts and in the public arena. A lot of the cases we win today came about because of public opinion that was molded years ago. What we do now to mold public opinion will have a positive effect on legal cases that arise in the future. It's a process."

"I just don't know if Amber can go through it."

Claire smiled with confidence. "Oh, Amber's a strong little soldier. She can do it. I was impressed with how she spoke right up and told everything to our staff, and Dr. Mandanhi, and even Mrs. Bledsoe."

Lucy was bitter. "*Amber*? You mean 'Amethyst,' don't you?"

Claire smiled and nodded. "Yes, you're right. But that doesn't matter. It's still Amber, really. Amethyst is a good friend for Amber because she bears the burden of what happened and speaks so freely, something Amber could never do as herself."

Lucy smiled a nervous smile. "But you know . . . I don't think I like Amethyst."

Claire laughed.

Lucy laughed too, hoping that statement would not be taken as seriously as she meant it. "I mean . . . Amethyst is just so brash and disrespectful . . . And I think Amber's getting away with a lot by blaming it on Amethyst."

"Well, you should put a stop to that, of course."

"But you see what I'm worried about? I think I would trust Amber to tell the truth . . . and I would know what she was thinking and feeling. But I just don't know about Amethyst. I never know what she'll say next!" Lucy shook her head to think she was even having such a conversation. "I need a set of reins for that little critter!"

Claire only laughed again. "Oh, don't be afraid of Amethyst. Inner guides are always trustworthy, and Amber needs that support and fellowship for what's ahead."

"Oh, I can see that."

But Lucy didn't feel any better, and Claire noticed.

"What else?" Claire asked.

"Since we're talking about Amethyst . . ."

"Yes?"

"Did you see that other article in the paper, about Sally Roe?"

Claire knew about it. "Lucy, really that's no concern of yours. You shouldn't even think such a thing!"

Lucy was close to tears. "But how can I help it?"

Claire stole several looks at Lucy as she drove. "Listen to me. It's not Amber's fault. I had some friends check out Sally Roe the moment you told me what happened in the Post Office. From what I've heard, Sally Roe was a deeply disturbed individual. She was tormented with self-doubt and guilt, and she could never break through . . . She was a karmic mess! Amber had nothing to do with her killing herself. She would have done it anyway."

Lucy shook her head and stared out the window. "But if you could have been there . . . if you could have seen that woman's face when . . . when *Amethyst* just tore into her. And I couldn't get her to stop. Amber just wouldn't snap out of it."

Claire patted Lucy's hand. "Let it go. Sally Roe is gone, fulfilling her own path wherever it takes her. You have your own, and so does Amber. You need to be thinking about that."

Lucy finally nodded. They were getting close to the Christian school, and she was feeling nervous. "I just hope this whole thing goes all right. I hope we know what we're doing."

Claire was firm. "I think it's something we must do. Religious bigotry is everyone's enemy. I think we would be denying our responsibility not to do anything."

There wasn't time to say any more. Claire was slowing the car down and signaling for a turn. There, on the left, stood the Good Shepherd Community Church, a simple brick building with gabled roof, traditional arched windows, and a bell tower. It was a landmark around Bacon's Corner, the home of several different congregations over the years; some had died out, some had moved on and new groups had come in, but it remained through it all for almost a century, a steadfast monument to tenacious Christianity. This latest congregation seemed to be setting a new record for endurance; it had been there in the church for almost fifteen years, and the current pastor had hung on for at least eight.

Claire pulled into the parking lot between the church and the Good Shepherd Academy, a simple, shed-roofed portable sitting on posts and piers. There were four vehicles parked in the lot at the moment. Two must have belonged to the school staff; the station wagon belonged to John Ziegler and Paula the photographer, and the large white van was clearly marked, "KBZT Channel Seven News."

"A *television* crew?" asked Lucy in surprise.

"Oh, right," said Claire. "I didn't tell you about that. The people from Channel Seven thought this would make a good news story."

The two men from Channel Seven were already prepared for Claire and Lucy's arrival, and bolted from the van as soon as their car pulled in. The cameraman set the camera on his shoulder and started watching the news with one eye. The other man, a young, athletic sort with suit and tie above the waist and jeans below, stepped up and greeted Claire as she got out of the car.

"Hey, right on time!" he said, shaking her hand.

"Hi, Chad. Good to see you again."

"This is Roberto."

"Hi."

Roberto smiled back, looking at her through the camera.

Lucy got out of the car a little hesitantly.

Claire introduced her. "Chad and Roberto, this is Lucy Brandon, the mother."

"Hi there. Chad Davis. This is Roberto Gutierrez."

"Are they going to take my picture?"

"Do you mind?" asked Chad.

"It'll be all right," Claire assured her.

Lucy just shrugged.

John Ziegler and Paula were there, ready to go. Claire greeted them, and Lucy just smiled.

The door to the portable opened, and a man looked out. At the sight of this band of people gathered in the parking lot, his face went pale; he looked sick.

He was, of course, Tom Harris.

Claire raised her hand in greeting, said, "Oh, hello there," and started walking toward the portable, the others following close behind.

No, Lord, no . . .

If I could just close this door and never come out, Tom thought. *If I could just call down fire from Heaven to clear these people out of my life, to make them go away . . . Haven't they done enough to me?*

Tom had been on the telephone most of the morning, riding the carousel of state bureaucracy while trying to teach his classes, and he still had not found his children. The last word he got was from the CPD, and they were emphatically refusing to tell him of the children's whereabouts. Pastor Howard still wasn't back, everyone else was at work, and nothing was happening fast enough.

Lord, I just wish these people would go away. I wish this day would end.

Tom looked back inside. Two kids, one third-grade, one fourth, were getting curious.

"Hey . . . TV!" said the little girl.

Tom was being recorded on camera this very moment. At least addressing the child would give him a chance to turn his back.

"Sammie, go sit down—this is none of your concern. Clay, are you finished? Well, put it on my desk and start the next page. I'll check it right after lunch, all right?"

"Mr. Harris?" said Claire, coming up the wooden steps.

"Yes?"

"My name is Claire Johanson. I'm a legal assistant for Ames, Jefferson, and Morris. I'm here representing Mrs. Lucy Brandon, whom you know. May we speak with you briefly?"

"This has been a very difficult day for me, Mrs. Johanson . . ."

"*Ms.* Johanson."

"I have nothing to say to any more reporters. I've had quite enough."

"This is a legal matter, Mr. Harris."

Oh terrific. What more could go wrong?

Tom knew better than to embark on any conversation in the presence of big-eared reporters and a television camera. "Why don't you come inside?" Then he made it clear. "You and Mrs. Brandon. These others can wait out here."

He stepped aside and let the two women come in, then closed the door against the reporters.

They were standing in a common lunchroom/coat room/library between two classrooms. Tom poked his head into the classroom on the right. A first- and second-grade class of about ten children was puttering away at some low worktables, coloring, pasting, and keeping the level of noise just below their teacher's established limit.

"Mrs. Fields?"

A plump, middle-aged woman stepped out of the classroom. Her cheeks were rosy and her hair tightly permed. Her eyes immediately showed alarm at the sight of Lucy Brandon and this officious-looking woman beside her.

"We have some important visitors," Tom explained quietly. "Could you please oversee my class for a few minutes?"

"Certainly," said Mrs. Fields, unable to take her eyes off the two women.

"They're doing their reading assignments right now, and should be finished by 10. Clay's on a special project I gave him; just make sure he puts it on my desk."

She nodded and crossed over to look in on the third- through sixth-graders.

"Let's step into the office," said Tom, and led the way to a small cubicle in the back of the building containing one desk, a computer, a copy machine, and two file cabinets. There was hardly room for three people to sit down. Tom offered the ladies the only two chairs and chose to stand, leaning against the file cabinets.

Claire wasted no time. "Mr. Harris, we're here to remove

Amber from the school. We'd like to have all her academic records."

Tom kept cool and businesslike. "I'll check with our secretary and have those prepared for you. You understand that all tuition payments must be current before the records can be released."

Claire looked at Lucy as she said, "All the payments will be taken care of. We'd like to process this as soon as possible."

"Certainly." Tom looked at Lucy. "I'm sorry that we weren't able to discuss this . . ."

Claire interjected, "There is nothing to discuss." With that, she rose, and Lucy did the same. "Now if you'll let Amber know we're here . . ."

The two women went out into the common room, and Tom followed.

Tom just wasn't satisfied. "Uh, this is a bit of a surprise. I take it we weren't able to resolve things to your satisfaction?"

Claire began to answer, "No, Mr. Harris—"

"The question was addressed to Mrs. Brandon," Tom said politely but firmly. He looked at Lucy. "It's been a month since we had that little problem. We talked it through, and I thought every-thing was settled. If you still had some doubts or misgivings, I cer-tainly would have welcomed another meeting with you."

"Would you call Amber, please?" said Claire.

Tom poked his head in the door of the classroom and quietly called, "Amber? Your mother is here. Better get your coat and your things."

There were eighteen third- through sixth-graders in the classroom, each seated at a small desk, and all the desks were arranged in neat rows. Posters of nature, astronomy, the alphabet, and tips on cleanli-ness adorned the walls. Against one wall a large aquarium gurgled, and nearby a donated telescope stood poised to probe the heavens. There were pots of pea plants all lined up and labeled on a table, and next to them a family of hamsters in a large, activity-filled cage.

At the second from the last desk, fourth row, was Amber Brandon, a bright, clever, slightly mischievous fourth-grader with a full, often wild head of blonde hair and large blue eyes. She was wearing a purple jumpsuit and pink tennis shoes, and on her shoul-der, a little pin of a toy horse.

She was surprised to hear that her mother had come, but also a bit excited. She hurriedly closed her workbook, gathered up her textbooks and her pencil box, and came to the door.

Lucy bent and gave her a hug. "Go get your coat, honey, and your lunchbox."

Those were the first words Tom heard from her today.

As soon as Amber was ready, Tom saw them to the door, open-

ing it widely for them to pass through. The reporters were still waiting outside, of course, and Tom could almost feel the one-eyed stare
of that television camera.

"Say, listen," he said to the reporters, "you people are on private property, and I think it would be best if you just move on, all
right?"

"Oh, Mr. Harris," said Claire, turning back and joining him in
the doorway. The camera caught a perfect two-shot. "I'm also here
to serve you this."

She took an envelope from her suitcoat pocket and placed it in
his hand. The camera zoomed in for a close-up. Paula's camera
clicked and whirred off several shots.

"We'll see you in court, sir. Good day."

She went down the stairs and walked with Lucy and Amber
back to her car.

Tom was frozen to the spot for a moment, which was fine with
Paula and Roberto. He stared down at the envelope, his stomach in
a knot, his heart pounding so hard he could feel it. The envelope
was starting to quiver in his hand. He looked at the newspeople.
They got some more shots.

"Please leave," he said, his voice hardly audible.

"Thank you, Mr. Harris," said John Ziegler.

Tom swung the door shut and then leaned against it, all alone
in the common room. He felt his legs would collapse under him and
he would sink to the floor any moment.

"Oh, God," he prayed in a whisper. "Oh, God, what's happening?"

From the two classrooms the quiet puttering and studying continued. Suddenly that was such a precious sound to him. He looked
around the common room and recognized the coats and lunchboxes
of all the children, all this dear little tribe. Before long they would
be having a prayer and going out for morning recess, filling the
swings and playground like they always did. Such simple, day-to-
day routines now seemed so priceless because of the envelope in his
hand, this invader, this cancer, this vicious, imposing enemy! He
wanted so fervently to tear it into a million pieces, but he knew he
couldn't.

Now everything was coming together. Now things were beginning to make sense. His eyes blurred with tears.

So this was why they took Ruth and Josiah!

Tal was there, his sword drawn, staying close to the building,
out of sight, watching the car and the news van pull away. Only a
few dark spirits had accompanied the visitors, and there were no

skirmishes, at least for now. The fact that Tom was well-guarded by two towering warriors helped keep things peaceful, plus the fact that Nathan and Armoth were atop the church in plain sight.

"No more harassments for the rest of the day," Tal instructed Tom's guards. "Let him heal up from this one first."

Then he spread his wings and reached the roof of the church in one smooth leap.

"So they've decided to go ahead with it!" said Nathan.

"The Strongman can be inflexible," said Tal. "I expect this will be a fight to the finish. It's—"

FOOM! A sudden explosion of wings! All three warriors immediately formed a close cluster, each facing outward, sword drawn, poised for battle.

"There!" shouted Tal, and they all faced the old bell tower.

It was Destroyer, standing tall and imposing, his expansive wings just settling, his glowing red sword drawn. A dozen warriors accompanied him, six on each side, almost as monstrous as he was. The hot yellow vapor from each demon's nostrils was already collecting in a writhing ribbon that drifted out over the parking lot like a slow, inquisitive serpent.

"If I mistake not, you are Tal, the Captain of the Host!" the demon called.

Tal, Nathan, and Armoth were sizing up this bunch. A fight would best be avoided.

"I am," said Tal.

The black, bristly lips pulled back in a mocking grin, unveiling long, amber fangs. "Then the rumors in the ranks were true!"

"And who might you be?"

"Call me Destroyer for now." Then he proclaimed proudly, "I am the one assigned to the woman!"

Tal didn't stir. Taunts never bothered him. He never fought until he was ready.

The demon continued, his sword ready. "I thought, before the battle begins, the two warlords should meet each other. *I* wanted to meet *you* to see if all the lofty words I've heard are true." Destroyer eyed Tal carefully. "Perhaps not." He waved his sword about. "But please look at this place, this little school! Is it really so much a prize as to be worth all your armies? Be assured, we want no more trouble in taking it as you desire in saving it. Captain of the Host, we could settle the matter sooner rather than later."

Tal answered, "The school is ours. The saints are ours."

Destroyer spread his arms with a flourish and made a pronouncement. "The Strongman has authorized me to give you the Christian schools in Westhaven, in Claytonville, in Toe Springs! You may have them! We will leave them alone!"

Tal remained stone-solid. "No."

Destroyer only laughed. "Oh. It must be the woman. Perhaps you are still bolstered by your recent victory in saving her. Consider that a gift, captain, our last blunder. Yes, you did save her life, but she lives for us. Her soul is ours!"

Tal said nothing.

"And not only the woman, but also all the power, resources, people, minds, money . . . *everything* we will ever need to trample you and your motley little flock of saints into the dust! You are too late, Captain of the Host! The time is past for you and your saints. *We* hold the power now! Surrender, cut your losses, and be content!"

"We will see you in battle," said Tal.

Destroyer looked at Tal for a long moment, shaking his head slowly, marveling at this angelic warrior's stubbornness. Finally he nodded.

"In battle then."

With another explosion of rushing, leathery wings, the demons rose into the sky, whooping and wailing, mocking and spitting until they were gone.

Only then did Tal put away his sword.

"Was that an attempt to frighten us?" asked Armoth.

"A strategic move," said Tal. "He was trying to steal our courage at the beginning."

"So now what do you think of our chances?" asked Nathan.

"Even," said Tal. "Maybe just even."

6

Chimon and Scion remained hidden on either side of Room 12 at the Rest Easy Motel in Claytonville. There were dark spirits about, apparently Destroyer's scouts—slimy, cowardly harassers, swooping down through the trees and power lines, zipping up and down the streets, looking into houses, through windows, down chimneys for the poor, bedraggled fugitive. The two angels were working hard to maintain a hedge about the woman, to screen her from their sight, and thus far they were able to keep her hiding-place a secret from any spirits sent to torment her.

But four spirits still followed Sally Roe wherever she went, and had been her close companions for so long that they could not be separated for the present. Chimon and Scion were just itching to stand in their way, to hack Despair, Fear, Death, and Insanity out of this world, to lessen the pain for that frightened, battered soul. But her life was such that they were there by right; and besides, the pain was necessary. The two warriors had to withhold their power.

Sally gave her head a good rub with a towel, and then straightened up for a look in the bathroom mirror. Her once-red hair now cascaded over her shoulders and down her back in wet, black strands. Well, maybe it would work—if they were only looking for red hair. But her face was still too distinctive; even with her hair dyed black and all pinned up, she still looked like Sally Roe. If she could hide all those freckles it would help. Maybe she could conceal her brown eyes with a pair of glasses, those stylish, tinted kind. Maybe she could wear a lot of makeup.

Her heart sank. This was all so futile, so childish. She was dreaming, groping for hope, and she knew it. If they ever spotted her, they would recognize her. She was finished, through, as good as dead.

She leaned on the sink, let her head droop, and just stayed there for the longest time, her mind failing her miserably; it just wouldn't function. It was tired, burned out, discouraged. All she could do was stand there, breathing one breath at a time. At least she could breathe; at least *something* was still functioning.

But why was she so glad about it? That bothered her.

Sally, you're too tired to think about it. Let it go.

But then her mind clicked on, just a little, and again, for the millionth time, she tackled the same vexing question: If life was so pointless, so futile, so meaningless, so empty, why was she trying so hard to hang on to it? Why did she want to keep going? Maybe it had something to do with how life evolved; nothing poetic or lofty, to be sure, just that mysterious, unexplained self-preservation instinct, the only reason we hung on long enough to beat the odds so we could walk upright and kill each other . . .

She snapped out of it. It was a waste of time trying to figure it out. It was a merry-go-round, an endless maze. *Keep it simple, Sally: somebody wants to kill you, but you want to stay alive. Those two propositions are enough for now.*

She leaned forward to check the cut in her shoulder. No infection, at least; that was good. For now the bleeding was stopped and the wound was closed, but just barely. She carefully bound it up with adhesive tape and gauze—a nice manual task, no heavy brainwork—then slipped carefully into her shirt.

She came out of the bathroom, sat on the bed, and started tinkering with the clasp on an inexpensive neck chain. It was a good buy down at the local variety store—provided it didn't turn her neck blue—and should do the trick.

She'd been shopping that morning, as quickly and quietly as possible, constantly hoping she would not be seen by anyone who might know who she was, or care. But she had to get that tape and gauze, the hair rinse, this chain, some clean clothes . . . and the morning paper.

The *Hampton County Star* was still spread out on the bed. She'd paged through it the moment she got back to the room. The front page carried some stories about a sewage plant, a local political scandal, and a county commissioner's thirtieth year in office, but no news from Bacon's Corner. The second and third pages didn't say anything either. She didn't find what she was after until the bottom of the last page of the news section.It was a tiny headline and about one and a half inches of story:

LOCAL WOMAN FOUND DEAD

Bacon's Corner—The body of a local woman was discovered last night in her home, an apparent suicide. The victim is identified as Sally Beth Rough, 36, an employee at the Bergen Door Company.

Her landlady, Mrs. Fred Potter of Bacon's Corner, made the discovery after noticing some of Rough's goats were loose.

"It's a real tragedy," she said.

It was a ridiculous piece of reporting. A run-over chicken would have gotten more copy, maybe even had its name spelled correctly. But that didn't bother Sally. That wasn't the point.

The story was not just wrong—it was incredibly, shockingly wrong.

They think the dead woman is me? *The woman who tried to* kill *me? They think she's* me?

She'd brooded about that all through her shower. It bothered her so much she had to read the instructions on the bottle of rinse three times.

At first she thought it could be good news. *They'll think I'm dead!*

But that notion soon faded. *They know I'm not. They have to know. They've lied to the paper, or the paper is lying.*

She finally got the clasp of the chain open and hung it around her neck. Then she reached over to the night table and picked up . . . that ring. She threaded the neck chain through it, fastened the clasp, buttoned up her shirt, and the ring was hidden.

They know who that woman was. They don't want anyone else to know.

And she knew she wasn't hallucinating. The ring around her neck told her that. It was one solid piece of evidence that would help her hold on to reality, bizarre as it may be.

Sally reached for her jacket and pulled another solid piece of evidence from the pockets—many pieces, actually.

Cash. She'd already counted it. Ten thousand dollars, in three bundles: one of twenties, one of fifties, and one of hundreds. The assassin's fee, most likely. Sally found it all in the woman's coat pockets and grabbed it. Why the woman was carrying it all on her person was a mystery, unless she carried the money for the same reason she wore the gold ring.

But the question still remained: After all these years, what had Sally done? How had she gotten in their way?

It had to be what happened in the Post Office. It was the only thing Sally could think of, a frightening experience and now a horrible memory. It was just like being caught, found out, discovered by an old enemy . . . a *savage* enemy! That little girl's eyes! Those taunting, hideous eyes! She could never forget that short moment when every fear, every nightmare from all her previous years came back in a torturous, merciless wave of recollection.

She had looked into the eyes of a devil. She could recognize it; she'd seen that look before, felt the stinging, mocking hate, heard the same vicious lying.

Sally flopped on the bed. No, she couldn't think about it. She was just too tired. She was frightened, her hair was black and looked strange, she couldn't think, she was a hunted animal, and she was just too tired.

Your hope is lost, worthless creature, said a voice in her head.

It's only a matter of time; a very short time, said another.

"Amber . . ." It sounded so much like her.

Now you can see how big we are, and how little you are!

You are dead, worthless creature! You are crazy!

Sally leaped from the bed and grabbed a pen from the table. She found some stationery in a drawer next to a Gideon Bible. She would write things down, that was it! Perhaps her mind wouldn't get scrambled if she put it all down on paper. She could record her thoughts before they melted away. She bent over the table, her pen poised over the paper.

But Despair was wounded, humiliated, indignant, and determined to redeem himself. He hung on her back like a coal-black leech, sucking out her will, whispering confusion to her mind. The other three spirits were with him, circling Sally, taunting her, jabbing her with their swords.

Insanity whipped his sword right through her brain.

Sally stared at the paper. Somehow she'd ended up on the floor. Nothing would come. What was that thought? She just had it, she was going to write it down, and now it was gone.

Give it up. Turn yourself in.

No one will ever believe you. You're crazy.

Crazy. It was a word. She wrote it down.

Insanity, cackling his witchy laugh, grabbed her mind between his two hairy palms and dug in his talons. Death joined in the attack.

Sally's mind went blank. The paper began to grow into a white screen that filled her eyes like a fog, a blizzard white-out. She was floating. She kept writing: "My name is Sally Roe . . . Sally Roe . . ."

She could hear voices in the room, taunting her, and could feel sharp claws tugging at her. They remained invisible, hiding from her, teasing, tormenting.

Then came Fear. Sally was overcome with a numbing, paralyzing fear. She was lost and falling, spinning, tumbling in space. She couldn't stop.

She willed to think, to form the word in her mind: Sally. Sally. Sally.

Come on, write it. Take the blasted pen in your hand and write it! We have you now. We will never let you go.

Sally. She could feel the pen moving.

The pen raced over the paper in circles, squiggles, jagged lines, crisscrosses.

It was gibberish. Nonsense.

She kept writing. She had to capture a thought, any thought.

Chimon and Scion had seen enough. It would have to be quick. Scion slipped outside to check the perimeter. Chimon crept like a shadow through the walls, moving in close.

All four spirits were clustered around Sally's head, whipping her consciousness into a myriad of senseless fragments. Chimon got a nod from Scion—he would be able to shield out the spirits outside. Now for these insects inside. It had to be just the right moment, just that one instant of opportunity.

Now. They wouldn't see it. Chimon whipped his sword in a quick, tight circle, a shining disk of light. *WHAM!* The flat of the blade smacked the demons senseless and shattered their tight little cluster. Despair went tumbling backward in a blurred spin and landed outside the motel; Fear, Death, and Insanity were interlocked and fell away together, their arms, legs, and wings a spinning, fuming, angry tangle.

The two warriors ducked back inside the walls.

Despair righted himself with a shriek and a huff, and only then realized where he was. With a flurry of wings, he shot back through the wall into the room. His three cohorts were just recovering. All four flung themselves at Sally's mind again.

But it was too late. She'd slipped from their grip like a bird out of a trap. Her thoughts, though sluggish, were moving in an orderly sequence through her brain.

Sally was suddenly able to read the words on the page. There were only six legible words at the top, "Crazy my name is Sally Roe." The rest of the page was filled with aimless, chaotic scribbles. She got up from the floor and sat at the table to try again. She had to keep writing, first one word, then a phrase, then another word—anything that would capture her racing, fragmented thoughts before they escaped her.

"Death and despair and fear and madness are back," she wrote, and then another thought: "Why kill me? I died years ago."

Sally kept moving that pen, whether her mind stayed on it or not. She was going to whip this madness. She had to. She was going to get her thoughts down on paper where they couldn't get away. She was going to win.

Ben was beginning to wonder about his gift for timing. He'd been out on patrol and just happened to stop in at the station to pick up some more highway flares. As soon as he stepped through the back door, he could hear Mulligan in his office, talking to someone on the phone, and using a hushed tone of voice that immediately roused Ben's suspicion. Since when did Mulligan ever get that quiet?

Ben got his flares from the supply room. The quicker he got out of there, the better.

Oh-oh! There went Mulligan's chair again, rolling back and hitting the wall. Ben ducked into the supply room, expecting Mulligan to come bursting through his door.

But Mulligan must have jumped up in anger. He stayed in his office, hollering at whoever was on the phone.

"No, Parnell, I'm telling you, there was nothing on either hand! That's what I said, nothing!"

Hmm. Parnell. That was the coroner.

Mulligan gave Parnell time to say something, and then dove into him again. "No, I didn't find anything in her pockets either! What kind of a jerk do you take me for?" Parnell got another two bits in, and then Mulligan answered, "Well, you just go back and

check around again! I'm doing my job, now you do yours!"
Another pause. "Hey, you're the one who got the body, not me. I
delivered it just like I found it. Why not ask the medics, if you've
got a problem? Yeah, Parnell, it's *your* problem, and I can make it a
bigger problem if you just say the word!"

He slammed the phone down and cursed.

Ben ducked back outside as quickly as he could. Even as he
closed the door behind him, he could hear the sergeant still hissing
and cursing under his breath.

7

James Bardine was a young, handsome lawyer with black, wavy
hair left long in the back and a voice with a lingering adolescent
quack. Normally, he was tough and decisive—his associates used
words like belligerent and rude behind his back—and in control of
his situation. He was ambitious, a real goal-grabber, and flaunted
his red Porsche at every opportunity. His suits were specially tailored to project an image of power. He'd perfected his own walk for
use whenever he went to court: a quick, intimidating clip, chin high,
spine straight, and lots of extra yellow legal pads under his arm. He
knew he'd go far. He had the grit for this work. He was good at it.

Right now, he was scared to death. He was sitting in an overly
soft couch in the outer office of his boss, Mr. Santinelli, waiting to
be called in for a conference. The room had high, twelve-foot walls,
dark-stained mahogany trim around, over, and under everything,
and a thick carpet your feet sank into. It was deathly quiet except
for the secretary's steady tapping on the typewriter and an occasional electronic warbling of a telephone. Bardine needed a
cigarette, but Mr. Santinelli forbade smoking in his office. The magazines on the coffee table were either old or boring, but it didn't
matter. There was no way he'd be able to read right now.

He was trying to compose a defense in his mind, something
persuasive. Surely Mr. Santinelli knew when he had a good man;
surely he wouldn't make a big thing out of such a little incident.
Surely he would consider the fine record Bardine had accumulated
in the past five years.

The big mahogany door opened like the seal of a crypt, and Mr.
Anthony stepped out. Anthony was Mr. Santinelli's aide and right-
hand man, a tall, thin, ghosty character, something like a cross
between a butler and a hangman. Bardine rose quickly.

"We're ready," said Anthony. "Won't you come in?"

Such a nice invitation to an inquisition, Bardine thought. He stepped forward.

"Are those yours?" Anthony asked, pointing to some yellow legal pads on the coffee table.

"Oh, yes, thank you."

Bardine grabbed them up and followed Anthony through the big door. It closed after them with a thud of finality.

This was the inner conference room adjacent to Mr. Santinelli's office. The ornate light fixtures were at full brightness, but the room still seemed gloomy. The dark woodwork and furniture seemed to absorb the light; the heavy, floor-to-ceiling, velvet curtains were drawn over the windows.

Mr. Santinelli sat at the other end of the oval conference table, looking over some papers before him and seeming not to notice when Bardine came in. He was an impressive figure, intimidating by his very presence. He was expensively dressed, gray, grouchy, and *in charge*. He was flanked by two of his closest and most powerful associates, Mr. Evans, a tight-faced, iron-fisted attorney who hadn't smiled in years, and Mr. McCutcheon, a man who had so much money the subject bored him. Near this end of the table sat Mr. Mahoney, Bardine's immediate superior, and not an impressive figure at all. One other man was present at the table, but unknown.

"Be seated, Mr. Bardine," said Santinelli, still not looking up.

Anthony showed Bardine to the chair at the nearest end of the table, the one directly opposite from Mr. Santinelli. This was going to be a real eye-to-eye meeting.

Bardine took his seat and arranged his legal pads neatly in front of him. "Good day, gentlemen."

Some of them muttered good day back. Some only nodded. None of them smiled.

Mr. Santinelli finally finished perusing his papers and looked up. "Mr. Bardine, let me introduce you to the gentlemen seated with us. Mr. Evans and Mr. McCutcheon I'm sure you know already."

Bardine nodded at the two men, and they nodded back.

"Mr. Mahoney is here as well, and we acknowledge his attendance. The other gentleman is Mr. Goring, from Summit, here to lend his assistance and expertise."

Bardine nodded at them, and they didn't nod back.

Mr. Santinelli leafed through the papers in front of him. "To quickly review our present situation, we find that a . . . complication . . . has developed, which at first seemed not so grievous as it now appears. Ehmmmm . . . and with each passing moment, the gravity of the complication increases . . ." Then Santinelli looked straight at Bardine and asked, "Mr. Bardine, are you familiar with the name Sally Beth Roe?"

Arrow Number One. Bardine could feel the question go right through him. "Yes, sir."

"And what about the name Alicia Von Bauer?"

That felt like several arrows. "Yes, sir."

"Would it be true to say, Mr. Bardine, that you are *extremely* familiar with the name of Ms. Von Bauer?"

"Well . . . I'm not sure what you mean by that . . ."

"We'll get to that later." Santinelli set that paper aside and perused the next sheet. "I'm sure you are aware by now that Ms. Von Bauer is dead?"

"Mr. Mahoney advised me of that this morning, sir."

Santinelli adjusted his reading glasses and studied the paper in front of him. "Sally Beth Roe . . . How interesting that she should pop up again, and in Bacon's Corner, of all places!" Santinelli looked at the men on either side of him. "Strange how things like this happen so often. You'd think there was an intelligent mind behind it, the hand of whatever god you may wish to imagine . . ."

It was no joke, and no one laughed.

"At any rate," Santinelli continued, "we have just recently learned that a plan was launched to have Sally Roe murdered, and, of course, to make it look like a suicide. Just whose idea was that?"

Mahoney spoke quickly and clearly. "Mr. Bardine's, sir."

Bardine looked at his superior in horror.

Santinelli asked, "You seem to be having a problem with his answer, Mr. Bardine."

Bardine's voice cracked as he said, "Uh, well, yes . . ."

"We'll get to that later," said Santinelli, looking at the paper again. "To continue my recounting—and please correct any flaws as you catch them—Alicia Von Bauer, a member of a Satanist organization called Broken Birch, was hired to perform this murder, and paid . . ." Santinelli bristled as he read the amount. ". . . ten thousand dollars as a retainer, with another ten thousand promised upon successful completion of her assignment. Am I correct so far?"

Mahoney just looked at Bardine. Bardine looked back at him. Neither man answered.

Santinelli continued, but watched both of them. "Apparently Ms. Von Bauer made her attempt on Tuesday night of this week, but found Ms. Roe to be more than her match. Ms. Roe was able to overcome her assailant and escape, leaving the dead body of her assassin behind, where, theoretically, she herself would have been found had the plan succeeded." He set the paper down flat in front of him, folded his hands on top of it, and looked at Mahoney and Bardine over the top of his reading glasses. "In other words, this ambitious, overly imaginative plot was a pitiful failure."

Mahoney looked at Bardine again. Bardine glared back at him.

Santinelli slid that paper aside and picked up the next one. "To further complicate matters, the, uh, planners of this scheme widened the circle of confidence beyond the key players and brought in a local peace officer named . . . uh . . . Mulligan, as well as the local medical examiner—the assumption being made, I suppose, that these two parties are steadfastly loyal to our cause, seeing that they were actually told in advance that there would be a suicide at the Potter farm and to handle it as quickly and quietly as possible."

Santinelli dropped the paper to the table and leaned back, removing his glasses. "Which, much to their credit, they are doing, or at least are trying to do, despite the fact that the deceased who is supposed to have killed herself is dead from an obvious act of violence and is, of course, the wrong person to begin with. By your silence I take it my account is accurate so far?"

Santinelli didn't need the answer he didn't get. He just replaced his reading glasses and went to the next sheet of paper. "Now for the complications—the *real* complications. First of all, the most obvious: Sally Beth Roe is alive . . . somewhere. She is living, breathing, walking about, and I'm sure totally cognizant that there was a ruthless attempt on her life. If she doesn't know who was responsible, I'm sure she has a very good idea. And how am I so sure? Let me tell you the next complication.

"According to a reliable source who shall remain nameless, Alicia Von Bauer was wearing a ring when she committed—excuse me, tried to commit—the murder. At our request, the medical examiner checked the body for that ring, and found that it had been removed from the third finger of the right hand with the help of cooking oil . . . uh, traces of the oil were still on the finger. We sent some people to check the murder site and the house, and the peace officer and medical examiner doublechecked the personal effects of the assassin. The ring is gone.

"And then there is the matter of the ten thousand dollars. That is also gone, without a trace. Von Bauer may have placed it in a secret account somewhere, but that is unlikely, knowing the delicate nature of her mission."

"Uh, sir?" said Bardine.

Santinelli lifted his eyebrows just enough to give Bardine the floor.

"The . . . uh . . . ten thousand dollars *was* laundered. It can't be traced to us."

The eyebrows went up again. "To *us*, Mr. Bardine?"

Bardine stumbled a bit. "Uh, to uh, the . . . to, uh, well, to us . . . myself, and . . . and uh . . ."

"It *is* gone, is it not?"

"Gone, sir?"

"Unless you can make a call or take a drive—just go and get it?"

"Oh . . ." Bardine stalled, but finally answered, "Yes, sir, I would say that the money is out of our reach now, irretrievable."

"But . . . laundered."

"Oh yes, sir."

Santinelli continued, referring to his notes. "The third complication embodies the first two: We have every reason to presume that Sally Roe has both the ring and the money. As such, she presents the greatest possible threat to us and to our plans." Santinelli paused for emphasis. "A greater threat, gentlemen, than she ever could have been had she been left alone."

Santinelli put his notes aside, removed his glasses, and looked squarely at Mahoney and Bardine. "Now, Mr. Mahoney and Mr. Bardine . . . let's return to an earlier question: Just whose idea was this assassination plot?"

Mahoney spoke first. "Mr. Santinelli, I'll have to claim some responsibility. When we heard that Sally Roe was in Bacon's Corner, we knew it could be a serious deterrence. We weighed many options, and I guess it became too high a priority in our minds. When Mr. Bardine presented the idea of an assassination to me, I guess I just wasn't firm enough in discouraging it. But by no means did I authorize the action, sir."

Santinelli could see that Bardine was quite agitated. "Do you have anything to add to that?"

Bardine looked from Mahoney to Santinelli and back again. "Sir . . . I . . . well, I understood that this undertaking had been authorized from the top down. I believed I was carrying out the plan with the full endorsement and authorization of my superiors." Bardine could feel the cold, icy wind blowing his way from Mahoney's countenance. He found himself at a loss for words—appropriate words, anyway. "The . . . uh . . . concept of a suicide, sir. This was not to be a murder, you understand, but a suicide, for all practical purposes. Done correctly, it would never be interpreted as anything else. Sally Roe was already a lonely and wasted individual with a terrible past and nothing ahead of her. Suicide seemed credible."

"I did not authorize it, sir!" said Mahoney. "He acted without my direct orders!"

Santinelli made no attempt to hide the smirk on his face.

"We'll get to that later. Mr. Bardine, I do have some questions about the involvement of the deceased, Ms. Von Bauer. How was she brought into this?"

"Uh . . . she . . ." Bardine felt like a badgered witness on the witness stand. "I, uh, was talking to her about this particular problem, and she . . . well, she proposed the arrangement."

"She proposed killing Sally Roe?"

"Yes, sir, for the price of twenty thousand dollars." Bardine quickly added, "As you know, this sort of thing *is* done now and then."

Santinelli's eyes narrowed. He was moving in for the kill. "You say you were talking to her about this particular problem?"

"Well, I . . ."

"Mr. Bardine, do you always discuss such highly sensitive subjects with such questionable characters?"

"No, sir, of course not!"

"You freely discussed top-level concerns with a *Satanist*?"

"Not a Satanist, sir—at least, not in a derogatory sense. She belongs to Broken Birch, yes, but they command much respect, even among our own ranks—"

"And just where did this discussion take place?"

"Well, I suppose . . ."

"Wasn't it in your home, Mr. Bardine? More specifically, in your bedroom?"

Bardine was silent. He was stunned.

Santinelli explained briefly, "We do keep up on things, Mr. Bardine." Then he started attacking again. "You were romantically involved with Alicia Von Bauer, weren't you?"

Bardine was trying to formulate an answer.

Santinelli hit him again. "You'd already had many clandestine trysts with Von Bauer even before this; you'd already revealed several of our secrets to her, and now, at the peak of your infatuation, when she had your complete confidence, you told her about this problem, and the two of you made a pact together, isn't that correct?"

Bardine decided to try honesty. "I . . . I thought it would be safe. I mean, she was involved in a bizarre group, she already had a criminal record . . . I thought that if something went wrong, we could always dissociate ourselves from her, claim no knowledge of her actions. She was . . . she was a disposable entity, purely utilitarian. I was sure it would work."

Santinelli placed both hands squarely on the table, as if bracing himself right before exploding. "I suppose, Mr. Bardine, you never considered what it could do to the reputation of not only yourself but this organization for you to be intimately associated with a convicted criminal?"

"Sir . . ." Bardine tried to lighten things up. "Our people are seen in the company of this kind of people all the time . . ."

"Not this kind, Mr. Bardine! Not Satanists! We do not wish to associate with them because we do not wish to *be* associated with them by the public, do you understand? This relationship of yours with Von Bauer was most imprudent!" Santinelli stopped, not satisfied with the word. "*Imprudent*? Mr. Bardine, it was *reprehensible!*"

Bardine could only sit there, silent and shot to pieces.

But Santinelli wasn't through. "Did it never occur to you that she could be a spy? Did it never once dawn on you that all the inside talk you were sharing with her—no doubt to impress her—would be immediately afterward shared with her cohorts in Broken Birch? Haven't you learned anything about the politics of power? Have you any idea how vulnerable you have made us to those despicable leeches?"

Santinelli was hot and rolling; there was no stopping him. "They want power, Mr. Bardine, just as we all do! They are no exception in this game! We all want it, and we all have our own little machinations and tricks to get it. But be sure of this, Mr. Bardine: power, real power, belongs to the select few, and *we* are that select few—do you understand?" He didn't give Bardine time to answer. "All the others, be they rich, be they royalty, be they gutter rats like these Satanists, will just have to get used to that fact and live by it. We will not allow any more petty power-grabbers to vie for leverage against us, and"—he leaned into this phrase—"we will not allow any more of our people to *give it to them*!"

Bardine's voice was barely audible. "I understand, sir."

Santinelli ignored the reply. "The ring taken from Alicia Von Bauer's finger . . . it was yours, wasn't it?"

Bardine tried to explain. "She . . . she stole it, sir! I did not give it to her! She had to have stolen it from the top of my dresser!"

"And this was, of course, after you had made your pact with her?"

"I . . . I suppose."

"So she took your ring, with your personal inscription on it, and placed it on her own finger, just in case—" Santinelli took a moment to breathe and cut some holes through Bardine with his eyes. "—just in case something went wrong, and we tried to dissociate ourselves from her and claim no knowledge of her actions and treat her like a disposable entity. With your personalized ring, don't you see, she would have some recourse against us, some proof that it was one of our own top-level attorneys who hired her and paid her that ten thousand dollars!"

Bardine looked down at the tabletop.

Santinelli had vented most of his anger. Now his voice softened. "Mr. Bardine, it is not my responsibility to think all these things through for you; it is your responsibility to do that, and to always keep the best interests of this organization foremost in your mind."

"Yes, sir. I'm sorry, sir."

"It's too late for that. The damage is done, and by another romantic entanglement! I hope you've learned—and it has been in the hardest way—how dangerous they can be."

"Yes, sir, I have."

"You're a good man, Bardine. I like your record of accomplishments. We're going to keep this quiet, and I expect you to keep it quiet, for your sake and ours too."

"Yes, sir. You have my word, sir."

"We will grant you a leave of absence to . . . pursue some further studies—and please come up with something convincing. In the meantime, we'll just have to see what we can do to straighten this mess out."

By this time, such a sentence was good news. "Yes, sir. Thank you for your kind considerations . . ."

Santinelli began to gather his papers together. "In the future, Mr. Bardine, you will show by your example how such actions as we've discussed are never a good idea for any man in your sensitive position."

"Yes, sir," said Bardine. "I will, sir!"

Santinelli only smiled. "Oh, I'm positive of that."

8

Ransacked. The place was a disaster, just like Mrs. Potter said.

Ben stood in the doorway of the Potters' little rental house and figured he'd better have a good look from here before he went inside. The small living room was scantily furnished with an old couch, a rocking chair, a small thin-legged lampstand, and one gray and brown rag-rug.

The cushions from the couch were tossed on the floor, the rag-rug was rolled aside and piled in a corner. In the middle of the floor were papers, books, small boxes, and several items of clothing, apparently the contents of some drawers somewhere, brought in and spilled out.

Ben checked his watch. Yes, he had time to linger a little longer. This sidetrip back to the scene of the so-called suicide was not official, to say the least, and he did have some other stops to make. But he had some nagging questions that drew him here, and he was hoping an answer, no matter how small, might turn up. Mrs. Potter was glad enough to see him again, and gave him the key after preparing him for what he would find.

He stepped inside the house and went into the kitchen. Every drawer had been pulled open and the contents scattered on the old trestle table: some unmatched bowls and plates, old army eating utensils, some aging dish towels, some cookware, and a half-empty box of Saltine crackers. The canisters on the counter were all open—someone had dug through the flour, the tea, and the sugar, spilling much of it. He checked the refrigerator—they'd gone through that too.

He found the bedroom. It was the messiest of all the rooms, probably because it held the most of Sally Roe's few possessions. Ben stood just inside the doorway a moment, noticing the intricate quilt now pulled from the small bed, the beautiful carved horse on the dresser, the pictures now hanging crookedly on the walls—prints of serene countrysides, grazing horses, hard-working farm folk. On the square table next to the bed was a small porcelain lamp, cracked, but decorated with hand-painted flowers and topped with an intricate crocheted lampshade. Apparently this was Sally Roe's favorite room, her private little world. It had received most of her attention and creativity.

The small closet had been rummaged through, but most of the clothes still hung there. Ben noted the blouses, the skirts, the dresses, the scarves. They were all clean, pressed, cared for, conservative. The closet smelled of lavender.

The room was flooded with sunlight that came through the south-facing window. Just below the window was Sally's old walnut desk, the drawers all pulled out, the contents scattered everywhere. Even so, Ben could easily picture how it used to be; a few books, a dictionary, and a thesaurus standing at attention on the left end, a small desk caddy holding a supply of pens and pencils on the right end, and in the middle . . . Well, whatever Sally used to have there, whatever she'd been working on, was now somewhere on the floor, or confiscated. But for a moment he could imagine her sitting in that heavy wooden desk chair with the casters on its feet, rolling this way and that, the sun warming her, the whole sun-washed, green, and growing countryside on continuous display through that window.

It wasn't a long, meticulous thought, just a quick impression, a simple conclusion: Mulligan hadn't captured all that Sally Roe was by such descriptions as "leftover hippie" and "loser."

Ben heard footsteps on the front porch and then Mrs. Potter's voice calling, "Officer Cole?"

"Yes, ma'am, I'm in here."

He made his way through the house to meet her, and found her in the living room, her arms crossed, shaking her head at the terrible mess.

"Just look at this! I've never been so disgusted!"

Ben was quite stunned himself. "These were people sent by *our* department?"

"That's what they said. Sergeant Mulligan said they'd be coming by to look for clues and things and to just let them in, so I did; and when they left, the place looked like this! Do you think I should complain?"

"Well . . . who were they? Had you ever seen them before?"

"No. They weren't from around here."

"Did they say what they were after?"

"No, I didn't think to ask."

"Well . . ." Ben looked all around, not sure what to tell her. "I'll, uh . . . I'll ask Sergeant Mulligan about it. I wouldn't worry. I'm sure they'll also take responsibility for cleaning the place up once they've finished their investigation."

She shook her head and started slowly for the door. "Well, I suppose they may as well box it all up and give it to a charity or something. I don't know what else to do with all the clothes and things with Sally dead. Poor thing. And tell me, just what am I supposed to do with her . . ." She stopped short, standing out on the front porch, looking up and down the drive. "Well . . . that's right! Her truck!"

Ben went out to join her. "Something wrong?"

She was still looking around. "Well, I was just going to ask you what I should do with her pickup truck now that she's dead, but now I remember . . . it isn't even here."

Ben took note of that. "That's . . . uh . . . that's unusual?"

"Well, she always drove it to work, and she always came home in it every day, and if she was home the other night, it just seems sensible that her truck would have been here. She would have had it parked right over there. See that brown grass? That's where she always kept it."

"Maybe it was already impounded. I'll check."

"But it wasn't here the evening I found her."

Ben made a curious face. "That is a little odd, isn't it?"

"Oh . . . who knows what's what anymore . . ." Cecilia looked through the doorway, surveying the living room again. "But I guess she was terribly lonely. Seemed like the animals were her only friends. I figured she was divorced, or separated, something like that. Can't see how else a beautiful redhead like that could be all alone and single."

Ben didn't think the question was that important when he asked it. "She was a redhead?"

"Sure. Had hair like the sunrise."

No. That didn't make sense; it didn't feel comfortable. "Umm . . . what *did* she look like, Mrs. Potter?"

"Oh . . . she was pretty, but tired, you know? Had freckles, big brown eyes . . . but lots of lines, lots of care in her face."

"How tall would you say she was?"

"Mmmm . . ." She held up her hand, palm down. "About there."

"Five five, five six . . . what about her age?"

"Well, she said thirty-four on her rental application, but that was two years ago, so I guess she's about thirty-six; that would be about right."

Ben doublechecked. "And red hair?"

She looked at him just a little impatiently. "Didn't you see her the other night?"

"Well, yes . . ."

But suddenly he wasn't so sure.

The red Porsche was traveling at better than ninety miles an hour when it failed to negotiate the turn, sailed off the freeway shoulder, and nosed into an embankment. Several cars stopped the moment it happened, and there were many witnesses.

"Yeah," said a retired vacationer, "he was doing fine there, passed my camper like I was standing still, and then, zingo! Right off the shoulder, just like that!"

"He was going too fast," said the wife, "just way too fast!"

The patrolman wrote it all down. There was an adequate crew on hand: two patrol cars, two aid cars, and even a fire truck, flashing their lights, setting out flares, and creating quite a spectacle. All the passing drivers were doing the usual rubbernecking, and traffic on the highway had slowed to a crawl.

The patrolman shouted, "Hey, let's get someone out there to handle that traffic! Get those cars moving!"

His partner came up the bank from the wreck. "Got an ID for you, Brent!"

"So, was I right?"

"Yep, it's James Bardine, the hotshot kid lawyer, your favorite."

"Dead, I take it."

"Oh yeah. Half his body went through the windshield, and he's wrapped up in the hood. They're going to have to cut up the car to get him out of there."

The patrolman scribbled it all down. "Well, now we won't be able to play tag with him anymore. Too bad."

The partner looked down into the gully where several men were cutting and winching the front of the car apart, trying to extricate the body. "Boy, the way he could corner in that thing! Never missed a move! He must have had a blowout or something."

"Probably fell asleep at the wheel."

"In the middle of the day?" The partner frowned. "Not him. He was a good driver. I'm kind of surprised."

"Aw, the other guys will figure it out, so don't worry about it. Let's just do our job and get out of here."

James Bardine was as crumpled and crushed as his car; his blood trickled to the ground even as the medics began to pull his body out of the twisted metal. It was tedious work, and they were taking it slow.

But during their grim task, no one smelled the odor of sulfur, or saw the yellow eyes peering from the rear of the car; they didn't hear the fiendish snicker, or the sudden rushing of black, leathery wings as the spirits soared away.

Lucy Brandon and her daughter Amber got home about 5 in the afternoon, and both of them were tired, cranky, and disoriented. Lucy's day had been traumatic enough with the filing of the lawsuit and everything that entailed, and she dreaded the thought of her face being on television that night. Amber's day had been a shambles; she'd spent most of the day at Claire's house instead of in school with her friends, and she still wasn't entirely sure why.

Lucy found some stew in the freezer. She could heat that up in the microwave and then make some salad, and that should take care of dinner for now. She was too tired and preoccupied to put any big effort into a meal tonight.

Amber took off her coat and plopped down on the floor in the living room among her dolls and toys. She picked up one doll, a blonde baby in a long, pink dress, and cuddled it, rocking it gently.

"Mommy?" she asked.

"Yes, honey," Lucy answered from the kitchen.

"Can't I go back to the school?"

Lucy didn't like that question. It made it all the more difficult to keep her mind made up. "No, honey, not the Christian school. We'll try to get you back into Miss Brewer's class. Would you like that?"

Amber rocked the doll and looked down into its little, painted eyes. "I want to go to the Christian school."

Lucy punched the buttons on the microwave and set it whirring. "We'll . . . well, we'll just talk about that later, Amber. It's been a confusing day."

Amber sank deeper and deeper into a melancholy mood. "I don't want to go back to Miss Brewer's class. I don't want to do those things anymore."

Lucy looked into the living room. "Amber, hang up your coat, please."

The little girl ignored her.

"Amber!"

She sat there very still, her blue eyes staring forward and blank. The doll had fallen from her arms.

Lucy approached her to give the command more emphasis. "Amber, I said to hang up your coat!"

"Aahhh!" the little girl squealed in delight, her face breaking into an ecstatic smile. She was looking at a little toy car on the coffee table.

Lucy froze where she stood. Oh no. It was happening again.

Amber rose to her feet, leaped in the air, and pawed the air like a jubilant show horse. She whinnied like a wild stallion, her blue eyes dancing; she tossed her head, causing her blonde locks to whip about her shoulders. "Indeed! All is well, Amber! Indeed, have no fear, for your friends do go before you!"

Lucy didn't know what to do. She was just getting so tired of this. "Amber, that's enough! You don't need to be Amethyst! I don't want you to be Amethyst! Now hang up your coat!"

Amber trotted up to the coffee table and grabbed the little car. "Varrooooom!" She raced it around the table, mimicking the sound of squealing tires.

Lucy was angry now. "Amber! Do you want me to—" She was going to say the word spank, but . . . now it didn't seem to fit.

"Faster," said Amethyst, "faster, faster . . . to your death, to your death!"

Then, with a final squealing sound and a powerful thrust of her hand, she sent the little car off the end of the table. It flew across the room and nosed into the carpet, tumbling end over end.

"And now you are gone, removed from that which is called life!" said Amethyst with a raucous laugh and another whinny. "You were just so clumsy!"

Lucy backed away as her daughter danced and pranced around the little upside-down car.

She took Amber's coat and hung it up herself.

9

"You did *what?*"

Attorney Wayne Corrigan had been patiently listening to Tom Harris's story up to this point and had hardly said a word. This was his first question.

Tom tried to back up a bit to explain. "She was . . . well, she was 'channeling' a spirit."

Corrigan rested his forehead on his fingertips and stared down at his desk, paging through the lawsuit as purely an emotional outlet. Looking down felt safer right now than looking Tom Harris and Pastor Mark Howard in the eye. "Channeling . . ."

"Well, yes. We used to call it mediumism; a person allows a demonic spirit to speak through him or her . . ."

"Well, yes, I know what it is, but . . ." And then Corrigan couldn't think of the right words for his feelings. He could only shake his head.

This was his last appointment of the day, and now it would probably be his worst. He was trying to be pleasant, but it was tough. Oh, what so many people expected of him! Here he was, in his forties, a small-town lawyer just scraping by, a reasonable man with a dear wife, four kids, mortgage payments, and a life of struggles and mistakes just like everybody else. But once again, someone with a need and no funds was sitting there looking for him to perform some miracle and suggest quick, simple answers to a case that was going to be complex and difficult. It just wasn't fair.

Pastor Mark decided to get into this. "Mr. Corrigan, I can assure you that Tom is a reasonable and truthful man. I believe what he's saying, and besides, Mrs. Fields can concur. She was there; she saw it too."

"All right, all right."

Corrigan stopped to think for a moment. Should he hear the rest of this? How far should he let these two go before he turned them down? Maybe he should just tell them how much defending a case like this would cost, and that would end this whole conversation. He wasn't too familiar with Tom Harris, but he knew Mark Howard and liked him. This gentle, genuine man in his fifties had that "gray head found in the way of righteousness" that the Bible talked about. Corrigan considered him a decent man of God, and most everyone agreed that the Good Shepherd Community Church was doing a lot of good for its people and for the community.

Corrigan shook his head. *It always happens to the good people*, he thought.

He leaned back with a sigh. "Okay, go on."

Tom wasn't sure he wanted to. "She . . . well, she came to our school just about three months ago. Her mother brought her in and signed her up."

"Did Mrs. Brandon agree to your Statement of Beliefs?"

"Well, yes. She signed her acceptance of them. She knows our doctrinal positions."

"What about the paragraph in the handbook about corporal punishment?"

"Well, I assumed that she'd read it."

"All right, go ahead."

Tom regathered his thoughts and picked up the story again. "Amber got along fine with the other kids for a while. It took her about a month to fit in. Then, during recess, she started teaching the children . . . how to relax."

"Relaxation techniques?"

Tom and Mark looked at each other with a ray of hope in their eyes.

"You've heard of it?" Tom asked.

"We had a case a year ago involving yoga being taught in a physical education class, and relaxation techniques were a part of it. Some parents—Christian parents—complained the school was teaching Eastern religion."

"So . . ." Mark was curious, "what happened?"

"We complained to the school district, but we didn't get the results we wanted. The school simply changed all the terms and sanitized the program so it wouldn't sound like religion, and then just kept doing it."

"So . . ." ventured Tom, "I guess you lost that one."

"We didn't exactly lose it. We dropped it. Let's hear the rest of your story."

"Well . . . I saw what Amber was doing and I asked her what was going on, and she told me that it was what she learned in Miss Brewer's class—that would be at the Bacon's Corner Elementary—and that it was fun because it helped you feel better and meet special friends, imaginary guides. I didn't know quite how to handle that, so I let it go. The other kids didn't seem that interested anyway.

"Well, then the kids started playing pretend games—you know how kids do. They were playing like they were in a horse show, and some of them were acting like horses and doing tricks while the other kids were the trainers. Kids play pretend games like that all the time—it was nothing odd, really.

"But then . . . Amber became the leader in the group, and her horse—the one she was pretending to be—was showing all the other horses how to prance, and do tricks, and how to . . . well, be good horses, I guess. And that was fine. But after recess, she wouldn't stop pretending to be a horse. She'd prance into the room and sit at her desk for a while, then prance over to the pencil sharpener, then prance up and down the aisles for no good reason, and she'd make horse sounds whenever I called on her, and we started having a real discipline problem. She was disturbing the class and disrupting things at every turn."

Mark prompted, "Tell her about the horse's name."

Tom recalled that part. "Oh yeah, right. I got after her once. I said, 'Amber, now you sit down and be quiet,' and she"—Tom made the motions with his hands—"pawed the air like a wild horse, and whinnied, and said, 'I'm not Amber. My name is Amethyst!'" Tom shrugged. "That was enough. I had to take her into the office with Mrs. Fields and have her paddled."

"Uh . . ." Corrigan looked at the document on his desk. "I think that's the second item on the complaint here."

"I think so. We followed the procedure clearly stated in the handbook and agreed to by any parent who enrolls his or her child. We use a paddle when a child decides to force his will against the teacher's will and we've carefully considered all the circumstances. We get alone with the student, we pray with them, we immediately try to contact the parents—"

"Could you contact Mrs. Brandon?"

"No. We tried her at home and at the Post Office, but she just wasn't available and the situation was getting pretty intense."

"Who spanked Amber?"

"Mrs. Fields. It's our policy that the girls must be spanked by a woman and the boys by a man."

"Oh, that's good. Did you have a witness?"

"Yes, our art teacher was there that day, and she served as a witness. We made a record of the whole thing, and then we finally contacted Mrs. Brandon that night and told her what had happened."

"So what was her reaction?"

"That's the strange part. She agreed with our action. She wasn't opposed to spanking Amber if Amber needed it."

Corrigan looked at the lawsuit again. "Mm. Somebody's changed her mind. But when did you . . . uh . . ."

Tom knew what Corrigan meant. "Just about a month ago. After we punished Amber, things went pretty smoothly for about three days, and then . . ." Tom stopped to think. "I think it must have started up again during noon recess. Amber became a horse again, just like before, and came back into class as . . . as

'Amethyst.' This time I wasn't about to tolerate it, and I got firm with her, confronted her, and then . . ."

Tom had to stop. He looked like he would cry. He forced himself to continue. "And then something came over that little girl. Her entire personality changed. She began to blaspheme, and curse, and mock the name of Jesus, and . . . and I had to get her out of there. The other kids were really being disturbed by it.

"I took her by the arm and had to physically drag her from the room—she was grabbing onto the desks and the chairs and even the other kids. Mrs. Fields could hear the commotion from clear across the hall, and she came running to see what was going on, and it took the two of us to get her out into the common room and hold her down. She was just having a real tantrum . . . no, worse than that. She wasn't herself. She wasn't Amber Brandon."

Tom stopped. Neither Corrigan nor Mark said anything. There were no questions. They were both waiting to hear the rest.

Tom pushed ahead, over the edge. "So, I . . . I discerned in my spirit that Amber was manifesting a demon, and I confronted this . . . this Amethyst in the name of Jesus; I ordered it to be silent, and to come out of her."

Corrigan slumped in his chair and exhaled a long sigh.

Mark interjected, "But she was all right after that, wasn't she?"

"She was herself again, yes."

Corrigan asked, "So naturally you assumed that this demon had left Amber, that you'd succeeded in casting it out?"

Tom was obviously embarrassed. "Yes. I guess so. But she must have told some real tales when she got home. Mrs. Brandon came in for a conference the next day, and by then she was beside herself, accusing me of physical abuse, terror, intimidation . . ."

Corrigan looked at his bookshelf, steadily slumping lower in his chair. "You tried to cast a demon out of a ten-year-old child . . ."

Mark protested, "Mr. Corrigan, you know what the Bible says about demon activity. You know demons are real, don't you?"

Corrigan flopped his arm over his desk and pointed it in Mark's face. "Do you think a jury will buy that, pastor? Go ahead! Pull a stunt like that and then try convincing any jury in this country that your behavior was appropriate!" Now he used both hands because he needed a bigger gesture. "A *child*, a ten-year-old child, and you tried to cast a demon out of her!"

"Well, what was I *supposed* to do?" Tom asked.

Corrigan sat up before he slid off his chair. He leaned over his desk and leafed through the complaint in front of him. "Well, to start out, you shouldn't have acted alone and you shouldn't have gone ahead with this . . . this act . . . without getting some counsel, even *legal* counsel."

Mark said, "He knows that now."

Then Tom protested, "But legal counsel? How was I supposed to know about that? Since when did Paul and Silas seek legal counsel before they—"

"They ended up in jail, remember?" Corrigan snapped, and for him to use a voice that was even a *little* loud had to mean he was upset. "They were beaten and thrown in jail for casting out a demon, and you're up against the civil version of the same thing. A civil suit isn't going to get you thrown in jail, but you're still going to need some kind of a Philippian earthquake to get you out of this. The American Citizens' Freedom Association has their fingerprints all over this thing . . . I suppose you know that."

Mark and Tom looked at each other. The ACFA, that infamous association—one could say conspiracy—of professional, idealistic legal technicians, whitewashed, virtuous, and all-for-freedom on the exterior, but viciously liberal and anti-Christian in its motives and agenda. Nowadays it was getting hard to find any legal action taken against Christians, churches, or parachurch organizations that did not have the ACFA and its numerous, nationwide affiliates behind it.

Mark said, "We thought maybe that was the case . . ."

Corrigan tapped the bottom of the first page of the complaint. "Ames, Jefferson, and Morris are members of the ACFA; they run the local chapter, and they've been the liberal, legal bullies around here for years. Why else do you suppose the press knew about your kids being taken away and were right there to hassle you at your home and in the police station? Why do you think they were right there to record you being served your summons? To create a scandal and smear you in the press, that's why. Why do you think your two kids were taken away in the first place? As soon as the ACFA heard about this case, they leaked the information—probably embellished quite a bit—to the Child Protection people and pulled them into it. They want this kind of spicy news. Now you're branded a child abuser, Tom, before you even get to court. The ACFA plays dirty.

"Well, just look at the complaint here against . . . uh . . . the pastor, the headmaster, the church, and the church board: 'Outrageous Religious Behavior Against a Child'—casting out the demon, of course, 'Physical Abuse by Spanking, Excessive Religious Instruction Harmful to the Child, Harassment, Discrimination, and Religious Indoctrination Using Federal Funds.'

"All this stuff is dynamite; it's going to make the case difficult because the ACFA will use all these hot issues to get the public's attention and stir them up.

"And did you catch those big key words, *federal funds*? That's what's going to get them through the door of the federal courts: 'violating mother's civil rights by teaching religion using federal funds—a violation of the Munson-Ross Civil Rights Act and the Federal Day-care and Private Primary School Assistance Act.'"

"Federal funds?" asked Tom.

"Lucy Brandon works at the Post Office, right? She's a federal employee, and under this Federal Day-care Act she receives a subsidy to help pay Amber's tuition. Didn't you know that?"

Tom was obviously surprised. "It's news to me. She didn't say a thing about it."

"Interesting. Maybe she didn't want you to know. Anyway, if you're getting federal funds, that means you can't discriminate or impose religion or spank or cause mental anguish by suggesting a child is demon-possessed, or whatever else the ACFA wants to test in a court of law. That's the whole point of this thing: they find a vague law and then work up legal cases just like this one to stretch that law as far as they can in the courts. This Federal Day-care and Private Primary School Assistance Act is a big, vague, anything-goes cloud of smoke, a clever move by Congress that most people never heard about. Now the ACFA's ready to get it defined through case law, legal precedents, maybe a Supreme Court decision.

"That's why they're going federal with this, citing federal law. Look here: 'You are commanded to appear at nine in the morning, two weeks hence, at the department of the Honorable Emily R. Fletcher of the *Federal* District Court, Western District, Room 412, *Federal* Courthouse, blah blah, blah.' This is a federal case, guys."

"So what do we do?" asked Tom.

Corrigan became quiet and then fumbled through an answer. "Well . . . I would say you need a lawyer, all right, but . . . um . . . I'm not sure whom you should consult on something like this . . ."

"You mean, you won't take this case?" Mark asked.

Corrigan gave a nervous chuckle and shook his head. "Well . . . no. No, I can't." He quickly blurted, "Now before you say anything or ask me why not . . ."

Then he stopped. *Oh brother, here I go again, having to explain this to another bunch of naive martyrs.*

"Listen, no offense intended, please understand. I mean, I can appreciate your position . . ." Corrigan pushed his chair back from his desk, waved his hands around a little, and looked at his bookcase as he tried to find the words. "But I've just about established a new policy in this office not to defend Christians anymore who can't pay for my services."

Mark thought the statement a little strange. "But . . . we didn't think you'd do this for free."

It wasn't a good enough escape for Corrigan to look down at

his desk—now he looked down at the rug. "Pastor Howard, you're the last guy on earth I'd ever want to turn down, but . . . Well, let me just share some depressing information with you.

"Okay, I'm a Christian and everybody knows it; the police know it, the local judges know it, the county prosecutor knows it . . . Worst of all, all the Christians around this county know it. That means, when the Christians get into a legal predicament, they call me, because I'm a 'brother in the Lord.'

"But then, because they're . . . Christians . . . they come into it having some convictions about how my services are going to be paid for, if paid for at all; they sit in my office and tell me about faith and God's provision and usually throw something in about God rewarding me for all my time and sacrifice; but in the meantime, my practice goes down the tubes from bad debts.

"But please don't get me wrong. I'm not blaming them. It's just the way the system works: The little people—the Christians—get into legal tangles because the state, or the ACFA, or some other rabid, Christian-eating secularist organization decides to pick on them, and those people always have all the power, connections, and finances they need to win any battle they want in a court of law. Not so with the Christians. They have to put on spaghetti dinners and car washes and jogathons just to hire some poor, minor-league attorney like me who supposedly has such a love for righteous causes that he doesn't care about the money."

Corrigan saw that Mark and Tom were listening without any signs of malice—at least not yet; so he proceeded. "Now that's half of the problem. The other half is that all too often Christians just aren't credible. You know, I've actually instructed some clients not to testify in court that they are Christians because in too many cases that information would damage their credibility! The world out there . . . the system . . . thinks it understands us. It has us pegged, categorized, defined. We believe in God; we believe in absolutes. Therefore, we can't possibly be credible!" He chuckled wryly. "When I was in law school it was the other way around. The perception was that people lacked credibility if they didn't believe in God. We've come a long way, haven't we?

"So anyway, I'm faced with two options: I can be retained by Christians and find out later they can't afford my services, or I can take their case for free or on a reduced basis—usually a drastically reduced basis. In this case right here, there would be about a zero chance of any contingency recovery. I could only hope to receive part of the settlement, but even then the system is already so stacked against me that I have no fair chance of winning, and therefore no chance of being paid that way either.

"Am I making this clear for you? To put it simply, I can't afford it, monetarily or reputationally. I've been too close to bankruptcy too many times to take another case like this. I think what you need is a fresh visionary, a brand-new horse who still has some miles left on him, somebody you can run ragged for next to nothing."

Corrigan stopped. He felt released now, but also a little ashamed. He looked at the wall where his eyes fell on his license to practice law, and concluded with, "Sometimes I almost admit to myself that I hate this job. Look what it does to me . . . makes me dump all my feelings on good people like you."

Mark looked at the legal torpedo on Corrigan's desk and sighed. "So where can we go from here? Tom's children are taken from him, and he still doesn't know where. Now the school is slapped with a lawsuit that . . . Well, it seems to me that our very freedoms are being threatened. There aren't any attorneys in Bacon's Corner; we could have gone elsewhere, but we came to Claytonville to see you because—and I'm not ashamed to say it—we knew you were a Christian. We knew you'd have the right perspective."

Corrigan looked at the minister just a little sheepishly. "Well, I guess I've blown that notion out of the water."

"But what about Tom? He could be bitter right now. He lost his wife in a car wreck just three years ago, his salary is pitiful, but he's stayed right here with his two children and served as the headmaster at our Christian school for four years now, doing an excellent job. And what thanks does he get? His children taken away and a lawsuit against the school that could jeopardize everything he and the rest of us hold dear. It isn't fair. It isn't right. Even so, he's remained true to his calling. He's a righteous man, a man of principle and conviction . . ."

"Hence the pitiful salary. Excuse me. Go on."

Mark was getting disgusted. "I'm through."

Corrigan sat quietly, rested his chin on his knuckles, thought for a moment, then nodded in agreement to his own thoughts.

"And to think it all started in Bacon's Corner. I guess it had to happen somewhere." He sat up straight and folded his hands on the desk. For the first time in several minutes, he looked directly at Tom and Mark. "Pastor, the ACFA isn't after your little school; Tom, they're not really interested in you either; as for this allegedly traumatized child, they couldn't care less about her. No, what they're really after is a legal precedent, something that's going to affect not just you, but everyone. They have all the money and skill they need to pull this thing off, and they know that you don't, and that's what they're counting on. That's why they chose a little place like Bacon's Corner and a little dirt-poor church like yours.

"And I guess they have me where they want me. I can just see those ACFA lawyers sitting in their office over at Ames, Jefferson, and Morris saying, 'Yeah, hit Bacon's Corner. That Wayne Corrigan is a burned-out tube, he'll never take the case.' Now wouldn't that be just peachy for them?"

He looked at the papers on his desk again.

"All right, I'll tell you what: I'll repent . . . sort of. I'll take this case, but I'll take as little of it as possible. That means you do the work, you do the hoofing, you do the research, you build the case. I'll tell you what to do, I'll write up the affidavits, I'll take the depositions, I'll plead the case and present the arguments, I'll advise you; but any information relating to this case is your responsibility. I suggest you get yourselves a private investigator to help you out. As far as my involvement, you'll get what you pay for, and . . ." He swallowed hard, came to a reluctant decision, and added, " . . . I'll reduce my fee by half, but you must agree to raise the other half."

Tom and Mark exchanged a quick glance and quickly agreed. "Okay."

"So what comes first?" Mark asked.

Corrigan leafed through the papers. "Number One, you've got a temporary injunction here that restrains you from just about everything named in the complaint. Uh . . . I think what it's going to boil down to is that you'll have to cease and desist from spanking and from any further 'outrageous religious behavior.' Guess that means you can't cast out any more demons until the court hearing in two weeks."

"What happens in two weeks?" asked Tom.

"We have to appear in court . . . 'to show cause, if any you have, why you and all persons acting on your behalf or on behalf of the school should not be immediately restrained from spanking, hitting, or otherwise having physical contact with children at the school for any reason whatsoever, and why you and all persons acting on your behalf in concert with you, should not be immediately restrained from any further religious behavior which could prove harmful to the mental, emotional, or social welfare of the child, or any excessive religious instruction, direct or indirect, of any kind, at the school or day-care facility, that could prove harmful . . .' And it goes on and talks about all this other stuff."

"Just what do they mean, 'excessive religious instruction'?" asked Tom.

"That has yet to be defined."

"What should we do?" asked Mark.

"Try to behave yourselves for the two weeks. Don't be outrageous, whatever that means. In the meantime, you need to give me some good arguments why you should be allowed to continue the above-mentioned activities. Then I'll file the briefs and affidavits with the court, and then we'll go in and see if we can turn you guys loose from this restraining order. That's the first thing."

"And then?" asked Mark.

Corrigan suddenly looked worried and careworn. "One bite at a time, pastor. You're going to be busy for a long, long time."

"What about Ruth and Josiah?" asked Tom.

"No easy answers there. It's going to be a tangled mess, and could be even worse, depending on whom you're dealing with in the system. I think you're entitled to a hearing within seventy-two hours to determine if the removal of your children has merit, but that's usually a rubber-stamp session where the judge approves the removal of the children based on the testimony of the social worker. You might be called to appear, you might be barred from the hearing altogether. It just depends on who's running the case. I'll look into it."

"But . . . won't I get my kids back?"

Corrigan hesitated to answer the question. "You'll probably have to go through a trial first, and that could mean a wait of six months or more."

Neither Tom or Mark were ready for an answer like that.

"That can't be all there is to it!" said Mark. "There have to be other options, something we can do!"

"You can pray," Corrigan answered. "Specifically, pray for some friends in the right places. You've got a fight ahead of you."

10

Sally would be staying at the Rest Easy another night. She had the whole ten thousand dollars to spend on this one room if she wanted to, if no better ideas came to her. Right now she had no better ideas.

She'd used up the afternoon and all the stationery in the room just scribbling thoughts down as they came to her. Now, as the day outside the windows gave way to evening, she sat at the table and leafed through page after page, her day's work.

The first page was no masterpiece: "Crazy my name is Sally Roe," followed by a full page of aimless lines and squiggles. Apparently she'd failed to capture her thoughts. But that was depressing. Maybe this *was* an accurate record of her thoughts. She didn't even remember doing it.

The next page had some scribbled words that looked like they might be "Death" and "Madness," but she couldn't be sure. After that, her writing broke down into chaotic scribbles again, and then at the bottom of the page she'd written her name several times, encircled by some strange, dark doodles. She remembered making those in a pit of depression when she didn't feel like thinking or writing anything. It just felt good to doodle, to pour her feelings onto the page without using any language.

The third page sounded so great when she'd first written it: "I am I: I think, I exist, but know nothing of the grasping of the essence of all that is under or over the abysmal attitudes that so wrack our awareness in the last autumns of mayhem upon the earth . . ." Now not even she could decode all that. Apparently her brain had been working while her mind was disconnected.

But she felt encouraged, not because her afternoon's project had produced such drivel, but because she could sit quietly now with her mind clear and *realize* it was drivel. She'd just come through some kind of spiritual storm, some raging, agonizing battle. *Just like the old days*, she thought. So many of the impressions, the hallucinations, the mindless wanderings were so familiar. Her mind had not slipped over the edge like that in almost ten years.

No doubt it was this new, mysterious terror that had brought it all back. She had stepped in the way of an old Evil, and she recognized it all too well. It must have recognized her too, and that was why it was chasing her now. With only a little imagination she could sense it still lurking outside the walls of the motel room, ready to pounce on her again should she ever rest.

But . . . what to do, what to do. What was the next step? How could she free herself?

She picked up that day's *Hampton County Star*. There was nothing new about her own death, and she figured there never would be. That story, her life, her name, were now buried, tucked neatly away in the archives to be forgotten.

She flipped to the front page and studied a large photo. Some blonde lady was handing a guy what looked like a summons. Well, this was more news from Bacon's Corner, a Christian school scandal. Tom Harris, headmaster at the Good Shepherd Christian School . . . accused of child abuse . . . accusations brought by local postmaster—

Sally's eyes froze on those last words. The local postmaster? She read the paragraph again.

" . . . the child's mother, the local postmaster, first became suspicious when her ten-year-old daughter was playing games of pretend and began to recount questionable behavior by her teacher at the school . . ."

Sally checked the time. A little after 5. Maybe there was something on television. She clicked it on.

Well . . . nothing much, just the sale of a pro football team to some unknown millionaire, a cleanup of hazardous waste in some small Midwest town, a new paint job for a historical building in the state capitol . . .

She let the television talk to itself while she finished reading the newspaper.

According to reliable sources, Tom Harris's two young children were taken from his home by child welfare workers yesterday afternoon . . . The CPD had what it felt was adequate reason to remove the children from the home . . . "If we must err, we must err on the side of the child," said the source . . . CPD is beginning an investigation into the alleged abuses of children at the school . . . Postmaster Lucy Brandon and ACFA lawyers have filed a suit against the school, charging the school with outrageous religious behavior against a child, physical abuse by spanking, excessive religious instruction harmful to the child, harassment, discrimination, and religious indoctrination using federal funds. The little girl reported that Harris tried to cast a demon out of her . . .

Oh! There it was on the television! Sally turned up the sound just as the on-the-scene footage began to roll. There was the little school, and there was Tom Harris, the headmaster, standing in the doorway. Yes, and there was the blonde lady, handing him the summons.

Chad Davis, reporter for Channel Seven News, was doing his voice-over narration. "The lawsuit on behalf of Ms. Brandon once again raises the question of how much religious freedom is too much, especially where young children are concerned, and calls for a limit to extreme fundamentalist practices that violate the laws of the state."

Next shot: Lucy Brandon, the postmaster, and . . . Amber! Neither of them said anything—they just went to their car and got in. Davis narrated, "The case could have implications at the federal level because federal funds were involved in the child's education at the school. The ACFA argues that the practices and teachings of the school are extreme, harmful, and clearly violate the laws concerning separation of church and state."

The blonde lady came on the screen. Her name appeared below her face: Claire Johanson, ACFA.

"We are concerned for the welfare of our children," she said, "and want to protect them from any more vicious and inexcusable abuse inflicted upon them under the license of religion."

Next came a quick interview with a Child Protection

Department lady, Irene Bledsoe. "We always investigate any reports that come to us," she was saying, "and we are looking into it."

Davis pressed a question from off camera. "Have Mr. Harris's children been removed from his home?"

"Yes, but that's all I can say."

"In the meantime," Davis continued in his voice-over, "the Federal District Court has handed down a temporary injunction against the school, barring any further spanking, religious teaching that could be harmful to children, or outrageous religious behavior, pending a hearing to be held in two weeks."

Back came the anchorman, staring soberly at the camera. "Thank you, Chad, for that report. We'll definitely keep working on this one and bring you more developments as they happen. Speaking on the lighter side . . ."

Commercial. Young bucks running and hollering and opening bottles of beer.

She turned off the television and sat on the bed, stunned. Irene Bledsoe . . . that same woman with the ratty brown hair and crinkled moonface. That same scowl.

The woman at the intersection! That was *her?* Those were *Tom Harris's* kids?

Lucy Brandon. Amber. Oh, and just when my mind was clearing up!

Thoughts began to fill Sally's mind with the bursting rhythm of popcorn, carrying it away in a tumbling flood, driving it forward like a wild automobile with no one at the wheel; it raced and swerved headlong from one thought to another, skipping over memories and colliding with replays, snagging and dragging scenes through her consciousness faster than she could watch them, flushing out conversations, facts, faces.

She clapped her hands to the sides of her head as if being attacked by a horde of noises. *Please, one at a time! I can't hear you when you're all screaming at once! Slow down!*

She looked at the news photo of Tom Harris again, standing in the doorway of the little school, getting his big white envelope from the blonde lady.

So he had met little Amber too!

Sally's hand went to the ring hanging under her shirt. It seemed that bad things happened to people who had run-ins with Amber Brandon.

She went to the table and found the first piece of paper she'd scribbled on that day. It was all she had; perhaps some legible writing would show up against all that nonsense.

Unless she just wrote more nonsense. It was going to be a struggle, but she would try again. She would try all night if she had to. Her head was boiling with scattered, unruly thoughts, and sooner or later they would have to spill out in some clear fashion.

Then suddenly, all around the motel, such an unexpected legion of harassing demons began to shower down that Chimon and Scion could no longer hide and had to throw any subtlety to the wind. They were in full glory, bright and visible, swatting and slashing as the demons swarmed around them like vile, biting bees. The intensity of the onslaught was shocking, surprisingly strong. It seemed each spirit would be swatted away only to be replaced by two more, and the air was filled with them. They were bold, brash, reckless, attacking with screams and shrieks, even grinning mockingly.

"For Destroyer!" they screamed as their battle cry. "For Destroyer!"

So that was it. The demonic warlord was trying a new tactic now, and this difficulty could only be caused by one thing: something had happened to their prayer cover.

"Well," said Judy Waring, "you just . . . you just never know about people. I always did wonder about him. We voted on your recommendation, we went along with it, and now what are we going to do . . ."

Mark was trying to end this telephone conversation and get back to the meeting. The parsonage telephone had been ringing all day, and he was about to pull the plug out of the wall.

"Listen, Judy," he said, "we're about to have an emergency board meeting about it right now, so I have to hang up. But let me assure you that Tom's handling this whole thing very well, just really open and forthright. I think we can trust him."

"Well . . . I'm hearing a lot of things . . ."

"Right . . . Let me say something about that before I hang up. I don't want any more gossip going around about Tom or the school or any of these matters. If there's anything to be settled, it will be settled at this meeting, with Tom present and able to speak for himself. Now please—"

"You *did* hear what the news said tonight—"

"Judy! Now listen to me! You don't need to get your information from the news, not when all this is happening to *us*, in our own church. Now you just sit tight and don't listen to any more rumors, and please don't spread any, all right?"

"Well, all right, but I don't know if we can keep Charlie enrolled at the school with this going on . . ."

"We'll have our meeting tonight, and then we'll take care of your concerns. Just be patient."

Judy was about to say something else. She always had the last word in any conversation. Mark quietly and courteously hung up before she could get rolling again.

Cathy Howard was nearby, making coffee for the men gathered in the dining room, and overhearing Mark's end of at least the twentieth conversation. Mark told her quietly, "Maybe you can unplug this thing, or leave it off the hook."

She made a questioning face.

"Or take the calls?" Mark asked.

"Just go ahead and have your meeting," she said with a chuckle. "I'll screen the calls for you."

That deserved a kiss. Cathy, a striking blonde with fine Nordic features, was remarkably serene. She'd kept her composure during this rough time, and Mark was thankful for her, more than he could say. Of course she didn't enjoy tribulation—who does?—but right now, when extra strength and resilience were needed, she was supplying them, and that gave Mark a quiet assurance that they would get through this crisis.

He stepped through the kitchen door and out into the dining room. The four church elders were gathered around the table, listening to Tom's account of what had happened up to this time.

"So what was it this spirit said?" asked Jack Parmenter, a hard-working, durable farmer with silver hair.

Tom didn't enjoy the memory of it. "Oh . . . it said we were all fools to worship Jesus, that He was only a liar, and not God at all, but just an illegitimate child—uh, the spirit used another word, of course—and then it went on to accuse Jesus of sexual perversions . . . in graphic terms."

"All that coming from a ten-year-old," said Bob Heely in disgust. Bob was a Viet Nam vet, a diesel mechanic who kept all the farm machinery around Bacon's Corner running. His hands were rough and grease-blackened.

"Sounds pretty weird to me," said Doug Parmenter, Jack's son and the spitting image of his father. "What do you think, Mark? I've never seen someone demon-possessed before."

Mark took his place at the head of the table. "I have, and I think Tom's impressions were correct."

Vic Savan, who ran the farm right next to the Parmenters', concurred with that. "Well, what that little girl—or that demon—had to say fits right in with everything else the Devil's saying nowadays about Christians and about Christ. Just look at all the slander he's been spreading in the papers and on the television, and I don't mean just our own situation. Seems like it's everyone else's civil rights and freedoms that matter, but when it comes to Christians, people—and I guess demons—can say and do whatever they want."

"Well," said Mark, "like Wayne Corrigan said, a lawsuit, a test of Christian freedom, had to happen somewhere. Looks like that somewhere is here in Bacon's Corner, and at our school."

"But isn't it just like Satan to use a child?" said Jack. "I mean, that's getting really low."

"Well, he can use God's own people, too. How many of you have heard some destructive talk about this before coming to the meeting tonight?"

Every man put up his hand.

Vic related, "I ran into the Jessups at the filling station, and they were wondering how many other kids got abused."

Tom cringed at that. "Abused? Just what do they mean by that?"

"You can fill in the blank, Tom."

"Well, we have the newspaper and KBZT to thank for that," said Jack. "They've been tossing that word around like it was a fact."

"And that's my point," said Mark. "We're the elders of this church, and we've got to keep a lid on this thing. There are going to be questions flying and a lot of accusations and gossip, and we'd better be thinking of how we're going to handle it."

Vic raised his eyebrows, shrugged one shoulder, and said, "Well, as far as the Jessups are concerned, they're taking their two kids out. They don't want any part of it."

"Neither do the Wingers," said Doug.

"And they said I was a fool for keeping my three in there," said Bob.

The phone out in the kitchen rang again. They could hear Cathy answering it.

Mark commented, "That's probably another family with the same concerns." He looked at Tom. "Well, Tom, let's get the first item covered and then we can go from there."

Cathy peeked in. "Ted Walroth's on the phone. He saw the news tonight, and he wants to know if we're going to have a congregational meeting."

"Tell him I'll call him back," said Mark. Cathy went to tell him, and Mark returned his attention to Tom. "You want to tell them?"

Tom didn't hesitate. "I'm stepping down as headmaster of the school; I'm going to take a leave of absence until this whole thing gets cleared up."

Jack was ready to debate that move. "Who says?"

"The school's in trouble because of me. If we're going to save it at all, I've got to get out of the picture."

He was right. Every man at the table hated to admit it, but he was right. There was a long, fidgety silence. They all looked at the table or out the window or around the room, and only occasionally at each other.

Mark decided to break the silence. "Tom and I talked and prayed about it, and we agreed that all of us have to face the facts as they are: the ruckus is over him; he's the center of the controversy. Now I know we're all standing with him, but the matter of his innocence is secondary. The biggest and most immediate concern right now is the confidence of the parents and the community. That confidence is taking a real beating right now, and it's going to be hard to get it back if we keep Tom in his position."

Jack fidgeted, looked this way and that, and then gave the table a pound. "But, Mark, we can't do that! It'd be like admitting Tom's guilty!"

Doug jumped in. "But, Dad, some people already think that! I've talked to some folks just today who are ready to give the whole thing up, just pull out of the school and let it die. They're knocked on their backs by this thing."

Mark cut in. "But that's part of the warfare, guys. Satan set this whole thing up so he could weaken us with gossip and slander. We need to do as much as we can to protect ourselves from that, or at least provide no fuel for the fire."

Tom explained, "If I stay at the school, we won't be able to convince anyone that we're truly concerned about all this. *I'm* concerned. I'm willing to step down in good faith until we can get all this trouble resolved."

"We'll do all we can to keep the academy open. Mrs. Fields will stay on and teach the remaining kids in her classes. I'll take charge of the remainder in the upper grades. Tom, what's the prospective enrollment?"

Tom had scribbled down a tentative list. "Um . . . I guess we should go for a worst case scenario . . . which would mean that Judy Waring will take out her son Charlie . . . and then there are the Jessups and their two . . . and then the Wingers with their three . . ."

"What about the Walroths?" asked Jack.

Mark answered, "I'll be calling him. I think I can talk him into hanging on for a while."

"So we'll leave those two children in?" asked Tom.

"For now."

Tom wrote them back in. "Okay. That means five kids are out of Mrs. Fields's class. Her enrollment's cut in half. My class is down by one. That isn't too bad."

"So for now we'll be able to survive," said Mark. "But tonight we'll have to talk about Tom's salary while he's out, plus some more volunteer help to keep things running—I won't have time to do all the bookkeeping and administrating. Then we'll have to reassign the bus route now that the Wingers are out and get someone else to organize the hot lunches now that the Warings are out."

"Donna Hemphile called today," Tom remembered. "She's very supportive of the school, and willing to put in any time she can spare when she's not tied up at the door factory."

"Who?" asked Doug.

"Donna Hemphile," said Mark. "She's a supervisor at the Bergen Door Company, a single gal."

"Yeah, she's nice," said Jack.

"Anyway," said Tom, "she says she'll take care of hot lunches, probably two days a week."

"Good enough." Mark wrote it down in his own notes. "Okay, other things to discuss tonight: We need to update you on what Wayne Corrigan told us, and what we have to do to fight this thing in court." Mark looked at Tom. "And there's also the latest report on your kids."

Tom looked tired. He'd been through quite a battle already over that issue. "Wayne Corrigan called this afternoon. He finally got in touch with someone at the District Court in Claytonville. They had the hearing today, in Judge Benson's court. It took about ten minutes, I understand. I guess I didn't miss anything; they would have barred me from the courtroom anyway. The judge approved the removal and set a date for the trial in October."

"October?" Jack exclaimed. "So what happens in the meantime?"

"I'm supposed to get some counseling, but from a court-appointed counselor. I'll be able to visit the kids, I don't know exactly when, and it'll be controlled; a social worker will have to be there . . ." Tom couldn't continue.

"Well, I say we fight this thing," said Jack. "Let the others run and hide. If being Christian is too tough for them, well, they can't say Jesus didn't warn them. But let's fight it! Let's go to our knees, and beseech the Lord to show us a way out of this. Our God is greater than any lawsuit or any bunch of social service bureaucrats! He'll stand with us, and that's . . . well, that's my final word on the subject!"

Mark looked around the table. "So how about the rest of you? Let me hear from you now, before we take another step."

"Let's fight it," said Doug.

"We're in this for the Lord," said Bob. "He'll help us."

Vic raised his hand to be counted. "Hey, if it had to happen to us, then it had to happen to us. Looks like we're first in line, guys. If we fall, all the other Christian schools are going to fall next. We'd better give them a good fight, with the Lord's help."

Mark felt the hand of God upon these men. He met Tom's eyes, and through Tom's tears he saw a quiet confidence.

"Then let's go to prayer," he said, "and let our agreement this night be settled in Heaven."

They joined hands around the table, making their covenant with each other and God.

High above the town, hovering between Heaven and Earth, his wings a soft, blurred canopy, Captain Tal overheard the transaction. The saints had bound themselves together in prayer according to the will of God; the Lord Almighty had received their petition. There was agreement, and that agreement was now sealed.

"Good," said Tal, "good enough!"

In Claytonville, the demons abruptly called it a day. The last of them swooped down, spit out some insults, and then soared off like a crazed swallow into the night, leaving Chimon and Scion alone on the roof of the motel. The sudden silence was jarring.

"Well," said Chimon, "did we get a prayer?"

"Looks that way," said Scion.

They sat on the roof, their swords resting on the shingles, their eyes scanning the sky. Below them, Sally Roe was lying down to sleep.

Perhaps now they would all have some peace for the night.

11

The Bergen Door Company was a noisy, dusty place employing about a hundred people, the only real industry to be found in Bacon's Corner. It was Friday morning, and during the regular work shift the planers, sanders, saws, and drills produced such a deafening din that ear protection was required and also a lot of lipreading.

Ben wore ear protection—little sponge-rubber earplugs—and also safety glasses as he walked through the factory. He'd never been here before, and found it a fascinating place, with the smell of sawdust filling the air, and doors, doors, doors everywhere, some stacked, some standing, some riding the forklift down to the loading dock; small doors, big doors, cheap doors, exquisite doors.

He was catching a few glances from the employees as he passed by. The sight of a uniformed police officer often roused curiosity, as if "something" was up. He just smiled cordially at the hefty women, the sawdusted men, the part-time students, the single mothers. He recognized many of them, including Donna Hemphile, busily supervising a big material sorting project. She recognized him and waved.

"Hey, Ben, what are you doing here?" she hollered.

"Oh, just a little business," he answered, probably not loud enough for her to hear him. He was hesitant to talk about it.

Up ahead, at the center of all the hubbub, was the enclosed office space of the floor supervisor, Abby Grayson. She spotted him through the office window and gave him a wave. The front office had already called ahead, and she was expecting him.

"Come in out of the racket," she said, throwing open the door.

He stepped inside the little cubicle and she closed the door after him, shutting out the noise.

"Have a seat," she said. "You must be that new cop. I don't think we've met before, and maybe that's a good thing, you know?"

They went through some friendly introductions. Abby was a homely but personable lady in her forties; she and her husband were real career people in this place. She'd just received her twenty year pin, and he his twenty-five.

"Well," she said, "we're all pretty shocked. Sally was a good worker. It's too bad she didn't open up a little more. We thought she might have some deep problems, but . . . Hey, we *tried* to be friends; what can I say?"

"I've heard from several people that she was reclusive," Ben said.

"Yeah, pretty much a hermit. We invited her to the last Christmas party, and I think she almost came, but then she found some excuse and stayed home. She didn't get out much as far as any of us could tell."

"You wouldn't have any photographs of her, would you?"

"Funny you should mention that. I guess she hated having her picture taken. We were all going to pose for a company picture . . . When was that? I think around Labor Day, and I remember she just kept hiding behind people and turning away. Ehh, some people are like that."

"So what kind of person was she really? What were some of your impressions?"

Abby took a moment to consider the question. "She was bright and intelligent, good with her hands, and caught on to the job right away, really easy to train. But there was always something a little strange about her." Abby smiled about a thought that came to her. "Well, I suppose I can say it now. You know . . . I think she was hiding something. A lot of us thought that."

"Hiding something?"

Abby shook her head and chuckled. "Oh, we came up with all kinds of silly notions, talking about her maybe being a fugitive from the law, or an ex-con, or a witch, or a hooker, or a lesbian . . . It was pretty silly, but when people are that secretive, that quiet, you wonder about them a little. It's only natural."

"Well?"

"Well what?"

"Was she any of those things to your knowledge?"

She laughed. "No. It was talk, nothing but talk."

"But still you think she was hiding something . . ."

"I don't know. She just acted like it, I guess."

Ben chuckled to keep the atmosphere relaxed. "Well . . . how about a description? What did she look like?"

"Oh . . ." Abby's eyes drifted about the room as she reconstructed an image of Sally Roe in her mind. "About my height, and I'm 5' 6". Red hair . . . long . . . I saw her brushing it out once; it went down to about the middle of her back. But she kept it bound up in a checkered scarf when she was working here, so you never saw much of it."

"Color of eyes?"

"Color of eyes . . . Boy, I never gave it much thought. Seems to me they were brown."

"How old was she?"

"Thirties. Maybe a little older."

"How about her weight?"

"Pretty good," and with that comment Abby laughed. "I don't know, she looked all right to me, enough to be jealous about, anyway."

Ben had heard enough for now. He stood up. "Well, thanks a lot. If I think of any more questions I'll give you a jingle. Oh . . ." He scribbled his phone number on a piece of paper. "If you come up with anything you think I'd want to know, just give me a call at home. It'll be fine."

"Sure thing." She stood and shook his hand. "Well, it was a real shock, just really tough news."

He nodded.

"And then that news this morning about the Christian school

and what that teacher was doing! What a world, huh? You just never know about people . . . It's kind of scary."

Ango was nothing significant, nothing to bow to, worship, revere, or dread. He was small, thin like a spider, and ugly. Oh, he knew it. He lived with it. He put up with the taunts of the other spirits who lorded it over him, ordered him this way and that way, took his glory, gave him their blame. Ah, it was all part of the warfare, all part of the master's plan for the earth, and each spirit had his own role, his own station, his own level of power. He knew his was a lowly station. To the rest of the demonic kingdom, what was the Bacon's Corner Elementary School? What did it matter among all the schools in the world?

His lips stretched open, and his jagged teeth clicked and gnashed as he hissed a giggle. Oh, this place *did* matter now! The other spirits had laughed and chided, but somewhere, seated loftily at the peak of power, the Strongman himself had chosen this place to begin the Plan. He had spoken the name of Ango as the spirit to be placed in charge! Now little ugly Ango had the Strongman's favor—and the other spirits' envy!

But why not? He deserved it. It took years to take control of this school—to oust the resisters, to implant the sympathizers, to blind the parents to what was happening to their children. It was no small task.

But it happened, and all because of Ango! Let the other spirits call him little and ugly. At this school he was *Ba-al* Ango, the beautiful and mighty. All the deceivers who flitted, darted, and hovered around that place were at his command, and through them many of the teachers, as well as the principal and the vice-principal. That was a precious power, a constant titillation, a marvelous reward for all those years and all that work. As he sat on his haunches on the expansive tar roof, he indulged himself in some hacking, sulfurous laughter.

He was thinking of all those young, impressionable children sitting in all those classrooms down there, and what they must be learning right now. As usual, most of his spirit underlings were occupied with that task. They were the best, and he reveled in the fact that for the past several years, ever since the laws had been changed, their job had been so much easier. Oh, how quickly men could accept the most outrageous of lies once the Truth was removed from consideration! Yes, there were still some bold saints of God lurking about like stubborn weeds in this otherwise flourishing garden, causing trouble with their protests, parent-teacher conferences, telephone babblings, and notes, notes, notes to the teachers, but . . .

Ango wheezed out another sulfurous laugh and rolled like a playful pup on the black tar. No matter. They were losing. Let them protest. *He* held all the power here.

Mota, strong, tall, and deep bronze, stood with his sword in his hand, his piercing eyes on the Bacon's Corner Elementary School, and his feet in about eight inches of chicken manure. His oriental friend and fellow-warrior Signa stood beside him, as deep into the same predicament. Were they not angelic spirits, it would have been most unpleasant. As it was, they were not disturbed by their surroundings, and the eight hundred cackling leghorns were not aware of their presence in this old chicken house.

It was Friday, and almost time for lunch and the noon recess.

"She's on her way," said Signa.

"Now," said Mota.

They were gone.

The bell rang for lunch. Ango could hear all the classroom doors opening and the mobs of children filling the halls. Recess would be an enjoyable time, just like always. What corruption the teachers could not spread in the classroom, the children could spread among themselves on the playground.

"Hail!" came a booming voice behind him.

"Aaaak!" Ango's sword was immediately in his hand as he spun to face the heavenly warrior. Oh, he was a big brute! A massive Polynesian, shining like lightning, with wings that scattered the fire of the sun. His sword was drawn, and it glimmered with a living light, but he held it downward, the tip resting on the roof.

"Forces!" Ango screamed, and fifty demons popped up through the roof like startled gophers with squawks and hoots of surprise and rage. They surrounded the big warrior.

"What brings you here?" Ango demanded.

But Mota wanted a little more space. He raised his sword, held it straight out at waist level, and began to sweep it in a wide circular arc around him. The seething, hissing spirits backed off when the tip of the sword passed under their chugging noses.

Now he was more comfortable, and spoke. "I'm looking for a petty little lizard called . . . Ankle . . . Inkle . . ."

"You seek Ango!"

Mota smiled and raised his index finger. "Yes! Ingo, that's it!"

"Ango!" the demon corrected.

Two guards were at their posts by the main door when Signa dropped out of the sky like a ball of lightning and knocked them both to the ground by his sheer presence.

"Forces!" they screamed, struggling to their feet, grabbing their swords. Twenty demons were immediately on hand, swords drawn, eyes gawking at this visitor.

One spirit shot out of the school in careless haste, not wanting to miss anything, his sword waving, his wings whirring. He got too close to the warrior.

Whoosh! The sword moved so fast it looked like a disk of light. Shredded particles of the spirit fluttered and floated in all directions, trailing red smoke and dissolving out of sight. The tip of the sword was now poised and ready for the next brazen attacker.

No one felt that brazen. They remained like statues, their eyes on this warrior. He remained motionless as well, watching them with his fiery eyes.

Sally Roe reached up and pulled the bell cord. The little bell at the front of the bus went *ding*, and the driver slowed for the next stop along the Toe Springs–Claytonville Road. She could see the Bacon's Corner Elementary School just ahead. She'd never been inside, but somehow she'd just have to find her way around without being seen by too many people. She'd done as much as she could to look unlike Sally Roe; she had her hair—black now—braided and pinned behind her head; she'd found some sunglasses that could pass for tinted eyewear, although they bothered her; she knew her old factory clothes would not be a good idea, so she'd managed to purchase a casual outfit—slacks, blouse, loafers. Apart from that, she could only hope that no one at this little school had ever seen her before or knew who she was.

The bus pulled to a stop, and she got off right in front of the school.

Mota still seemed unsure. "No . . . it cannot be Ango. I see no one here who fits what I have heard of him. I seek Ango the small, weak, and pitiful."

Ango could feel the stares of his subordinates. Of course they wanted to see what he would do. He raised his sword, and they all did the same. "The Ango you seek is mighty! He is Ba-al of this place!"

"Ba-al?" Mota asked. "A spirit with only half a heart, and less of a brain?"

"Gaaaa!!" Ango cried, raising his sword over his head. "*I am Ango!*"

He brought his sword down in a red, glowing blur. The huge sword of the warrior was there instantly and took the blow.

Mota was surprised. This little demon could strike hard, with much greater strength than Mota expected. He hid his concern, however, and only acted as if he finally realized whom he was addressing. "Ooohhhh . . ."

"Forces—" Ango screamed.

Mota thrust his sword right under Ango's nose. "Before you attack . . ." Ango swallowed the order. "I would like to state my business with you."

Signa had the attention of the guards in front of the school and at least half the demons from inside it.

"And now," he said, "we'd like to take a look inside this school."

The guards spit sulfur at him, and for a moment he was blinded. He raised his sword in defense and tried to clear his eyes, stumbling backwards out onto the school lawn. The guards followed him, pushing him back, waving their swords. The other spirits felt a new courage, and moved in closer, hissing, spitting, holding their swords high.

They were not watching the door.

Sally walked briskly up the front walk and through the door. The clock in the main hall said she was on time; it was 11:50, time for lunch break. Now to find Miss Brewer's classroom, Room 105. It was either to the left or the right, but first she'd have to pass by the school office. There was a receptionist standing behind the counter, and several office personnel working at desks behind her. *Well*, she thought, *if I just look like I know what I'm doing, maybe they won't ask to help me.*

She headed for the hall, walking by the reception counter, keeping her eyes ahead, not slowing her walk, not looking bewildered. *Come on, Sally, make it convincing.*

"Don't you move!" said the demon behind the counter. "Don't you come one step closer to me!"

Chimon and Scion had come in with Sally, and were now standing at the counter, their wings unfurled, totally blocking any view of the hallway. Their swords were drawn, but at their sides. They didn't speak, but just looked at this slimy creature yelling at them.

"How did you get in here?" the demon demanded. "Guards!"

Suddenly Scion's hot blade rested right between the demon's yellow fangs. He thought it best not to pronounce another word.

The receptionist looked at the clock. Hmm. Miss Brewer was expecting a visitor today; the receptionist thought she'd heard someone come in, but there was no one in the hall. *Well, the visitor must be a little late.*

Sally took a left turn down the hall, disappearing around the corner. It had to be a miracle that that lady behind the counter had not seen her. Oh well. Now to find Room 105.

Good! Here was Room 103, and now Room 104, and bingo! Room 105!

She stood in the open doorway and knocked on the jamb.

Miss Brewer, the young and pretty fourth grade teacher, rose from her desk with a welcoming smile and extended her hand. "Hello. You must be Mrs. Jenson!"

Sally took her hand and replied pleasantly, "And you are Miss Brewer."

"Please come in."

I can't believe I'm doing this, Sally thought. She immediately stopped thinking such things—it could ruin her act.

Miss Brewer motioned Sally to a chair beside her desk and then continued to the bookshelf behind it. "So how are things at the Association?"

Sally sat down and kept her eyes on Miss Brewer. "Well, just wonderful so far. I'm really glad to be working for them now."

"Well," said Miss Brewer, pulling a loose-leaf binder from the shelf, "we've certainly enjoyed this curriculum, and the kids really take to it. Most of our parents are very pleased."

She set the binder on the desk in front of Sally, and Sally smiled as she picked it up. On the cover were the words, "Sexual Understanding and Family Life, Fourth Grade." At the bottom was the name of the publisher, Freeman Education Associates. She began to leaf through it.

"Could I help you find what you're looking for?"

"Oh, don't take your lunchtime to help me. I have a whole list of revisions . . . Let's see, this is the newest edition, isn't it? All right, that should make it easier, not quite as much to doublecheck."

"Just what was the problem?"

Sally had her story well rehearsed. "Well, the quotes are accurate enough, but the sources didn't feel the attributions were clearly enough stated, so now I have to prepare a reply and . . . wouldn't you know it, I left my copy in the last town. Well, such are the hazards of being on the road."

"It must be exciting, though, servicing so many schools around the state. Has the curriculum been well received in other school districts?"

"For the most part, yes."

Miss Brewer paused to think, then chuckled, sitting on the edge of the desk. "Having trouble with the right-wing fundamentalists?"

Sally chuckled back and nodded. "That's one reason I have to review all the attributions, to make sure everybody's legally covered."

"Oh, what a world!"

Sally took a chance. "Speaking of fundamentalist problems, I understand Amber Brandon was in your class?"

Miss Brewer smiled with curiosity. "Now how did you know that?"

"Well, yours is the only fourth grade class, and the paper said that the child involved in the lawsuit was in the fourth grade, and I learned somewhere that the child was Amber, so . . ."

Amber's former teacher nodded sadly. "Isn't it awful? I'm glad they're taking this thing to court. We've just got to stop all this harassment and censorship. Enough is enough."

"Listen, don't let me keep you from lunch!"

Miss Brewer set out for the door. "Can I bring you anything?"

"Oh, no, don't worry about me. I won't be long anyway."

"Fine. Just take your time."

And with that, she was out the door and down the hall.

Sally waited just a moment, then closed the binder and placed it back on the shelf it came from. Then she looked among the other binders, books, and materials for the title she was after. The kids in the class had drawn pictures of strange faces, weird animals, gods, and bizarre cartoon characters, and the drawings were still displayed on the walls, along with several complex, mesmerizing pattern studies. The curriculum had to be here.

She found it.

Ango began to curse at Mota as his demon warriors became steadily braver. "Out! Begone, you! This is our territory, and none of your concern!"

Mota decided to push this demon a little. "Oh, is that what you think?"

He made a move toward the roof, ready to pass through it and invade their little operation.

"Attack!" Ango screamed, and every demon rushed forward, red blade flashing. "Away with him!"

Mota shot skyward, drawing a horde of spirits after him. He stopped, flipped, faced them. His sword became a continuous ribbon of light.

The first demon became two halves that passed by Mota on either side and then sank into oblivion. The second and third he swatted aside. He kicked and bowled down a cluster of eight. But they just kept coming, faster and faster, swinging and slashing with more and more strength. Mota had planned on putting on an act to keep them following him, but suddenly he found he was no longer acting. This fight was real.

The next wave of spirits surged upward. He backed away, his wings reaching higher and higher. He couldn't let this end too soon, but he was beginning to wish he could.

To the west he saw Signa involved in a similar skirmish, taking some real attacks, whipping his sword about and drawing the guards away from the school. He was backing away, about to be surrounded.

Chimon and Scion could hear the commotion all around the outside of the school. The demons sounded rather jubilant.

"YAAA!!" Suddenly four huge demonic thugs exploded through the walls on every side, their teeth bared, their talons ready to tear.

Chimon and Scion shot through the roof of the school like two rockets, retreating, totally surprised, and angry about it.

"Where did they come from?" Chimon hollered.

Scion was too busy defending himself against their swords and sharp teeth to answer. It was like being chased up a huge tree by a foaming pack of rabid dogs.

They backed away, higher and higher, trying to stay clear of those whistling red blades. What horrible situation had they walked into?

Sally's hands were shaking and she was afraid to open the three-ring binder now in her lap. The title sounded harmless enough: *Finding the Real Me—Self-Esteem and Personal Fulfillment Studies for Fourth-Graders.*

She flipped the cover open and quickly perused the title page. She didn't recognize the author's name, but the name of the publisher immediately turned her stomach: The Omega Center for Educational Studies. With great effort, she turned several more pages, skimming the contents. She found a particular index tab and skipped far forward to a later chapter.

Her heart was pounding as if she'd sprinted up a hill, and her hands were getting slick with sweat. They were shaking.

The old torments! Her mind was beginning to race again. She could hear the voices calling, mocking, cursing. There were spirits in the room!

She had to get out of there.

She carried the binder to the shelf and tried to put it back. A large atlas fell over, blocking the slot. She almost whimpered out loud as her fingers dug after the fallen atlas, trying to get a grip on it. She lifted it, it slipped out of her fingers, she lifted it again, tried to hold it in place while she jammed the binder in. The binder got hung up on a bulging manila envelope and wouldn't go in; she pressed the envelope aside with her palm.

The binder slipped back into place. As soon as her fingers let go of it, her nausea began to ease.

I've got to get out of here. Right now!

She dashed for the hallway and then ran down to the north entrance, pushing her way outside as if running from a fire.

Above and all around the school, the demons were just returning from a glorious rout. They had chased those pesky warriors of Heaven away at last, and now the territory of the glorious Ango was safe again.

Far above the school, a safe distance away, Mota, Signa, Chimon, and Scion gathered to update each other.

"What happened down there?" Chimon wondered.

"Ango and his imps were never this strong!" said Signa, still rubbing the burning sulfur out of his eyes.

Scion was checking a good-sized cut in his leg as he said, "We were all playing the fool to go into that thinking only of a diversion. They meant business!"

Far below, looking as small as an insect on the vast green terrain, Sally was running back to the Toe Springs–Claytonville Road. She would probably run to the next bus stop instead of waiting in front of the school where she might be seen. At least five taunting, torturing spirits were following her, buzzing about her head like angry hornets.

"They'll follow her to her next destination," said Signa.

"When they're clear of this place we'll take them out," said Mota. "We can't fight them here."

"Cree and Si are already at Omega. They have no idea what's in store for them!"

They all knew the problem without anyone having to say it. Mota finally did. "The prayer cover. We're losing it!"

Tom Harris pushed his grocery cart up and down the aisles of the PriceWise grocery, making his weekly rounds. He was having a little trouble with his shopping list; with Ruth and Josiah gone, he wasn't sure what items he should restock and which he should just skip for now. He crossed off the breakfast cereal—there was still plenty of that. The milk in the refrigerator was going sour. He decided he would pour it down the sink and just buy a quart today instead of the usual two half-gallons.

"Hey, Mr. Harris!"

Oh! It was Jody Jessup, the little fifth-grader. It was strange seeing her here in the store during a school day, but then, Tom wasn't usually in the store during the school day either. In any case, he was happy to see her bright smile again.

"Hi, Jody! How're you doing?"

She came running down the aisle past the cornflakes and oatmeal, her long brown hair flying. "I'm with my mom. I get to help her buy groceries."

She pressed against his side, and he gave her a little hug around the shoulders. "Well, it's great to see you."

"It feels funny not being in school anymore."

Tom agreed. "Yes, it sure does."

Then came an alarmed voice from down the aisle. "Jody! Come here!"

It was Andrea Jessup, Jody's mother, pushing her shopping cart with Jody's younger brother Brian by her side. Tom was shocked and incredulous at the coldness in her eyes.

He waved. "Hi, Andrea. Good to see you. Hi, Brian!"

Andrea ignored him. "Jody! Come here right now! I don't want you talking to Mr. Harris!" Jody hurried back to her mother. Andrea bent and barked the order directly into Jody's face. "You stay with me now, and don't talk to strangers!"

Jody started to object, "But that's Mr. Harris!"

"Don't argue with me!"

And then they were gone around the corner; Tom could hear their conversation moving down the next aisle.

"You stay away from that man," she was saying. "Don't you go anywhere near him! And that goes for you too, Brian!"

Brian started asking questions, but Andrea hushed both her children and continued down the aisle.

Tom's life came to a halt, right there next to the breakfast cereal. The Jessups used to be such good friends, and so supportive. He'd shared dinner with them on several occasions, he'd played with their kids, they'd gone together on field trips with the whole school. Jody and Brian were—used to be—two of his best students.

No more. Everything had changed. Tom tried to think of a good reason, but couldn't. He tried to think of what he had to buy next, but he couldn't think of that either.

Lord, he finally prayed silently, *I haven't done anything! Why did Andrea treat me like that?*

Then he began to wonder how many more of his own brothers and sisters in the Lord felt the same way about him.

Andrea kept pushing her cart along, grabbing pickles and relish off the shelf with hardly a glance, and moving on. She wanted to get out of the store before she saw that man again, before her children saw him again. She'd never been so upset at anyone in her life. The nerve of that man!

A small spirit, Strife, followed Andrea. He had nervous, agitated wings that never stopped quivering and a blaring mouth that more than made up for his size. He ran along the tops of the jars and boxes, hurdling the Saltine crackers and leaping over the paper towels.

He lied to you all along! he shouted to her. *And you know, Pastor Mark is lying too, trying to protect him! You don't know half of what went on in that school!*

On the other side of the aisle, rushing through the flour and sugar and somersaulting over the cooking oil, Gossip filled in all of Strife's pauses. *Sexual! He has problems with sex! It has to be sexual! You'd better ask around and see if anyone knows anything! You just never know about these people! Talk to Judy Waring! She might know!*

Andrea got more enraged, the more she thought about this

whole Christian school scandal. *That Tom Harris needs prayer*, she thought.

But she hadn't done much praying.

Mulligan's ears were so red they almost glowed.

"Cole! You are just that far from being canned!"

Mulligan towered over Ben's desk like a rotting tree about to fall, and Ben felt he should stand up to keep from being crushed, except that Mulligan might interpret that move as aggressive.

Mulligan pointed his finger—it seemed a bit red too—right in Ben's face. "Were you out at the Potter place the other day?"

"Wednesday afternoon, sir," Ben replied, noting that he'd called Harold "sir." *Wow, I must be scared.*

"And just who ordered you to go out there?"

"The visit was voluntary, sir. I had a little free time, so I—"

"So you thought you'd snoop around without authorization, isn't that right?"

Ben drew a breath and then released it slowly before he said another word. He had to be careful now because he was upset. "I was not aware, sir, that the Potter residence was off-limits to a law officer, especially when his presence there was with the full invitation and welcome of Mrs. Potter herself."

"So how about that little visit out to the door factory? What about that?"

"They were glad enough to have me there."

"And I say you misused your badge!"

Now Ben did stand up, tall and straight. "You might be interested in what I've found out, Sergeant Mulligan, *sir*."

"If it's about Sally Roe, forget it! That case is closed because I said so!"

"The descriptions of Sally Roe that I got from Mrs. Potter and from Abby Grayson at the Bergen Door Company were consistent. Sally Roe was in her mid- to late-thirties, about five six, with long red hair."

"What of it?"

"The woman we found in the goat shed was younger, and had black hair, probably shoulder-length, but no longer."

Mulligan smiled a smile of pity. He put his big hand on Ben's shoulder and spoke condescendingly. "Cole . . . come on. It was dark in there. You only saw the body for a second. I don't know what's gotten into you."

"Harold . . . why was the house ransacked? Did you authorize that?"

"Sure I did. We were looking for evidence."

"Evidence of what? You said it was a suicide."

"Standard procedure. Isn't your shift about over?"

"I do have a message for you from Mrs. Potter. She'd like to have that mess cleaned up by whoever it was that made it."

"That's taken care of . . . Don't worry your little head about it."

"And whatever happened to Sally Roe's pickup?"

Mulligan looked at him just a little funny. "What pickup?"

"Sally Roe always drove a '65 blue Chevy pickup. I let Mrs. Potter go through our vehicle ID book yesterday, and she pointed out the make and model to me. The truck's nowhere around the property. Roe had to have driven it home from work the evening she allegedly killed herself. I was wondering if the same people who ransacked the house may have made off with her truck."

Mulligan looked a little worried. "I don't know anything about that."

"And since we're on the subject, I'm still wondering about that bloodstained shirt we found. Did the coroner ever check the blood type? That scene was full of signs of violence. And the body . . . That woman didn't hang herself!"

Mulligan turned his back on Ben, stomped into his office, and returned with some papers in his hand. He slapped them on Ben's desk. "There! The county coroner's report on the death of Sally Roe! Read it for yourself! Death by asphyxiation from hanging. Not murder, not a struggle, not anything! Now if you disagree with the coroner, why don't you come up with another body for him to examine?"

"There might be one."

Mulligan actually grabbed Ben's shirt in his fist. His eyes were wild, and he hissed the words through jaws locked shut in anger. "Stop right there! Not another word!" Ben said nothing, but he didn't back down either. Mulligan didn't like that at all. "Your shift is over for today, Officer Cole, and if I hear one more word about this from you, your *job* is going to be over, you got that?"

Mulligan let go of Ben's uniform with a feisty little shove. Ben did what he could to straighten out the wrinkles. "I'll be watching you, boy, I mean really watching you. You drop this Sally Roe thing, you hear? One more false step from you, and I'm going to have myself some real joy ripping that badge right off your chest!"

12

Well, those guys mean business, I guess.

Wayne Corrigan sat at his desk after-hours, drinking one last cup of coffee from his thermos and looking through several pages of notes Mark Howard, Tom Harris, and the church board had compiled in answer to the temporary injunction against the school.

All the usual arguments for corporal punishment were clearly laid out—the Scriptures from Proverbs about the rod, of course, and a definitive procedure for spanking clearly outlined in the *Student-Parent Handbook.* Lucy Brandon's signature on the enrollment agreement constituted her agreement with the handbook, so that wasn't going to be hard to argue. It was obvious the church board had done their homework many times over in this area.

As for their argument against any restraint from "further religious behavior which could prove harmful to the mental, emotional, or social welfare of the child, or any excessive religious instruction that could prove harmful," they did a pretty good study on that, with Scripture after Scripture declaring the existence, purpose, behavior, and "casting out" of demons, as well as a general apologetic for the basic gospel message. This was definitely a matter of religious belief, supposedly protected by the Constitution, sure . . .

But an exorcism perpetrated upon a ten-year-old child? A minor, with no parental consent? Where was that provided for in the handbook? When did Mrs. Brandon agree to that kind of treatment for her daughter?

He stopped cold. This case was too big and the stakes were too high. It was more than he could handle.

Yeah. Those ACFA guys found just what they were looking for; the way they would handle the case, the Constitution would be just so much toilet paper when children were involved.

Well, Corrigan, you did it again: you said yes too easily. Now the hearing's in twelve days. Better do something.

"Lord God," he prayed, "I'm in over my head again. I need Your help to bail me out . . . to bail *all of us* out."

He started scribbling out a brief for the court, trying to cover the items in the complaint. Misuse of federal funds was easy to refute, and Discrimination and Harassment were basically a walk in the park, but then came the tricky stuff, and he began to pray in earnest as he wrote every line.

On Monday morning, a week after Ruth and Josiah were first hauled from his home, Tom got a call from an unidentified lady at the Child Protection Department. Without consulting him, and with no prior notice other than this call, an appointment had been set for him to visit with his children for one hour under the supervision of a child welfare counselor. The appointment was for 11 that morning, at the courthouse in Claytonville.

He barely made it in time, pulling into a visitor parking slot at the courthouse at 10:52. He doublechecked his appearance in the visor mirror, straightening his tie, smoothing down his hair, his hands trembling and his stomach queasy from the anticipation. He grabbed a brown bag of things for the kids, locked up the car, and bounded up the concrete steps of the old stone building.

The inside hall was cold marble, tall, gray, and imposing. Every footstep echoed like a public announcement, and he felt naked in this place. Lawyers, clerks, and other just-plain folks passed him on every side, and he found it hard to look them in the eye. What if they had seen his face in the paper or on television? They probably wouldn't want his autograph.

The girl at the information desk took his name and offered him a seat on a hard wooden bench against the wall.

"I'll let them know you're here," she said.

He sat there and slowly scratched his chin, looking down at the marble floor. He felt angry, but he knew he couldn't let it show, he couldn't let it come out, or he'd only make things worse.

He prayed repeatedly, *O Lord, what can I do? I don't even know what to say . . .*

He naturally thought of Cindy, now gone for three years. Difficult times such as this reminded him of how much he always needed her, and how much he had lost. He'd recovered from the initial grief, yes, but sometimes, when life was at its darkest and the struggle was the most uphill, out of habit he would reach for her, think of her, rehearse the words to share his pain. But then would come that same, persistent reminder, the realization that she was gone, replaced by a closely following shadow of sorrow.

Cindy, he thought, *you just wouldn't believe what's happening down here. I guess it's the persecution Jesus and the apostles warned us about. I guess it always seemed like something far away, maybe in Soviet Russia, or during Roman times, but not here, not now. I never thought it would actually happen to me, and I sure didn't think it would happen to the kids.*

He pulled his handkerchief from his pocket to wipe his tears away. He couldn't let the kids see him like this—and what would the state people think?

"Mr. Harris?"

He sucked in a breath and immediately, even desperately, tried to compose himself. *Tom, whatever you do, be cordial! Don't give her anything to use against you!*

He was looking up at none other than Irene Bledsoe.

"I'm sure you remember me?" she said, sitting near him on the bench.

"Yes." He figured that would be safe.

"Before I take you upstairs to see your children, I need to remind you that this visitation is a privilege that can be revoked at any time. We expect you to remain on your best behavior and to comply with my instructions at all times. You are not to touch your children, but remain on your own side of the conference table. You cannot ask them anything about where they are staying. Any other questions that I may deem inappropriate will be disallowed, and the meeting can be terminated at any time if I find it necessary. Is all that clear to you?"

"But . . . Mrs. Bledsoe, are we going to have a chance to talk this thing out? I want to get this whole mess cleared up and get my children back home with me where they belong."

"That won't be possible at this time; our investigation is still in progress."

"What investigation? I haven't heard a thing from anyone, and I haven't even been able to get through to you."

"We have a very heavy caseload, Mr. Harris. You'll just have to be patient."

Tom felt an anger, even a hunger for revenge rising inside him, something totally un-Christian, he knew, but it was irrepressible. He just couldn't think of any words that would be civil.

Irene Bledsoe asked him again, more firmly, "Is all that I have said clear to you?"

All he could do was give her the right answer. "Yes."

"What is this package?"

Tom opened it for her to see. "I brought some things for the kids. They don't have their Bibles, so I brought them, and some pens and stationery."

"Fine." She took the bag. "Come with me."

She took off at a hurried, efficient pace, the *pock, pock, pock* of her heels telling everyone on the floor she was passing by. Tom just tried to step quietly; this kind of attention he didn't need.

She led him up the winding marble staircase to the second floor, along the balcony overlooking the front entry, and through a heavy, uninviting door with big brass hinges and a knob that had to weigh twenty pounds. They passed through a cold and bare antechamber with one tall window letting in grayish light. A security guard stood by an archway to the right, looking just a little bored, but manning his post. Tom followed Mrs. Bledsoe past the guard and through the archway.

Tom's heart leaped into his throat, and tears flooded his eyes.

There, seated on the other side of a large table, were Ruth and Josiah. They were on their feet in an instant at the sight of him, crying "Daddy," their voices shrill with excitement. They ran for him.

Irene Bledsoe stood in their way and blocked them with her arms. "Sit down! Sit down at the table!"

"I want to see my dad!" Josiah cried.

"Daddy!" was all Ruth could say, her hands outstretched.

He couldn't take them in his arms. He couldn't touch them. All he could do was cry. "Sit down now. Do like Mrs. Bledsoe says."

Ruth began sobbing, almost wailing. "Daddy . . ."

"I love you, Ruth! Daddy loves you. Go ahead. Sit down. Everything's going to be all right."

Irene Bledsoe encouraged the children to sit down with a firm hand on their arms.

"Mr. Harris, you may sit in this chair facing your children. Let me remind you of what we discussed downstairs."

We didn't "discuss" anything, Tom thought. *You gave the orders, I sat there and listened.*

He slowly slid the chair out and sat down. He couldn't waste this time crying. He tried to sober up, and pulled out his handkerchief to wipe his eyes again.

"How are you two?"

"I wanna go home, Daddy," said Ruth, still sobbing.

Josiah was trying to be brave, and wiped his eyes like his father. "We miss you."

"Is Mrs. Bledsoe taking good care of you?"

Mrs. Bledsoe answered that one. "Your children are in very good hands, Mr. Harris, and I think that should be the last of that sort of question."

Tom glared at her. He couldn't hide his anger. "Then I'd like to ask you some questions afterward."

She smiled pleasantly in the children's presence. "We can discuss that later."

Tom noticed the bump on Ruth's head the moment he saw her. Now he was ready to ask about it. "What happened to your head, Ruth?"

Bledsoe cut right in on that question, even rising a little from her chair. "We can't discuss that! I'm sure you understand!"

"I bumped it in the car," said Ruth.

"Ruth! Don't you talk about that or I'll take you away!"

She started crying in anger now. "How come?"

"It's all right, Ruth," said Tom. "We don't have to talk about it." He turned to Josiah. "So . . . uh . . . what have you guys been doing?"

Josiah was unhappy and made no attempt to hide it. "Nothing. We sit around and watch TV."

Tom was unhappy to hear that, but he didn't show it. "Oh, does Mrs. Bledsoe let you watch TV?"

"No, Mrs. Henley does . . ."

Irene Bledsoe was right on top of that. "Josiah, we can't talk about who our foster parents are. That's a secret."

Tom tried to get the conversation back into safe territory. "So . . . how about reading? Have you read any good books?"

"No," said Ruth.

"They have some video games," Josiah volunteered. "Those are kind of fun."

"So . . . are there other kids around to play with?" Tom cringed even as he asked the question, but Irene Bledsoe let that one go.

"Yes. There's a boy named Teddy and another boy named Luke. But I don't like them."

"Oh . . ."

"They're bigger, and they pick on us."

"They pick on you?"

"Yeah, they push us around and use bad language. They're not Christians."

Ruth stuck her lower lip out and said, "Luke calls me names."

"Oh, Ruth, that's too bad. Have you tried to be friends?"

She looked at him, and her eyes flooded with tears again. "I want to go home!"

"I want you to come home too."

Tick, tick, tick. Irene Bledsoe was tapping the table with her fingernail and glaring at Tom.

Josiah must have caught that signal. He was a sharp little nine-year-old. "Ruth bumped her head on the side of the car."

"Now that's enough!" said Mrs. Bledsoe.

Tom looked at Irene Bledsoe and tried to keep his face calm. "What car, Mrs. Bledsoe?"

Mrs. Bledsoe looked at him with her eyebrows raised and her head tilted forward, so condescendingly. "Mr. Harris, we've found that children will usually concoct stories to protect their parents."

Tom caught her meaning. He had to choose—seriously, *strenuously* choose—to stay calm and cordial. "And just what story did both Ruth and Josiah concoct, Mrs. Bledsoe?"

She raised her chin and appeared to look down at him. "Mr. Harris, I can understand how you would be concerned about the injury to Ruth's head. But you should know, so are we. I'm sure that, given time to get over their fears and prior conditioning, your children will be ready to tell us the truth. For now, I think this visit is concluded." She rose from her chair. "Children, say good-bye to your father."

"We just got here!" said Josiah.

"I don't wanna go!" Ruth wailed, her face filling with fear.

"Children, we are going!" said Mrs. Bledsoe.

"Just one moment!" said Tom. The meeting was shot anyway. He dove for the opportunity. "Josiah, go ahead. Tell me how Ruth got that bump on her head."

"We almost got in a wreck . . ."

"John!" Mrs. Bledsoe yelled.

The security guard walked into the room and just let his presence be known. Tom didn't want any trouble; he made no moves.

Bledsoe grabbed both children by the arms. "Mr. Harris, I warned you to control yourself, and you can be sure that your behavior will go down in my report!"

"Which part didn't you like? When I bit the chair leg or when I broke out all the windows?"

She started hauling both kids toward the door. Tom was on his feet, ready to do something. The guard stood in his way—just like Mulligan had stood in his way a week ago. It was happening all over again, right before Tom's eyes. Mrs. Bledsoe was pulling Ruth and Josiah by their arms, taking them away screaming. She reached the archway. He wanted to stand in her way; he wanted to reach out and stop her.

He couldn't. All he could do was watch it happen.

"What wreck, Josiah?" he asked.

"Children, come on!" Bledsoe shouted, pulling them into the antechamber.

"I hit my head," Ruth repeated. "She stopped too fast and I hit my head."

Josiah went for broke. "She went through a stop sign and almost hit a blue pickup truck! Ruth hit her head on the door of the car!"

"She? You mean Mrs. Bledsoe?"

Irene Bledsoe had Ruth through the door and jerked Josiah through before he could complete an answer. But he was nodding a firm yes as he disappeared.

"Kids, I'm proud of you! Real proud of you! I love you!"

They were gone.

"Give 'em a few minutes," said the guard, not letting Tom follow.

Tom sat at the table again. The guard went to the door to make sure Mrs. Bledsoe was in the clear.

Tom noticed the brown paper bag on the floor. Irene Bledsoe

had left the package behind, and the kids had not gotten their Bibles or stationery. He couldn't touch them in this way either.

"Okay," said the guard, "you can go now."

His job completed, the guard went out the door and on to other business, leaving Tom alone in the cold, vacant room.

"O Lord . . ."

Tom broke. The tears ran down his face.

But they weren't entirely tears of grief, and they certainly were not tears of despair. He'd seen his kids, and they had shared something, despite Irene Bledsoe, despite the guard. He knew that their souls had touched, that their hearts were still together. It was not enough, of course, to see them for just those few minutes. Such a cold and regimented visit could never be enough. But for right now, it was enough to know they loved him. They loved their daddy. They wanted to be with him.

Now his doubts were gone. Amid all the pain and challenge, the smearing, the soiling of his name, he'd found himself wondering where he really stood. There were voices in his mind telling him horrible things he'd never thought about himself. He tried not to give place to such lies; but still, because the voices were so relentless, he'd wondered if there was something wrong with him, something he'd been blind to. Maybe, the voices would say, he deserved what was happening to him.

But now he knew. He still had his integrity, and before God he still had the hearts of his children. Right now, it was just so wonderful to know that for sure.

Ben and Leonard quickly ducked into Don's Wayside, trying to look casual, even though they were in full uniform, carried their nightsticks, wore their guns, and had their portable radios on their belts, hissing and squawking. Every eye in the place was instantly drawn in their direction.

It was a bust! It was something for everyone to watch and then talk about at home. The contractors sitting at the counter and the truckers sitting at the tables looked up from their lunch and wagged their stubbly jaws only enough to finish the last bite of soup and sandwich. Some kept talking only to look natural, but they were watching, all right.

The name was muttered around the room by several, and rose above the general hubbub: "Krantz. Yeah, the Krantz boy. He's still at it."

At the end of the counter, Kyle Krantz sat under the watchful eye of bald and chubby Don Murphy, the proprietor, and two blue-jeaned farmer's sons who were well-built for hay-bucking, steer handling, and cornering shoplifters.

"Hey, Kyle," said Ben. "What are you up to now?"

"Caught him dipping into the cash register," said Don. "Then he took off for the door trying to get away. Bub and Jack were just coming in and held him until you could get here."

"How much did he take?" asked Leonard.

"Eighty-five dollars," said Don, indicating a wad of bills on the counter.

Leonard gave Kyle a careful visual scrutiny. The boy was only fifteen, skinny as a rail, with shaggy, unkempt black hair and pimples. His face was dull and expressionless, and his eyes were red and watery.

"You know, son," said Leonard, "I think I have cause to believe you might be carrying something illegal. I'd like you to empty your pockets for me."

Kyle hesitated.

"You heard the man," said big Jack, tilting his hat forward to emphasize his lean toward the boy.

"We can help you if you're unable," said Bub.

Kyle began emptying his pockets. First he set some change on the counter, then some cigarette papers.

"Jacket pockets," directed Leonard.

Kyle hesitated, then wilted in surrender, dug into his jacket pocket, and produced a plastic bag full of ground green leaves.

The front door opened.

"Ehh . . ." said Don, sorry to have to miss the rest of this. "Customer."

Ben glanced at the man who had come in. He was middle-aged, handsome, well-dressed. Ben recognized him: Joey Parnell, the county coroner.

Leonard was handling the Krantz boy okay. Ben said softly, "Hey, uh . . . you've got it under control; maybe I'll have a word with Parnell over there . . ."

Leonard shrugged. "Go for it."

Ben walked to the other end of the counter where Parnell had taken a stool and was perusing the simple menu.

"Excuse me," said Ben. "Joey Parnell?"

Parnell looked up and smiled. "Yes."

Ben introduced himself. "Can I join you for just a minute?"

Parnell was agreeable. Ben took the stool next to him and tried to think of where to start.

"Just off the record, unofficially . . ." he began, and felt a little sheepish even saying that. "I wanted to ask you what your findings were in that Sally Roe suicide case."

Parnell looked at the menu again, a clear signal that he wasn't interested in talking about it. "I handle a lot of cases, Officer Cole. Just what is it you want to know?"

"Well . . . now I know this may sound a little strange, but . . . were you able to make a positive identification of the body?"

Parnell looked at Ben as if he were joking. "Well, I should hope so. I wouldn't be a very good coroner if I couldn't even determine whose remains I was examining."

Ben knew he was looking foolish, but he tried to press on. "Well, what about that plaid shirt with the blood on it? Did you get that?"

Parnell didn't answer right away. He seemed to be having trouble remembering. "Uh . . . yeah, I think I got that."

"Did the blood types match?"

"What do you mean, did the blood types match?"

"Well, did the blood on the shirt match the blood of the deceased?"

Parnell broke into a grin and eyed the menu again. "Well, I don't know. I guess I never checked that. Why should I?"

"Was there a wound on the deceased that could explain where the blood on the shirt came from?"

"I . . . I don't remember that there was."

"And what was the cause of death? I think you said asphyxiation by hanging in your report?"

"Mm. That's right. I do remember that."

"I was there on the scene, Mr. Parnell, and what I saw indicated a violent death, not at all what you would expect in a suicide. Also . . . the body wasn't hanging. It was thrown violently to the floor, and there was no rope around the neck."

Parnell just looked at him, listening, without comment.

Ben pressed some more. "Could you tell me . . . just so I know for sure . . . a description of the deceased?"

Don came down the counter, and Parnell ordered a beef sandwich and some soup. Parnell took his time, and seemed to enjoy not having to talk to this young, inquisitive cop.

Ben waited politely. Finally Parnell turned to him and with a wry smile said, "No, Officer Cole, I couldn't."

That didn't sound right to Ben. "That's . . . privileged information?"

"That's right."

"Well, what about the color of the hair? I recall seeing a woman with black hair, in her twenties, medium height . . ."

"How about asking me something else?"

Ben stopped, considered, and then asked something else. "According to what I've seen around the station, and then at the

Potters' rental, something's missing, perhaps something that belonged to the dead woman. Would you have any idea what everyone is looking for?"

Parnell was clearly getting impatient. "Now that question I don't understand at all."

"Well, Sergeant Mulligan sent someone to the house to search it, and I know he was asking you about something—"

"No comment, sir!" Parnell was visibly upset.

Ben figured he'd better retreat from that line of questions. But now what? "Uh . . . well, just one more question."

Parnell was emphatic. "One more."

"Is it still possible to see the body?"

Parnell chuckled at that. "Afraid not. It's been cremated. Now, is that going to do it for you?"

Ben smiled. "Sure. Thanks a lot, Mr. Parnell. Sorry to bother you."

"All right."

Parnell unfolded a copy of the *Hampton County Star* and gave it his full attention. Ben joined Leonard, who now had Kyle Krantz in custody, and they went out to the squad car.

13

Sally Roe was far from Bacon's Corner, sitting on a hard bench in a bus depot in another town, looking the part of a wayward, hitchhiking vagabond, dressed in her old jeans and blue jacket, her dyed hair braided and tucked under a wool cap, her nicer clothes hidden in a large duffel bag on the bench beside her. She was oblivious to the passing travelers and their whining children, the used sections of newspapers strewn on the benches, the gum wrappers on the linoleum floor, and the occasional squawking announcements of departures and arrivals over the public address. Her bus would be leaving in one hour. She would spend that hour writing in the spiral notebook in her lap. It would be a letter, her first, to Tom Harris.

> *Dear Mr. Harris,*

She stopped. *How do I start this? He doesn't even know me. Guess I could say that.*

> *I don't know how to start this letter; after all, you don't even know who I am. But let me introduce and*

explain myself, not just in this letter, but I hope in many more to follow. Perhaps by the time I have written my last letter to you, everything will be clear to both of us.

My name is Sally Roe, formerly a planer-sander at the Bergen Door Company. You may have read the recent news story about my death by suicide. I assure you, I am the Sally Roe the news story talked about, and obviously, I am alive.

Let me tell you what really happened . . .

Sally could see it all happening again, even as she searched for the words to recount it.

The day had been perfectly normal and downright boring. Working at the factory always was a bore, especially working in the sanding department, operating power sanders that hummed, whirred, and vibrated until it seemed they would make a milkshake out of your brains. After a full day and a quota of twenty-five doors, she finally drove the old blue pickup down the gravel driveway to her house. She was tired, tasting sawdust, and had no other plans than to shower, grab dinner, and go to bed.

But then there were the goats, Betty the doe and her two kids, Buff and Bart. Pets, mostly. Sally inherited a buck and a doe from a lady at the factory who couldn't afford to keep them. Sally sold the buck, kept the doe, had her bred, and now had the mother and two babies who were the cutest in the world and good company, always glad to see her come home.

Sally parked the truck and headed for their pen. She would greet them first, give them some feed, have her usual one-sided conversation with them about her day, and then go inside and collapse.

The goats were excited, but not with happiness. They were glad and eager to see her again, but mostly because something was disturbing them.

"Hey . . . settle down there . . . Momma's home . . ."

She dug a pail of rolled ration from the feed bin beside the house and stepped through the gate into the goats' pen. Betty circled her, happy but upset. The kids just kept bleating and bounding back and forth along the fence.

Sally shook the pail to get their attention. "Come on, get some treats!"

She went to the shed, hoping they would just follow her and calm down. The neighbors' dog must have been around. He often got a real kick out of terrorizing her goats.

She stepped into the shed. "Come on now, it's all right—"

Shock! A rope came over her head from behind and began crushing her windpipe before she even knew what it was! The pail of feed fell and spilled on the ground. With incredible strength, an unseen assailant heaved on the loop of rope, jerking her body backward, lifting her feet off the ground. She kicked, she grabbed at the rope. No air.

Her feet found the wall, and she pushed. She and her attacker fell back against the feeder, and it cracked. The rope went slack and she wriggled free, dropping to the floor, rolling in the straw, pulling in air.

A woman in black, eyes wild with hate, a knife! The killer pounced like a leopard, Sally ducked to one side, the knife caught Sally in the shoulder with searing pain.

Sally tried to wriggle out of the corner in which she was trapped, kicking and clawing the straw and dust. The woman's knee came down on her chest and held her there. The rope fell across her neck again. Sally kicked the woman with one free leg.

WUMP! Just that fast, like a rag doll, the woman crashed against the opposite wall of the shed, her head and limbs slapping against the boards, as if a giant had grabbed her and thrown her there. Sally had hardly made contact with her kick and felt some amazement, but at least the woman was off her. She scrambled out of the corner, her eyes on her assailant. The assassin slid down the wall to her feet and stumbled forward, her eyes blank and wandering, her jaw hanging.

OOF!! Something struck the woman with such force, it lifted her off her feet. She flopped into the straw, her arms limp and flailing, her head crooked, her body lifeless, the rope still in her hand.

> *I didn't take any time to look. I just got out of there, still trying to breathe, totally occupied with just staying alive. I remember getting through the gate and then falling to the ground and retching. I can't blame Betty and the kids for running away. Maybe it was a good thing they did.*

Sally leaned back from her writing and absentmindedly tapped the pen on the notebook, just thinking. It was a pretty bizarre way to open a letter. Maybe if she just kept writing, she would seem more credible as her story progressed. Well, all she could do was try.

> *What can I say, Tom? How can I qualify myself as a reliable witness? If you were to ask me who I am, I would have to reply that I don't know. For years I have asked myself the same question and now I wonder if, in the writing of these letters, I might be reaching out for an answer.*
> *You see, Tom, I want to help you. In my own way, and drawing from my own experience, I can relate to your situa-*

tion and I know how you must feel. As one lost entity with-out source and without destination in a universe that is ulti-mately meaningless, I can't tell you where my concept of "wrong" ever came from. Call it sentiment, call it "the way I was raised," figure I'm just taking a desperate stab at meaning through antiquated morality, I still feel it—what is happening to you is wrong, and I'm sorry for your pain.

She looked up at the big clock above the depot door. Her bus was scheduled to leave in half an hour. Soon the public address would be squawking out the announcement.

If you would indulge me, I would like to at least act as if something matters. I would like to do one "right" thing. I might be concocting my own concept of "good deeds" in an effort to run from despair, to convince myself that life isn't futile after all, but I have nothing to lose. If despair is the final truth we all face, then let me hide from it, just this once. If hope is a mere fiction of our own making, then let me live in a fantasy. Who knows? Maybe there will be some meaning in it somewhere, some purpose, some reward.

At any rate, I'm going to retrace some old steps and find some things out, for your sake and for mine. I hope to share some useful information with you before long—infor-mation sufficient to get you out of trouble and, most of all, bring your children back to you.

Please keep this letter, even if it sounds strange to you, even if you don't believe it. I'll write again soon.

I remain sincerely yours,

Sally signed her full name, "Sally Beth Roe," carefully took the pages from the spiral notebook, and folded them. She had a box of envelopes in her travel bag. While in Bacon's Corner, she'd looked up Tom Harris's home address and written it in the front of her notebook. She now copied that address onto the envelope and stuffed the letter inside. She didn't seal it yet, but rose from the bench and walked over to the small depot cafeteria to get some dimes. If she hurried, she could get this letter mailed before she left for the next town.

Chimon and Scion walked beside her, wings unfurled, swords drawn. For now, the demons were hiding.

Chimon looked down at the letter in Sally's hand. "'The word of her testimony,'" he said.

"That's one," said Scion.

Terga, Prince of Bacon's Corner, was glad for some good news, and was ready to share a rare smile with Ango, the little Prince of the Bacon's Corner Elementary School.

"Chased them away, eh?" said Terga, strutting up and down the school's tar roof with Ango at his side.

Ango was ecstatic with this great honor. To think that all his underlings were now seeing him in the company of the Prince of Bacon's Corner! Before this, Terga had never even known his name.

Ango was rising to the occasion and giving his report like a real commander-in-the-field. "It was a brazen onslaught, my Ba-al. An incredibly large heavenly warrior challenged me on the roof, and another challenged my guards at the front door. Two warriors were caught inside, but were immediately chased away."

"But you overcame them all?"

"Not without a deadly struggle. I am most proud of my warriors, who showed themselves brave, fierce, and daring!"

"And I am proud of you, Ango, for proving to me that Bacon's Corner is still secure for our operations."

"Thank you, Ba-al."

"With my commendations to you and your warriors, I leave you now . . ."

Terga stopped in midsentence. Both demons heard a familiar sound, and began searching the eastern horizon. From somewhere beyond the treetops, a low, droning rumble reached their ears, growing steadily louder, closer.

"Now who could that be?" Ango wondered.

The deceivers and guards in and around the school heard the sound as well and paused in their duties, buzzing and flitting out into the school yard for a look, or popping up through the roof for a better view.

Terga's wings billowed and lifted him from the roof. He drew his sword as he peered toward the east. Then he tensed just a little and called down to Ango and his troops, "They are ours!"

"But who?"

Terga looked grim, and shook his head in dismay. "I believe it is Destroyer, with fresh forces from the Strongman."

That word brought a mutter of fear from all the ranks below.

Then the visitors appeared, still a mile away, approaching like a low-flying squadron of bombers. There were at least a hundred, flying in an arrowhead formation and coming closer, closer, closer. Now the red glow of their swords appeared against the dark shadowy blurs of their wings.

Terga set down on the roof again. "Ango, prepare your forces to greet some honored guests!"

"Forces!" Ango yelled. They fluttered up out of the school and school yard. He ordered them to assemble in orderly ranks on the front lawn. They formed the ranks immediately, a motley, sleazy crew of some three hundred—tiny spirits of anger, hatred, rebellion; huge, lumbering giants of violence, vandalism, destruction; clever deceivers with their wily ways and shifty eyes. They looked sharp, all lined up in neat rows, the tallest in the back, the shortest in the front, and every demon's sword held across his chest.

Destroyer's squadron came over the town, casting a spiritual shadow upon the entire length of Front Street and putting a chill in the air that the humans down there could feel. The shadow passed over the fire station and then the row of homes along the Strawberry Loop, and dogs all over the neighborhood began to howl.

Terga, Ango, and all the assembly of demons could now see the squadron's leader well in front, at the tip of the arrowhead. They could see the yellow glint of his eyes and the red glimmer of his sword. They all bowed low.

Destroyer and a terrifying battalion of the Strongman's hand-picked best descended on the school like a cloud of monster locusts, their wings producing a roar that could be felt and stirring up such a wind that some of the smaller demons on the front lawn blew over and rolled like leaves across the grass.

Destroyer alighted on the roof of the school with twelve hideous captains surrounding him. The rest of the battalion took positions all around the perimeter of the school grounds. The wings settled, the roar subsided. Now Terga and Ango found themselves in the presence of a spirit so evil that neither of them could look up for stark fear.

Destroyer took a moment to look all around. He gazed with narrow, fiery eyes at the troops gathered on the lawn. He wasn't impressed. He walked slowly toward the two bowing princes of this place, his toes settling into the tar, his talons gripping tightly with each step. He stood in front of them, his captains standing on either side like tree trunks.

"So, Terga," he asked in a voice as cold as ice, "it seems you have reason to be giddy?"

Terga straightened, said, "I have, my Ba-al," and then bowed again.

With numbing fear, Terga suddenly felt the hot edge of the Ba-al's blade under his chin. He followed the blade's prompting and raised his head.

"Who is this beside you?"

"This is Ango, the prince of this school, a brave leader."

The burning sword raised Ango's chin. "You are prince of this place?"

Ango tried to speak in a strong voice, but couldn't keep it from quivering. "Yes, my Ba-al."

Destroyer leaned close to Ango's face. "I have received word that you had a confrontation here with the Host of Heaven."

Ango smiled faintly. "It was my duty and joy to please such as you, and drive the heavenly warriors away."

"How many heavenly warriors?"

"Four, my Ba-al. One assailed me on the roof, one attacked our guards at the front, and two launched an attack from inside. We chased them all away immediately."

Destroyer pondered that for just a moment. He had no immediate compliments for Ango's actions. "What else happened that day?"

Ango wasn't at all prepared for the question. "What else?"

"Did you have any unexpected human visitors to the school?"

Destroyer was staring, waiting for an answer, and now Ango could feel a stare from Terga. But he couldn't come up with an answer. "I . . . I know of none."

"Can you give me any good reason why four—only four—of the enemy's hosts would suddenly appear here, only to allow themselves to be chased away by spirits as petty and weak as you?"

Ango shuddered. This conversation was taking a bad turn. "They . . . they came to spy on us, to invade the school . . ."

"That is your explanation?"

"That is . . . Yes, that is what I know."

Destroyer sheathed his sword, and everyone breathed a little easier. "Go back to your duties, Ango the Terrible, you and your warriors. Do your worst with these little children. Terga, I'll have a word with you."

Terga followed Destroyer to the other end of the roof, while Ango dismissed his demons to return to their duties. When Destroyer came to a stop, satisfied with the place, the twelve captains surrounded him and Terga like a castle wall.

Terga was worried.

Destroyer glared down at him—angry, but calculatingly controlled. "She was here."

Terga, of course, did not want to believe it. "How do you know, my Ba-al?"

"Where did she go from the motel in Claytonville?"

"I . . ."

"Did your petty pranksters follow her? Did they have her under their careful watch at all times?"

Terga felt he would melt right through the roof. "The . . . the Host of Heaven . . . We were confounded . . . They got in our way . . . We couldn't see her anymore . . ."

"You lost track of her! She eluded you!"

Terga knew full well that Destroyer's own ravagers were following the woman too, but now did not seem an appropriate time to remind him. "Uh . . . yes. But . . . she wouldn't come back *here*, to the place of greatest danger—"

"Danger?" Destroyer's voice was as sharp as his blade. "What danger, when you and such as this Ango are responsible for it?"

"But why would she come here?"

Terga didn't even see Destroyer's huge hand before it struck him, dashing him to the roof. Terga made no move of retaliation; he never had any intention to do so, and besides, twelve huge swords were only inches from his throat. All he could do was look up at the furious face of Destroyer as the wicked spirit unloaded his venom.

"You fool!" Destroyer shouted. "Why wouldn't she come here? This is where our Plan began, or don't you recall all our years of development, our infiltration of this place? You were here, you were a part of it. Did you think we carried it all out with no object in mind?"

"I'm sorry, my Ba-al."

Destroyer's foot caught Terga under the ribs and kicked him several feet in the air. Terga's body struck the immovable chest of one of the captains and then tumbled down to the roof again.

"You're sorry . . ." muttered Destroyer mockingly. "You let her elude you in Claytonville, you let her sneak into this school under your very nose, you let her escape again, to disappear until she pops up again to do more damage, to uncover more of our Plan, we know not where, and all you have to say is, 'I'm sorry'!"

Terga wanted to say he was sorry again, but knew that would not be accepted. Now he had no words left to say.

"Go!" said Destroyer. "Take care of your little town. Leave Sally Roe to me."

One of the captains, built like a bull, took Terga by one wing and flung him into the sky. Terga tumbled and fluttered skyward until he could recover control of his wings, then shot away in shame.

Destroyer watched until Terga was gone, then spoke in low tones to the twelve demons with him. "The Strongman does have all his players in place and a strong network ready to be used, but we have seen ourselves how vulnerable the Plan can be, especially when the Host of Heaven are interested in our enterprise, and most certainly interested in Sally Roe. They are trying to set up a hedge around her, screen her from our eyes, accompany her. They have a plan too."

One hulking spirit reminded Destroyer, "But the Strongman will not turn away from his Plan; he is committed to it."

"An easy position for him to take," Destroyer hissed spitefully, fingering the handle of his sword. "If the Plan should fail, it will not be his head that rolls, but ours. He will see to that. We must succeed."

He stopped to think for a moment, his black talons pulling like hooks at the stiff hairs on his neck.

"I am learning more and more about this Tal; he is quite the strategist, a master of subtlety. Thus far the Host of Heaven have been effective and yet largely invisible. Tal is waiting, maneuvering. He is a layer of traps, a setter of snares."

Another spirit, scarred and grotesque, growled, "I was there in Ashton. I saw the ambush."

Destroyer spit sulfur and let his anger rise. "So you know that Tal waited until our forces could wait no longer and flew headlong into his patient trap, brash and unaware. We had only our confidence, but Tal was *ready*. We will not make that mistake again."

Destroyer scanned the town from this rooftop perch. "If Tal is so subtle, we will be even more so. If he depends on the prayers of God's people, then we will work all the harder to keep God's people from praying." He chuckled a sulfurous chuckle. "You don't know about the little imps I requested from the Strongman: Strife, Division, Gossip, and a host of others flooding this town at this very moment! These humans are only of flesh, of mud, and I suggest there is one force stronger than their zeal for God: their own self-righteousness! We will make them proud, pure in their own eyes, vindictive, unjust judges over each other, and stir up such a noise among them that the simplest prayer will not be uttered!"

The warriors were impressed and muttered their awe and approval.

"In the meantime," Destroyer continued, "let us not forget that *our* people are praying as well, devoting much time and worship to our lord, and he is responding with great favor toward us, sending more and more forces to bolster our ranks and confound our enemies! Time is on our side!" Then he stopped and grinned. "So, if Tal is a master of waiting, we will be the same! Though Tal may dangle Sally Roe like a carrot before our noses, we will not assault her too soon. We will not fly into another ambush." Destroyer's eyes narrowed with cunning. "We will wait, as Tal does. We will watch, we will follow, until our moment is right, until this mighty Captain of the Host is not so mighty, but is confounded, stripped of his power by the saints of God themselves!

"And then sometime, somewhere, Sally Roe will have her Gethsemane. She will be alone. Her escorts will be unaware, unready, small in numbers. The moment will be ours to take her."

"But how will we know?" asked a fourth demon.

"We will know, just as before, because a Judas will tell us. All we have to do is find him." Destroyer hacked a hideous chuckle. "Such a marvelous thing, betrayal!"

14

Ben would be getting out of the station and out on patrol a little earlier this morning. He had plans to sit behind the trees at the west end of the Snyder River Bridge and nab speeders for a while, maybe get his citation quota up a bit.

But first . . . if he could do it quietly enough, he thought he'd use the police teletype to request a crime check on Sally Roe. It just might turn something up.

"Cole . . ."

It was Mulligan, and there was something strange about the tone in his voice.

"Yes, sir."

Mulligan came out of his office and over to Ben's desk. He leaned on it with his big fist and cut into Ben with his eyes.

Ben was ready to talk, but not to be stared at. "Something wrong, Harold?"

Mulligan was almost smiling. "You been snooping around again?"

"Snooping?"

"Leonard tells me you were bothering Joey Parnell, the coroner."

Ben was a little stunned to hear that such a report had come from Leonard, of all people. "If Leonard told you I was *bothering* Mr. Parnell, I would have to disagree with his terms. I don't think I was bothering Mr. Parnell at all. I sat next to him over at Don's and just asked a few questions. It was all very casual."

"Didn't I tell you to drop this Sally Roe thing? What's wrong with your memory, Cole?"

Ben had been a wimp long enough. He stood to his feet and faced Mulligan eye to eye. "There is nothing wrong with my memory, Harold, Mr. Sergeant, sir! I have never been able to forget what I've seen pertaining to this case and the way it's been handled. I've been bothered by it, I've lost sleep over it, and quite frankly I've been very disappointed by the incompetence I've seen on the part of some duly elected public servants who should know better. If we must discuss memories, I found that Mr. Parnell's memory is no better than your eyesight in regard to the dead woman we found and her true identity. Forgive me for speaking so freely, sir."

Mulligan leaned toward Ben so that their faces were only an inch apart. "I thought you and Leonard were supposed to be doing a drug bust at Don's. I don't see any contraband, Cole. Where is it?"

"Leonard took care of that, sir."

Mulligan called, "Leonard?"

Leonard was doing something in the back. "Yeah?"

"Did you bring any contraband back from that drug bust?"

"Yeah. About a quarter kilo of marijuana. Ben took care of it."

Ben made a face and smiled a bit at the mixup. "Leonard, you handled that whole case, remember? I was over talking to Parnell."

Leonard came into the room, his face filled with astonishment. "Ben, have you slipped a gear? I gave that pot to you to file as evidence."

Ben was incredulous. "No way!"

Mulligan looked back and forth at the two men. "Guys, we are missing some pot. Now where is it?"

"I gave it to Ben to file as evidence," said Leonard.

"No," said Ben. "Absolutely not!"

Mulligan smiled cunningly. "How's about we just take a look in your locker, Cole?"

"Sure thing."

But even as Ben said that, it occurred to him what might be happening. As they went down the hall to the lockers, he knew he wouldn't be surprised if . . .

Mulligan threw open the locker. The plastic bag of marijuana fell out and landed on the floor.

Mulligan raised an eyebrow. It was no secret that he was getting a kick out of this. "Looks like you filed it in the wrong place, Cole."

Ben nodded with full knowledge of what was happening. "Yeah, right, right." He looked at Leonard. "Next time I'll have to get a lock on my locker instead of trusting the people I work with."

Leonard countered quickly, "Careful what you say, Ben. This could be serious."

"Serious? Guys, this is *pitiful*!" Ben reached for his chest. "Hey, how about it, Harold? I'll bet you have a spicy report written up already. Don't worry. You won't need it. Guys, the game stops here. I'm not playing." He removed his badge and held it out for Mulligan to take.

Mulligan took it. "Turn in your uniform by tomorrow."

"You got it."

Ben went quietly to his desk, removed his gun, radio, and other gear, and set them down. He opened the drawer, removed a New Testament and some other personal items, then slid it shut.

As he put on his jacket, he realized he had mixed feelings about what had happened—he felt sorrow and anxiety over losing his job, but at the same time elated and relieved. At least he was losing his job for the right reasons. Hopefully the Lord would bless him for that.

Mulligan and Leonard stood in the hall together, watching him go. He examined their faces for just a moment, and then went out the door.

The two weeks were up. The hearing convened on schedule, at nine o'clock in the morning, in the department of the Honorable Emily R. Fletcher of the Federal District Court, Room 412, the Federal Courthouse, in the city of Westhaven, some sixty miles south of Bacon's Corner.

Tom and Ben rode with Mark and Cathy. They challenged the freeway, waited for the lights, made the correct turns, and arrived in Westhaven with just enough time to park in a multistoried concrete parking lot, get their parking stub, dash across the street to the courthouse, and catch a crowded elevator up to the fourth floor where they finally found Room 412.

Right away, they knew the whole experience was going to be imposing, foreign, frightening, and inscrutable. It was bad enough being in this vast building with heavy marble walls that seemed to close in on you. It was worse to know next to nothing about what was going to happen and how your fate was going to be decided by so many three-piece-suited professionals you'd never seen before. It was even worse than that to find no less than a hundred people crammed into the hall outside the courtroom trying to get in. Who *were* they, anyway?

Tom cringed. Many were reporters. They weren't allowed to bring their cameras in, praise the Lord, but they were certainly gawking at him and muttering, swapping information, scribbling in their notepads. Some artists were there, easels and chalk ready to sketch a quick portrait of these strange Christians from an obscure little town.

Where was Wayne Corrigan? He said he would meet them here. Oh, there was his hand, waving in the air above a tight circle of reporters. He elbowed his way out of the circle and hurried up to meet them, the reporters following him as if connected to his body with string.

"Let's get inside," he said, sounding desperate. "It's a zoo out here."

They pressed forward into the crowd, and somehow, one step at a time, they made it to the big wooden doors and pushed through.

Now they were in a cavernous courtroom, with deeply stained woodwork, a thick green carpet, tall, draped windows, and a bench that rose like a mountain in front. The gallery was almost full.

Corrigan showed Tom and Mark to the defendant's table; Ben sat with Cathy in the front row of the gallery. Mrs. Fields was already seated there and doing some cross-stitch. Three board members, Jack and Doug Parmenter and Bob Heely, were ready to testify as well.

Corrigan spoke to Tom and Mark in muffled tones. "The judge may not take any oral testimony, but it's good to be ready in case. It's a real circus, let me tell you. The ACFA is here in full force, and the press, and I think some people from the National Coalition on Education. We're in the hot seat. It's—"

Lucy Brandon entered the courtroom, wearing a blue dress and looking very formal. She was flanked by the blonde Claire Johanson and a tall, youthful-looking man, obviously her attorney.

"That's Gordon Jefferson, Brandon's attorney. He's ACFA."

In came an older attorney, his chin high, holding a black briefcase in front of his stomach.

"Wendell Ames, Brandon's other attorney, senior partner at Ames, Jefferson, and Morris. His father was the state founder of the ACFA back in the thirties."

The four sat at the plaintiff's table without looking their way.

"*Two* attorneys?" Tom asked.

"They're out to win. What can I say? I did the best I could with the brief. It only came to twelve pages. The affidavits—the sworn statements of yourselves and Mrs. Fields—seem effective enough, but our Scriptural arguments are going to have trouble standing up against psychological reports. They've hired a shrink, you know, some child psychologist named Mandanhi. That's him sitting in the second row over there."

They looked and saw a balding, dark-skinned man of apparent East Indian descent.

"What did he have to say?" asked Mark.

"What do you think? He has Amber diagnosed as a sick and traumatized little girl, and it's all your fault, naturally."

"Naturally," muttered Tom.

"We'll see how we do, guys. Just remember, it's only the first battle, not the entire war."

A door to the left of the bench swung open.

The bailiff stood to her feet and declared, "All rise."

They all rose.

"Court is now in session, the Honorable Emily R. Fletcher presiding."

Judge Fletcher was a dignified woman in her fifties with close-cropped blonde hair and a pleasant facial expression. She took her place behind the bench and spoke in clear tones. "Thank you. Please be seated."

They sat.

"The case is *Brandon v. The Good Shepherd Academy*. Today is a hearing on a temporary injunction issued by this court two weeks ago restraining The Good Shepherd Academy from . . ." She perched her reading glasses on her nose and referred to the documents before her. "'Outrageous Religious Behavior Against a Child, Physical Abuse by Spanking, Excessive Religious Instruction Harmful to the Child, Harassment, Discrimination, and Religious Indoctrination Using Federal Funds.' Are counsel ready to proceed?"

She looked toward Lucy Brandon and her two attorneys.

Ames stood to his feet. "Yes, Your Honor."

She looked toward Tom, Mark, and Wayne Corrigan. "And the defendants . . . are you ready?"

Corrigan rose and replied in the affirmative.

She looked over her reading glasses at the crowded courtroom. "This case is obviously one of great public importance and intense public interest. If there are no objections from counsel, the court is prepared to grant permission for the use of cameras and recording devices by the press."

Gordon Jefferson stood up immediately. "No objections, Your Honor."

Corrigan noticed the immediate headshake from Tom and Mark. He stood. "Your Honor, the defendants would request that no cameras be allowed."

Jefferson countered, "Your Honor, as you have observed, this case does reflect matters of great public interest. I think the public would be well served through firsthand information that television can provide."

Corrigan whispered to Tom, "The ACFA loves to try cases in the press. They're going for this one."

Judge Fletcher didn't take long to ponder the issue. "Mr. Corrigan, the court sees no harm in such camera coverage, certainly not so much harm that the importance of public awareness does not outweigh it. Cameras will be allowed."

Several reporters bolted from the courtroom to grab their gear.

The judge flipped to the next page before her. "I have read the briefs and affidavits presented by both sides in this case. Well done, excellent on both sides, and as one might expect, in sharp dispute. In light of the short time frame, and in the interest of expediency, we will avoid oral testimony if counsel agrees, and hear this case on the basis of the affidavits and oral argument of counsel."

Wayne Corrigan whispered to Tom, "It's okay. It's to our advantage. They have to meet a higher standard of proof if there's no oral testimony." He spoke to the judge. "We have no objection, Your Honor."

Ames and Jefferson were still whispering to each other. They didn't seem too happy about the court's suggestion. Finally Ames answered, "Uh . . . no objections, Your Honor."

The judge seemed pleased with the progress they were all making. "Well then . . . if counsel are ready, Mr. Ames or Mr. Jefferson, you may proceed with your argument."

Jefferson rose, buttoning his jacket. "Thank you, Your Honor."

He walked forward and began to form his argument, wandering back and forth, studying the carpet, waving one hand in the air as if leading a choir. "Your Honor, this is not a difficult case; as the court has seen in the brief and affidavits, the complaints against the Good Shepherd Academy are well-founded. We do believe in religious freedom, of course, and far be it from us to suppose we can infringe on that sacred right. But how, Your Honor, does a child of ten have the power to decide freely in such matters when surrounded by a coercive and repressive environment such as we have found at the Good Shepherd Academy?"

Tom listened raptly to Jefferson's speech. The guy was being slanderous, he thought, but selling it all very well. The press was going to eat this up for sure.

"You have seen the report by Dr. Mandanhi, a distinguished psychologist well-acquainted with emotional trauma in children. He has clearly stated that young Amber has been severely traumatized by the outrageous religious behavior of these people, and has demonstrated such symptoms as illness, headaches, loss of appetite, and bed-wetting, not to mention severe religious delusions and even . . . uh . . . personality disorders which can be attributed to the curriculum taught and example set by the leadership at the Good Shepherd Academy. I must also inform the court that Mr. Harris is currently under investigation by the CPD for possible child abuse, and that his own children have been removed from his home pending that investigation."

Corrigan bolted out of his chair. "Objection!"

"Sustained," said the judge. "Mr. Jefferson, Child Protection Department matters are strictly confidential and are not to be discussed in open court. You will restrain from any further mention of it."

"And in light of just such tactics as this," said Corrigan, "may I again request that cameras and recording devices be barred from the courtroom?"

"The request is denied," said the judge, but then she looked toward the members of the press. "But the press is ordered not to publish anything about that revelation."

Corrigan said, "Thank you, Your Honor," and sat down. He whispered to Tom, "Jefferson knew what he was doing."

Jefferson continued, unruffled. "As for the 'outrageous religious behavior,' the details are clear in the court file, of course, and I hardly need to comment on the behavior described, that of attempting to cast a demon out of Amber, and even suggesting to an impressionable child that she is possessed by a spirit. Your Honor, this is a most unusual twist, a new and obviously bizarre form of child abuse; this must fall outside the protective umbrella of religious freedom, and we would ask the court to so rule.

"The physical abuse by spanking is clear enough as well, and even the defendants admit that the spanking did occur. As the court well knows, this practice is already forbidden by the state in any foster homes and in the public schools, and we would suggest that the precedents in law and in society are clear on this issue. This is not proper behavior toward a child, but is another form of abuse, and should also be extricated from under the umbrella of religious freedom."

Tom and Mark could see the case forming; this clever lawyer was whittling away at something he repeatedly termed "the umbrella of religious freedom." It was clear to them that umbrellas had little to do with it—religious freedom itself was the object of his attacks. But Jefferson was good at what he did, they had to admit that. His oratory was forceful, well choreographed, and persuasive. The disturbing thought now was, *Is Corrigan going to be able to top it?*

"As for excessive religious instruction," Jefferson continued, "who can object to teaching basic virtues such as honesty, self-esteem, the Golden Rule? Our difficulty is in the pervasive fundamentalist idea that we are all feeble, despicable, worthless sinners, incapable of any good in ourselves, but dependent on some outside 'savior' to lift us out of our personal morass, and without whom we have no hope at all . . . an idea we must suggest is destructive to the mental health and well-being of any child, and Dr. Mandanhi's report reflects this.

"To quickly close the matter, and not take any more of the court's time, the above-mentioned offenses do necessarily constitute a form of harassment and discrimination because no opposing view of these fundamental beliefs is allowed; this is intolerance, of course, and the seedbed of bigotry.

"But, of course, an even greater legal issue here is that these teachings and indoctrinations are being supported and paid for by federal funds, since Mrs. Brandon is a federal employee and is receiving a child care subsidy under the Federal Day-care and Private Primary School Assistance Act, part of which she has used to pay her daughter's tuition."

Judge Fletcher interrupted. "Counselor, it is the court's understanding that Amber has now been removed from the school."

"Yes, Your Honor, for her own well-being, of course. But we submit that the issue of separation of church and state is still viable since federal funds were used in the religious indoctrination of Amber while attending the school, which would bring the school into accountability to the state. This is covered in detail in our brief on the applicability of the Munson-Ross Civil Rights Act and the Federal Day-care and Private Primary School Assistance Act. While Congress intended to assist working parents with child care, no one in their right mind would argue that federal funds should be used for religious instruction. Our brief shows how legislative history and prior case law make this abundantly clear.

"Finally, we would ask that the court consider not only Amber, who was fortunate enough to be removed from the school and therefore saved any further harm; we would ask the court to also consider the children still there, still subject to this excessive behavior and instruction, still very much in harm's way. We don't know who the other children in the school are and whether or not federal funds are being used to supplement their tuition as well. That is why we are asking the court to order that the defendants produce the name of each child and any financial information concerning the child's enrollment in the school, in addition to continuing the restraint.

"Your decision here today will affect the future well-being of the other children also, and therefore we are sure the court will rule in their favor."

Jefferson sat down as every television camera in the room followed him to his chair and cameras clicked away.

Tom and Mark looked at Corrigan. He was hurriedly going over his scribbled notes, apparently hoping for an inspiration. It didn't seem to be coming to him.

"Mr. Corrigan?" said the judge.

Tom gave Corrigan an encouraging pat on the shoulder. "Godspeed, brother."

Corrigan rose to his feet. This was his moment. He buttoned his jacket as well, not to signal his determination to do battle, but because his nervous hands needed something to do. It also gave him a moment to pray.

"Your Honor, counsel for the plaintiff has taken great pains to paint a bleak and gruesome picture of the Good Shepherd Academy. We can assure you that things at the school are much different than they've been made out to be.

"First of all, we haven't had a chance to meet with Dr. Mandanhi and discuss his findings, and therefore we can't be certain that Amber's problems are entirely due to her attending the school. As we've tried to show in the affidavits, she came to the Good Shepherd Academy with some problems already, and I suggest it would not be fair or accurate to attribute all her problems to the environment at the school. We should have the opportunity to have our own expert examine Amber, as I'm sure another expert could balance the report of Dr. Mandanhi.

"As for corporal punishment, this is certainly not the anachronism that the plaintiff is trying to make it out to be, and we are not going to resolve that issue in this case. Spanking, when administered by loving parents, or by a Christian school headmaster following agreed-upon procedure, is not abuse at all, but proper discipline, and as we have shown in our court file, a matter of Biblical doctrine, a matter of deep religious conviction.

"Also, I would remind the court that the guidelines for corporal discipline are clearly spelled out in the Academy handbook, and that Mrs. Brandon signed a letter of agreement to those guidelines. Both items are included in our brief, and speak for themselves.

"So I think this issue of spanking is not at all settled, especially when there can be no doubt that Amber's punishment was properly and lovingly administered. It would not be fair or accurate to label it as child abuse. To do so would invade the privacy and convictions of millions of parents across this country who still believe in spanking, and yes, there is the matter of religious conviction and religious freedom. These must be protected and should not be infringed upon.

"We must also object to the plaintiff's accusation of 'excessive religious instruction.' What the plaintiff refers to is a fundamental part of the gospel, but I must remind the court that the gospel is the Good News, not Bad News. The message of the gospel does not leave us all condemned . . . or as counsel for the plaintiff stated, 'feeble, despicable sinners.' We believe . . . that is, the doctrinal position of the Good Shepherd Academy is . . . that yes, man is a sinner. He is separated from God because he has transgressed God's righteous law, and, by himself, has no salvation from his predicament. But this message is never forced or imposed on any child without the positive side of the message, that God sent His Son to pay the price of our sins with His own life, and thereby save us and reconcile us to God.

"Now, I realize I may sound like a preacher here, but this is, after all, one point of contention raised by the plaintiff, and I must answer it." Corrigan brightened a bit as a thought hit him. "But maybe it would be appropriate for me to point out right here that clearly this is a religious matter. Your Honor, we are discussing religious *doctrine*, and in a court of law! Yes, Your Honor, we do challenge the plaintiff's contention that any excessive religious instruction has occurred that would be harmful to Amber. But also, we remind the court that through this complaint, the plaintiff has asked the state to rule on the propriety of a particular religious belief, and this is something the state is constitutionally barred from doing."

You got them there, thought Tom.

"We also deny any harassment or discrimination, and as the court file shows, even though the plaintiff has obtained the professional opinion of Dr. Mandanhi regarding alleged trauma to the child, the plaintiff has failed to prove any specific allegations of excessive or outrageous behavior."

The judge looked up from her notes with a quizzical expression. "Counselor, your brief included at least a cursory reference to the alleged 'outrageous religious behavior' cited by the plaintiff. Do you now deny the plaintiff's allegation that Mr. Harris attempted to cast a demon out of the child?"

Tom and Mark were certain that Corrigan would be cornered on this one, but he didn't seem to balk at the question. Apparently he'd done a lot of thinking about it. "The allegation is open to challenge, Your Honor, inasmuch as there could be many different interpretations, many different definitions of the word 'demon.'"

The judge leaned forward, lowering her chin to just inches above the bench. "Would it be fair to suppose a Judeo-Christian or Biblical interpretation of the word 'demon' in this case?"

Tom could feel his heart pounding and his stomach turning into knots.

Corrigan drew a breath and came back with his answer. "I suppose it would, Your Honor, but then, even within the parameters of a Biblical interpretation, you would have to decide between . . . uh . . . whether it would be a liberal, allegorical interpretation of the word, or the more fundamentalist, literal interpretation . . ."

The judge smiled just a little. Someone in the courtroom snickered. "I suppose we could belabor that point, counselor, and indeed enter into a theological argument. Please proceed."

Tom looked at Mark. Was that a good or bad sign? They couldn't help trying to guess what the judge was thinking.

Corrigan tried to cap off his argument. "We are here today, Your Honor, to show just cause why we should not be restrained from certain activities. Well, first of all, I would argue that these allegations of activities are spurious and unfounded at best, and that the plaintiff in this case has fallen sadly short of proving the truth of any of them. This being the case, a restraining order against the school is simply uncalled for, and I would suggest entails a violation of the separation of church and state, in that the state is encroaching on the free exercise of religion by the Good Shepherd Academy by placing itself in a position to decide for the Academy what is acceptable religion and what is not. I hope that we will not find that kind of a situation developing here, and that this restraining order will be removed. It is appropriate here for the court to remove the restraint because the plaintiff is no longer affected by the school's policies, and no other student is a plaintiff and therefore this case is moot. Thank you very much."

With that, Corrigan sat down.

"Thank you, Mr. Corrigan," said Judge Fletcher.

Then came the long, second-by-second wait. Judge Emily R. Fletcher leafed through her notes, scribbled some notes next to her notes, and then stared at her notes as a tense silence fell over the great chamber.

15

Finally Judge Fletcher set down her pen and spoke, alternately looking through her reading glasses at the papers in front of her and then looking over them at the lawyers, litigants, observers, and television cameras.

"I doubt that either side will be entirely pleased with my decision, but contrary to Mr. Jefferson's opening assertion, this *is* a difficult case, and it puts me in an even more difficult position, where I'm called upon to balance, as it were, the Constitution and the best interests of a ten-year-old child. In trying to achieve that kind of balance, it's inevitable that both sides in this dispute are going to lose something and find their respective desires not totally satisfied.

"I've read the file and heard the arguments of counsel. I believe this is a case where some injunctive relief is warranted. However, there are some strong and some weak arguments on both sides, and some issues that seem to me to be, at least at this point, unarguable. I'll address the separate complaints one by one.

"To go down the list . . . pertaining to 'Outrageous Religious Behavior Against a Child,' I agree with the Constitution that there is a place for individual religious persuasion and practice. But I hold that there is certainly a place for proper restraint, and no place at all for any violation of the laws of the state. The complaint of the plaintiff is clear and direct, that Amber was harassed and effectively branded as someone possessed by a spirit, a demon, whatever the definition of that word might be. I do believe the propriety of such behavior should be called into question; I think this protection should remain. Therefore, the restraining order against such behavior shall issue until the matter is resolved in trial.

"I will say the same for any further spanking of any child at the Academy. The state has an interest in protecting its children, and there have been many cases where corporal punishment has been found to be inappropriate. While religious conviction has its rightful place in our society, the possibility of child abuse still exists, and therefore I think it is appropriate that a restraining order should issue along the lines requested by Mrs. Brandon, and that the matter proceed to trial.

"As for the next three complaints, 'Excessive Religious Instruction Harmful to the Child,' 'Harassment,' and 'Discrimination,' I would agree with Mr. Corrigan that these are rather vague complaints that have not been established to the satisfaction of the court as harmful to the children. The court agrees that these are religious matters, and it is clear that the religious position of the Academy was well-advertised and clearly stated so that Mrs. Brandon was aware of the religious nature of the Academy before enrolling her child. If the plaintiff argues that such beliefs and teaching are inappropriate for any child, then let counsel build a case and present it in trial.

"As for the final complaint, 'Religious Indoctrination Using Federal Funds,' Mrs. Brandon has removed her daughter from the school, and as long as no further tuition is paid to the school out of Mrs. Brandon's salary, there is, in my opinion, no further violation of the law, and no further harm done until this matter can be decided in trial. The restraint is moot, then, and therefore removed.

"I will sign the appropriate written order when completed by counsel. Counsel should discuss the appropriate bond to be placed in the order. If you cannot agree, call my clerk.

"I am withholding a ruling at this time on the production order plaintiffs seek. I'm concerned about that. Further argument may be needed, or it may be moot, but it is an important issue.

"By this order I'm not saying the plaintiff's claims are unfounded, just that all the restraint requested pending trial is not warranted. The whole matter will proceed to trial in due course." She picked up the gavel and rapped it sharply. "This court is in recess."

"All rise," said the bailiff, and they all rose, and the muttering and mumbling started as Judge Fletcher left the room.

"Now what?" Tom asked.

"Now we dodge the reporters and get out of here," said Corrigan.

"How did we do?" asked Mark as Cathy took his arm and listened.

"Well, we still have a long battle ahead of us. To review, your school can stay open and you can keep teaching your normal curriculum, but spanking is out and casting out demons is taboo. The judge says you don't have to produce the names and financial records of any of the other kids, so that's one hassle avoided. I would say we did pretty well, considering how it could have gone. Let's get out of here."

Mrs. Fields and the Parmenters were full of questions too.

"Can the school stay open?" Mrs. Fields asked.

"Yes, it's all right," said Tom.

Cathy gave her a hug and said, "We're going to have a meeting with everyone and explain it all."

Jack Parmenter was still itching for a fight. "We've got to get that . . . that Jefferson punk. We don't have to stand for that kind of talk!"

"Let's talk about all that somewhere else," said Corrigan.

He led the way, and the others followed in a single file through the courtroom doors.

The camera lights were blinding; it was like daylight in the hall outside.

"Mr. Harris!" came the first reporter. "What is your reaction to the judge's ruling?"

"No comment," said Wayne Corrigan.

"What about your children?" asked another reporter. "How long have they been removed from your home?"

So much for the judge's order, Tom thought.

"Is it true that you tried to exorcise a demon from the child?" said a lady, shoving a microphone in Tom's face.

Corrigan grabbed the microphone. "We intend to try our case in a court of law, not in the press. Thank you."

More questions.

"Let's go," Corrigan said to Tom and the others.

They kept moving, even slinking, through the crowd.

They passed a cluster of reporters and cameras gathered around Lucy Brandon and her two lawyers. Jefferson was holding forth with quite a comment for the press. ". . . The judge's decision was just what we expected. While we can't believe that anyone would allow their children to be subjected to this kind of curriculum and the harsh treatment it requires, I can understand why the judge was reluctant to rule on the abbreviated evidence that one can produce for a short-notice hearing such as this. We are, however, pleased that the judge chose to protect the children of Bacon's Corner from further physical abuse at the hands of Tom Harris and his staff . . . these fundamentalists."

Tom heard all that and turned. He had to say something. He couldn't let that get into the press.

"Come on, let's just go," said Corrigan, tugging at his arm.

They hurried from the courthouse.

The Wednesday night prayer meeting at Mark and Cathy's house was packed. Attendance wasn't that bad on any normal Wednesday night, but this night was not normal at all, and there weren't enough chairs for everyone.

All the board members were there along with their wives, as were some of the people on the prayer chain: Donna Hemphile, Lester and Dolly Sutter, Tim and Becky Farmer, Brent and Amy Ryan, and the widow Alice Buckmeier. Ben Cole was there with his wife Bev; Mrs. Fields was there, even though she regularly attended the local Baptist church on Wednesday nights. Wayne Corrigan was there as well and would probably be the center of attention.

The one person noticeably absent was Tom Harris. He'd taken his leave of absence, and felt compelled to keep his distance. Besides, Mark felt the evening's discussion would be freer and any grievances could be more easily voiced if he was not there, and Tom agreed with that.

Some other absences were a little unsettling to Mark, who, being the pastor, was more prone to notice. Andrea and Wes Jessup, who usually attended the midweek meeting, were absent, as were the Wingers. Mark knew why they were gone. There were still some disgruntled people out there who needed to have their fears and false information cleared up, and naturally, being the ones who needed most to be here, they were not. Dealing with them was going to be a tough and unpleasant project.

In all, the house had to be holding no less than fifty people. This had to be a crisis indeed.

But the house was also filled with other visitors, no less than fifty, almost an even match in attendance. Tal was there, along with Guilo, recently returned from his surveillance near the mountain town of Summit; Nathan and Armoth were ready at Tal's side, and at their command was a formidable troop of warriors. Mota and Signa, having completed their assignment at the elementary school, were in attendance and overseeing the hedge of guards now surrounding the house. This would be one meeting uninvaded by any marauding spirits.

"Messengers are ready," Nathan reported. "All they need is a word from you."

Tal looked around the room and managed a grim smile. "Maybe we'll get a better idea where the trouble is, and where our prayer cover went. May the Lord grant His people a special portion of His wisdom tonight." He took one more look around the room and then said, "The messengers will wait for my word."

"Done."

"What of Sally Roe?"

Chimon stepped forward. "Scion and I have just delivered her into Cree and Si's care. They're escorting her to the Omega Center."

"Good. Go immediately to Bentmore and prepare the way for her there."

"Done."

Chimon and Scion vanished to their next assignment.

Wayne Corrigan stood to address the group and field their questions.

"I would say it was about a fifty percent victory," he said, "which is a positive way of looking at it. The Academy should be able to run smoothly without too much interruption—"

"Until some of those kids find out you can't paddle 'em," said Tim Farmer, who *was* a farmer, showed a missing tooth whenever he grinned, and had his boy in the Academy's fifth grade. "Whatever you do, don't tell Jesse about this!"

They all laughed. They were glad it was Jesse's father who'd said it.

"You will be under a handicap, certainly," said Corrigan. "You'll have to come up with some other means to deal with discipline problems."

Judy Waring, always the hearer and bearer of bad tidings, was bursting to say her piece. "Well, I want to know what got us into all this trouble to begin with! Just what is Tom Harris doing with our kids?"

"Judy!" Mark cut in. "We're here to cover that to everyone's satisfaction, don't worry."

Amy Ryan asked a simple question. "Mark, could we hear it from you? Did Tom try to cast a demon out of this little Brandon girl?"

Mark knew he was going to have trouble as soon as he said it. "Yes, he did. She was—"

"Now there was a dumb move," piped Brent, Amy's husband. He was a muscular public utilities contractor who considered his areas of competence to be natural gas, the Word of God, and dumb moves. "How did he know if it was a demon or not?"

Judy Waring was more than ready to whip that horse. "He didn't have any idea what he was doing, and now he's gotten our school into hot water it'll never get out of!"

Mark tried to restore order, and had to speak in firm tones. "All right, everybody. Now before we all run off in a hundred different directions, let's just be quiet and first hear what Wayne has to say. Direct your questions to him, one at a time!"

"We've done something wrong," Judy insisted. "We wouldn't be in court if we didn't do something wrong."

"Judy!"

She closed her lips, but with a defiant expression.

"Come on, saints," said Tal, "you can do better than that!"

Guilo muttered, "You were wondering where our prayer cover went?"

Wayne Corrigan tried to start again. "I want to give you an accurate picture, but also I don't want to sound too negative. We *are* in the middle of a lawsuit, but it's not the end of the world . . . or of the school. It's possible we can pull through this thing and come out unscathed with the help of the Lord and everyone who can pitch in. For right now, the school is under a restraining order forbidding the use of spanking or of any religious behavior that could be construed as harmful to children."

"Casting out demons . . ." Brent muttered under his breath. Everyone heard him.

"No, now let me comment on that right now. You have to realize how the system works, and how the ACFA works. Casting out demons isn't the ultimate point of all this. It's just the issue that keeps moving to the forefront because it's sensational in nature and mostly because it involves a child. The ACFA knows that and they're playing it for all it's worth, making it the rallying point.

"But it would be better to follow and watch the phrase, 'outrageous religious behavior.' You see, what could happen in this case is that the courts—for the sake of a child—will have to rule that some particular action by a religious group constitutes outrageous religious behavior; once that legal precedent is set, it can be used in future cases to widen the original definition of just what kind of religious behavior is outrageous and can be legally challenged, whether a child is involved or not. We would ultimately open the gate for the courts to establish what kind of religious belief is acceptable and what is not, to put it bluntly."

"But what about religious freedom?" asked Lester Sutter, one of the senior citizens of the congregation. "Since when does the government tell us how to live our lives and how to raise our children?"

"Exactly. That is the real issue here, and I want all of you to understand that. This lawsuit is not about spanking or demons or anything else. The ACFA is behind this whole thing, and you can be sure they are working to set some legal precedents that will give the federal government the power to control religion and religious schools."

"They can't do that!" said Amy Ryan.

"They're doing it," said Brent.

"But what about the Constitution?"

Brent shrugged. "What about it?"

Corrigan stepped in. "Brent's aware of my point. The popular notion these days is that the Constitution is a 'living document' that can be reinterpreted by the courts as society continues to evolve morally."

"Or *decay* morally," said Frank Parmenter.

"Or *spiritually*," said Mark. "Listen, people, this isn't just some kind of legal battle. This is a spiritual battle, don't forget that."

"Yeah," said Brent, showing a slight turn-around in his attitude. "What if it *was* a demon? Pretty soon it's going to be against the law to cast one out."

"But who says we have to do what the government says?" asked Tim Farmer. "What about the apostles? They didn't obey the Jewish rulers when they were told not to preach about Jesus."

Corrigan replied, "That's an important point, and something you all need to consider seriously: you may choose to be civilly disobedient as the apostles were, and to obey the Law of God rather than the law of man . . ."

"Let's do it!" said Frank Parmenter.

"But," Corrigan was quick to add, "remember that the apostles went to prison, were beaten, tortured, and martyred for their stand. And as I've said before, Paul and Silas cast out a demon in Philippi and ended up in prison for it. Civil disobedience is not without a price." Now the room was quiet. Corrigan continued, "And that price could also mean extreme damage to your credibility in this lawsuit. Your arguments on appeal will be harder to sustain. Now of course you must follow your conscience before God, and there is Scriptural precedent for civil disobedience—the Hebrew midwives who violated Pharaoh's orders to kill the male Hebrew children, Rahab who hid the spies, the apostles who preached in the name of Jesus when ordered not to. But my advice to you is to work through the system first, the old Romans 13 approach. It will go better for you in the trial."

"What if we lose?" asked Brent.

"Then . . ." Corrigan hesitated and considered his answer. "Then you'll just have to do what you have to do." He hurriedly added, "But please remember, the legal process takes time. You must be patient and not do anything rash that could hurt your chances of winning in court. Remember, the ACFA plans to go national with this case, as far as it can go, with national media attention and as much negative publicity as they can generate. They're using the Day-care Act to get into the federal courts as well, so this case could easily have damaging precedents that could affect every other church, every other Christian school in the country. You're not just making choices for yourselves tonight, but for your brothers and sisters everywhere. You're the first domino. Remember that."

"The first domino," Brent said quietly, and then shook his head at the thought. "Looks like the persecution's started, folks."

Mark stepped in. "So what's coming up next, Wayne?"

"The hardest part of all, I suppose. We'll have to send interrogatories to the other side, take depositions from them, and build a defense. For those of you who don't know what those words mean, an interrogatory is simply a list of questions, things we want to find out from them. We want to know what their grievances are and what they know, so we can counter whatever their argument is going to be. The depositions are similar. We will meet with the witnesses who will be testifying against us, and they will answer our questions under oath with a court reporter there to take down a verbatim record of what they say. The other side is going to do the same with our witnesses, and supposedly both sides will know what testimony and evidence are going to be presented so they can prepare their arguments for the courtroom."

"So what can we do to help?" asked Jack Parmenter, and every face in the room agreed with the question.

"Well . . ." Corrigan looked at the ceiling for an answer. "Any lawyer is only as good as his information, and as I've already discussed with your pastor and with Tom Harris, I'm hard-pressed as far as the availability of my time to do all the homework. I . . ." He wasn't sure if he should say his next thought. "Well, with some reservation let me just say this: obviously we're up against some aggressive people, very organized, highly motivated, with contacts and assistance all over the country as near as their phone. They mean business, they mean to win, and their methods are not always above board . . ."

"They're a bunch of crooks, in other words," said Brent.

"Well . . ." Corrigan tossed up his hands. "I guess I won't debate that opinion. What I'm trying to say is, you need an investigator; someone who can dig after the facts that our opponents are going to do their best to hide. I've dealt with the ACFA before, and they do not cooperate when it comes to supplying any information in answer to interrogatories. They're sneaky, conniving, stealthy, and ruthless. Within Christian propriety, of course, you need someone who can be just as ruthless and find out what you need to know even if the ACFA is trying to hide it. That takes time, skill, and experience; you need someone who can help you with that."

"So who do we call?" asked Jack Parmenter.

"I don't know of anyone nearby who'll do it for any price you can afford."

Suddenly Ben Cole spoke up. "Well, maybe I can work on that. I'm out of a job right now; I have the time, for a while anyway."

Amy Ryan leaned forward to see Ben around several other heads. "Ben, I didn't know you were out of work. What happened?"

Ben shrugged. "It's a long story."

Bev looked at him for just a moment. "You gonna tell 'em?" Ben hesitated, so Bev jumped in. "You wanna talk about shady dealings goin' on, I think Ben got caught stickin' his nose where certain people didn't want it. He was onto somethin', I know."

Ben was apologetic. "Well, that's off the subject."

But Bev didn't drop it. Tall, lean, and athletic, she was no weakling and could be very persistent when it came to fighting for the truth. "It might be right on the subject. You know that suicide that happened a couple weeks ago?"

Some did, some didn't. Few could see what it had to do with anything.

"Ben thinks it was a murder, but the cops are covering it up. I think he was getting too close to finding something out and that's why they fired him."

Ben held up his hands and smiled apologetically. "Hey, it's a great story. I'll tell it to everybody later."

Mark said sincerely, "Ben, we'll pray about all that tonight."

Ben nodded. "Thanks. Anyway, all I wanted to say was that I'll be happy to do what I can. I'll do some of the hoofing; just tell me what to do."

Mark thanked Wayne Corrigan and then stepped to the center of the room. "Let's go to prayer. I think we're going to have a real mountain of things to do, and all kinds of battles to fight on the natural level; we'll be fighting against the schemes of men, against all the curveballs hiding in the law courts, against the financial challenge this is going to be. But none of the battle is going to succeed if we don't fight first of all where the real battle is taking place, and that's in the spiritual realm."

"Pastor," said Donna Hemphile, "may I just say something?"

"Go ahead."

Donna Hemphile stood to her feet and addressed the group. "I feel a real spirit of defeat in the group tonight, and I just want all of us to know that we don't have to accept any of this! God is our Victory, and He's already won for us! All we have to do is move in and take that victory, just pick it like ripe fruit!"

"Right on," someone said.

"Amen," said Jack Parmenter.

Donna kept talking along those lines. An address from her to the congregation usually took longer than was necessary, but her words were always encouraging, so they all learned to bear with it.

Tal could feel the Spirit of God speaking, and noticed Cathy Howard hearing the Lord's gentle voice.

Cathy leaned over and whispered in Mark's ear, "Honey, I feel a check. I don't trust her."

He squeezed her hand to acknowledge her words.

Donna kept going. "We have the right to speak what we want and see it happen. We need to search our own hearts for the strength that's ours!"

Okay, that was enough. Mark quickly, very courteously got the floor back from Donna and continued, "Let's call upon the Lord tonight, and ask Him to help us and guide us through this thing. Like Jonathan said, the Lord is not constrained to win by many or by few. If God is on our side, He'll bring things around just the way He wants them. Let's pray."

The saints joined together in prayer, a genuine concert of praise and petition. They agreed from their hearts, and as a body they were one in purpose. They asked for the Lord's special guidance for Wayne Corrigan as he worked on the case, and cried out to the Lord for the sake of the school. Jack Parmenter prayed for the kids still in the school, that their education and spiritual training would continue with strength and clarity; Mrs. Fields prayed for Tom, that the Lord would give him strength and reunite him with his children; Brent Ryan prayed for Lucy Brandon and the others who were suing them; Mark prayed for Ben and his job situation.

Tal could feel a good concert of prayer here—but he was also distracted by a bad presence in the group. Somewhere, somehow, Destroyer had planted an invisible, insidious infection, and Tal could feel it growing. Destroyer had done well; on the surface, the infection was almost impossible to notice; it was going to be hard to expose, and even if the Heavenly Host could reveal it, the hearts of the people themselves would have to change before the germ could be rooted out.

But in the usual way, unaware of the undercurrents, the saints continued to pray, and for now it was enough.

Ben prayed for help, any help, that the Lord could bring their way—someone who would know what to do, where to look, how to fight.

And Tal got his order from Heaven.

"Go!" he said.

Nathan passed the command to two messengers waiting just outside the house: "Go!"

The two messengers instantly exploded into brilliant figures of light and shot into the sky with a rushing of jeweled wings. They soared higher and higher, the town of Bacon's Corner shrinking to a cluster of tiny lights below them, lost in the center of a vast, flat table of patchwork farmlands. Then they streaked toward the east, passing over green hills and forested mountains as if with one instantaneous leap, the winding rivers, rural roads, and gray interstates appearing ahead and vanishing behind in an eye's twinkling.

And then they arrived at their destination, another cluster of lights, though much larger than Bacon's Corner, in the middle of farmlands and countryside. They dove headlong for that cluster and it grew before them, becoming a distinguishable grid of streets, alleys, neighborhoods, a new mall, and a quaint college campus. Automobiles were still moving steadily up and down Main Street, dark little bugs with red lights on their tails and headlights peering into the pools of light they formed on the street ahead of them. The streetlights glowed in warm, welcoming amber. Up the hill above Main Street, porch lights glimmered on all the houses where families were tucked away for the evening with homework, after-dinner dishes, perhaps a football game on television.

The two messengers pulled out of their dive and shot up Main Street, etching two brilliant trails between the streetlights. Then they slowed to a hover above a small storefront office between the new bakery and a bicycle shop. They dropped through the roof and landed in the front office area.

The place was deserted; it was after-hours. They paused a moment to look around. This humble little home of the town's newspaper hadn't changed much since they were here the last time. The three old desks were still there, but now one of the two typewriters was replaced with a word processor, and the telephone system had been upgraded from one line to two.

The glass-enclosed office of the editor was still the same—still out of place in this cluttered, cramped building, and still a bit messy. On the wall above the desk was a small calendar indicating all the games in the upcoming season of the editor's favorite football team, and on the desk, in a special corner undisturbed by any papers, galleys, photographs, or scribbled notes, were framed photographs of a lovely redheaded woman and what had to be her daughter, also lovely and also redheaded.

Just behind this enclosure was the teletype room. The messengers checked the recent news releases. They found just the right one, separated it neatly from the other wire copy, then carried it into the editor's office and set it squarely in the center of his desk.

Then they waited. He was going to see it. They were there to make sure he did.

At precisely eight o'clock, a key worked in the front lock, the door opened, the little bell at the top of the door *ding-a-linged*, and the editor came in, switching on the lights, raising the thermostat, hanging up his coat, and heading for the coffeemaker. He poured in the grounds, filled it with water, and plugged it in, then stepped into his office.

The two messengers were there, watching his every move. He wasn't looking at his desk yet, but instead started fumbling with some scribbled notes on the bulletin board above the filing cabinets, muttering some unintelligible words of frustration against someone who didn't do what they were supposed to do when they said they were going to do it. He dropped some of the bulletin board pins, so he had to pick them up; and then, having removed some of the items from the bulletin board, he found he finally had enough pins to hold each item up there without doubling up the items, and that pleased him.

Then he went to the phone on his desk and picked up the receiver. His eyes fell on the wire copy the messengers had placed there, but he didn't take much notice of it.

The Lord spoke.

The messengers heard His voice clearly and wondered if the big, red-haired fellow had also. He wasn't dialing the phone yet, but was holding the receiver next to his head and not moving. He stayed that way for just a moment.

He jerked his head a little—his way of shrugging that was smaller than a shrug—and then started to dial the phone.

The Lord spoke again.

He stopped in mid-dial and hung up the receiver. The messengers drew closer for a better look.

Yes, he was reading the news item. It was about the recent hearing in the city of Westhaven, and about the Christian school scandal that was rocking a tiny, obscure farming town called Bacon's Corner.

The Lord spoke. The big man sat down at the desk and listened, holding the news item in his hand, reading it again slowly.

Finally, with a low, husky, morning-voice, he said, "Well, Lord . . . what do You want me to do?"

16

Near the East Coast, up in the green hills above a picturesque river, people from all over the world had found a special place to gather; with devotion, vision, and sweat they had worked to convert an old YMCA camp into a special campus, a center for learning, personal enrichment, and community. The Omega Center for Educational Studies was now in its fourteenth year of existence and growing steadily every year, supported and enhanced by teachers, professionals, scholars, artists, intellectuals, and spiritual pilgrims from all walks of life and many nations of the world. Their binding, motivating spirit: a vision and hope for world peace and community; oneness with the rhythms of nature and the eternal expansiveness of the universe; the accepting of the impulse to change; the challenging of the unknown.

Among its neighbors, the Omega Center was described in many terms of varying shades, from such labels as "a real vanguard in human potential" to such accusations as "a Satanic cult." The people who worked, lived, and studied at the Center took it all in stride. They knew not everyone would understand their mission and purpose right away, but they clung to the dream that, given time, the unity of all mankind would manifest itself. They were dedicated to seeing that happen.

It was early on a Friday morning. Cree, his wings spread and motionless like the wings of a gull, dropped over the tops of the bordering maples and glided just above the glass-smooth surface of Pauline's Lake, silently passing the small summer cottages, diving rafts, floating docks, and beached canoes. He would come up behind the Center, hopefully avoiding any spirits that might be on watch near the main Administration Building.

He slowed, rose from the lake, and drifted to a silent, stalled landing on the swimming beach. The sand was wet with dew, and a mist rose from the lake. Rowboats lay on racks belly-up; the roped swimming area reflected the boat dock like a flawless mirror. To one side, back among some trees, was the equipment shack. He ducked through its walls and found a hiding-place among the canoe paddles, volleyballs, and tennis rackets.

Then he listened. There was no sound. The timing was right; the Center was almost deserted now. It was a short time between two educational retreats. The weekday group had finished, packed up, and left Thursday night; the weekend group was due this evening.

Most importantly, the prince over this place was away, feeling lax and confident during the lull, probably on some errand of mischief along with the bulk of his demonic hordes. The prayers of those faithful few saints in faraway Bacon's Corner were having their effect; the prayer cover was slight, still decaying, but enough for now, provided Cree and his warriors timed things just right.

The heavenly troops were here to find one particular resident faculty member, a lady who lived in the faculty dorm.

Cree, in appearance a Native American, with powerful bronze arms and long, ebony hair down to his shoulders, had all the stealth and cunning of a skilled hunter. His sharp eyes peered through the window and out across the lake. He drew his sword and let just the tip shine through the window.

From trees nearby, from boats on the lake, from cottages and boathouses, from the thick woods across the lake, tiny points of light answered, the tips of hundreds of angelic blades.

All warriors were in place. They were ready.

Cree waved a quick little signal with his blade. A warrior appeared from behind a rowboat, skimmed across the water, zigzagged through the trees, and joined Cree in the shack. Another warrior emerged from a boathouse, shot across the water, ducked behind the swimming dock, then made it to the shack as well. Two more, darting from tree to tree and flying low, completed the number Cree wanted. They remained for a moment in the shack, tight against the walls, listening, watching.

"She'll be awakening soon," said Cree. "She'll have four guarding her. They aren't strong, but they do have big mouths. Don't let them cry out."

They drew their swords and set out across the campus, working their way from building to building, tree to tree, smoothly, steadily.

"'Course now, the drones aren't much good for anything after they've gone flying with the queen, so they just get thrown out of the hive with the garbage. Heh! I know a lot of men who are just like that, only good for eating and mating."

Mr. Pomeroy, a jolly retiree in jeans, flannel shirt, and workboots, was talking about bees, his hobby and obsession, and Sally just let him talk; the more he talked, the less she would have to, and the less questions she would have to answer about herself.

They were riding in Mr. Pomeroy's old Chevy pickup with the rack over the bed and the dented right side—he'd run over a stump trying to pull out another one and he told her all about it. He was just on his way up to a fellow-beekeeper's house to check his hives when he spotted this lone, wandering gal out on the highway, dressed in jeans and an old blue jacket, a blue stocking cap on her head, and a large duffel bag over her shoulder. He was a neighborly sort and didn't like to see a woman hitchhiking alone; so he pulled over, picked her up, gave her a short lecture about the dangers of hitchhiking, and then asked her where she was going.

"The Omega Center," she said.

She almost expected a negative reaction from this local, traditional thinker, but apparently he'd grown used to the Center being around and had no hard feelings, just curiosity.

"Must be an interesting place up there," he said.

"I don't know. I haven't been there in years."

"Well . . . we're all searching, aren't we?"

Sally didn't want to get into any deep discussions, but she answered anyway. "Yeah, we sure are."

"You know, I've found the God of the Bible to be a terrific answer to my questions. You ever thought about that?"

Sally noticed the bee helmet and veil behind the seat and used that to change the subject. "Hey, you take care of bees?"

And that was what got Mr. Pomeroy started about workers, drones, queens, hives, honey, extractors, and on and on. Sally was glad. It got them off the uncomfortable subjects and excused her from having to talk.

"That Center's just up the road here a few more miles. I can drop you off right at the front gate . . . How about that?"

The faculty dorm was a new structure, two-storied, with twenty units. The dark-stained, grooved plywood siding and shake roof matched the general motif of the campus—rustic, woodsy, but functional. Cree and his warriors found plenty of places to hide in the thick shrubbery just beneath the rear windows.

At one end of the building, a dark, slick-hided arm hung through a closed window pane and dangled outside, the silver talons walking absentmindedly, playfully back and forth along the wall. Yes, there were enemy spirits about. This one must belong to another resident faculty member. That was his room.

The opposite end of the building was a blank wall, void of windows and flanked by some large trees. Cree appointed a sentry, and then, as the sentry watched from the bushes, the other four warriors ducked around that end of the building, floated up the wall, and disappeared into the attic space. Then the sentry followed.

They crouched just under the rafters, their feet in the pink fiberglass. Now they could hear a faint, whining sound, not unlike a violin in the hands of a beginner. It was coming from one of the rooms not too far from them. They moved forward, the roof bracing passing right through their chests as they walked. Now they were above the sound.

Cree pitched forward, sinking slowly through the fiberglass and ceiling joists until he could look into the room.

Yes. They'd found the room of Sybil Denning, a kind and matronly educator of many years, just dozing in her bed, not quite awake. She was apparently enjoying some half-dreams still playing in her head, and was not ready to open her eyes just yet.

Sitting beside her on the bed, a playful, elfin spirit moved his finger about in her brain as if stirring a bowl of soup, singing quietly to himself, giggling a little between his singsong, scratchy phrases as he painted pictures in her mind.

"You will enjoy this one," it teased in a crow's voice. "Go ahead . . . leave your body and touch the moon . . ."

There were three other spirits in the room, one hanging from the wall like a bat, one flat on his back on the rug with his clawed feet in the air, and one lying on the end of the bed as if asleep. They reminded Cree of young delinquent boys hiding in some forbidden hangout, gleefully committing sin in secret.

"Oh, don't give her·*that* one again," said the spirit hanging from the wall.

"Why not?" said the dreampainter. "She always believes it."

"I can do one better."

"Tonight will be your turn."

Cree looked up at the warriors. They were ready.

The dreampainter's yellow eyes danced with delight at his own cleverness. "Oooo, remember this place? You've been here before. It is a part of you!"

A blinding flash! Four angels, four demons! Flashing swords, red smoke!

Mrs. Denning awoke with a start.

Oh. It was morning. What had she been dreaming? Walking on the moon, touching it, knowing it as if she'd made it. Yes. How beautiful. Maybe it was true, just buried behind a veil of forgetfulness. Someday she must analyze what it could mean.

She sat up. She felt rested, but not energetic. Somehow her usual inspiration wasn't with her. Maybe the previous week's work had drained her power.

Cree and his warriors regrouped in the attic to watch her. The room was empty now except for her.

She got up, got dressed, and went down the stairs. Perhaps a short walk on this crisp, clear morning would reawaken her inner potential and get the creative juices flowing. It always worked before.

"Yeah, here it is," said Mr. Pomeroy, pulling over next to a wide, gravel drive that wound back into the woods. Just next to the road was an attractive, sand-blasted sign: OMEGA CENTER FOR EDUCATIONAL STUDIES.

Sally swung the door open and hopped out. "Thanks a lot."

"God bless you now," said the kind man.

More traditional thinking, Sally thought. "Sure. Take care of yourself."

He nodded and smiled. She closed the cab door and pulled her duffel bag from the truck's bed. She gave him a wave, and off he went, apparently with bees and hives on his mind.

The sound of the old pickup faded away, and then there was only the quiet of this mountain morning. Sally stood motionless for a moment, just looking at that sign. She figured they had probably repainted it at some point, but apart from that, it was still the same. The gravel drive looked the same as well. How many years had it been? At least ten.

She was afraid, but she just had to take the chance. She started walking up that gravel drive, watching carefully on all sides. She tried to remember what it was like, where everything was. She was hoping nothing would escape her notice and surprise her.

Mr. Pomeroy's old pickup roared up the mountain road and around a long, steady curve. When the road passed behind a thick grove of trees the sound of the truck faded quickly, replaced by a whispered rushing of silken wings.

Where the road reappeared, Si, a dark East Indian, was aloft, his wings unfurled and his sword in his hand. With a burst of power he went into a steep climb and circled back toward the Center.

Mrs. Denning felt a little better out in the fresh air, walking on the smooth, asphalt path between the classrooms and meeting halls. Soon the campus would be full of people again and this restful solitude would be ended. It was certainly pleasant now; there went a chipmunk up that tree, and how the birds were chattering!

Oh, what was this, an early arrival? Just beyond the sports field, a young lady was coming up the main road into the complex. Their eyes met.

Cree touched Mrs. Denning's eyes. *Easy now . . . don't see too well.* Then he darted into the trees and out of sight. Somewhere the other warriors were present, ready and invisible.

Sally looked carefully at this woman she was approaching. She wasn't sure who she might be. She was afraid they may have known each other before. She kept walking.

Finally the two women came face to face in front of the quaint Log Cabin Cafe.

"Hello," said Mrs. Denning. "And who might you be?"

Sally smiled, but her mind was instantly far away, more than eighteen years away.

I know this woman.

The woman before her, dressed in gray pants and a casual Omega Center sweatshirt, was eighteen years older, grayer, with more lines in her face. But the gray eyes still had that same sparkle, the head still had that same playful tilt when she spoke. This was Sybil Denning!

Sally found her tongue and the name she'd decided to use. "Um . . . I'm Bethany Farrell. I was just passing through the area, and someone told me I might find a place to stay up here."

Mrs. Denning smiled. "Oh, you just might. We have overnight camping here, and some nice cabins. We're expecting people to arrive for a weekend retreat this afternoon, but they're a small group. I'm sure we'll still have some rooms empty. What did you have in mind?"

"Oh . . . just a warm place out of the rain, some blankets, maybe a mattress."

Mrs. Denning laughed. "Oh, we can do better than that! Listen, the office doesn't open for a few more hours. I think the Galvins are up by now; maybe they'll open the cafe and we can get a cup of coffee, all right?"

"All right."

Mrs. Denning turned toward the Log Cabin Cafe, and Sally followed her.

"By the way, I'm Sybil Denning."

"Pleased to meet you."

"Excuse me. What was your name again?"

"Bethany Farrell."

Mrs. Denning paused on the large patio in front of the cafe. "Bethany Farrell . . ." She stared at Sally for a moment. "Don't know why you seem so familiar to me. How do you spell your last name?"

"F-a-r-r-e-l-l."

Mrs. Denning shook her head just a little. "No . . . that doesn't sound familiar. Tell me, have we ever met before?"

Sergeant Mulligan drove over to the Post Office the moment he got the call. He parked the car quietly, went up the steps quietly, and quietly found Postmaster Lucy Brandon, then just about broke a blood vessel containing himself.

"Hi, Lucy," he said, probably too loudly.

"Oh hi, Harold," she replied from behind the counter. She was helping a patron decide whether to send something first or fourth class, and the little lady couldn't seem to make up her mind. She turned to Debbie, who was just handing a giddy junior-higher a box of baby chicks. "Debbie, could you finish helping Mrs. Barcino?"

Debbie stepped over and began checking the weight of the package on the scale. "Fourth class?"

Mrs. Barcino still wasn't happy. "Well, I don't know . . . That's kind of slow, isn't it?"

Lucy hurried to the back room and opened the Employees Only door for Mulligan. He stepped inside, his hand on his hip and his feet shuffling nervously. Lucy said nothing, but quickly stepped behind a partition for privacy. Mulligan followed her, and when they were both safe from any watching eyes, she showed him a letter, still in a sealed envelope.

He took it in his big fingers, read the address and the return address—actually just a name, and said nothing. He couldn't think of what to say.

It was a letter addressed to Tom Harris. The name in the upper-left corner was Sally Roe.

"When did this come in?" Mulligan asked.

"Today. And look at the postmark: just three days ago."

Again Mulligan couldn't think of what to say.

Lucy was quite troubled. "I don't understand. I guess it could have gotten lost somewhere, or rerouted, I don't know, but . . . there's only one postmark, and that's . . . that's halfway across the country."

Mulligan murmured, "Somebody's being a real sicko. It's a joke."

"Well, there's no address to return it to. I just don't know . . ."

"Can we open this thing?"

"No, we can't tamper with the mail . . ."

"Mmm."

"It's kind of scary, though. The postmark is after Sally Roe's suicide. What if Sally Roe is still alive somewhere?"

Mulligan didn't handle that question very well. "She isn't! That's crazy!"

She put her finger to her lips to shush him.

Debbie's attention was caught, however, by that outburst. She was finished with Mrs. Barcino and could see just a little of what was going on behind the partition.

He struggled for an answer. "Well . . . listen, I don't know what this is all about, but let me take this with me and check into it."

"But . . . it's mail!"

He held his hand up. "Hey, we're only delaying it, that's all. We need to check into this."

"But—"

"If Tom Harris ever got this letter . . . You never know, it might hurt your lawsuit."

Lucy hesitated when he said that. "But I'm concerned about the law . . ."

"Don't worry about it. We'll cover for you. I'll just have some friends check this out, and we'll get it back to you."

"You're not going to open it . . ."

"Don't worry. Just don't worry."

He put the letter in his pocket and got out of there, leaving Lucy troubled, curious, nervous, and yes, worried.

When he put the letter in his pocket, Debbie saw him do it. She didn't know what it all meant; she just thought it might be something worth remembering.

Debbie wasn't the only one who saw it. Two little spirits were following Mulligan, flitting about his shoulders like oversized mosquitoes, carefully eyeing that letter, snuffing and hissing in a frantic, secret conversation.

Mulligan climbed into his car and cranked the engine to life. He would have some phone calls to make when he got back to the station.

The two spirits had seen enough.

"Destroyer!" hissed one.

"He will reward us for this!" slobbered the other.

They shot up the street, careening over the tops of the trucks and cars, dodging the utility poles, darting this way and that between and through the stores and businesses. Destroyer must still be nearby; they would find him.

Just beneath them, unnoticed, a brown Buick eased down Front Street. The big man driving the Buick was taking it easy going through town, just getting a feel of the place. It wasn't much of a place. On the one side was the only gas station in town, boasting cheap prices and fixing flats for ladies free. Next to it was the Bacon's Corner Mercantile, a sagging old veteran of many a hard season, just like the old rusted tractor parked alongside in grass as high as the hubs.

On the other side of the street was the Myers Feed and Farm Store. That place seemed to be getting a lot of business—there were a lot of weathered pickup trucks parked around it and a lot of John Deere hats around. Then came the grain elevators, the towering sentinels that were visible for miles and bore the name of the town for anyone who might be wondering what all these little buildings were doing out in the middle of nowhere. The PriceWise grocery seemed out of place—it needed a mall around it to look right.

"So where now?" the big man asked his wife.

She sat next to him, at least as radiant in real life as she was in that picture he always kept on his desk. "What was that church we passed back there?"

"Methodist, I think."

"Oh, here's a Lutheran."

"Yeah. Very nice."

"So where do you put a Community Church?"

"We're running out of community, Kate. We'll have to turn around."

"Guess we'd better ask somebody."

He pulled over in front of Max's Barber Shop, much to the interest of the two easygoing retirees sitting in their wooden chairs on the front porch.

"Hello there," he said, and they both stood and came closer.

"Well, hi," said Ed.

"Yeh," said Mose.

"I'm looking for the Good Shepherd Community Church."

The two grayheads looked at each other and exchanged a silent, inside joke with their eyes.

Ed leaned against the car and just about put his head through the window. "You another reporter?"

Well . . . in a way, he was. "Uh, not exactly."

Mose stood behind Ed to ask his question, even while Ed just stayed there, his nose almost through the window, looking this big fellow over. "Don't think anyone's there now. The school's in session, though, and maybe the pastor's there, but he and that other lady . . ."

"Mrs. Fields," said Ed.

"Yeah, they'd be up to their gizzards in kids right now. But Tom Harris is the real hot item. If you want to see *him* . . ."

The man looked at his wife. She already had one eyebrow raised. This thing *was* big news around this town. He turned to Mose—and Ed, who was unavoidable. "Okay. Where can I find Tom Harris?"

"You're almost there. Head on up to the bank there, turn right. That's Pond Road. You go about half a mile, and you'll see the church first, on the left, and then Tom Harris's place is just the other side of the pond, on the right, a little white house with a glassed-in south side."

"Where you from?" asked Ed.

"You've never heard of the place."

"Just wondering."

Ed stood away from the car and gave a little wave as the Buick drove away. Mose just watched with a smile on his face.

Ed nodded with great conviction. "He's a reporter, Mose. I can tell."

Tom was reading through some notes he'd made for some upcoming interrogatories. Wayne Corrigan said the ACFA probably would skirt having to answer most of them, but he was going to ask them anyway. He had a lot of questions to ask those characters, and it was going to start right here.

There was a knock on the door. He closed the folder and tucked it away on the bookshelf.

Then he opened the door. His first thought was that he was facing another set of reporters, but these two were probably married, the way they stood next to each other. The man was tall and strong-looking, about middle-aged, dressed casually. His wife was attractive, also dressed casually, but exuding a quiet dignity.

"Tom Harris?" the big man asked.

"Yes," he answered, and made no effort to hide his wariness of these two strangers. "And just who are you?"

"The name is Marshall Hogan, and this is my wife Kate. We've come a long way, and we'd like to talk to you."

17

Tom made a lunch of it. He invited Mark and Cathy, Ben and Bev, and Wayne Corrigan. Corrigan was in court and couldn't make it, but the others got right over there. They pooled their sandwiches, chips, salad, and soft drinks and met with the two out-of-towners in Tom's backyard for a meeting of the minds, a serious checking-out of this Marshall Hogan. Sure, he was a Christian, and sure, he'd been through an interesting spiritual battle himself, but he was also a member of the press, and by now the press was not considered friendly or trustworthy.

They sat in a circle of chairs in the yard, munching on sandwiches and talking seriously. Marshall recounted in crisp, newscopy fashion the adventure he'd had in the town of Ashton. They were amazed. Naturally, the occult-based conspiracy to take over Ashton and the thwarting of that conspiracy went unreported in the national media. No one sitting in the yard that day had ever heard of the place or what happened there.

"And I never would have heard of you people either," he said, "if the whole thing didn't have such scandal potential. Hey, this kind of stuff the press calls news. It sells papers, and that's how it got to me, over the news wire. From what I read in the wire copy—reading between the lines, of course—you folks are up against the same thing we were facing, only worse."

Mark asked, "So you weren't disillusioned by the reports of our 'outrageous religious behavior'?"

"Maybe you *are* outrageous. Maybe you're like too many Christians who see a demon under every doily. Maybe you deserve the lawsuit and the press you're getting." Marshall looked every one of them in the eye as he spoke. "Or maybe this whole thing is legit. If it is, then I might stick around and do what I can to help you out. I've got a young gal who can run that paper while I'm away; I can take care of my own expenses up to a point. I'm a good snoop, I know how to dig things up, and I know how to fight. If this thing is what it looks like, then I'm ready to make myself available, and so is Kate."

Could this be an answer to prayer? Mark was willing to explore it further, and the others agreed. They decided to tell Marshall the details of the lawsuit and the strange incident with Amber Brandon that started the whole thing. Marshall listened intently to the whole story, and he appeared to believe it.

Then Marshall asked, "So did Amethyst ever show up again?"

Tom thought about that question. "Not in the same way. Amber stayed quiet, but she was still really strange—depressed, edgy, unattentive. She couldn't sit still during our morning devotions, and she couldn't stand hearing the Word of God. Now we know why. Amethyst wouldn't manifest at the school anymore, but she never really left."

"A tougher case than you figured on, I suppose?"

Tom turned to Cathy Howard. "Why don't you tell him about what Alice Buckmeier told you?"

"Alice Buckmeier's a widow who attends our church. She's a dear," Cathy explained. "It wasn't too long ago, just about the same time this lawsuit began, that Alice was in the Post Office mailing a package when she heard this big commotion and saw Amber screaming at a woman patron. Lucy Brandon—the postmaster—came out of the back room and tried to quiet Amber down, but she just kept screaming, and Alice says Amber was prancing like a horse again, just running circles around the woman and screaming at her and scaring her to death. The woman ran away really frightened, and Alice was just . . . she just stood there, just blown away."

"Who was the woman?"

Cathy shrugged. "Alice didn't know; she never saw her before. Anyway, Lucy Brandon chased Amber around the Post Office lobby for a long time, and I guess Amber finally calmed down and acted like nothing happened, like a total personality switch. Now that sounds . . . well . . ."

Marshall whistled at the story. "This is getting more convincing all the time."

Tom shook his head sadly. "Just try convincing the rest of the world."

"Right." Marshall pulled some news clippings from his attaché case. "The *Hampton County Star* seems to have you all figured out."

"And most of the big papers too," said Mark. "It's gone out over UPI and AP. I imagine the whole country's buzzing about it now."

"Oh sure. I see they're cashing in on the child abuse angle: 'Child Victims of Bizarre Fundamentalist Behavior.' Nice. Or how about this one from the East Coast: 'Religion as Abuse: Behind the Doors of a Private School.' Oh, I was going to ask you about this one: 'Christian School Responds to Court Order.' It says here that you still hadn't decided if you would obey the court order or not. Where's that quote? Oh. '"We must obey the laws of God rather than the laws of men," said Pastor Mark Howard.'"

Mark nodded and had to laugh. "Yes, I did say those words, but I think my entire statement was that we had heard from both sides of the question, and that some said we should obey God's appointed authorities, and some said we must obey the laws of God rather than the laws of men. I guess they caught the last part of my statement but not the first."

"So what did you decide?"

"For now, we'll submit to the court order. We figure it would be in our best interests until this lawsuit is settled. Then we'll just have to look at the question again."

Bev piped up, "Just goes to show how people with the power can decide what we know and what we don't know. It's just like what happened to Ben."

"That's nothing . . ." Ben started to say.

Bev was indignant. "Nothin'? It's got you out of a job, babe, and I don't call that nothin'!"

Cathy was in Bev's camp. "There's some other hanky-panky going on right in the Police Department. A lady was killed a few weeks ago, and they're calling it a suicide, but Ben thinks it was a murder, and now they're just covering it all up."

"And the Star's coverin' it up too," said Bev. "Did you see that little puny article calling the whole thing a suicide?" Marshall only began to shake his head. "Well there. See, you didn't see it either. They didn't want anyone to see it."

Marshall got a question in. "Ben, what happened to your job?"

"They canned him," said Bev. "He knew too much."

Ben laughed and put his arm around Bev. "That's the way I see it, yes."

Marshall considered that. "Okay. Maybe we'll talk some more about that later. But let's get back to the core of this problem, and that's Amber. Tom, you said something about her claiming to have learned all this stuff in her class at the elementary school . . ."

"Right. Miss Brewer's class. I can believe it. The schools have been experimenting with a lot of new curricula. It could be that some kind of thinly cloaked occultism got in."

"What do you know about Miss Brewer?"

"Zilch. I think she's new this year."

Cathy confirmed that. "Yes, she's new. I have some friends who know her."

"All right, we'll have to talk to them and see what they know. Miss Brewer may have brought a curriculum in with her, or maybe the school board's trying out something new. In any case, it would be nice to know how Amber got the way she is, and to be able to prove it. How about it, Kate? Feel like paying Miss Brewer a visit?"

She looked up from her notes and smiled at the thought of the adventure. "Looking forward to it."

"Now . . . people of like interests tend to clump together, just like we're doing right now, and that's called networking. Once they get networked, they start working together, and that gives them a lot of clout they didn't have before. I'd like to know how much this town is networked by any occult or cosmic-type groups. They might already be in the schools. Maybe they've infiltrated into other areas of power as well."

"There's LifeCircle," Mark said.

"Some kind of occult fellowship?"

"Oh yes. You hear a lot about them around town, and they sell herbs and mystical, holistic literature down at the Mercantile. They call themselves something like, 'a supportive circle of friends devoted to personal growth and evolvement.'"

"Who belongs to this bunch?"

They all started looking at each other. No one knew for sure who was involved in it.

"I don't know anyone right offhand," Mark explained. "They don't function much in public; they're not very visible."

"What about Miss Brewer?"

No one knew.

"How about Lucy Brandon?"

No answer.

"Well, we'd better find out then. We can't see anything yet, and it may not be just this LifeCircle outfit, but what we're looking for is some kind of connection, some kind of link-up between these ACFA guys, Claire Johanson, Lucy Brandon, Miss Brewer, and ultimately Amber. We've got to know the enemy before we can deal with him." Marshall finished the last few drops of root beer. "And I guess you know this is a spiritual battle. How are things in that department? Do you have some good prayer warriors?"

The reaction wasn't immediately affirmative. There was doubt all around, on every face.

Mark tried to explain. "It's been tough because of the lawsuit, because of the accusations leveled at Tom. The people here today are all praying, but the church is really struggling with this whole thing, and there are a lot of very unhappy people. I'm still trying to get a handle on all the talk going around."

"So they're talking and not praying?"

Mark nodded. "That's about it."

Marshall thought about that and nodded. "Sounds like a smart move on Satan's part. If he can divide the church and split you into camps, his job will be a picnic."

"Well," said Mark, "we can sure pray now, just us. I know *we're* together on this thing."

"Yeah, let's do it," said Ben.

They prayed, and took quite a bit of time at it. Marshall and Kate joined them, and that meant a lot to everyone. There was definitely a unity here, a oneness of spirit. This big man from far away and his wife were not strangers at all, but fellow-combatants. This was the hand of God.

Not long after Mark said the final "Amen," Marshall popped the final question. "So how does it sound to you? You want to deal us in, and see what develops?"

By now they were ready. Mark extended his hand, and he and Marshall shook on it. "We have fellowship, brother."

"All right, then. I've got a few projects in mind already. Cathy, see what your friends can tell us about Miss Brewer, and then Kate will drop in and visit her in person. Bev, we'll need to talk to Alice Buckmeier about that incident in the Post Office and hopefully get some more details from her; maybe then we can find out where Amber got this little horse friend and what we're really dealing with. I'll see if I can check out this LifeCircle bunch and find out who's involved."

It sounded good to them all.

The group began to break up. Cathy and Bev started clearing plates from the picnic table. Mark and Tom started folding up the furniture.

"Oh, Ben . . ." said Marshall, and Ben joined him by the back fence. Marshall leaned on the fence and looked out over a wide, green pasture bordering Tom's yard. "You were a cop, huh?"

"Yes. *Was.* They let me go about two weeks ago."

"Because you were getting too close to something they were trying to cover up?"

Ben smiled apologetically. "Well . . . in retrospect, I don't know for sure. It just seemed fishy to me."

"Let's say you *were* onto something. Tell me what."

Ben looked out at some Holsteins grazing lazily in the distance. "I've no idea, Marshall. It was simply that the deceased, a woman named Sally Roe, was killed quite violently—at least that's how the evidence looked to me. There were signs of a struggle, a shirt stained with blood, some spilled goat feed—the body was found in a goat pen, the body itself was flung on the floor as if there had been a violent struggle. The medical examiner attributed the death to asphyxiation by hanging, the same as Sergeant Mulligan's initial conclusion, but I don't think that conclusion matched the situation found at the scene. When the landlady, Mrs. Potter, found the body, it wasn't hanging from the rafters; it didn't have a rope around its neck, nor was any rope tied to the rafters. The deceased did have a rope in her hand. And the body was flung in the straw, just as we first found it. I'm also bothered by the fact that when the call first came in, Sergeant Mulligan referred to it as a suicide before we even drove out there, and I know I gave him no information at the time to that effect.

"Add to that a disturbing development that I uncovered by talking to some people who knew Roe before her death: the description they gave me of Sally Roe doesn't match the description of the woman we found in that goat shed, which raises some frightening implications. The whole thing doesn't make sense at all, and I'm still disturbed about it."

"I see you have moles in this part of the country too," said Marshall, pointing out some new molehills in the yard.

Ben was a little disappointed. Apparently his concerns were unimportant to this man who claimed to be so interested in the problems he and his friends were facing. "Well . . . yeah. They're tough to get rid of. When they come up in my yard, I just keep scooping up the hills so they don't kill the grass. It's about all you can do."

Brother, thought Ben, *what a stupid conversation this is becoming.*

"Looks like the neighbors have them too." Marshall pointed at several molehills out in the pasture.

"Yeah, they get around," said Ben, ready to end this letdown of a conversation, starting to look around.

"Two different pieces of property here," said Marshall, looking up and down the fence. "Tom has a mole, and the farmer over there has a mole." Then Marshall looked at Ben for a moment, waiting for Ben's full attention. "How much you wanna bet that the molehills in this yard and the molehills in that pasture were made by the same mole?"

Ben stopped any other thoughts and paid attention. This guy was making a point that sounded interesting.

Marshall enhanced his point. "Ben, from up here on top of the ground, we think in terms of property lines, of separate domains. Tom has his yard, the farmer has his pasture, and the two domains are separated by this fence. But what about the mole? The fence doesn't stop him; he just goes wherever he wants and pushes up his little hills, and as far as he's concerned, it's just one big piece of ground."

"Keep going," said Ben.

Marshall smiled, his eyes squinting a bit in the sun, the breeze blowing his red hair. "The Good Shepherd Academy has a problem, and you have a problem. The Academy has a mole, and you have a mole. I'm suggesting that it might be the same mole. We're talking spiritual warfare here; spirits don't care about whose yard it is, or where our fences might be."

"So what are you saying?"

"I'm saying I'll feel a whole lot better if you and I can find out all we can about this Sally Roe."

Ben felt better. "You know, I was hoping someone would see it this way."

"I think Bev already did."

Ben carefully considered that. "She sure did." Then he dug up a buried idea. "I was going to run a criminal check on Roe before I got fired. I think I could still run a check; I have a friend with the police in Westhaven who could do it for me."

Marshall looked at the molehills again. "Can't wait to see it."

18

S ybil Denning was a kind and sociable person, and she never seemed to be at a loss for words and topics. She and Sally spent the better part of the morning wandering about the grounds of the Omega Center for Educational Studies as Mrs. Denning pointed out all the buildings, their purpose, and what new projects were currently underway.

"This plaza should be ready in a few weeks," she said, pointing to a large patio the size of a basketball court, but without any markings and bordered by newly planted hedges. "The Tai Chi Chuan program has gained such popularity that we thought it fitting to create an effective space for it."

They walked further. "This is the performance theater. It seats about four hundred, and is our showcase for any performing arts such as music, movement, dance, poetry, drama, and so forth. Oh, and down here . . ." They came to a large stone-and-glass structure. "This is our healing arts center. We've had our various workshops in classrooms all over the campus, but since last year we've tried to consolidate the research in one building. We're trying new holistic approaches to the immune system, as well as nutritional therapy, and then homeopathy, crystals, vibrational healing, even Tibetan medicine—that's a course I plan to take while I'm here. Listen, are you hungry? It's almost time for lunch, and I'm sure the Galvins will have something ready."

"Lead on," said Sally, alias Bethany Farrell.

They sat down to a tasty vegetarian lunch. Sally ordered the rice and stir-fried vegetables; Mrs. Denning ordered a large green salad.

"Obviously," Mrs. Denning continued, not skipping a beat from the entire morning's lecture, "the goal of education, true education, is not simply teaching generation after generation the same amount of academic content as a preparation for life—just the same old basics, as they say. The human race is evolving too fast for that. What we are more concerned with in education is the facilitation of change. We need to change the upcoming generations to prepare them for a global community. That means a lot of stubborn old ideas about reality are going to have to be cast aside: such notions as nationalism, accountability to some Supreme Being, even the old Judeo-Christian dogma of absolute morality. In their place, we purpose to implant a new worldview, a global scheme of reality in which our children realize that all the earth, all nature, all forces, all consciousness are one huge, interconnected, and interdependent unity. And we're no longer alone in that goal; even the National Coalition on Education has taken up the cause."

She continued to munch on her salad like a happy rabbit. "So, we bring all wisdoms of the world to this place, all systems of belief, all mystical traditions, and we bar almost nothing. Through it all, the truth can be found by each person where he finds it."

"Human potential," said Sally.

"Oh, yes, that, and spiritual wholeness, universal consciousness, all of the above!" Mrs. Denning laughed with delight. "It's been such a rewarding time for me . . . well, for many years of my life, actually. I used to teach high school English until six years ago when I came on staff here."

Sally knew that. Though her memory of Mrs. Denning the English teacher went back nineteen years, she could see it as if it were just yesterday. A scene began playing in her mind. There stood a much younger Mrs. Denning, with more brown hair than gray, scowling at her, angry at being interrupted. Sally was much younger too, a junior in high school with a drab green sweater, a thigh-high skirt, and long, straight, red hair down to her waist.

"Who are you and why?" Mrs. Denning demanded. It was a stock question she always used; she must have thought it was clever. Sally thought it was rude.

Obviously, Mrs. Denning was not feeling well at the moment. She was trying to lead a remedial reading group, and most of the students were the shaggy, acid-dropping, spit-on-the-floor type who couldn't read and didn't care if they ever did. Mrs. Denning was definitely not in her element, much less in her best mood.

Sally wasn't feeling well either. Her mother, whom she hadn't seen in almost twelve years, had just died, a pitiful alcoholic. Sally felt no remorse, but the event did deepen some attitudes she'd been developing in that high school—attitudes of fatalism, cynicism, and gloom.

Now Sally was only doing her job as an office assistant during fourth period, and trying to bring Mrs. Denning a sign-up sheet on a clipboard, a typical list of participants in an upcoming volunteer whatever-it-was. She didn't ask to be snapped at. Mrs. Denning's question hit a lot of raw nerves.

Who am I and why? Good question.

She looked down at the teacher scowling up at her, and answered quite directly, "I don't know, and you teachers have convinced me that I never will."

Well, of course Mrs. Denning got irate. "Young lady, I don't like your attitude!"

At this point in her life, Sally didn't care what Mrs. Denning liked or didn't like. "Mrs. Denning, I came into this classroom because Mrs. Bakke would like to get your signature on this sign-up sheet. I'm just doing my job, and I don't deserve to be treated rudely."

Mrs. Denning stood to her feet, ready to take up the challenge. "What is your name?"

"Roe. Sally Roe. That's R-o-. . . Got a pencil?"

Mrs. Denning had a pencil.

"R-o-e. I'm sure you'll remember it."

"I'm surprised they let you work in the office. Mrs. Bakke is going to hear about this!"

Sally held the clipboard out. "Will Mrs. Bakke be able to count on you as a volunteer?"

Mrs. Denning grabbed the clipboard and hurriedly signed it. "Now get out of here!"

"Thank you for your time."

Sally was just reaching the door when Mrs. Denning had some parting words for her. "This *will* be counted against you, young lady!"

She stopped and looked back at this teacher, this figure of authority. "Well, you're the teacher; you have the power. Right and wrong are situational and law derives from power, so I guess that makes you right." Then Sally thought it best to footnote her comments. "Mr. Davis, Humanities 101, sixth period."

Mrs. Denning meant to report Sally's behavior, but never did. Something about that brief encounter stuck with her, and no, she did not forget Sally Roe's name.

Sally's mind returned to the present, and she chased a mushroom around her plate as Mrs. Denning continued to prattle. Sally had to smile at how different their conversation was compared to their first.

"Of course, I was involved here long before I actually came on staff. I'd be here almost every summer, working on continuing education credits and helping with the Young Potential program." Sally was just about to ask, but didn't need to; Mrs. Denning went on to explain what that was. "Several of the teachers acquainted with Omega regularly took part in a program to recruit young people from the various high schools we represented around the country, young people who showed real potential for future leadership, who displayed special ability. I recruited several young people myself from the high school where I taught. These Young Potentials, as we called them, would be a part of our summer program here at the

Center, and several came back for intensive training over several summers, even after they started college."

Sally smiled. She could remember the Mrs. Denning of nineteen years ago, sitting at her desk in her empty classroom during the lunch recess, strangely pleasant.

Sally, still the skinny and stone-faced upstart, had paused outside the classroom door to get her nerves good and steely before she stepped inside. When Mrs. Denning smiled and offered her a chair, she was quite surprised and a little suspicious.

"As you have probably figured out," she said, "I didn't report that confrontation we had a few weeks ago."

Sally said nothing. She was here because Mrs. Denning had asked her to come; let Mrs. Denning carry the conversation.

Mrs. Denning rested her elbows on the desk and folded her hands just under her chin. "I apologize for being so crabby. I considered what you said, and yes, I believe I was rude to you."

Sally wasn't feeling talkative yet. "Okay."

"Sally, I've talked to Mr. Davis, and also to Mrs. Bakke and Mr. Pangborn, and we've all come to agree that you show great promise; you've risen above some real obstacles in your life and excelled academically and intellectually. Now the other teachers tell me you're asking some incisive questions and digging into the material much more deeply than the courses require."

"I want it to be *about* something," Sally said.

Mrs. Denning was impressed and nodded with a smile. "Yes. The meaning behind it all, isn't that right?"

Sally was in no mood to waste words. "I've excelled. I've learned. I've kept a consistent 4.0 average. But if I'm nothing more than a cosmic accident, then I don't see any point in all that I've done, and to be honest, I'm getting quite bored with it."

Mrs. Denning reached for a brochure and handed it to her. "You might be interested in this."

Sally looked it over as she listened.

"It's a special summer program for exceptional students. I've been involved as a summer advisor for several years now, and I'm always looking for new Young Potentials. I think you would fit the qualifications."

"What would I learn?"

Mrs. Denning was delighted to give such an answer. "The meaning behind it all."

The meaning behind it all. Now, nineteen years later, Sally couldn't hold back a bitter smile. Fortunately, Mrs. Denning didn't notice.

"Would you like any more tea?" the teacher asked.

"Yes, please."

Mrs. Denning poured the green, herbal concoction into Sally's cup.

Sally asked, "So how have all these Young Potentials turned out?"

"Marvelous! We've had an impressive record, with our Young Potentials going on to become educators, psychologists, doctors, even statespersons. You see, the strength of Omega is in the upcoming generations we educate. When we mold them in their younger years, they then mature to be the future change agents in our culture, bringing all the masses closer and closer to the ultimate goal of world community. It starts in the classroom.

"And that's what's so exciting about the changes that have occurred in recent years. Our material and curricula are gaining a much wider acceptance now. Educators and schools all over the country are attending our seminars and signing up for our programs. I think one factor would be the dissolving of the old traditional worldview, the Christian factor, that's been such an obstacle for so many years. People are starting to wake up to themselves and the need for global community. It's the only way our race can survive, of course. Now that we're educating new generations totally free of the old traces of Judeo-Christian bigotry, our success rate is rising exponentially."

Cree was hearing it all, hiding in the attic of the little cafe. But he was getting edgy; it was getting later all the time, and before too long, more people would start showing up, more teachers, more leaders, more gurus and shamans, and with them, more demons than he or his warriors wanted to face. Worst of all, the prince of this place would be back as well, and he would be most upset to find these saboteurs lurking about.

He heard a special whistle. It was Si, signaling trouble. He shot down the length of the attic, out the end of the building, and into the concealing branches of a large maple.

There was a tiny sparkle of light coming from the trees near the front gate—Si's signal. He was alerting all the warriors.

And there was the trouble! The demons appeared first, swirling and hovering in a flock of at least a hundred, following about twenty feet above an unseen vehicle. They weren't too large, probably not front-liners, but deadly nevertheless. Cree had to cringe just looking at those flashing fangs and clicking, razor-sharp talons. Assailing that bunch would best be avoided.

Then the vehicle appeared, a large van, lumbering toward the campus, stirring up the dust. It was full of weekenders—and full of demonic warriors as well.

The window of opportunity was rapidly closing. They had to get Sally out of there!

"Say," said Sally, as if she'd just remembered something, "would it be the Omega Center that published that curriculum I saw . . . *Finding Me . . .* ?"

Mrs. Denning's eyes brightened. "*Finding the Real Me*! Yes, that's a popular curriculum for grades 1-6; we have different programs for every grade, but the easiest implementation so far has been with fourth-graders. You know, we've had that curriculum available for about ten years, but never got into the schools until just a few years ago—the old Christian roadblocks again. We're having great success with it now, however. It still works, and that says a lot for the staff that put it together."

Si whistled again, and Cree got the signal. More vehicles were coming up the road: a fifty-passenger bus, full of high-schoolers, several cars, another van.

The first van was pulling up in front of the registration office, its escorting cloud of demons beginning to disperse, all cackling and chattering, some roosting in the trees, some alighting on the top of the van, some just flitting about the grounds looking for mischief.

No! Cree hadn't seen these two yet. From within the van, like huge, hulking dinosaurs, two demon warriors emerged and stood guard, their swords ready at their sides, their yellow eyes darting about with great wariness. They were searching the grounds, the trees, every possible hiding-place, looking for any intruders.

Then a man stepped out of the van and stretched a bit. He was dressed in a navy-blue jogging suit and wore dark sunglasses. He was middle-aged, but obviously a real health enthusiast. His face had a strange, stony expression; the muscles seemed tight.

Cree recognized him immediately.

Steele. The mysterious Mr. Steele, overseer of the Omega Center! No wonder there were such monstrous demon guards along!

Four other men got out of the van, each with at least four demonic escorts clinging to him. These were vicious characters indeed. There was something about these four; Cree could sense that they were something even more insidious and evil than Mr. Steele.

Mr. Steele paused by the registration office to chat with some old friends who had just arrived in the school bus. He waved at all the high schoolers still waiting to pile out.

Cree could no longer signal anyone without being seen. He and his warriors would soon be boxed in.

Both ladies had finished their lunch and now sat over their cups of tea, relaxing.

Sally figured the time was right for her next question. She began to pull the neck chain from inside her shirt.

"Say . . . in all your travels, I was just wondering . . . have you ever seen a ring like this?"

She brought the ring out into the open and let Mrs. Denning have a good look at it.

Mrs. Denning put on her reading glasses for a closer look. "Hehhh . . . what is this symbol on here?"

"I've always tried to figure that out."

"Where did you get this?"

"A friend."

Mrs. Denning turned the ring over, this way and that, studying it. "Well . . . this face could be a gargoyle, but so triangular . . . like a combination of ghoulish face and triangle . . . Fascinating."

"But you've never seen anything like this before?"

"Oh no, not that I know of."

Steele was heading for the cafe. Cree looked across the grounds. His warriors were hiding themselves well—so well that even Cree could not see them. He wasn't sure where they were, or if they were there at all.

Oh no! Beyond the lake, just over the tops of the trees, a large detachment of demons approached like a swarm of bats, appearing as a long, thin, charcoal smudge across the sky. The Prince of Omega was returning, ready for more evildoing. Soon he and his horde would be right over the lake.

Cree ducked back into the attic of the cafe to check on Sally.

Mr. Steele went into the Log Cabin Cafe and immediately greeted Mr. Galvin who stood behind the counter polishing a long row of drinking glasses along the back shelf with a soft white towel.

"Hey, Mr. Steele, you're back already!"

Mr. Steele didn't remove his sunglasses, but he did allow a smile to cross his tight lips. "Wanted to be here for the weekend, Joel."

"What'll you have?"

"Coffee, please."

"Got a fresh batch."

Mrs. Denning heard Mr. Steele's voice and turned in her seat. "Oh, Mr. Steele! What a surprise!"

He smiled at her and came their way.

Sally looked down at the table immediately, trying to get the horrified expression off her face. Was her heart beating? For a moment she thought it had stopped.

"So how has the week gone, Sybil?" said Mr. Steele.

"Mr. Steele, I'd like you to meet a visitor we have today. This is Bethany Farrell, a traveler from Los Angeles just looking for a change, a little bit of a challenge."

Mr. Steele removed his sunglasses. Sally looked up at him. Their eyes met.

They knew each other.

Cree drew his sword, trying to concoct a plan. With Sally cornered in the cafe he might have to call for a full assault. In any event, they only had minutes to spare now. Demonic forces were gathering on every hand. What about Si—

ROOAARRR! Cree ducked as the blazing sword slashed right over his head! Teeth! Yellow eyes! Gaping jaws!

Cree's wings exploded into a brilliant blur. He shot through the attic toward the gable end, the demon's sword like a shrieking buzz saw at his heels.

YAUGHH! The other demon guard appeared in front of him like a bomb blast, yellow teeth bared. Cree couldn't stop in time; he whipped his sword in a fiery arc.

The demon's head and Cree went sailing through the end of the building; the head dissolved, and Cree shot skyward, letting out a desperate shout that echoed over the campus and across the lake.

The remaining demon guard, a hideous monster, grabbed at Cree's feet. Cree shot upward with another burst of speed. Another demon from above swooped down like a hawk and lunged with its sword. Cree blocked it and sent the demon spinning crazily away.

The guard's blade came at his midsection full-force. Their swords met in an explosion of fiery sparks, and Cree tumbled into the trees.

Mr. Steele's lips were even tighter now, and his eyes were piercing. He extended his hand in greeting. "I'm pleased to meet you, uh . . . Bethany."

Sally took his hand, and he gripped it so tightly it hurt. For the longest time he just wouldn't let go, but held her hand and gazed at her.

"I'm pleased to meet you," she said as soon as she could find her voice.

He hasn't changed at all! He still looks the same!

Mrs. Denning was still her jovial self. "Mr. Steele is the director of the Omega Center. He's a tremendous man." Then she told Mr. Steele, "I've been showing her around the Center, just acquainting her with what we're about . . ." She just kept going on and on.

Oh, Mrs. Denning, please shut up. You're going to get me killed.

"So you've seen everything, have you?" asked Mr. Steele.

"Well, not *everything* . . ." He was hurting her hand.

He was the same way when he taught the summer classes here at the Center years ago. Sally was afraid of him then. She was afraid of him now. There was a sinister power, a presence, about him. He could hypnotize with those eyes of his.

Si shot out of the trees along with about fifty warriors at that end of the campus, taking the demons by surprise. One cluster of them was just coming onto the grounds with another automobile full of weekenders. The heavenly warriors flooded over them before they knew what was happening and removed that complication immediately.

In answer to Cree's shout, the remaining hundred warriors swept in a fiery sheet across the lake, divided into many streams, and rushed through the campus like a flood. Demons spun about, then shot forward from the trees, buildings, and vehicles with piercing cries and vicious wails. Swords clashed, wings roared, sparks flew. The angels were engaging the demons' full attention, fiercely battling two, three, six demons at once, but they were not prevailing. The evil spirits were standing their ground.

Cree shot and zigzagged through the trees, this way, that way, in, out, up, down, feinting, darting.

CRUNCH! The guard came at him, and their swords met again. This demon couldn't be shaken!

The expansive cloud of spirits beyond the lake heard the cries and saw the battle. Out front, his fangs protruding past his chin and his head bristling with spikes, Barquit, the Prince of Omega, roared a command and drew his sword. With an echoing, ringing, flourishing of red, glowing blades, the returning warriors dove for the campus.

Mrs. Denning wasn't about to stop until she had told Mr. Steele everything. "Oh, you know what? She has a strange ring she ought to show you."

Mr. Steele let go of Sally's hand. He leaned closer. She thought she felt heat from his face. "A ring?"

Sally shook her head and tried to smile, to chuckle the whole thing aside. "Oh no, it's nothing."

He was still leaning so very close. "Oh, yes. I'd like very much to see it."

The guard came down from high in the trees like a meteor. Cree shot sideways and just barely avoided being cut in half. He gave another mighty burst of his wings and headed for the sky.

The guard had his heel! Cree pulled with his wings, but the beast jerked him down!

ZZOOOSH! Si! God bless him!

OOF! Cree's heel was free.

In a long streak of light, Si dropped out of the sky and rammed the guard full-force. Both went tumbling in a grappling, snarling ball of fire. Cree flipped over and dropped earthward again, sword ready.

The guard had Si by the throat, his big sword raised.

Cree hurled his sword, and it went through the guard's torso like a missile. Si wriggled free and cut the thing in half. It dissolved in a choking cloud of red smoke.

Cree regained his sword. He could see the Prince of Omega descending like a storm. "Let's get her out of here!"

Sally drooped her head.

"Is something wrong?" asked Mrs. Denning.

"I think I'm going to be sick." She wasn't lying.

Mr. Steele grabbed her wrist. "Let me help you to the restroom."

He lifted her from her seat.

"No, let me go alone . . ."

Mrs. Denning was a little startled by Mr. Steele's forward behavior. "Mr. Steele, maybe she can go alone . . ."

He didn't seem to hear her. He was signaling through the window to the four men who had come with him in the van. They were watching. They saw the wave of his hand and started toward the cafe.

Cree and Si had made their chance.

"No guards," shouted Cree. "He's open!"

Barquit and his demons were diving across the lake, heading for the campus, swords ready.

Sally could see four men hurrying to the cafe. They could see her through the window, and the sight quickened their step. Mr. Steele was making no effort to get to the restroom. He wouldn't let go of her.

This wasn't a man. This was . . . something else.

"I'm going to throw up!" Sally threatened.

Cree banked sharply, made a tight turn, and dropped like a missile toward the end of the cafe, his wings roaring. The wall of the cafe filled his vision, slapped past him. He was inside, careening over the tables, along the counter, sword extended.

Joel Galvin ducked, his arms over his head, and Mrs. Denning shrieked as the entire row of drinking glasses shattered from one end to the other.

Mr. Steele ducked too, pulling Sally down with him.

Cree was out the other end of the cafe, pulling up into the sky just as Si shot like a bullet through the front of the cafe and right through Steele.

"Ahhh!!" Mr. Steele's hand went to his eyes.

"Mr. Steele!" shouted Galvin.

Sally was free. She ran for the door.

Si's sword had been there. The four men didn't see her, and neither did the spirits attached to them. The spirits were fluttering about, looking for their attacker; the four men stood there squinting, shading their eyes, trying to figure out which direction the sun was coming from.

The Prince of Omega and his hordes descended on the campus, flushing out a blizzard of brilliant warriors who scattered in all directions, fleeing like frightened birds. The demons shrieked and gave chase. This was the kind of sport they were hoping for. Barquit kept looking for the leader of this marauding host, but did not see him.

Retreat! Retreat! The angels fled, leading the demonic hordes further into the sky, further from the campus, further from the trouble below.

"Good!" said Cree, following Sally.

Sally ran down the gravel road, passing more cars arriving with more people.

"Hey," somebody called, "which way to registration?"

"Just keep going," she replied. "You'll find it."

They kept going. So did she.

The Prince of Omega and his demons cheered and wailed as they chased countless angelic warriors across the sky. They had the power and they had the numbers. They would purge their territory of these brilliant troublemakers, and that would be that.

Cree and Si just kept close to Sally, trying to force her under trees and out of sight. She seemed to know what to do, where to run, how to hide. They flew headlong just above her, swords drawn, rolling steadily to look skyward, earthward, skyward . . .

They didn't know how many they'd lost in this battle. But they still had Sally Roe . . . for now.

Good. Run, girl, just run.

19

Mr. Steele stood, but his hands were still covering his eyes. Mr. Galvin and Mrs. Denning hurried to his aid.

"Hey, easy now! Get glass in your eye?" Galvin asked.

"Must be, must be."

The four men hurried inside, still seeing spots in front of their eyes. One stayed by the door. Another checked the back door.

The third took hold of Mrs. Denning's arm. She protested, "Ouch! I beg your pardon!"

"That's Mrs. Denning!" Mr. Steele snapped.

The man let go of her. "What happened?"

The fourth man helped Mr. Steele to his feet. "Man, look at the mess!"

"Mr. Steele, you all right?" Galvin asked.

His eyes cleared. Galvin looked at them closely.

"I don't see anything, Mr. Steele. You feel anything?"

Mr. Steele was concerned about something else. "Did you see her?"

The fourth man answered, "Not clearly, just through the window."

"Did you see her *leave*?" he demanded.

"No."

"We didn't see a thing," said the third man. "The sun was right in our eyes."

Mr. Steele sat in anger and disgust. "The sun . . . !"

Galvin was curious. "Who was that woman, Mr. Steele?"

Mr. Steele suddenly smiled as if she were a pleasant subject. "An old friend, Joel. I hadn't seen her in years."

Mrs. Denning's eyebrows shot up in surprise. "You *know* Bethany Farrell?"

He looked at Mrs. Denning quite flustered and didn't answer.

"How are your eyes?" she asked.

"They're fine, thank you."

Mr. Galvin got a broom to sweep up the broken glass. Steele got up and motioned his four men outside.

As soon as they stepped onto the porch, Steele cautioned his men, "Nobody hears about this."

"Right," they answered, "you got it."

He spoke rapidly and quietly. "She's got a dye job now, her hair's black, and she's wearing tinted glasses. She has the ring, all right."

"She can't get very far," said the first man.

Steele whispered to the fourth man, "I'll give you some work right away if you wish."

The fourth man understood. He whispered some quick orders to the other three. "Check up and down the road right away, and then check around Fairwood."

Mr. Steele suggested, "They might check at the Schrader Motor Inn in Fairwood. She used to stay there."

The fourth man nodded and gave one final order. "If you find her, take care of her cleanly and quietly."

The three other men snapped into action.

Mr. Steele looked back toward the cafe. "Mrs. Denning will have to be interviewed. Goring will be coming from Summit on Monday, and Santinelli said he'd be here by Monday evening. We'll talk to Mrs. Denning as soon as Goring gets here. I think you should be at the interview as well."

The fourth man nodded. He was dark and lean, dressed all in black, with a sharp nose, deep brown eyes, and strange, pointy eyebrows.

"Looks like your energies hit a critical mass in there," he said. "That was quite a disturbance."

"Maybe." Mr. Steele was unwilling to admit it. "Roe might be into some new kind of power . . . She *might* be." Then his voice took on a strange, sinister tone. "But she's dealing with *us* now, so she won't last forever. The real power is ours, and it's going to stay that way!"

"No," said Ted Walroth, starting to raise his voice. "June and I have talked about it, we've prayed about it, and we just can't go on with this. Listen, Mark, we've gone astray from the will of the Lord having this school. I've always thought that, and now we're just finding it out the hard way. The Lord just isn't blessing this thing!"

Mark and Ted were in the little school office; Mark had gathered all the records for the two Walroth children, Mary and Jonathan, and had them ready to hand over to Ted, but he was still hoping against hope that he could talk Ted into keeping his children in the school.

"But, Ted . . . if you'll be honest with yourself, with June, with Mary and Jonathan, you'll have to admit that the school's done them a world of good. Their scores are up, they're close to the Lord, their self-esteem is great, they're happy . . ."

"Oh, are they?" Ted challenged. "For how long? How long is it going to be, Mark, before something happens to them too?"

Mark had heard that kind of talk too many times before, and he was getting tired of it. "Ted, I don't know who you've been talking to, but there are a lot of outright lies going around, and I hope—"

"I don't care about the lies or the gossip, I know about all that nonsense. But I believe that behind all the talk and the fear there is a definite element of risk—"

"There is no element of risk!"

Now Ted was openly angry. He pointed his finger at Mark and looked down that finger with cold blue eyes. "Now that right there is a problem in itself! You've lost your objectivity in this thing, Mark, totally and completely! If there was a problem, even a serious problem, I don't think you'd admit it! You've taken Tom's side in this thing, and I think that's unacceptable for the pastor! You don't know what kind of person Tom is when you're not around! None of us do! And if you're going to be his advocate in these matters, then I don't think we can trust you either, and I don't think we can remain under your pastorship!"

Mark took a moment to be quiet and break the momentum of this building confrontation. He spoke softly. "Ted . . . Satan is busily at work among us, trying to split us up, trying to cause division . . ."

Ted agreed. "I'll say! You can't see the Lord's will anymore, Mark, even when it's as plain as day, right in front of you! This school is a colossal mistake, a wrong step we never should have taken, and now we're paying for it, and you're just refusing to see that."

Mark tried to clarify what he meant. "I meant . . ."

"I know what you meant! And I'm saying you're wrong, dead wrong. You've been stubborn, you've been blind, you've come to the defense of a man that we simply can't trust, and now we're all under a lawsuit and push has come to shove. June and I want no part of it, and we certainly don't want our kids dragged through it." He grabbed the knob and opened the door. "I've got to go."

Mark handed him the records.

"Thanks."

Ted walked hurriedly, angrily, to the main door.

"See you Sunday?" Mark asked.

"No," Ted replied, not turning around. "Don't expect that. I don't think the Lord is happy with this church right now."

And with that, he was gone.

Tal, Nathan, and Armoth stood just outside, watching him go.

"It's spreading," said Nathan. "First in the school, and now in the church. They're at each other's throats."

Tal fell back and leaned against the school building. "Destroyer! With no change in direction, the saints here won't have a school left to defend."

"And we won't have the prayer backup to succeed in . . . in *anything!*"

"But what about the spirits responsible?" demanded Armoth. "Surely we can root them out!"

"No," said Tal, and he was quite angry and frustrated. "They have a right to be there. They were invited. The saints have given themselves over to this fight, and until their hearts break, until they repent, this cancer will never slow its spread."

"So what now?" asked Nathan.

"Mota and Signa are working to find a breach in the enemy's ranks, some weak spot in Destroyer's plan that we can expose for the saints to find. In the meantime, all we can do is keep the core group praying, fighting. The Lord will move according to his purposes. He'll—"

They drew their swords.

No, it was no demonic army, not even a formidable spirit, only a small, ugly messenger, brazen enough to fly right over their heads, waving its empty hands to show it was not an aggressor.

"Ha haaaa!!!" it called. "Are you Captain Tal?"

"I am," said Tal.

"Destroyer has a message for you!" The little imp hovered high above them, calling out its message with a high, grating voice. "He says, 'I have cut you down, great captain! Omega is mine, and ever shall be, and your army is routed and scattered! Send some more! My warriors are hungry!'"

The imp darted away like a little fly.

Tal did not smile as he said, "Sally Roe is safe. Had they destroyed her, that would have been Destroyer's message." He sheathed his sword. "We'll find Cree and Si, and make sure of their welfare. I've sent Guilo ahead to aid Chimon and Scion at Bentmore. We three will take charge of Sally's next stop. We must keep her alive."

"We are weakened, captain," said Nathan.

Tal nodded. "Gather all the forces you can spare, Nathan. We'll do our best."

Sally remembered a side road when she came to it, but couldn't remember exactly where it went. She took it anyway, just to get off the main highway. There was a red farmhouse not too far down on the right, with a gully in front and a classic-looking red barn. That registered. She'd seen it before, perhaps while bicycling. This road should eventually lead her back to Fairwood.

She heard a vehicle approaching and ducked into the woods. It was just a farmer in his pickup.

She decided to wait for just a while. She pulled out her spiral notebook and added some quick notes to another letter, first recounting her recent narrow escape, then trying to summarize her troubled, churning memories.

> *I'm remembering, Tom, piece by piece. The Omega Center has grown a lot and is double the size it was when I was last there. But the spiritual forces are the same, as are the philosophies and the goals of those people.*
>
> *It all seemed so utopian eighteen years ago. I can recall the classes in Eastern philosophy and the long sessions in the meadows, sitting for hours in meditation, feeling such a unity with all life, with all that is. What bliss that was. I can remember the special spirit-guides who came to me during my last summer. They opened my consciousness to realize my own divinity, and revealed worlds of experience and awareness I'd never known before. It was like an endless carnival ride through a world of enticing secrets, and my guides promised to remain with me forever.*
>
> *But the joy of those days eventually soured like warm, aging milk. The bliss of meditation became more and more a form of insanity and escape; the spirit-guides did not remain with me as they promised, but decayed into illusions, ghostly images, tormentors. I had gone to Omega to*

*find, as Mrs. Denning put it, "the meaning behind it all,"
but found instead a world of mindless credulity and wishful
thinking, a floating, aimless quest for experience in place of
rationality. Meaning? No, only self-aggrandizement. And
whether a person is a small cosmic accident or a god who
fills all that is, that person is still alone.*

*So it was futile. I can see that now, but of course
"now" is too late. I am so much older, and so many fruit-
less years have passed. Looking back, I find it so very sad
to count the years I devoted to that place and what it
stands for. I find it even sadder to think that it is still there,
still drawing more and more Sally Roes into its nets. I wonder, someday will those bright-eyed and optimistic teens
look back across the years and find the futility that I find
now? From a better vantage point, will they assess their
lives and find as little value?*

*Those were, as I have said, days of madness. But I
must REMEMBER, whatever it takes. There is still more to
the story, and I must remember who these people are,
where they are, and what they intend. I must remember
who I am, and what I am—or was—to them.*

I'll keep writing as often as I can.

"Yeah, and some very hot places are going to freeze over before
I'll believe that! You heard me!"

Wayne Corrigan slammed down the phone and fumed, "They
won't answer my interrogatories! They're stalling, playing games!"

"Surprise, surprise," said Marshall.

Corrigan, Marshall, Ben, and Tom were sitting in Corrigan's
office comparing notes and going over the case.

"How many interrogatories did you send out?" asked
Marshall, sitting on the other side of Corrigan's desk, looking
through a stack of copies.

"Just the preliminaries, the basics," said Corrigan. "But they
won't even answer those, they won't return my phone calls, and
even if I do get through, they stonewall it. You may have noticed
the response I got from Brandon's lawyer just now, that Jefferson
character."

"I noticed the response he got from *you.*"

"Well, I was upset."

Ben was leaning against the windowsill, just listening to the
conversation. "You did just fine. They had it coming."

Marshall concurred. "They're just looking out for their own behinds. It won't hurt to go after them a bit, keep them off-balance."

Corrigan tried to explain his frustration. "But they keep saying their records are too personal and confidential, and then Jefferson told me they haven't even assembled their discovery materials yet, and I think that's baloney. On top of that, I think they're stalling on taking depositions from our side. They want us to go first so they'll have more ammunition. I can't stall like that; we just don't have the time."

"Looks like they aren't going to give you anything without a court order."

"Yeah, tell me all about it."

"Hey, listen. Kate's asking around about this Miss Brewer at the elementary school, and she's already made an appointment to visit the class on Monday. Maybe when she gets back she'll have some goods on this Miss Brewer, and you can use that in some depositions."

"Well, that's what I need: more leads, more players in this thing. So far I'm in the dark about what the other side is up to."

Marshall tossed the interrogatories back on Corrigan's desk. "Well, it's bigger than it looks, I know that."

"Moles," said Ben.

"Huh?" said Tom.

"Get Marshall to explain it to you sometime. It's a great parallel."

Corrigan was ready for another topic. "So how about your kids, Tom? Are you going to be able to see them again?"

Tom wasn't happy about his answer. "Pretty soon, but I'm not sure when. It's all up to this Irene Bledsoe lady, and she's . . . well, she's quite ruthless. I try not to think about it too much."

Corrigan shook his head and leaned back in his chair, making the springs squeak. For him, leaning back and examining the ceiling was a typical expression of frustration. "She's feeling her oats, if you know what I mean. Tom, if you were rich and powerful, you'd probably have your kids back by now. But Bledsoe knows she has all the power she needs, and without some real pressure from people in important places, she can do whatever she wants. The laws are just vague enough to allow a lot of leeway from case to case."

"But she's so unreasonable!" Tom moaned. "She's guarding my kids like . . . like she's afraid to let them out of her sight, like she wants to control them."

"She is and she does," said Marshall.

"But you heard about that bump on Ruth's head, didn't you?"

Marshall was sitting in a swivel chair. With a simple kick he swiveled around to face Tom. "No. Tell me."

"Last time I visited the kids, Ruth had a big bump on her head, and both of them said she got it when Bledsoe just about got into a wreck driving them away from our house! Bledsoe's trying to blame that bump on *me*, suggesting that *I* did it!"

Marshall was hearing some shocking news, it seemed. "A near-wreck?"

"Yes. You should have seen how Mrs. Bledsoe tried to keep the kids from saying *anything* about that, but Josiah told me about it anyway. He said she went through a stop sign and almost hit a blue pickup truck. She stopped too fast, the kids must not have been belted in, and Ruth—"

Ben interrupted. "Wait a minute! Did you say a blue pickup truck?"

"Yes, that's what Josiah said."

"When was that?" Ben started thinking back.

"I'm not sure . . ." Now Tom started recalling. "Evidently the evening when she came and took them away . . ."

Ben brightened with recollection. "The same evening when we checked out that so-called 'suicide' at the Potter place! Listen: Cecilia Potter told me that Sally Roe drove a blue pickup truck—a '65 Chevy, to be exact—and when I was there checking out the scene later on, the truck was gone. We were wondering about that."

"The truck was gone?" asked Marshall.

Ben was getting excited. "Gone. Now listen. According to Mrs. Potter, Roe always drove that truck to work and came home in it every day. So if Sally Roe did commit suicide like Mulligan and the medical examiner said, who drove her truck away?"

"Whoever Mrs. Bledsoe almost ran into, that's who!" said Tom.

Marshall was sitting up straight in his chair. "Did your kids see who was driving that truck?"

"I don't know. I suppose . . . somehow . . . I could ask them."

Marshall looked at Ben. "You ordered that criminal check, right?"

"I've got Chuck Molsby working on that. He's that friend of mine with the police in Westhaven."

"I hope we get a mug shot or something."

"I hope she's a criminal," said Tom.

"Yeah," said Marshall, "there is that little detail. But if we can get a photo of her, and if we can get it to the kids and have them identify her . . ."

"The fur would hit the fan!" said Ben. "It would prove Sally Roe is still alive, that it wasn't her suicide that we found!"

Marshall stood to his feet. "Moles."

"There's that word again," said Tom.

Corrigan straightened up in his chair and leaned over his desk. "Hey, guys, anytime you want to explain all this to me, I'd be glad to listen. I *am* supposed to be your lawyer, you know."

Marshall took a piece of scratch paper from Corrigan's desk. "Just like a mole in your yard and somebody else's yard . . . well, in three yards, actually. Three molehills, but all the same mole." He took out his pen and drew a small circle. "Here's the first molehill: the lawsuit against the Christian school, Lucy Brandon, the ACFA, that whole ball of wax." He drew another circle. "Here's the second molehill: The ACFA uses the child abuse hotline to report Tom and get the CPD into it. Irene Bledsoe gets the pickup order and takes the kids. That connects the two molehills . . . sort of." He drew a connecting line between the two circles.

"Maybe," said Corrigan. "I mean, you know it and I know it, but proving it is another thing."

"That comes later," said Marshall. "But now . . ." He drew a third circle. "Here's the third molehill: the mysterious death of Sally Roe—or somebody else. Somehow, possibly, the real live Sally Roe crossed paths with Irene Bledsoe right after the point in time when she was supposed to be dead." He drew another connecting line between the second and third circles. "Now you have two kids who might be—*might be*—witnesses to that, and so . . . possibly . . . Irene Bledsoe is withholding them, hiding them, dragging her feet all she can, to keep them quiet. Now she might just be protecting her own position, waiting for Ruth's bump to heal, or for both kids to forget what happened. Or . . ."

Ben took his own pen and connected the third circle with the first, forming a closed triangle. "Or she's helping to cover up whatever happened at the Potter farm, which means this Sally Roe thing could be in some way connected with the attack on the Christian school, which we know is connected with the taking of Tom's kids."

"None of which you can prove," Corrigan reminded them again.

"That comes later," said Marshall again. He smiled. He felt good. "But that's what's happening. We've got moles—spiritual powers and human counterparts—under all this, and they've pushed their way to the surface in these three areas."

Tom stared at the three circles. "If you want to talk about underground spiritual activity . . . how about the mileage Satan's gotten out of this whole CPD deal? They've got me branded as some kind of child abuser, and the whole church is falling apart over it. We can't win any fight of any kind in the shape we're in."

Marshall nodded. "Exactly. Now you're catching on."

Tom wanted to believe it. "But . . . I don't see any *direct* connection between what happened to Sally Roe and what's happening at the school. There's nothing there."

"There is," said Marshall.

"There isn't!" said Corrigan. "You can't prove a bit of this!"

"We will. Call me a fanatic, but I think God's showing this to us. He's giving us the outline; all we have to do is fill it in."

Ben was getting stirred up. "You've got something, Marshall!"

"But nothing *I* can use!" said Corrigan.

Marshall put his pen back in his pocket and just looked at that little diagram. "We'll get you something, Wayne. I don't know what, but we'll get it."

The music was soft, steady, compelling, with a relaxing rhythm and tone. Miss Brewer, a young and pretty teacher with a disarming smile, read from a script in a soothing, almost hypnotic voice.

"Feel the breeze drifting through your hair, feel the warm sun on your skin, the firm, inviting earth under your body. You're just a rag doll, totally limp, filled with sawdust . . ."

Kate Hogan sat quietly in the back of the classroom, trying to surreptitiously jot down notes as she watched the twenty-three fourth-graders go through the exercise. The desks were arranged to provide floor space for an activity area at one end of the room, and now the children lay flat on their backs on the floor in that area on blankets, pillows, or coats, their eyes closed, their breathing slow and deep, their arms limp at their sides.

"First the sawdust drains from your head . . . then from your neck . . . then from your chest . . . You just start sinking, sinking, sinking toward the ground . . ."

Kate watched the clock on the wall. So far they'd been lying on the floor for ten minutes.

The music kept playing. Miss Brewer came to the end of her soothing, lilting monologue. She paused, looked around the floor at every child, and then proceeded with some softly spoken instructions.

"Do you hear a babbling?" Then she whispered, "Listen! Do you hear it?" She took a moment for the kids to listen. "It's coming closer now, isn't it? It's your new friend, your wise person; they've come to talk to you. Let your friend appear on your mental screen. What is your friend's name?"

Kate scribbled just a few words to guide her memory. Most of the details of what she was now witnessing were familiar to her.

"Pick a room for your friend; make up a room in your mind to be your new friend's house. Make it something just right for them. Now talk to your friend, your very own wise person. Remember, your friend knows all about you . . . how you feel . . . what you like . . . what you don't like . . . all your problems and hurts . . ."

The exercise lasted another fifteen minutes or so, and the silence in the room was impressive for this age group. At last, after a predetermined amount of time, Miss Brewer counted to five slowly and then snapped her fingers. The children seemed to wake up from a trance, and sat up.

"Very good! Now we'll all take our seats and the monitors will pass out some paper. We'll draw our new friends."

The children folded the blankets, put away the pillows, hung up the coats, then returned to their desks. One child from each row passed out drawing paper. Under Miss Brewer's firm but kind guidance, the children got out their crayons and began to create portraits.

Miss Brewer walked up and down the rows, surveying each child's progress. "Oh, what a nice-looking friend! What's that on his head? Stars? He must be a marvelous creature!"

Kate took a short tour herself. The children were drawing ponies, dragons, princes and princesses, and some rather frightening monsters as well. They all received praise and compliments from Miss Brewer.

One little fellow showed Kate his picture. "This is Longfoot," he said. "I'm going to keep him in my mental basement."

The picture was typical fourth-grade artwork, but recognizable as a giant, lumbering figure with large feet.

"Look at his huge feet," Kate said playfully. "What does he do with those big feet?"

"He stomps on my mom and dad and all the big kids."

"Oh my."

A little girl turned to join the conversation, holding up her drawing for Kate to see. "See my friend? He's a dragon, but he doesn't breathe fire. He spits out jawbreakers!"

"Oh, and did you meet him today?"

She shook her head a little sadly. "No. He already lives in my head; he's been there a long time, and we're friends. I couldn't see my new friend today. I heard him, but I couldn't see him."

"Look at my picture!" said another little girl.

Kate walked over to take a look. Then she took a longer look.

The child had drawn a big-eyed, chubby-cheeked pony. The drawing was exceptional.

"This is Ponderey," she said. "He's my inner guide."

"A pony . . ." said Kate in wonder. She smiled. "That's a wonderful picture, honey. You draw very well."

"Ponderey helps me. He loves to draw."

Kate took her seat again in the back of the classroom and jotted down a few more notes, even though her hand was a little unsteady. She was so upset, she feared losing her quiet, professional manner.

Before long it was time for recess; the children filed out in a neat line until they reached the door to the playground. Then they abandoned the building like sailors from a sinking ship.

Miss Brewer sank into her chair at her desk and sighed with a big smile. "Well, that much of the day is over!"

Kate approached her and found a chair nearby. "They're a wonderful group."

"Aren't they, though? This is a great year for me; the kids in this town are really special!"

"The creative exercise was something special too; it evoked a lot of response."

Miss Brewer laughed out of pleasure and pride. "It's an adventure every time. Kids can be so creative, and there's just such wisdom and insight locked up in each one of them. You never know what they'll uncover."

"And what do you call this? Isn't it like Whole Brain Learning?"

"Sure. That's part of it. But most of the concepts and exercises are from the *Finding the Real Me* curriculum. It's a tried and tested program, and it includes the best of the proven theories now in use. It's very comprehensive."

"Well, what's the underlying principle to all this?"

Miss Brewer smiled. "You're not a parent, are you?"

"No, just a curious citizen. Like I said on the phone, I've heard a lot about what you're doing here, and I thought it would be interesting to watch."

"Sure. Well, of course our perspective is that each child should be free to achieve his or her own highest potential, and that takes a certain measure of creative and intuitive freedom. Too often an educator can stifle that potential by imposing a particular rule of behavior or truth upon the learner when the learner should be experiencing his own realities, creating his own concept of the world.

"We've found that relaxation and visualization exercises are a real key to untying each child, setting him free to start his own process of becoming. Human consciousness, even in a child, carries an incredible wealth of knowledge that no traditional classroom could ever cover even in a lifetime. That knowledge is available to each child from his own inner wisdom. We don't teach the child how to feel or how to perceive truth. All we have to do is show him how to unlock his own wisdom and intuition, and the rest just happens."

"And that's what you were doing today?"

"Well sure, exactly. We only use about two percent of our brain anyway. When we teach the children how to tap into the vast resources hidden in the rest of their brain, the sky's the limit."

"So where do these 'inner guides' and 'wise persons' come into all this?"

Miss Brewer let her eyes search the heavens as she formulated an answer. "To put it simply, there is a vast storehouse of knowledge locked up in our own hidden consciousness, and one of the ways to access it is to personify it, dress it up as a person, a character familiar to us. So, say I'm a little girl with fears about big people, grown-ups, maybe my own parents. Actually, I already have within myself all the knowledge I need to cope with whatever situation I encounter. I only need to learn it from myself. So, to facilitate that, I relax, let my mind go, and imagine—visualize—a favorite image, a character, a friend. Did you notice the pictures the children drew? Every one of those drawings was the child's expression of an inner friend, an inner guide, a personification of their own wisdom with which they feel free, unhampered, and comfortable. Once they create this image, it takes on a life of its own, and can talk to them and give them the advice and counsel they need for whatever they're having to deal with. In essence, they are learning from themselves, from their own buried consciousness."

"And this is all contained in this *Finding the Real Me* curriculum?"

"It's all in there, all organized, categorized, and graded. It makes the whole task a lot simpler."

"But—if I might play the Devil's advocate for a moment—what are they actually learning from this? Is there any academic achievement connected with the time you spend going through these exercises?"

Miss Brewer paused to formulate an answer. "I think what you're alluding to is the kind of argument we hear a lot, that we're not really teaching the kids anything, but are programming them, or using them for guinea pigs. But really, what is education? It's training and equipping children to live their lives, to survive in this world, to have the right attitudes and life skills to adapt to a rapidly changing social environment."

"And . . . I take it, of course, that reading, writing, mathematics, social studies, subjects like this have their place in this overall definition of education?"

Miss Brewer made a strange face. "Well . . . basic academic training is one thing, but it won't bring about the necessary change . . ."

"Change?"

"Well, reading, English, arithmetic, and those other subjects are in another category. They can't be applied in an affective, clinical sense . . ."

Kate hesitated. This young gal was enthusiastic about her job and her teaching style, but also vague with her answers.

"Okay . . ." she said, looking over her notes. "You used the word 'clinical.' So you see your role as more than just a teacher? You see yourself also as a therapist of some kind?"

Miss Brewer smiled and nodded. "That's a fair way to put it, I think. It's not a complete education to just fill their heads with the same old ideas that were taught to their parents. We need to equip them to rise above whatever knowledge came before, and to search out their own truth and personal values."

Kate was tired of generalities. "Even if it means training young children in shamanism and Eastern meditation?"

Miss Brewer laughed as if she'd been told a joke. "You make it sound like there's some kind of religion going on here. That's a common objection we hear all the time. There were some parents who came to me with that conception, but we cleared it up. This isn't religion; it's purely scientific."

"I understand those same parents withdrew their children from this school because they were convinced you were teaching religion here, something contrary to their own beliefs."

Miss Brewer nodded. She remembered it. "I guess that's how we cleared it up. Sounds like you've already talked to them."

Kate nodded back. "Yes."

Miss Brewer was still pleasant and all the more confident. "Well, I have no misgivings about what we're doing here. I think the school board and all the teachers they hire are more than qualified to judge what is helpful and constructive for the children. And the courts have stood behind the education community in that regard. If parents don't feel they can trust highly trained professionals to be competent in handling their children, then I guess withdrawing their children is their only real option. We aren't here to cater to fringe elements who insist on living in the past."

"You referred to the school board. I take it they selected and authorized the *Finding the Real Me* curriculum?"

"Yes, unanimously. You really should meet them before you draw any final conclusions. They're a wonderful group of people. I'm proud to be working with them."

"Well, I'm sure they are. But tell me . . ." Kate was ready to ask the question, but didn't know if Miss Brewer was ready to answer it. "Wasn't Amber Brandon in your class this year?"

Oh, Miss Brewer received that question like a revelation. She closed her eyes and smiled a long, showy smile as if to say, *Aha!* "So . . . is that what this visit is all about?"

Kate decided to try some education rhetoric herself. "Well, let's just remember that we all believe in freedom of thought, freedom of information, and above all freedom from censorship for those who have a right to know." Then she tried a straight answer. "For your information, I'm a friend of Tom Harris's, and I'm doing some research for him."

Miss Brewer was truly an admirable person. She remained strong and sat up straight. "I don't mind. I don't have to make apologies or hide anything I'm doing in this classroom. In answer to your question, yes, Amber Brandon was in my class, and as a matter of fact, she's back once again to finish out the year."

"Was she here today? I don't think I saw her."

"No, and it's understandable. Due to the trauma she's going through, she just isn't willing to attend this part of the class anymore. She spends this time in the library, and then returns to class after lunch."

"Then can you tell me about Amethyst the pony?"

Miss Brewer rose from her desk and pointed out a crayon picture posted high above the chalkboard. "Here she is, right here."

Kate walked closer for a better look.

It was an eerie experience, like getting the first look at a night-stalking burglar, or seeing the face of a serial rapist for the first time.

So this was Amethyst!

She was a little purple pony with shining pink mane and tail; her eyes were large and sparkling, she had a five-pointed star on her cheek, small white wings grew from her shoulders, and she stood tall and alert under a rainbow arch. She was beautiful, a remarkable drawing for a ten-year-old. In the lower-right corner, Amber had carefully printed her name in dark pencil.

"She drew this about a month before she transferred to the Christian school," Miss Brewer explained. "She was having some remarkable experiences during our exercise sessions. I've never seen such progress in a child."

Kate swallowed. Her mouth was suddenly dry.

"And you . . ." she began, but had to clear her throat. "You hold that this . . . this image . . . is a . . . uh . . ."

"A visualization of Amber's own inner wisdom."

"I see." Kate took a moment to formulate her next question. "So . . . as you probably know, the current case against Tom Harris stemmed from a confrontation between himself and . . . and Amber as Amethyst."

Miss Brewer smiled. "Well . . . all I can give you is my opinion."

"Please do."

"Whenever a child is thrust into a situation that is intolerable, such as a case of abuse, it's not unusual for the child to bury the memory of it or any thought of it to avoid the pain and trauma of the event. Many child abuse counselors have found that one way to bring things back out into the open is to allow the child to project the memory into a neutral object, such as a figure or doll or puppet.

"In Amber's case, you have a little pony who is bright, confident, and pristine, and who has the strength to deal with such problems where Amber doesn't. When it comes to what really happened at the Christian school, Amber can't talk about it, but instead lets Amethyst come forward and do the talking for her."

Kate digested that for a moment. "But would that explain why Amethyst appeared and caused a disruption even before Tom Harris confronted her?"

"Well, we don't know everything that happened, do we? There could have been some abuse before the events that Tom Harris told you about."

"What if Amber came to the school already manifesting herself as Amethyst? Would that suggest that there had been some kind of abuse before Amber ever met Tom Harris or ever spent one day in the Good Shepherd Academy?"

Miss Brewer shook her head. "I doubt it. Amber comes from a very loving home."

Kate nodded. "All right. Say, would you have a copy of that curriculum around? I'd like to look through it."

"Certainly."

Miss Brewer went to the shelves behind her desk and scanned all the titles. "Well . . . no, umm . . ." She straightened and turned. "Well, it isn't here . . ." Then she remembered. "Oh, that's right, I'm sorry. The principal, Mr. Woodard, asked to borrow it. He was supposed to bring it back, but obviously he hasn't yet. But if you care to, you can always order a copy from the publisher."

That idea intrigued Kate. "And who might that be?"

"The Omega Center for Educational Studies. I think I have the address here somewhere."

Miss Brewer combed through some binders on her desk.

Kate had another question, a stab in the dark. "Isn't there a support group of some kind in Bacon's Corner? Some group called LifeCircle?"

Miss Brewer looked up from her search. "Oh, yes. They're a wonderful group of people."

"What is it exactly?"

"Oh, just a loosely organized fellowship of people with like interests—the arts, religion, philosophy, ecology, peace, that sort of thing."

"Do you belong to that group?"

"Yes, I do."

"Then you must know Lucy Brandon personally?"

"Uh-huh." She caught herself and smiled. "That's right; you're probably finding out all about her."

Kate smiled and shrugged. "Of course."

"Oh, here's the address." She scribbled it down on a scrap of paper.

"Then that other woman, the legal assistant for Ames and Jefferson . . . ?"

"Claire Johanson."

"Yes."

"She must be involved in that as well."

"Oh yes. She's one of the leaders. But a lot of people belong to it."

"Like who?"

Miss Brewer stopped, tapped her chin as she thought a moment, and then answered, "Maybe you should ask *them*."

20

Barquit stood his ground, his nostrils chugging sulfur straight down over his burly chest and his yellow eyes steadfast, unflinching. He was the mighty Prince of Omega, and had done more mischief and won more victories for his master than this pompous, swelled-headed upstart that now stood before him, spewing threats and abuse.

Destroyer was not about to be ignored. He drew his sword and flashed it about, ready for a test between the two of them. "You blind, bumbling sloth! Revere me now, or challenge! I will abide either course!"

They hovered high above the Administration Building on the Omega Center campus, surrounded by their respective guards, escorts, and aides.

The escorts on either side of Barquit began to beseech him, "No, do not assail him, Ba-al! He is sent by the Strongman!"

"He calls me a sloth!" Barquit hissed through clenched teeth.

"*And* a bumbler!" said Destroyer. "You were away from your post, and allowed that woman to roam and learn freely!"

Barquit drew his sword so fast it whistled. He held it forth to strengthen his reply. "And where was the word I never received, that this wretch would be entering my domain? If you are so intent on capturing her, why was I never told?" He continued with an added edge, "And how is it that she is still alive at all, and free to harass us? Wasn't she supposed to be destroyed in Bacon's Corner?"

The two swords almost touched.

Just then a human voice broke in. "Gentlemen, if you'll just have a seat . . ."

The spirits in the air froze. Business was calling. The humans below were starting their meeting.

Barquit sheathed his sword. "The heavenly ranks were routed, and we still hold our territory. I'll put this behind us."

Destroyer put his sword away as well. "I'll put aside past blunders . . . for now."

They dropped through the roof of the building to join the meeting, taking place in a small conference room. Mr. Steele sat at the head of the table; at his right sat the dark man dressed all in black; at his left sat two other men. At the other end of the table, looking nervous, sat Mrs. Denning.

Mr. Steele led the proceedings. "Sybil, we'd like to thank you for coming. Let me introduce everybody. Obviously, Mr. Tisen you know. Gentlemen, this is Gary Tisen, the faculty head here at Omega." Tisen was a bearded man in his thirties, a likable sort of guy. "This gentleman here on my right is Mr. Khull, a free-lance journalist and photographer. On my immediate left is Mr. Goring, from the Summit Institute." Goring was an older man with probing eyes, meticulously combed white hair, and a neatly sculpted beard. He wore several strings of beads around his neck. "Gentlemen, this is, of course, Sybil Denning, a member of our faculty for several years now."

Everyone nodded at everyone else. Mrs. Denning smiled a little, feeling like this meeting might not be as serious as she once thought.

Mr. Steele maintained a smile, but there was something cutting in his eyes. "Now, Sybil, we had some questions about this woman who came to the Center last Friday. What did she say her name was?"

Sybil was a little taken aback by that question. "Well, Mr. Steele, that was Bethany Farrell, from the Los Angeles area, remember? You said you knew her."

Mr. Steele chuckled sheepishly, and then he lied. "I thought she was someone else. What we're trying to find out now is who she really was. Did she give you any other identification, any other proof of who she might be?"

"Well . . . no."

Mr. Steele paused at that answer. "So . . . Sybil, you see what happened? A total stranger walked onto our campus, gave you nothing more than her name and the claim that she was from Los Angeles, and that was all she had to do to get a carte blanche tour of the Center." Mrs. Denning didn't know what to say. Mr. Steele just smiled. "Well, Sybil, that's what I've always liked about you: you love people, you trust them, you reach out to them, and that's what Omega is all about, isn't it?"

She brightened just a little. "Well, of course."

"Did she say anything else about herself?" Mrs. Denning tried to remember. "Is she married, for instance?"

"No, she's divorced. She said she was just hitchhiking around the country, trying to find herself. She was looking for a place to stay, as I recall."

"And so you gave her a tour of the campus."

"Yes. I took her for a walk and talked about the Center and what we do here, and what our goals are."

Mr. Steele and Mr. Goring each drew a breath and held it a moment. Then Mr. Steele spoke. "Uh . . . Sybil, that's the sort of thing I was alluding to. To put it simply, you shouldn't have done that. We don't know who this woman was, or what her intentions were, and I'm sure you realize that there are many interests out there that are hostile to us. Our goals could be severely jeopardized if we aren't careful choosing whom we give information to. What goals did you discuss with her?"

She probed her memory, and it was painful to admit anything she found. "Uh . . . our goals for change through education . . ."

That brought an audible sigh, and Mr. Tisen even tapped the table.

"What else, Sybil?"

"Our programs, our curricula, our working into the public education system . . ." Her emotions started to show. "I'm sorry. I just didn't know . . ."

"What else?"

"Umm . . . I know we talked about the Young Potentials program . . . and our quest for global community . . . and our clinical approach to education . . ."

Mr. Goring asked a brief question. "Did you discuss the *Finding the Real Me* curriculum?"

Mrs. Denning was a little surprised that Goring knew about that. "Why . . . yes, we did. But I think it was because we were already talking about getting our curricula placed in the public schools, and apparently she'd seen it somewhere, and wondered if we were really the ones who had published it."

"Mm. Now, I understand she showed you a ring?"

"Yes. She had it on a chain around her neck. She wondered if I'd ever seen a ring like it before."

"Had you?"

"No."

"What did the ring look like?"

"Oh . . ." She tried to draw little images with her hands as she described it. "It was kind of large, like a class ring . . . It was gold . . . There was a strange, mythical-looking face on it, like a gargoyle, but triangular."

The men were keeping a poker face, with obvious effort.

Mr. Steele asked, "And you're sure you've never seen her before?"

That question suggested the possibility. "Um, well, I don't know. Should I have known her?"

Goring butted in. "No, of course not."

But Mrs. Denning thought about the face again, and that first meeting, and that woman spelling her name, "F-a-r-r- . . ."

Goring decided they'd asked enough questions. "Don't worry about this, Mrs. Denning. Obviously there was no harm done. We know you'll be cautious in the future."

A memory was emerging. Spelling a name. Who was that girl who did that? She was really sassy when she did.

Mr. Steele also tried to close out the conversation. "You've done a wonderful job here, Sybil, and we're glad to have you on board. Thanks for your time."

But Mrs. Denning kept remembering. She saw the face; freckled, stone-hard, long red hair. "R-o-e . . ." said the girl.

Mrs. Denning's eyes popped open wide, as did her mouth. "Roe! It was Sally Roe!"

Mr. Goring didn't seem to hear her. "Thank you very much, Mrs. Denning. Gentlemen, I'm ready for some coffee."

Mrs. Denning was awestruck, her mind awash with the memory. "She was a student of mine years ago! She was here at the Center in the Young Potentials program! *Now* I remember her!"

Mr. Steele cut in. "Sybil . . ."

"Whatever was she *doing* here? Why didn't she tell me who she was?"

"Sybil!"

She gave him her quiet attention.

Mr. Steele looked grim. "Save your excitement. I can assure you, it wasn't Sally Roe."

Now that was hard for her to swallow. "It wasn't?"

"Sally Roe is dead. She committed suicide a few weeks ago."

That silenced her. She was shocked, confused, speechless.

Mr. Steele dismissed her. "Thank you. I think if you hurry, you can get to your first class right on time."

She stood and left the room without a word.

Destroyer was spitting sulfur, grabbing and clawing at Steele while Barquit tried to hold him back. *You fool! Haven't you done enough damage? I'll cut out your tongue!*

Goring glared at Steele. "Not exactly a prudent line of questioning."

Mr. Steele tried not to look embarrassed. "Mr. Goring, we can rehash our slip-ups or we can talk about what we're going to do."

Goring moved on, but unhappily. "Mrs. Denning is now a liability. You and I both know she's suspicious that Sally Roe is still alive—and we both know why."

"No," said Tisen, "I wouldn't worry about that. She has a marvelous and deep loyalty to the leadership here."

Mr. Steele turned away from that issue. "She's not a problem. What I'm wondering is where will Roe turn up next, and should we forewarn anyone before she can get to them and milk them for information as she did Mrs. Denning?"

Destroyer stood back and glared at Mr. Steele. *Bungler! Fool! Idiot!*

Goring rolled his eyes. "Do you actually propose that we forewarn everyone to be looking out for a woman who is supposed to be dead? Just how far down the ranks should that information go? Don't be a fool, Steele! Once such information leaves this room, it will be beyond our control. Besides that, whom would we tell? How do we choose which direction Roe will go? We don't know what she's thinking, and obviously you had no idea she would appear here!"

Barquit stood between Mr. Steele and Destroyer before the angry predator did something rash. "I remind you, great warrior, that we received no warning! You could have foreseen she would be here, and we would have been spared this difficulty and embarrassment!"

Destroyer calmed just a little. "All right. Granted. For a time, the Host of Heaven hid her from us, responding to the prayers of the saints of God. The saints in Bacon's Corner do have quite an interest in this battle. But their prayers are weakening now. They are preoccupied with other things." Just the thought of that cheered Destroyer, and he became more pleasant. "We will find her, Barquit, but by stealth and craftiness rather than force." Destroyer could see someone approaching the room. "Ah! Behold this! We've just gained another advantage the Heavenly Host have not thought to contain."

"An advantage?"

Destroyer only smirked and looked toward the door.

There was a knock.

"Who could that be?" Mr. Steele wondered.

"We weren't to be disturbed," said Tisen.

"Who is it?" Mr. Steele demanded.

The door opened a crack, and a young student assistant stuck his head in. "Excuse me, Mr. Steele. I have a special item for Mr. Goring."

"I'll take it," said Goring.

The young man entered the room with a manila envelope.

Two spirits entered as well, quite gleeful, trying not to cackle too loudly. Destroyer ordered them to stand just behind him. They obeyed instantly.

"Very punctual," he said to them.

They tittered and cackled their delight at such a compliment.

As Destroyer and Barquit watched the young man hand the envelope to Mr. Goring, Destroyer explained, "These two messengers happened upon an interesting development back at the Bacon's Corner Post Office. I decided to reward them and secure their future services."

The young man exited. Mr. Goring opened the envelope and pulled out the contents with a puzzled expression. A small letter-envelope and a three-page cover letter fell to the table.

Almost at the same time, all four men saw the name on the upper-left corner of the envelope: Sally Beth Roe.

Goring read the cover letter. "It's from Summit. This letter from Sally Roe arrived last week at the Bacon's Corner Post Office. Lucy Brandon discovered it and referred it to the peace officer Mulligan. He checked with LifeCircle and Ames and Jefferson, the lawyers on the case. They sent it on to Summit. The people at Summit opened it and thought I should see it immediately."

Goring picked up the much-traveled letter from Sally Roe, addressed to Tom Harris. All four men looked at it with shock, awe, and then a steadily increasing jubilation.

Goring spoke first. "So . . . Sally Roe is writing letters!"

Mr. Steele was almost smiling widely. "To . . . to *Tom Harris*?"

Goring was skimming the letter from Summit. "Brandon is reasonably sure that this is the first letter." He dug Sally's letter from its already opened envelope; it was a document handwritten on three-ring spiral notebook paper. He quickly perused it. "Yes. This sounds like the very first letter. She's introducing herself . . . Oh no! She's describing her encounter with Von Bauer!"

At that, they all gathered to look over Goring's shoulder.

Mr. Steele read the account, taking great interest in how Von Bauer suddenly died. He then recalled what happened in the Log Cabin Cafe. He looked at Khull. "She *is* into some kind of tremendous psychic power. *Something's* protecting her!"

Goring wasn't entirely impressed. "And yet she still seems lost, confused. Look at her here, going on and on about morality, meaning, despair. The woman is a mess!"

Mr. Steele read ahead. "Mm. 'I'm going to retrace some old steps and find some things out.' That's why she was here. She's hunting for information."

"And she found it," said Goring in disgust.

Another thought was sobering. "If Tom Harris had actually received this letter . . ."

Goring looked up. "Of course. It could have spelled the end of everything, including Brandon's lawsuit." But Goring's mood began to lighten. "But as it now stands . . . Sally Roe has virtually betrayed herself to us. See here? She plans to write more of these letters, and that could be the key to finding her, predicting where she'll be, finding out what she knows, and just what she has planned!"

The four men looked at each other. It just might be that.

"If we can continue to intercept these letters, observe the postmarks, derive clues from their content, I would say we would have a remarkable advantage," Goring summarized.

"But can we trust Brandon to intercept the letters?" asked Mr. Steele. "Won't she buckle under the legalities?"

Goring smiled. "No, not Brandon. She has too much to lose by not cooperating, what with the lawsuit now in progress. Besides, if we can persuade her that it would be in her best interests to cooperate with us, then . . . we will have all the more leverage for controlling her with each letter she tampers with."

The men exchanged glances and nodded. It sounded like a workable plan.

Goring concluded, "We'll consult with Santinelli when he gets here. If he's agreeable, we'll send word back to LifeCircle to persuade Brandon to continue intercepting the letters and sending them to Summit. Eventually, most certainly, Sally Roe will tell us where she is, and . . . you, Mr. Khull, will then be of value to us."

Khull smiled, relishing the thought.

The two messengers behind Destroyer cackled and slobbered in delight.

"A Judas," said Destroyer. "Someone who will betray Sally Roe into our hands: Sally Roe herself!"

Claire Johanson and her live-in boyfriend Jon Schmidt shared a large, white house on the outskirts of town. The house was once the center of a large ranch, but the ranch had been divided into several smaller farms, and now the house remained as a comfortable, manageable estate for Claire and Jon's purposes. She was, of course, a legal assistant for Ames, Jefferson, and Morris; Jon was an architect and painter.

But most of all, they were the founders and facilitators of a movement, a fellowship, a gathering known to its members as LifeCircle.

Today was a LifeCircle meeting, not too formal an occasion, but rather a time to share, to combine interests, to discuss new discoveries and insights. There were plenty of cars parked on both sides of the road that ran in front of the house, and the house was full of people, not only from the immediate Bacon's Corner area, but from other communities as well.

In the living room, the fine arts enthusiasts enjoyed a miniconcert of mind-expanding music by a popular instrumental trio consisting of flute, guitar, and string bass. The president of the local grange was there, in a strange daze as he listened; Mr. Woodard, the elementary school principal, was also there with his wife, relaxing to the lilting sounds. Some young farmers were in attendance as well, some enjoying the music, and some thinking of moving on to another activity elsewhere on the grounds.

Upstairs, in a bedroom that was totally empty except for cush-

ions everywhere on the floor, young men and women participated in
a yoga workshop, humming and droning like a beehive, sitting in
the lotus position. They were everyday people—a rancher, a carpen-
ter, a UPS truck driver, a teacher of "special needs" children, a couple who ran a day-care center, and Miss Brewer, who taught fourth
grade at the Bacon's Corner Elementary School.

Outside the back door, sitting in comfortable chairs under a
vast grape arbor, a discussion group of some dozen people was taking time to share ideas and hear the opinions of a visiting author
regarding the application of Zen to farming.

In a corner of the backyard, not too far from a swing set, several young children cavorted on the grass, pretending to be ponies.
Leading them all was Amber, now Amethyst, jumping, prancing,
and spouting words of wisdom.

"It is as you see it to be," she was saying. "If you see yourself as a
black horse, that is what you are. If you see before you an open prairie,
that is where you are. Create your own world, and run free in it!"

So, the kids created their own world and ran free in it—as far
as the back fence, anyway.

In Claire's office on the main floor, behind closed doors, a meeting of great importance was in progress. Claire sat regally behind
her desk; Gordon Jefferson, the ACFA attorney, sat at one end of
the desk, his briefcase at his side; opposite them sat Lucy Brandon.
Next to the door, in a neutral position, sat Jon, Claire's live-in. He
was blond and handsome, like a male model for running shoes, and
had a quiet, confident demeanor.

Another woman was present, a short-haired, thin, female attorney from Sacramento, who'd brought a brief from another case the
ACFA had finished there.

"You'll find a lot of useful parallels in this case," she said,
handing it to Jefferson. "If you have any questions, Mr. James will
be happy to offer his time and services."

"Splendid!" Jefferson replied, taking the materials. "I understand Mr. James was able to uncover some persuasive case law in
this one."

"And it's yours to use as well."

Claire smiled with gratitude. "Thank you, Lenore. I suppose
you know the people in Chicago are watching this one?"

The woman named Lenore smiled. "Oh, of course. So if you
find yourselves in any need at all, we're ready and waiting to send
you more manpower, more documents, anything."

Jon chuckled and clapped his hands. "We're off and running!"

"And that reminds me," said Claire, "we've been getting a little
low on news items; John Ziegler and the folks at KBZT are always
open for more news if we can find it."

Jefferson responded, "Well . . . the case is pretty much in limbo until the trial."

Jon asked, "What about Harris's troubles with the child welfare people?"

Claire shook her head. "We can't go near that, not yet. The judge ordered the press to stay away from that, and if they try to dig anything up it will look too much like a violation of her order."

"Well," Jefferson thought out loud, "if we could find something outside that order, it would help. We need to keep the Christians on the run, keep them hiding."

Jon joked, "Maybe we could use the child abuse hotline again and get Harris in trouble with someone *else's* kids."

"No . . ." said Claire, though she knew Jon wasn't serious. "We don't want to start looking obvious, and Irene Bledsoe's under enough of a load as it is."

"Well, be patient," said Lenore. "It's a gradual process, one case at a time. The consolation is that once we gain the ground, we never lose it again."

"So time is on our side," said Jon.

There was a lull in the conversation. All eyes began to drift toward Lucy Brandon, who sat silently, listening to them all.

She returned their gaze, and smiled nervously. "You're asking me to do a lot."

Claire chuckled disarmingly. "Oh, it's not as serious as all that."

Jon patted her hand. "Don't worry. There's too much power represented here for you to be in any real jeopardy. Isn't that right, Gordon?"

Gordon Jefferson jumped right in. "Of course. Listen, Lucy: these letters are not legitimate mail. They're from some crank, some sick person who's been following the case in the media. It happens all the time. Letters like that shouldn't be delivered anyway."

Claire added, "But in the meantime, we never know just what or who might be behind them, and we can't afford to take any risks."

"That's right," said Jefferson. "We don't know what the letters contain, but we can be sure that your case will not be helped in any way if Tom Harris should ever receive them."

Lucy sat there thinking about it, but still seemed unconvinced.

"Well," asked Claire, "how many have there been now?"

"The second one came in just yesterday."

"What did you do with it?"

"I still have it 'on hold'. I wanted to talk to you first."

"That was smart."

Jefferson concurred. "Real smart. You see, Lucy, we could be dealing with some pretty shady people in this case. You never know what kind of stunt they might try to pull." Then he added in a slightly quieter voice, "Also, consider the stakes involved. If you should win this case, there would be quite a bundle of money in it for you."

"But money aside," Claire added, "think of all the children this case could affect in the future. If we're ever going to build a future of peace and world community, we must deal with the Christians; we must remove their influence upon the upcoming generations. It's for their own good, for the good of humanity."

"But what about Amber?" Lucy asked.

Jefferson was quick with an answer. "You know, Lucy, I don't think you even have to worry about that. Dr. Mandanhi can present reports and testimony on Amber's behalf, and she'll never have to go anywhere near the courtroom. We'll be able to insulate her from this case altogether."

"That would be nice."

"Well, we'll just play it that way."

Claire spoke with great sincerity in her voice. "Really, if we thought this was going to be harmful to Amber, we wouldn't pursue it. It's the children we're concerned about, after all."

"Right, absolutely," said Jon.

Lucy finally smiled and nodded. "All right. I just wanted to be sure, that's all."

"No problem," said Claire.

"We understand," said Jon.

Jefferson doublechecked. "You do have the address for forwarding the letters?"

Lucy thought she remembered. "The Summit Institute, right?"

"Right."

"I have it in my private files. I'll send the letters off as soon as I get them."

They all nodded their approval. "Excellent, excellent."

The music played on, the discussions continued, the humming and chanting made the windows buzz. All in all, LifeCircle was having a fruitful day.

So was Marshall Hogan. It hadn't taken him too long to drive slowly by the house and past all those parked cars, chattering into a small tape recorder in his hand. "GHJ 445, HEF 992, BBS 980, CJW 302 . . ."

In just two passes, he had them all.

21

Dear Tom,

I want to know something for sure. Right now I don't.

Blame it on pride. When I first entered high school I relished what I was taught: that I was the ultimate authority in my life, the final arbiter of all truth, the only decider of my values, and that no prior traditions, notions about God, or value systems had any authority over my will, my spirit, my behavior. "Maximum autonomy," they called it. Such ideas can be very inviting.

But there was a catch to all this freedom: I had to accept the idea that I was an accident, a mere product of time plus chance, and not only myself, but everything that exists. Once I bought that idea, it was impossible to believe that anything really mattered, for whatever I could do, or create, or change, or enhance, would be no less an accident than I was. So where was the value of anything? Of what value was my own life?

So all that "maximum autonomy" wasn't the great liberation and joy I thought it would be. I felt like a kid let loose to play in an infinitely huge yard—I started to wish there was a fence somewhere. At least then I would know where I was. I could run up against it and tell myself, "I'm in the yard," and feel right about it. Or I could climb over the fence, and tell myself, "Oh-oh, I'm outside the yard," and feel wrong about it. Whether right or wrong, and with infinite freedom to run and play, I know I would still stay near the fence.

At least then I would know where I was. I would know something for sure.

Sally was in the town of Fairwood, a small burg along a major river, a fairly busy shipping port for that part of the state. Even though the Omega Center was only a half-hour, winding drive into the hills above the town, she had lingered and hidden here for the weekend, getting to know the place again, walking its streets by day and spending the cool nights in the woods down by the river.

The town had not changed much in ten years. There was a new mall at the north end of the main thoroughfare, but every town has to have a mall sooner or later. As for the city center, all the stores remained the same, and even the Stop Awhile Lunch Counter was still there, with the same jukebox and ugly blue formica-topped counter. The menus were new, but only the prices were different; every page still carried the same logo and the same meals.

She was remembering things. She was bringing it all back. The park in the middle of town was just the way she remembered it. The wading pool was empty and dry, waiting for warmer weather, but kids were playing on the swings and monkey bars, and Sally considered how the playground was the same but the kids were different; it wouldn't be too long before the children who were there ten years ago would be sending *their* children down to the same park to play on the same swings.

It's really not a bad town. I can't blame it for the feelings it evokes in me, the strange conflicts I feel. In this one place are hidden my happiest and my most bitter memories, side by side. Both have been buried so long, obliterated by drugs, by delusion, by altered states of consciousness, that I've forced myself to remain here to revive them. I must remember.

She was being followed by friends. From atop the First National Bank building across the street, Tal, Nathan, and Armoth kept watch as she sat on a bench in the park, writing another letter.

"She hasn't found it yet," said Nathan. "I don't think she wants to. She's been down every street but the right one."

"She wants to find it, but at the same time she doesn't, and I don't blame her," said Tal. "But we'll have to help her. With our present tactics, we can only hold that motel room open for today."

"She's moving again," said Armoth.

Sally was putting her notebook back in her duffel bag and preparing to move on.

Nathan surveyed the skies over the town. "Destroyer's scouts are still around. They must know we're here."

Tal agreed. "They simply aren't afraid of us. But I consider that an advantage. I would prefer them to be very confident." Then he saw Sally turning to the right on Schrader Avenue. "Oops! No, Sally, not that way."

They unfurled their wings and leaped from the building, floating down over the tops of passing cars, banking silently around the corner, and settling to the sidewalk on either side of this singular, weary traveler. She seemed a little perplexed, not knowing which way to go.

Nathan spoke to her, *No, Sally, you've already been this way. Turn around.*

She stopped. *Oh, brother, I've already been down this street, and it was a bore.*

She turned around and followed Schrader the other way, crossing several streets, passing other pedestrians, always looking over her shoulder.

The three warriors walked with her, staying close.

Sally looked around as she walked. No, she hadn't been this way yet. Some of the storefronts looked kind of familiar. *Oh! That flower shop! I remember that!*

Then, finally her eyes caught a sight she hadn't seen—or wanted to see—in ten years. Up ahead, on her side of the street, was a large, rectangular sign, SCHRADER MOTOR INN, and below that a smaller sign, KITCHENS, DAILY, WEEKLY, MONTHLY RATES. She stopped dead in her tracks and gazed at that sign, spellbound.

It hadn't changed. That motel was still there!

Tal came up close behind her. *Steady, Sally. Don't run.*

She wanted to run, but she couldn't. She didn't want to face this memory, but still she knew she had to.

If you want to know the truth, said Tal, *you must face it even if it's painful. You've run long enough.*

She stood still in the middle of the sidewalk as if her shoes were glued to the pavement. She began to remember more and more of this place. She'd walked down this sidewalk before, many, many times. She'd visited that flower shop. There was a True Value Hardware on the corner, but now she remembered it used to be a variety store.

She started walking again, slowly, drinking in every sight. These planters were new; it used to be just a bare curb here. That parking lot across the street had undergone a change in management, but it was still a parking lot.

The Schrader Motor Inn was the same, a large, sixty-unit motel of three stories, L-shaped, with parking in front and around the back. It wasn't a high-priced place, nothing fancy, no swimming pool. The motel may have been painted; she wasn't sure about that. The entrance to the office looked the same as she remembered, and still had the large breezeway jutting out across the entrance.

She looked up at the third story, and scanned all the blue doors facing the iron-railed balcony. Yes. She could see Room 302 down near the end.

It had been her home for almost ten months. Such a short period of time, and so long ago!

Even as she passed under that breezeway and stepped up to the office door, she felt she was being a bit irrational. What purpose could such an action serve? Why dig up the past? None of this was necessary.

She was going through with it. She had to see it all again; she hadn't paid attention the first time.

She pulled the door open.

It was meant to be, came a memory from somewhere in her mind. It was her own voice. Now she remembered saying it. *My higher self ordained it.*

"Hello," said the nice lady behind the counter. "Can I help you?"

Sally could still hear her own voice echoing from the past: *After all, there is no death; there is only change.*

She knew she'd been asked a question. "Uh . . . yes. I was wondering if you had a kitchen unit available."

The lady checked her register. "Hm. You're in luck. Yes, that fellow moved out just this weekend. It's on the third floor . . . Is that all right?"

"It's fine. Uh . . . would it happen to be 302?"

The lady's eyebrows went up. "Why, yes, as a matter of fact. Have you stayed there before?"

Sally was looking this lady over carefully. No, they'd never met, she was sure. She must be a new owner, or employee, or something. "On occasion."

The lady slid the application across the counter to her, and Sally filled it out. She gave her name as "Maria Bissell," put down a totally fictional address in Hawthorne, California, then claimed to be driving a '79 Ford Mustang with a California license plate, and she made up the license plate number as well. All she could hope was that this lady would appreciate the color of her money and not question her credentials.

The lady did appreciate the color of Sally's money, receiving a week's rent and damage deposit in cash. She handed Sally the key.

The stairway had new green carpet now. Sally could remember the worn, brown carpet it used to have.

She reached the third floor and walked along the balcony overlooking the parking lot and beyond that, the Nelson Printing and Bookbinding Shop, still there, the offset presses still rumbling inside.

She placed her hand on the railing and noticed her wrist was unhampered. The last time she ever saw this railing, she was handcuffed, and she was not free.

Out of her buried memory came the image of squad cars parked in the lot below, their lights flashing. Then she recalled the other tenants watching through their windows, peeking around the drapes, curious and anonymous. She could feel the pain of big hands holding her arms, pushing her along this balcony.

There was an aid car down there too, and some medical personnel running around. She could just barely remember them.

She came to the door. With held breath and a turn of the key, she opened it. The chain-lock was repaired now, and apparently the doorjamb had been replaced.

Some things were different. The couch was new, but still sat in the same place. The picture on the wall just above it used to be a sailboat, and now it was a surrealistic vase of flowers. She liked the sailboat better.

The kitchen looked the same, and the cabinets hadn't changed a bit. The sink still had that brown crack. The pots and pans were in the same cupboard just to the left of the sink.

Through an archway at the back of the room was the bedroom. She knew where the bed would be, and she knew the room had a large closet. She didn't bother going in to look.

Next to the bedroom was the bathroom. She didn't want to go in there at all.

Ben was almost beside himself when Marshall came pulling into the driveway. He ran out to the car to meet him.

"Man, where have you been?"

Marshall was feeling pretty good himself. "Got some license numbers from the cars belonging to our local LifeCirclers. That'll give your friend in Westhaven some more to do, running some Motor Vehicle Reports."

"Chuck's already done a *lot*," Ben exclaimed, fidgeting on the sidewalk. "Come on in!"

Marshall hurried inside and followed Ben into the dining room. Bev was there, her eyes gawking, studying some documents spread out on the table.

"*Oh, Lord . . .*" she said.

Ben wasted no time, but pointed to a grainy, black-and-white, front- and left-profile mug shot. "That's the lady. That's Sally Roe!"

Marshall picked up the photo and studied it carefully. "Man, she's wasted!"

Indeed she was. The tired, gaunt, and dazed woman in the photographs looked every bit the part of a half-drunk or half-drugged tramp. Mug shots never were very complimentary, but even so . . .

Ben grabbed Marshall's shoulder in his excitement and started jabbing his finger at the photographs. "Marshall, that is *not* the dead woman we found at the Potter farm! But it's Sally Roe, all right! I've already been by the Potters' and the Bergen factory to talk to Abby Grayson. Both of them confirm that this is Roe."

"They must not have been too happy . . ."

"They were shocked. Yes, very shocked." Ben went on to explain. "Chuck requested a Records Check from the National Crime Information Center and the State Information Section. Sally Roe was only arrested once, ten years ago. He got the rap sheet on that, then followed that up with the local police in the town where the arrest occurred."

"Fairwood, Massachusetts . . ."

"Right. They supplied the photographs."

Marshall hesitated. He was bothered about something. "Fairwood, Massachusetts . . . Fairwood . . . I'd better check with Kate about that." He took another look at the photographs. "And we'd better get some copies of these pictures."

Bev piped up, "I'm gonna do that right now; I'm goin' down to use the church's copier."

"Great. Kate's going to need one, I know." He looked over the other documents. "Okay, now what did she do?"

Ben pointed out the crime record. Marshall stopped short. He turned the paper toward him, so he could read it better.

"Isn't that a kicker?" said Ben.

"This thing is getting juicier all the time! Any details?"

Ben pointed out a short police bulletin. "It's bizarre; nothing like I expected."

Marshall read the bulletin as his face filled with horror and disbelief. All he could say was, "Why? This is crazy."

"We've got to find out more, Marshall."

Marshall stared at the photograph again. "I've got a friend in New York, name's Al Lemley. That guy's a real friend, and he can produce. Maybe he can get us something more on this."

Ben had a thought. "You might want to stop in at Judy's Secretarial Service. It's in that little storefront at the four-way stop. She has a fax machine, and you could get the stuff right away."

"Yeah. For sure." Marshall looked at the crime record again and shook his head. "First-degree murder!"

"You're nothing but bloodthirsty killers, as far as I'm concerned," said Mr. Santinelli, warming himself in front of the fire in Mr. Steele's private lodge. He'd put his full and hectic schedule on hold and caught an afternoon flight from Chicago to get here. Now he was tired and cranky, and not at all happy with some of the company he was keeping.

His statement was addressed to the dark and mysterious Mr.

Khull, who sat comfortably on the couch, swirling a gin and tonic about in a glass, making the ice cubes tinkle. Mr. Khull was not in the least ruffled by Santinelli's blunt statement.

"We are all that way, Mr. Santinelli—if not in deed, at least in heart. You did, after all, hire me."

Mr. Goring, relaxing in an overstuffed chair before the fire, quipped, "A decision we have all regretted, Mr. Khull."

Santinelli took an indignant puff from his cigar. He didn't like the tone of Goring's comment. "I should like to remind you, as I'm sure Mr. Khull will be happy to boast, that he already had a controlling interest in our organization, thanks to the romantic adventures of the man he eventually eliminated, our boyish upstart, Mr. James Bardine."

"James Bardine . . ." Mr. Khull seemed to have a lapse of memory. Then it came to him. "Oh yes! He died in that tragic automobile accident! I believe he fell asleep at the wheel . . ."

"Everyone believes that," said Santinelli. "My compliments."

"Thank you. We try to be thorough."

Santinelli sat down in a chair opposite Khull, making no effort to hide his disdain. "All you Satanists are thorough, I'm sure. You worship on the run, don't you, always looking over your shoulder?"

Khull leaned forward, his drink in his hands, his head drooped between his shoulders, his eyes piercing. "No. Actually, we have yet to be chased."

Mr. Steele, listening to it all from his own chair directly facing the fire, intervened. "Gentlemen—and Mr. Khull—we know how we feel about each other, so that matter is settled. We don't trust each other, and that's the way we want it."

Santinelli added, "What is also settled is that a liability has been removed—namely, Alicia Von Bauer and James Bardine and their little love nest. Such relationships can be an extreme embarrassment, and from this point forward I hope we've made a clear enough example to our subordinates that any more relationships with these Broken Birch people will not be tolerated."

Khull took a sip from his drink and leaned back into the soft couch. "Especially by those who know as much as Mr. Bardine did."

Santinelli fumed, "As much, I'm sure, as you do now, thanks to the lecherous Ms. Von Bauer!"

Khull laughed. "Such are the politics of power."

Goring responded, "And the reason you are even allowed in our company!"

Mr. Steele was eager to finish their unsavory business. "All right, whether we like it or not, Broken Birch is now part of the

Plan. Let's get the ledger balanced, so Mr. Khull can go away satisfied and be about his business."

Santinelli produced a check and handed it to Khull. "There. While in our employ, and admittedly due to our negligence, Ms. Von Bauer was killed. We gave you freedom to kill our own Mr. Bardine, and here are your damages as you have required."

Khull examined the amount on the check and nodded his approval. He folded it and slipped it into his pocket. "That's settled."

"Good," said Mr. Steele. "Now get that ring back."

Mr. Khull sipped from his drink again. "Your credit is good with us, of course, but . . ."

This time Mr. Goring produced a check. "As we discussed, here is your first half to commence the job. The second half is payable upon recovery of the ring and the elimination of Sally Roe."

Khull took that check and pocketed it. "As you know, this Roe has been very elusive."

"And we are paying you to make her vanish altogether."

Khull swirled his ice cubes. "And, naturally, her blood would be on *our* hands. How convenient for you."

Mr. Steele objected, "Your hands are already bloody."

"And yours aren't?" Khull laughed at them. "Ah, don't worry. I understand. We kill regularly, as a form of worship; it's a sacrament to us. If you kill . . . well, it's only through hirelings like us. It keeps your hands clean. You don't plunge the knife, so you don't feel the pang of conscience." He laughed again. "Maybe you are still too Christian!"

Mr. Santinelli hated this man's taunts. "If I may remind you, Mr. Khull, you are serving your own interests in this as well, perhaps more so than we. If Sally Roe should ever be found alive, if she should ever tell her story, you and your followers could easily be implicated with murder. And unlike human sacrifices that vanish without a trace, this victim is alive, walking, and talking. At least our suicide cover story has bought us all some time. I would say you owe us something for that."

Khull was only mildly impressed. "Yes, we both have something to lose if she remains alive. But how much we have to lose depends on how much we've invested, doesn't it? What is Broken Birch, compared to you and your Plan?"

"Not much," said Mr. Steele, supposedly admitting something, but actually using it as a taunt.

Khull ventured a sneer. "You're no better. Someday you'll realize that. What we are now, you are rapidly becoming. If you hate us so much, perhaps it's because you see yourselves in us!"

Santinelli barked, "*I* will see *you* to the *door*!"

Alice Buckmeier was a marvelous hostess, of course, and loved to have company. So what Kate had planned as a short interview turned out to be a delightful visit over tea and pastries in the widow's dining room, surrounded by knick-knacks, doilies, crystal, and pictures of sons, daughters, and grandchildren.

"You must be everybody's grandma," Kate said.

Alice laughed. "A title I wear proudly. I don't just have my own grandchildren, you know, but I'm Grandma Alice to all the kids at church, too!"

"That's wonderful."

"I love children, I really do. Sometimes it's hard to understand how people treat their children. I know it breaks the Lord's heart." She warmed up Kate's cup of tea and continued, "I've wondered about that little Amber ever since I saw what I saw at the Post Office. What must she be going through at home?"

Kate got her notebook ready. "Bev Cole says you have quite a story."

"Oh, yes. It was very disturbing. I was mailing a package off to my son—well, actually, to my grandson, Jeff. I knitted a sweater for him, and I was trying to get it there in time for his birthday. Well, I was just standing there at the counter, and that other young lady, Debbie, was weighing my package and stamping it and all that . . ."

Judy Balcom stuck her head into Don's Wayside and called, "Mr. Hogan! Al Lemley's on the phone!"

Marshall got up from the counter, paid for his coffee, and hurried next door.

Judy Balcom ran a tight little secretarial service, typing letters, making and answering calls, making copies, doing word processing, and relaying messages—to name just a few tasks—for many of the local businesses around the town. For a reasonable fee, she let Marshall call Al Lemley in New York, and now Lemley, true to his style, had wasted no time in finding what Marshall needed.

"Hello from New York," came that same East Coast voice.

"Al, are you going to make me happy?"

"No, buddy. I'm going to make you sick. Got the fax ready?"

Judy was ready.

Marshall gave Al the go-ahead.

Alice continued her story. "Now, I didn't even notice who was over in the lobby where all the mailboxes are. I never pay attention to that unless it's someone I know. But all of a sudden I heard this commotion out there like some child was getting rowdy—you know, misbehaving, and I remember thinking, Now where are that child's parents? They shouldn't let her carry on so!

"Well, Debbie was all finished with my package, so I went out into the lobby, and then I could see the whole thing. Here was this woman, just standing there in the middle of the lobby . . . She had some mail in her hand, so I guess she'd come to get her mail . . . And then, here was this little girl, this Amber, just screaming and shouting and . . . and prancing like she was a little horse, and that poor woman was just terrified!"

The fax machine started to hum and roll out some documents. Marshall picked each page up as it dropped into the bin. There were police reports similar to what he already had, and then there were some news articles from the local newspapers. One article carried another photo of Sally Roe, this time in handcuffs, in the custody of two uniformed officers.

"And what that child said!" Alice exclaimed.

"What did she say?" asked Kate.

"She pranced, then she hit the woman, and she screamed, and just kept hitting the woman, and she was saying, 'I know who you are! You killed your baby! You killed your baby!' The poor woman was just terrified; you'd think she was being attacked by a vicious dog or something.

"Well, finally the woman broke free and ran out the door like a scared rabbit. Amber ran after her as far as the door, still shouting at her, 'You killed your baby! I know you! You killed your baby!' Then Mrs. Brandon came out of the back room and grabbed her daughter and tried to pull her back inside, but she wouldn't go with her mother, she wouldn't go at all, and so they had a big tugging match right there in the lobby, right in front of me, and Mrs. Brandon was shouting, 'Stop it, Amber! Stop that right now! No more of this!'"

Kate asked, "Did Mrs. Brandon ever use the name Amethyst?"

A light bulb went on in Alice's head. "Why, yes! I do remember that! She was calling Amber Amber one minute, and Amethyst the next. She was saying, 'Amethyst, Amethyst, you stop that now! You stop screaming and calm down!' I didn't understand what she meant; I thought it was just a nickname or something."

Another news article dropped out of the fax machine. Marshall skimmed it. Sally Roe had been arrested after police broke down the door of her motel room in Fairwood. Inside, they found Roe in the bathroom in a seemingly drugged stupor, and her infant daughter, less than two months old, drowned in the bathtub. Roe was subsequently charged with first-degree murder in the drowning death of her child.

Kate could hardly wait to ask her next question. The incident in the Post Office could have been coincidence, but in a small town like this, that was unlikely. She dug in her briefcase and brought out the mug shots of Sally Roe, placing them before Alice. "Is this the woman you saw that day?"

Alice's eyes grew wide, and then she gave a slow, awestruck nod. "She looks so awful in this picture . . . but this is her. Sally Roe, huh?"

"That's right."

"Is she a criminal?"

"Yes."

"What did she do?"

"Well . . . she did kill someone."

Marshall walked slowly to his car, got behind the wheel, and then just sat there for a long while, reading through the news articles and police reports Al Lemley had sent. It was fascinating stuff, full of potential leads, but also very, very tragic.

"Tramp," the prosecutors had called her. "Diabolical witch, self-centered, self-seeking, contemptible, child-killer."

The police report said that Sally Roe was soaking wet when she was found on the floor in the bathroom. The tub was overflowing. The child was in the tub, dead. She'd told the police at the time that she'd killed her baby, but when questioned later, claimed she had no recollection of what had happened.

During the trial—and Marshall found this interesting—Sally seemed detached and unremorseful. "It was meant to be," she said. "My higher self ordained this should happen. Rachel's higher self wished to die at this time, and Jonas was there to carry it out. We all determine our own fates, our lot in life, when we are to die, and what destiny we are born into the next time. There is no death; there is only change."

Jonas. A spirit-guide, according to Sally. She admitted drowning the child at first, but later seemed to change her testimony by blaming her spirit-guide. "He took control," she said, "and he did the drowning."

The jury didn't buy it. They found her guilty, and Sally was later sentenced to thirty years in prison.

As for the father of the child, he never came forward and was never found. Sally never identified him. She was simply portrayed as a tramp and her child as illegitimate.

It all happened ten years ago.

22

Drip. Drip. Drip.

The faucet seemed to mark off segments of time, announcing the passing of a moment, and another moment, and another moment, and another moment, like a clock, never stopping, never slowing—steady dripping, moments passing.

Traffic flowed by outside the bathroom window, but Sally didn't hear it. A siren wailed once, but she did not stir or take notice. She had no strength, no will to rise from her place there on the bathroom floor—her back against the pale blue wall, her hands limp upon her lap, her head resting against the hard plaster, but not turning away from the discomfort.

She just sat there, staring vacantly at that tub, listening to the faucet drip, watching each drop build on the tip of the spout and then, stretching with weight, break free and disappear.

Drip. Drip. Drip.

"Ms. Roe, did you think there was no law higher than yourself?"

"There is no higher reality, sir, than what I myself have created."

Drip. Drip. Drip.

"You honestly don't recall picking up your child, holding her under the water, and drowning her?"

"I told you before, I wasn't there; it was Jonas."

"But you admitted drowning your daughter!"

"Jonas performed the act. My higher self willed it, he carried it out . . ."

Drip. Drip. Drip.

"We found the defendant in the bathroom . . . She seemed dazed . . ."

"And what did she say to you?"

"She said, 'Oh no! I've killed my baby.'"

Drip. Drip. Drip.

" . . . ladies and gentlemen of the jury, you have heard an account of the unthinkable . . . This vile creature, void of conscience, without remorse . . ."

Void of conscience, without remorse. Void of conscience, without remorse. Void of conscience, without remorse.

A child in an infinite yard with no fence. The creator and arbiter of all reality. The center of her own universe. No right, no wrong. Only self. *I am all that matters.*

At least, that's how it used to be.

Sally shifted just a little. The hard linoleum floor reminded her of where she was: her glorious universe. Yes. A small, cold, echoing bathroom with a dripping bathtub faucet, inhabited by a murderer, a vagabond, a tramp, a failure, an empty jar drained steadily over ten years of pointless, aimless existence, a discarded piece of flesh nobody wanted.

Now she sat on the linoleum, her head against the wall, her elbow resting on the toilet, beside the bathtub where she'd taken the life of her daughter.

Her universe. Her destiny. Her truth.

She had no tears. She was too empty to cry; there was no soul within her. She continued to breathe, but not because she wanted to. It just happened. Life just happened. She just happened, and she didn't know why.

The spirits had found her: Despair, Death, Insanity, and now Suicide. They dug at her, whispered to her, scratched away her soul one layer at a time. *Murderer*, they said. *Worthless, guilty murderer! You can never do good! There's nothing good in you! You can't help anyone! Why don't you give it all up?*

It's lonely in this universe, she thought. *It's supposed to be my creation, but now I'm lost in it. I wish I could know something for sure. I wish I could find a fence at the end of this yard.*

Ah, but it is too late for that now.

Her hand fell from her lap and thumped gently against the side of the tub.

A fence.

No, it wasn't a big thought; it wasn't a stirring idea, and it didn't cause the slightest change in her breathing or pulse. It was just a notion, an inkling of a possibility, a simple proposition to toss around: this tub could be a fence.

She looked at the tub; she touched the cold, blue-green porcelain. *I could pretend,* she thought. *Just for the sake of discussion, I could pretend that this is a fence, a limitation, a boundary.*

A boundary I crossed over, and shouldn't have.

She let her thoughts continue on their own and just enjoyed listening to them huddle together and confer in her head.

What if what happened here was wrong?

Ah, come on, according to whom? There are no absolutes; you can't know anything for sure.

What if there are, and what if I can?

But how?

Later, later. Just answer the first question.

What if it was wrong?

Yeah.

Then I'm guilty. I made a wrong choice, I jumped the boundary, I did wrong.

But I thought boundaries exist only in your mind!

I did wrong. I want to think that, just once.

Why?

Because I need a fence. Even if I'm on the wrong side of it, I need a fence. I need to be wrong. I need to be guilty.

What for?

Because . . .

Sally stirred. She pressed her hand firmly against the side of the tub where her child had died. She mouthed the words, then she whispered them, then she said them out loud, "Because at least then I'd know where I am!"

Apparently she'd awakened a dormant emotion; pain came upon her suddenly, an aching deep in her soul, and with gritted teeth and a stifled whimper, she pounded the side of the tub. "*Oh, God!*"

She rested against the hard plaster wall again, panting in hurt, anger, and despair. "O God, help me!"

Despair slipped and fell. His talons had lost their grip.

There. She'd said it. She'd followed the proposition through to its conclusion, had her little fit, and now she was finished. She didn't know if she felt better. She felt a little foolish for talking out loud to herself—or to God, whatever the case may be. It didn't matter.

For some reason she felt a weight around her neck, against her chest. Her hand went to the ring hanging there. She pulled it out and looked at it again. The ugly little gargoyle bared its teeth at her.

And then a memory hit her. It hit her so hard and so suddenly that she was amazed it had stayed hidden so long.

"The ring! *Owen's* ring!"

Irene Bledsoe was visibly uncomfortable. "Mr. Harris, your friends will have to remain here."

Under the circumstances, Tom never felt better. He was sitting on the same hard wooden bench in the same cold, echoing, marble hallway in the courthouse in Claytonville; he was here for another prearranged visit with his children, and once again Irene Bledsoe was in charge.

But this time he was flanked by . . .

"Mrs. Bledsoe, this is my pastor, Mark Howard, and my attorney, Wayne Corrigan."

Both men offered their hands, and she shook them out of necessity, but she was not entirely cordial. "Hello. As I said, Mr. Harris will only be allowed to see his children alone."

Corrigan was in great form. "We are here upon Mr. Harris's invitation, and we will accompany him during his visitation. If you refuse to allow it, you'll be required to appear in court to show just cause." Then he smiled.

Bledsoe was indignant and actually had to search for her words. "You . . . This is . . . this is a private meeting! Mr. Harris must see his children alone!"

"Then I'm sure you'll be happy to remain here with us while he does so?"

"That's not what I meant and you know it! The visitation is to be between Mr. Harris and his children with a social worker in attendance."

"Meaning yourself?"

"Of course!"

Corrigan got out his notepad. "By whose order?"

She stalled. "I'd . . . I'd have to look it up."

"If it's all the same to you," said Tom, "I'd like to see my kids. They're waiting for me, aren't they?"

"One moment," she said with a raise of her hand. "Have you brought the questionnaires I sent you?"

Corrigan had something to say about that as well. "In light of the pending civil suit, I've advised my client to defer filling out any psychological surveys or other tests for the time being."

Her answer was cold and threatening. "You do realize, of course, that this will delay our releasing the children back to Mr. Harris's custody?"

"According to CPD records, you've never released any children back to their parents without first having a trial anyway, so at the moment we're resigned to that. Now, if we could proceed with the visitation?"

She gave in. "All right. Won't you follow me?"

She started walking toward the big marble staircase again, the *pock, pock, pock* of her heels echoing through the hall as an announcement of her authority, and perhaps an expression of her indignity as well. They reached the second floor, went through the big, uninviting door and into the antechamber where John the guard was stationed once again. He seemed a little surprised to see three men instead of just one, but since they came in with Bledsoe, he figured it must be okay.

"Hi, kids!"

With cries of delight, Ruth and Josiah ran to their father. Tom dropped to one knee to embrace them, and for some reason Irene Bledsoe did not come between them. Josiah was really tickled to see his dad again; Ruth just started crying and wouldn't let go of him. All the hugs went on for quite some time.

"Poor, abused kids," Corrigan whispered to Mark.

Bledsoe took her seat at the end of the table and offered chairs to Mark and Corrigan. They sat down quietly on Tom's side of the table.

"Okay, kids," Tom said finally. "Go ahead and sit down."

They went to their chairs on the other side of the table, and just then noticed Mark. "Hi, Pastor Howard."

"Hi. How are you?"

"Okay."

"We have forty minutes," Bledsoe said, mostly to remind everyone that she was still in charge.

For the next thirty minutes Tom visited with his kids, getting caught up on mostly trivial matters. The kids were trying to read more, and seemed to be getting along better with the other kids in the foster home, although Tom couldn't be sure if it was the same foster home as last time. They weren't doing any schoolwork, though, which meant they would have some catching up to do during the summer, if that happened at all. Ruth's bump had healed well and was barely visible.

But as the time grew shorter, there was one thing Tom knew he must do before leaving, while he still had the chance. Above all else, he knew he must pray with his kids.

"Hey, Daddy has to go pretty soon, so let's pray together."

He reached across the table and took their hands. They were a family again, just for that moment, and he was the spiritual head, the leader and example he was meant to be.

"Dear Lord, I just pray now for my children, and I ask You to place a hedge of protection around them. Protect their hearts and their minds, and may they never doubt that You love them and that they are in Your hands. Help them to always be good kids and live the way You want them to. I pray, dear Father, that we will all be together again."

Mark and Corrigan joined in the prayer, and listened as little Ruth prayed for her daddy and her brother, and even for Mrs.

Bledsoe. Then Josiah prayed, declaring his love for Jesus and his desire to be a good child of God.

None of this was an accident. They were doing battle in this room, for even though the state might erect insurmountable walls of red tape around these children, the prayer of each child, offered in simple faith, would be enough to tear the walls down. This was where the victory would begin. They all knew it, and as the kids prayed, they could feel it.

"Amen," said Josiah.

"Amen," they all said—all except for Irene Bledsoe.

It was almost time to go. Tom opened a paper sack. "Here. I meant to give these to you last time."

"Hey, all right!" said Josiah, receiving his Bible.

"Thank you, Daddy!" said Ruth, hugging hers to her chest.

Tom also brought them some of their favorite books and the stationery they didn't receive the last time. He could see Irene Bledsoe eyeing everything he brought out of the sack, but he proceeded slowly and openly, having nothing to hide.

Well, almost nothing. Josiah was thumbing through his new book about whales when he found some photos inserted between the pages.

Tom, Mark, and Corrigan tried not to look at him too directly, lest they draw Bledsoe's attention.

"Like your book, Ruth?" Tom said, reaching across the table to help her find his little note to her on the title page. That physical gesture helped; Bledsoe watched him closely. "See what I wrote? It says, 'To my darling daughter Ruth. Jesus thinks you're precious, and so do I!'"

"Hey!" said Josiah. He was looking at the photos. "The lady in the pickup truck!"

That got Bledsoe's attention immediately. She saw Josiah holding the pictures, studying them with wide-eyed recognition. Her face went visibly pale.

Corrigan asked, "What do you mean, son? Have you seen that woman before?"

Bledsoe jumped to her feet. "Mr. Harris!"

Tom responded calmly. "Hm?"

"How dare you! How *dare* you!"

Corrigan pressed Josiah for an answer. "Do you recognize her?"

"Sure," said Josiah. "She's the lady that was driving that truck we almost hit. She always looks kind of sick, doesn't she?"

Bledsoe stomped around to where Josiah sat and grabbed the pictures from him. She took only a moment to look at them in outrage, and then defiantly she tore them in half, in quarters, in eighths, and then crumbled them up and pitched them into a wastebasket.

Then she stood there, shaking, glaring at Tom. "Just what are you trying to prove here?"

Mark spoke gently. "Mrs. Bledsoe, you're upsetting the children."

She pointed her finger in Tom's face, and her voice trembled with rage. "You have committed a serious offense! I can make things very hard for you! Don't think I can't have your children taken away permanently!"

Tom replied calmly—mostly for the children's benefit, "Then what are you so afraid of?"

She fought back. "Oh, I am not afraid, Mr. Harris. You don't scare me!"

Tom gave her a statement he'd rehearsed in his mind for quite some time. "Mrs. Bledsoe, it's been quite clear to me that you are not as concerned with the interests of my children as with your own interests. In any case, I think you're abusing your power—and my children, and me—and I intend to find out just whom you're trying to protect."

She tried to keep her voice down; after all, shouting was unprofessional. "Why, you—!" With great effort, she relaxed, assumed a professional demeanor, and announced, "This visitation is over. I think your betrayal of my trust was deplorable, and I will keep it in mind when I consider the date for our next meeting."

"It'll be sooner than you think," said Corrigan. He walked around the table, took her hand, and slapped a subpoena into it. "Try not to tear this up. Good day."

Dear Tom,

I feel different today, and I don't know if I can explain it. Undoubtedly it stems from my fanciful proposition of the morning, the possibility of my guilt. Being guilty, or even feeling guilty, is not pleasant, of course, but the mere suggestion of it seems to have weakened another nagging emotional companion of mine: despair. It makes me think of a clown hitting his thumb with a hammer to get his mind off his headache: now that I feel guilty, I don't feel as much despair.

But—and this is purely for the sake of discussion—it could be said that the reasons go deeper than that. As I've said before, an all-out plunge into humanism and its total lack of absolutes can leave you groping for fences, wondering where you are, wishing you could know something for sure. Now that's despair.

Then suddenly, guilt—well, the possibility of guilt—has come upon the scene, and I find myself playing with the thought that I might be standing in the wrong, which means I could have violated a standard somewhere, which means there might be a standard to be violated, which means there might be something out there somewhere that I can know for sure.

So, I guess I said all that to say this: If I really can be guilty, if I really am guilty, then at least I know where I stand. Suddenly, after all this time, I've found a fence, a boundary, and just the thought of that dispels that old cloud of despair, so much that I've noticed it.

Just consider, Tom, what great lengths I've gone to all through my life to quell despair. The Young Potentials program at the Omega Center presented a possible escape; I dove into everything they offered: yoga, TM, diet, folk medicine, altered states, drugs, and a lot of mental trips about my own divinity and ability to create my own reality. It was a long excursion into insanity, I admit it. What good did it do to make up my own truth? I was lost and drifting to begin with, and any reality born in my head could be no better off. I and the universe I created were lost and drifting together.

And then there was Jonas, my "consummate friend." He was a marvelous salesman with a lot of good lines, remarkably skilled in flattery. We took many long walks together during my yogic trances, and he did have me convinced that all reality—including death—was an illusion to be manipulated, and that I, being God, could form reality to be whatever I wanted it to be.

And for a crucial season, I believed that. I believed I had formed a reality to serve me and supply what I wanted. I believed I had formed a man who gave me pleasure without guilt. I believed I had formed a child that asked me to send her on to her next life, leaving me free to continue where I left off.

But did I form the prison bars too? I was talking about fences, wasn't I?

I lived behind that fence for seven years, and Jonas never came to visit me. I did resent that. I did blame him for Rachel's death. It was, in my thinking, his idea. He was the one who took control of my body and snuffed out her life. He committed the act. He was to blame.

But I don't think that now. I changed my mind at some point; maybe it was this morning.
"Amethyst" was right; I killed my baby.

Sally put away her notebook and went out, her mind full of thoughts, turning things over, sorting things out. She felt a change coming, though she had no idea what it could be or which direction it would go. But this walk of hers right now was going to be part of it; she was going to track down a memory and find another missing piece to the puzzle of her life.

As near as she could remember, it was an old red brick building not far from the motel, and there was an alley, an old, cobblestoned alley with a stream of water running down its center and a grate over a drain. Oh, where was that?

Tal followed right behind her. Nathan and Armoth hovered just above, swords drawn, eyes looking warily about. Destroyer was getting close. Time was short.

Keep going, Sally, said Tal. *You're getting warmer.*

She turned down a side street. This sidewalk looked familiar; these potted elms seemed to match the memory, though they were much bigger now.

A noisy garbage truck roared and rumbled out of an alley behind an old brewery, nosed its way into traffic, and then growled through its gears, heading down the street.

Sally headed for the alley.

This had to be it! The same, narrow, cobblestoned alley, the same, towering, red brick walls of the old brewery! She was walking into the past. The drain was still there, the moss on the brick walls was still the same, the smell of garbage was right out of her memory. She quickened her pace. It was somewhere along here, a loose brick in a windowsill . . . She was remembering more and more as she ran along, looking carefully at each window, hoping for any detail that would trigger a memory.

Tal could see the angelic sentries ahead, guarding the spot. There were four of them, bold and brilliant, all grim with dedication, their swords ready. They'd been at this post, watching it, preserving it for ten years. At the sight of Sally Roe approaching, they raised their swords and let out a cautious, muffled cheer.

She approached the rear corner of the building. It had to be here somewhere; she seemed to remember it being near the corner.

There was one last window, and the brick sill was at eye-level. She stopped and looked around. She was alone in the alley. She touched the sill, ran her fingers along it. It had to be the same one. Was that loose brick on the right side or the left? She put her thumb under the brick on the left end and gently pressed upward.

It budged. For the first time in ten years, it budged. The light of day flooded the cavity underneath it.

Sally's heart leaped. She could see a faint glint of gold. She lifted the brick further.

There lay the ring. It was like a miracle. Sally's emotions rose to such a pitch that a faint cry escaped from her. She reached into the niche and grabbed the ring between her thumb and forefinger. She pulled it out into the light, and let the brick sink back into place.

Ten years later, the ring was still remarkably clean except for some gray spiderwebs. She rubbed it against her shirttail, and the shine returned. She pulled the first ring out of her shirt and held the two together.

Yes, they were the same. Now there were two little gargoyles, snarling at her with identical expressions.

Tal dismissed the sentries.

Sally leaned against the brick wall and thought about the day when she planted the ring in this hiding-place. She was desperate, afraid she would be betrayed. Perhaps it was a stealthy, conniving act to steal that man's ring and hide it here, but as it turned out, she *was* betrayed, and now, ten years later, this ring could be a key to reopen the past, to view it all again, to find out what went wrong.

She thought of Tom Harris and those Christians at that little school in Bacon's Corner.

Have I done wrong? If so, then let me do something right, *just this once.*

She unclasped the chain around her neck and placed the second ring beside the first.

Back at the Schrader Motor Inn, the office door swung open; the electric eye beeped that someone had come in.

The lady behind the counter looked up. "Hello. May I help you?"

Mr. Khull smiled most pleasantly. "Good morning. I'm looking for my wife. She said she'd rented a room here . . . uh, number 302?"

"Oh!" She pulled out the registration. "Are you Mr. Rogers?"

Khull broke into a wide grin. "Yes, yes! All right, I finally found her!"

She was curious. "Well, how did you know where to look?"

"Oh, we've rented the room before. We love it. We stay here every time we come through. I was detained at home for a few days, but she called me and said she'd found the same room. I was hoping it was the one I was thinking of."

"Well . . ." She found a problem. "Uh, she only rented it to herself. I guess she misunderstood."

Khull got out his wallet. "Yeah, that's a mistake. Let me make up the balance. Is she up there right now? I think I might surprise her."

"Well, no, I think she went out. But I can give you a key."

"Great."

"Why don't you fill out another form here so I can get my records straight?"

"Sure."

He filled out another form and gave their names: Mr. and Mrs. Jack Rogers. He had a good size wad of bills as well, and paid her the balance still owed.

She looked at the address he gave. "So how are things in Las Vegas? Is it as wild as they say?"

"No . . ." He laughed. "Well, in certain places it is, I suppose. But it's not a bad place to live."

"Well, here's your key . . . Oh dear. I guess she has the only duplicate. Well, come on, I'll just go up and let you in."

"Thanks. Hey, don't tell her I'm here. She isn't expecting me until tomorrow!"

Across the street, crouching atop the hardware store, and across the motel parking lot, hiding on the roof of Nelson Printing and Bookbinding, squads of filthy warriors puffed a cloud of sulfur when they saw Khull follow the lady up to Room 302.

Destroyer watched from his vantage point above the flower shop. "They guessed right," he hissed. "She's here!"

23

"Praise God," said Tom, so excited he couldn't sit still. "I can't believe it! Progress!"

"Well, a hundred different pieces maybe," said Marshall. "But give it time—it'll fall together."

Tom, Marshall, Kate, and Ben were having another powwow with Wayne Corrigan in his office, not too long after that rather explosive meeting with Irene Bledsoe.

Ben had gotten over his excitement. Now he was pensive, probing. "She's alive. Sally Roe is alive, and Mulligan knows it."

"And Parnell too," said Marshall. "I've got him on my list."

"But what are they trying to pull, and why?" asked Kate.

"That's what I'm still waiting to hear," said Corrigan. "I love all this stuff, guys—I'm really enjoying it, but sooner or later—and let's hope sooner—it's got to add up to something. We need a case we can present in court, and so far I don't see anything that directly applies to the lawsuit."

"Right," said Marshall, looking through some notes. "So far it's all indirect, peripheral stuff. But we're getting closer. Here are the names of the people I got from that Motor Vehicle Report on the license plates. The following people are possibly involved in this LifeCircle outfit, and some of them fit right into this: Mr. Bruce Woodard, the elementary school principal, and, no surprise, our plucky Miss Brewer."

Kate inserted, "And as for Mr. Bruce Woodard, I talked to him on the phone again today, and he still assures me he'll find that curriculum so I can look at it. But if you ask me, he's stalling."

"If he is, try these names: Jerry Mason, Betty Hanover, and John Kendall, three members of the Bacon's Corner school board, all three most likely connected with LifeCircle."

"Hence the *Finding the Real Me* curriculum at the elementary school," said Tom. "It fits right into their worldview."

"And their agenda," said Marshall. "These people are just as evangelistic about their religion as we are, and they're wasting no time." He raised an eyebrow at the next set of names. "Jon Schmidt and Claire Johanson. Schmidt doesn't impress me yet, but Johanson is big stuff, a direct connection with the ACFA. Oh, and who was that other guy? Oh yeah. Gordon Jefferson was there too, so now we have a link-up with the ACFA for sure, not to mention . . ." He scanned down the page. "Lenore Hofspring, from California. Check the ACFA California roster, Kate. I'll bet she's on it. They're bringing in some bigger guns from out of state."

"It isn't fair!" said Tom.

"Have faith. We've caught so many fish today our nets are breaking. Here's another fish right here . . . Surprise, surprise. Lucy Brandon. What a recipe. Take a mother involved in this cosmic mystic group, add the cosmic mystic group controlling the school board and pumping cosmic mystic curricula into the local school, then get a well-meaning, crusading teacher fresh out of . . . what was that teacher's college?"

Kate answered, "Bentmore."

"Right, one of America's finest, they say. Miss Brewer learned everything she knows from them, and now she's cramming it into the kids. These people have the whole system sewn up from the top down.

"Anyway, throw it all into the pot, stir it all up, and what do you get? A little girl channeling a spirit just like all the moms and pops and uncles and aunts out there at the big white house.

"We're talking about a lot of moles, a lot of demons connecting this whole thing: Lucy Brandon, LifeCircle, the school board, the school, the ACFA, and even the little girl."

Ben was puzzled. "But . . . are you saying they purposely enrolled Amber in our school just to force a confrontation?"

Marshall laid the notes on the desk and thought about that. "No. Maybe Lucy Brandon really wanted something better for her kid. Maybe the trouble that popped up was something the others—LifeCircle, the ACFA—saw as an opportunity. What do you think, Tom?"

Tom was intrigued with the notion. "When she first enrolled Amber, she seemed concerned about the changes Amber had gone through since being in Miss Brewer's class. At the time, I honestly thought that Lucy Brandon wanted a more basic, 'traditional' education for her daughter."

"That's the feeling I get," said Marshall. "It'll be interesting to talk to her and find out what she's really thinking, and if she's doing her own thinking at all."

Kate reported, "Alice Buckmeier told me about Debbie, the girl who works with Lucy at the Post Office. Debbie was there that day and saw the confrontation between Amber and Sally Roe. She might be able to tell us something more about Lucy."

"Sounds good. And now . . ." Marshall spread some sheets of paper out on Corrigan's desk as the attorney watched. "Here's the best part, I think. It could make this case bigger than just Bacon's Corner . . . and it could blow it wide open. We don't know yet."

The others gathered around.

"That address bothered me, the location of the Omega Center that published that curriculum. That was in Fairwood, Massachusetts, right?"

Kate had that information. "Right. I got the address from Miss Brewer."

"Ben, where did you get that arrest record, the one that included the mug shots of Sally Roe?"

Ben was stunned as he doublechecked the document. "Fairwood, Massachusetts!"

"So . . . a lady gets arrested for murder clear across the country, but then shows up in this little place for no apparent reason. In the meantime, a curriculum is published in the same town where she was arrested and finds its way here . . . Maybe it's just a coincidence, except for some more molehills: a little girl who ends up demonized, most likely because of that curriculum, later confronts

Roe in the Post Office, and the little mole sticks its head up out of the ground and says, 'I know you, you killed your baby!'" Marshall smiled and shook his head at his own conclusion. "That demon was in Fairwood; it knew about Sally Roe."

"And then . . ." said Ben; he was figuring it out.

Marshall verified his thought. "And then somebody comes along and tries to kill Sally Roe . . ."

"The very same day my kids were taken!" said Tom.

"*And* the very day before you got your summons."

"I love it," said Corrigan. "But what does it really mean?"

Marshall looked over all the notes one more time and answered, "I don't know. We have molehills all over the place, and demons tunneling everywhere, maybe even across the country, but . . ." He sighed. "No case. We can theorize that Sally Roe's so-called suicide has something to do with the lawsuit against the school, but . . . what? And so what? There just isn't any visible connection—yet."

Ben turned away, frustrated. "We've got to find out who that woman was, the one we found dead in the goat shed!"

"Parnell's the one to talk to."

"Well, he wouldn't talk to me! He and Mulligan are in this together, that's obvious, and they're looking out for each other."

"And I'll guess somebody higher up is watching them closely, if you get my drift."

Corrigan piped right up. "I don't get your drift."

"Humor an old reporter," said Marshall. "I'm guessing they both belong to some kind of secret group, maybe a lodge, maybe something occult, who knows, something like LifeCircle, something tied closely to it, maybe even a part of it, but not nearly as nice. Hidden. Powerful. Something has a really short leash on those two."

"But you're guessing," said Corrigan.

"Keep on guessing," said Tom. "You're a good guesser."

Marshall ran his fingers through his hair. "I'm in your camp, Wayne; a guess is only good if it pays off. We'll just have to find some levers to pull, some way to squeeze these people. Oh, Kate, speaking of levers, forget waiting for Woodard to get you the curriculum. Go to the school board, those three people . . ." He checked his list again. "Uh . . . Jerry Mason, Betty Hanover, and John Kendall. Just see what they say, but don't wait for them either. If they stall, write to Omega for it. I want to see that curriculum."

Corrigan rested his chin on his knuckles and stared at all the notes. "Man, where is Sally Roe?"

Marshall said grimly, "I imagine somebody else is wondering that too."

A rustling went through the demonic ranks surrounding the motel; black wings began to quiver, and red glowing blades appeared.

Sally Roe was returning to the motel, walking briskly up the street, alone and unprotected.

"Remain in place," said Destroyer. "Don't move."

Immediately there was a hissing and an agitation among the ranks. The officers on either side of Destroyer got fidgety.

"She is ours!" said one.

"Alone!" said another.

"Remain in place," said Destroyer.

Sally felt no anxiety, no fear. If she felt anything, it was a new kind of exhilaration. She still couldn't believe the incredible recovery of that second ring. She considered herself extremely lucky, or fortunate . . . She wasn't ready to say "blessed."

She rounded the corner, passed under the breezeway, and started up the stairs to Room 302.

"We should saturate the building!" said the monster at Destroyer's right. "Khull and his men need our power!"

"You must reinforce the demons of Broken Birch!" said the beast at Destroyer's left.

Destroyer watched, still silent, as his warriors fussed and hissed all around him, itching to get in on the kill.

Sally reached the first landing and was starting up the second flight of stairs.

Khull was in the room, waiting. One of his men, dressed as a repairman, remained near the soft drink machine at the other stairway, ready to block any escape that way. Another man, looking like a casual vacationer, took his post at the bottom of the stairs Sally had just taken.

A third man, dressed in dark clothes and smoking a cigarette, started up the stairs after her, quietly, surreptitiously.

Sally was just on the second flight of stairs when she didn't feel right about something.

Tal was beside her. *Stop*, he said. *Wait.*

She stopped. She'd seen that one man standing near the office door when she came around the corner, and now she was sure he was coming up the flight of stairs below her. When she stopped, he hesitated. Now it was ominously quiet.

Tal remained beside her; Nathan stood at the top of the stairs, Armoth at the bottom. They were making themselves clearly visible.

Tal drew his sword slowly and let its light flicker against the wall of the building for all to see. Nathan and Armoth did the same. Now they could see the demonic response: from rooftops all around the motel, the sky lit up with the red glow of enemy swords, and the air was filled with the clatter and rustling of black wings.

There was a standoff.

A taloned hand grabbed Destroyer's arm.

"Will you not attack? There are only three guarding her!" said the warrior. The demons all around squawked their eager agreement.

"Only three?" Destroyer replied. "You mean you *see* only three." He pointed his crooked finger at the warrior that had grabbed him, then at another whiner, and then at one more overly anxious fighter. "Very well. You, you, and you, attack! Do your worst!"

They shrieked, raised their swords, and shot from the roof like skyrockets, swooping down toward the motel. They would give Broken Birch all the power they needed, and Sally Roe was as good as dead!

Tal shot from the stairway in a brilliant explosion of wings, and met the three attackers over the parking lot. Two were instantly shredded; the third went careening and fluttering over the print shop, trailing red smoke from what was left of him. Back on the stairs, Nathan and Armoth closed in on Sally Roe, their wings outspread, their swords ready.

KAWOOOM! Bursting instantly out of hiding, at least a dozen warriors appeared all around the motel, their wings spreading to form an impenetrable wall.

"Oh, Mrs. Bissell!"

It was the office lady. Sally was relieved to hear her voice. "Yes, I'm up here!"

"Could I see you for a minute?"

The man on the flight below dropped his cigarette and crushed it out with his toe. Then he hurried back down and ran across the parking lot. Sally went to the balcony railing and saw him ducking around the corner.

"Hmm," said Destroyer. "How many more warriors do you suppose he has hidden in there?"

No demon would venture a guess.

"Maybe none at all . . . maybe thousands! Would anyone like to find out?"

The lady in the office brought Sally's travel bag out from behind the counter.

"I hope you won't think me too forward for doing this," she said, "but before you go up to your room, you'd better know that there's a man up there waiting for you. He said he was your husband."

Sally was horrified. "What?"

"Is he?"

Sally backed toward the door. "I don't have a husband."

"Don't go out there, not yet."

Sally stopped.

"What about that other man, the one following you up the stairs?"

Sally was amazed. She looked out the windows. "He's . . . I saw him running away." Then she backed away from the window, afraid of being seen.

"I don't know who you are, or who he is, but I ran a check and there's no such thing as a '79 Mustang with the license number you gave, and no such thing as a Buick Regal with the license number he gave. Maybe two people can be married and have different last names, but when you say you're from Hawthorne, California, and he says you're both from Las Vegas, I just don't like the looks of it."

Sally didn't know what to say. "I'm sorry."

"I got your bag out of the room when I let him in; I told him the previous tenant left it there. Is there some kind of trouble? I don't want anything weird going on in my motel."

Sally took the bag. "Thank you."

"Should I call the police?"

"Uh, no. No, I'll just leave. Keep the rent money—it's okay."

"What about 'Mr. Rogers' upstairs?"

Sally was backing toward the door. She looked out the window to make sure he wasn't lurking about. "Uh . . . yes, call the police."

Destroyer and his army could see Sally slip quickly out the front door and run down the street, completely surrounded by the angelic guards.

A demon hissed and pointed. There went Khull, sneaking out of Room 302, hurrying down the back stairs with the "repairman." The casual vacationer had also disappeared. Somehow they knew the jig was up. Perhaps it was that timely interruption by the lady in the office; maybe they'd felt Sally Roe's great "psychic power" in the place. Perhaps they could feel their demonic escorts being stalled by the angelic guard. Whatever the case, things did not feel right, and they were calling it quits.

Destroyer blew a stream of sulfur from his nostrils. "Remember," he said to his warriors, "this Tal is a layer of traps, a setter of snares. No little human as dangerous to us as Sally Roe is going to walk down the street uncovered and alone. He was there. His warriors were ready." He laughed. "But that will change."

He looked down the street in time to see Sally Roe disappear around a corner, still heavily guarded. "No, Captain of the Host! Not this time. You are still too strong, but time is on my side! I have your saints in *my* hands. This game will be *ours*. *We* will set the rules, *we* will pick the time."

Judy Waring wasn't spending as much time home schooling her son Charlie as she promised herself and everyone else she would. At the moment, her plucky little third-grader was doing whatever he wanted out in the yard while she tended to some pressing matters on the telephone.

"Well, that's what I heard," she said. "He's had sexual problems ever since Cindy passed away, and I think they were even having trouble in their marriage because of it. Did you ever notice the way he'd always stand so close to Cathy Howard? Maybe she was next on his list, I don't know."

Then the other party talked for a while, and Judy kept busy snipping coupons out of the shopping news.

Judy's turn came again. "Well, that's what I think too. I mean, how can we be sure what really went on in that classroom? Mrs. Fields is busy enough with all the kids in her class; she can't possibly be watching Tom all the time."

Gossip sat on her shoulders, dangling his skinny fingers in her brain while Strife sat on the table and watched.

"A marvelous idea!" said Strife.

"You know," said Gossip, "this woman will believe anything!"

24

"He was harsh, belligerent, and frightened the children on many occasions," said Irene Bledsoe, her face defiant, her spine straight as a rod.

She was flanked by the two ACFA attorneys, Jefferson and Ames, sitting in a conference room adjacent to Wayne Corrigan's office. Across the conference table from her sat Wayne Corrigan, Tom Harris, and Mark Howard. At the end of the table was the court reporter, taking down everything spoken.

Wayne Corrigan scanned his notes. This lady was a tiger for sure, and he was wishing he had more to go on. With the little information he had so far, it was going to be a short deposition.

"But this is based solely on the word of Amber Brandon, is it not?" he finally asked.

"Yes, and she is a bright, truthful, and responsible little girl."

"But you yourself never saw Mr. Harris displaying any of this behavior?"

"I certainly did: the first time he came to visit his children. He violated the rules we had agreed upon, he was rude, and he was belligerent."

"Belligerent. You've used that word twice. Now, is that your word or Amber's?"

Jefferson spoke up. "What kind of a question is that?"

Corrigan didn't have to tell him, but he did. "I'm trying to figure out what Amber Brandon said and get around any embellishments from Miss Bledsoe." He went to the next question. "So what about Amber's testimony to you? What specifically did she say Mr. Harris did?"

Bledsoe leaned forward just a little, but kept her spine straight. "Amber told me that Mr. Harris and the other children made fun of her, harassed her, and tried to impose their religious views on her."

"Could you be more specific? How did they make fun of her?"

Bledsoe hesitated. "Well, they . . ."

"Did they call her names?"

"I suppose so."

"Well, did they or didn't they?"

"Amber wouldn't cite any specific names, but I'm sure if we asked her, she could tell us exactly."

"All right, we'll do that." Corrigan moved on. "Now what about harassment? How did Mr. Harris harass Amber?"

Bledsoe laughed at that question. "Oh, how indeed! I suppose you consider it normal to be branded as demon-possessed, to be forbidden to play with the other children . . ."

"Mr. Harris forbade Amber to play with the other children?"

"Oh yes. She was forced to stay inside at recess and write a page from the Bible."

Corrigan made a note of it. "And did Amber say just what the reason was for that?"

Bledsoe shrugged just a little. "Oh, apparently Mr. Harris wasn't happy with her views in a particular matter, and so he decided she needed some more intense indoctrination."

"Are those the words Amber used?"

"No . . ."

"That's just your interpretation?"

"Well, yes."

"What exactly did Amber say?"

"She said that Mr. Harris wouldn't let her go out for recess, but made her stay inside and copy from the Bible."

"Did she suggest that she was being punished for an infraction of the school rules?"

"I didn't gather that from what she said."

"Did it happen once, for one recess, or was it a constant, daily practice?"

"I'm not sure."

"And again, you were not a direct witness to any of this?"

"No, of course not."

"Was anyone?"

"Well, Mr. Harris, but . . ."

"Mm-hm." Corrigan flipped to another page of notes. "Let's talk about Amethyst the pony. Is that the correct name of this . . . uh . . . alter ego?"

"I don't know. She does identify herself as Amethyst, and I understand she is a pony, a mythical character."

"So you've met Amethyst yourself?"

Ames jumped in on that one. "Excuse me, Mr. Corrigan—I don't think that question is very clear."

Corrigan asked Bledsoe, "Is the question clear to you?"

"No."

"Have you ever dealt with Amber when she was acting like Amethyst?"

She shrugged, unruffled. "Of course."

"And nothing about it seemed strange to you?"

"No, of course not. Children have been known to dissociate into alternate personalities, or make up imaginary friends in dealing with severe trauma. It's very common."

"And what severe trauma are we talking about?"

Miss Bledsoe tried to compose a clear answer. "There was severe trauma all through Amber's experience at the Christian school: harassment, discrimination, stress, imposing of Christian dogma . . . It all led to Amber resorting to a false personality to cope with it. Mr. Harris could have responded properly and dealt with the real source of Amber's trouble, but instead he compounded the trauma by branding Amber as demon-possessed, which I think is just horrendous."

"But you were not a direct witness to any of this?"

"No."

"This is all according to what you learned from Amber?"

"Yes."

Corrigan jotted some notes and went to a fresh page. "Let's talk about the Harris kids. What first brought the situation in the Harris home to your attention?"

She hesitated. "I believe . . . we received a complaint."

"You mean a hotline complaint?"

"Yes."

"So you don't know from whom?"

"No."

"It was not from the attorneys for Mrs. Brandon?"

Jefferson was right on top of that. "Objection!"

Corrigan pointed his finger at Jefferson. "This isn't a courtroom, and you aren't the judge, Mr. Jefferson!"

"I resent the question!"

"Do *you* want to answer it?"

"Don't be impertinent!"

Corrigan turned back to Miss Bledsoe. "Miss Bledsoe, to the best of your knowledge, did you receive the complaint from anyone connected with this lawsuit?"

"Absolutely not!" she said with great indignity.

"Not from any of the attorneys for Mrs. Brandon?"

"No!"

"How about Mrs. Brandon herself?"

"No!"

"All right. Now, I'm sure you've had abundant opportunity to talk to Ruth and Josiah?"

"Oh yes."

"Have they reported any abuse of any kind from their father?"

"Yes, they have."

Tom looked up at that remark.

Corrigan pressed it. "Okay. What abuse?"

"Frequent spankings with a wooden spoon."

"I take it you had reason to believe that these spankings were not administered in a loving and controlled manner?"

"They were administered, Mr. Corrigan, and that to me is abuse."

"All right. Any other abuse toward the children?"

"He doesn't let them watch television."

Corrigan remained deadpan, and scribbled that down. "Were you aware that Mr. Harris doesn't even own a television set?"

"Yes. His children told me."

"Were they complaining about it?"

"I think they were. I took it that way. They're captivated by the simplest programs as if they've never seen anything like it before. They know so little about what's going on in our culture. Their lives are far too sheltered for their proper social development."

"And that is your professional opinion?"

"Yes, of course."

"And what about direct evidence of any physical abuse? Did anyone see any bruises on the children, any signs that something was amiss?"

"Well, of course! Ruth had a large bump on her head!"

It was all Tom could do to remain quiet.

Corrigan asked, "I take it the anonymous hotline caller reported that bump?"

"Of course."

"Did Ruth ever say where she got that bump?"

Miss Bledsoe assumed an even stiffer posture and answered, "We're still investigating, and until that investigation is complete, the matter is strictly confidential."

"I would think the bump is a matter of public record," said Corrigan. "You realize, of course, that the children have told their father, in your presence, where that bump came from."

"But remember, Mr. Corrigan, that it was their father they were talking to. Out of fear, a child can tell a tale to avoid further abuse."

Corrigan indulged in a quick sigh of frustration. "Ms. Bledsoe, why do I get the impression that you don't really have a concrete reason for holding the children in custody in a strange home and environment, away from their own home and father?"

Miss Bledsoe made a visible effort to keep her cool. "We have suspicions, Mr. Corrigan, and suspicions are enough reason. We are still working with the children. We have ways of drawing out the truth eventually. The children do want to tell us everything, but are often afraid."

"So you do believe that Ruth and Josiah mean to be truthful?"

"Yes."

"And yet you won't accept Ruth and Josiah's account of your near-collision with a blue pickup truck, and their claim that it was in that near-mishap that Ruth sustained the bump on her head?"

She grimaced in disgust at the question. "That's an entirely different matter! You can't trust children to be reliable witnesses in such things."

"So they are reliable witnesses only when their testimony confirms your prior suspicions?" Jefferson started getting ruffled. Corrigan spoke first. "You don't have to answer that."

Corrigan pulled out a photograph and placed it in front of her. "Have you ever seen this woman?"

Bledsoe looked at the picture of Sally Roe and did her best to draw a blank. "No, I don't think so."

"Any chance that she was the driver of that pickup?"

"Objection!" said Ames. "You haven't established that there even was a pickup."

"Miss Bledsoe, did you have a near-miss encounter with a blue pickup while driving the Harris children away from the Harris home?"

"No, I did not!"

"With any vehicle of any color?"

"No!"

Corrigan pointed at the picture of Sally Roe. "You said you've never seen this woman before. Have you ever seen this picture before?"

She hesitated. "I may have."

"Where?"

"I don't recall."

"Do you recall tearing up some photographs that were in Josiah Harris's possession during the children's last visit with their father?"

She was clearly uncomfortable. "Oh . . . I tore something up, I'm not sure what it was."

Corrigan took back the picture. "Let's talk about your driving record. Any moving violations in the past three years?"

Now she hesitated. "What do you mean?"

"Traffic tickets. Citations."

"I believe so."

"According to the Department of Motor Vehicles, you've had five speeding violations in the past three years. Is that true?"

"If that's what they say."

"You've also been cited twice for failing to stop at a stop sign, correct?"

"I don't see what this has to do with anything!"

Corrigan insisted, "Correct?"

She sighed. "Yes."

"You've had to change insurance companies three times?"

"I don't know."

Jefferson blurted, "I think you're badgering the witness, Mr. Corrigan."

"I am through with this witness, Mr. Jefferson." Corrigan folded up his notes, relaxed, and smiled. "Thank you very much for coming, Miss Bledsoe. Thanks to all of you."

Bledsoe and the two lawyers felt no need to hang around socially, and the court reporter had another appointment. In no time at all, Corrigan, Mark, and Tom were alone in the conference room.

"Well?" asked Tom.

Corrigan wanted to be sure Bledsoe and the others were gone. He leaned over to look out through the door. The coast was clear. He sat down and thought for a moment, looking through his notes.

"Well, she's lying like a rug, and it shouldn't be too hard to trap her on the witness stand."

Mark asked, "What about Marshall's theory? She's connected to this whole thing, isn't she? She's working for them."

Corrigan thought for just a moment, and then nodded. "The evidence is still circumstantial, but there's a connection, all right, and she's working hard to cover it up. That's one reason she's being so stiff-necked with your kids, Tom. They're witnesses. If you want to hear my latest theory, I'd say she was brought in just to discredit you, but then crossed paths with Sally Roe with the children as witnesses, which complicated everything. Now she not only has to keep the kids quiet about seeing Sally Roe, she also has to keep them quiet about having that near-accident in the first place, and Ruth's bump isn't going to make that easy."

"My children are like hostages!" said Tom angrily.

Mark was fuming as well. "She's connected with Mulligan, then; she's helping him protect that whole suicide story."

Corrigan leafed through his notes. "The more we get into this, I think the more we're going to find that everybody's connected with everybody else. And don't forget Parnell, the coroner. In order to get the whole thing dismissed as a suicide, he'd have to be a part of this too."

Mark looked at his watch. "We'd better pray for Marshall and Ben. They're talking to him right now."

Joey Parnell was not happy at all when he opened his front door to find Marshall Hogan and the recently jobless Ben Cole standing there.

"Hi," said Marshall. "Sorry to bother you at home. Apparently you forgot our appointment."

He had trouble looking them in the eye. "I'm sorry. My secretary was supposed to call you. I'm sick today."

"She did tell us that," said Ben, "but only after we sat there and waited for half an hour."

"Oh, I am sorry. Well, perhaps some other time . . ."

"You'd better have your secretary call the Westhaven Medical Association too," said Marshall. "I saw the ad in the paper, and I just talked to them. They're still expecting you to speak at their conference in an hour."

"Is that why you're wearing your dress shoes and slacks?" asked Ben. "Looks like you're getting dressed to go somewhere."

Parnell became angry. "What business do you have snooping into my daily affairs?"

Marshall reached into a manila envelope. "This might help to answer that." He produced a photograph and showed it to Parnell. "Mr. Parnell, to the best of your knowledge and expertise, is this the woman who committed suicide at the Potter farm several weeks ago?"

He didn't want to look at the picture. "Listen, guys, I do have some other things to do and I have to get ready. Now if you'll excuse me—"

"Just give us a minute," said Ben. "Please."

Marshall showed him the picture again. "Take a good look. We've checked around with several witnesses who have positively identified her; we have fingerprints, a rap sheet, the whole thing. Is this Sally Roe?"

He looked at the picture for a moment. "Yeah, sure it is. I remember her. Death by strangulation. She hung herself."

"Just checking," said Marshall.

Parnell turned away from the door. "Now if that's all . . ."

"Mr. Parnell," said Marshall, "that was a picture of my sister."

Parnell's face went blank and suddenly pale. His hands were starting to shake.

Marshall continued, "I figured since you live here in Westhaven you probably wouldn't know what the real Sally Roe looked like, and now it's obvious you've never seen her dead either."

Parnell was speechless. He kept looking down, then at the door, then inside the house, then at Marshall and Ben. The poor guy was acting like a cornered animal.

Ben asked, "Can you tell us who the dead woman really was?"

"I can't tell you anything!" he finally blurted. "Just go away—get out of here!"

He slammed the door.

Marshall and Ben walked back toward their car.

"Did you see that?" asked Marshall.

"That guy is *scared*!" said Ben.

Kate's afternoon had been, in a way, informative; at least she was being informed in a most frustrating way how difficult it was to ever see a bona fide copy of the *Finding the Real Me* curriculum for fourth-graders.

She stopped by the office at the elementary school to meet with Mr. Woodard, the principal, and look at the curriculum. Mr. Woodard wasn't there. She found him down the hall, whereupon he had a sudden recollection of their appointment.

Then the curriculum was nowhere to be found, and he couldn't understand whatever happened to it. He told her to talk to Miss Brewer. Miss Brewer was with her class and could not be disturbed, but would call her. Miss Brewer never called.

Then Kate called Jerry Mason, a member of the school board and most likely a member of LifeCircle.

"Well, I think the teacher should have a copy," he said.

Kate was getting tired of that line. "No, she doesn't. I've already checked with her and she referred me to Mr. Woodard, who then referred me back to Miss Brewer."

"Well, I don't have a copy."

"I was just wondering if you might, since you did approve the curriculum for the elementary grades."

"But do you have a child taking that curriculum?"

"No, I'm just trying to see a copy of it."

"Well, there aren't that many around, and I don't think anyone who wants to can just drop in anytime and see it. We prefer to work with only the parents. You probably should make an appointment."

Kate ran around the mulberry bush a few more times with Jerry Mason, and then called Betty Hanover, another school board member.

"Say, listen," Betty said, "we've been through all this before with the . . . the religious fringe. The community has decided they like the curriculum, and we'd just as soon have some peace now, all right?"

John Kendall was no better. "Did you ask Miss Brewer? It's the teachers who are supposed to be in charge of it. They ought to be able to help you out."

Kate put down the phone and checked off another name. Then she let out a mock scream.

If for no other reason, that curriculum had to be worth seeing simply because so many people were going to such great lengths to keep it hidden.

Another letter! It was just like the other ones—same envelope, same handwriting, same thick letter inside on lined notebook paper! Lucy grabbed it out of the pile of incoming mail and slipped it quickly into her pocket. Where were all these letters coming from? If this was a joke, it was certainly a long-lived joke, and not at all funny.

If it wasn't a joke, and these letters really were from Sally Roe . . .

She didn't want to think about that; it was easier not to consider it at all, and go on trusting all the people she now trusted.

Debbie was nearby, sorting through the mail in another mailbag. She'd stopped working, and seemed to be looking carefully at a mailing label on a magazine, but . . . To Lucy, it seemed like Debbie was watching her, but trying not to look like it.

"Something wrong?" Lucy asked.

"Oh, no . . . nothing," Debbie answered, turning away and shoving the magazine into one of the mailboxes.

They went on sorting the mail, and nothing more was said.

But Debbie had seen the whole thing.

25

Wayne Corrigan had read Dr. Mandanhi's detailed report on Amber Brandon's condition. Most of it was so technical it would take another expert to refute it, if it was refutable. One thing was clear to even a lay reader of the document: Mandanhi held the Good Shepherd Academy responsible for Amber's troubles, and had a low opinion of Christianity. This deposition would not be easy.

Mandanhi was a gentle man, however, and not unpleasant to deal with. He was in his forties, of East Indian descent, well-dressed, well-mannered, professional. Attorneys Ames and Jefferson sat on either side of him, as they did Irene Bledsoe, but didn't seem quite as edgy for his sake as for Bledsoe's. Apparently they were sure Mandanhi could take care of himself.

Corrigan started with some basics. "So could you review for the record Amber's basic symptoms of trauma?"

Mandanhi brought a few notes, but didn't seem to need them. "Amber's behavior is typical of any child her age who has undergone extensive emotional trauma: bed-wetting, moodiness, occasional nausea, and frequent escapes into fantasy . . . a loss of reality, paranoia, the fear of unseen enemies—spooks, bogeymen, that sort of thing."

"And you attribute all this to the environment at the Christian school?"

He smiled. "Not entirely. There could well be other factors, but the pervasive religious overtones of the school's curriculum would be, in my opinion, sufficient to exacerbate Amber's preexistent emotional turmoils. The Christian doctrines of sin and of a God of wrath and judgment, as well as Christianity's imposition of guilt and accountability, would immediately assimilate into the child's preestablished identity structure, producing a whole new set of reasons for her to be insecure and fearful of her world."

"Have you discussed any of this with the pastor of the Good Shepherd Church, or with the headmaster of the school?"

"No, sir, I have not."

"So do you know for a fact that the school was imposing any kind of guilt or fear upon the child?"

"I have examined the child, and I know she went to the school. A clear connection is not hard to draw."

Corrigan made a few marks in the margin of his copy of Mandanhi's report. "Now . . . about this Amethyst, this little pony that Amber becomes . . . What was that term you used?"

"Dissociative disorder, or hysterical neurosis, dissociative type."

"Uh . . . right. Could you explain just what that is?"

"Basically, it is a disturbance or alteration in the normally integrative functions of identity, memory, or consciousness."

"I'm going to need that in simpler terms, doctor."

He smiled, thought for a moment, and then tried again. "What Amber is displaying is what we call Multiple Personality Disorder; it's a condition in which two or more distinct personalities exist within one person. This disorder is almost always brought on by some form of abuse, usually sexual, or severe emotional trauma.

The onset is almost invariably during childhood, but often is not discovered until later in life. Statistically, it occurs from three to nine times more often in females than males."

"I wanted to ask you about some of these complications you listed."

Mandanhi consulted his own copy of his report. "Yes. Complications, difficulties that can arise when this disorder manifests itself."

Corrigan scanned the list. "External violence?"

"Yes. A total break with social norms of behavior, social inhibitions. Blind rage, injury to others . . ."

"How about screaming, kicking, resisting authority?"

"Oh yes."

"Suicide attempts?"

"Very common."

"How about Amber?"

Mandanhi thought for a moment, then shook his head. "Her case seems rather mild in that area."

Corrigan found another new word. "What is coprolalia?"

"Violent, obscene language, usually involuntary."

Corrigan stopped on that one. "Involuntary?"

"The victim has no control over what he or she says; the utterance is spontaneous and can include animal noises, growls, barking, hissing, and so forth."

"Uh . . . how about blasphemy?" Corrigan felt a need to explain that. "Uh . . . railings, obscenities, slanderous statements against a Deity?"

"Yes. Quite frequent."

"And then there are . . . altered states of consciousness?"

"Yes, trance states."

"And according to your experience, this sort of thing is usually—or almost always—brought on by severe emotional trauma or sexual abuse?"

"That is correct."

"And this is your assumption regarding the Good Shepherd Academy?"

"It is."

"But you haven't talked to the school personnel about this?"

"No."

"I see." Corrigan jotted some notes and read a few more notes. "The press seems to have some firm opinions about what went on at the school, and they've said some pretty rough things about Tom Harris. Have they gotten any of their information from you, doctor?"

"I have not spoken to them personally, no."

Corrigan raised an eyebrow. "But it's reasonable to think that your opinions, in some form or another, have gotten into the hands of the press?"

He didn't seem too happy to have to answer. "I believe so."

"How about the Child Protection Department?"

Mandanhi looked at the lawyers. They didn't seem too distressed. "The CPD received a complete copy of my report, and I have consulted with them on a regular basis."

To Corrigan that was not a complete surprise, but he could still feel a tinge of anger. "So . . . they must think the Academy's quite a dangerous place for children."

"You would have to ask them."

Corrigan's voice rose just a little. "What did you tell them?"

Mandanhi balked at the question. "What did I tell them?"

"You've regularly consulted with them. Have you led them to believe the school is a dangerous place for children?"

"I can't tell you what they believe."

Corrigan let the question go. "Then I suppose by the same token you can't explain why there hasn't been an all-out investigation of the school and its personnel, and of every parent who has their child enrolled there?"

Mandanhi only shrugged. "That is not my responsibility to know. I don't make the decisions."

"Would the CPD representative you've regularly consulted with happen to be Irene Bledsoe?"

"Yes."

Corrigan said nothing in response to that; he just wrote it down. "Have you ever heard of a Miss Nancy Brewer, fourth grade teacher at the Bacon's Corner Elementary School?"

"No, sir."

"Have you ever heard of the *Finding the Real Me* curriculum that Miss Brewer teaches to her fourth-grade class?"

"No, sir."

"Then you are not aware, doctor, that Miss Brewer regularly teaches the children to relax, achieve susceptible states of consciousness, and contact inner guides?"

The question grabbed Mandanhi's interest, but he still had to reply, "No."

"Were you aware that, prior to Amber's enrollment at the Christian school, she was a student in Miss Brewer's class and went through that curriculum?"

That grabbed Mandanhi's interest even more. His expression became a little grim. "I was not aware of that."

"Are you familiar with a local organization called LifeCircle?"

"Yes."

"Are you aware that they regularly practice consciousness-altering techniques such as yoga, meditation, and . . ." Corrigan paused and then hit the term with emphasis. ". . . trance channeling?"

"I am aware of that."

"Are you aware that Lucy Brandon and her daughter Amber are both closely involved with that group and its practices?"

"Yes."

Corrigan wasn't expecting all these affirmative answers; he was a little shocked. "Then can you please explain to me, doctor, just how you can be so sure that only the Good Shepherd Academy is to be blamed for Amber's abnormal behavior?"

He smiled. "I do not blame the Academy for Amber's behavior; I blame it for the trauma that precipitated the behavior."

Corrigan had to get a grip on himself. This man was starting to bother him. "But in light of what is happening at the elementary school and at LifeCircle, can you agree that such behavior as Amber's can be taught and conditioned in a young child *without* severe trauma?"

Mandanhi laughed. "Since you are asking me, I will tell you that I do not recognize the validity of anything that may be happening at the elementary school or at LifeCircle. I look upon these things as highly subjective, even religious matters, something I prefer not to approach clinically."

"So Amber's behavior, in your opinion, must indicate severe emotional trauma as its only cause?"

"That is what I have written, and that is my opinion."

Corrigan stopped for a moment. He was frustrated, but tried not to show it. He went back to some other notes he'd jotted on the report. "So, doctor, between the Christians, the LifeCirclers, Miss Brewer, and even Amber, it looks like we have a lot of different opinions as to what this Amethyst really is."

"I am not responsible for any opinion other than my own," the doctor interjected.

"Would you agree that Amber is able to communicate with this . . . whatever it is?"

"That is not untypical for a dissociative. The different personalities are often aware of each other, will often converse, and sometimes even disagree and argue."

"And it's normal for Amber to blink out and not remember the passing of time when Amethyst is manifesting herself?"

"That is quite typical."

"How about special knowledge? Is it possible for Amethyst to know information that Amber could not possibly know or have prior opportunity to learn?"

Mandanhi hesitated. "I'm not sure I can answer that. The disorder does present a lot of questions at times . . ."

"Such as?"

"Oh . . . My colleagues and I have always been mystified by that one trait you mentioned, special knowledge—some would call it clairvoyance or ESP. But another phenomenon we often find in this disorder is an actual physiological change in the person affected. The normal personality may not need eyeglasses at all, while the alternate personality does; or both may wear glasses, but the prescription will be quite different. The blood pressures can be different, or the reaction to certain medications; the bleeding and clotting rates can be different, and we've even noted a clear and measurable change in the blood composition."

Corrigan wrote it all down. "Any explanations, doctor?"

Mandanhi shook his head and smiled. "There is still much we do not know about ourselves, Mr. Corrigan."

Corrigan had heard enough. He was ready for the next witness. "How would you feel if I talked to Amber about all this? Would she be willing to talk about it?"

Mandanhi considered that. "I don't see that it would do any harm, provided you limit yourself to reasonable questions and behavior toward the child."

"Well, I was thinking I'd like to have our own psychologist examine Amber as well."

Suddenly Jefferson jumped on that. "No, Corrigan. Forget it. That isn't going to happen."

Corrigan knew he'd hit a nerve somewhere. "Hey, come on. Dr. Mandanhi doesn't seem to think it'll hurt."

Ames was really hot about it. "You're not going anywhere near that child! She's suffered enough!"

Corrigan turned to Dr. Mandanhi. "How about it, doctor? Think it'd be okay?"

Mandanhi looked at the attorneys and caught the meaning in their eyes. "Well . . . I suppose not, Mr. Corrigan. I suppose it would be harmful."

"You suppose?"

"It *would* be harmful."

"Forget it!" said Jefferson.

Fat chance, thought Corrigan.

26

B efore Sally noticed, she was writing by the light of the overhead lamp above her seat, and not by the daylight coming in through the window. It was getting late. The hazy red twilight was giving way to the deepening gray of night, and now the farms and fields rushing by outside were beginning to hide behind the reflection of her own face. The rhythmic rocking of the railcar and *click-click-clacking* of the tracks had a lulling effect, a dulling effect, and she was feeling sleepy.

It would be another day or so before she would reach her destination and revisit old Bentmore University. Her stomach turned with fear at every thought of it. These would be the powerful people, the influential ones, the molders of education and educators. If the people at Omega remembered her, undoubtedly she would be remembered at Bentmore. But still she had to go. She had to see that place again.

So, my stay in Room 302 in Fairwood was suddenly ended, and I am on the road—riding the rails, actually— once again, with only my duffel bag and my life as possessions. I don't mean to sound flippant, but running for my life is a whole new experience for me. First of all, I've never done it, and secondly, I never thought I would be running from the people I once trusted and admired so deeply. One of the hardest lessons I have had to learn is that the utopian dream of a new world order is not without its dark side, its powermongers, schemers, manipulators, and killers. Behind all the Mrs. Dennings and Miss Brewers who dream of refining and guiding mankind, there are the Mr. Steeles who dream of subjugating and controlling mankind. The Dennings and Brewers work hard to prepare all mankind for a global community; the Steeles look forward to running it.

And then there are the Sally Roes who get caught in the middle, disillusioned by the idyllic dreams of the Dennings and Brewers and trying to stay out from under the crushing boot of the Steeles. Perhaps they are the ones the Steeles fear the most: they know all the tenets, but no longer believe in the faith. They can get in the way more effectively than anyone.

She paused, and looked at her reflection in the window, a tired face with the blackness of night behind it, and it occurred to her what sorts of allegories she would have drawn from such a picture only a few days ago, or even yesterday. She could have written about the blackness of her soul, or the great void that lay beyond the visible Sally Roe, or the transience of her life, nothing more than a fleeting reflection on a thin pane of glass—here during the night, but gone by morning.

Oh, it was great stuff, but for some reason she just didn't feel that way. Something deep inside her was still changing, like a gradual and steady clearing of the weather.

Tom, remember my last letter, when I talked about guilt? I haven't forgotten any of those thoughts; as a matter of fact, they are still churning in my head, and I don't know where they will eventually carry me.

Since I last wrote, I did come up with one challenging proposition about guilt: that it could be a fact, and not just a feeling.

I'm sure you know how much the rest of us despise that one aspect of Christianity: the classic "guilt trip." If I recall the jargon correctly, we are all "sinners," we are all guilty. Religion has always been, in my perception, one big guilt trip, and no one wants to feel guilty. That is why my friends and I spent so much time and energy concocting a universe in which right and wrong did not exist—if there is no right or wrong, there is no need to feel guilty about anything.

Now for the wrench in the works, first thrown in this morning: the possibility of guilt as a fact and not just a feeling. If—and I emphasize the word if—there is a fixed standard of right and wrong—a fence, as I've said—then it is possible to be guilty of an offense, all feelings of guilt aside. I can be on the wrong side of the fence and be in the wrong regardless of how I feel about it.

Please bear with me if I state the obvious; I have the distinct fear that you got all this clear in your own mind when you were a child and are getting bored, but please bear with me. I have to think it through, and it helps to do it on paper.

Let's say I rob a bank. That makes me guilty of robbery. Let's say I don't feel guilty about it. If robbery can be established as wrong, then I'm still guilty of robbery, regardless of how I feel.

The feeling—or lack of feeling—does not change the fact.

So, reflecting on what I've learned through the years in the humanist and mystic camps, I see that much of it was an attempt to escape from guilt through philosophy, meditation, drugs, etc., etc. But now I have to ask, what exactly have I been trying to escape: the feelings or the fact? I have been able to escape the feelings—for a season. The feelings you can bury, suppress, deny, or talk yourself out of.

But what can change or erase the fact? So far I haven't thought of a thing.

Wayne Corrigan had mixed feelings about Thursday's deposition; he felt prepared in some ways, and in other ways he was sure he and his volunteer crew of investigators had not yet scratched the surface of what Lucy Brandon and her lawsuit were really all about. But here she sat, the plaintiff herself, dressed up in a gray pantsuit, flanked by Ames and Jefferson, ready to hold forth and looking nervous.

Mark and Tom were present again, and Corrigan had plenty of notes for reference.

They went over old ground first, rehashing the offenses against Amber at the Christian school. Lucy seemed to have a much better grasp of the details than Irene Bledsoe displayed.

"He would often grab Amber by her shoulders and shake her until she produced the answer he wanted," she said.

"Can you give us an example?" Corrigan asked.

"Well . . . she told me once about Mr. Harris trying to get Amber 'saved,' and he was quite forceful about it, shaking her, insisting that she say that Jesus was her Savior. She just wanted to say that He was her example, or her friend, or her guide, but that wasn't good enough for him. He shook her, yelled at her, and really upset her. Then he made her stay in during recess until she changed her attitude. It was horrible; she cried about it all that evening. It was all I could do to get her to go back to the school the next day."

Tom jotted a note to himself. This testimony was a blatant lie, but it was not surprising. He'd heard Amber use the same truth-stretching whenever she tattled.

"This is, of course, Amber's account?" asked Corrigan.

"Yes, it's what she told me."

"And you were not a witness to this?"

"No, but I believe my daughter."

"Did you ever discuss this with Mr. Harris?"

"No, I didn't."

"Why not?"

She had to search for an answer. "Oh, I guess my mind was on other matters, and it didn't seem important at the time."

"But it seems important now?"

"Why, yes."

Corrigan showed her a document. "This is your signature on this Parental Agreement Form, correct?"

She looked at it. "Yes."

"And if you'll notice paragraph nine on this form, it states that you have read the Student/Parent Handbook and agree to all it contains. Did you read the handbook, and did you agree to all it contained?"

Lucy was quite reluctant to answer. "Yes."

Corrigan checked some records. "Is it true that Amber was paddled on . . . March 25th, and that Mr. Harris informed you about it that evening by telephone?"

"Yes."

"And is it true that at that time you approved of the spanking?"

"Yes."

"To the best of your knowledge, has Amber ever been spanked since then?"

"No."

"So, just to make sure I have this straight, you are suing the school for physical abuse by spanking, but as far as you know there was only one incident of spanking, and you approved of it beforehand when you signed the Parental Agreement, and also at the time the spanking was administered? Do I have that right?"

She was unhappy, but answered truthfully, "Yes, that's right."

"Were you aware of the infraction for which Amber was spanked?"

Lucy thought for a moment. "I think she was being disruptive in class."

Corrigan didn't want to go into the next subject, but he had to. "Do you recall the nature of the disruption? Do you remember Mr. Harris describing it to you?"

Lucy stumbled with an answer. "She was . . . being noisy, um, playing at her desk . . ."

Corrigan dove in. "Well, let's just go ahead and talk about Amethyst."

Lucy brightened with recollection. "Oh . . ."

"Do you recall now that Amber was spanked because she was portraying Amethyst in the classroom and disturbing the class, and not heeding Mr. Harris's orders to stop that behavior?"

"Yes."

"Mrs. Brandon, we've heard a lot of opinions about who or what Amethyst really is. Who or what is Amethyst in your opinion?"

Lucy looked down at the table, thought about the question, even laughed just a little, and then shook her head. "I'm not sure. I guess she's just a character that Amber made up, but . . . Well, Dr. Mandanhi said it's possibly an alternate personality, but I don't know . . ."

"Are you affiliated in any way with a fellowship group in the Bacon's Corner area called LifeCircle?"

"Uh . . . yes."

"Isn't it true that that group holds to a belief in channeling and spirit-guides?"

She laughed, but it was a nervous laugh. "Well, we embrace a lot of different beliefs; we all have our opinions about channeling. I guess ultimately we don't question it, we just experience it."

"Would you say that Amber was channeling Amethyst?"

"Oh, she could be channeling, or she could be pretending she's channeling, or . . . I don't know. There are many different views. It's really something to be experienced for what good can be derived from it; it's not to be questioned."

"Have you ever considered that Amethyst could be a spirit?"

The term seemed to shock her. "A spirit?"

"Yes, a spirit-guide, or an ascended master, or a disembodied entity from the astral plane. Those are familiar terms to you, aren't they?"

She smiled, impressed. "You know a lot about this sort of thing, don't you?"

Corrigan smiled back pleasantly. "Well, I try to do my homework. But do you think Amethyst could be a spirit-guide? Is that possible?"

She furrowed her brow and looked down at the table, struggling with such a thought. "Some believe that. I still don't know what to think."

Corrigan scribbled in his notepad. "At any rate, on March 28th, Mr. Harris and Amethyst had a confrontation. Do you recall hearing about that?"

"Yes. Mr. Harris called me at the Post Office. It sounded serious, so I came over."

"Did he tell you what happened?"

"Yes. He said that Amber had been . . . Oh, I can't remember how he put it, but he basically told me that they thought she had a demon and tried to cast it out of her. I was outraged. I'd never heard of such a thing."

"You've never heard of casting out demons?"

She answered bitterly, "That's strictly a Christian idea, an invention of organized religion, and I resent that it was imposed upon my daughter! Channeling is a gift, a special ability; it has nothing to do with religion!"

"But you do understand that the Bible teaches otherwise?"

Lucy was angry and hurt. "Mr. Corrigan, she's just a *child*, a child with a special gift! She doesn't have to explain her gift to me, or defend what she's experiencing. I've never singled her out or harassed her; I've just loved her, accepted her, and just let her have her gift for whatever good it can do for her and for the rest of us. She's just a child, not a theologian or a scholar or a priest or a lawyer, and what power does a ten-year-old child have to stand up against—" she hesitated, but then spewed out the words "—against hard-nosed, prejudiced, religious adults in that school who abuse their power and their size, who have no tolerance and no understanding, who just . . . attack her, pounce on her, scream at her, and accuse her of being possessed . . ."

She buried her face in her hands for a moment. Corrigan was just about to call for a recess, but then she recovered and finished her statement. "They just had no right to treat my daughter that way, to single her out and persecute her just for being different."

Corrigan figured it was time to go on to the next question. "When you came to the school, what did you find? How was Amber?"

Lucy thought for a while, recalling it. "She was . . . she was sitting in the school office, and she looked awful. She was very tired, and I remember she was wet with perspiration and her hair was all uncombed. She was upset . . . moody. When I took her home, I found that her body was bruised in several places like she'd been in a terrible wrestling match. I was just shocked." Lucy's emotions began to rise. "I couldn't believe such a thing could happen to my daughter, and at a Christian school where . . . Well, I once believed that a Christian school, of all places, would be a good place for Amber, a safe place. I didn't think that Christians would stoop to such behavior. But they did."

Corrigan spoke gently to her. "Mrs. Brandon, was it Amber as Amber who remembered the incident? Could she tell you what happened?"

Lucy was still composing herself. "I don't think she's ever been able to talk to me directly about it. She has to be Amethyst to talk about it."

"So it was Amethyst who told you what happened?"

"Amber pretending to be Amethyst, or channeling Amethyst, yes."

Corrigan thought for a moment. "Mrs. Brandon, whenever Amber becomes Amethyst, after she stops being Amethyst, does she remember anything that Amethyst said or did?"

Lucy smiled a little sheepishly. "Well . . . she says she doesn't."

"All right. At any rate, that incident occurred on March 28th, but you didn't take Amber out of the school until April 20th. Can you explain why, after such an outrageous incident, and such selective, prejudicial behavior toward Amber, you still kept your child enrolled at the school?"

"I . . ."

"Obviously you consulted a lawyer during the interim?"

"Yes."

Corrigan produced a photocopied, handwritten record. "Part of the discovery materials included this photocopy of a journal you kept. Do you recognize it?"

"Yes."

"So, between March 28th and April 20th, you kept detailed records on the school . . ." Corrigan leafed through the many photocopied pages. "You kept track of all the lessons, the Bible verses for each day, the discipline problems, the Bible projects . . . quite a detailed account."

"Yes."

"So isn't it true that you kept this record all this time, with Amber still enrolled, because you fully intended to bring this lawsuit against the school?"

Jefferson jumped on that. "I object, counselor. That's a matter of speculation and conjecture; there's a total lack of foundation."

"So let's get some foundation. Mrs. Brandon, some time after March 28th, didn't you consult a friend at LifeCircle for legal advice regarding these matters?"

Lucy even shrugged a little. "Yes."

"Was it Claire Johanson, legal assistant to Mr. Ames and Mr. Jefferson?"

"Yes."

"And what was the result of that conversation?"

"The result?"

"Didn't you decide at that time to pursue a lawsuit against the school?"

"I think so."

"You think so?"

"Well, yes, I did."

"And in preparation for the lawsuit, you began keeping this detailed record of everything happening at the school, correct?"

Lucy was chagrined. "Yes."

"All right. Now, having established that, let me ask this question: Since you kept Amber enrolled at the school despite the outrageous behavior demonstrated against her, is it possible that gaining more material for your lawsuit was more important to you than your own daughter's well-being?"

"I'll definitely object to that!" said Jefferson.

"And I'll drop the question," said Corrigan, unruffled. He looked at his notes. "Does Amber still become Amethyst from time to time?"

Lucy smiled as she reluctantly admitted, "Yes, she still does."

"Was she displaying this kind of behavior even before she enrolled at the Christian school?"

"Yes."

"Is it true that she learned to . . . create or visualize Amethyst in her fourth-grade class at the Bacon's Corner Elementary School, a class taught by a Miss Brewer?"

"Yes. Miss Brewer is a wonderful teacher."

Corrigan paused. "Then why did you transfer Amber to the Christian school?"

Lucy seemed a little embarrassed. "Oh . . . I thought her time in the elementary school had served its purpose. Amber was fulfilling her potential and discovering herself, yes, but . . . she wasn't learning much else."

"A little weak in academics?"

"A little. I thought some balance would be good for her; a wider realm of experience."

"I understand." Corrigan went to another matter. "Do you recall an incident at the Post Office several weeks ago when Amber, as Amethyst, had a confrontation with a patron in the lobby?"

Lucy was visibly disturbed by that question. "How did you find out about that?"

"Do you recall it?"

"Yes."

"Does Amber recall it?"

"No. She was . . . Well, she was Amethyst at the time, and now she doesn't remember any of it."

"She doesn't remember it?"

"No."

"Is it true that Amber, as Amethyst, became very aggressive toward the patron?"

Lucy was sickened by the memory, and perhaps by the question. "Yes."

"She circled the patron, struck her several times?"

"I . . . I did see her hit the lady, yes."

"Did Amber, as Amethyst, make loud, screaming accusations against the lady?"

"Yes."

"Would you say that Amber's behavior was violent, uncontrolled?"

She didn't want to admit it. "Yes."

"So violent that the lady was forced to flee from the lobby?"

Lucy was getting upset; the memory was a painful, perplexing wound. "That's what happened. I couldn't get Amber to stop. I was just so embarrassed."

"Did Amber know this woman?"

"No. I just don't know how she could have."

"And as far as you know, the woman did nothing to provoke this attack?"

"No."

"Do you recall what Amethyst was screaming?"

Lucy's eyes dropped to the table; she rested her forehead on her fingers. "She was saying . . . something about the woman's baby . . . saying, 'You killed your baby.'"

"Do you know who the woman was?"

"I don't know . . . I think so."

Corrigan took out a photograph and showed it to her. "Is this the woman?"

Jefferson jumped in. "Really, I don't see what this has to do with anything!"

Corrigan just gave him a correcting look, and he remained quiet.

"Is this the woman?"

Lucy stared at the grainy photograph. Her face answered the question before she said it. "Yes."

"Do you know who this woman is?"

She seemed to give in. "Her name is Sally Roe. She was a patron at the Post Office. But that's all I know about her."

"And she committed suicide just a few weeks ago, isn't that true?"

Lucy lashed back, "That wasn't Amber's fault!"

Corrigan paused just a little at that outburst, then said, "We're not saying it was. Now, you heard Amethyst—Amber, whatever—accuse Sally Roe of killing her baby, correct?"

"Asked and answered," said Jefferson.

"Just trying to be sure," said Corrigan.

"Yes, I did," said Lucy.

"Were you aware that Sally Roe had a criminal record?"

It was obviously news to Lucy Brandon. "No."

Corrigan produced some documents. "This is a copy of her criminal record, and here are some news clippings. You'll notice the highlighted areas: she was convicted of first-degree murder ten years ago. As you can see here, and here, and on this news story here, she was found guilty of the drowning death of her baby daughter."

He waited for it all to sink in, and watched the blood drain from Lucy Brandon's face.

"Obviously your daughter, as Amethyst, was correct in her accusations against Sally Roe in the lobby of the Post Office. To the best of your knowledge, was there any way that Amber could have known about Sally Roe's past?"

Lucy could hardly speak. "No. *I* didn't even know about it."

"Can you explain, then, how *Amethyst* knew about it?"

Lucy took time to answer only because it was difficult. "No." She tried to do better. "Psychic ability, maybe."

"On whose part, Amber's or Amethyst's?"

Lucy shook her head, quite flustered. "I don't know. I don't understand these things. But it can happen in channeling."

"So Amber was channeling?"

"Yes, I guess she was."

"And apparently this special gift of hers has a rather violent side to it?"

"I don't know . . ."

"You did have quite a wrestling match with Amethyst, didn't you? It was several minutes before you could get your daughter under control?"

"Yes."

"And when the incident was finally over, would you say your daughter was wet with perspiration, probably disheveled, tired, moody, maybe even bruised a little?"

Lucy was reluctant to answer that.

Corrigan pressed it. "Wasn't that her general condition?"

"I suppose so."

"And during the scuffle, didn't you refer to your daughter as Amethyst?"

She looked puzzled.

Corrigan asked it another way. "Didn't you wrestle with your daughter, and say words to the effect, 'Amethyst, you stop this . . . Amethyst, calm down'?"

Lucy's voice was barely audible. "I suppose I did."

"Just who were you talking to?"

Lucy didn't appreciate that question. "My daughter!"

"Which one?" Lucy hesitated, so Corrigan built on the question. "You've already stated that Amber has no recollection of the incident, and normally does not remember anything that Amethyst says or does. You have admitted that Amber was channeling. Would it be correct to say that it was Amethyst, and not Amber, who was displaying all this aggressive behavior?"

"But it was my daughter . . ."

"But a different and separate personality, correct?"

Lucy stared at him. She was thinking about it. Corrigan could sense Ames and Jefferson getting more and more tense.

"Correct?" Corrigan asked again.

"Yes," she said finally. "I think that's correct."

"So . . . if someone—even yourself—should ever confront Amethyst, they would actually be confronting a personality other than your daughter?"

"I guess so. Maybe."

Ames and Jefferson did not like that answer. No doubt they would have quite a conference with Lucy Brandon when this was over.

Corrigan decided it was time for a provocative benediction. "So, does it seem so strange to you now that Mr. Harris might also have had a similar encounter, not with your daughter Amber, but with Amethyst, a separate personality: a violent struggle, a wrestling match, a demonstrative confrontation? Can you imagine what it must have been like for him to have Amethyst behave in the classroom as she behaved in the Post Office lobby, screaming, hitting, and producing information that Amber—as Amber—could not possibly know? Can you understand now what conclusion a Biblical Christian would come to when confronted with a violent, uncontrollable, alternate personality in a young, innocent child?" He didn't need an answer, and he didn't wait for one. "Thank you, Mrs. Brandon. I know this has been difficult for you. That's all for now."

27

Bentmore University was nestled—almost hidden—within the tight, red-brick grid of a major metropolis. In every direction, it was just across the street from the noise, litter, traffic, and growing pains of the city. It had outlived the rise and fall of a low-income housing project on its north flank; on the west side, the delicatessens, tailors, and cleaners were now owned by third generations; on the east, the tugs still pulled their barges up and down the murky river, the rumble of their engines audible across the campus when the wind was right; on the south, several new apartments had become the only view in that direction, and now the streets down there were filled with big old cars driven by retired folks who drove slowly.

In the center of it all, Bentmore lived on, standing firm and steadfast in red brick and white stone, its halls, dormitories, libraries, and labs evenly dispersed on the lawned terrain, its patterned brick sidewalks radiating like spokes from every entryway, crisscrossing and networking like trade routes to every point on the campus.

To the human eye, Bentmore seemed an oasis of peace, reflection, and learning amid the hubbub of its surroundings; in the spiritual realm, the real trouble was within its borders, not outside them.

Guilo met with Tal and his top warriors on the roof of the old North American Can Company, located just across the river from the campus. Beneath their feet, soup cans, juice cans, fruit cans, and sardine cans took shape and clattered by the windows in an endless, rolling parade; across the river, still veiled by the morning mist, old Bentmore was ominously quiet.

Guilo stood beside Tal to give his report. He was nervous, agitated, ready for a fight, his hand resting on the handle of his sword. "Some of their best are there. The great deceivers, the great builders of the Enemy's coming kingdom, all supervised by a behemoth who calls himself Corrupter."

"I've heard of him," said Tal. "He has power and great deceptive ability, but not much speed or wit in battle."

"An advantage, to be sure. If we remain stealthy, there is a lot we could do before he becomes aware of it."

Nathan peered through the mist and thought he saw some hulking spirits gliding occasionally between the structures, but most of them were unseen. "They remain hidden, tucked away inside the buildings."

"Very occupied," said Armoth. "Classes are in session."

"Corrupter is a bit comfortable at the moment, and off-guard," said Guilo, "but Destroyer is going to be another problem. He is on his way now, with all his forces. Then old Bentmore will be like a hive of hornets at rest. Merely shake the tree, and . . ."

"They will overrun us," said Tal. "Destroyer's troublemakers in Bacon's Corner are doing well at this point; our prayer cover is as weak as it's ever been, and we're left with seriously depleted numbers. Direct confrontations are going to be risky. We'll have to lean heavily on stealth and strategy . . ."

Guilo allowed himself a quick, stifled chuckle as he eyed the campus. "I remind you all: they could eat us alive."

The benches here and there on the campus were still wet with dew and mist, but Sally found a comfortable desk hidden away in the stacks of the Research Library. So far she hadn't seen library staff that she recognized, and that set her a little more at ease. Thanks to a small cleaning shop on the west side of the campus, her better clothes—slacks, blouse, dress jacket—were cleaned and pressed; she'd replaced her wayfaring-stranger ensemble with a more presentable outfit, and stashed her duffel bag, replacing it with a less obtrusive carry bag. She could recall looking sharp and professional twelve years ago, with carefully coordinated outfits and her hair tightly pinned. Today the best she could look was casual and twelve years older, with tinted glasses and dye-blackened hair pinned up as best as she could arrange it. She just had to hope she looked different enough from the Sally Roe people would remember.

Oh, I must have been so proud of my calling as an educator! As I sit here and observe the graduate students around this place, working toward their Master's degrees just like I did, I can see the same pride in their faces, I can sense the same highbrow demeanor. To be honest, I see myself as I was back then. The old Bentmore mold has not broken. I can guess what they're thinking: they are world conquerors, missionaries for a bold message of global change.

And I would say they are correct. Bentmore is still turning out great educators, great agents of change. They will be the teachers, the administrators, the principals, the authors, the lobbyists. A nation will follow them; they will restructure an entire culture.

Sally checked her watch. It was after 9 in the morning; someone should be in Professor Lynch's office by now, either his secretary or Lynch himself. This would be the greatest risk of all, but she must contact him. Of all people, he should have some of the answers she needed.

She'd checked for his name and number in the campus directory, and surprising as it was, after twelve years Samuel W. Lynch was still head of the School of Education. As she remembered him, he was definitely fit for the position, always an imposing man of great knowledge, stature, and strength.

A tall, athletic undergrad had just finished using the pay phone on the wall behind her. She grabbed the opportunity. She would try to get an appointment with Lynch, perhaps during his office hours. All she could hope was that the man was not as brilliant as she remembered him to be; perhaps he wouldn't recall who she was.

Wayne Corrigan and Gordon Jefferson, the ACFA attorney, were never going to be good friends, that was readily apparent.

"Mr. Jefferson, I'm simply saying that we have the right to confront our accuser!" Corrigan was feeling very forceful, and had his mouth so close to the receiver that Jefferson heard a roar every time Corrigan pronounced an *s* or an *f*.

Jefferson came back just as firm, and even a little snide. "Your accuser, Mr. Corrigan, is Lucy Brandon, not Amber, and you have already deposed Mrs. Brandon in such a harsh manner as to cause her terrible distress! We wouldn't think of putting Amber in the same situation."

"We do not wish to cause Amber any grief—none at all! We'll work within restrictions, we'll be gentle. But so far everything we've heard, all the testimony, all the grievances, have come through either Lucy Brandon or Dr. Mandanhi. The real complainant in this case is neither of these people, but Amber herself."

"Amber is not going to testify or be forced to go through a deposition. We will fight that, sir!"

"We must have Amber's direct testimony concerning the complaints brought against my clients."

"It would be too traumatic for her. She's already so deeply wounded by these unfortunate events, we simply cannot allow her to be traumatized further by being put through the stress and pain of a deposition and a trial!"

"Then we want our psychologist to examine her. At least then we would have our own expert testimony to balance the testimony of Dr. Mandanhi."

"Absolutely not! Amber is not to be involved in this case in any way. She must be kept separate from it; she must be protected from any further abuse and intimidation!"

Corrigan sighed and looked across his desk at Marshall, who was closely listening and watching Corrigan's side of the conversation. Marshall made a wringing motion with his hands as if twisting an invisible arm and whispered, "You stick it to 'em!"

"I'm afraid we can't back down in this matter," Corrigan told Jefferson. "If you won't change your mind, then we'll ask the court to compel her availability and testimony."

"We're prepared for that," said Jefferson.

"Very well, then."

Corrigan hung up, and then he thought for a moment. "Maybe I pushed Lucy Brandon too hard. Now they're hiding Amber under a bushel."

Marshall nodded an emphatic nod. "Sure. Irene Bledsoe, and Lucy Brandon, and this Dr. Mandanhi character can say all they want, but Amber's the key to this whole thing. As long as Amethyst is doing her—its—stuff, Amber's going to be a real risk."

"Sure, if we can just get her on that stand, or get our own

expert to examine her. I mean, if we can just get Amethyst to manifest once, we could build an argument that Tom's behavior in confronting Amethyst was justified." He smiled. "Wouldn't it be great if we could get Amethyst to tear up the courtroom? We could *win* this case!"

"They know that."

"Well, we *do* know what happened in the Post Office, and that has them scared. We need to beef up that defense; we have Alice Buckmeier's eyewitness account, but another witness would sure be nice, especially if Lucy decides to squirrel out of her deposed testimony somehow."

Marshall answered, "Well, there's still that other gal, Debbie, who works at the Post Office with Brandon. Alice says she was there, but I'm wondering where her loyalties might lie."

"We'll just hand her a subpoena and find out."

"And then there's the victim of Amethyst's attack."

Corrigan nodded. "Our greatest unsolved mystery. She's like a ghost, you know? We have pictures of her, eyewitness accounts of her, facts and information about her, but as far as what she has to do with this case, she's like a mirage, she simply isn't there."

"So push this Amber thing. Go ahead and ask for a hearing. The ACFA could use a dose of their own medicine. If it doesn't do anything else for us, it'll buy us time. You never know when something big will break."

Corrigan was captivated by the thought. "Amber, we've got to get you on that stand!"

Claire Johanson got Dr. Mandanhi on the phone only minutes after Jefferson had hung up on Wayne Corrigan.

"Doctor, your report is too weak."

Dr. Mandanhi was nonplussed, and also a little impatient. "Now . . . which report is that, the first one or the second one, or the second version of the first one?"

Claire made a disgusted face only because Dr. Mandanhi would not see it over the phone. "The first version of the second report, the one establishing that Amber is in too delicate a mental condition to be deposed or to testify."

"And what do you mean when you say it is too weak?"

"It just doesn't have enough persuasiveness; it would be too easy for the defense to play down. Corrigan is going to ask for a hearing to decide whether or not Amber should be made to testify, and we need something stronger to present to the court."

Mandanhi paused a moment. He was clearly unhappy. "Ms. Johanson, we've been down this path before. You didn't think my first report was strong enough either!"

"Well, it's the way things go—"

"Ms. Johanson, when you first brought me into this, I gave my fairest, most objective opinion regarding Amber's condition. I agreed with you and with the child's mother that the child had suffered harm. Why wasn't that enough?"

Claire was feeling the pressure from above and now from this doctor below. "Because, Dr. Mandanhi, in a court of law an argument has to be forceful, it has to have overwhelming power to persuade. Your first version was too . . . too . . ."

"Too factual?" Mandanhi suggested. "You would rather I lied and fabricated additional trauma just to win a court ruling?"

"Not fabricate, doctor. Enhance maybe, just make your opinions more forceful."

"Well, I feel I did that with my first report. I gave you what you wanted, and I think more than the facts warranted. Now you want me to do that again?"

Claire hesitated. Then she snapped, "With the facts at hand your second report could be enhanced. Make it stronger, make it persuasive! It shouldn't be too hard to show how the stress on Amber would cause her permanent psychological harm."

"Are you asking me to lie?"

"I'm asking you to use the facts, be an advocate, and protect Amber. She must not testify!"

Sally got her appointment with Professor Samuel W. Lynch, and made it to his office on time at 6 in the evening. It was an odd hour, but he was usually in his office at this time anyway and would be happy to see her.

He had a new office now, on the second floor of Whitcombe Hall, the main hub of the Bentmore School of Education. Whitcombe Hall was a newer structure of steel, marble, and glass and towered ten stories over the rest of the campus. Apparently Bentmore was proud of its contributions to education and wanted to display that pride in a big way.

Room 210 was more than just a room; it was the whole north end of the floor, divided off by a wall of glass with impressive double doors. The secretary was working late as well, and could look through that glass wall from where she sat and see anyone coming down the hall. She saw Sally the moment Sally got off the elevator, but she didn't seem to linger on the sight too long. That was comforting.

Sally pushed through the doors and tried to address the secretary from a distance. "April Freeman to see Professor Lynch."

The lady smiled and nodded. "Yes, the woman from the *Register*?"

"That's me."

"All right, fine." She picked up her telephone and pressed a button. "The lady from the *Register* is here to see you." She looked at Sally. "He'll be right with you. Go ahead and have a seat."

Sally stood near the couch in the waiting area, but did not sit in it. She was too uncomfortable to sit, and apt to run. The fib about being a reporter from the campus newspaper was working so far, but if anyone should think to call the *Bentmore Register* office to check on any of this, her disguise was history. Besides that, a man was already sitting there, and she'd caught him looking at her once, even though he was supposedly reading a magazine. Maybe he was reading that magazine, but maybe he wasn't. What was he doing here at 6 in the evening? The way she felt right now, every person in that place was a potential killer.

Her heart was pounding; if her hands shook much more, it would show. She tried to take some deep breaths to steady herself.

"Miss Freeman!"

That voice! After twelve years she still remembered it. She turned.

There stood Professor Samuel W. Lynch. Oh! That tremble was so great, it had to show! She stiffened her body to remain steady, forced a smile, and extended her hand. "Hello."

He shook her hand. "A pleasure. Come this way."

He turned, and she followed him back toward his office.

This wasn't right. It wasn't twelve years later. It had to be twelve years *ago*. He hadn't changed. He was still the same, distinguished, overweight, gray-haired gentleman, the same articulate pedagogue she'd admired. She would have recognized him anywhere.

Was she as familiar to him? Hundreds of students must have passed through his life since she was last here; surely her face would be lost behind all the others.

He led her into his office and offered her a comfortable, padded chair. She sat immediately and found herself looking up at just about everything. The booklined walls in this room towered so high overhead that she felt she was sitting in the bottom of a deep well. The room was dead silent, like a crypt.

Lynch took a seat behind his desk and relaxed for a moment, studying her face, his hands clasped in front of his chest.

She looked back at him and tried to smile. She was beginning to feel the silence. This wasn't right. Someone should be saying something by now.

"So you're with the *Register*?" he asked, still relaxed, leaning back in his chair.

"Yes, I just started this quarter."

"And what is your major?"

"Um . . . economics."

He smiled. "Good enough. What do you think of Professor Parker?"

Oh-oh. Was this a test? Who was Professor Parker? Was it a he or a she? Was Parker even alive?

Sally fumbled. "Oh . . . I still get the profs mixed up. I just transferred in . . ."

He laughed. "No matter. You'll get to know them, and I'm sure they'll get to know you. You'll find we're a cordial institution, one big family. Where are you from, anyway?"

She was using a phony accent. "Oh, uh, Knoxville, Tennessee."

Sally opened her notebook just for something to do, something to fill the awkward, empty time. Her mind had suddenly gone blank as if a dark cloud had entered it. One moment she knew what she was going to say, and the next moment she felt that part of her brain had died.

And Professor Lynch was just sitting there, not saying a word. Silence filled the room like deep water; the warm, stuffy air pressed in on all sides.

"Uh . . . I just wanted to ask you some questions . . ." Sally said, pulling a notebook from her carry bag and leafing through it. Where were the questions? She'd written several down, but now . . . "I'm just trying to find my questions; I had them here somewhere."

"Don't be nervous," said Lynch. "I won't bite you."

She laughed. So he'd noticed! "Thank you. I'm still a bit new at this." She found the questions. "Oh! Here we go. I thought it would be interesting to track down a Bentmore success story and do an article about Owen Bennett."

He smiled. "Ahhh . . . That would make an interesting story. Owen Bennett is a fascinating man."

"He was a professor here for many years, I understand."

"Oh, yes! But say, would you excuse me for just a moment?"

"Certainly."

He rose from his chair and hurried from the room, leaving her alone in the bottom of this dark, oppressive well.

The silence closed in again, heavier than ever. She had trouble breathing, as if her chest were collapsing, as if the air were too thick to inhale. It had to be her imagination, the stress, the nervousness.

She closed her eyes and opened them again. The room still seemed dark. Maybe darker.

High above her, the walls holding hundreds of books on all those shelves looked like they were leaning more and more toward the center of the room. It was a wonder all the books—and some of them were massive—weren't sliding off the shelves and crashing down on her. At the same time, the ceiling, distant as it was, seemed to be receding even further away, making this well, this pit, this trap all the more deep.

Sally closed her eyes. She did not want to believe that her old tormentors were lurking about. She could not accept that she might be trapped in this pit with them, with no escape, helpless, with no choice but to wait for the first clap of their invisible jaws.

But try as she could, she could not shake this . . . this *presence*. No, it wasn't the walls and the books that were closing in. These illusions were only born out of a devouring, inner terror. There was something else oozing into this room, something from her childhood nightmares—that steady, unrelenting, slowly advancing *thing* of terror, that bogeyman, that monster, that unseen, voracious, undefeatable enemy she could never run fast enough to escape from. It was here somewhere, hiding behind the books, maybe wriggling through them, staring at her, watching her shrink into the chair, watching her tremble and sweat.

Her palms were leaving wet patches on the arms of the chair. Her skin was crawling.

She had to get out of here. She'd made a mistake; she'd walked into a death trap. This room was alive with evil, about to crush her.

She saw it! A cry escaped from her throat before she could stop it. Just behind the desk, directly opposite from where she sat, a row of angry, golden eyes glared at her from the bookshelf. Her own eyes blinked shut. She thought better of that, and opened them again.

They were still there, not moving. But . . . no. They were not eyes. She exhaled slowly and tried with all her might to steady her emotions and her thoughts. She looked at them deliberately; she gazed at them, even challenged them.

They were four golden symbols on the spines of four ornately bound volumes. They still seemed to be staring at her. She tried to stifle her imagination. She had to be objective about this.

She leaned toward them. They were faces. Ghastly, triangular faces, all staring, all seemingly snarling at her. Little gargoyles. Deep, vacant eyes, almost like sockets. Bared teeth. High, shining foreheads.

Her heart began to race. Her mouth dropped open, and she stared transfixed. With fingers numbed and fumbling, she pulled at the chain around her neck. The two rings emerged from hiding and she held them side by side in front of her face, looking at them and then beyond them at the faces on the four volumes.

Identical.

28

When Lynch returned to his office, he found his guest looking quite wilted and noticeably white.

"Are you feeling all right?" he asked.

She smiled weakly. "Oh, to be honest, I think I'm battling a little bit of flu or something."

"Oh, I'm very sorry. Let's try to proceed with this interview as quickly as possible, then."

Sally didn't feel like proceeding, but she did. She got out her pen, and prepared to take some notes.

Lynch started talking without any questions. "As you must know, Owen Bennett was a law professor here for several years, and a good friend to all of us. He was adventuresome, innovative, intelligent . . ."

This moving tribute to Owen Bennett continued for several minutes. Sally wrote it all down as best she could, hoping desperately to find some point where she could just cut it off, thank Professor Lynch, and get out of there.

Professor Lynch had been sitting in his chair, turned slightly away from Sally, looking at the books on the wall and speaking in fluid sentences, his fingers spread and his hands bouncing against each other, fingertip to fingertip. Now, with hardly any pause at all, but with a strange, ominous change in his tone, he turned his chair toward Sally and continued his comments. "Now, it was in that particular year that Owen, having completed the initial structuring of the Law Advisement Council and having entrusted its administration to capable hands, took up another, even more pioneering challenge, that of serving on the advisory board for a new visionary effort: The Omega Center for Educational Studies, located in Fairwood, Massachusetts."

Sally wrote it down. She noticed that he stopped to watch her write it down.

"This came as a surprise to some people. They asked, 'What interest could you possibly have in that place?' For a man of Owen's professional stature, such a role on the advisory board of an obscure, metaphysical institution seemed a condescension.

"But they didn't know Owen as his closer friends did. Those

who knew Owen well knew that he was a master of the politics of power; he understood that power can be a commodity to be sold in exchange for favors and more power, a bribe that can be slipped to the right people to accomplish a certain agenda, and even a lever to control the wills and purposes of underlings or professional enemies. He was already welcome in the company of legislators and judges, corporate executives and politicians, all the *right* people who could make the right things happen in the right places for anyone who had enough influence with which to bargain. Owen had influence, but taking this position gave him even more.

"The Omega Center, you understand, is a center for the facilitation of change in our society. As a man thinks, so is he. Change the way he thinks, and you change the man. Change the way a society thinks, and you change the society. The Omega Center is dedicated to changing the way our society thinks, and hence changing our society, beginning with its most vulnerable and moldable segment: its children.

"That, Ms. Freeman, was the kind of thing that could attract Owen as honey attracts bees. If such an institution as the Omega Center can actually play a part in controlling what our society will become, then it would be most beneficial to be one of the people who control the Omega Center. Owen Bennett became one of those controllers, a controller of a controller! Now he had something others would want."

Lynch turned his chair so that he was facing Sally directly. "But of course you know all that. It's one of the simplest principles of survival in this world: if you want to get ahead, have friends in high places." His eyes narrowed, and a grin—it looked malicious—slowly spread on his face. "As an example, I can recall a student I had some time ago, an extremely bright young lady who actually spent several summers at the Omega Center before she started her studies here at Bentmore. She came here with a high recommendation from the Omega Center, and we were happy to give her special attention. She remained here until she earned her Master's degree in education and then, wouldn't you know it, she desired to return to the Omega Center and be a part of that dream.

"Fortunately, she and Owen Bennett were the closest of friends, and by that time he was on the Omega advisory board, so her position with the Omega Center was an instant reality." He laughed and leaned on his elbows. "So you see, even as I have taught my students, it does help to have friends with influence to offer, especially in a field where you may be changing a society against its will."

Sally smiled and jotted down some notes. He just kept staring at her.

She was finished. *Very* finished. All she wanted was to get out of there. "Thank you so much for your insights. I'd like to take this home now and organize it. Perhaps I can call you again?"

"Oh, just one more thing!" he insisted, gesturing for her to remain seated. "Yes, friends in the right places are important, and power is definitely a tool, but you must remember never to be too close to your friends, because any weapon, any lever you may use to gain power over others, can also be used to gain power over *you* unless you take necessary precautions. I know of one man, a skilled, upcoming young attorney, who allowed a lady friend of questionable background to know him just a little too well, and she later attempted to use that knowledge as a lever against him. It created a most ticklish situation! Do you understand?"

She was on the edge of her seat, ready to stand and walk out of there. "Well, yes, like blackmail, I suppose."

He brightened at her correct answer. "Yes, that's it exactly! In gaining power over others, you never want to rule out blackmail as one lever to get what you want or to protect yourself!" He suddenly reached into his pocket and brought out a small jewelry box. "This is why I stepped out of the office momentarily. I knew you'd be interested in this."

He flipped it open and showed her the contents.

It was a gold ring. The same gargoyle.

Professor Lynch's voice grew quiet and somber. "This young lawyer hired his lady friend to kill someone. Yes, that's right, *kill* someone, and he paid her a large sum of money to do it. But she was subtle and clever; she stole a very personal item of his, his sacred ring, knowing that forever afterward she would be able, should she have the need, to prove that she had had an alliance with him. She wore the ring on her person when she tried to carry out the grisly deed, and we have good reason to believe she carried the money on her person as well so that, should something go wrong, she would be found with it and a connection could be made to the one who hired her. At any rate, the ring was identical to this one and, with the money, was a perfect lever to blackmail and manipulate him."

He let her view it for just a moment, and then abandoned all cordiality when he demanded, "You do have the ring in your possession, don't you?"

She rose to her feet but wobbled there, feeling faint, light-headed with terror. Words wouldn't come. There weren't any words.

"I . . . Thank you, sir," she said, nausea washing over her. "I need to go now."

She hurried to the door and threw it open.

The man from the waiting area! He was no longer reading a magazine—now he filled the doorway, blocking her escape!

Lynch spoke to her coldly. "This is Mr. Khull, a highly motivated individual now in our employ. We knew there was a probability you would be here next, and so we invited Mr. Khull to be on hand should it happen. Why don't you have a seat again so we can complete this interview . . . Sally Beth Roe?"

Khull leaned toward her. She backed away until she bumped into her chair, then sank into it.

Lynch sat down and glared at her for several moments.

"So what do you hear from Jonas these days?" he finally asked.

She looked at him for the first time since she sat down. There seemed to be no reason to carry on her act. The Tennessee accent vanished. "He's gone. I haven't channeled him since I went to prison."

Lynch smiled. "I imagine he felt there were more respectable people to work with, not vile, pitiful baby-killers."

She looked down in shame and defeat. She no longer knew how to defend herself.

"Yours is a pitiful story," said Lynch. "I had such great hopes for you. I groomed you, I honed you myself, I made you what you are—excuse me, *were*. You were a born leader, Sally. We were counting on you. Owen was counting on you. Such marvelous potential, such incredible spiritual connections!" He paused just to look at her forlorn frame. "But oh, how you toppled! Oh, how you fell!"

Perhaps it was hate that gave her the strength to say, "I didn't fall far enough, I guess. That woman you were talking about, who stole the man's ring—I take it she's the one who tried to kill me?"

He was not at all disturbed about it. "So I've heard. But that brings us back to my original question: What did you do with the ring you took from your attacker's finger?"

She couldn't think of a good enough lie, so she said nothing.

He nodded in response. "Of course. You're not going to tell me. As we've already discussed, you took it for insurance, for . . ." He couldn't help laughing. "For leverage! Oh, Sally, as your teacher I feel condemned!" He reached over and picked up the little jewelry box, eyeing the ring inside it. "Fine, fine. You don't have to tell me. Now that we have you, the ring doesn't matter. But really . . ." He looked at her and laughed as if he'd seen a joke. "Why do you want to help that pitiful little teacher in Bacon's Corner? What good could you possibly do?"

Now he circled his desk and stood above her, making her feel even smaller. "Do you feel guilty perhaps? Now, that would be so unlike you, Sally." His voice went down in tone, and every word cut like a knife. "Since when does guilt mean anything to you, a murderous wench bereft of conscience? As for Tom Harris, you will never find a more insignificant nothing! He is garbage, like you! And what can garbage offer to garbage? Who would believe a word you said? Who would give you the time of day?" He laughed, genuinely amused. "But I can understand your infatuation with the man; you make a perfect pair: a child killer and a pedophile!"

He was trying to cut her down, and even through her weakness and torment she was beginning to resent it. "What happens now?"

He circled back around to his chair and sat down, letting her wait for an answer. "First, some advice which will probably go unheeded, but maybe not. I strongly suggest, Sally, that you abandon this escapade of yours, whatever your intentions. Find another little farm somewhere near another obscure little town, and disappear—forever."

He seemed so relaxed. A moment passed, and nothing happened. Nothing was said.

Sally looked at him, then at the sinister Khull, and then back at Lynch again. She felt too weak to get out of the chair; she was helpless regardless of the answer to her question. "Are you going to kill me?"

He smiled. "You are one scared little waif. Well, it will be good for you. It will provide incentive for you to seriously consider your options. There are only two: Find a deep, deep hole somewhere, Sally, and disappear into it. Let us not see your face again in this life. Or, consider your life ended altogether, perhaps today, perhaps tomorrow, but most certainly."

He nodded to Khull, who stepped away from the door. With a glance back at Sally, he released her to go.

She reached down and picked up her carry bag. Then she pushed her way out of the chair, found strength for the first step, then the next, then enough strength to get to the door.

"Sally!" Lynch called.

She wasn't about to stop. Khull made sure she did.

"Don't ever blame Jonas for what happened. *You* did it, Sally. *You* are the one to blame!"

"I know that, sir," she replied.

"Disappear, Sally. Disappear!"

She went through the door, then found new strength to quicken her step down the hall to the big glass doors. She got through them.

Then she ran. Tears started to blur her eyes. With her renewing strength she realized how terrified she was. She could never wait for the elevator. She took the stairs.

Tal had some special warriors busy at a dairy far away. He needed to shake things up in a home near the Bentmore campus.

Marv and Claudia Simpson were just starting to enjoy this short stay with their daughter and son-in-law when the phone rang.

"It's Mack, at the dairy," his daughter Jessica said.

Marv scowled and took the phone. "Okay, Mack, break it to me gently."

"Marv," said Mack, "you'd better get back here. Lizzy's getting ready to drop that calf now!"

"Now? She's a week early!"

"And the milking machine is on the fritz too. I don't know what's wrong with it!"

Marv grimaced. "Oh, great!"

"And that stupid tractor won't start for anything!"

"Doggone! Ed and I were planning to go to the ball game tonight!"

"Well, it's your dairy. Do what you want."

"Oh, right, sure, some choice I've got!" He looked at Claudia, who only shook her head in sad resignation. "All right, we'll get going right away, but we're going to have to drive all night."

"Well, I'll try to hold down the fort until you get here. Sorry to interrupt your visit."

"Yeah . . ."

Marv hung up, questioning why God would allow such things to happen at such inopportune times.

Mota stood in the room, making sure things happened. *Come, Marv, be quick about it!*

Khull took a moment to relax in the same chair where Sally had sat, and listened to Professor Lynch's side of a long-distance conversation.

"Mr. Goring, I was disappointed. She was hardly the formidable foe she seems to be in her letters. A breeze would have knocked her over. That's right." He listened for a moment, then forwarded a question to Khull. "How many men do you have tailing her?"

Khull answered quickly. "Five around the building, five more on the main campus walks."

Lynch brought back an answer. "Well covered. After today, the saga of Sally Roe will be over. Yes. I'll bring you word as soon as I know. Oh, and will you want the ring back?" He chuckled. "I guess I can always flush it down the toilet. Then Bardine and his ring will be together!" He took some time to laugh at that wisecrack, and apparently Goring was laughing at it too.

Khull laughed for about half the time, then stopped abruptly.

Lynch started his good-bye. "Very well, then. Happy to be of service. Yes. Give my regards to everyone at Summit. Yes, I'll see you all at the conference. All right. Good-bye." He hung up the phone and leaned back in his chair. "Oh, such a nasty business!" He looked at Khull. "But I suppose you Satanists take it all in stride?"

"We are *all* killers at heart, Professor Lynch."

"Well, I hope you just do it quickly, and spare me the details!"

"It's too bad you let her go."

"Don't be silly. I don't want it happening anywhere near here. I can't let anyone in this office suspect I had anything to do with it."

"Well, maybe you thought she was weak and helpless, but it looks like she was still clever enough to rip you off."

Lynch looked toward Khull, then followed his gaze to the bookshelf behind the desk.

Khull announced even as Lynch noticed it, "Looks like she took your rosters."

The four volumes that bore the strange symbol of the snarling gargoyle were gone, leaving a distressing gap.

"Destroyer!" said Tal, and all the warriors looked. Yes, there he was, swooping over the campus like a huge, black hawk. "He'll take her this time!"

Guilo pointed with his sword to a huge, black shape rising from the Administration Building. "Corrupter! He's slow, but he sees well!"

"Keep him busy and out of our business!" Then Tal started barking orders as warriors shot into the sky in all directions. "Scion, decoys! Chimon, stay with her. Signa, back him up! Nathan, Armoth, block the bus stop! Cree and Si, set screens!"

Lynch grabbed Khull's arm. He was desperate. "Khull, make sure your men succeed! They must succeed!"

Khull looked at Lynch, then at the gap in the bookshelf, and smiled a wicked smile. "Hm. You must be pretty scared."

Destroyer could see a tiny, frightened figure bursting out of Whitcombe Hall. "Hmm. So how strong are you now, Captain Tal? We will make you show us." He called to his captains, "Take her!"

"There she is!" said one thug to his partner. He'd spotted Sally running from Whitcombe Hall, heading south toward the nearest bus stop. It was dark. They could take her into any of the gardens, alleyways, or groves and finish her instantly.

They were large, burly men, heavily tattooed; one had a deep scar on his left cheek; both wore a large earring in one ear. Beneath their dark leather coats, they carried the shining silver tools of ritual death.

The second one put a portable radio to his jaw and muttered, "She's—"

He was about to say which direction she was going, but suddenly she was gone.

Both men bolted from their hiding-place and stood in the middle of the walkway. Sally Roe had vanished.

Cree and Si stood directly in front of them, wings outstretched. Behind them, Sally continued to run south.

A shriek from the sky! The two warriors shot a glance south. Sally was dashing down some steps, dropping out of sight. Above them, four demon warriors dropped like falcons. Cree and Si bolted, one this way, one that, disappearing in a flash of light into the buildings on either side of the walkway. The demons went after them.

"The woman!" screamed Destroyer from the sky. "Get the woman!"

The demons spun in tight circles, their red blades streaming fire, and kicked the two men in their backs. *Move! This way!* Then they shot down the campus, the walls, windows, and walkways a blur on either side, their black wings screaming.

The two thugs ran after them.

"She was heading south," the man barked into his radio.

Corrupter rose above the campus with the agility of a hot air balloon, watching the incredible spectacle on every side. He spotted Sally and pointed. "There! There—do you see her?"

A bolt of light came from somewhere, delivering such a blow to his head that he tumbled backward, end over end, like a helpless, spinning beach ball, wailing and howling.

Guilo knew he'd be out of the way for a while. He darted away with other things to do.

Sally took only a few seconds to duck into some shrubs and retrieve her hidden duffel bag. She jammed her carry bag into it and continued running.

She rounded a corner near the Psych Library, saw the bus stop illuminated by an amber street lamp, dashed that way, slipped and stumbled to a stop, and dashed back the other way.

The bus stop was covered. Somehow she knew who those two men were.

Run! said Nathan. *The other way!*

Armoth took the blows from the two demons guarding the bus stop just long enough to slow them down. They didn't want him—they wanted Sally Roe.

Two more normal-looking killers were at their post by the Memorial Fountain. One saw through the vertical jets of water and spotted the woman running north toward the Sculpture Garden.

"Heading north!" he barked into his radio. "The Sculpture Garden!"

Sally was heading west—not north—toward the Physical Sciences Building when she ducked behind a tree to hide from four fierce-looking characters running north toward the Sculpture Garden. As soon as they had passed, she headed west again.

"Where'd she go?" a killer asked, looking this way and that.

The Sculpture Garden contained plenty of weird sculptures in stone and steel, but no fleeing woman.

Scion, looking like himself again, took wing and swooped out of the Sculpture Garden with four black bats hot on his tail. As soon as he cleared the roofs, still trailing a stream of light, Si crossed that stream with a searing trail of his own and drew aside two of the demons. At least these buzzards would be busy for a while.

Sally ran past the Physical Sciences Building, over a plaza, and then down a long flight of concrete stairs to the busy street below. A taxi was approaching. She waved furiously. "Taxi! Taxi!"

Two men, looking like any other university students, spotted her and started her way.

The cab driver thought he saw someone trying to flag him.

Two demons dropped through the roof and clawed through his brain.

Huh? Eh, she isn't there . . . Now where was I going, anyway?

The taxi drove by, swerving from lane to lane, not slowing. Sally bolted into an alley.

It was a blind alley—sheer concrete walls and no escape.

The two men closed in behind her, silent, skillful. If they moved quickly enough, they could finish her before she had a chance to scream. One had a long scarf in his hands, the other held a gleaming knife.

Filthy spirits were there too, whooping and frothing, bouncing off the walls like golf balls down a gutter. This was it!

Mota rode on the roof of Marv Simpson's ranch wagon as it rolled lazily down Hannan Boulevard on the south end of the Bentmore campus. When it came to a corner, Mota's wings burst forth like fireworks and the next thing Marv knew, he was in a right-turn-only lane and had to turn right, heading up the campus's west side.

"Doggone," he muttered.

"Weren't we supposed to go the other way?" Claudia asked.

But he was looking this way and that and trying to change lanes, getting more and more frustrated. "Now how do we get out of *here*?"

Sally backed away until she came up against the sheer, featureless concrete at the end of the alley. So much for flight. Now for fight. She raised her duffel bag to shield herself.

No sound, only shadows blurring in the street lights. The scarf hit her face, her head hit the wall, one eye was covered, she couldn't see.

A knife flashed!

Chimon was there and parried.

The knife deflected and lodged in the duffel bag.

A blow to her neck! She pitched forward, grabbing the knife man. He pulled the blade free and plunged it at her again.

The knife ripped through her coat. Her scream was muffled inside the scarf.

A searing blade opened Chimon's shoulder. Two demons caught his backhanded sword and dissolved.

The knife slashed Sally's coat open, but missed her flesh.

Scion came in low, ducked under a cluster of lashing, hacking spirits, and rolled into the knife man's legs. He fell backward. The knife clinked on the concrete. Scion had rolled into the middle of a death trap. Twisting and spinning, he was able to fend off most of the demons' blows, but one wild blade caught his leg, cutting it deep.

Chimon had a screaming, flopping, slobbering demon by the feet. He batted Scion's attackers away in one powerful swing, then whipped the flailing body over his head and smacked the scarf man in the face.

The scarf slipped away. Sally could see again. She lunged forward and broke free.

The knife man grabbed her coat sleeve.

Signa dropped out of the sky, tracing an exclamation point of light. His sword caught the seam at Sally's shoulder and the sleeve tore away.

She ran. Alive!

The knife man was looking for his knife. The scarf man couldn't tell where he was in the dark.

Chimon, Scion, and Signa were cut, bruised, and limping, but they grabbed hold of Sally and got her out of that alley.

Destroyer saw it all, and screamed for his hordes. The spirits gathered from every corner of the campus, swords burning, wings roaring, ready for a kill. With Destroyer at the point of a massive arrowhead formation, they dove toward the street.

In Bacon's Corner, Lucy ran into Amber's bedroom expecting blood, bruises, an accident, something horrible.

It was nothing of the kind. The child was beside herself, screaming, cursing, pounding the walls.

"Amber, what's wrong?" her mother cried, trying to embrace her.

She spun around like a vicious animal and stood apart from her mother, her fingers curved like claws, her eyes wild and glaring, darting about the room as if watching distant events. "Cut her up! Grab her, take her, cut her up!"

Lucy backed into the wall and remained there, speechless. There was no stopping Amethyst when she was like this. She'd tried before.

Destroyer and his hordes were screaming out their war cry, their sulfurous breath forming yellow streamers that etched the sky like comb's teeth.

Marv Simpson was looking for a place to turn around and getting more and more frustrated. He hardly noticed that woman running out of the alley.

"Oh my," said Claudia, "what's going on here?"

Tal dropped through the roof and filled the whole backseat with his massive frame. *Stop and pick her up!*

Marv saw her again. She was actually running into the street.

"Oh!" Claudia exclaimed, "she's coming toward us!"

"Oh, man, a nut case! We've got to get out of here—"

Tal grabbed Marv's head in his two huge hands and forced him to look toward the woman. *PICK HER UP!*

"Let's pick her up," said Claudia.

He pulled over.

Guilo shot into the sky, flanked by Nathan, Armoth, Cree, and Si. They intercepted Destroyer and his henchmen like a clap of thunder over the campus. The demons were like an irresistible wall, and the angelic warriors went tumbling and spinning aside. Destroyer and his horde resumed their course, dropping toward that station wagon; the five warriors recovered, circled, and dove down on the demons' backs like falcons. The vile spirits fought them off, but they had to take precious time to do it.

"Need a ride?"

Sally pulled the door open and clambered into the backseat. "Please. Get me away from here!"

Four men appeared on the sidewalk, two with radios. They saw her get into the car and quickly disappeared.

Marv was still lost. "How do I get out of here?"

"Left, up at the corner," said Sally, "and then go under the tunnel."

"Tunnel?"

Destroyer and his warriors skimmed over the top of the Physical Sciences Building and dropped toward the street, closing in on the station wagon. Tal and Mota clung to the car's roof, swords ready, wings covering the passengers inside. Then Guilo shot out from a side street, Nathan and Armoth whipped around a bank building, Scion dropped from an overpass, Chimon and Signa weaved among the cars only inches above the pavement, Si came up through a manhole, and they all pounced on the car, covering every square inch of it, their drawn swords making it look like a glowing porcupine.

This would be it, a direct, power-for-power battle!

But suddenly, surprisingly, Destroyer pulled out of his dive and followed only twenty feet above them, passing through the traffic lights, telephone lines, and street signs, keeping an eye on them, sizing them up. The sight of the small band of warriors clinging to the vehicle, swords drawn for a last stand, made him laugh. It made his henchmen laugh.

Finally he shouted to them, "Call it a victory, captain! *I* call it progress! You are weaker than ever now, and the next time will be ours. The fruit will be ripe, and we will pluck it down with ease! And don't concern yourself with hiding her. We will always know where she is!"

They climbed into the night sky and were just disappearing into the darkness when the car went into the tunnel.

"What now?" Chimon asked, holding his wounded shoulder.

"Name it, cap," said Scion, holding his useless leg. "We'll do it."

"We are spent," said Tal. "Even though we confused Khull's men, Destroyer could have taken us, and it's only by the hand of the Lord that he didn't know it. It's time we hid her in Ashton."

"And let her hear of the Cross!" said Nathan.

"We'll get her there and let the Spirit speak to her." Then he added with an unabashed anger, "While we get back to Bacon's Corner and root out this prayer blockage once and for all!"

"Uh," asked Marv, "where you headed?"

Sally was gasping for breath, sick with terror, and dripping with sweat. She was not entirely rational. "I don't care. Anywhere. Anywhere away from here."

Claudia looked over her shoulder at the pitiful creature slumped over in the backseat, weeping, panting, dripping with sweat. "You poor dear!"

Marv looked at her through the rearview mirror and could see the fear in her eyes. The Lord spoke to his heart. Yep, it was no accident that he'd picked her up. "Well, you just take it easy and try to rest. We'll get you far away from here. I know just the place."

29

Lucy Brandon was feeling weak and ill, but trying not to show it, even as she scribbled a forwarding address on still another letter from Sally Roe and slipped the letter into the bag of outgoing mail. She didn't want to do it, but she could see no alternative. Her lawyers were pressuring her, her friends at LifeCircle were smiling and encouraging her, Sergeant Mulligan was watching her, the lawsuit was moving full speed ahead, and the momentum was overpowering, carrying her along like a runaway train.

But after no less than twenty of these letters, she'd seen enough. She was afraid, she was ignorant of legal strategy, and perhaps she was a little too trusting and gullible, but she wasn't stupid. There was no question in her mind that Sally Roe was alive.

The more she thought about that, the more devastating it became. Gradually, just one small idea at a time, she was allowing herself to think the unthinkable: something more than a lawsuit was in progress and she was being lied to by someone, maybe everyone. If she was being lied to, she was probably breaking the law for all her friends and not for herself. If all that were true, then—she'd tried to bury this thought for weeks—she was being used.

She had no question that her daughter Amber was being used, if not by these legal eagles, then certainly by that once-cute little pony Amber had befriended in Miss Brewer's fourth-grade class. The laughter, the fun and games, the cartoon-character charm were all things of the past. Amethyst was no friend of any kind.

But now Lucy was in so deep, how could she back out? What direction could she turn? How—

The bell rang at the front desk. Debbie was on her break, so Lucy hurried to the front.

This big man looked familiar. She'd seen him around town, but he wasn't from around here. She immediately felt uncomfortable.

"Can I help you?"

"Hi. I'm Marshall Hogan. I'm a friend of Tom Harris, and I just got a letter here from the Omega Center for Educational Studies in Fairwood, Massachusetts . . ."

He acted like he was giving her a cue, but she didn't catch whatever it was. "Yes? Is there a problem?"

"Well . . . I suppose you know that they're the publishers of the *Finding the Real Me* curriculum that Miss Brewer uses at the elementary school?"

"I still don't see your point."

"Well, I wrote to the Omega Center to order a copy of the *Finding the Real Me* curriculum, and they tell me here in this letter that they only make that curriculum available to educational institutions, and not to the general public. Don't you think that's a little strange?"

Lucy knew she didn't want to talk about this. "I'm not the Omega Center, sir, and I'm not responsible for their policies. Now unless you have some business with the Post Office . . ."

Marshall looked behind him. No one else was standing in line. "I'll just be a second. Let's talk about that local group, uh, LifeCircle. I understand that LifeCircle is a major force in education around here: three of the school board belong to it, the principal of the elementary school—Mr. Woodard—belongs to it, Miss Brewer belongs to it, and you belong to it. The school board adopted the Omega Center curriculum, Mr. Woodard implemented it, Miss Brewer's teaching it, and your daughter Amber contacted her inner guide, Amethyst, because of it."

Only a week ago Lucy would have felt invaded, and very angry. Today was different. "What about it?" She really wanted to know.

She was trying to look strong and unshakable, but Marshall caught the curiosity in her eyes. "Let me ask you this: Why do you suppose Miss Brewer couldn't produce the curriculum when we asked to see it, and neither could Mr. Woodard, and neither could the school board, and now the Omega Center itself won't allow me to order a copy of it? When I consider how all you people are connected, it sure makes me wonder if your lawsuit against the Good Shepherd Academy might have something to do with it. Do you suppose there's something in that curriculum your friends don't want us to see?"

Lucy didn't answer for a long moment. She'd never thought about the question before. She wanted an answer herself. "I don't know, Mr . . ."

"Hogan. Marshall Hogan."

"What are you, an investigator or something?"

"Sure, something like that. Mostly just a friend of your opponents in this lawsuit."

"Well, obviously I can't talk about any of this."

"I understand. Thank you very much for your time."

"You're welcome."

He left the building, and Lucy returned to her work, or at least tried to return to it. If she was pensive and troubled before her visit with this Mr. Hogan, now she was totally distracted. What else did that man know, and why didn't she know it?

Marshall got back to Ben and Bev's, and placed a collect long-distance call.

Back at his newspaper, a young, pretty, bespectacled brunette answered the phone from inside Marshall's glass-enclosed office. "*Ashton Clarion*, Bernice Krueger speaking."

"Hey, Bernice, this is Marshall."

"Well, well!" She closed the office door against the outside clamor and plopped down at his desk, ready for the latest. "Can any good news come out of Bacon's Corner?"

"Well . . . the walls of the fort are getting thin, but no break-throughs yet."

"Keep digging."

"That's why I called. You remember I told you about that curriculum at the elementary school?"

"Right. The kids getting into alpha mind control and spirit-guides. Did you ever get a copy of it?"

"No dice. They're stonewalling it, as far up the ladder as Omega itself. Are you still in touch with that guy in Washington, what's-his-name . . . ?"

"Cliff Bingham. Sure. He got me some inside stuff on the last election."

"I'm wondering if he couldn't check with the Library of Congress and find an original copy of this thing."

Bernice grabbed a pen and started writing herself a note. "I'll call him. What exactly do you want?"

"*Finding the Real Me*, a curriculum for fourth-graders."

She wrote it down. "Published by Omega Center . . ."

"Uh . . . Omega Center for Educational Studies, Fairwood, Massachusetts."

"Any idea what year?"

"Beats me."

"Okay. We will see what we will see."

"Okay, now let's talk about the Tuesday edition. Pull that malt shop story; John likes it, but his wife will have a fit . . ."

They talked business. Bernice took notes, pulled files, read copy over the phone, and got orders from her boss.

Outside, the midweek, midday business in the town of Ashton was in full swing; people, grocery carts, and vehicles were circulating through the parking lot at Carlucci's Market; the fire fighters were hosing down the apron at Station Fifteen and shining up the pumper; Clyde Sodeberg and his sons were beating the still-green concrete off some forms over at the new Midwest Savings and Loan project.

Driving past it all, and then stopping at the second of four lights along Main Street, Marv and Claudia Simpson introduced Sally Beth Roe—they thought her name was Betty Smith—to their town.

"It's a great place to live and do business," said Marv. "At least it is now. We've had our share of trouble, but things have settled down quite a bit, and I think we're having a turn for the better."

The light turned green and Marv piloted the big station wagon further down the street, past the small stores, the True Value Hardware, the local newspaper . . .

"That's the *Ashton Clarion*," said Marv. "It comes out on Tuesdays and Fridays, and the editor's a saint. I think he's been out of town for a while; I don't know what he's been doing."

They drove past the high school. It was new this year, because enrollment was up.

Marv turned left at the third light and drove up a gradually graded street into a quiet neighborhood with massive oak trees lining the street, small, garishly painted bicycles leaning against the oaks, and orange basketball hoops on every other garage. The lawns were neat, the sidewalks were clean, and the cars all seemed to know their proper parking places.

Marv turned left again and came to a row of large, turn-of-the-century homes with white, beveled siding, large chimneys, massive roofs, cozy dormers, and wide, roomy front porches. He pulled over and parked in front of the third house on the right, probably the most inviting house of all, with a perfectly manicured lawn, colorful planted borders, a pillared front porch, and an inviting porch swing. In front, just beside the walkway, was a small, unpretentious sign: Sara Barker's Boarding House.

"Here's the place I told you about," said Marv.

"It'll be just right, I think," said Claudia. "You'll have time to think things through and get your head clear."

Sally took their hands and held them tightly. "You've done me a wonderful kindness. Thank you very much."

"You're welcome," said Marv. "We'll have you out to the dairy sometime."

"I'd love that. "

"Oh, here's Sara now," said Claudia.

"Sara's a good gal; you'll like her."

Sara was, and Sally did. The house actually belonged to Sara and her husband Floyd, but they thought using just her name on the sign would be more charming. Floyd was a tall, thin man of few words who had recently retired from the grain business and was now trying his hand at being a writer when he wasn't serving as the handyman for the boarding house—which he was at the moment. He was glad to meet her and shook her hand warmly. As for Sara, she impressed Sally as everyone's idea of the perfect grandma, a short little woman with close-cropped gray hair, little round glasses, and a cute story about most everything.

"We used to have eight kids, and now they're gone, so we have all these rooms empty and ready for the right people," she explained, showing Sally through the big house. "We've had mostly single women here; some have troubles at home and need to stay away, some are on their way somewhere else—you know, between things—and the two that are here right now are here for keeps until they get married, I suppose."

The living room was old, classic, with a high ceiling, finely milled wainscoting, inviting, comfortable, antique furniture, and even an old pump organ from Ashton's first pioneer church. The dining room was large and well-suited for a big family, or for a houseful of boarders.

"Now, we have a downstairs bathroom, but it's being worked on . . . "

They were in the central hallway just below the big staircase, and they could see a toolbox jutting into the hall through the bathroom door and hear the clunking and tinkering of work going on.

Sara stepped around the toolbox and then out of the way, so Sally could look in. "When we get the plumbing fixed, things should be back to normal."

Sally looked into the bathroom. It was large, and during normal times it was probably very nice. Right now it was a mess; the carpet was rolled back, there were tools and pipe fittings on the floor, a glaring work light hanging from the vanity mirror, and, strangest of all, a young man in coveralls on his knees in front of the toilet—he seemed to be hollering down into the bowl.

"No," he shouted, "come back up! You're going the wrong way!"

A muffled voice—it was Floyd's—came from below somewhere. "Who put all this stuff down here, anyway?"

"You put it in, Floyd; don't blame me!"

Then the young man noticed Sally watching him. "Oh, hi there."

"Hi."

Sara leaned in. "Hank, this is Betty Smith, a new boarder. Betty, this is Hank Busche, our pastor."

He waved a wrench at her. "Pleased to meet you. I'll be happy to shake your hand later." It was clear to see that his hands were quite dirty at the moment.

Sally was fascinated. This was a pastor? "Why are you yelling down the toilet?"

He thought that was funny. "Well . . . that's Floyd down there. Have you met Floyd?"

Floyd's voice came from under the floor. "Yeah. That's Betty, right?"

Hank hollered back. "Yeah."

"We've met."

"She's here to inspect your bolting job."

"Oh, I'm in trouble now!"

Hank explained, "Floyd used the wrong bolts to put this toilet in fifteen years ago, and now we can't get the nuts loose underneath."

Sally's smile was a weary smile, but it felt good.

Sara said, "You're tired. Come on upstairs and I'll show you your room."

But Sally hesitated just a moment. "You don't look like a pastor."

Hank smiled, brushing some hair away from his forehead with his forearm. "Thanks."

Why not go straight to the horse? Sally thought. "I suppose you know God?"

"Sure, I know Him."

He was so matter-of-fact about it. He didn't even hesitate with that answer. Sally tried a tougher question. "Can you prove He exists?"

Hank sat back from the toilet and just looked at her for a moment. "Got a Bible?"

Sally was about to say no, but Sara said, "There's one up in her room."

Hank was thinking. He almost looked like he was listening. "Tell you what. Read Psalm 119, and just ask God to speak to your heart while you read it. See what happens."

"Psalm 119," Sally repeated.

"Right."

"Good luck with the toilet."

"Thanks. And nice to meet you."

Hank sat there a moment after Sally and Sara were gone. The Lord had spoken to him about this woman named Betty.

Floyd's voice came from below, "Psalm 119? What kind of Scripture is that for getting somebody saved?"

Hank was puzzled himself. "I don't know. It's the Scripture the Lord told me to give her."

"The longest chapter in the Bible . . ." Floyd muttered.

Hank prayed, right there. "Lord God, please make Yourself real to Betty Smith. Show her how much You love her."

"Amen," said the voice under the toilet. "Now can you flush me a smaller wrench?"

Atop the house, Tal consulted with the two angelic princes of Ashton, Krioni and Triskal.

"We are honored to see you again, captain," said Krioni. "We'll always remember the victory achieved here."

Tal scanned the horizon and could see the thick hedge of angelic warriors that surrounded the town, sealing it off from demonic invasion. They were there to serve the saints within, responding to their prayers, widening doors of opportunity to minister. The town was not perfect, not without problems; it still had its taverns and turmoils, its scrapes and its sins. But the Lord was working in Ashton, its saints were praying, and for Sally Beth Roe it was safe.

"I leave her in your hands, Krioni. I see Hank is planting the right seeds already."

Triskal smiled. "The Spirit of God is continuing to draw her."

"Care for her in the meantime. Make sure she meets Bernice, but don't let Bernice know who she is until the right time."

Krioni gave Tal a knowing look. "Once again you have a plan. How is it unfolding?"

Tal looked grim. "Steadily, but miserably."

Krioni nodded. "You and the others are going to need some time to heal up, I see."

"Destroyer learned from what we did here. He got to the saints first. He and his demons are wreaking strife and division that church hasn't seen in years, and every day our situation grows more precarious. I'm going back to Bacon's Corner to stop that campaign. Nothing else can proceed until I do."

Triskal's face wrinkled with concern. "But is there time, captain?"

Tal answered simply, "No. We'll just have to do what we can. If you can use this crisis to arouse specific prayer from the saints here, so much the better."

Triskal smiled. "Count on it. They will pray."

Krioni added, "But it sounds like Sally Roe is headed for even greater jeopardy."

Tal nodded, with regret. "We cannot bring the plan up short, or spare her every last step. We will win all . . . or we will lose all."

Krioni and Triskal embraced him. "Godspeed."

Tal drew his sword to rally his warriors, and they shot into the sky, bound for Bacon's Corner.

"Lost?" Destroyer roared. "You dare to tell me you lost her?"

Six loathsome spirits stood before him on the roof of Whitcombe Hall at Bentmore University. They'd locked their eyes on the thick, rolled roofing and refused to look up. They were silent, with no fitting words of explanation. Destroyer and Corrupter were not too far from shredding them this very moment.

Destroyer wanted an explanation, and right now. He grabbed one demon by the hair and jerked his head upward so their eyes would meet. "I knew *you* would never lose her, but follow her to the ends of the earth so we could choose our time, taunt the Host of Heaven, pick the fruit when it was ripe, and now . . . you have lost her? Tell me how!"

"We followed her," the thing said.

"And?"

"She went west with the dairy farmer."

"*And?*"

The spirit looked at his comrades. They wouldn't even return his gaze, lest Destroyer think they knew something. "The farmer took her to Ashton."

Destroyer gave the demon's hair a painful yank, twisting his neck backward. "*Ashton?*"

The demon winced with pain. "We followed as long as we could, but we were turned back."

Destroyer's eyes burned with fury. "The Host of Heaven?"

The warrior was almost falling over, squirming in Destroyer's iron grip. "They hold that territory, they and the saints of God!"

Destroyer released the demon's hair and the warrior dropped to the roof, rotating the kinks out of his neck.

Destroyer and Corrupter moved away to consult privately.

Destroyer was turning the air yellow with his frantic, anxious panting. "That slimy, slippery, subtle Captain of the Host! I should have anticipated this! He is hiding her in a stronghold we cannot penetrate!"

Corrupter muttered, "She is free, and alive, and now has *both* the ring and the rosters."

"The rosters are *your* fault!" Destroyer insisted.

"And her disappearance? Is that not yours?"

"If we lose track of her now . . ."

"That is not an option."

" . . . the Strongman will take both our heads from our bodies with his bare hands!" Destroyer spit sulfur in a new burst of rage. "Never! The Captain of the Host will not defeat me! I will not be humbled by these feeble saints!"

He screamed to his henchmen who stood guard nearby. They snapped to attention.

"Gather your hordes! We return to Bacon's Corner! We will finish this business and decimate the saints, silencing their prayers once and for all!"

Claire Johanson hung up the telephone in her office and then stared at it, motionless, deep in thought.

Jon knew that look on her face. "What is it?"

"That was Mr. Goring, from Summit. Sally Roe showed up at Bentmore. She was right in Samuel Lynch's office."

Jon rose from his chair, anticipating an answer he would not like. "She didn't get away?"

Claire sighed, letting her hand fall to the desk with a slap. "She did. Khull and his men chased her all over the Bentmore campus, but she managed to hitch a ride with some stranger and they lost her."

Jon threw up his hands in anger. "Great. That's just great! I'm really starting to wonder about this Khull. He's had two chances now and came up empty both times!"

Claire cautioned him, "Please keep your voice down. Some LifeCirclers are in the house."

Jon tried to calm himself, but couldn't sit down or relax at all.

"She has the rosters," Claire added.

Jon looked at her curiously. "What rosters?"

"Professor Lynch's membership rosters."

Jon stared at her blankly. He couldn't bring himself to believe it. He shook his head. "Now that has to be a mistake. Somebody's wrong. That isn't true."

"It's true."

He shook his head again, harder. "No, it is not true! It's too unthinkable to be true!"

"Lynch stepped out of the office to get his ring and contact Khull. She must have snatched them from his bookshelf while he was gone. He didn't notice until after she left."

Jon shouted at that. "She *left*?"

Claire shushed him, feeling defensive for Lynch. "He couldn't have her killed right there in his office! Khull's men were supposed to take care of her elsewhere, secretly."

Jon fumed and huffed and paced around the office. "Is Professor Lynch still alive?"

"Of course he is."

"Why?"

Claire looked away impatiently. "Jon, what would that solve?"

Jon was having trouble keeping his voice down. "That old codger is a liability! He should be eliminated, and Khull as well!"

Claire sighed and rested her chin in her hand. "Maybe they will be, I don't know. I don't control such things."

"So, when is that hearing?"

"Nine o'clock Monday morning."

Jon cursed. "We should have known by now! There are other forces working on Roe's behalf, directly opposing us. I can feel it. No doubt they're working against this lawsuit as well. We could get a wrong ruling."

Claire was about to disagree, but then decided she couldn't. "I believe that is a possibility."

Jon stopped to give Claire a good look in the eye. "If we lose in this hearing, and they can put Amber on the stand, or even depose her . . ."

Claire agreed. "I'll call the others."

"And Hemphile too. I want her in on this. We have to hit that church!"

"We already have . . ."

"I mean hit them harder! Something right up front!"

Claire stood, her finger to her lips. "Someone might hear you."

He tried to quiet himself. They could hear a LifeCircle yoga class going on upstairs, right above their heads.

Claire had another caution. "You know that with any overt action we'll be risking exposure . . ."

Jon chuckled at that. "Come on. They're old-fashioned, fringe, fanatic Christians. Who's going to believe them?"

She acquiesced. "All right."

"We'll curse the church, and we'll curse Sally Roe. Can we get anything she owns?"

"Well, I guess the rental house still has all her belongings in it."

"Anything alive?"

Claire thought for a moment. "Oh, yes. As a matter of fact, I think she did have some animals."

Jon smiled and calmed a bit. "Good. Good."

30

It was quiet at Floyd and Sara Barker's after dinner. Floyd and Sara were settling into the couch downstairs for some reading; Michelle, the young college girl, was in her room studying; Suzanne, a young attorney just new in town, was out meeting a prospective partner.

Sally was fed, bathed, warm, and secure in her little corner bedroom, snuggled in the soft bed under one of Sara's handmade comforters, her back supported by an ample supply of large pillows.

For the first time in so many years Sally had trouble calculating the number—she finally figured it had to be about twenty-five—she held in her hands a volume she had blamed for the world's woes, belittled as an overrated anthology of myths, resented for its narrow views of morality, condemned as oppressive and authoritarian, and ignored as an outmoded, stagnating lead weight around the intellectual ankle of mankind.

It was one of Sara Barker's Bibles.

She found the book of Psalms immediately. It was in the middle of the Bible.

"Just open your Bibles right to the middle," came a voice from her past. "Psalms is right there in the middle."

What was that woman's name? Oh, Mrs. Gunderson, that's right. She was an older lady. She was old as long as Sally ever knew her, as if she'd hit a peak in years and just stayed there. Every Sunday morning, Sally would clump down the church stairs with all the other seven- and eight-year-olds and gather in Mrs. Gunderson's Sunday school class in that cold church basement, in that small, echoing classroom with the hard wooden chairs and the chalkboard that still bore the unerasable traces of lessons from weeks ago.

Then Mrs. Gunderson would tell them a story, placing paper Bible characters on the same green-grass-and-blue-sky flannel background. Even now, as Sally lay in the bed with the Bible in her lap, she could remember those stories: the wee little man who climbed the sycamore tree, the fishermen who fished all night but caught no fish, the disciple—she thought it was Peter—who walked on the water to meet Jesus, the man named Lazarus whom Jesus raised from the dead, Moses, Noah, and of course Jonah who was swallowed by the fish.

Strange. She'd put those stories out of her mind as far back as junior high school, but now, at thirty-six, she remembered not only those stories, but also the deep feelings of conviction and morality she always had after every Sunday school: I want to be good. I want to do good things and love God. I want Jesus to come into my heart.

Such old memories, such long ago feelings. But the memories were pleasant, and the feelings they evoked were warm and comforting, which caused her to pause and reflect. How many pleasant memories did she really have? Not too many. Maybe these, some of her oldest, were her happiest.

Psalm 119. Hmm. It was a long chapter. She read the first verse. "Blessed are they whose ways are blameless, who walk according to the law of the Lord."

That first verse was enough to grab her attention, and she read on.

Verse 3 said, "They do nothing wrong; they walk in his ways."

Verses 4, 5, and 6 continued the same theme: "You have laid down precepts that are to be fully obeyed. Oh, that my ways were steadfast in obeying your decrees! Then I would not be put to shame when I consider all your commands."

How did that pastor know? She'd asked him the toughest question she could think of, but he came back with the answer she needed, the one perfect for her situation, right here and now, the very next step in her musings.

She continued to read, and the words spoke to her over and over again about something she'd fled from for years, denied, fought against, and finally lost . . . but perhaps needed most of all.

Absolutes. A genuine right and a genuine wrong. A fence, a point of reference, a way to know something for sure.

She couldn't let these ideas get away from her. She hopped out of bed and hurried to the closet for her duffel bag. The few clothes she had were in the laundry at the moment, so the bag was a lot emptier, containing a still frightening amount of freshly minted cash, her notebook, which she set aside, and . . . the rosters from Professor Lynch's office.

She felt sick at the sight of them, as if there was an evil attached to them, as if an invisible, poisonous stowaway had come along to haunt her. They frightened her; they gave her the same stomach-turning fear and disgust one feels while waiting for something horrible to jump out in a late-night horror movie.

Unseen by Sally, though she could sense them, the same little quartet of demons still lurked about, watching her, looking for opportunities. They had followed her everywhere she went, and could pass through any angelic hedge because she carried them with her. Despair was enjoying his job less and less; the more Sally continued in her quest, the less of his poison he could sow in her mind. Fear had had much to do and a lot of fun doing it, and was glad to have those rosters along, but Death and Insanity were getting frustrated. Sally had found some new purpose somewhere; Death was no longer welcome in her thoughts, and her thoughts were becoming too clear and rational for Insanity to scramble.

All four reached out for her, but at the moment there was nothing to grab.

Sally closed the duffel bag, leaving the rosters hidden and confined. *Not now, rosters; I'll deal with you later. I don't want to feel sick, I don't want to struggle. Just give me a break. Let me rest awhile.*

The demons slinked away to wait.

She grabbed up her notebook and pen, and hopped into the bed again.

Good feelings, don't go away. Let me meet with you awhile, study you, figure you out; let me think things through.

She began another letter to Tom Harris.

I'm working my way through Psalm 119, and if I understand the message correctly, there are at least two absolutes being presented, two things I can know for sure:

1) There is a right: to obey God's laws and follow His ways.

2) There is a wrong: to disobey God's laws and not follow His ways.

How am I doing so far? I hope you're keeping up, because now it's going to get tougher.

Psalm 119 also talks about two human conditions that are the direct result of the two absolutes:

1) Do what is right, and you'll be happy and blessed.

2) Do what is wrong, and you'll be put to shame.

Now is that simple or what? Too simple, I suppose; too basic to be believed and accepted by people like me who insist there is no reality higher than themselves.

But, Tom, I do believe I have been put to shame. Even the vicious, cutting remarks of an enemy, Professor Lynch, make that clear to me. He was trying to destroy me, I know, but there was nothing he said that wasn't true. I couldn't argue with him. The truth is, my life is in ruins.

But can I accept the Bible's explanation for it? Dare I trust this Book? If the Bible is trustworthy, and if I did choose to believe it, then I could, once and for all, determine who and where I am: in the wrong, outside of God's favor, put to shame.

Not a comfortable thought, but at least I would have an immovable rock under my feet.

Despair flopped to the floor beside the bed, holding his stomach and moaning. Death and Insanity weren't feeling very well either, but took it out on Despair.

"You're losing her, leech! You're the one in charge of this mission! Do something!"

Fear volunteered, "Perhaps I could think of something to frighten her."

Despair hissed at him, "You've done that, and driven her closer to the truth!"

Sally felt sleepy at last. For now, her questions were resolved, her thoughts were recorded, and she could rest. She set the notebook on the bedside table, put all the pillows aside except one, and clicked off the lamp.

As she lay there in the dark, she noticed how peaceful she felt. This was the first night in a long time that she did not feel afraid. Instead, she felt . . . what was this? Hope? Yes! This had to be hope. It felt so foreign, so different.

Out of her distant past, she could recall once again those old feelings and thoughts from Sunday school: I want to be good. I want to do good things and love God. I want Jesus to come into my heart.

She fluffed her pillow and let her head sink into it. Hm. Jesus. Now what does He have to do with all this?

Very early on Sunday morning, Ben Cole stood in the gate to Sally Roe's goat pen, incredulous, sickened, wary of proceeding inside. This couldn't be real. Things like this just didn't happen, not around here.

He looked back toward the field between the Potter home and the rental. Mrs. Potter stood in the middle of the field, nervously wringing her hands and watching, but refusing to come any closer.

He looked back toward the goat pen. Buff and Bart, the two kids, were still alive, but disturbed and jittery. As for Betty, the doe . . .

Ben finally entered the pen, closing the gate behind him, stepping carefully through the dirt and straw, searching the ground for any clues. He approached Betty's dead and butchered carcass. She hadn't been killed too long ago. It had to have been the previous night.

He turned and shouted to Mrs. Potter, "Did you hear anything?"

"No," she replied.

Ben looked around the carcass. No clues. No footprints. The dirt did seem to be disturbed, however, probably brushed and raked to erase any clues.

Mrs. Potter came closer, but still wouldn't look.

"Have you called the police?" Ben asked.

"Well, I called you."

He smiled. "I'm no longer with the Police Department."

"I know. But I wanted you to come. I don't trust Sergeant Mulligan. I don't think he'd do anything about it."

Ben backed away from Betty's carcass and joined Mrs. Potter near the fence. He was wishing he had a camera to record this.

"Well," he said, drawing his first full breath. "*I'm* going to do something about it."

Betty lay in the straw, her throat cut, her body totally drained of blood, and all four legs cleanly and skillfully removed, missing without a trace.

The morning air was chilly, but Ben could feel a chill that had nothing to do with the weather. In his spirit, he could feel some real trouble approaching.

Well, maybe I should, Sally thought. *It's one thing I haven't tried yet. It could provide more information that would round out my perspective. It might clarify some of the old memories I haven't been able to fully recall. It would be an interesting glimpse into middle-class American religious culture. Perhaps it might—*

"Get your coat, then," said Sara Barker. "Floyd's warming up the car right now."

Sally answered a little late, "Well, sure, I'll go. Why not?"

And that's how she found herself standing in front of the little white Ashton Community Church, a half-mile up Morgan Hill on Poplar Street, on a warm and beautiful Sunday morning. People were already filing inside, talking, laughing, hugging like old friends, guiding their small children by the hand and calling to the older ones to come on and hurry up, church was starting.

Sara spared no pains to make sure Sally met everyone. "Hi, Andy, this is Betty Smith. Edith, how are you? I'd like you to meet Betty Smith, our new boarder. Cecil, it's great to see you're feeling better. Have you met Betty Smith?"

Sally smiled and shook the hands extended to her, but with only half her attention. The sight of a little girl in a Sunday dress, holding her mother's hand and carrying a Bible, triggered a memory.

Thirty years ago, that was me.

Sally could remember wearing a pretty dress and a matching ribbon in her hair. She could remember carrying a Bible too, a gift from the lady who held her hand back then, her guardian, Aunt Barbara. Sally's mother, lost to alcohol, had never been much of a positive influence. Aunt Barbara, on the other hand, always took her to Sunday school. Aunt Barbara took religion seriously, and in those days Sally respected that. It was good for Aunt Barbara, and yes, it felt right for Sally too.

"Well, we'd better get in there," said Sara, her words jolting Sally from her reverie.

They went up the front steps, through the double doors, and into a small foyer where a few clusters of people—Floyd was part of one cluster—were still getting caught up on each other's week.

Oh, there was the Sunday school attendance posted on the wall. She remembered that. She remembered always bringing an offering, too; that was important in those days.

The people around her were of all kinds. Some were well-dressed, some were in blue jeans; there were older folks and many younger; there were plenty of young children about, suggesting a middle-class, Protestant baby boom.

Sally quickly had to admit to herself that, Christianity itself notwithstanding, there was little reason to be uncomfortable in this place. Her lack of acceptable attire could have been a reason—she had only her slacks and blouse and could not wear the jacket because of the knife holes in it, not to mention the missing sleeve—but now she saw that attire had little to do with acceptance, and neither did ethnic background or social status.

Well . . . I guess I won't be uncomfortable.

She followed Floyd and Sara to a place in a wooden pew near

the back and sat down. Her feet could touch the floor. The last time she sat in a pew, her feet dangled. That was when . . . Tommy Krebs! Yes, now she remembered him, that little snotty kid with the crewcut and the marker pen without a cap. She finally tattled on him and that brought some peace for a while, but not before he'd blackened her knee. Yes, that all happened in a pew just like this one, during the Sunday school's opening exercises. Oh! What was that song she and all those other little moppets used to sing? "Jesus loves me, this I know, for the Bible tells me so . . ." Oh, yes. That song had to be one of the oldie-goldie hits of American Protestantism; obviously *she* never forgot it.

She tried to relax, and looked around the small sanctuary at the backs of all those heads. Oh, there was the pastor, Hank What's-his-name, closing off a conversation and taking a chair on the platform. Now he looked a little more like a pastor, with a suit and tie, but she knew she'd never forget that guy wrestling with a toilet back at the boarding house.

This was becoming quite an experience. There was so much to see and remember, so many feelings to sort through, she hadn't become bored yet. Rather, she was captivated.

But . . . what am I doing here, really? she wondered. *Is it just because Sara invited me?*

No, not really. The invitation was as good an incentive as any, but not the real reason. Sally did want to be here, even though it was only now that she realized it.

Is it a matter of curiosity?

No, more than that. Curiosity was one thing, hunger was another.

Hunger? For what—fond memories? Nostalgia?

No, more than that. It was more a haunting sensation that she had come full circle after thirty years and found, just as strong as ever, a truth, a treasure, a special matter of the heart she once held but lost. She couldn't recall her life being as shaky during her Sunday school childhood as it had been ever since. There was just something about the convictions of this culture, the solid certainty of everything.

Maybe that was part of it. Maybe those experiences of long ago were the last solid ground Sally had ever walked on.

Yes, things were so different then.

Sally, Sara, and Floyd all scooted over a little to make room for a young lady to sit next to Sally.

"Hi," she said, offering her hand. "I'm Bernice Krueger."

"Um . . . Betty Smith." She had to be sure she remembered the right name.

"She's our new boarder," said Sara.

"Oh, great," said Bernice. "You new in town?"

"Yes."

"What brings you here?"

"Oh . . . just traveling."

"So how long have you been here?"

"Uh . . . I just got here yesterday." Sally was hoping this wasn't going to be a long interview. She decided to get the subject off herself. "So what do you do?"

"I work for the local newspaper. I'm a reporter and assistant editor, and I also wash the coffee cups and empty the wastebaskets."

"Oh, that's interesting."

Bernice laughed. "Sometimes it is. Well, it's great to have you here."

"Thank you."

There was a slight pause. Bernice looked forward and Sally thought the conversation was over, but then Bernice turned to Sally again with an additional thought.

"Say, if there's anything I can do for you, please let me know."

The offer was a little abrupt and unexpected. It made Sally wonder what this Bernice Krueger was thinking. *Do I seem that pitiful?* Sally did appreciate the compassion, but knew she could never accept it. "Thanks. I'll remember that."

The service began, and it was a real study in middle-class fundamentalism. Sally decided she would be an objective observer and take mental notes.

The content of the songs was worth noting: in every case, the lyrics spoke of love, worship, adoration, and reverence for God and for Jesus Christ, and it was readily apparent, as expected, that the people believed and practiced with great conviction the sentiments expressed in the songs.

As the service progressed through the songs and then a time of sharing inspirational personal anecdotes, Sally found it easy to get caught up in the very phenomenon she was observing. She was enjoying it. These people were happy, and even though the form and process of worship seemed a little odd and foreign to an outsider, Sally knew and reminded herself that next to her own yoga techniques and trance channeling, this stuff was tame, normal, even downright bland.

The time came for prayer, and Pastor Busche opened the floor for prayer requests. An elderly man was having trouble with a pulled muscle and asked for prayer, as did a young lady concerned for her husband who "didn't know the Lord," a young father who needed a job, and a lady whose sister had had a child born prematurely.

Then the young lady who worked at the newspaper, Bernice Krueger, spoke up. "Let's remember to pray for Marshall and Kate while they're away. I guess things are getting pretty difficult, and they're encountering a lot of spiritual resistance."

"Right," said Pastor Hank, "we've all been following that. We'll be sure to pray about it."

And then the pastor led the congregation in prayer, glorifying and praising God, and then asking God to supply all the requests that the people had made.

"And we remember Marshall and Kate as well, involved in spiritual warfare . . ."

That topic caught Sally's interest. Spiritual warfare. Wow! If these people only knew what *she* was going through.

31

"'**B**ut he was pierced for our transgressions, he was crushed for our iniquities; the punishment that brought us peace was upon him, and by his wounds we are healed.'"

Bernice Krueger read the words in a soft voice from her Bible as Sally followed along in the Bible she'd brought from Sara Barker's. They were sharing a booth at Danny's Diner on Main Street, not far from the *Clarion*. They'd ordered their lunch, it was on the way, and now, over coffee, they were taking a second look at Hank's sermon text for the morning, some verses from Isaiah 53.

Bernice read the next verse. "'We all, like sheep, have gone astray, each of us has turned to his own way; and the Lord has laid on him the iniquity of us all.'"

"Sin and redemption," said Sally.

Bernice was impressed. "Right. So you know *something* about this."

"No, nothing really. It's a phrase I've heard in some circles, apparently a quick way to define the typical Christian view of things. We always hated the idea."

Bernice sipped from her coffee. "Who's 'we'?"

Sally brushed off the question. "Just some old friends."

"And what did you hate about it?"

Sally sipped from her coffee. It was an effective way to buy time to formulate an answer. "The notion of sin, I guess. It's hard enough for anyone to feel good about himself, and it seemed so negative and oppressive to teach that we're all miserable, no-good sinners. Christianity was the curse of mankind, enslaving us and holding us back from our true potential." She felt a need to qualify that. "Anyway, that's what we thought."

"Okay, so that's what you thought about the sin part of it." Bernice smiled, and tapped the passage from Isaiah 53 that still lay open under Sally's nose. "But did you catch the redemption part? God loves you, and He sent His Son to pay for that sin with His own death on the cross."

Now Sally remembered Aunt Barbara and Mrs. Gunderson telling her that. "So I've heard."

"But getting back to what the Bible says about sin, since when is that such a shock? Mankind has been proving for thousands of years the kind of stuff he's made of. Listen, man's problems aren't due to politics or economics or ecology or levels of consciousness; man's problems are due to his ethics—they're lousy."

Sally heard that. It sank in. That was putting it simply enough, and hadn't she demonstrated the truth of those words in her own life? "I guess I'll agree with you there. But let me just confirm something: I take it the Bible is the ethical standard by which we determine what's 'lousy'?"

Bernice gave an assertive nod. "*And* what's good, what's righteous."

Sally pondered that. "That being the case, I imagine this standard puts us all on the wrong side of the fence."

"I think you'll find that idea acceptable if you're honest with yourself. You've lived long enough to know what we as human beings are capable of."

Sally even chuckled. "Oh, yes indeed."

"And here's God's answer for it." Bernice pointed out the phrases and reviewed them. "'He carried our infirmities and our sorrows . . . he was pierced for our sins and crushed for our iniquities . . . the Lord has laid on Him all our sins.'"

"Why?"

Bernice thought for a moment. "Well, let's talk about justice. You do something wrong, you end up in prison, right?"

Sally definitely agreed. "Right."

"Now, in the ideal sense, all legal loopholes aside, there are only two ways out of there: change the rules so that what you did isn't wrong so you aren't guilty, or pay the penalty."

"I've tried changing the rules," Sally admitted.

"Well, in God's scheme of things, rules are rules, because if they weren't, they wouldn't be worth much, and right and wrong would be meaningless. So what's left? The penalty. That's where God's love comes in. He knew we could never pay the penalty ourselves, so He did it for us. He took the form of man, took all our sins upon Himself, and died on a Roman cross two thousand years ago."

Sally examined the passage again. "So tell me: did it work?"

Bernice leaned forward and said, "You be the judge. The Bible says that the penalty for sin is death, but after Jesus paid that penalty He rose from the dead on the third day, so *something* was different. He conquered sin, so He was able to conquer sin's penalty. Sure, it worked. It always works. Jesus satisfied divine justice on that Cross. He bore the punishment in full, and God never had to bend the rules. That's why we call Jesus our Savior. He shed His own blood in our place, and died, and then rose from the grave to prove He'd won over sin and could set us free." Now Bernice started getting excited. "And you know what thrills me about that? It means we're special to Him; He really does love us, and we . . . we *mean* something, we're here for a reason! And you know what else? No matter what our sins are, no matter where we are or what condition we're in, we can be forgiven, free and clear, a clean slate!"

The lunch came—two soups and two salads. Sally was thankful for the pause in the conversation. It gave her a chance to think and to wonder, Who gave this young lady the script anyway? How was it that she could say so many things that spoke directly to Sally's situation?

Well, Bernice did go to Pastor Hank Busche's church, and *he* had a way of hitting the nail on the head. His suggestion to read Psalm 119 was perfect, and his morning sermon on Isaiah 53 was just more of the same perfectly tailored message, exactly what she was ready to hear.

But there was still a snag in all this. Sally took a few bites of her salad while she considered her next question, and then she formed it as a comment. "I don't feel forgiven."

Bernice answered, "Have you ever asked God to forgive you?"

"I've never even believed in God, at least not in the traditional sense."

"Well, He's there."

"But how can I know that?"

Bernice looked at Sally and seemed to know her heart. She replied simply, "You know."

"So . . ." Sally stopped short, and ate some more salad. She couldn't ask the question she had in her mind. It would seem too silly, too childish, like a dumb question already answered. But still . . . she had to hear a direct answer, something she could carry away without any doubts. "Well, I hope you'll indulge the question . . ."

"Sure."

"It's easy to speak in comfortable, generalized, generic terms . . ."

"Be as specific as you want."

"Did . . ." She stopped again. Where was that emotion coming from? She pushed it down with another bite of salad. Now she felt all right. It seemed safe to ask. "Did Jesus die for *me*?"

Bernice did not answer lightly or flippantly. She looked Sally in the eye and gave her a firm, even reply. "Yes, He died for you."

"For me, for . . ." She had to remember her alias. "For Betty Smith? I mean, Bernice, you don't know me . . ."

"He died for Betty Smith just like he died for Bernice Krueger."

Well, she got her answer. "Okay."

That was the last item on that topic. Bernice could sense her lunch guest was getting uncomfortable, and didn't want to make things worse. Sally was afraid she'd opened up just a little too much to an innocent stranger, and dared not risk dragging this nice woman into her troubles.

Bernice resorted to purely social conversation. "So how long have you been on the road?"

Sally was even afraid of that question. "Oh . . . about a month or so, something like that."

"Where are you from originally?"

"Does it matter?"

After that, conversation was difficult, and both regretted it. Except for small talk and purely social conversation, the lunch was more important than any more words. The salads disappeared, the soup bowls went empty, the minutes slipped by.

"I enjoyed meeting you," said Bernice.

"I guess I'd better get back to Sara's," said Sally.

"But listen . . . why don't you come by the *Clarion* when you get the chance? We could have lunch again."

Sally's first impulse was to refuse, but finally she allowed herself to relax, trust just a little, and accept the invitation. "Well . . . sure, I'd like that."

Bernice smiled. "Come on. I'll drive you back to Sara's."

The old farm outside Bacon's Corner had been deserted for years, the barn empty and graying. Ever since the owner had died, no human was ever seen in this place, not a sound was heard, not a single light glowed—except for certain nights no one was supposed to know about.

On this night, the dull orange glow of candles appeared through the cracks in the clapboard siding and through the chinks in the weather-warped door of the massive old barn. Inside, human voices muttered, murmured, and rumbled through rhythmic chants and incantations.

There were about twenty people inside, all clothed in black robes except for one woman who wore white, standing around a large pentagram etched in the bare earth floor. In the center of the pentagram, two front legs cut from a goat lay crossed in an X, and a candle burned at each of the pentagram's five points.

At the head of the circle, the woman in white led the meeting, speaking in low, clear tones, a large silver cup in her outstretched hands. "As from the beginning, the powers will be brought forth through blood, and restitution by our hand will balance the scales."

"So be it," the others chanted.

"We call forth the powers and minions of darkness to witness this night our covenant with them."

"So be it!"

Demonic wings rustled in the rafters as dark, destructive spirits began to gather, looking down with gleaming yellow eyes and toothy grins, basking in all the adoration and attention.

In the peak of the roof, clinging to the rafters and overseeing it all, Destroyer could mouth the ceremony even as he listened to it.

"May their fury be kindled against our enemies, against all who oppose. May their favor be with us as we dedicate this offering."

"So be it!"

"May the woman be found."

"So be it."

"So be it," agreed the demons, exchanging glances.

"It will be," said Destroyer. "It will be."

"May she be driven from hiding, and crushed as powder," declared the woman.

"So be it," chanted the others.

The demons nodded and cackled in agreement, their wings quivering with excitement. More spirits arrived. The rafters, the hayloft, the gables of the roof were filling with them.

"Defeat and division to the Christians, ill health, ill will."

"So be it."

Destroyer spoke quickly to the gathering demons, pointing to this one and then that one, assigning hordes to every task as the spirits murmured their acceptance.

"May they grant a court decision in our favor! We give to them the heart and mind of Judge Emily Fletcher!"

"So be it."

Destroyer looked around their group and finally settled on a larger, hulking spirit roosting on a diagonal brace. He'd handled courtrooms before; he would be in charge of that.

"And now . . ." The woman drew the silver cup to her lips. "Through blood we seal the success of the powers, the death of Sally Beth Roe, and the defeat of the Christians!"

"So be it!"

The demons all leaned forward and craned their necks, wanting to see. They giggled, they slobbered, they gave each other happy pats and pokes. Destroyer became drunk with exhilaration.

The woman pulled back her hood and took a drink from the cup. When she withdrew the cup, the stain of fresh goat's blood remained on her lips.

Claire Johanson, high priestess of the coven, passed the cup to Jon, who drank and passed it on to the next person, and every witch, male and female, drank to seal the curses.

Then, in chorus, their arms shooting upward, the witches let out an eerie wail: "So be it!"

"Go!" said Destroyer with a clap of his wings and a point of his crooked finger.

The marauding spirits shot out of the barn, pouring from the roof like black smoke from a fire, like bats from a cavern. They dispersed in all directions, howling and cackling, full of lustful, destructive mischief.

On Monday morning, the day of the hearing in Westhaven, Pastor Mark Howard was thankful he'd arrived at the church earlier than everyone else. Hopefully he would be able to clean up the mess before any of the school kids saw it.

He'd already opened the school building and turned up the heat; so the facility was ready, and he still had about forty-five minutes before the parents started dropping off their children. He hurried down into the church basement, opened his office, and grabbed the telephone.

His voice was quiet and somber as he spoke, almost afraid of being heard. "Good morning, Marshall. This is Mark. Sorry to wake you up so early. Please come to the church right away. I'm going to be calling Ben, and I hope to have him here as well. Yes, right away. Thank you."

He opened the utility closet under the stairs and grabbed a mop and bucket. He was so upset he forgot he would need a garbage can as well. With his heart racing, he ran upstairs and out onto the front porch of the church.

The blood on the front door was dry. It would take some scrubbing to get it off.

Oh! I've got to get the garbage can! No, not yet. I'd better wait until Marshall and Ben get here. I hope they get here before the children do. O Lord Jesus, we pray for the covering and protection of Your shed blood over this place!

Come on, guys, hurry up! I can't leave these things here!

At Mark's feet, crossed like an X and staining the church steps red, were two hind legs from an animal, most likely a goat.

At nine o'clock that morning, representatives of the press, the ACFA, the National Coalition on Education, and even a few churches converged on Room 412 at the Federal Courthouse in Westhaven, the courtroom of the Honorable Emily R. Fletcher.

Wayne Corrigan and Tom Harris were already seated at the defendant's table; Gordon Jefferson and Wendell Ames, Lucy Brandon's attorneys, were seated and ready for combat, with Lucy seated between them. In the first row of the gallery, Dr. Mandanhi was waiting to testify.

KBZT Channel Seven News reporter Chad Davis was there, prowling about for any news tidbits or comments while Roberto Gutierrez set up the television camera.

John Ziegler was there as well, and Paula the photobug had already snapped some pictures—uninvited—of Tom and Corrigan.

The bailiff stood to her feet. "All rise."

They all rose.

"Court is now in session, the Honorable Emily R. Fletcher presiding."

The judge took her place behind the bench. "Thank you. Please be seated."

They sat. So far everything was going the same as last time, and just like last time, the judge perched her reading glasses on her nose and looked over the documents before her.

"The defendant has requested today's hearing to determine whether or not the child in this case, Amber Brandon, should be excused from any deposition or testimony. It is the court's understanding that counsel for the plaintiff strenuously opposes any deposition or testimony from the child, and so the court has been asked to rule on the question." She looked up and seemed just a little impatient with the whole matter. "Mr. Corrigan, please proceed."

Corrigan rose. "Thank you, Your Honor. Our request is simple enough, and not at all irregular. The complaint against my client includes charges of harassment, discrimination, and outrageous religious behavior. But may I remind the court that thus far, any testimony pertaining to these charges has not come from the plaintiff's key witness, Amber herself, but secondhand, through Amber's mother, Lucy Brandon, and from the plaintiff's expert witness, Dr. Mandanhi. We've made many requests to talk to Amber, to have our own psychologist visit with her so Dr. Mandanhi's opinions can be balanced with those of another expert witness. But counsel for the plaintiff has adamantly refused to cooperate, and we are concerned that my client's right to confront his accuser is being infringed. Also, with no opportunity to question Amber and hear her testimony for ourselves, we have no assurance that the indirect testimony coming through Mrs. Brandon and through Dr. Mandanhi is not in some way colored, tainted, or embellished.

"Counsel for the plaintiff has insisted that Amber is in too delicate a condition, at too fragile an age to go through a deposition or a court trial. But we can assure counsel that we would not in any way resort to harsh tactics.

"Also, the record is clear that Amber is a strong-willed child and has stated conflicting facts, even to her mother. In addition to that, Amber's mother has testified in deposition that there are other influences affecting Amber's life which she was exposed to outside the school. Only Amber herself can answer the many unanswered questions that arise in these areas.

"All we're asking is that we be allowed to hear the details from Amber herself, and that our own psychologist be allowed to examine Amber to verify or refute the findings of Dr. Mandanhi."

Corrigan took his seat, and the judge recognized Wendell Ames.

Ames wasn't quite as exciting to watch as the younger Jefferson, but he did exude a dignity of experience that was in itself persuasive. "Your Honor, this entire case is being brought to court because of severe damage done to an innocent child, the extent of which is clearly shown in the affidavitts and the reports of Dr. Mandanhi. As attorneys for the plaintiff, we wish to right a wrong, to redress a grievance, and to somehow undo the harm that has been done. It was never our intention, as responsible human beings, to only increase Amber's pain by putting her through the trial process, dredging up all her old wounds, and putting her hurts on public display.

"We have presented an additional opinion from Dr. Mandanhi, detailing for the court Amber's current emotional condition and establishing that it would not be in her best interests to be made to testify or give a deposition. If the court so requires, Dr. Mandanhi is here to testify in person as to Amber's fragile state of mind and emotions at this time."

Judge Fletcher looked at Mandanhi and then at Ames. "Would the doctor have additional statements to make not included in his written opinion?"

"I'm sure he could clarify for the court any items the court may need clarified."

The judge quickly perused Mandanhi's report. "I think it's clear enough. Any further oral testimony would most likely be cumulative."

"Very well."

"Anything else?"

"Yes. Even though there are strong arguments on either side, we would hope that common sense and decency will speak more loudly and persuasively than any argument, and that the court would spare this innocent child the pain and grief of reliving her hurts, of being challenged and doubted by the defense, of being put on display, as it were, in open court.

"We understand the legal process, of course. We understand that the defendant does have a right to confront his accuser. But we remind the court that we are dealing with a case of child abuse, a fact the defendants have already admitted."

"Objection," said Corrigan. "The defense has made no such admission."

Ames responded, "Your Honor, I was simply referring to what has already been established, that spanking does occur at the school, and that the school does teach pervasive and imposing doctrines . . ."

The judge was a little impatient. "The affidavitts are clear on what the school practices and teaches, Mr. Ames. If the defendants want to stand by their practices, this in no way constitutes an admission of guilt. The objection is sustained."

Ames regathered his thoughts and continued. "At any rate, Your Honor, we hold that Amber is a child of tender years who needs to be protected. That is, after all, the motivation behind this suit in the first place. Given that, we must plead that the court spare Amber any further pain and trauma by ruling that she need not be deposed and she need not testify, or go through any more grueling examination by still another psychologist."

Ames sat down.

The judge looked at Corrigan. "Anything else?"

Corrigan stood. "I suppose it might be effective to point out why I don't have anything else I can say. If, as the plaintiff argues, Amber Brandon is in such a pitiful state of mind and emotion that she simply must not be allowed to testify or participate in the trial, we are left with having to take counsel's word for it, with no way of knowing how true these claims are. Amber could actually be in this bad a condition, but we could never confirm that. The plaintiff might be conducting a clever, purposeful cover-up, but we could never know that either. Counselors for the plaintiff obviously think they know all they need to know about Amber and what she allegedly went through at the hands of the defendants, but the defendants and their counsel know virtually nothing apart from the filtered hearsay provided thus far. Without Amber we are being restricted, expected to present a persuasive defense, but forbidden to cut through to the real heart of the matter, to the real source of these complaints. I repeat again, we do not want to hurt Amber in any way or add to her trauma—if there be any trauma. We simply want to get to the facts so we can prepare to answer the charges. You have our brief as to the law which shows that Amber must be made available."

Corrigan sat down, and the judge looked at Ames and Jefferson. "Anything else?"

"No, Your Honor," said Ames.

"Court will recess, then, and reconvene at 2 this afternoon for my ruling."

"All rise," said the bailiff, and they all rose, and out went the judge.

Tom whispered to Corrigan, "How do you think we did?"

Corrigan wasn't very happy. "I have no idea. I think that's the weakest argument I've ever presented for anything." He fretted, fumed, replayed the hearing in his mind. "I should have stressed the law more; it's supposed to be on our side . . . Did you see her reaction to Mandanhi's affidavitt? She took it as gospel!"

"How about some lunch?" Tom asked.

Corrigan followed him out of the courtroom, still muttering to himself.

32

The spirits were aloft and rampant, goaded on by goat's blood and blasphemy, by rage and conspiracy, by Destroyer's reckless indignation and thirst for immediate victory over the subtle Captain of the Host and his prize, the elusive Sally Beth Roe.

Infested by lying demons, the Warings (Ed and Judy) and the Jessups (Andrea and Wes) were meeting for lunch at the Warings' home to prayerfully discuss the latest news hot off the prayer chain: June Walroth had just heard that Tom regularly beat his daughter Ruth, and always dressed her in long sleeves so no one would notice; someone else—they didn't know who, but the person had to be reliable—was concerned because Pastor Mark and Cathy were having some marital problems, most likely because Mark had been unfaithful years ago; the Christian school was actually in terrible debt because Tom and Mrs. Fields were pilfering some of the money.

Andrea was aghast. "Are you sure about that? I can't believe Mrs. Fields would do such a thing."

"Well," said Judy, "do you know how little money she makes teaching at that school? It would be a real temptation, let's face it."

"But who told you about this?"

Ed was reluctant to reveal their source. "It's . . . Well, let me just say that it's someone close to the church board, someone I've really come to respect, all right? But this is all in strict confidence!"

Wes was immediately angry. "So why hasn't the board told the rest of the church?"

"The party I spoke to is concerned about the same thing. She's in a real fix: she doesn't want to violate the confidence of the board, but at the same time she's hurt because so much of this is being kept secret."

Judy piped in, "I think we need to have a congregational meeting, that's what I think!"

Andrea concurred. "And get this stuff out in the open once and for all!"

Ed nodded. "Well, I've talked to Ted and June Walroth, and they're ready for one."

Wes just shook his head and even laughed to vent his nerves. "This is all going to come out in that trial, you know. Somehow those ACFA guys are going to dig this up, and they're going to sue the ever-loving buns off our church!"

Gossip, Slander, and Spite thought that was funny, and shrieked with laughter. What wouldn't these people believe?

At the school, Mrs. Fields and Mark had just broken up their third fight, and now eight kids—six who were fighting and two who were urging them on—were staying inside for noon recess, cleaning the blackboards, dusting the furniture, and sweeping the floor. It had been a trying day.

Mrs. Fields plopped into her chair and heaved a deep sigh. "Pastor, what's happening around here?"

Mark wanted to say they were under spiritual attack, but he steered clear of that out of concern for Mrs. Fields. She was a sensitive woman, and it would have been distressing for her to learn what he'd found on the front steps that morning.

He finally just asked her to pray with him, and that is how they spent their noon hour—in between peacekeeping missions on the playfield.

Dreaming, dreaming . . . little baby girl . . . Rachel . . . pink and fat, laughing . . .

"Come on, sweetie, time for your bath."

Water running in the tub, just the right temperature.

Let her play in the running water. "See that? Isn't that fun? Time to get all clean."

Jonas. He's calling.

Not now. I'm giving Rachel a bath!

Pulling, pulling, yanking me from my body . . . No, not now . . .

Sudden blackness, floating, no feeling, no sounds, no pain, nothing but sweet love, bliss, oneness . . . A long, long tunnel, a bright light at the end, getting closer, closer, almost there, I've got to get back! What's happening to Rachel?

SLAP! A hand across her face!

"Come on, lady, snap out of it! Get up!"

Water everywhere, all over the floor. I'm sitting in it, I'm soaked. Who's this guy?

"Can you hear me? Get up!"

He's a cop! What's wrong?

"Aw, she's stoned, man, bombed to oblivion!"

Where's Rachel? "Where's my baby?"

The tub, filled to the brim, running over, water everywhere, cops, medics, the landlady, everything a blur.

A piercing, stabbing horror slowly rising. The unthinkable invading her mind. "Oh no! I've killed my baby!"

"Ma'am, I need to advise you of your rights. You have the right to remain silent . . ."

Up off the floor, held in strong arms, her hands bound behind her. "Where's my baby?"

"Get her out of here."

"Where's my baby?"

"Your baby is dead, Sally. Come on."

The quickest image, only appearing for a second: a tiny bundle on the kitchen table, medics all around, covered in a white cloth . . . one little pink hand showing.

"Oh no! Rachel! I've killed my baby! Jonas!"

Pain from handcuffs, her arms twisting, soaking wet, shoved out the door.

"Rachel!!"

"Come on, Sally, let's go!"

AAWW! Sally jolted awake in the darkened bedroom, almost falling off the bed. Her four tormenting companions were all over her.

Forever, forever, said Despair, *you will be condemned forever. You are what you are, you can never change it.*

Insanity piped in with renewed vigor, *It's all in your poor twist-ed mind, you know. You're a very sick lady!*

Death always follows you, said Death. *Everything you touch, everything you love, will only die.*

And they'll get you for this! said Fear. *All the spirits you've ever crossed are waiting to get you!*

Sally rolled over and buried her face in the pillow. "O God, help me!"

He can't help you . . . you've offended Him, He'll never hear you . . . we have you now . . .

Sally looked toward the window. The daylight was still visible around the edges of the drawn curtain. She checked the clock beside the bed. Four P.M. She flopped onto her back and tried to calm down, steady her heart, slow her breathing.

She told herself, *Easy now, girl, it was all a dream, a nightmare. Calm down.*

Her heart was still pounding and her face was slick with sweat. *Some nap this turned out to be; I feel worse.*

She tried to sort it all out. Yes, the dream was like a videotape; that's the way it happened. She hadn't had that clear a memory of it in years. *O God, what did I do, what did I do? How could I let this happen to me, to my daughter?*

Jonas, my wonderful counselor and friend, my infinitely wise spirit-guide!

The thought of that spirit made her sick.

I trusted him! I gave him my life, my thoughts, my spirit, my mind, and now . . . now I find out how evil he was. Or is.

Evil. Well, there's another absolute. Jonas is one incredibly evil spirit, and no one's going to convince me otherwise.

What had she just been reading? She rolled slowly off the bed, planted her feet on the floor, and went to the window. She pulled back the curtain and had to squint in the daylight that flooded the room. There, on the table under the window, was Sara's Bible, still opened to the Gospel of Mark. She'd just started reading it before she got sleepy and lay down. There was something it had said, and at the time she only gave it a passing thought.

She sat at the table and looked that passage over again. Here it was, in chapter 1: "Just then a man in their synagogue who was possessed by an evil spirit cried out, 'What do you want with us, Jesus of Nazareth? Have you come to destroy us? I know who you are—the Holy One of God!'

"'Be quiet!' said Jesus sternly. 'Come out of him!' The evil spir-it shook the man violently and came out of him with a shriek. The people were all so amazed that they asked each other, 'What is this?

A new teaching—and with authority! He even gives orders to evil spirits and they obey him.' . . .

"That evening after sunset the people brought to Jesus all the sick and demon-possessed. The whole town gathered at the door, and Jesus healed many who had various diseases. He also drove out many demons, but he would not let the demons speak because they knew who he was."

Demons. They're demons. Sally believed it. She'd never given this Bible much credence since her Sunday school days, but right now, sitting in that room, having awakened from as clear a lesson as she could ask for, she believed what this Book said about these spirit entities. The whole thing was a sham, a deception, a spiritual con game. These things were as evil as evil could be.

Where's that notebook? I've got to write to Tom.

Tom, you know this already, and that's why you're in all this trouble, but let me assure you as one who has been on the other side, you are correct. Amber Brandon has contacted a spirit-guide, and now that thing is controlling her life, her thoughts, her behavior. I had Jonas, now Amber has Amethyst, and if I haven't said it clearly enough before, let me say it clearly now, because now I know it clearly: these spirits are evil; they are out to destroy us. Just look at what Jonas did to me. I don't blame him entirely; I asked him into my life, I gave him my mind and body. But I found out too late what his real agenda was.

And what about Amber? I suppose for her it was all fun and games to begin with. Now I'm almost sure she's into something she would rather be out of, but can't escape it. To be honest, I'm not sure that I have escaped it.

But if the Gospel of Mark is correct, and this Jesus of yours can order these spirits around and rescue people from their power, then I hope you have enough faith in your Savior to get His help.

And, Tom, while you're at it, please put in a good word for me.

Destroyer's spirits were laughing themselves silly as they fluttered out of the courthouse.

The judge rose, everyone in the courtroom rose, and then she went out, leaving the ACFA attorneys feeling pretty cocky while Wayne and Tom could only stand there with their mouths open.

Corrigan was so upset he could hardly keep his voice down as he muttered to Tom, "We are absolutely going to appeal this one. I've never seen a more obvious, ludicrous breach of justice or denial of due process in my career!"

Tom didn't know whether to have hope, or put up a fight, or give it up, or go home and die, or what. "Okay. If you think that will work."

"I don't know if it will work or not, the way these courts are getting so stacked, but we might have better luck with a different judge. Ultimately, it has no bearing on the decision to appeal. I'd be as remiss as the judge if I didn't appeal her decision. Come on, let's get out of here."

Just outside the courtroom, Wendell Ames was basking in the floodlights and catering to the microphones as he delivered a prepared statement to the press. "We are certainly gratified that a person of the stature of Judge Fletcher acknowledges that children of tender years still need protection from admitted child abusers, even in a court of law . . ."

"That's all," said Corrigan. With a sudden, uncharacteristic anger, he forced his way right into the circle of reporters. "Gentlemen and ladies, I will have a statement for you as soon as Mr. Ames has completed his statement."

He got their attention right away. They were hungry. They flooded him with questions, many of them quite loaded.

He brushed all the questions aside and said what he wanted to say. "First of all, to correct Mr. Ames, this case centers on constitutionally guaranteed freedom of religion and not on child abuse. No admissions of any kind have been made, and try to get that right when you run your stories. If spanking is child abuse, then let's put half the country in jail right now!

"Secondly, seeing as the attorneys for the plaintiff continually insist on trying this case in the press, let me just throw this into the mill for your consideration: a) Everything we've heard in this case has been filtered through Amber's mother and the attorney-appointed child psychologist, Dr. Mandanhi, and we insist we have the right to confront our accuser, who is Amber, and just get to the truth. b) We do not intend to be harsh toward Amber or abuse her in any way. We will accept reasonable restrictions, and we will work with the judge and with the plaintiff's attorneys accordingly.

"Now, as to this ruling of Judge Fletcher: it is clearly erroneous and absolutely contrary to the law, and we have no choice but to appeal to the Court of Appeals without delay. Now try not to edit that too much."

With that, and with more questions still being hollered at them, Corrigan and Tom hurried down the hall to the elevators.

Back in Bacon's Corner, little Amber Brandon was giddy and laughing when she got off the school bus, and had been so disruptive on the bus that the driver was only minutes from writing her a discipline slip to give to her mother. But Amber's stop came first, and so the driver was satisfied with just getting Amber and her playmates off the bus.

Her playmates were used to seeing Amber acting like a pony, and some had even played the pretend game with her. But today Amethyst was not a fun pony to play with. She pushed her friends, she teased them, she stole their books and threw them about, she jumped, pranced, somersaulted, and mocked them.

All Amber's friends went home angry at her, vowing never to play with her again.

But Amethyst just kept laughing and prancing, and she didn't care a bit.

It was definitely time to get all the team together. That evening, Mark and Cathy opened up the church and the core group gathered—the Howards, Ben and Bev Cole, Marshall and Kate Hogan, Tom Harris, and Wayne Corrigan—along with the elders, Don Heely, Vic Savan, Jack and Doug Parmenter, and their wives. Push had come to shove. God was moving in their hearts and they could all feel the threat from outside; it was time to do some serious business with the Lord.

They sat in a close circle on the pews and some pulled-up chairs at the front of the sanctuary, ready to compare notes, talk it out, pray it through.

"I figured we should meet here tonight," said Mark. "This seems to be the center of Satan's attention right now, the center of his attacks. We need to pray a hedge around this place."

"Let's meet the enemy!" said Ben.

"It's high time we did!" said Jack.

Mark smiled, encouraged. "I want to tell you, the battle is getting thick out there!"

"So how did your deposition go last week?" Doug Parmenter asked.

Mark sighed; Corrigan rolled his eyes a bit. Mark answered,

"Ames and Jefferson are laying a trap of some kind, that's obvious. They were just so kind and yet . . ."

Corrigan completed the thought. "They were trying to milk Mark for anything they could find to use against him, to set him up for a fall." He looked at Mark. "I think you did all right, though, pastor. You came out squeaky clean, and they didn't like that."

"Well, praise the Lord for that. 'He who walks in integrity walks securely.'"

"Right on," said Bev.

Mark turned to Corrigan again. "Wayne, since we're on the subject, why' don't you tell all of us what's next in the legal process?"

Corrigan looked a little tired and depressed. "Well, of course, Tom and Mrs. Fields are scheduled for depositions in the next few weeks. But in the meantime, we're going to appeal today's ruling to the Court of Appeals, and then we'll have to wait and see. We may not win there either, but at least it will buy us a little more time. Mind you, this is just a minor detail in the whole lawsuit, only one little skirmish in a long and costly war." He looked at Marshall. "We'll have to hope that something else breaks in this case. It just feels like we're so close!"

"How about that curriculum?" asked Kate. "I'm convinced now that the school system isn't going to let us see it without some real legal pressure. They're stalling."

Corrigan nodded. "I wouldn't be surprised if they were hoping they can outlast the court system and hide that curriculum until we're already in court. Well, with today's ruling and the appeal process starting, that's going to be hard to do. I'll definitely issue a subpoena for that curriculum tomorrow."

"As far as something else breaking," said Marshall, "we just might have it, or a part of it, or an inkling of how we might track down a corner of a part of it. I'm talking about the curse put on the church this morning."

Bob Heely asked, "Did you go to the police about that?"

Ben replied, "Are you kidding? I'm about 90 percent sure that Mulligan's in on this thing! Those goat legs came from Sally Roe's goat, and you know how Mulligan's been covering up that attempt to murder her. He's got to be a part of this curse too, or at least helping whoever it was that did it."

Jack Parmenter had to ask, "Are you really sure about that?"

Marshall stepped in. "Not yet. But the point I'm making is that now we have concrete evidence that there's some witchcraft or Satanism in the area, some organized, heavier form of occultism like a coven, a secret society, whatever. And that means there are people—and I mean normal-looking, everyday people you'd never suspect—that belong to this group. And in a town this size, they can pull a lot of weight and intimidate a lot of people. Mulligan and Parnell the coroner might be under the control of these people, or they might belong to the group themselves.

"But don't miss this point: Whoever these people are, they've clearly spelled out that this church and Sally Roe have something in common: we are their enemies, and they mean to do us harm. They killed Sally's goat and drained its blood, probably for use in their ceremonies. Now that's a contact point for them, something that belonged to the person they want to curse. They took off the legs and left the front ones here at the church. That includes us in the curse they've leveled at Sally Roe. I'm guessing that the hind legs are still with the witches somewhere as a contact point at their end."

"Why the legs?" asked Corrigan.

Marshall guessed, "Well, you can't run far without them, and right now Sally Roe is running, I'm sure of that."

Tom's wheels were turning rapidly. "So there are your moles again, Marshall! They've tried to put Sally Roe and us under the same curse; so even though we can't see it yet, there has to be a connection: Sally Roe has something to do with our situation, with this case, and they know it."

"You've got it."

Corrigan clenched his fists and looked toward Heaven with mock drama. "Oh, if only we could prove all this! If only we knew who these weird people are!"

"I don't know about you, but I have some suspects," said Marshall. "We would do well to take some careful second looks at Sergeant Mulligan and Joey Parnell. They've been close to this whole Sally Roe thing, and we know Parnell is scared spitless right now."

Ben was more blunt. "Parnell's in it, no doubt."

"And I'll even throw in Irene Bledsoe, the CPD lady, as a suspect. She's working with the whole Brandon/ACFA camp, and she's being anything but objective."

"Oh, man, I hope not!" said Tom.

"How're the kids?"

"I saw them on Friday. They're hanging in there. The foster home sounds pretty rough, but at least they're not in Bledsoe's daily care. A witch taking care of my kids, that's all I need!"

"And there might be still another suspect," said Mark. They turned to hear who, but he fell silent and thoughtful, exchanging a look with Cathy. "How do we know that one of these witches, or Satanists, or whatever they are, hasn't come right into this church?

We've been having no end of trouble, and I've never seen so much division as long as I've pastored here."

Cathy added, "I feel that we do have some kind of poison working directly among us, no question."

"It does happen," said Marshall. "They do infiltrate churches; they know all the Christian lingo, they know the Bible, they make it a serious business to pass for Christians and stir things up from the inside."

That stopped them all cold. Suddenly they found themselves looking at each other like all the suspects in a "whodunit." It was a downright creepy feeling.

Jack asked Mark and Cathy, "Any idea who?"

Mark shook his head. Cathy answered, "No . . . but listen: we have one. We have a demonic mole in this church. I just feel that from the Lord."

Marshall nodded. "That's a distinct possibility."

They pondered that for only a moment, and then, without a further word, Mark slid from his chair and sank to his knees right there. The others did the same. It was spontaneous. They knew what they had to do.

"O Lord God, have mercy," Mark prayed. "Where we have sinned, forgive us. Grant us wisdom to know what we're doing wrong, and repentance from that wrong. Have mercy on us, Lord God, and restore us."

His prayer continued, and the others prayed right along with him. Tears started to flow, unbridled weeping before the Lord.

Ben prayed, "Lord, help us to sort this whole thing out. Protect us from our enemies, and give us a victory for what's right."

"We pray for all the children," said Cathy. "This is their battle too, maybe even more than ours. Satan wants our kids, and we just can't let him have them."

Mark declared, "We just pray now for a hedge of angelic warriors to surround this place and guard it. Surround Your people, Lord, and protect us all from any curses leveled against us. We plead the shed blood of Jesus over ourselves, our ministry, our children, the school . . ."

"Protect Ruth and Josiah," prayed Tom. "O Lord, please protect my kids."

"Bring an answer, Lord," said Marshall. "We have enough hunches and theories to fill a warehouse, but we need an answer, something solid, something positive, and we need it fast. Please break through the walls the enemy has put up; break through, Lord God, and bring us an answer."

"And, Lord," said Jack, "if there is an invader in our church, a demonic mole, we just put chains on that person right now, we bind the demons associated with him or her, and we ask, Lord, that this person be exposed."

Outside the church, Nathan and Armoth set up the hedge, a regiment of the best warriors available for the job, all standing shoulder to shoulder around the church property, swords ready, alert, ready for a fight.

Tal was pleased with this little bit of progress. "That should hold things together for a while. Now to root out that mole!"

"It looks like we'll be ready," said Nathan, regarding the prayers from the people inside the church.

"Of course," said Tal. "And it was nice of Destroyer to get so reckless. He's exposed the breach we needed!"

33

It was Tuesday morning and the *Ashton Clarion* was out on the stands, in the grocery stores, and on the front porches all over town. That used to mean it would be a little calmer around the *Clarion* office; Cheryl the cub reporter could relax and catch up on advertising clients, Tom the paste-up man could go fishing or work at home in his yard, and George the typesetter could sleep in.

Well, this Tuesday things were a little different. The *Clarion*'s tough, whip-cracking editor was gone on an assignment—he never was clear about its exact nature—but that didn't mean there would be any vacation. Actually, because Marshall was such a hard worker, it meant more work than before, and Bernice Krueger, now filling Marshall's shoes, could be just as tough, demanding, and efficient as her boss.

So, Tuesday was rolling along at a brisk pace, everyone was there, hard at work, and Bernice never seemed to be in one room or chair for any more than two minutes at one time. With papers, galleys, or a cup of coffee in her hand, she was constantly running to the front to check a traffic revision story Cheryl was trying to get out of the county road crew, then charging to the back with more copy for George to typeset, then running into Marshall's glass-enclosed office to answer phone calls, then running up to the front desk to wait on a customer because Cheryl was busy taking an ad over the phone.

I am going to visit with Betty Smith, Bernice kept telling her-

self. *So help me, when my lunch comes, or before that, or during
break, or sometime, I'm going to sit down and visit with her; she
must think I'm so rude, inviting her here just to ignore her!*

But so far "Betty Smith" was not feeling slighted or snubbed.
She was sitting in the teletype room, watching the news stories
come clattering in over the news wire. For the last half-hour it had
been interesting—for the last few minutes it had been riveting. She
now held a particular news story in her hand, and she was devouring the news.

"WESTHAVEN—Federal District Judge Emily R. Fletcher
today ruled that a ten-year-old child, key witness in the much publi-
cized Good Shepherd Academy child abuse case, would not be
required to testify or be examined by defense psychologists, agree-
ing with the plaintiff's attorneys that such further questioning and
examining of the child could prove harmful.

"Citing expert evaluations offered by psychologist Dr. Alan
Mandanhi, Judge Fletcher concluded that the mental state of the
child is in such a tender and vulnerable state because of the alleged
abuses that any further recounting of them would do even greater
damage.

"'We are here to speak for the children,' she said, 'and protect
them from abuse. We cannot justify even further abuse in the cause
of preventing it.'"

Several daily newspapers from around the country lay ready on
the table for Bernice's perusal when she got the chance. Sally
reached for the one on the top of the stack, a large newspaper from
the West Coast. She found nothing about the case on the front
page, but the second page did carry a story, along with a nonflatter-
ing courtroom photograph of Tom Harris and his attorney. The
description under the photograph identified them as "alleged child
abuser Tom Harris and attorney Wayne Corrigan."

It was all bad news for the Good Shepherd Academy.

She found an editorial in the second newspaper. The ACFA
could not have written it better.

"This will be a precedent-setting case, interpreting the Federal
Day-care and Private Primary School Assistance Act, and defining
whether the state may breach the wall of separation in order to protect innocent children from harm done in the name of religious freedom.

"Freedom of religion is part of our heritage, but freedom of
religion does not mean freedom to abuse. It is our hope that this
case will establish once and for all a binding legal and social man-
date that religious practice, though free, must never violate the laws
of the state, but be subject to the state for the good of all."

It sounded so virtuous, so American, so right. But the writer had never met Amber Brandon. None of the journalists across the country had ever looked into those demon eyes and heard that mocking, accusing voice. They'd never been a victim of the wrath and ruination Sally's former associates could dish out. Instead, as if on cue, they were writing, reporting, selecting, and interpreting the same ideas and opinions, as if the same instructor taught them all.

I can't stay here, Sally thought. *I have to move on. I have to finish.*

"Hey, Betty!" It was Bernice, standing in the doorway looking a bit frazzled. "I'm sorry it's such a madhouse around here, but I think I'm caught up for the time being. Are you keeping yourself occupied?"

Sally set the newspaper down. "Oh, I was reading the newspaper and the items coming in over the wire. It's been interesting."

Bernice could tell she was bothered about something. "How are you doing?"

Sally evaded the question. "I think there's a bus leaving in an hour. I need to be on it."

"Moving on so soon?"

"Could I have . . . Would it be okay if I had your address and telephone number? I'd like to be able to contact you later on."

"Sure thing." Bernice wrote it down on a slip of paper.

"Oh, and the *Clarion*'s address too?"

Bernice wrote that down as well, and handed it to her. Then she looked for a moment at the trouble in Sally's eyes. "Is there anything else I can do?"

Sally thought for a moment with a timid smile on her face. "Well . . . you could pray for me. You never know, it might work."

Cheryl called from the front, "Bernice, it's Jake's Auto Repair on the phone . . ."

"I'll call them back."

"He's leaving in ten minutes. He needs to talk to you now."

Bernice was obviously frustrated, and looked at Sally apologetically. "Listen, after this call we'll just get out of here. I'll take you to lunch, all right?"

Sally smiled. That was all. "Um . . . is there a Post Office around here?"

"Sure, just two blocks up the street on the right-hand side. It's on the way to the bus station. I can drop you by there."

"Great."

"Give me a second, okay?"

Bernice hurried into Marshall's office and took the call from Jake's Auto Repair. Jake could talk and talk about the same thing over and over as if he had nothing else to do with his time and no one else did either. "Okay, sure, we'll change the ad in Saturday's issue, all right?" He went back to the beginning and started the conversation all over again, and Bernice mouthed the words, "No, listen, you already told me that. We'll take care of it for Friday." He started squawking. "Well, that issue's already out, it's history, we can't change that now." She pounded the desk with her fist. This guy was impossible! "All right, listen, Jake, you know our deadlines just like everybody else; don't give me that! You'll get the change on Friday. Yes, that's a guarantee. Hey, didn't you tell Cheryl you had to leave in ten minutes? You're late. Good-bye."

She hung up and bolted from the office, grabbing her coat. "Okay, Betty, let's get out of here! Betty?"

She went into the teletype room. Betty was gone. She stepped into the hall. "Cheryl?"

"Yo!"

"Where's Betty?"

"She left."

That stung. Bernice's first question to herself was, *What did I do? Oh brother, it's what I didn't do! That poor gal. I don't blame her. I shouldn't have invited her into this madhouse!*

She dashed out to the street, but Betty Smith was nowhere in sight. Bernice's initial thought was to run after her, or get the car and try to find her, but then that thought melted away as a more practical one took its place: *This is probably the way she wants it. It's just the way she is, poor thing. Oh well. Maybe she'll write or call sometime.*

Maybe. Bernice felt terrible.

She went back inside.

Tom came out from the back room. "Say, what about that ad for Jake? Cheryl says you talked to him."

"We're rewording it. Cheryl has the new copy, so tell George to set it right away."

"All right. But what about that aluminum can drive? Are you sure you want that on page 3?"

Bernice kept moving down the hall, her mind occupied. "Change Jake's ad first, and then I'll take a look at page 3."

"Well, I need to know—"

"Just give me a second, will you?"

Tom turned on his heels and headed toward the back again. Bernice ducked into the teletype room knowing she owed Tom an apology.

She plopped into the chair Betty Smith had sat in, and took just a moment to pray. *Lord, I could have done better. I could have given her my time. I should have done more to tell her about You . . . Doggone! What a lousy way for this to end!*

Her eye caught the wire copy lying on the table, an item from Westhaven . . .

Westhaven? She snatched up the wire copy and scanned it. Yes. It was the latest news on the Good Shepherd Academy case in Bacon's Corner!

The warrior Triskal stood in the teletype room with her, just watching. He had his orders, and now the time was right. He gently touched her eyes.

Okay, Bernice. Time for you to see.

Bernice saw the newspaper opened to the editorial page. She saw the editorial. Good Shepherd Academy. Bacon's Corner.

Betty had been reading about that case! Is this why she seemed so troubled, so secretive? A lone woman, traveling, elusive . . .

It was like a stab through the heart. Hadn't Marshall told her about some woman they were trying to find?

She bolted from the room and dashed into Marshall's office.

Bev Cole turned off her vacuum cleaner and answered the phone. "Hello?"

Bernice was frantic. "Is this the Cole residence?"

"Yes, it is."

"Is Marshall Hogan there? This is his assistant at the *Ashton Clarion*, Bernice Krueger."

"Oh, he's out right now. I can have him call you."

"Well, who am I talking to?"

"This is Bev Cole."

"Do you know anything about the Good Shepherd Academy case?"

"Oh boy, do I!"

"What about that woman that's missing? Do you know anything about that?"

"Oh, you mean Sally Roe?"

Bernice recognized the name. "Yes! That's the one! Do you know what she looks like?"

Bev stumbled a bit on that one. "Well . . . we've never met her in person. All we have is a bunch of police and newspaper photos, and they aren't very good . . ."

"Does she have long, black hair?"

"No, I think her hair's red."

"What about her age?"

"I think she's about thirty-six now."

"Can you send me those pictures?"

"You want me to mail them to you?"

"Can you fax them? I need them right *now*."

Bev was getting flustered. "Well, the only fax machine is down at Judy's Secretarial, and Ben's gone with the car."

Bernice gave Bev the *Clarion*'s fax number. "Get them to me right away, as soon as you can, all right? Send me everything you have on her. And have Marshall call me."

"Hey, what's happening over there?"

"I've got to go. Please get that stuff to me!"

"Okay, you've got it."

Bernice hung up and then ran into the front office. "Cheryl, get your keys! We've got to find Betty!"

Cheryl half-rose from her desk, still wondering what was going on. "What . . ."

Bernice grabbed her purse and dug for her own keys. "You go down to the bus station and see if she's there. I'll check at the Post Office. If you find her, stall her and call my pager."

Cheryl got up and grabbed her coat. She had no idea what this was all about, but Bernice was so frantic, it had to be important.

Lucy Brandon unlocked her front door and stood back to make sure Amber went inside. "Go ahead, Amber." No response. "Amethyst, go inside, and quietly."

Amethyst complied, moving rather stiffly, a pout on her face. She went to the stairway in the front entry and sat down on the first step, her chin in her hands. Then she glared at Amber's mother as Lucy closed the door and hung up her coat.

"How dare you bring me home!" she said finally in a low, seething voice.

Lucy was angry enough by now to directly face this creature. "I had to, and you know it! Miss Brewer refused to have you in the class anymore."

Amethyst bared Amber's teeth in an animal-like snarl. "She knows not what she wants! First I was invited, and now I am rejected! Miss Brewer is a turncoat and a fool!"

Lucy bent low over Amethyst and spoke directly to her. "And you are a filthy, destructive, disrespectful little imp!"

Amethyst snarled at her.

Lucy slapped her soundly across the face. "Don't you snarl at me, you little monster!"

But Amethyst began to laugh a fiendish laugh. "Why are you slapping your *daughter?*"

Lucy wilted a little. She didn't know what to do. "I want you to get out of my daughter. I want you to leave her alone!"

Amethyst smiled haughtily. "Your daughter is mine. She invited me in, and now I have her. She is mine." Then she pointed her finger right in Lucy's face. "And you are mine as well! You will do as I say!"

Lucy felt a terrible rage and even raised her hand, but had to stop.

Amethyst taunted her. "Go ahead. Slap her again."

"No! You won't do this to us!" She called, "Amber! Amber, wake up! Amber, answer me!"

"She can't hear you."

A formula, a tradition from Lucy's past, came to her mind. "In the name of Jesus Christ, I command you to come out of her!"

Amethyst raised her eyebrows in mock horror. "Oh, now you're throwing that name around! Ha! What is He to you?"

Lucy didn't know why she grabbed Amber's body. It was an unthinking, desperate act. She was trying to find her daughter in that little body somewhere. "Amber!"

SMACK! Lucy stumbled backward, her hand to her face, stunned. Like a wild animal escaping from a cage, Amethyst bolted from the hallway. Blood trickled from Lucy's nose; she dug in her pocket for a handkerchief as she ran around the corner into the dining room, bumped against the table, recovered, went through the kitchen doorway. She could hear silverware rattling to her right.

Amethyst had opened the cutlery drawer. Amber was holding a knife to her own throat. "Stop or I'll—"

But this was Amber's mother, wild with rage and maternal instinct. Lucy clamped onto the arm holding that knife and jerked it away with such force that Amber's entire body came up from the floor as Amethyst screamed. Lucy slammed into the counter behind her, bruising her spine. The hand would not release the knife.

The drawer flew open; butcher knives, steak knives, utensils all shot across the kitchen and clattered against the opposite cupboard doors.

Amethyst snarled, cursed, spit in Lucy's face. Her strength was incredible.

Lucy worked the knife loose. It fell away, hung in midair, spun, came at Lucy point-first.

"Aaww, Mommy!" came Amber's voice.

Lucy spun away as the knife went past her and dug into the dining room carpet. She fell to the floor with Amber still in her arms.

Amber screamed a long, anguished scream of terror. "Mommy
. . . Mommy!"

Lucy held her tightly. The blood was still dripping from Lucy's
nose. She wiped it away with her hand.

"Mommy . . ."

"I love you, Amber." Lucy wept in pain and fear. "I'm right
here, honey. I have you."

"Mommy, why do I do bad things?"

"It's not you, sweetheart. It's not you."

"I don't know why I'm bad!"

Lucy held her tightly. For now, she had her daughter back.
"Shhh. It wasn't you. It wasn't you."

Bernice and Cheryl returned to the office two hours later with
nothing to show for their frenzied efforts. Bernice had checked
with the Post Office, but the clerk on duty knew nothing of any
strange woman coming through; another clerk may have seen her,
but was now gone for lunch. Cheryl searched the bus station and
even waited for the mysterious Betty Smith to appear, but there was
no sign of her. There was, however, an eastbound bus that left only
moments before Cheryl got there. Both ladies had searched up and
down the streets between the *Clarion* and the bus depot, but Betty
Smith/Sally Roe was gone.

As soon as Bernice came in the door, Tom and George were full
of questions.

Bernice talked as she hung up her coat. "Paste Jake's ad on
page 4 and shove over the Insurance box; just yank those personals
and put them alongside the classifieds this time. Go to twelve point
instead of sixteen for that notice, and change 'howl' to 'bark,' we'll
get a pun out of it."

"Yeah," said George, "I thought of that."

They were content for now. Bernice checked the fax machine,
nestled against the wall in the front office, next to the photocopier.
They'd received a transmission—the long ream of paper poured out
of the machine and lapped upon itself several times on the floor. She
carefully tore it off and then found the first page.

Cheryl was there to see it too. There, looking vacantly over her
ID number in a police photo, was Betty Smith, alias Sally Beth Roe.

"I'd better call Marshall," Bernice said in a weak voice. "He's
going to love me for this."

Cheryl asked, "What about Sara Barker? Sally Roe stayed in
her boarding house. Maybe she knows something about Sally's
plans."

"Call her."

Bernice contacted the Cole residence in Bacon's Corner. Ben Cole was there this time.

"Did you get that fax?" he asked.

"Yes, Ben, thank you very much, and thank Bev too. I need to talk to Marshall."

"Well, he's still out, hunting for information."

"Well, I have some for him. Have him call me, will you? I'll either be at the *Clarion* office or at home."

At the elementary school, Mr. Woodard was all smiles and pleasant as he handed the *Finding the Real Me* curriculum across the office counter to Kate Hogan. "There. Actually, a subpoena wasn't necessary. I know we would have found it sooner or later."

"Well, it never hurts to jog somebody's memory a little," said Kate. "Thanks a lot."

She hurried to her car, the thick binder under her arm. That she actually had possession of this document was almost beyond believing. Now the question was, would it answer any questions or confirm any hunches?

As soon as she got into her car, she flipped the curriculum open to the title page.

The publisher: Omega Center for Educational Studies, Fairwood, Massachusetts.

The title: *Finding the Real Me: Self-Esteem and Personal Fulfillment Studies for Fourth-Graders.*

The authors: Dee Danworth and Marian Newman.

She read every word on the title page, and quickly skimmed the introductory pages for any leads, anything that might tie in Sally Roe. So far, nothing.

Well . . . if it was there, she was going to find it. She started the car, and headed back to the Coles' house.

When Bernice called Hank Busche, she was close to tears. "She was right here, Hank, right under my nose, and I didn't see it; it never occurred to me! Her life is in danger, and we could've helped her, and I let her get away!"

Hank was just as shocked and dismayed. "It's incredible. I talked to her when I was over at Barkers', and I could feel a tug from the Lord then. I just knew she was here with a real need."

"We've just got to pray that we find her, that she writes to me or calls or *something*!"

"I'll get on the phone. We'll get something going."

Triskal and Krioni soared high over the town of Ashton, their wings rushing, shedding rippling, sparkling trails of light. The prayers were beginning all over the town, and the Spirit of God was stirring up even more.

"There now," said Krioni. "This should make a difference in Bacon's Corner!"

"Let's just hope it isn't too late!" said Triskal.

All over Ashton, with one accord, the saints knelt wherever they were—beside their beds, at couches and chairs in living rooms, in a garage next to a jalopy, next to a television that had been turned off for this important moment, over a sink where dishes were soaking in suds. Some were visiting friends, and they all sought the Lord together; school kids paused in their homework to say a quick word; grandparents and relatives across the country joined the prayers by telephone.

They prayed for this woman, this unknown, mysterious, and troubled stranger named Sally Beth Roe. They prayed for her safety and that she would find whatever she was seeking.

Most of all, they prayed that she would turn to God and meet Jesus Christ.

They prayed for a place they'd never heard of before: Bacon's Corner. They sought the Lord on behalf of the believers there, and asked for a real victory in their time of siege and struggle. They bound the demonic spirits in the name of Jesus and by His authority, forbidding them to do any more mischief among those people.

Bernice skipped dinner so she could fast that night. She spent the time sitting on the couch in her apartment, praying and waiting for the phone to ring. It finally did at just about seven o'clock.

"Hello?"

"Bernie, this is Marshall."

"Marshall!" Then Bernice choked up.

"Hello?"

She blurted it out. "Marshall, she was here!"

Marshall knew immediately what Bernice meant, but he didn't want to believe it. "Are we talking about Sally Roe?"

"She was here, Marshall, right here in Ashton!"

"Where is she now?"

Bernice slumped on the couch, heartsick. "I don't know. I didn't know who she was until she left town on the bus. She was staying at Sara Barker's . . ."

Bernice told Marshall everything she knew: how she'd met Sally Roe in church, had lunch with her, and tried to visit with her at the *Clarion,* but just got too busy.

Marshall had to be the most frustrated man in the world right now. Bernice could hear him trying to hide it, trying to remain calm and civil. "We've got to find her, Bernie. We've got to find her."

"I know."

"Did she say anything about the case?"

"She's following it, Marshall. She was reading the wire copy that came in today, and some newspaper stories about it. She seemed pretty upset about that recent ruling."

Marshall paused again. Bernice could just envision him chewing up the phone book. "Well . . . was she coherent?"

"Very coherent, intelligent, articulate. And I think very hungry spiritually. We talked about Jesus and the Cross at lunch on Sunday. She didn't seem to buy into it, but she understood it." Then she added, "But she was elusive about herself. Secretive. She wouldn't talk about herself at all."

"That sounds like every other report I've heard about her. You got those mug shots from Ben?"

"Yes, over the fax. It's her."

"I finally saw the *Finding the Real Me* curriculum today."

"Oh, man, don't tell me . . ."

"I won't. There's no visible connection. But the content is solid confirmation of what Miss Brewer is doing with the kids in the class, along with all the usual humanist, cosmic stuff: collectivism, global consciousness, altered states, relativism . . ."

"All the usual 'isms' . . ."

"But no mention anywhere that Sally Roe had anything to do with it. So we still don't know what this whole attempted murder thing is about, or what Sally Roe has to do with this case, and I've used up a lot of precious time."

"She did get my phone number and address from me."

"No kidding!"

"So there's still hope."

"Yeah, and we've got a lot to hope for. Keep praying."

"Oh, we're all praying for you, Marshall, right now. The whole bunch of believers over here."

"Great! We need something to break, and real soon!"

34

The prayers reached to Heaven from Ashton, from Bacon's Corner, and everywhere in between, and it was as if the Lord God was waiting for just this moment, just this particular cry from His people. He began to move His sovereign hand.

Tal got the report from a courier in the early hours of Wednesday morning. "Guilo!"

Guilo was at his side in an instant.

Tal's voice was strained with excitement. "The Lord has spoken! She's ready!"

"Praise to the Lord!" said Guilo. "Where? When?"

"She's left Ashton and is almost to Henderson. It'll only be a matter of hours. We'll meet her there with everything we can muster! If we can get her through before Destroyer and his minions find out, we may be able to tip the scales at last!"

Guilo drew his sword with a metallic ring and a flash of light. "A turning point!"

"Mota and Signa will remain here with their warriors ready, watching that breach." Tal smiled for the first time in weeks. "They just might get some real action today!"

Dear Tom,

I arrived by bus about seven o'clock this morning, and I imagine I'll get a room soon enough. For now, I'm quite comfortable just sitting in Lakeland Park near the city center. The sun is warm, the bench is dry, and the nearby pond is placid and full of ducks.

I would not call the city of Henderson an inviting place, but it does have some major advantages: it is a large, metropolitan city, and therefore easy to hide in, and it has an immense downtown library, an excellent place for finding certain information. I'll be going there today, or

tomorrow, or whenever I finish a more immediate matter
demanding my attention.

A more immediate matter. Sally was a little surprised at her
detached, businesslike tone, as if she were going to type a letter or
make a purchase. In reality, she was about to enter into a relationship that could potentially alter the course of her entire life, totally
restructure her worldview, and bring into consideration every moral
issue, every act, every decision, and every attitude of all her previous years; her deepest scars and emotions, the most personal and
guarded areas of her life, would be laid bare. The relationship
would be confrontational, perhaps devastating.

At least, that is what she expected from the arrangement, and
for that reason she'd pondered the move all through the night,
weighing the pros and cons, considering the costs, testing and elimi-
nating the options. It became clear to her that she would have to
pay an enormous price in terms of ego and self-will, and that the
arrangement would carry with it staggering implications for the
future. But every second thought was entertained and answered,
every objection received a fair hearing, and in between the fierce
and heated debates Sally conducted with herself on the floor of her
own mind, she slept on it.

By the time the light of day peeked through the bus windows,
she'd settled in her mind that, with all things considered, such a
major commitment would be the most logical, practical, and desir-
able thing to do, with advantages that far outweighed the disadvan-
tages.

It was quiet in the park, with few people around besides a
matron walking her poodle and a few yuppies jogging to work. She
moved to another bench closer to the pond, out in the full morning
sun, and sat down, her duffel bag beside her.

Then she took a good long look at herself. Dressed in her jeans
and blue jacket, with a stocking cap on her head and a duffel bag
beside her, she looked like a homeless vagabond.

She was.

She looked solitary and lonely.

She was.

She also looked small and insignificant in a very large world,
and that carried more weight in her mind than anything else. What
must she look like to a God big enough to have created this huge
globe on which she was sitting? Like a microbe on a microscope
slide? How would He even find her?

Well, all she could do was make some noise, call out to Him,
cause a disturbance, send up some verbal flares. Maybe she could
catch His eye or His ear.

She placed her notebook in her lap and flipped to a page of notes she had prepared. Now . . . where to start?

She spoke softly, just barely forming the words on her lips. She felt self-conscious and she was willing to admit it. "Uh . . . hello." Maybe He heard her, maybe He didn't. She said it again. "Hello." That should be enough. "I imagine You know who I am, but I'll introduce myself anyway. It just seems the thing to do. My name is Sally Beth Roe, and I guess one refers to You as . . . God. Or maybe Jesus. I've heard that done. Or . . . Lord. I understand You go by several titles, and so I hope You'll indulge me if I grope a bit. It's been a long time since I've tried to pray.

"Uh . . . anyway, I would like to meet with You today, and discuss my life and what possible role You might wish to play in it. And thank You in advance for Your time and attention."

She stared at her notes. She'd gotten this far. Assuming she'd secured God's attention, she proceeded with the next item. "To quickly review what brought this meeting about, I guess You remember our last visit, approximately thirty years ago, at the . . . uh . . . Mount Zion Baptist Church in Yreka, California. I want You to know that I did enjoy our times together back then. I know I haven't said anything about it in quite a while, and I apologize. Those were precious times, and now they're favorite memories. I'm glad for them.

"So I suppose You're wondering what happened, and why I broke off our relationship. Well, I don't remember what happened exactly. I know that the courts gave me back to my mother, and she wasn't about to take me to Sunday school like Aunt Barbara did, and then I went to live in a foster home, and then . . . Well, whatever the case, our times together just didn't continue, and that's all . . . Well, I guess it's water under the bridge . . ."

Sally paused. Was there some kind of awakening happening inside her? God could hear her. She could sense it; she just knew it somehow. That was strange. It was something new.

"Well . . ." Now she lost her train of thought. "I think I do sense that You're listening to me, so I want to thank You for that." She got her thoughts back again. "Oh, anyway, I guess I was an angry young woman, and maybe I blamed You for my sorrows, but . . . at any rate, I decided that I could take care of myself, and that's basically the way it went for most of my life. I'm sure You know the story: I tried atheism, and then humanism with a strong dose of evolution thrown in, and that left me empty and made my life meaningless; so then I tried cosmic humanism and mysticism, and that was good for many years of aimless delusions and torment and, to be honest, the mess I'm in right now, including the fact that I'm a convicted felon. You know all about that."

Okay, Sally, now where do you go from here? You may as well get to the point.

"Well, anyway, I guess what I'm trying to say is that Bernice, back in Ashton, was right, at least as far as Sally Roe is concerned. I have a moral problem. I've read some of the Bible. Uh . . . it's a good book . . . it's a fine piece of work—and I've come to see that You are a God of morals, of ethics, of absolutes. I guess that's what 'holy' means. And actually I'm glad for that, because then we can know where our boundaries are; we can know where we stand . . .

"I'm beating around the bush, I know."

Sally stopped to think. How should she say it? Just what was it she wanted from God?

"I guess . . ." *Oh-oh. Emotion. Maybe this is why I can't get around to it.* "I guess I need to ask You about Your love. I do know it's there; Mrs. Gunderson always talked about it, and so did my Aunt Barbara, and now I've had a brief glimpse of it again in my talks with Bernice and that pastor, Hank the Plumber. I need to know that You'll . . ."

She stopped. Tears were forming in the corners of her eyes. She wiped them away and took some deep breaths. This was supposed to be business, not some emotional, subjective experience she might later doubt.

"Excuse me. This is difficult. There are a lot of years involved, a lot of emotion." Another deep breath. "Anyway, I was trying to say that . . . I would like very much for You to accept me." She stopped and let the tightness in her throat ease. "Because . . . I've been told that You love me, and that You've arranged for all my wrongs, my moral trespasses, to be paid for and forgiven. I've come to understand that Jesus died to pay my penalty, to satisfy Your holy justice. Um . . . I appreciate that. Thank You for that kind of love.

"But I . . . I want to enter into that kind of relationship with You. Somehow. I have wronged You, and I have ignored You, and I have tried to be a god myself, as strange as that may sound to You. I have served other spirits, and I have killed my own offspring, and I've worked so hard to lead so many astray . . ."

The tears were coming again. Oh, well. Considering the subject matter, a few tears would not be inappropriate.

"But if You will have me . . . if You will only accept me, I would be more than willing to hand over to You all that I am, and all that I have, whatever it may be worth." Words from thirty years ago came to her mind, and they captured her feelings perfectly. "Jesus . . ."

She couldn't stop the emotions this time. Her face flushed, her eyes filled, and she was afraid to go on.

But she did go on, even as her voice broke, as tears ran down her cheeks, as her body began to quake. "Jesus . . . I want You to come into my heart. I want You to forgive me. Please forgive me."

She was crying and she couldn't stop. She had to get out of there. She couldn't let anyone see her like this.

She grabbed her duffel bag and hurried away from the pond, turning off the walkway into the nearby trees. Under their sheltering, spring-fresh leaves, she found a small clearing and sank to her knees on the cool, dry ground. With a new freedom that seclusion brought, the heart of stone became a heart of flesh, the deepest cries of that heart became a fountain, and she and the Lord God began to talk about things as the minutes slipped by unnoticed and the world around her became unimportant.

Above, as if another sun had just risen, the darkness opened, and pure, white rays broke through the treetops, flooding Sally Beth Roe with a heavenly light, shining through to her heart, her innermost spirit, obscuring her form with a blinding fire of holiness. Slowly, without sensation, without sound, she settled forward, her face to the ground, her spirit awash with the presence of God.

All around her, like spokes of a wondrous wheel, like beams of light emanating from a sun, angelic blades lay flat upon the ground, their tips turned toward her, their handles extending outward, held in the strong fists of hundreds of noble warriors who knelt in perfect, concentric circles of glory, light, and worship, their heads to the ground, their wings stretching skyward like a flourishing, animated garden of flames. They were silent, their hearts filled with a holy dread.

As in countless times past, in countless places, with marvelous, inscrutable wonder, the Lamb of God stood among them, the Word of God, and more: the final Word, the end of all discussion and challenge, the Creator and the Truth that holds all creation together—most wondrous of all, and most inscrutable of all, the *Savior*, a title the angels would always behold and marvel about, but which only mankind could know and understand.

He had come to be the Savior of this woman. He knew her by name; and speaking her name, He touched her.

And her sins were gone.

A rustling began in the first row of angels, then in the next, and then, like a wave rushing outward, the silken wings from row upon row of warriors caught the air, raising a roar, and lifted the angels to their feet. The warriors held their swords Heavenward, a forest of fiery blades, and began to shout in tumultuous joy, their voices rumbling and shaking the whole spiritual realm.

Guilo, as brilliantly glorified as ever he was, took his place above them all, and swept his sword about in burning arcs as he shouted, "Worthy is the Lamb!"

"Worthy is the Lamb!" the warriors thundered.

"Worthy is the Lamb!" Guilo shouted more loudly.

"Worthy is the Lamb!" they all answered.

"For He was slain!"

"For He was slain!"

Guilo pointed his sword at Sally Beth Roe, prostrate, her face to the ground, still communing with her newfound Savior. "And with His blood He has purchased for God the woman, Sally Beth Roe!"

The swords waved, and their light pierced the darkness as lightning pierces the night. "He has purchased Sally Beth Roe!"

"Worthy is the Lamb who was slain," Guilo began, and then they all sang the words together with voices that shook the earth, "to receive power and wealth and wisdom and strength and honor and glory and praise!"

Then came another roar, from voices and from wings, and another flashing of hundreds of swords. The wings took hold, and the skies filled with warriors, swirling, shouting, cheering, worshiping, their light washing over the earth for miles around.

Miles away, some of Destroyer's demons covered their eyes against the blinding light.

"Oh no!" said one. "Another soul redeemed!"

"One of our prisoners set free!" wailed another.

A quick, sharp-eyed spy returned from taking a closer look.

"Who is it this time?" they asked.

The spirit answered, "You will not like the news!"

Tal and Guilo embraced, jumping, spinning, laughing. "Saved! Sally Beth Roe is saved! Our God has her at last!"

They remained, along with their warriors, keeping the hedge about her strong and brilliant, making sure her conference with the Lord would proceed undisturbed.

Time passed, of course, but no one seemed to notice or care.

Later—she didn't know how much later—Sally pressed her palms against the earth and slowly lifted herself to a sitting position, brushing dry leaves and humus from her clothes and using a handkerchief to wipe her face. She had been through an uncanny, perfectly marvelous experience, and the effect still lingered. A change, a deep, personal, moral restoration had taken place, not just in her subjective perceptions, but in fact. This was something new, something truly extraordinary.

"So this must be what they mean by 'getting saved,'" she said aloud.

Things were different. The Sally Roe who first ducked into these woods was not the same Sally Roe that now sat in the leaves, a trembling, awestruck, tear-stained, happy mess.

Before, she had felt lost and aimless. Now she felt secure, safe in God's hands.

Before, her life had no meaning. Now it did, with even more purpose and meaning yet to be discovered.

Before, she had been oppressed and laden with guilt. Now she was cleansed. She was free. She was forgiven.

Before, she was so alone. Now she had a Friend closer than any other.

As for her old friends, her tormentors . . .

Outside that hedge, thrown there like garbage into a dumpster, Despair, Death, Insanity, Suicide and Fear sulked in the bushes, unable to return. They looked at each other, ready to squabble should any one of them dare to say the first word.

They were out. Vanquished. Through. Just like that. Somehow, she'd no sooner become a child of God than she began to assert her rights and authority as such. She didn't say a lot, she didn't make it flowery. She simply ordered them out of her life.

"She learns fast," said Despair.

The others spit at him just for saying it.

"This is marvelous," she said to herself, chuckling in amazement and ecstasy. "Just marvelous!"

Tal and Guilo were watching, enjoying every moment.

"'The word of her testimony and the blood of the Lamb,'" said Tal.

Guilo nodded. "That's two."

"Captain Tal!" came a shout. A courier dropped from the sky like a meteor, snapping his wings open just in time to alight directly in front of Tal. "Mota sends word from Bacon's Corner! The prayers have brought a breakthrough! They've opened the breach, sir! They're ready to expose Broken Birch!"

Tal laughed with excitement. "Well enough! The kindling is

stacked, and"—he looked at Sally—"we now have the match to start the brushfire! Nathan and Armoth!"

"Captain!" they replied.

"Sally's ready. Follow her from here on, and be sure Krioni and Triskal are warned to secure Ashton from invasion. When she lights the brushfire, sound the signal for Mota and Signa in Bacon's Corner."

"Done!"

"Cree and Si, establish your armies at the Omega Center. When the fire reaches there, send it on to Bentmore."

They were gone immediately.

"Chimon and Scion, prepare armies at Bentmore; be ready to send the fire on to Summit."

They soared away.

Tal turned to the courier. "Tell Mota and Signa that they have the prayer cover and can proceed closing the trap. After that, have them wait for the signal from Nathan and Armoth."

The courier flew off with the message.

Tal put a brotherly hand on Guilo's shoulder. "Guilo, the Strength of Many, it's time to position the armies at the Summit Institute!"

"YAHAAA!" Guilo roared, raising his sword for the other warriors to see. "Done!"

Tal unfurled his wings with the sound of a crashing ocean wave. He raised his sword high, and they all did the same so that Lakeland Park was flooded with the flickering light. "For the saints of God and for the Lamb!"

"For the saints of God and for the Lamb!"

Mota got the word from Tal, and not too soon. He and Signa were just then hiding in the ventilation ducts at the Bergen Door Factory, looking for an opportunity to throw a wrench into Destroyer's clever, unseen assault on the saints of Bacon's Corner.

Signa was pointing out supervisor Abby Grayson, moving among the router tables with her ever-present clipboard in hand, just keeping things running smoothly as she had done for the last twenty years. "They've never brought their intrigues and manipulations into this place, at least not so much as to be seen. Abby has no idea what's been happening."

Just then, a pimple-faced youth came down the main aisle through the plant, catching a few stares from some of the workers and looking very uncomfortable.

"All right," said Mota, "here we go. Hopefully Abby's going to have her eyes opened."

"Come on, Abby. Pay attention."

The kid walked up to Abby looking hesitant, embarrassed, but determined to have an audience with her. No voices could be heard above the roar of the machinery, but Abby's lips weren't too hard to read: "So what can I do for you, Kyle?"

Come on, said Signa. *Tell her.*

Two angels immediately stood by Kyle Krantz's side, dressed like factory workers—the people couldn't see them, but any demons might. Kyle—wayward, oft-busted, former pot-smoking Kyle—needed all the encouragement he could get. He was just plain scared.

Come on . . . Mota urged.

Kyle leaned close to Abby's ear and said what he had to say before he lost his nerve completely. Abby seemed a little puzzled, maybe even shocked at his words.

"Let's get inside my office," she said.

The two angels looked up toward the ventilation ducts and gave strong, affirmative nods.

"Done!" said Mota.

"Better surround that office. Those two need to talk!" Signa added.

Only an hour later, Abby Grayson gave Ben Cole a call from her little office cubicle. Ben could still hear the muffled noise of the factory in the background.

"Well hi, Abby! This is a pleasant surprise."

"Oh, this crazy world's full of surprises. I heard you were fired. Is that true?"

The question seemed rather blunt, but very much like Abby.

"Well, yes, it is. It's a long story . . ."

"I'm going to make it longer. I've just heard some information you ought to know."

Ben sat down on the sofa. "Go ahead."

"I just had a long talk with Kyle Krantz—remember him? You've busted him a few times for carrying pot."

"Yeah, right."

"He was working here and doing all right until he got fired yesterday. The word among the supervisors was that he was peddling drugs around the plant, and we have strict rules about any of that stuff, so out the door he went. But he got brave and came to see me today, and . . . Well, normally I wouldn't believe him, but considering everything else that's happened, maybe this time I do." She hesitated.

Ben figured he'd better make it easier for her. "Hey, don't worry. I'm with you so far."

"Well, Ben . . ." She had to build up the nerve to ask it. "What would you say if I told you that we have some witches in town, and some even working here in this plant?"

Ben sat up straight, his whole body full of attention. "I would be very interested to know about that."

"So you don't think it's crazy? I did say *witches*."

Ben's memory still carried vivid scenes of a goat dismembered and its two front legs crossed and bloody on the front steps of the church. "No, Abby. We've seen quite a few strange things lately. I don't think it's crazy at all."

"Then maybe you'd better hear what Kyle has to say. Will you be free after four o'clock?"

Does a duck swim? "You just name the place."

35

It was about four-thirty, and there was a cold wind blowing across the long-neglected, weed-infested fields of the old Benson farm. The white paint on the farmhouse was turning a gritty gray and beginning to peel like a sunburn; the windows were broken out, the shakes on the roof were beginning to splinter away in the wind; the apple and pear trees in the front yard were blossoming, but now reached skyward in a wild profusion of unpruned trunks and unsightly suckers. The Benson farm had been deserted too long and was simply not surviving, but fading steadily into decay and ruin with every passing season.

A heavy chain blocked the driveway, and Marshall could drive the Buick no further. A NO TRESPASSING sign hung from the chain and swung forward and backward in the wind, right above the Buick's grill.

"Is this the place?" he asked.

Kyle Krantz, the young delinquent who couldn't seem to stay out of trouble, sat in the seat beside him, nodding his head and looking scared. In the backseat, Abby Grayson and Ben Cole looked at the dismal scene before them, and found it easy to believe what Kyle had told them about it.

Kyle pointed. "That's the barn right back there. That's where it was."

"I take it they were trespassing, just like you were?" asked Marshall.

Kyle had grown dull toward such loaded statements. "They were here, man."

Marshall looked at the others. "So, I guess we'll have to trespass too."

They got out of the car and took a moment to look the place over. As near as they could tell, they were the only living beings here. There were no sounds except for the wind and the occasional cheep of the swallows nesting under the eaves of the farmhouse.

Marshall ducked under the chain, and the others followed. The driveway wound around the farmhouse, went past a garage and toolshed, then opened into a wide, graveled area in back—a turnaround and access for farm machinery, supplies, and livestock that were no longer there. On the far side of this open area stood the old gray barn, weathered but intact, the main doors shut.

"Just what were you doing here anyway?" Marshall asked the boy.

"Billy and I were looking for a good place to have a kegger. We always do that 'cause we find good spots no one knows about."

"So this barn must have looked pretty inviting."

"Yeah, back then it did. Now it doesn't."

"How did you manage to get this close without anyone seeing you?"

"It was dark, and we snuck in around the other side of the house. They weren't watching for us anyway; they were too busy doing all their weird stuff."

They reached the doors.

"Have you ever gone inside?"

"No way. Billy and I just wanted to get out of here, and that's all."

The big door swung open with a long, aged creak. The inside of the barn was cool, dim, and expansive. No one entered. Marshall was waiting for his eyes to grow accustomed to the low light.

Finally they could all make out the dirt floor. It seemed plain enough—just smooth dirt. They saw nothing out of the ordinary. They looked at Kyle. He was immediately uneasy and defensive.

"I saw it, man. They were here."

"Okay," said Marshall, "show us what you saw."

Kyle went into the center of the floor and turned in a circle, his finger extended out and toward the floor. "They had a big circle carved in the dirt right here, and a big pentagram in the middle of it." Then he pointed to a spot toward the back wall. "There was a big bench there, like an altar, and there was blood on it, and there were about twenty people standing all around the circle with robes on and hoods over their heads, and they were all chanting and shouting, and there were candles around the circle. They had candles at all the points of the pentagram."

Marshall looked around the barn. "What cracks did you and Billy look through to see all this?"

Kyle pointed to the side of the barn. "Right over there."

The daylight was now plainly visible through two large spaces between some loose boards. Marshall went to where the cracks were, crouched down to their level, and looked back. He was satisfied—the cracks provided a wide, clear view of the area in question.

"You say they had hoods on their heads?"

"Yeah. Black robes and hoods, and they were barefoot."

"So how do you know who they were?"

"'Cause some of them were facing this way. I could see their faces turned right at me." Kyle was offended and edgy. "I don't know why you don't believe me!"

Marshall held up his hand to calm the boy. "Hey, I didn't say I didn't believe you. But listen: you've got plenty of reason to get back at Mulligan, or any cop for that matter."

"Not to mention getting your job back," said Abby.

"I'm not making it up, man! I saw Mulligan. He was standing right here, with a robe and a hood on, and chanting just like all the others."

Ben was inspecting the spot where Kyle claimed an altar had stood. "Marshall."

Marshall joined him. Ben had scratched in the dirt with his finger and uncovered some brown stains. He was able to pick up some clumps of stained dirt in his fingers. "Could be blood. I'll take a sample."

"See?" said Kyle.

Marshall asked, "Tell me about that blood you saw. What were they doing with it?"

"They were drinking it out of a big cup, a big silver cup. They were passing it around."

"How do you know it was blood?"

"The lady said it was."

"What lady?"

"Well, the leader, I guess. She was standing right there, and she said something about making some woman die and beating all the Christians. Uh . . . she said, 'Defeat to the Christians!' And she drank from the cup and passed it around, and they all drank from it." Then Kyle remembered something else. "Oh yeah, man, get this: they had some animal legs right here in the middle of the circle."

Oh-oh. Kyle could tell he'd impressed them with that. Hogan and Cole were looking at him, dead serious and ready to hear more.

"Tell me about the animal legs," said Marshall.

"They had to be goat legs. They were crossed right here, like an X." He saw something. "Hey!"

"Hold it!" said Marshall, touching Kyle to stop him from disturbing the dirt at his feet. "Ben."

Ben crouched for a close look. "Yeah. More blood. And here are some hairs."

"Goat hairs," said Kyle. "That's what they are."

"So they wanted to defeat the Christians, huh?" asked Marshall.

"Yeah, they were really hollering about it." Another memory. "Oh, and they were saying something about a courtroom, winning in a courtroom."

"And they were after some woman too?"

"Yeah."

"Did they say her name?"

The name meant nothing to Kyle, but he remembered hearing it. "Uh, Sally on Death Row, or something like that."

He was batting a thousand now. He could see it all over their faces.

Marshall dug into his jacket pocket. "Did you see any of the other people's faces?"

"Sure. The woman leader took her hood off, and I could see her."

Marshall produced some color photographs he'd taken with much care, stealth, and a telephoto lens. He showed Kyle a picture of Claire Johanson.

"Yeah! Yeah, that was her!"

"The woman who led this whole thing?"

"Yeah."

Marshall showed Kyle a picture of Jon Schmidt.

"Yeah! He was here too."

Marshall slipped in a picture of his sister.

"No. I've never seen her before."

A photo of Irene Bledsoe.

"Uh . . . no, I don't think so."

Officer Leonard Jackson.

"No."

Bruce Woodard, the elementary school principal.

"Naw, not Mr. Woodard. Man, where'd you take all these?"

Marshall put the pictures away. "Kyle, I think you're giving it to us straight. Now listen, I'm not a cop, and whatever you tell me I'm not going to take it to the cops. I just need the information. It's important. I want you to tell me the real truth: did you have any marijuana on the job at the Bergen Door Company?"

Kyle raised his hand as if taking an oath. "None, I swear. Hey, Cole knows I've had some here and there, but not on the job. My old man would kill me, and besides, I need the work bad."

Abby cut in. "So you're saying that you were set up just to get you fired?"

"You got it. I didn't put that marijuana in my locker."

Marshall looked at Ben and could tell he was recalling a similar incident involving marijuana in a locker.

"Any idea who put it there?"

"Who do you think? I saw her here, and then opened my big mouth about it in the lunchroom, and so she must have found out about it. She gave me some pretty dirty looks after that, and then, bam! *She's* the person who says they ought to search my locker, and then they find the pot. Real handy, you know?"

Ben added sympathetically, "And considering your reputation, there wasn't much point in denying it."

"You got it."

Abby objected, "But Donna's been with Bergen almost as long as I have. I can't believe she'd pull a stunt like this."

"She was here," Kyle insisted. "She was standing right next to Mulligan. I saw her, and she knows it, and that's why I got fired." Kyle then recalled bitterly, "Then Mulligan comes down to the factory and tells me he'll let it go this time if I behave myself and 'make the right choices,' he said. I know what he was doing. He was telling me to keep my mouth shut or he'd bust me for good."

Marshall reviewed it all in his mind. "So . . . looks like we might have a real club here: Claire Johanson, Jon Schmidt, Sergeant Mulligan, and . . ."

Kyle resented Marshall's hesitation. "She was here! I swear it!"

Marshall completed the sentence. "Donna Hemphile, Kyle's supervisor at the Bergen Door Company, and a member in good standing at the Good Shepherd Community Church!"

Thursday afternoon, Officer Leonard Jackson had some unwelcome visitors. He was sitting in his squad car, cleverly hidden in the trees at the west end of the Snyder River Bridge, just watching for speeders and having a pleasant day building up his citation quota, when suddenly, without prior notification of any kind, a big brown Buick swung off the road and into the trees, pulling right up alongside him.

Now who in the world was this? Leonard felt invaded. This was a desecration of a sacred place.

A handsome black man rolled down the window on the passenger side of the Buick. "Hey, Leonard, how's it going?"

Ben Cole.

Leonard tried to be sociable. "Not bad, I suppose. What can I do for you?"

Ben looked toward the driver of the Buick. "Have you met Marshall Hogan?"

Leonard had seen him around town and never felt good about him. "No, we've never met."

Marshall called a greeting. "Hello, Officer Jackson."

"Hello."

Ben said, "We'd like to have a brief word with you."

"Well, I'm on duty . . ."

"How's your quota so far?"

Leonard realized Ben would know everything about his job, so bluffing wasn't going to be possible. "Well . . . I guess I'm doing all right. I've logged twelve so far."

Ben was impressed. "Hey, you're way ahead of the game! How about taking a short break for a little conference?"

"I promise you'll find it interesting," said Marshall.

At Summit, five demon messengers gathered just outside the dark, musty, secret chambers of the Strongman, each with an urgent message for Destroyer.

The first demon said to his fellows, "I bring word that Broken Birch has been breached!"

The second demon nodded in acknowledgment and added, "I bring word that Hogan and Cole are about to corner Officer Jackson!"

The third demon gasped at that news and growled his own. "I bring word that they will be seeing Joey Parnell again and may frighten him into talking!"

The fourth said, "I bring word that Pastor Mark Howard is rooting out the division in his church even now, and the Enemy is healing all the damage we've done!"

The fifth said, "I bring word that Sally Roe has—"

Oh. The ground suddenly quivered with a roar that came from inside the Strongman's lair. Apparently Destroyer and the Strongman already knew about that.

Destroyer dared not draw his sword—such an aggressive move would only worsen the Strongman's fury. So he dashed to and fro, grabbing the air in violent, desperate wingfuls, his arms covering his head and face, as the Strongman came after him with flying blade and swinging fist, his mouth foaming with rage, his jowls flopping, his rancid breath turning the air yellow.

"A reversal!" the Strongman screamed. "She was ours, and now you let them have her!"

"I allowed no such thing!" Destroyer countered. "I was biding my time—"

Contradicting the Strongman was a poor idea. It earned Destroyer a violent swat across his head from the flat of Strongman's blade. "Lazy, unmoving, blind idiot!"

"She is ours, my liege!" Destroyer shouted over Strongman's roaring. "Tal and his hordes grow weaker by the day!" *SMASH!* A huge fist in the neck. "Soon they will fall away from her like over-ripe fruit—" A clawed, scaly foot to the rump. "—from a tree, and we will take her!" *OOF!* A knee to the stomach.

"You were going to take away Tal's prayer cover!" yelled the Strongman. "What became of that?"

"As I've tried to tell you, we have been whittling it away!"

"*Whittling* when you should have been chopping, dashing, shredding, *slaughtering*!"

"You will see it!"

"I wish to see her destroyed, bumbling spirit! Live up to your boastful name! Pierce through a chink in her armor! Let her own sins rot her away!"

"Her sins are gone, my Ba-al! She has come to the Cross—"

WHAM! A folded wing against the midsection. Destroyer tumbled and fluttered sideways across the room.

"NOOO!" the Strongman screamed. "You will not mention *that!*"

"But we can still take her . . ." Destroyer insisted, although rather weakly.

"We will not . . . turn . . . back!" the Strongman roared, waving his sword in a fiery, rushing arc with each word. "I have a plan—I will see it unfold! Let the blood of the Lamb defeat the others—it will not defeat me! I will tread upon it, march around it, assail it and bury it, but I will not surrender to it!"

"I know we *will* take her!" Destroyer insisted again.

"YAAAA!" The Strongman brought his sword down with immeasurable fury, trailing a long, crimson streamer of light.

Destroyer drew his own blade in an instant and blocked the razor edge with a shower of sparks. The power of the blow slammed him into the wall, and the Strongman held him there like a ton of fallen earth.

Now they were eye to eye, the yellow, glowing orbs almost touching, their sulfurous breath mixing in a putrid cloud that obscured their faces. The Strongman's arm did not weaken; he did not lessen the weight that held Destroyer motionless.

"You will do it," he said finally, his voice a low, panting wheeze, "or I will feed you to the angels myself—in tiny pieces!"

With an explosion of arms, wings, and one blade that seemed like several, the Strongman cast Destroyer from the room, and he tumbled into the five demons still waiting for him outside. They bowed before him—as soon as they could crawl out from under him.

"We bring word, Ba-al!" they said.

"What word?" he asked.

They told him.

He cut them all to pieces.

Tom, I am free. I could just see that Cross so clearly, just as it must have looked on that bare, forlorn hill two thousand years ago, and I was flat on my face before it, so weighed down with my wrongs, my boasts, my choices, my SELF that I couldn't rise an inch. All I could do was lie there, admitting and confessing everything and reaching out to that rough-hewn piece of wood like a drowning man reaches for a lifeline, and grabbing hold for my very life.

And how can I describe it? I apologize, but the words will not capture the experience: I had nothing to offer Him, no incentive at all for Him to forgive me, not the slightest item of value with which to barter or cajole. All I had was what I was.

But he accepted me. I was so surprised, and then relieved, and then, with the steady realization of what had happened, ecstatic! My offering—nothing other than myself, Sally Beth Roe, pitiful, failing, and wayward—was accepted. I was what He always wanted in the first place, and He received me. He lifted the load from my heart, and I could feel it go; I could just sense it all drawn away from me and rushing up to that Cross. I felt so light, I thought I would be carried away by the slightest breeze.

I was able to raise my head, and then saw the closing of our transaction: a trickle of blood running down the wood and puddling on the ground. The payment. Such a gruesome sight, such a discomforting thought, but really, to be honest, quite appropriate considering what Jesus, the Son of God, had just purchased.

I am free. I am ransomed. I've never felt this way

before, like a slave set free who was born a slave and never
knew what freedom was like.
    I want to get to know this Jesus who has ransomed me.
We've only just met.

Sally lay her pen down on the small motel room desk, and
wiped some tears from her eyes. She was still shaking. Just beside
her notebook, a Gideon Bible lay open to the Gospel of Matthew,
chapter 11:

"Come to me, all you who are weary and burdened, and I will
give you rest. Take my yoke upon you and learn from me, for I am
gentle and humble in heart, and you will find rest for your souls.
For my yoke is easy and my burden is light."

36

That night, Marshall and Ben found County Coroner Joey
Parnell at his home in Westhaven. As usual, he wasn't glad to
see them, nor was he willing to chat.

"Now get out of here and don't come back!" he ordered
through his barely cracked front door.

"Mulligan's controlling you, isn't he?" said Marshall. "He
knows about that hit and run, and he's been hanging it over your
head."

The door didn't close. "Who told you about that?"

"A source close to the Bacon's Corner Police Department. You
struck a deal with Mulligan, and he's owned you ever since." The
door started to close. Marshall talked fast. "You hit a high school
girl named . . . uh . . . Kelly Otis, and Mulligan tracked you down,
and you were just then working on a case of suspected homicide,
some female transient, and Mulligan made you a deal: falsify the
cause of death of this female transient, and he'd let the hit and run
slip by. Am I right so far?"

The door cracked open a little more. "Just what do you want
from me?"

Marshall tried to sound compassionate despite the urgency that
kept making his voice tense. "How much longer do you want this
to go on? You can be their puppet for the rest of your life, or you
can help us put a stop to it."

Parnell was silent for a moment. Then he opened the door wide
enough to pass through. "Come inside before somebody sees you."

Parnell's wife was beside him. She was dark-haired, stout, and looking as troubled as he was. "This is Carol. We can talk freely in front of her; I've told her everything."

"Would you like some coffee?" she said quite mechanically. It was clear she didn't know what else to do.

"Yes, thank you," said Marshall, and Ben accepted as well.

"We'll sit in the dining room," said Parnell, leading them through the house.

They sat around a large table under a dimly glowing chandelier. The low, somber lighting seemed to match Parnell's mood; he looked worn, tired, at the end of his strength.

Without cue or question, he started talking as if he'd saved this story for years. "The transient was a thirty-two-year-old woman named Louise Barnes—she was homeless, a scavenger, no family. She was found dead in the woods along the Snyder River, about six miles north of Bacon's Corner. I remember the details perfectly because I want so much to forget them." He paused to gather his thoughts and control his emotions, then continued. "Her body was found hanging by the ankles from a tree limb, the blood drained. There were abundant signs of bizarre, ritualistic murder that I won't go into. The hunters who found her had apparently startled the killers, who fled before they could dispose of the body altogether.

"I received the remains and finished the autopsy. I found the cause of death to be homicide, of course. But then . . . as you have already heard, I did get into a mishap near the high school on my way home. I didn't see the girl, Kelly Otis, until she stepped from behind a tree and into the street, and . . . and I hit her. I slowed just enough to look, to see that she was still alive though injured. Some other people were running to help her. I . . . I just couldn't let the incident damage my career. I'd just gotten the coroner's job, and you know how the political world is, how fragile a reputation can be. I fled.

"Sergeant Mulligan came to my office the next day, and we met in private. I expected him to question me about the hit and run, but he immediately asked me about the body of Louise Barnes and what my findings were. I told him, and that's when he made the offer to let the hit-and-run incident pass, just bury it, if I would alter my findings and not report the real cause of death." Parnell just stared at the table, his face etched with pain. "I accepted his offer, filed the cause of death as accidental, and it was the worst decision of my life.

"There have been three ritual murders since then that I know of, and I'm sure many more that no one will ever know of. The three brought to me I quickly wrote off as accidental deaths. They were unknowns, possible runaways. I was hoping they would not be missed, but simply buried and forgotten, and that's what happened.

"But you see, I knew Sergeant Mulligan and his friends would be watching me. I knew I would have to perform to satisfy them, and so, with each murder I concealed, I fell deeper and deeper under their control, and that's where things stand at the present time."

Marshall asked, "Just who are these people? *What* are they?"

Parnell reached into a cabinet and pulled out a file folder, then set it before him closed, his folded hands resting on top. Carol brought the coffee and sat down beside her husband, putting her hand on his arm and saying nothing.

"If you want a name to call them, you can use the term Broken Birch. It's a secret label they share among themselves. They're a coven of witches, Satanists, occultists, whatever you wish. They're linked with hundreds of other such groups across the country. And taken together, these people wield incredible power, mostly through terror."

"And they're responsible for those ritual murders?"

Parnell looked at the telephone hanging on the wall. "You should know that right now I can pick up that telephone, call any one of six different phone numbers, and have both of you dead within twenty-four hours. The other side of that, however, is that there are other parties who can make the same call regarding me, and I could be dead just as quickly, and may very well be if they find out I've talked to you. Unknowns and transients are used for ritual sacrifices; people who are known and would be missed are . . . Well, fatal accidents are arranged for them."

"Can you tell us who belongs to this bunch?"

Parnell shook his head slowly for emphasis. "First of all, I don't know all of them. Secondly, I wouldn't tell you if I did. I can only confirm what you already know: Sergeant Mulligan is involved, and has been for years. As I understand it, he and some of the men from the local lodge checked it out and found the transition very easy. Because he holds such power in town and is head of law enforcement, they were quite willing to include him."

"Can you confirm Claire Johanson?"

Parnell hesitated, and then answered, "Yes."

"What about her boyfriend, Jon Schmidt?"

"Yes, he's part of it."

Ben wondered, "So what about all those people involved in the LifeCircle fellowship? Do they tie into this?"

Parnell shook his head emphatically. "They aren't supposed to know about it. All those well-meaning people being pulled into the LifeCircle group are simply being used and manipulated; they have no idea that Broken Birch is at the core of it, and they have no idea what their leaders are really up to."

Marshall asked, "What about Donna Hemphile? Is she a part of Broken Birch?"

"I believe so. It's hard to be sure sometimes, they hide it so well." Parnell drew a breath to change gears, then opened the file folder. "Here's what you really want to know, and all I really want to tell you."

He distributed the contents of the folder on the table in front of Marshall and Ben. With great interest, the two men examined several police mug shots and the rap sheet on a young, beautiful, black-haired woman.

"Not Sally Roe, obviously," said Parnell.

Ben recognized her. "The dead woman we found in the goat shed."

"I did some checking on my own. Her name is Alicia Von Bauer, twenty-seven, a Satanist, a member of Broken Birch. You'll note her criminal record: animal mutilations, public nudity and perverse behavior, prostitution, pornography. I might add to that list ritualistic murder, but who could ever prove it?"

Marshall asked, "So you think this Sally Roe thing was another ritual murder, or at least an attempt at one?"

"Exactly. It's clear to me that her death was arranged, and it was supposed to appear to be a suicide."

"That's how you recorded it, anyway," said Ben.

Parnell nodded. "With an unforeseen additional service: identifying the body of Alicia Von Bauer as that of Sally Roe. I do what I'm told, Mr. Cole. But obviously, something went terribly wrong, and all I can figure is that Sally Roe—or something else—overpowered Von Bauer, and Roe escaped."

"That's our theory," said Ben. He picked up the most recent photograph of Alicia Von Bauer for a closer look. The deep black eyes seemed to stare back at him from the page. It was eerie.

Marshall asked, "Where's the body now?"

"Cremated. We did that as soon as possible."

"Disposing of the evidence?"

"Exactly."

Marshall didn't know if he'd get an answer to the next question. "Mr. Parnell, we have a lot of reason to believe that this attempted killing isn't just a Broken Birch affair. What about the big people Claire Johanson and Jon Schmidt are connected with? Would they have something to gain?"

"I think you're on the right track. I'm sure the order for the murder came from someone higher up."

"How do you know?"

Parnell even smiled a little. "Because it's the first time I've seen Sergeant Mulligan afraid. Not long after I collected the body, Mulligan called me, asking if I'd found any personal effects on the body, which I hadn't. I could tell he was getting pressure from someone much higher, much more powerful than him or his Broken Birch friends. He was desperate enough to tell me what to look for, something missing that should have been there."

"Yeah," Ben recalled, "I asked you about that. Somebody even ransacked the rental house."

"So what was missing?" asked Marshall.

"A gold ring," Parnell answered. "Someone took it off Von Bauer's finger with cooking oil. I found traces of the oil still on Von Bauer's finger. The other thing missing was ten thousand dollars in cash."

Marshall and Ben looked at each other. They both had the same thought.

Ben spoke it. "Somebody hired her."

"Who?" asked Marshall.

Parnell shrugged. "I'd advise looking for someone rich, influential, and very powerful."

Ben responded, "A mighty big mole, Marshall."

Marshall had no comment. Right now he was overwhelmed with a sudden, flesh-crawling fear he hadn't felt since a few years ago in Ashton, when it seemed all the evil in the world was about to crash down on him. A mole? Suddenly the analogy was inadequate. What Marshall felt was more like a dragon, a monster—dark, insidious, clever, and big enough to fill the sky, with jaws gaping just above them, dropping to the kill, closing like a vise.

Far away from Bacon's Corner, and still hidden from her enemies, Sally Roe sat among the floor-to-ceiling shelves at the downtown library in Henderson, flanked on every side by invisible angelic guards, and paging through a massive National Bar Association directory of attorneys. She had a hunch, only a guess, but in her thinking it was the strongest possibility.

At her elbow sat Volume IV of the four rosters she had stolen from Professor Samuel W. Lynch's office, its full title: *A Continuation of the History and Roster of the Royal and Sacred Order of the Nation.* Each of the four volumes contained about two hundred pages. Most of the pages were devoted to weird, esoteric, ceremonial mumbo-jumbo, secret rites and initiations, minutes of meetings, and bylaws. At least fifty pages in each volume were dedicated to the names of members. The pages of names held her attention for the time being; she'd been scanning them for hours.

She now had another volume lying across Volume IV to hold it open to page 68, *The 168th Brotherhood of Initiates*. Like the 167 pages in this and the three volumes that came before, this page listed the names of new members brought into the Order of the Nation in one particular year, and contained two columns of fifteen names each. The column on the left contained bizarre, esoteric names like Isenstar, Marochia, and Pendorrot. The column on the right contained real names, some of them even familiar. Two-thirds of the way down the left column, she'd found the name she had looked through several years' worth of pages to find: Exetor.

At first, Exetor was just a mysterious word she'd found engraved on the inside surface of the ring she'd taken from the finger of her would-be assassin. Until she stole the rosters and studied them, the engraving made no sense at all. When she finally found page 68 in Volume IV of the rosters, it made a lot more sense. Exetor was a secret name or title, ninth on the list of fifteen. Directly opposite the name Exetor, in the right column, was the real name of the man who had received the title.

"James Everett Bardine."

James Bardine. He'd been initiated into the Sacred Order of the Nation along with fourteen other men twelve years ago, and upon his initiation had been granted the secret Brotherhood name of Exetor and his Ring of Fellowship bearing his secret name.

Very impressive, even spooky, and not to be scoffed at. The Nation could have been just another lodge or fraternal organization, some secret society or club where all the good old boys could get together, have a secret meeting with its oaths, handshakes, funny hats and rituals, and afterward down some beers and be rowdy. Almost every town had a lodge or secret order of some kind.

But the Nation went beyond that. It bound a lot of familiar names together and gave them at least this society in common. She'd found the name of Samuel W. Lynch among the 129th Brotherhood of Initiates—he'd been initiated into the Nation fifty-one years ago, and as he showed her in his office, still kept his cherished Ring of Fellowship.

The second ring in her possession—the one she'd hidden for ten years under the brick windowsill in Fairwood—bore another secret name, Gawaine, but she already knew whose ring it was. She quickly found his name at position seven, opposite the name Gawaine, in the 146th Brotherhood of Initiates: Owen Jefferson Bennett, initiated thirty-four years ago when a senior at Bentmore University.

Good old Owen. There were so many things he never told her.

All this was fascinating, of course, but first and foremost in Sally's mind at this moment was the name of James Everett Bardine.

The Nation was a strictly male organization, but a female assassin was wearing his ring. What was the connection? Who was Bardine in the first place?

Perhaps it was the current lawsuit causing all the stir in Bacon's Corner that made her think Bardine might be an attorney; perhaps it was the fact that the Nation seemed to have no ordinary, blue-collar people in its membership, but only bankers, businessmen, educators, attorneys, and statesmen—purveyors of power.

Whatever the case, she was now narrowing her search in the "B" section of the Bar Association directory, and getting closer.

Barcliff . . . Barclyde . . . Barden . . . Bardetti . . . Bardine. James Everett Bardine.

Bingo. This guy was an attorney. The listing was current, published this year. Bardine was working for a big law firm in Chicago: Evans, Santinelli, Farnsworth, and McCutcheon. They were members of the American Citizens' Freedom Association.

Sally had to sit back and think about that. *James Bardine is a member of the ACFA . . . The ACFA is bringing the lawsuit against the school . . . The killer was wearing Bardine's ring.*

Did this mean a connection between the ACFA and Sally's would-be killer? Sally thought so. She would be looking up more names, that was certain. She couldn't wait to write to Tom and tell him.

But who in the world was that fiendish woman in black?

Friday morning, Pastor Mark Howard found his way through the noisy, busy, bustling Bergen Door Company, protective eyewear and earplugs in place, dodging the forklift, ducking around the doors being stacked, being sanded, being moved. He engaged a clipboard-carrying foreman in a brief, shouting conversation, and got directions to the small cubicle office of Donna Hemphile, Finish Supervisor. Mark could see Donna through the glass enclosure. He stepped up and tapped on the door.

"Yeah, come in!"

Mark stepped inside.

Donna Hemphile swiveled around in her desk chair and stuck out her hand. "Hey, Mark! What a surprise! What brings you here?"

Mark had no time for sweet-and-easy, beat-around-the-bush phrases. "Some pretty serious matters, Donna."

Donna looked at the clock. "Well, you know, I have to be out of here by—"

"I already talked to Mr. Bergen. He has someone else handling that new band saw. He said I could have an hour with you."

Donna had to digest that for a moment, and then relaxed back in her chair. "Okay. Have a seat."

Mark wheeled the only other chair around and sat facing Donna. "I've been running all around town since Wednesday night trying to nail some things down, and I haven't slept much. You know the kind of trouble we've been having in the church since this lawsuit came up. I've felt like a seaman trying to patch the leaks in a sinking ship before it goes down completely."

Donna nodded. "Yeah, it's been rough."

"Anyway, I finally got three families together for a conference: the Warings, the Jessups, and the Walroths. It was a pretty good meeting, I guess. Ed and Judy Waring are still disgruntled, but the Jessups and Walroths might be coming around." Mark paused. He was going to change directions. "But I wanted to ask you about something they all told me, and you know, I never thought about it before this. You're on the prayer chain, and your name comes before the Jessups, the Walroths, and the Warings."

"Mm-hm." Donna just sat there listening.

Mark plunged in. "So, let me ask you point-blank: Did you tell June Walroth that Tom Harris beats his daughter Ruth, and that's why he puts long sleeves on her so often?"

Donna chuckled at that. "No."

"Did you tell Judy Waring that Cathy and I are having marital problems because I was unfaithful and had an affair a few years ago?"

Donna smiled and shook her head. "No."

"Did you tell Ed Waring that the school was in bad debt because Tom and Mrs. Fields were stealing the school's money?"

"No."

"Did you tell Andrea Jessup that Tom's had some real problems with sexual deviancy ever since Cindy died?"

"No."

Mark was finding Donna's extremely brief answers a bit jarring. "You don't have any other comment about all this?"

Donna smiled and shook her head in seeming incredulity. "Why should I say anything, Mark? Those people are gossiphounds. This is the kind of thing they'd come up with."

"Why do you suppose they all came up with the same source for their information?"

She tossed up her hands. "Beats me. They must have something against me, I don't know. So what else do you have on the list?"

"Well . . . somebody who doesn't even go to our church. Kyle Krantz, the kid who got fired on Tuesday for having marijuana in his locker."

At that, Donna rolled her eyes. "Oh, brother!"

"Well, he has an interesting story to tell, and you know, a lot of what he has to say checks out. I guess you know his side of the story, right? That someone planted that bag of pot in his locker to set him up?"

"Oh yeah, I've heard it, all right. He could have come up with something more original. All the kids use that line."

"I've heard it before myself, from Ben Cole. Somebody planted some confiscated marijuana in his locker at the police station, and Mulligan fired him. Of course, it was Mulligan, according to Kyle, who came down to the plant here and struck a deal with Kyle and didn't book him for possession, isn't that right?"

"That part of it wasn't my concern. I just fired him according to company policy."

Mark slowed down a little for emphasis. "Kyle says Mulligan told him he'd let it go if Kyle kept his mouth shut about some things he knew."

Donna got just a little tense. "Well, listen, Mark, what goes on in this plant is my business, and none of your concern."

Mark didn't back off, but kept going. "Somebody killed Kyle's dog too; they cut it open and left it on the front seat of his car. Maybe they were trying to give him a little reminder to watch himself."

Donna leaned her elbow on her desk, propped her hand under her cheek, and gave every appearance of patiently humoring a childish, assuming, overimaginative minister.

Mark kept going. "That was weird enough in itself, and I don't know if I would have believed Kyle if something similar hadn't happened to us, right at the church. Monday morning, somebody splashed goat's blood on the front door and left two goat legs crossed on the porch. It was some kind of curse, or maybe it was a warning, I don't know. But just the day before, on Sunday morning, Ben Cole went out to the Potter place to investigate the killing of a goat that used to belong to Sally Roe. All the blood had been drained out, and the legs cut off.

"Then, according to Kyle, on that Sunday night he and a friend were out at the Benson farm and saw a witch coven holding a ritual in the barn, and wouldn't you know it—the witches, or Satanists, whatever they were, were drinking goat's blood and were standing in a circle around two more goat legs, calling for the defeat of the Christians and for the death of Sally Roe."

That finally evoked at least a small comment from Donna Hemphile. "Heh. Pretty bizarre."

Mark hit her squarely with the next sentence. "And Kyle says *you* were there, that you were part of that group holding the ritual, along with Sergeant Mulligan, Claire Johanson, and Jon

Schmidt—probably Tom Harris's, and our church's, worst enemies right now."

Donna said nothing. She just leaned back in her chair and kept listening, surprisingly detached.

"We also checked with Kyle's friend and gave him quite a thorough testing with some photographs Marshall had of the people Kyle claimed were there, as well as some photographs of people who were not there, and some phony information we claimed Kyle had told us. The friend checked out on every detail. I'm convinced we have two reliable witnesses."

"And a pretty wild story," Donna reminded him.

"Well . . . after all we've been through, and everything we've seen and learned, it isn't that wild. It's disgusting, it's tragic, it's bizarre, but at this point I find it incontrovertible, especially since Mulligan—and perhaps yourself—have stooped to such terror and intimidation tactics to keep the boys quiet about it." Donna didn't look like she had any comment to that, but Mark didn't wait for one. "Donna, you said that what happens here at the plant is your business and none of my concern. Well, what happens to my church is my concern, so let me just get down to the direct question: Were you there at the Benson farm on Sunday night?"

"No," she said simply.

"Are you involved in witchcraft or occultism?"

"No."

"Are you trying to destroy my church with gossip and division?"

She chuckled, and the chuckle had a note of mockery in it. "Of course not. Hey, you're going through difficult times. If you don't all stick together, you won't make it."

"What about Sally Roe?"

"Never heard of her."

An unplanned question occurred to Mark. "What about the social worker for the CPD that took Tom's kids, Irene Bledsoe? Is she purposely working against us, trying to destroy Tom's reputation?"

Donna laughed. "Hey, as far as I know, she's just doing her job. If you ask me, Tom's a sick man, and I think she can see that."

"What about that time you saw Ben Cole first visiting Abby Grayson here at the plant? Did you report that to Sergeant Mulligan?"

"You mean, did I snitch?"

"Whatever."

"I don't really know Mulligan. Why would I go out of my way to tell him about one of his own cops?"

Mark looked at Donna, and Donna returned his gaze. There was no question remaining between them.

"Donna . . . you don't lie very well."

She smiled that same subtle, mocking smile. "On the contrary, Mark—you did approve my application for church membership."

Mark nodded. "So I did. So I did." He'd heard enough. "Well, I could go through the Biblical pattern and come back with some witnesses to go through all this again with you, but . . . what do you think? That probably isn't worth the trouble, is it?"

Donna just kept smiling. "No need, really."

The phone rang. Donna picked it up. "Yeah. Okay. I'll be right there." She hung up. "Well, sorry, that was Mr. Bergen. He wants to meet with me right away."

"I know," said Mark, rising from his chair. He let himself out the door, and walked down the aisle. Donna was not far behind him.

Mr. Bergen's office was about halfway down the floor. Mark looked through the window; Abby Grayson, Kyle Krantz, Kyle's friend Billy, and Marshall Hogan had already been there quite a while. Mr. Bergen, a stern-looking man in his sixties, was pacing about the office, waiting impatiently, visibly angry.

Mark cracked the door open and stuck his head in long enough to catch Mr. Bergen's eye. Bergen looked his way immediately; he was expected.

"It's all true," said Mark.

Then he closed the door and went on his way, pausing just long enough to look back and see Donna Hemphile go into the office of her boss.

37

Lucy Brandon could feel her scalp crawling and her stomach twisting into a knot. This was her second such phone call today, interrupting her work at the Post Office and scaring her to death.

"Don't talk to Hogan," said her once-kind friend Claire Johanson. "Don't say a word to him, or to any of those people! It could go very bad for you if you don't protect any knowledge you have!"

Lucy tried to keep her voice down so Debbie wouldn't overhear. "Claire, what's happened?"

"Nothing has happened!"

"I got a call from Gordon Jefferson just like yours. He wasn't kind at all. He kept telling me I'd be in legal trouble if anything leaked, and I didn't even know what he was talking about . . ."

Claire didn't answer right away. She was working on a reply that was safe—or downright deceiving. "The hearing before the federal Court of Appeals is coming up soon, and things are getting critical, that's all. I think it has all of us on edge."

"So why come down on me?"

"It's not just you. We're clamping down on everyone, even ourselves. Too much information is getting out, and it could ruin our case. We have to be careful. I'm sure you understand that."

"This all seems so sudden."

"Well, it just seems that way. Don't worry about it. Just keep quiet, and keep things to yourself from now on. I have to go."

Click.

I'm going to explode, Lucy thought. *I'm just going to go crazy, stark raving mad. I can't take this anymore!*

Ding!

A patron was at the counter. *No, I can't see anyone, I can't talk to anyone. I just want to get out of here. But where could I go? How would I explain my daughter? What about the trouble I've gotten myself into?*

Ding!

Oh, where's Debbie? Lucy looked at the clock. *Oh, wonderful! She's on break, probably across the street buying some sugarless gum or something.*

"Coming."

She gathered herself, trying to calm down, and stepped to the front.

The patron was Tom Harris.

Both of them immediately felt awkward and even shied back a little.

"Oh, I'm sorry," said Tom. "I mean, I don't have to—"

Lucy looked this way and that. There was no one else in the lobby. "Well, I can wait on you."

Tom stood back from the counter. He extended his arms to lay some packages in front of Lucy. "I wanted to send these to my folks."

Lucy pulled the packages toward her, turned them around, turned them around again, read the addresses, read them again, still didn't know what she'd read. She just couldn't think. Was she supposed to weigh them? She set all three on the scale at once and fumbled with the sliding weights. No, no, this wouldn't work, not all three . . .

She set the packages down and without looking up tried to say, "I'm sorry any of this ever happened," but her voice was too weak and trembling.

Tom heard her anyway. "Sure. So am I."

She tried to concentrate on the packages. "Well, I guess we aren't supposed to talk about it."

"I understand."

"Do you think Amber's possessed?"

The question didn't just slip out—Lucy pushed it out. She wanted to know.

But Tom Harris was muzzled, and acted like it. Even though he wanted to answer, he could only look at her in obvious frustration. "You know I can't talk about that."

"*I* need to know. For *me*."

He shook his head sadly, painfully. "I can't talk about it. But listen . . ."

She listened.

"Uh . . . Jesus Christ conquered the spiritual forces of evil on the Cross. The Bible says He disarmed them and made a public display of them. He has all authority over them, and He's given that authority to His people, the true believers in Him. He's the answer. That's all I can say."

"Have you ever seen someone possessed?"

Tom took back his packages. "I wish I could tell you all about it. Maybe when this lawsuit is over, huh? I'll . . . Listen, no offense, okay? I'll mail these later."

He hurried out the door, leaving Lucy with her questions unanswered.

"Evans, Santinelli, Farnsworth, and McCutcheon," said the receptionist.

"Mr. Bardine, please," said the woman's voice on the other end.

The receptionist hesitated. "Uh . . . I'm very sorry to inform you, but Mr. Bardine is deceased. Did you have any current business with him? We can arrange for someone else to complete that."

The other party was understandably shocked by the news. "Did you say Mr. Bardine was deceased?"

"Yes, I'm sorry to tell you that. He was killed in an auto accident several weeks ago. It was a real blow to all of us here at the firm."

"Well, I'm . . . I'm shocked to hear that myself."

"I'm sorry. Perhaps you'd like to talk to Mr. Mahoney, Mr. Bardine's superior. Perhaps he can help you."

"Oh, thank you, no. Let me sort things out first."

"Fine. Thank you for calling."

"Good-bye."

The receptionist hung up the phone and went back to typing a letter on a sophisticated electronic typewriter, sitting at a massive, dark oak, brass-fitted desk, in a plush carpeted office with twelve-foot-high, wood paneled walls and ornate lighting fixtures, as gray-haired senior partners, junior partners dressed for success, aggressive legal assistants, ambitious secretaries, and powerful incognito visitors moved tight-lipped and chin-high up and down the halls with their briefcases, legal files, or yellow legal pads.

The Chicago offices of Evans, Santinelli, Farnsworth, and McCutcheon were more than a palace; they were a citadel of power and legal technocracy, where knowledge and power were synonymous and time was money—lots of money. Here the czars of case law and the architects of legal precedent groomed the future by challenging, bending, stretching, and even crossbreeding the law, turning it their way as far and as often as their money, skill, connections, and power would allow.

These were the offices of the elite: the promoters of the favored and the deposers of the dispensable, the guarantors of success and the instigators of ruin.

Atop this ivory tower, at the pinnacle of the pyramid, strode the ruthless and powerful Mr. Santinelli.

"Good afternoon, Mr. Santinelli," said the receptionist.

"Good afternoon," he replied with a faint, obligatory smile, extending his hand to receive the newly typed letter. "I'll be having a special meeting for the next half-hour; there will be no calls, no disturbances."

"Yes, sir."

Santinelli continued down the aisle to a tall and imposing mahogany door. An aide swung the door open just in time for him to pass through it, and then closed the door after him like a slab over a crypt.

Santinelli was in the private conference room adjacent to his office, a soundproof, secret, and rather gloomy place. The woodwork still seemed to absorb the light, and the floor-to-ceiling, velvet curtains were still drawn over the windows.

Three men stood in a tight cluster at one end of the room, talking in hushed voices. They nodded a greeting when Santinelli came in.

One of them was Mr. Khull, the man entrusted with the elimination of Sally Beth Roe.

Santinelli made some quick introductions. "Gentlemen, allow me to formally introduce Mr. Khull, who will be assisting us in the present pressing matters. Mr. Khull, I present to you Mr. Evans, a partner in this firm, now fully devoted to our present legal concerns, and Mr. McCutcheon, our director of administration and finance."

"A pleasure," said Khull.

"I've spoken with Mr. Goring at Summit and Mr. Steele at the Omega Center," Santinelli reported. "It's clear to all of us that Sally Roe has been tracking down the owner of that ring she slipped from Von Bauer's finger, and using Von Bauer's fee to finance her cross-country sleuthing. They agree with us that the rosters are enough to lead her to the late James Bardine, which means she'll have to come here, though we can't be sure when. Mr. Khull has secured the building for that eventuality, and of course we have your assurance, Mr. Khull, that the failure at Bentmore University will not be repeated?"

"Last time we were a little too discreet, I would say. I have twice the personnel here as I had stationed at Bentmore, and our techniques will be much more direct this time."

"The hearing in the federal Court of Appeals is on Monday," Santinelli fumed. "A ruling in our favor will not be much consolation if Roe is still at large. When she comes, you may bring her to this room and kill her right here, as far as I'm concerned."

Khull stifled a laugh.

Just across the conference table, Destroyer and the twelve grotesque warriors who flanked him did not stifle their laughter at all, but thoroughly enjoyed the thought of killing that woman.

Destroyer's laugh was a brief indulgence, however. He still bore the bruises and shame from his recent meeting with the Strongman, and now his exhilaration at the thought of Sally Roe's impending death was mixed with desperation.

You will take her this time! he growled, his wings flared in anger, his crooked finger pointing across the table. *You will take her and kill her!* Then he shouted to his warriors, "Surround this place, and post sentries over the city! She will not evade us this time!"

The warriors swooped out of the room with a thunderous war cry, almost crazy with a thirst for blood.

Destroyer glared at Khull, and muttered to himself, *Come to us, Sally Roe. Whatever your condition, Cross or no Cross, this time nothing will stop us. Nothing!*

On the outskirts of Chicago, Sally Roe sat in a dismal, musty room at a cheap motel, staring at the telephone and wondering what to do next. So James Bardine was dead! She'd spent no small amount of time preparing herself to confront him face to face, to bring it all to a head, and she had come so close, but now what could she do? Well, there was no point in visiting Evans, Santinelli, Farnsworth, and McCutcheon. The man she sought was no longer there.

But obviously Bardine wasn't the only player in this game; there were other players and strategists, from the clumsy police in Bacon's Corner to the mind-molders at Omega, to the highest levels of the educational establishment at Bentmore University, and even beyond that. They all knew about her, they all wanted that ring, and they all seemed quite determined to kill her.

With reluctance, she brought back an old thought she'd entertained several times in the past few weeks and went over it again. There was one final ploy she could try, one do-or-die way to find and identify the people who were responsible for this whole nightmare. Did she say do-or-die? It would most likely be die, if God didn't see fit to spare her.

Funny. Before she encountered the Cross, she saw no reason to live but feared death. Now she had a reason to live, but did not fear death at all. It was an odd kind of peace, a fascinating sense of rest and stillness deep in her soul. Someday she would have to analyze it and clarify just what had happened to her, *if* she lived long enough. If not . . . Well, maybe she'd lived long enough already.

She got out her notebook again, and began to compose her very last letter to Tom Harris.

Nathan and Armoth were tense with anticipation and preoccupied with strategy, but they were there by Sally's side when she started that letter.

"'The word of her testimony, the blood of the Lamb, and she does not love her life so much as to shrink from death,'" said Nathan.

"That's three," said Armoth.

Sally's pen glided over the paper.

> *Tom, this will be my last letter to you. I have told you all that I have done, and all that I know, and I've shared with you my encounter with the God and Savior you serve. What more could remain but to see you face to face and finally bring this trouble to an end?*
>
> *There is no doubt in my mind that the ACFA has pulled some big strings, or vice versa, and are connected with the attempt on my life, which must be connected with the attack against you and your school. I now have the gold ring taken from my would-be assassin as well as the four volumes of the History and Roster of the Royal and Sacred Order of the Nation which prove the ring belonged to the now deceased James Everett Bardine, an attorney in*

high standing with the ACFA. I also have other informa-
tion, much of which I have provided in many letters, that
should prove invaluable to you in your defense against this
lawsuit.

All that remains now is for me to return to Bacon's
Corner to aid your attorney in building his defense, and
ultimately to testify in open court on your behalf.

I believe it's time I heard from you. Please contact me
at the Caravan Motel.

She gave Tom the address and telephone number, then closed
her notebook. If she hurried, she could get the letter photocopied
and mailed.

But first, there was one more letter to write. She flipped to a
fresh page in her notebook—she'd used up the pages in two note-
books by now, and was starting into her third—and began her first
and last letter to Bernice Krueger, c/o the *Ashton Clarion*. She wrote
hurriedly, saying only what was essential.

The young clerk at the Post Office was just bagging up the mail
for the evening pickup when a lady in jeans and a blue jacket came
to the counter with some more. He was in a hurry; the truck was
coming any minute. He took care of her quickly, applied the necessary postage, and threw the rest of the mail into the mailbag.

There was the truck! He grabbed the bag and headed for the
back door.

The lady went out the front door, glad she'd made it in time.

In the rush, one letter fell from the mailbag to the floor under
the front counter and lay there facedown.

It was addressed to Bernice Krueger, c/o the *Ashton Clarion*.

38

On Monday morning, without prior warning and totally unexpected, the fax machine in the *Ashton Clarion* office warbled
its electronic ring and was barely heard over the prepublication
bedlam that usually marked Monday mornings. Bernice didn't hear
it at all; she was in Marshall's glassed-in office trying to convince
Eddy's Bakery to buy just two more column inches so she wouldn't
have to keep filling in that space with stupid one-liners.

"Hey listen," she said, "we'll make the donut bigger, and then
make the coffee mug bigger, you know, show more steam coming out
or something. The readers will grab right onto it. Sure they will!"

"Bernice!" Cheryl called through the glass. "You're getting a fax!"

Bernice looked up at Cheryl. "What?"

Cheryl said something back, and all Bernice could hear through the glass was the word fax. The rest was meant for lipreaders.

A fax? From who? So far she was drawing a blank.

The phone squawked in her ear. She had to give a reply. "Oh, yeah. Well, think about it, will you, Eddy? I'll give you a deal on it. Well, let *me* think about *that*. Okay, good-bye."

Cheryl knocked at the door lightly, cracked it open, and tossed the sheet of paper in, hot off the fax machine.

Bernice grabbed it before it floated to the floor and gave it a once-over.

Oh! This was from Cliff Bingham, her contact in Washington, D.C.! She'd forgotten all about him. Well, well! He'd found the *Finding the Real Me* curriculum for fourth-graders at the Library of Congress and sent her the title page with a note scribbled at the top: "Bernice, is this the one you're after? —Cliff."

She smiled. *Well, Cliff, you did all right, but Marshall's seen the curriculum already; you're too late. Thanks anyway.*

She went to her Rolodex to find Cliff's number, found it, and picked up the telephone. She punched in the number, and looked over the title page again as she waited for the ring and the answer.

Then she saw it. She slammed the phone down. She scanned the page again to make sure. She checked the publication date.

She picked up the phone and pounded out the number for the Cole residence in Bacon's Corner.

"Hello?" It was Bev Cole.

"Hello, Bev. This is Bernice Krueger in Ashton."

"Oh, hi! What do you know?"

"I've got to talk to Marshall right away!"

"Hooo, well he isn't here, and I don't know where he is."

"I've got to—oh, nuts! Did he say when he'd be back?"

"No, he runs around so much I never know where he is, he and Ben."

"Bev, listen, I'm going to fax him something. He should be able to pick it up at Judy's, right?"

"Oh yeah, if she's open."

"I'm going to fax it to Judy's Secretarial Service right now, and you tell him to get over there right away and pick it up, all right?"

"Okay, I'll tell him. Hey, you sound excited."

"Oh, I'm a little excitedseeyoulatergood-bye!"

She scrambled out of the office and made a beeline for the fax machine.

Marshall, where are you?

Lucy Brandon was going through the morning mail, sorting it, slipping it into all the Post Office boxes and assigning it to the four different carrier routes. She was ill, nervous, overwrought, and exhausted, and now she was beginning to hate her job, especially when letters came in from "S. B. Roe."

Like this one, fresh out of the bag, no sooner thought of than in her hand! How many did this make? It had to be more than thirty. Thirty-plus envelopes, all stuffed with several thicknesses of the same lined notebook paper, all written in the same, fluid handwriting just visible through the envelope, and all addressed to Tom Harris.

So I guess when I forward this one, I'll be violating federal law over thirty times. What a thought. What if I just delivered it to Tom Harris? What if I slipped it into his carrier's box, just one of these letters, just once?

"Good morning, Lucy!"

She literally jumped, dropping the letter to the floor.

Sergeant Harold Mulligan!

"Sergeant! What are you doing back here? You scared me to death!"

He stooped and picked up the letter from the floor. "Ah, another one, eh?"

She tried to take it from him. "Yes, thank you kindly—"

He wouldn't let go. "Naw, now just hold on, Lucy. I've got orders regarding any further mail from Miss You-know-who."

She didn't care. "I'll take that letter back, sergeant! It's United States mail!"

What? He actually grabbed her arm with painful force and pushed her against the wall! He hurt her, and she just couldn't believe it!

He spoke to her in a low, threatening voice she'd never heard from him before. "And just what do you think you're gonna do with it, huh, Lucy? Are you thinking you just might mail it where it's supposed to go? Huh?"

"You let go of me!"

"You listen to me, little lady! Any more mail from Roe, you put it right in my hand, right here, see? You don't mess with it, you don't even think about it, or you are gonna have one big, ugly pack of troubles!"

She was getting scared. "I'm doing what I'm told, Harold, you know that. Please let go of me!"

"Just wanna make sure we're clear on this—"

"Excuse me," came a voice from the front.

It was Marshall Hogan.

Oh man, how much of this did he see? Mulligan immediately

turned his aggressive posture into a teasing one and let Lucy go. "Okay, Lucy, take care!"

He went out the back way with the letter in his pocket.

Debbie stepped up to the counter to help the big, red-haired man. Lucy hurried forward. "I'll take care of him."

Debbie backed away, but could see Lucy was in no condition to help anyone. Too late, though. They couldn't talk about such a thing in front of a customer. She went back to her sorting, but kept an eye on her boss.

"I'd like a book of stamps," said Marshall gently.

She reached into the drawer under the counter. Her hands were visibly shaking, and she couldn't look up.

"Are you in trouble?" Marshall asked.

"Please, I can't talk to you," she said on the verge of tears.

"Just sell me some stamps then," he said. "Do that first."

She finally found a book of stamps and set them on the counter.

He had something else on the counter as well. "This is County Coroner Joey Parnell's report on the woman who committed suicide, supposedly Sally Beth Roe. See the description? Black hair, in her twenties. Here . . . look at this." He set a photograph in front of her and continued to talk in quiet, gentle tones. "This is a police mug shot of her. She had a criminal record. Now I know you know what the real Sally Roe looks like; you identified a picture of her at your deposition. But this is the woman who was found dead. She was a member of a secret coven of witches who call themselves Broken Birch, and when she tried to kill Sally Roe, she was working for someone—she was carrying ten thousand dollars."

Lucy looked down at the picture, still shaking but listening.

Marshall continued, "Now that cop who just roughed you up back there has done all he can to cover this up and make it look like a suicide, and we think we know why: he belongs to that coven; he's in on the whole thing. As a matter of fact, that coven lays claim to some pretty big wheels in LifeCircle—some of your own friends, including Claire Johanson and Jon Schmidt."

Marshall waited just a moment for that to sink in, and then concluded, "As for Sally Roe, we have good evidence that she's still alive somewhere, probably hiding for her life. So the question I'd like you to consider is this: Why would the same friends who are helping you in this lawsuit want Sally Roe killed?"

Lucy didn't say a word. She could only stand there stone-still, staring at the photographs as tears filled her eyes.

Marshall got his answer from her face. He took back the coroner's report and photos and slipped a piece of paper to her. "This is where you can reach me, at Ben and Bev Cole's house. Call me anytime."

He paid for the book of stamps and walked out. Lucy still didn't move, even as Marshall's money for the stamps sat on the counter in front of her.

Debbie saw the whole thing. Now she was finished with just watching. She was going to do something.

The mail . . . I forgot the mail!

Bernice got into her Volkswagen Beetle and zipped over to the Ashton Post Office a little late this morning. In all the excitement, her daily mail pickup had slipped her mind.

She went into the lobby, said hello to Lou, the young mail clerk, and opened the *Ashton Clarion*'s Post Office box.

Krioni stood beside her, as interested in the morning mail as she was. He was looking for an important letter from Sally Roe.

Bernice flipped through the junk flyers, the bills, the letters to the editor . . . Ah, here were some checks in payment of advertising and want ads; those were always nice.

Nothing unusual, everything routine. She dropped all the mail into her large plastic shopping bag and headed out the door.

This was a horrendous development! Krioni shot through the roof of the Post Office and met Triskal high above.

"Nothing!" he said.

Triskal wasn't ready for that report. "Nothing? No letter?"

They could see Bernice getting back into her little car, far too calm and unruffled.

"It didn't get here," said Krioni, agitated, frustrated, and thinking fast. "It's lost. . . It's misplaced . . . I don't know! We'd better get word to Nathan and Armoth. If we don't get the fire started in time, Sally Roe is as good as dead!"

Sally's last letter to Tom Harris lay open on Claire Johanson's desk, and Claire was on the telephone.

"The Caravan Motel," she said. "I think our magic worked after all; this is the first time Roe has ever revealed her whereabouts. Apparently she'll be there for a while; she's waiting for Tom Harris to contact her." The party on the other end was elated. "Well, I'll breathe easier when we have her, before she writes to anyone else. And I'll breathe easiest of all when she's dead." More elated squawkings from the other end. "Yes, I'm sure Mr. Santinelli will be pleased. Give him our regards."

Claire hung up, rested her chin on her knuckles, and smiled at Sergeant Harold Mulligan. "Harold, help yourself to a drink."

Nathan shot through the roof of the Post Office near Chicago and flew over the heads of the busy staff, looking this way and that, banking and swooping over the tables, counters, and carts, then ducking under the tables, flying just inches above the linoleum, his sharp eyes scrutinizing every scrap of paper, every piece of junk mail, every—

There! Just under the front counter, facedown, lay the lost letter to Bernice Krueger. It was going to take some special measures to get it to Ashton in time. He grabbed it, arched upward, and looked around the room for the right mailbag to put it in.

Snatch! The letter was gone from his hand! He spun about in time to see a brazen little imp holding the letter in his claws, grinning a toothy grin, hovering on blurred black wings.

"Ooo," said the demon, "and what have we here?"

Nathan didn't have time for this. His sword was instantly in his hand.

OOF! A kick from a black, clawed foot! Another spirit came at him from the side, sword ready!

Nathan dashed the demon's sword aside with his own, then kicked the demon back, sending him through the wall of the building.

Another spirit dropped from above; Nathan shot sideways to dodge a plunging sword, then mowed the spirit in half.

Where was that imp? There! Hiding behind the sorting bench!

Two more spirits! They must have heard there was a fight in here. Nathan dove for the first, his sword raised, but the other spirit grabbed his ankle and jerked him backward. His sword cut through space, and that was all. The first demon was ready now with his own sword, laughing and drooling. The ankle-grabber was still pulling, his claws digging in.

Well, use what you have, Nathan figured. His wings roared with power, pulling him forward. With incredible strength and perfect timing, he swung his leg in a high, sweeping kick, giving the ankle-grabber a thrilling ride until Nathan brought him down with skull-crunching force on his partner. They were out.

There went the imp with the letter! Nathan shot sideways and caught him in the belly. The legs drifted to the floor while the imp dissolved. Nathan caught the letter, made a quick search, then slam-dunked it into the right mailbag. It would go out on the next truck.

As for the demons, Nathan knew there could be trouble—some of them had gotten away with the knowledge of this letter.

In the sealed conference room at Evans, Santinelli, Farnsworth, and McCutcheon, Santinelli hung up his private line and looked across the table at the anxious Mr. Khull.

"Mr. Khull, I've just been given some good news. You'd better gather your choice personnel."

That "good news" went out through the demonic ranks like a shock wave, and as Destroyer flew up through the roof of the law office building to gather his hordes, he suddenly found he had all the friends and yea-saying lackeys he needed to finish the job, especially the demons from Broken Birch. They were swarming in from every sector of the sky, whooping and hollering, wanting to be a part of this glorious moment.

"I knew it!" he gloated, and with no small measure of relief. "I knew it would work! Our Judas has come through at last, and now Sally Roe will have her Gethsemane! We will take her!" Then he added under his breath, "And I will throw her as a gift into the Strongman's face!"

The demons were muttering, nodding, and rumbling their approval and admiration of Destroyer's great wisdom as they came to rest on the roof, hovered overhead, buzzed in tight circles around the building, and even tripped over each other.

This motley, bloodthirsty swarm needed to be brought to order. Destroyer soared into the sky where every gleaming yellow eye could see him, and waved his glowing red sword in wide circles to get their attention. Most of them settled down and listened. The others were too busy hooting, hollering, and sparring.

"Forces!" Destroyer called.

His twelve captains converged immediately.

"We need to weed this garden and select the best! Choose warriors for our mission, and send the rabble to Summit. Let the Strongman put them to work!"

The captains soon had the spirits thoroughly sifted; the best warriors stood ready, swords gleaming. The pranksters, imps, and harassers were ordered to Summit, and left with much grumbling.

Destroyer was satisfied. He addressed the great horde. "We will prepare the way for Broken Birch! Death to the woman!"

"Death to the woman!" they shouted as one, and with an explosion of wings they rushed into the sky.

From miles away, Tal, Nathan, and Armoth saw the demons rise like a swarm of shrieking, whooping bats over Chicago, heading south. This was an armada of death for Sally Roe, a black cloud of doom.

Tal had received Nathan's news about Sally's last letter. "Then it's going to be a day late. Our fire is delayed, and Sally will soon be in their hands!"

"Can we stop them?" asked Armoth.

Tal shook his head. "Everything is in motion now. We're committed."

"We do have warriors posted to monitor everything," Nathan assured his captain.

"But Destroyer will take her," Tal replied, his voice weakened with the pain of it. "And he will do what he wants with her . . ."

Marshall no sooner got back from his trip to the Post Office for stamps than he was out again, this time heading for Judy's Secretarial Service, quite curious and adequately baited by Bernice and her maddening flair for suspense. To hear Bev Cole tell it, the fate of the world depended on Marshall picking up whatever Bernice was going to fax to him.

Sally Roe remained in her musty little room at the Caravan Motel, sitting in the only chair, reading from a Gideon Bible.

"Who shall separate us from the love of Christ?" she read. ". . . I am convinced that neither death nor life, neither angels nor demons, neither the present nor the future, nor any powers, neither height nor depth, nor anything else in all creation, will be able to separate us from the love of God that is in Christ Jesus our Lord."

She closed her eyes, gave thanks, and kept reading, just waiting hour by hour in her little room.

Marshall pulled into the small parking area in front of Judy's Secretarial. Well, was anybody there? The lights were on inside, but there was no sign of Judy. Hm. That looked like a note taped over the OPEN sign hanging in the window. He got out to have a look.

Outside Chicago, two cars turned off the main thoroughfare, came down one block, and slowed long enough for the people inside to get a good look at the Caravan Motel.

"Hm, so this is the Caravan," said Mr. Khull, giving the old motel a quick once-over. "Roe isn't operating on much of a budget."

"What a dump," said one of Khull's three favorite killers, a young, wiry woman with long, blonde hair who could have passed for a college student.

The Caravan Motel was no joy to behold. Long ago, before the freeways diverted all the interstate traffic, this place probably did a profitable and respectable business in housing weary travelers for the night. Now times had changed, the fourteen little cabins were run down, the lawn had surrendered to weeds, and most of the business here was probably the disreputable kind.

"Which cabin is she in?" asked a tall, youthful-looking man. He'd gotten within a knife's blade of Sally Roe on the Bentmore University campus. He still had his knife, and he was looking forward to a longer, more satisfying encounter.

"Fourteen," said Khull, "right on the end near the road. We won't have to pass any of the other rooms. She's making it easy."

Khull parked the car just past the motel, and the other car pulled in behind. Altogether, eight people got out of the two cars. Khull gave the four men from the second car a slight nod, and they scattered immediately up and down the street, covering every avenue of escape from the motel.

"Okay, babe," said Khull, "check and make sure."

The young woman went ahead of them, walking into the motel office.

Khull and the other two just stood on the sidewalk, talking and looking casual.

She came out again, and pointed discreetly at Number 14.

"Let's go," said Khull.

"Oh, hi," said Judy. "Been waiting long?"

"No, not long," said Marshall. "About ten minutes, I guess." He'd seen the little note she'd taped in the window, "BACK IN TEN MINUTES."

"Had to get a new typewriter ribbon. I can hardly read my letters anymore." She had a small sack in her hand, which meant her trip must have been successful.

"I think I have a fax waiting for me."

"Oh yeah, you do."

Judy unlocked the door and let him in. "It came in not too long ago. I think I put it . . . Let me see, where did I put it?"

The young blonde knocked on the door to Number 14.

Sally tensed, closed her eyes, and prayed a quick prayer. Then she rose from her chair and approached the door. "Yes?"

"Maid," said the woman.

Judy finally found the sheet of paper that had come out of the fax machine. "Oh, here you are."

Marshall took it and thanked her. Now this looked familiar. It was even disappointing. Hadn't he told Bernice he'd already seen the curriculum? What was the big deal? All the way over here to Judy's for this?

But what was Bernice's note at the top? She'd written it in bold marker pen.

"Okay, just a minute," Sally said, and looked around the room one last time. She was ready. She went to the door and put her hand on the knob.

"Marshall," said Bernice's note, "have you seen this? Call me."

From the note, a huge arrow drawn with a wide-tipped marker pen bled down the page to a glaring circle at the bottom.

Within that circle was the name of the curriculum's author—its *real* author.

Sally Beth Roe.

WHAM! The door burst open and almost caught Sally across the face. Khull was all over her, then two more blurred figures. Arms grappled and grabbed, the room spun around her, she fell to the floor, her face smacking the worn carpet. A sharp knee gouged into her back, pinning her down so hard she thought her ribs would crack. They grabbed her arms and twisted them behind her until she cried out in pain, then bound them with loop upon loop of tight, cutting rope.

AAW! Khull grabbed a fistful of her hair and wrenched her head up from the carpet. She couldn't breathe. He held a glimmering, silver knife to her throat. "Make a sound, and this goes in."

She closed her mouth tightly, trying to contain the cries of pain and terror she just couldn't help.

The room was full of people, searching every corner, every drawer, under the mattress, dumping out her duffel bag, going through all her possessions.

"You know what we're looking for," said Khull right into her ear. He grabbed one of her bound hands and forced her index finger open. "Tell us where the ring is and where those rosters are, or I start cutting."

"If I tell you, you'll just run off with them yourself!" said Sally. The knife came against the base of her finger. She gushed the words out. "I'll tell the people who sent you! Turn me over to them!"

The knife remained in place.

Sally blurted, "You want to get paid, don't you?"

The knife stayed where it was; Khull's grip on her finger never loosened. She could feel the edge of that knife against her skin, and she prayed while an eternity passed.

Destroyer stood in the room, not at all willing to lose the prize once he had found it.

Take her to Summit, he said to Khull.

Khull leaned over Sally, longing with every fiber of his being to run his knife through her heart. He hesitated, breathing hard.

Destroyer put his hand on his sword. *You will take her to Summit, to the Strongman, and you will do it now!*

After the longest, most agonizing moment, for no apparent reason, Khull took away the knife and let her finger go.

Sally thought she would faint. She was close to vomiting.

"Get her up!"

She was snatched from the floor in an instant by no less than four huge thugs, and held tightly, unable to move. Now she could see Khull's face leering at her, the eyes full of hate. Demon eyes.

SLAP! His hand felt like iron across her jaw, cheek, and nose. She almost blacked out. Warm blood began to trickle from her nose and down over her mouth.

Khull grabbed a fistful of her hair again and held his knife right under her nose. "We're going to take you to our friends. They are going to get the whole package right in their laps, and listen to me now: you'd better give them everything they want when they want it, because I will be right there, and if they don't get what they want, they are going to give you to me. To *me*, understand?"

"I *will* cooperate."

"Not a sound from you!"

"Not a sound."

Khull looked at her with all the lust and murderous intent of the Devil himself, and then gave the order: "Let's go."

The young blonde woman stuffed everything Sally owned into Sally's duffel bag, and a thug grabbed it up.

In broad daylight, like a gruesome parade, Khull led his band of rogues and their captive, bound with rope and her nose still bleeding, out of Number 14 and to the street. Sally could see some curtains cracked open across the courtyard, but no one dared show their face. Even the owner of the place, an ugly, chain-smoking woman in her fifties, caught just a glimpse of them and then turned away, being careful to mind her own business.

They took Sally to the first car, shoved her into the backseat between two men—one of them was the young knife-wielder she'd met at Bentmore—and drove away unhurried, unhampered, and unchallenged.

The Caravan Motel was almost invisible under a crawling, hissing swarm of evil spirits. Every person in every building was motivated by fear, self-interest, and even self-delusion. No, they didn't see anything. It wasn't what it looked like—it just seemed that way. It wasn't their problem. A lot of that kind of thing happened around places like this; so what?

Destroyer and his twelve key warriors flew just above the two automobiles, wary and braced for any angelic resistance. The resistance never came. They did see some heavenly warriors, but the warriors made no moves against them; they were intimidated by the great demonic numbers, no doubt.

"Ha!" Destroyer laughed, elbowing his closest warrior. "What did I say? Their strength is gone! Tal has no more numbers to boast in, and . . ." He was delighted with his own craftiness. " . . . I do believe we have surprised them all! Before they could muster any new strength, we have snatched their new little saint right from under their noses!"

As the two automobiles turned onto the main thoroughfare and sped away, many of Nathan's prize warriors were on hand to watch, hiding in the shadows, crouching behind trees, parked cars, and houses. They kept a close watch, but they did not intervene. The word had spread quickly and clearly among them all: This was Destroyer's moment, and Captain Tal's biggest risk ever.

Out on the interstate, a U.S. Mail truck sped along, heading southward from Chicago toward the easy rolling hills of the Midwest and the quaint little college town of Ashton.

On board, in a mailbag, just a little dirty and wrinkled by now, was that letter addressed to Bernice Krueger.

39

Marshall was impatient, and that made him anxious, and that made him irritable. Ben Cole just kept pacing around the house trying to think of what else to do, Kate sat next to Marshall at the dining room table, flipping through all their accumulated files for any information Marshall might need, and Bev Cole just kept watching it all and praying softly, "Lord Jesus, we need You now!"

Marshall was on the phone with John Harrigan, a friend and contact with the FBI. "Oh yeah, she wrote it, all right. I got back to my reporter, and she'd already gotten back to this Cliff Bingham guy, and he verifies the edition he found was recent, published only two years ago." Marshall rolled his eyes and gritted his teeth. This conversation wasn't bringing results fast enough. "So that means the curriculum the school gave to us was doctored; Sally Roe's name was deleted and substituted by two other names, and that fits right in with the cover-up I told you about. No, I don't have a case yet. I thought you guys were the ones who are supposed to investigate these things. Well, I'm close, real close, and I do think it's something for you guys to handle. The Omega Center's in Fairwood, Massachusetts, and Sally Roe was almost murdered clear over here in Bacon's Corner, for crying out loud! Now is that across state lines or what?" More talk from the other end. "All right, listen: can you give me a number where I can reach you anytime, I mean, right in the middle of the night if I have to? I won't call unless I've got some real stuff for you, but when I do get it, time will be that much shorter for Sally Roe." He got an objection. "Come on, I'll owe you one. Just remember that lead I got you in that cocaine operation." Marshall grabbed his pen. "Good man!"

He got several numbers, said good-bye, and hung up.

Everyone in the house converged on him. "Well? What did he say?"

"He'll be on call. I've got phone numbers to reach him at work, at home, at church, and I've also got his paging service, so he's covered. But what he's waiting for is some firm information to justify the FBI getting involved."

Ben was indignant. "What's wrong with all that stuff you gave him?"

"Eh, it was enough to make him interested, but not enough to make him stick his neck out."

"What about Wayne Corrigan?"

Kate answered, "I left a message at his office. He'll get what we have."

"O Lord Jesus, protect Sally Roe!" said Bev.

Guilo had returned to his post in the mountains above the picturesque town of Summit, and though the surroundings were as strikingly beautiful as ever, the invisible evil was even worse. Educators, statesmen, jurists, entertainers, corporate moguls, and financiers from all over the world were gathering just a mile up the valley from Summit at the Summit Institute for Humanistic Studies. Their semiannual conference was just getting underway, and as these global planners gathered, demon lords and warriors of the most conniving sort gathered with them, filling the valley with a swirling, sooty, steadily thickening cloud of spirits. The demons hovered, hooted, sparred, and jostled, more numerous, riotous, and cocky than ever before.

"They are expecting a real party," said Guilo.

Mr. Santinelli, kingpin of the law firm of Evans, Santinelli, Farnsworth, and McCutcheon, Mr. Goring, the lord and administrator of the Summit Institute for Humanistic Studies, and Mr. Steele, the ruthless ruler of the Omega Center for Educational Studies, were together again, enjoying a brandy by the fire in Mr. Goring's rustic chalet on the Summit Institute campus. This meeting brought back the memory of their last meeting at Omega, when things were not so rosy; they could recall the indignation of having to endure the very presence of that most undesirable of personalities, Mr. Khull—and, of course, at that time Sally Roe was still at large.

Now they clinked their glasses together in a toast of victory. Indeed, with the news that came in earlier today, things were definitely different.

"To the future!" said Santinelli.

"To the future!" echoed Goring and Steele.

They sipped from their drinks, smacked their lips, and even allowed themselves a chuckle or two.

As they relaxed into Goring's soft couch and easy chair, Santinelli addressed the pressing matters before them. "I've sent our private jet to bring Mr. Khull and his personnel. They should arrive here with the prize in a matter of hours."

"Have you ever met her?" asked Steele.

Goring and Santinelli exchanged glances.

"Not I," said Goring, "but I'm looking forward to it."

Santinelli agreed. "An outrageous fish story can never compare to actually seeing the fish hauled in. Actually, I'm impressed that Khull was able to restrain himself and deliver her to us alive."

Goring spoke with great anticipation. "I'll be fascinated to meet her. I have many questions, to be sure."

"Oh," said Santinelli, "we'll all have questions for her—serious questions."

"Any word on the ring or the rosters?" asked Steele.

"None. But with Sally Roe in our custody, I can't imagine that will be a problem."

Goring cautioned, "But just remember, there are many delegates and visitors about. Our present business would be quite distasteful to most of them, I'm sure; so our guests must never know about it."

"Agreed. And I have instructed Khull to preserve Roe's appearance, just in case she may be seen by someone."

"Now," said Goring, "there is that other matter that we discussed . . ."

"Of course," said Santinelli, "the whole matter of Khull in particular and Broken Birch in general."

"Mm," said Steele, nodding. "I've thought about that too. Now that they're in bed with us, they won't stop until they control the bed."

"I've consulted with Mr. Evans and Mr. Farnsworth, and they have some of their best people looking into it. If we move carefully, and lay a thoroughly thought-out plan, we could accumulate some damning evidence against Broken Birch while keeping ourselves clean. Evans and Farnsworth are quite sure that the whole lot of them can be arrested for crimes totally unrelated to our enterprise."

Goring smiled and nodded. "Excellent. I've already consulted with my board, and they think such a plan would be feasible. We'll be able to call in some favors from our corporate and governmental resources, and I'm sure they'll be most willing to see what we want them to see and to look the other way when it would be . . . worthwhile."

"Then we must proceed on this without delay," said Santinelli. "Khull and Broken Birch have finally done their job, but upon delivery of Sally Roe we must erase any association with them."

Goring added, "Any *memory* of them in *any* circles, if we can help it!"

Santinelli raised his glass. "I'll drink to that!"

And so they did.

The van had been driving along the winding, climbing, meandering highway for what seemed hours, and Sally finally nodded off, her chin on her chest, sitting between two of the four surly, burly escorts that came with Khull and herself on the plane. The flight had lasted several hours, the driving even longer, and now it was night.

She looked a little better. At least Khull figured she couldn't escape from a flying jet plane, and, reciting Santinelli's order to "preserve Roe's appearance," untied her and let her use the cramped little washroom to wash the dried, caked blood from her mouth and chin, change from her bloodstained shirt to a clean but sadly wrinkled blouse, and brush out her hair. She looked a little better—for a totally exhausted, manhandled, soon-to-die fugitive.

They were heading into the mountains, through tall forests of pine and fir that became monotonous after a while. Sally slept fitfully, jolting awake every few moments, but only long enough to see more trees going by the window, and then she would nod off again.

Some time later—she didn't know how much later—she awoke to morning light. The van was slowing down; Khull and his cohorts were looking around, trying to get their bearings. They were entering a village.

Khull, sitting in the front passenger seat, turned around to tell her, "Welcome to Summit."

Sally rubbed the sleep from her eyes and looked out the windows at a quaint-looking little town surrounded on all sides by snow-covered, sawtoothed peaks and thick, unblemished forests. Out the left window, just above the A-framed roofs of some ski lodges, the morning sun turned a distant waterfall into golden tinsel; out the right window, through a gap in the small inns and storefronts, the mountainside dropped sharply away to a flower-strewn alpine meadow. Patches of snow still remained everywhere, dripping and glistening in the low-angled sunlight.

Why have we come here? Sally wondered. It hardly seemed the setting for such gruesome business, and people like Khull and his bunch just didn't fit at all.

But then again, maybe they did. Sally began to notice some of the establishments and institutions in this village; she began to read some of the signs.

Taoist Retreat Center. Valley Tibetan Project and Monastery. Temple of Ananta. Library and Archives of Ancient Wisdom. Native American School of Traditional Medicine. Karma Triyana Dharmachakra. The Temple of Imbetu Agobo. Babaji Ashram. Mother's Temple Shrine of Shiva. The Children of Diana. Temple to the Divine Universal Mother. The House of Bel. The Sacred and Royal Order of the Nation.

She leaned toward the window. The big escort put his ham-sized palm in her chest and shoved her back. She twisted and looked out the rear windows as the building passed.

The Sacred and Royal Order of the Nation. The little gargoyle snarled at her from the front door of the black stone temple and from the building's facade. She could just hear it screeching, Welcome to Summit!

Destroyer had followed the hunting party clear from Chicago, and now, as the van came through the valley and entered the village, he was going to milk this moment for all it was worth. He dropped from the sky, alighted on the roof of the van, and stood there, his sword held high in victory, his wings trailing like banners behind him, his twelve captains forming his honor guard. Driving under the thick mantle of spirits was like entering a dark tunnel under a towering mountain; on every side, and thousands of feet above, demons cheered and waved their swords in a thunderous display of admiration.

Destroyer reveled in his victory and newfound fame. These vile hordes once ignored him, mocked him, cared not to know his name. Now listen to them! Let the *Strongman* listen to them! A better announcement of his arrival could not be asked for.

Guilo turned at the sound of wings behind him. The captain had arrived.

The cheers of the demons echoing out of the valley could only be for one reason. "They've brought her," Guilo reported.

Both he and Tal stayed low among the trees with their warriors. The swarm of demons below was nothing to tangle with before the right time.

Guilo pointed. "There! That blue van just entering the Summit Institute!"

They could see it only intermittently, as small as a grain of sand, appearing through the thinner parts of the demonic swarm and then disappearing again. It reappeared just long enough for them to watch it turn off the thin, gray ribbon of highway and slip out of sight under the mantle of spirits covering the Summit Institute.

"Well, now she's alone," said Tal. "We can't break through that."

"What about the fire you were going to start?" Guilo asked. "If ever we needed something to happen, it is now!"

Tal shook his head. "It will be a day late. For now, all we can do is wait for Nathan's signal and hope it comes soon."

The semiannual Global Consciousness Conference was getting underway; so the van's driver had to drive up and down the large, black-topped parking lot several times before he could find an empty parking place. Sally spent that time observing the Summit Institute for Humanistic Studies. It reminded her a lot of the Omega Center, except that it was newer and the architecture more modern. Stone was an abundant building material around here, and so was used in the construction of the offices, lecture halls, walkways and gardens. True to their religious devotion to Mother Earth, the designers of the campus did not supplant the natural environment, but let the campus merge with it, almost hiding it among the trees, rocks, and hilly terrain.

The hour was still early, so there were no people out walking. How fortunate for Sally's captors.

Khull turned to Sally, holding up his knife as a reminder. "All they paid me to do is deliver you here. If you get cut up in the parking lot, it's your fault and not my problem, understand?"

She nodded.

"Let's get her into Goring's place."

An observer standing at a distance would have thought an

important dignitary had arrived and was now surrounded by Secret Service agents. Sally was barely visible within the tight cluster of bodies that formed outside the van's side door and then began moving up the path toward Mr. Goring's chalet.

Sally made a concerted effort to see around the backs and shoulders of her escorts and study the layout of this place. Right now they were passing through an expansive, meticulously arranged herb garden with sculptured hedges, stone pathways, and eye-pleasing reflection pools. In the middle of a carpet of moss, one lone man sat almost naked in the early-morning cold, eyes shut, legs crossed in the lotus position, totally entranced.

Leaving the herb garden, they rounded a corner, followed a narrow, natural stone stairway with tall evergreen hedges on either side, and then broke out into the open. To the right, the ground dropped away into a natural amphitheater, and beyond the amphitheater, a heart-stopping view of the mountains spread wider and higher than the eye could take in.

In the center of the amphitheater, a sizable group of people stood in neat, concentric semicircles around a blazing firepit, chanting, droning, and tossing flowers, grain, and fruit into the fire. On a small platform at the head of the circle, gawking down into the fire as if mesmerized by it, seven stone deities received the offerings and worship of these adoring early-risers while a gaunt, white-haired woman in a yellow robe sang a haunting song in Sanskrit.

Sally remembered the song and still knew some of the words, even though she hadn't heard it in ten years. She couldn't remember all the names of the seven little deities, but they were secondary gods anyway. This ceremony was to invoke the blessing of the Universal Mother first of all, and secondly to appease these seven dwarfs.

Then she caught a glimpse of some of the faces as they lifted toward the morning sun. No! There was Mrs. Denning from the Omega Center, and two of the Omega faculty! And was that Mr. Blakely, her counselor at Bentmore Teacher's College? She thought she recognized his face, and then his cracking, squawking chant identified him for sure. Close to the fire, her face washed with red light, was Krystalsong, a witch, scholar, and mother of four from the West Coast; she and Sally had worked together on a holistic preschool program.

Quite a homecoming for us all, she thought.

On the highway to Ashton, the mail truck continued to roll along, right on schedule. The morning mail shipment would be at the Ashton Post Office the moment they opened the doors.

"That has to be it!" said a spirit to his friends.

They were whirring and rushing along above the highway, keeping pace with the truck and eyeing it curiously. The spirit leading them had been in a terrible fight; his wings were tattered, his flight was wobbly, and his face was misshapen.

"This time," he slurred, "we won't let any heavenly warrior stop us!"

"Destroyer will reward us!" said another.

"We will stop the truck and get that letter!"

They swept their wings tightly behind their shoulders and dropped like torpedoes toward the truck, cutting through the thin layers of morning mist, the wind whistling through their wings and whiskers. This should be easy enough. They could foul the engine, break the steering, flatten a tire. They could—

LIGHT! SWORDS! WARRIORS! The truck was full of them!

Nathan shot into the air and met the battered demon.

"You again?" they both said.

The demon dissolved into red smoke. Nathan spun to take out another one.

Armoth tore three spirits apart with one sword swipe, and then spun in a blur to bash two more with his heel.

A dozen warriors had burst out of the truck and now swirled around it, swatting and hacking.

Their picnic ruined, the remaining spirits fled like flies and the truck kept rolling.

40

The saints were on their knees. The division was fading. Mark had devoted multiplied hours of his time and large measures of his personal concern to healing and restoring the hurting and wounded among his flock, steadily, prayerfully undoing the tangled mess that Destroyer and his hordes had created in the church. It had taken some real breaking, some repenting, some forgiving on all sides, but it happened, and was still happening, one heart at a time.

The Jessups were so hurt and dismayed that it took careful, loving appeals from the Walroths for them to come back into fellowship; Judy Waring was carrying a lot of bitterness against the likes of Donna Hemphile who had used her—and her mouth—to hurt God's people. But she had to admit that it was, after all, her mouth and her heart, and she started her turnabout with those two areas of her life.

Every one of them had to totally reevaluate their opinion of Tom Harris, and they were still in that process even as they prayed.

It wasn't an easy restoration for any of them, but in the face of their revealed enemy they had a clear choice: rejoin God's army and fight the evil that was even now destroying them, their families, and their Christian faith, or . . . proceed with being destroyed.

They rejoined the army—with a vengeance.

The angels kept quiet, stayed low, and didn't talk much as they secretly placed themselves at strategic points around the country, waiting for Tal's "brushfire" to start.

Mota the Polynesian and Signa the Oriental had many points to cover all around the Bacon's Corner area, but they now had more than enough warriors, so carefully, methodically they covered them. Terga, the tender-egoed prince of the town, was getting edgy about the sudden tide of prayer coming from the reunited saints, but so far he did not sense the activity all that prayer was bringing about. Besides, he'd heard the news from the powers above him: the woman had been captured; the danger was over.

Cree the Native American and Si the East Indian had returned once again to the Omega Center for Educational Studies, and were now planting angelic warriors like explosive charges in just the right places all around the campus. It was tedious, dangerous work, the greatest danger being discovery. While they crawled along or under the ground, moved under the surface of the lake, stole from tree to tree, or spent hours totally motionless under rocks, boats, or buildings to avoid discovery, they could always see Barquit, the Prince of Omega, soaring to and fro, his eyes everywhere, laughing and exulting in any progress made in the classes and workshops, then growling and spitting at any clumsy moves by his demons or by his puppet-people below. He was still very much in charge and ruling his demon hordes with an iron hand. Now that the woman was captured, he felt no fears or worries at all, and obviously planned on remaining at his post forever.

On the surface, Bentmore University looked like the same old red-brick, permanently established alma mater it had always been, and classes were in full swing as usual.

In the spirit realm, however, Corrupter, Bentmore's rotund master of disinformation and fleshly indulgence, moved like a blimp over the campus, seeking out any damage the school may have incurred from that recent, violent exchange with Heaven's warriors. Ha! Destroyer was nothing but a status-anxious worrywart! Damage? There was none to speak of. Professor Lynch had been a bit ill lately, but he was getting old anyway, and there were plenty more where he came from. With the woman captured, the future was wide open.

Across the river, atop the North American Can Company, Chimon the European and Scion of the British Isles were back, hiding behind one of the factory's many ventilator stacks. Things looked quiet at Bentmore right now, but when Tal's brushfire started, there would be noise enough.

Chimon and Scion were looking for hiding-places and sending troops to fill them. The warehouse by the river could hold a myriad or so; the wharf on the Bentmore side would also serve very well, being closer to the campus. The troops moved silently and quickly. One false move, one ill-timed glint of light, could endanger them all.

At every point along Sally's journey, at every stronghold of Satan, the angels moved into position and then waited for the signal.

But they all knew they were waiting longer than expected.

In the peaks above Summit, Tal and Guilo watched and listened for any hint of what might be happening inside. Behind them, a hidden army lay in waiting, ready.

"Any time now," Tal said more than once. "Any time."

In purely a physical sense, Mr. Goring's chalet was an inviting A-framed structure built with rough-hewn timbers and a full-height glass front that commanded a marvelous view of the mountains. It could have served so well as a ski lodge or mountain getaway.

In a spiritual sense, it was a churning, frothing hornets' nest of evil, and Sally could feel it even before her captors led her through the front door. She knew she was being watched from every direction; she could discern the oppressive, smothering hate that covered the place like a leaden fog.

Destroyer was already in the chalet, shoving his way into the living room, brushing aside the Strongman's demons and attendants with rude boldness. Into the Strongman's lair he went, strutting down a narrow aisle formed by two straight lines of demon lords from all over the world, until finally he stood in the presence of the Strongman.

"My Ba-al," he said loudly, with a rather showy bow, "I bring to you Sally Beth Roe!"

The Strongman had heard the demonic cloud in an uproar, and now he could see Khull and his party bringing Sally Roe to the front door. He nodded in carefully measured approval. "So you have. So you have."

The demon lords raised their swords to begin a cheer.

The Strongman growled, his arms outstretched, "Hold!" They froze and stared at him. "First we will see if there is anything to cheer about."

The heavy plank door closed behind Sally and her captors. They were standing in Mr. Goring's spacious, comfortable living room. At one end was a massive stone fireplace; at the other end, a wall of glass brought in the mountains; the open-beam ceiling soared above them to the roof's apex, and from the massive ridge beam, rustic iron chandeliers hung on long chains.

Three men rose from their places by the fire. Sally recognized Mr. Steele, and it was obvious by his satisfied grin that he recognized her.

It was Goring who ordered, "Bring her here and sit her down."

Khull was after some glory. He grabbed Sally's arm and pulled her forward, keeping her constantly off-balance, then, with a cruel grip that bruised her arm, flung her down into a sofa. With just a few small gestures, he ordered his four thugs to stand guard around her.

"Gentlemen," he said arrogantly, "I bring to you Sally Beth Roe."

The three men stood before her, staring at her with great interest. The gray-haired man with the perfectly trimmed beard and the bone necklace looked at the tall, silver-haired executive type, and then both of them looked at Mr. Steele.

"This is she," said Steele. "Well done, Mr. Khull. We will settle our account with you immediately. However, if you are agreeable, we may still have need of your services."

Khull smiled, giving Sally a leering, sideways glance. "It would be my pleasure."

"Then please remain for a time, you and your staff. We'll try to settle this business as quickly as we can."

"Take your time."

With Sally placed securely on the sofa and under capable guard, the three gentlemen relaxed and took their seats—the two older men in another sofa facing Sally, and Mr. Steele in a large easy chair between the two sofas, facing the fire.

Steele opened the conversation. "Sally, let me introduce my two friends." He indicated the man with the perfectly trimmed beard. "This is Mr. Emile Goring, presently Director of Finance of the Mannesville Association, an international humanitarian and environmental think tank and mobilizer of global projects. He's a major stockholder and director in over forty global corporations dealing in oil, gas, transportation, exports, mining, and so forth."

Sally looked toward Goring, who nodded back at her with a grim but still fascinated expression.

Steele wanted to be sure Sally was impressed. "Consequently, what Mr. Goring desires to do, he has the means to do. He and his associates are major contributors and underwriters for such endeavors as the Summit Institute; this institute is part of their vision, and it wouldn't be here at all if not for their efforts.

"The other gentleman is Mr. Carl Santinelli, Senior Partner at Evans, Santinelli, Farnsworth, and McCutcheon, one of the most powerful law firms in the country and, in a sense, the flagship of the ACFA. He is a man of great causes in law and jurisprudence, a legal activist of the highest order, and definitely not a man to be tampered with."

Sally looked at Santinelli, and got a cold, probing stare back.

Then Mr. Steele turned to Goring and Santinelli. "Mr. Goring and Mr. Santinelli, I introduce to you Ms. Sally Beth Roe, former Director of Primary Curriculum Resources at the Omega Center for Educational Studies, convicted murderer, former convict, production worker at the Bergen Door Factory, and most recently, vagabond."

Goring and Santinelli continued to study her as if looking upon a real oddity.

Steele relaxed in his chair and studied her himself. "It has been quite an adventure, hasn't it?"

"It has," she answered.

"I see your hair roots are beginning to grow out. I do miss seeing your fiery red hair. And since when do you wear tinted glasses?"

She sighed and removed them, rubbing her tired eyes. "All a disguise, of course." Then she bitterly admitted, "And quite futile."

"Quite futile," Steele agreed. "But you do understand, don't you, why we had to track you down?"

The question angered her. "It is my impression, Mr. Steele, that you and your associates want me dead, and I would like to know why."

"Oh, come now!" said Santinelli. "A person of your brilliance and experience should have no trouble seeing how much you are in our way. As for that initial attempt on your life, we will not mince words. It was a blunder, an unfortunate fiasco perpetrated by some incompetents who thought they would please us. We were not pleased. Killing you in such a way was never our original intent."

"So what was your original intent?"

Santinelli smiled. "Our original intent was the lawsuit against the Good Shepherd Academy in Bacon's Corner, your current town of residence. Your stumbling into the middle of our project was a total surprise to all of us."

Sally needed to confirm what she thought. "*You* are the people ultimately responsible for the lawsuit against that Christian school?"

Santinelli nodded. "Lucy Brandon first contacted our local ACFA affiliate, the affiliate contacted the state chapter, the state chapter contacted us, and we decided the case could prove profitable. We immediately put our strength and influence behind it."

"But not for the child Amber's sake, of course?"

Santinelli exchanged a glance with the others. This woman was as sharp as Steele had said she was. "Obviously you have no illusions about our concern for the safety, rights, and welfare of children, especially since the ACFA regularly defends the interests of child pornographers and molesters." He sat back with his chin high, tapping his fingertips together, watching her eyes for a response.

She forced one corner of her mouth to stretch upward and nodded.

"As you may well imagine, the real object of that lawsuit is not the awarding of damages to the plaintiff, but legal precedent, the molding and shaping of law, even the rewriting of law, through an ideal test case."

Steele contributed, "Ms. Roe is quite familiar with our agenda for social change through state-controlled public education. She was a major contributor to that effort at one time."

Santinelli nodded, impressed. "So you do realize how great a deterrent to our cause the Christians are as long as they are allowed to raise and educate their own children according to their Biblical beliefs. Even before your years at Omega, we were seeking legislation and legal precedent that could be used to stifle that deterrent. It's taken this long for that to develop."

"But it did," said Goring with a gloating smile.

Santinelli indulged in the same smile and continued, "The latest legislation for our use was the Federal Day-care and Private Primary School Assistance Act, and the Munson-Ross Civil Rights Act, each a rather muddled stack of laws that—as we had hoped—would require testing and clarification in the courts. The Good Shepherd Academy case seemed tailor-made for that purpose. It not only involved federal funds spent in a Christian school, and therefore government intervention and control, but also included the useful, inflammatory child abuse angle, something we could use to incite support in the media and in the public mind, getting them all on our side regardless of the real issues. And that, of course, was the object. With the public outraged and preoccupied with the protection of innocent children, we would be seen as no less than champions for children in establishing through case law the right and duty of the state to control religious education." He couldn't resist a laugh of delight. "Even after the initial trauma—real or concocted—against the child fades into the past and is forgotten, the laws will still be on the books, and the government firmly planted within the walls of the church.

"As you yourself taught and were taught, once such control of religious instruction is established, the methodical, gradual elimination of religious instruction altogether is only a matter of time. And then such people as you once were will have tremendous, far-reaching power to control and mold every segment of the next generation without resistance."

Sally nodded. She'd learned this catechism.

Goring picked up the narrative. "Well, it did look promising, of course. But that was before you happened along. You can imagine what a shock it was to learn you were out of prison and living in the very town where we'd brought the lawsuit. Worse than that was the way we found out: Our little prize, the very child in question, supposedly the pristine, totally innocent victim of Christian bigots and abusers, suddenly chose to demonstrate her true colors one day in the local Post Office. Ah! I see you remember the incident! Of all people to witness such an outburst, it had to be you!

"When Mrs. Brandon brought the incident to her attorneys' attention, they passed the word to us, and, knowing who you were, we saw a substantial risk that you would recognize the child's condition, especially since you wrote the very curriculum that caused it. We were aware that you could severely jeopardize our case should you decide to step forward."

Santinelli allowed himself a mournful chuckle. "But really, we hadn't yet decided what our course of action would be before a misguided member—uh, former member now—of our staff took matters into his own hands and secured the services of an assassin."

"That part you are quite familiar with," said Goring.

"Oh, yes," Sally answered.

"And that," said Santinelli, "brings us to why we've all been on this merry chase. Ms. Roe, had you died then, we could have absorbed the error and continued with our plan, none the worse for our friends' impulsiveness." He sighed. "But impressive person that you are, you not only lived, but a) you killed the assassin and left her there to create all kinds of questions should she be found, and b) you made off with a ring the assassin was wearing on her finger, a ring that could eventually link the whole wicked affair with us."

Sally said nothing, and tried to keep her face from saying anything.

"The assassin was a crafty sort. She was a paramour of that former member of our staff, and pilfered his ring, we believe, for the purpose of blackmail and manipulation. That ring could have told anyone who its owner really was—all it would take would be the securing of the Nation's rosters in which all the code names are listed. Both items are now, we believe, in your possession?"

"I'm prepared to bargain," she replied.

They all stifled a laugh and exchanged glances.

Steele ventured a question they all felt was unnecessary. "So . . . you are willing to relinquish the rosters and the ring in exchange for something? Just what would that be?"

Sally looked them all in the eye and spoke clearly. "Abandon the lawsuit. Leave the Christian school alone, and let Tom Harris have his children back."

This time they didn't stifle their laughter at all, but enjoyed her appeal thoroughly.

"And then," Goring asked, "you will release the ring and rosters back to us for our disposal?"

"We can certainly talk about it; I'm sure we can arrange something."

Santinelli leaned forward. "Is that a chain I see around your neck?"

Khull found out for sure. He forced her head sideways and grabbed at the chain, yanking it from under her blouse.

The gold ring dangled on the end.

With a vicious jerk that pulled her from the sofa and gouged her neck, he snapped the chain and tore it from her. She landed on the rug with a cry of pain, only to be gathered up by the thugs and flung on the sofa again.

"Here now, enough!" said Goring. Then he pointed to her bleeding neck. "Put a cloth on that. I don't want it staining the sofa."

One of Khull's men placed his handkerchief around Sally's neck.

Khull dangled the ring above Santinelli's palm, and then dropped it.

Santinelli examined the ring. "Mm-hm. The Ring of Fellowship in the Royal and Sacred Order of the Nation. A sacred object, to be sure." He glared at Sally. "Too sacred to be in your possession . . . and no longer in your possession."

Sally held the handkerchief to her neck, stunned and deflated in her spirit and wincing from the searing pain from her wound. "I see you belong to that group."

Santinelli looked at the gold Ring of Fellowship on his own hand. "Oh, the Nation consists of many brothers, all in vital places: in government, in banking, on the federal bench, on college boards and regencies. You were quite familiar with Owen Bennett, of course, and I'm sure you've already read an impressive list of names from those rosters you stole. Like any other secret society, we help all our initiates get established in the right places, and we see to each other's interests—provided, of course, that each man's interests conform to the interests of the society."

"Apparently James Bardine's interests did not."

Santinelli smiled. "Ah, yes, that 'former member of our staff' does have a name. Then it was you who called our office? I understand our receptionist recently informed an anonymous female caller of his untimely death." He dropped the ring back and forth from hand to hand. "Brotherhood is one thing; violation of sacred blood oaths of secrecy is another."

He looked out the windows toward the mountains. "There are some things that are best kept sealed, Ms. Roe. If you could have toured these grounds, or walked through the town of Summit and met some of the people that are here this week, you would have found many different esoteric organizations represented, as well as some very . . . unique . . . individuals. We're all one global family, you know; that is the unifying cry of every heart. We proclaim that idea here and everywhere, just as you yourself have proclaimed it, and we teach that all are equal." He paused for effect. "But we keep to ourselves the fact that some are more equal than others, and far more fit to rule."

He set the ring on the glass coffee table and then looked directly at her. "I trust that now you fully appreciate what the stakes are here, how ruthless and determined we are, and how desperate your situation is. We are not here to bargain, Ms. Roe, but to put an end to the threat you pose to us. Exactly what process will be necessary to accomplish this will depend largely on yourself." He looked toward Khull. "I'm sure you'll find little comfort in the fact that Mr. Khull and his four accomplices are members of the same secret order to which your assassin belonged, a Satanic cult known as

Broken Birch. They're a ruthless bunch who thrive on bloodletting, torture, human sacrifice. Quite unsavory." He looked back at Sally. "Ms. Roe, we are decent men, and we desire no more discomfort for you than you may make necessary. To be blunt, your fate depends on your performance."

Nathan the Arabian and his small band of sentries continued to ride shotgun in the mail truck as it drew closer and closer to Ashton. Armoth the African had flown ahead to warn Krioni and Triskal, the watchcaring angels of the town—it was only a matter of time before Destroyer heard about the letter aboard that truck.

In the herb garden not far from Goring's chalet, a group of about thirty conferees gathered in the crisp, scented air for a morning workshop led by a well-known recording artist. The young, blond-haired man had his guitar along, and some songs were planned before his talk on "Ecology: The Merging of Earth and Spirit."

There was a certain giddiness in the group. These people had never been this close to such a famous person before, and he was not the only famous person sitting there amid the rosemary, thyme, and lamb's ears. Two newsmaking clergymen of global stature were also in attendance, as well as a director of mystical science fiction films whose name was a household word and whose film characters were now plastic toys in every kid's room in this country and abroad.

The blond singer strummed his guitar, and they all began to sing one of his well-known ballads. The moment was magical.

The demons among them were enjoying it as well. Such worship and attention as they were now receiving was like getting a good back rub, and they even twitched and squirmed with delight at every bar of the song's carefully shaded double meanings.

Huh? What was that? The demons twisted their heads around to look toward a disturbance.

Two demonic warriors were gliding in over the top of the Goring Pavilion, apparently heading for Goring's chalet. They carried between them the drooping, limp form of a battered demon, still whimpering and wailing in agony. With a soft, rustling sound, they passed right over the herb garden and then disappeared beyond the tall evergreen hedge.

The demons in the herb garden fidgeted, stirred, and muttered to each other. *What was that? Who was that? What has happened?*

Some psychics were in attendance, and the demons attached to their brains were just as stirred up as the others. The psychics could immediately sense it.

The blond man even stopped the song. "What is it?"

"A disturbance," said a woman attorney and psychic.

"Yes," said a fifth grade teacher, his eyes closed. "Some kind of bad energy. Something's wrong somewhere."

In the chalet, Destroyer was relishing the entire conversation, as was the Strongman, though the Strongman was getting impatient.

Why wait so long? he growled. *Make her talk, and then finish her! The Plan is waiting!*

"Destroyer!" came a gravelly voice outside the building. It was one of Destroyer's henchmen. "A warrior brings news!"

"Not now!" Destroyer barked, wanting to watch what happened to the woman.

"Go!" said the Strongman.

He went, ducking outside the chalet to hear from a most pitiful-looking spirit.

"What happened to you?"

The demon sat on his haunches on the ground, his wings spread like tattered black tarpaulins, wrinkled, limp, and full of holes. His head was battered, and he braced himself to keep from falling over. "We attacked a mail truck on its way to Ashton."

Destroyer stooped low. "*Ashton,* you say?"

The demon started to topple.

Destroyer grabbed him by the neck and jerked him upright. "Did you say *Ashton*?"

The demon slurred a faint answer. "Ashton. A letter is bound for Ashton, and the Host of Heaven guard it."

Destroyer shot a glance into the chalet. The Strongman was still watching the interrogation of Sally Roe. He was still impatient. He wanted results. If he didn't get results, and fast, certain heads were going to roll.

Destroyer could just feel his head rolling. He let the demon flop to the ground, then motioned to his captains who gathered around him. "There is a letter bound for Ashton, guarded by the Host of Heaven. They do not guard it for nothing!" His face crinkled grotesquely at the thought of it. "Sally Roe may have written to someone there."

The captains gawked at each other.

"Well?" Destroyer demanded. "Did you hear me?"

"Ashton!" exclaimed one.

"We can't go back there!" said another.

Destroyer shushed them with a quick gesture. "Just look into it, and do it quietly. I'm sure it's nothing to worry about, just one little letter."

They looked back and forth at each other. "Which of us should go?" they wondered.

Destroyer held back a scream and hissed instead, "How about *all* of you? And take some spare warriors with you."

They all went, gathering as many demon troublemakers as wished to go.

Destroyer hurried back into Goring's chalet. The Strongman was intently listening to Sally's interrogation and didn't ask what the interruption was about.

Destroyer had no intention of telling him.

In Ashton, Krioni and Triskal could see the mail truck entering the city limits, right on time. Unfortunately, the precious letter inside was one truckload and one day late.

Triskal looked toward the west. "All clear so far."

Krioni was not optimistic. "They'll be here."

41

Santinelli leaned back, relaxed, and with an instructive glance at Goring and Steele encouraged them to do likewise. Then he looked at Sally and became suspiciously cordial.

"Sally, I have always considered myself a gentleman, a man of dignity and honor, and respectful of the dignity of women. I sincerely desire an intelligent, productive dialogue with you, and I'm sure, given the alternative, you desire the same."

"I would prefer it," Sally admitted.

Santinelli nodded. "Then, having agreed on that, it might be well for us to consider your credibility as a witness against us. It seems to me that you've forgotten what you are."

Sally answered simply and directly, "I'm an adultress, a baby killer, and a convicted felon." They looked uncomfortable. She'd answered that question a little too easily. "I've been reminded of that constantly since the day it first happened, by seven years of prison, by spirit tormentors, and by my own conscience."

Steele said, "Sally, that's a shameful and disgusting set of labels."

She smiled, and that even surprised her. "Actually, those labels are marvelous and beautiful because . . ." She hesitated.

Goring completed her sentence. "Because of the Cross?"

She brightened at that question. "Yes, Mr. Goring. I'm surprised you would know about that."

Goring sneered a little. "We know about a lot of things, Ms. Roe."

Sally gave that statement no reaction, but went on. "I'm far from competent in Christian theology, but I do know I've met this Jesus personally, and I know I've been forgiven. Considering what my deeds were, I find that fact exhilarating, inspiring."

They didn't like that answer at all.

The Strongman didn't like it either, and let out a roar that filled the building and set the demons stirring. He shot a sideways glance at Destroyer, who looked away.

Santinelli tried to keep cool, but his face was getting a little pink. "So are we to understand that you've turned to antiquated religion in one final attempt to expunge your past?" He laughed derisively. "That, Sally, is a marvelous delusion for the fainthearted and weak-minded. The notion that your sins are forgiven is as much a fable as the sins themselves. You are God, Sally; you are accountable to no one."

"Then I should be free to go, shouldn't I?"

"That's a side issue," said Goring with a wave of his hand, "having no bearing on our present purpose. Sally, let me be blunt: Even if sins were real and this Jesus could save you from them, what you must face at this moment is that He cannot save you from *us*."

"I wouldn't presume that He should."

Now Santinelli even raised his voice. "Ms. Roe, I'm sure you know that this conversion of yours has placed you in even greater jeopardy. You could have done no better in assuring enmity between us, and even your own death, than by becoming a Christian!" He leaned forward and with a controlled rage pointed his finger in her face. "You have established yourself as a supreme enemy of this enterprise, deserving of our hatred!"

Just like Amber, Sally thought. *Steele, Santinelli, and Goring are showing the same demon eyes, the same diabolical hatred.*

She acknowledged Santinelli's words. "I know."

The Strongman could see the peace in her eyes, and it incensed him. *Strike her!*

Santinelli slapped her across the face. "You will tell us where the rosters are! What did you do with them?"

Krioni and Triskal greeted Nathan and his warriors as the mail truck reached the Ashton Post Office.

"So you've had some trouble?" asked Krioni.

"A little," said Nathan.

"Well, we're expecting more," said Triskal.

Armoth followed the driver into the building and watched intently as he set the mailbag with some others on a receiving cart. Soon the mail would be removed and sorted, and that would be the most critical time of all.

A sooty, motley band of imps and troublemakers, led by Destroyer's loathsome twelve, made their way toward Ashton, flying low to the ground, pouring on speed, their swords drawn, their eyes bulging with anxiety. This battle would be their last, thought the twelve. It may as well be their best.

At the *Ashton Clarion*, it was time to get the morning mail; Bernice had her coat on and her car keys in her hand, but wouldn't you know it? She no sooner put her hand on the front door knob than the phone rang, and it was Eddy from Eddy's Bakery. The guy was a paragon of pickiness!

"Yeah, Eddy, we can give you those two inches. Well, yes, for free, but that's just for a one-month trial basis." More questions. "To decide if you like it that way and if we like it that way. We've never done it, and I thought we should try it." He kept talking. She shifted her weight toward the front door. "No, I think we can just blow up that coffee mug a little larger and it'll work out fine. Right, you won't have to change your logo." She made a face and rolled her eyes. "Listen, why don't you talk to Cheryl about it? Yes, she knows all about it."

He didn't want to talk to Cheryl.

ATTACK! The black spirits threw fear and caution to the wind and descended on Ashton in a torrent of chaos and evil, wings roaring, sulfur streaming, blotting out the light, clashing with angelic warriors all over the town. Up and down the streets they soared, tumbling, clashing, hacking with swords of fire and heat at Heaven's warriors, dashing through traffic, ambushing at corners, streaking through buildings and wreaking confusion, shrieking their war cries, fully abandoned to keeping the angels on edge, in battle, no matter what the cost, no matter what the loss. While the imps, harassers, and troublemakers stirred up the town like a whirlwind, Destroyer's twelve went for that letter. '

Bernice got to her little Volkswagen bug at last, but the door wouldn't open. The key wouldn't even turn in the lock.

WHOOOSH! A streak of light cut across the demon who had fouled the lock. He dissolved.

The key turned at last. Bernice climbed in.

Down the street, the traffic light jammed on red and the cars began to back up.

A small sedan eased to a stop right beside Bernice's car, and immediately a pickup rear-ended it. Both drivers climbed out of their vehicles and began to engage in a long battle of apologies.

Six angels flew abreast down 6th Avenue while four more dove out of the sky and shot up Miller Street. They converged in an explosive clash just above the traffic signal, hurling dissolving demon saboteurs in high arcs that created a fern of red smoke trails.

The light turned green.

But the traffic still wasn't moving, thanks to the fender bender. Bernice decided to walk.

Sally tried to sink deeper into the sofa, but there was no way to lessen the pain of the big thug's bruising, crushing grip on her shoulders. He was hurting her and enjoying it.

Steele was speaking slowly and deliberately to make sure she heard him; at the moment she seemed rather preoccupied with her agony. "I'm sure you're familiar with Satanic rituals, so I shouldn't have to go into the details. Sally, we don't want to see it happen; but if we have to, we'll turn you over to Mr. Khull and his people and let them do their worst until you tell us what we want to know."

Sally was about to answer, about to say they were going to kill her anyway, but she was stopped when something happened to her eyes, as if they'd opened for the first time, as if a dark curtain had been pulled aside. Maybe the pain was causing her to hallucinate.

She could see the spirits behind these men. They were towering, warted, ugly things, glaring at her with murderous hatred. Throughout her occult experiences, good and bad, she'd never seen them so clearly; she'd never discerned such evil or such hate.

But she could tell their hatred was not for her. It was for the Savior within her.

And then she knew. She just knew, and she spoke, whether aloud in the present world or in her spirit in another dimension, she couldn't tell. "You were there! All of you were there! You gave him your worst . . . you killed Him!"

That troubled the spirits. They looked at each other, indignity and outrage wrinkling their faces.

"And He defeated you by dying! He won!" The big, hulking spirit hovering high above bared his teeth and roared indiscernible curses at her, his wings billowing. She looked into those burning, yellow eyes, and to her great surprise she saw fear. In her spirit she laughed. "And whatever you may do to me, *I've* won!"

She cried out. She could feel all the pain again. The thug was about to break her neck. The spirits faded away with the rest of the world. She no longer saw, she no longer heard. She was sinking into a dream, into bottomless darkness. Santinelli yelled something, and the thug let her go. She thought she would float up from the couch. The pain lessened.

In a moment she could see and hear again, and she realized she was almost falling over. Her shoulders were throbbing. Santinelli was saying something about killing her.

Then Goring said, "The conference day is going to start; people might walk by the windows. We'd better continue this downstairs."

"Wait!" Sally said, and they all froze. She had their attention. She raised her head, gathered her strength and courage, and feebly muttered, "I do have an additional bargaining chip. You should know that I've corresponded on a regular basis with Tom Harris in Bacon's Corner. I've told him everything I know and everything I've done. If anything happens to me, somebody will know."

Goring smiled, and reached into a briefcase beside the sofa. "Oh, you must be referring to these." By handfuls, three at a time, four at a time, one at a time, Goring pulled the letters from the briefcase and set them in a pile on the coffee table, giving Sally a slow, torturous revelation. When she had turned a satisfying shade of white, he continued, "We've put a great amount of preparation into our plan, and fortunately we were able to exert enough influence on the plaintiff in the lawsuit who is also the local postmaster. She's been forwarding all your letters to us; so needless to say, Tom Harris and his friends never got them. They have no idea of your whereabouts, or what you might know."

Santinelli added, "And yes, we have been watching them, and it's obvious that they have little information about you and are shooting in the dark. I would say they're getting rather desperate. But that doesn't matter now, does it? We have you, and we will deal with you as we see fit, as we find necessary."

Goring pointed to the coffee table. "So, we have you, we have all your letters, we have the telltale ring; it's time we firmly dealt with those stolen rosters. Gentlemen?"

Suddenly she was hanging from her arms. She pushed with her feet to lessen the pain, and stood on her own.

"This way," said Goring.

The men of Broken Birch forced her along, taking her toward a stairway that led down into the cold, concrete belly of the chalet. Goring led the way, turning on the lights and guiding them down the winding steps.

Steele followed behind, and after him Santinelli. Khull followed at the rear of the procession, reaching into his coat for his knife.

Then Khull hesitated. "I'll make sure the front door's locked," he said.

He went upstairs again, but passed by the coffee table to take a good look at all those letters. *Hmmm. Excellent!*

There, I made it! Bernice checked her watch and found it only took about ten minutes to walk to the Post Office. That wasn't so bad.

Now to get that mail.

High overhead, Destroyer's twelve henchmen saw her. They also saw the canopy of angels over that building. They let out a cry and dove to the battle, their wings screaming, their nostrils trailing sulfur.

WHOOSH! Three of them swept five angelic warriors from the Post Office roof and engaged them, tumbling, rushing, spinning, hacking. They would be busy for a while.

Two henchmen shot through the north wall. Nathan and Armoth ducked as they passed, swatted them soundly, and sent them through the south wall.

OOF! Four more dropped through the roof and struck the angels down with bared talons. The demons got a faceful of fiery wings and then saw the swinging blades too late.

Red smoke.

The young mail clerk carefully emptied the mailbag, sorting out the packages, envelopes, junk mail, magazines.

"Hi, Al!" came a call from the lobby.

"Hi, Bernice! The mail's a little late."

"Oh, that's okay, so am I."

Ah, here was some mail for the *Clarion*. He slipped it into the *Clarion*'s box, then looked to see if there was more.

Four henchmen exploded through the wall, wings a blur, Krioni and Triskal hot on their heels.

A red sword swept downward.

The letter fluttered to the floor.

Bernice gathered all the mail out of the *Clarion*'s box and dropped it into a shopping bag. She looked through the opening and called, "Is that it?"

Al looked through the new mail that had come in. "Yeah, I think I got it all."

"Okay."

Bernice closed the door of the box and turned to leave.

Krioni took one spirit by the heel, but the thing was so strong it dragged him through the Post Office wall and he had to let it go.

Triskal took a nasty blow from one monster, slashed away at another one, and kicked a third out over the counter.

Bernice didn't see the spirit sail right past her as she reached to push the door open.

Nathan ducked for the letter.

A black, taloned foot caught him in the chest and propelled him as high as the ceiling. Two more spirits closed in on him. He spun, sword extended, dividing one, catching the parry of the other with a burst of sparks.

Krioni was back, saw the letter, and went for it. Armoth covered for him, pushing two spirits backward, right into Nathan's blade.

Krioni slipped his sword under the letter and flipped it into the air.

Al didn't see Krioni punching two demons out of the mail clerk's way, but he did see the letter just coming to rest on the floor, address up. "Oh, hey, Bernice!"

The door was just about to close behind her. She heard him call and turned back, opening the door again and reentering the lobby.

Good! Now the warriors could concentrate on the demons. There shouldn't be too many more—just the biggest and strongest.

Al handed Bernice the letter over the counter. "Kinda thick. Might be a card in there or something."

Bernice's heart almost stopped when she saw the return address: S. B. Roe.

In Bacon's Corner, Kate handed Marshall the phone. "On your toes, Marshall," she whispered.

Ben and Bev heard that and got close. "Who is it?"

Marshall spoke into the phone, "Yeah, this is Marshall Hogan."

"Mr. Hogan," said the voice on the other end, "this is Debbie Aronson. I work at the Post Office with Lucy Brandon. I need to talk to you."

The Post Office lobby filled with red smoke as Triskal shot sword-first right through two spirits and through the wall to the outside, shaking the dissolving spirits from his shoulders and wings.

Bernice tore the letter open and found a Post Office box key inside. Box 203. Here? In this Post Office? She quickly scanned the letter from Sally Roe.

She may not have noticed, but she began to bounce up and down on her toes.

Marshall grabbed a pen while Kate got him some paper, and he sat down at Ben and Bev's dining room table. "I'm glad you called, Debbie. I'd be happy to talk to you."

"Well, I don't have that much to say. I'm on my break, over at Don's Wayside."

"Can we get together somewhere, sometime?"

"No, I don't want to risk being seen with you. Listen, just let me tell you what I know, and then we'll pretend I never talked to you, all right?"

"All right."

Bernice found Box 203. She could see a large stack of mail through the glass panel. She put the key in the lock, and it fit perfectly, turning the latch.

"Lucy's been intercepting some mail; she's been forwarding letters that I'm sure aren't supposed to be forwarded. I've seen her doing it for weeks now, and I think Sergeant Mulligan is scaring her into doing it."

Oh man, oh man, oh man. Lord God, is this it? Marshall tried to keep his voice calm. "Okay. Do you know who the letters are for, or who they're from?"

Bernice opened the mailbox door. What were these? Manila envelopes, smaller envelopes, a plain brown package, a little box wrapped in paper.

"They've all been addressed to Tom Harris . . ."
Marshall could feel his eyes getting big.
" . . . and they've all been from that woman who's supposed to be dead . . ."
Marshall kept from saying the name. Debbie had to say it herself. "What woman, Debbie? Do you know the name?"
"Um, that Roe lady. Sally Roe."

Bernice's hands were trembling as she dug every last item out of the mailbox and stuffed it into her shopping bag. She couldn't wait to get back to the office.

Nathan ducked under a violent sword thrust of one remaining beast, then came back hard and fast with his own blade. The thing backed through the wall, and Krioni met it outside.
Red smoke. That was the last of them.
The rest of Ashton was safe as well. The attack, centered on the Post Office, had been met and defeated.

Marshall hung up the phone gently, then leaned back in his chair, threw his head back, and let out a roar that shook the windows. He didn't know what to say, what to do, how to express how he felt, so he just hollered while Kate, Ben, and Bev tried to get him to talk.
"Marshall!" Kate insisted. "What is it?"
He just hollered again, raising his hands toward Heaven.
The phone rang again. Marshall picked it up in trembling hands. "Yeah?"

The voice on the other end could hardly speak, and the pitch was ceiling-high. "Marshall, this is Bernice! Sit down whatever you do!"

Sally had lit the brushfire at last.

Nathan was the first to have his hands free. He shot into the sky over Ashton, cutting a brilliant swath through the ebbing smoke of the battle now ending, and put a golden trumpet to his lips.

The signal carried over the farmlands, over the prairies, from one end of the sky to the other; every angelic warrior could hear it and knew what it meant.

Still they waited. Not yet. First Bacon's Corner, and then the rest. They listened again. The signal from Bacon's Corner should come soon enough.

At the Summit Institute, the demons heard the faraway signal, and it was unnerving, like a deeply buried memory too horrible to face. Too many of them had heard that sound before and now bore the scars that came immediately after hearing it.

The Strongman cocked his head around for a moment. "Wait! Be still!"

Destroyer heard it, but didn't want to admit it. He immediately thought of his twelve henchmen and the hordes they'd led into Ashton. Wasn't that the direction the sound was coming from? Oh no.

Out in the herb garden, the psychics were gasping with fear.

"No . . . no!" said the demon atop the woman attorney.

"No . . . no!" echoed the woman.

"What is it?" said the blond singer.

The demon atop the fifth grade teacher concocted an answer he didn't believe himself. The teacher echoed, "It is fear and ignorance, bigotry and hatred, still rife in the land! The winds of change must blow it aside; we must stand before it and prevail!"

"Yes, yes!" they all replied. The singer strummed his guitar, and they began to sway with the melody of still another song of global peace and perfection.

In Bacon's Corner, Mota and Signa burst from hiding with a shout, swords flashing, wings unfurling like the crashing of waves, white light burning like the sun.

"For the saints of God and for the Lamb!" they shouted as the cornfields, the silos, the store buildings, the barns, the forests, the roads all around Bacon's Corner exploded with the white light of Heaven's legions.

Mota shouted, somewhat with glee, "Stand ready! We will begin with Amethyst!"

42

The sound of Nathan's trumpet was still ringing in the Strongman's ears. He knew something was going wrong somewhere. *Get on with this! Cut her, burn her, do what you must, but delay no longer!*

Khull spoke softly to the dignified, honorable, respectable men who were paying him for his services. "We can make her sing loud and long. Just say the word."

Santinelli took only a furtive, sideways glance at Sally, now bound and held in a hard wooden chair in the middle of the basement, weak with exhaustion, pain, and fear. She was surrounded by Khull and his four cutthroats, who now brandished their implements of ritualistic torture and were all too eager to begin.

"Sally, to think it would ever come to this!" Santinelli muttered. "You should never have mentioned that Name; you should never have aligned yourself with our enemies!"

Goring reminded him, "We have much at stake here, Carl. I would say the situation forces our hand."

Santinelli replied in a voice hushed by his own disgust, "So now we have become butchers!"

Khull smiled. He almost laughed. "No, Mr. Santinelli. You pay *me* to do that. I'm not as dignified and respectable as you are. I'm just a plain little rotten Satanist."

The Strongman gave Destroyer a shove, and Destroyer spoke quickly to Steele's mind.

Steele offered, "We're talking about a commodity here. Sally Roe's only value is in what use she is to us. Let's get that information and be rid of her."

Khull did chuckle a bit this time. "How about it, Mr. Santinelli? It's your decision: do you want her tortured?"

Santinelli glared at Khull. "Do *I* want her tortured?"

Khull smiled. He loved to see a big man like Santinelli squirm. "Okay, I'll tell you what: Add two extra grand to my fee and I'll pretend that it wasn't you that hired me." Then he tilted his head the other way, his eyes full of mocking. "Maybe you're still a little too Christian, huh?"

Do it! shouted the Strongman. *Just do it!*
Sally closed her eyes and prayed.

"I can't come to work!" Lucy cried into the phone. "It's Amber again! She's beside herself! I'll call later!"

She slammed down the telephone and went after her berserk little daughter, following a trail of chaos and destruction: in the kitchen, the drawers were yanked open and the contents spilled all over the floor, including the knives Lucy had tried to hide; in the dining room, the tablecloth had been yanked from the table and the azalea centerpiece now lay broken on the floor, the potting soil strewn everywhere.

From the front of the house, the shrieking voice of Amethyst the pony continued to rant and rail against unseen enemies. "No! No! Leave me alone! My master will destroy you! Leave me alone!"

Lucy ran into the living room. The coffee table was upside down, the books and magazines flung everywhere.

Amethyst's voice came from the front entryway. "She is mine! I have a right to be here! Go away!"

Lucy ran and found her daughter cowering in the corner on the floor, her arms covering her head, screaming in fright.

"Leave me alone, leave me alone!" the pony screamed.

Lucy stopped in her tracks and observed for a moment. Had she ever heard Amethyst frightened before?

Mota and Signa stood in the entryway near Lucy, swords drawn, in full glory, their light washing out any darkness around them. In the distance, the dull thundering of angelic wings grew louder and louder, and the light of Heaven's Host began to stream through the windows.

They had chased and cornered the imp, the teaser, the liar named Amethyst—and Amethyst was not a cute little pony. She was a small, crinkled, warty lizard with toothpick arms and legs and a dragonlike face, cowering in the same corner, her body superimposed over Amber's, her arms covering her head.

"She is mine," Amethyst insisted, even pleaded. "She invited me in!"

Mota held his sword right under Amethyst's flaring, chugging nostrils. "Saints of God are coming, and they will deal with you."

"No . . . please . . ."

The doorbell rang. Lucy's first thought was: *No! Not now of all times! God, how can You be so cruel to me?*

But she could see the outlines of her visitors through the frosted glass of the front door. She threw the door open.

Marshall and Kate Hogan.

"Hi," said Marshall, "we're—"

Amethyst screamed, "No, go away! Go away!" Then she began to curse.

Lucy stepped back from the door and motioned for them to come in. "You may as well know everything!"

They stepped through the door.

At the sight of them, Amethyst leaped to her feet, her back flat against the wall, her eyes bulging with terror. "Stay away from me! I'll kill you! I'll kill *her*!"

It took only a split second for the Spirit of God to tell them what they were facing.

"You be quiet!" said Marshall.

Amethyst's head bumped against the wall as if she'd been thrown a punch. She glared at them through wide, glazed eyes, hissing through tightly gritted teeth like a muzzled, rabid dog.

"Just stay there now, and be quiet."

Kate stood by Lucy and held her. Lucy clung to her without reserve.

"Amethyst?" Kate asked.

Lucy nodded.

Marshall and Kate couldn't help staring. This was the initial cause of it all; the lawsuit, the heartache, the mystery, the gossip and division, *all* the trouble began with this imp now trembling and cowering before them. It was like isolating a virus—or cornering a rat.

"Amethyst," said Marshall, "it's all over."

Amethyst glared back at him defiantly. "She's mine. I won't let her go!"

Marshall spoke evenly and firmly. "Spirit, my Master has defeated your master. He has disarmed all the powers and authorities, right?"

Amethyst drooled in defiant silence.

"The shed blood of Jesus Christ has taken away your authority, right?"

"Yes!" Amethyst hissed.

"And my Master, the Lord Jesus Christ, has granted me His authority over you, hasn't He?"

"Yes!"

"And *you* are defeated, aren't you?"

Amethyst put his clawed fingers over his own mouth and refused to answer.

Mota flipped the hand away. "You answer him!"

Amethyst could hear the angels everywhere, could feel the heat of Mota's blade, and could not back away from the authority of this believer in Jesus. It was no use resisting.

"Awww!" Amethyst cried. "I hate you! I hate all of you!"

"Come out of her."

"No!"

"I'm binding you right now, in Jesus' name!"

Amethyst cried out, writhing, struggling against unseen shackles that held her arms and legs. She couldn't move.

"Let go of this little girl. Come out, and go where Jesus sends you."

One claw at a time, Amethyst began to let go of the little girl, her eyes darting back and forth from Marshall to the angels and back again. Mota and Signa began to close in.

With an anguished scream she dropped the girl and made a break for it, shooting through the roof of the house. Mota and Signa made no attempt to chase her.

It wasn't necessary. Amethyst had no sooner cleared the roof of the house than she saw an incoming wave of white fire rolling over the town, heading her way.

The Host of Heaven!

She let out a squeal and shot across town, heading for the big white house. *The spirits at LifeCircle! They got me into this!*

Amber slumped toward the floor as if in a faint, but Marshall caught her. Lucy and Kate knelt beside them.

"Mommy . . ." said the girl, dazed and exhausted.

Marshall gave the girl to her mother. "She's all right, but we'll have some praying to do. We'll have things to talk about."

Amber fell into her mother's arms, and then nestled there with no desire to leave. That was fine with Lucy. She had her daughter back, and she wasn't about to let go.

With tearful, weary eyes she looked at these two rescuers and whispered, "I'm sorry."

Marshall and Kate were in a terrible rush, but they had to be gentle about it.

Kate started. "Can you help us?"

Lucy couldn't answer. She was torn and confused, pulled from all directions.

Marshall spoke gently but quickly. "Listen to me, Lucy. We know Sally Roe is alive, that she's been writing letters, and that you've been intercepting those letters from some people who want to kill her. The last letter she wrote gave away where she could be found. If she isn't dead by now, she soon will be if you don't help us."

Lucy looked down at her daughter, peaceful though shaken. "It's been just awful."

Kate asked, "Where did you send those letters, Lucy? Please tell us. Sally Roe's life could depend on it."

Lucy looked at them, then at her daughter. Her mind was so confused; it was just so hard to know what to do anymore.

Destroyer was filling Khull's mind with some marvelous inspirations as Khull held his knife in plain sight, always sure that Sally could see its clean, keen edge. "Might as well face it, *gentlemen*. We're all made of the same stuff. All our hands are dirty, and we're all killers at heart. You want power, we want power, and we walk on the disposable people to get it. That's the name of the game."

Santinelli looked at Sally. Her face was still red from where he had struck her. "I will not have your blood on my hands, Ms. Roe. What follows will be your doing, not mine."

Sally spoke for the first time since being bound in the chair. "The responsibility is *yours*, sir. I appeal to you in the name of decency itself, in the name of all that is right."

"Law derives from power, Ms. Roe, not from morality. Spare me your newfound beliefs."

"The rosters, Ms. Roe," prompted Goring.

Do it, said the Strongman.

"She'll turn state's evidence, John. Yeah, and she's got an earful for you."

Marshall was sitting at Lucy Brandon's dining room table, on the telephone with John Harrigan, his friend in the FBI. Lucy, Kate, and Amber sat in the living room; Lucy was still holding Amber, who hadn't made a sound. Pastor Mark Howard was there as well, at Lucy's invitation.

"Ever heard of the Summit Institute? Well, let me give you the location. Sally Roe's letters went there, and now she's probably there too, if she's still alive."

Lucy spoke up from the living room couch. "They'll kill her. They want her for no other reason."

Marshall liked what he was hearing from Harrigan. "Yeah, right, those agents shouldn't be too far from there right now. That's good. Well, get them over there, and I mean now! Yeah, right."

Lucy told Kate and Mark softly and bitterly, "LifeCircle! They got me into this! The whole lawsuit was their idea! Claire Johanson and Jon Schmidt—the whole lot of them! They've done nothing but threaten me and coerce me since this whole mess started, and now where are they? Well, I'm not going down alone!" She called to Marshall, "Tell them I'm ready right now."

Marshall heard her. "John, you can send somebody over here right now. She's ready to talk."

This was it! The brushfire was catching on! From here it would burn upward—hot, hungry, inextinguishable!

Mota took a golden trumpet in his hand and shot through the roof of the house, soaring through the white light of his warriors still rushing over the town. Upward, skyward, slowly spinning, wings afire, he put the trumpet to his mouth.

In the mountains above the Summit Institute, the signal reached Tal's ears loud and clear.

"Done!" he cried, leaping to his feet. "They've set the fire in Bacon's Corner!"

"Better late than never," Guilo said with a shrug.

"It will reach Summit soon enough," said Tal, drawing his sword. "Prepare to attack!"

Amethyst was getting close to the big white house, the home of LifeCircle. The roar of Heaven's wings thundered in her ears. She whimpered, she cried, she fled before them. *My masters in LifeCircle! They will save me!*

Santinelli smiled a bitter smile as he looked long and hard at Mr. Khull, still brandishing the knife. "I believe you're right, Mr. Khull. I do see myself." He looked at Sally. "Power is power, whether it be wielded through legal decisions or . . . from the edge of a knife. And as for our gentle followers . . ." He looked upward, thinking of the hundreds of peace-seeking conferees now gathered from around the globe. "We *are* equal. We are devils, all."

He stepped back and took his place by the wall, out of the way. Goring and Steele joined him. He crossed his arms and with chin jutted out resolutely, said, "Teach us, Mr. Khull. We will learn."

Destroyer clicked his talons, and the spirits of Broken Birch moved the five Satanists like puppets.

Khull smiled with diabolical pleasure and nodded to his men. Two of them immediately looped a chain over a beam and affixed a hook to it. The other two released Sally from the chair and yanked her to her feet.

The Strongman, Destroyer, and all their wicked lords and commanders gathered, moving in close, ready for the triumph.

Sally knew there was no more time. "The rosters are in Ashton!"

"Too late," said Goring. "Please proceed, *gentlemen*!"

They bound her hands in front of her.

"The rosters are in Ashton!"

Where? growled the Strongman.

"*Where* in Ashton?" demanded Santinelli.

"I sent them to a Post Office box!"

Santinelli put up his hand. Khull looked disappointed, but he motioned for his men to stop.

Santinelli stepped forward. "What Post Office box?"

Sally really did try, but . . . "I . . . I can't remember the number."

"Proceed, gentlemen."

They grabbed her arms and started lifting her.

"I planned all those letters!"

Santinelli held up his hand again, and Khull's men set her down. Santinelli exchanged encouraged glances with Goring and Steele. "My, how the revelations are beginning to flow!"

Destroyer didn't like the subject matter. He nudged Steele.

"She's lying," said Steele.

"I remember the mail room, Mr. Steele!" Sally cried with a trembling voice.

Steele only leered at her. He didn't know what she was talking about.

"I used to work in the mail room at the Omega Center, remember?"

Steele didn't leer this time. He remembered.

Sally spilled it out rapidly, desperately. "You told me how to intercept mail you didn't want the staff to read. You said it wasn't wrong because it protected our purposes. You said your people did it all the time! Remember that, Mr. Steele?"

Goring and Santinelli looked at Steele. He was silent because he did remember it.

The Strongman suddenly grabbed Destroyer around the neck, but he didn't start squeezing. Not yet. He was waiting to hear the rest.

"Go on," said Santinelli.

"It was the only way to find you. I figured whoever tried to kill me would have to keep anyone from finding out I was still alive, so they'd have to intercept my letters; and I knew from the papers that you were using the postmaster in Bacon's Corner for your lawsuit, so that's where I sent them, and . . ."

"And you addressed them all to the defendant in the lawsuit, Tom Harris . . ."

"I knew you couldn't let *him* see the letters."

Santinelli smiled. He was impressed. "So your letters were to be a trail to the people ultimately responsible for your . . . alleged death!"

"Professor Lynch knew about my concern for Tom Harris, and Khull knew exactly where to find me, and you all knew without my telling you that I'd embraced Christianity. That was confirmation enough that you'd stolen my letters, but of course . . . now you've shown them to me. You have them. Every one of them."

Destroyer tried to force a leering, cocky smile as he choked and gargled out, "So what?"

Goring stepped in. "Marvelous! Yes, the letters are all here, and so are you. Now you have the satisfaction of knowing who your would-be killers are. But you recall, of course, that no one else has seen those letters, and the world has lost all track of you!"

"That's why I made copies."

There was a strange delay, as if that sentence took a few seconds to reach their ears and register in their minds. They all looked at her dumbly.

She drew a breath and went for broke. "The copies are in the Post Office box too, along with the rosters and James Bardine's ring, the one I took from the finger of that woman who tried to kill me. The ring you took from my neck is the one I got years ago from Owen Bennett. You can doublecheck his code name, Gawaine, on the inside of the ring if you like."

Santinelli came close, and he was even shaking a little. "What Post Office box, Ms. Roe?"

"It's empty by now anyway. I sent a letter to a lady who works at the *Ashton Clarion*, and I enclosed the key."

Now the Strongman applied the pressure, and Destroyer had to struggle for breath. "I never heard of any such letter! What do *you* know about it?"

Destroyer tried to answer. "I sent the twelve captains to Ashton to look into it—"

The Strongman began shaking him, making Destroyer's eyes look like horizontal, yellow blurs. "Where are those twelve?"

"They . . . they . . ."

"Wasn't the intercepting of those letters *your* idea?"

Suddenly Destroyer thought he was reliving his first feelings of doom; he was hearing the sound of a trumpet again, just like before. But this time it was louder. It was reverbrating all around them. It was so loud he couldn't be imagining it.

He wasn't. The Strongman heard it too, and let out a growl that shook the room.

Then they heard a resounding shout from so many voices it sounded like waves of the ocean. "For the saints of God, and for the Lamb!"

The Strongman roared again and threw Destroyer to the floor. "The enemy! We are discovered!"

The hundreds of demons in the room—the Strongman's aides, the bloodstained murderers of Broken Birch, the lofty and conceited deceivers controlling Santinelli, Goring, and Steele—flew into a panic, reaching for their swords, jostling each other, shouting and shrieking.

The floor and walls began to shake with the rumble of heavenly wings descending from above like a violent storm.

It was exhilarating, thrilling, reviving, rewarding—everything an angelic warrior was made for!

The Host of Heaven had waited so long and had built up such fervor that when the signal finally came, they broke over the crests of the mountains on every side like a violent, shimmering ocean wave and showered down like hail upon the dark cloud of demons in the valley, scattering them like dust before the wind, routing, battling, swinging, and pushing down, down, down toward the Summit Institute.

Tal, at the crest of the wave, dove like a hawk, his wings straight back, his sword a needle of light at the end of his outstretched arm. His war cry could be heard above all the tumult, and his sword was the first to strike.

They flew into the heart of the black cloud, like piercing a black, boiling thunderhead. The swords of spirits clashed, wings slapped and fluttered, red smoke fogged the air. Tal kicked, cut, spun like a scythe, and fought his way downward, downward. He could hear the roar of Guilo, the Strength of Many, just above and to the left, batting at demons and mowing them down, flipping them sideways to meet other blades, kicking and grabbing what hides he could find, cutting a widening swath, gutting the cloud at its core.

The Strongman slapped his demon lords about the room to bring them to their senses. "Are you commanders or not? To your posts! Defend us!"

The demons scattered to their posts, leaving the room almost empty except for the demons of Broken Birch.

The Strongman glared at Destroyer. "The woman has lit a fire that will consume us. There is nothing more we need from her. Finish her before *we* are finished!"

Destroyer shot a glance at Khull's demons.

Khull raised his knife.

"Mr. Goring!" came a cry from upstairs. "Mr. Goring! Something terrible is happening!"

Footsteps! People were in the chalet!

Khull grabbed Sally from behind, clapped his hand over her mouth, and poised his knife at her throat. His message was clear.

"Mr. Goring!" came the shout again.

Santinelli pushed Goring. "Answer them! Stop them before they find us!"

"My word," said Goring. "Those letters! They're right up there on the table!"

He hurried to the stairs, turning off the basement lights.

"Mr. Goring, are you here?"

He ran up the stairs. "Yes, right here! What is it?"

Amethyst cupped her wings open and came to an abrupt halt just short of the big white house. LifeCircle was under attack! Angels were everywhere! The spirits there, her masters, were fleeing!

Claire and Jon scurried about the office, finding documents, papers, anything and everything that might connect them with this miserable lawsuit and everything it entailed. They would deny everything, of course. It was all they could do. Maybe they'd get through okay, maybe they wouldn't—they didn't know, they couldn't think about it, they could hardly think at all; they were just too scared.

They'd gotten the tip-off: Lucy was talking; there were copies of Roe's letters in the wrong hands. The lid was coming off!

Jon jammed papers into a trash can until it was full, muttering angrily, "I knew we should have gotten out of this long ago! We've overreached ourselves!" He ran to find another container.

Claire had the telephone propped on her shoulder. She was talking to Miss Brewer, Amber Brandon's fourth grade teacher. "That's right. You'd better come up with some good explanations for what happened to Amber. Lucy Brandon's done an about-face, and she's blaming it all on you. Hey, don't blame *us*! You didn't have to select that curriculum; that was entirely your own choice, and we had nothing to do with it! No, I never heard of any Sally Roe; that's your concern, not ours!"

She slammed down the phone just as Jon rushed back into the room with a garbage can. "Jon, what about that curriculum? Can that be traced to LifeCircle?"

Jon found some documents and held them up for Claire to see. "Not after I burn these!"

Overhead, the swarm of survivors from the LifeCircle rout turned tail and fled before a wall of angels. They flew toward the elementary school. Ango the Terrible would be there with all his mighty hordes! He would know what to do!

Goring reached the upstairs and found the two psychics from the morning discussion group all in a dither.

"Here now," he said, "what's all the commotion?"

"Bad energy," said the woman attorney. "I can't explain it, but all the psychic energy around here is horribly disturbed!"

The fifth grade teacher nodded in agreement, his eyes wide with horror. "We're being invaded! That's the only word I can think of to describe it!"

In the basement, Sally, Khull, and the others stood in the dark, overhearing the conversation. Sally tried not to stir; she could feel Khull's blade against her throat.

Goring was trying to calm them. "Well, just take it easy. Let me encourage you to combine your insights with others around the campus. Perhaps we can all learn and benefit from this experience."

"It's scary!" said the lady.

"I'm so disoriented," said the man.

Khull pulled Sally's head back so hard, she thought her neck would snap. He huffed into her ear, "They're feeling *you*, lady! You and your filthy Jesus!"

The cloud of evil spirits closed ranks and drew in tight, swords ready, as all around angelic warriors continued to thunder down the mountainsides like an avalanche and swirl around them like a cyclone. The Host of Heaven struck the cloud at the base, and it collapsed downward to fill the gap; they assaulted the pinnacle and it shriveled, bleeding a shower of stung demons; they shot like fatal bullets through its center, and the cloud's mass began to thin. They harried it, struck at it, sliced it into weaker segments. The cloud was thick, tough, and tenacious, but it was weakening.

Tal hacked an attacker, mowed through four more, spun and kicked another spirit aside, and then spotted a sudden, instantaneous gap in the demonic mantle just over Goring's chalet. He folded his wings above his head and dropped through it.

Sally and the others could hear Goring having a bit of trouble with his distraught psychics.

"Now, if you'll excuse me," said Goring, "I do have some urgent business to attend to."

"What could be more urgent than this?" said the man, his voice coming close to the basement stairway.

"Please!" said Goring, coming after him. "Use the front door! Go out the way you came in!"

Maybe, just maybe, that man would hear her. Sally steadily filled her lungs.

"Wow!" said the woman. "What are all these letters? Fan mail?"

Sally screamed, pushing the sound against Khull's hand with all the diaphragm she could muster. The scream came through Khull's thick hand a pitiful, muffled moan. No one heard it.

Khull had his excuse. He dug in with the knife.

"AWWW!"

"Khull!" said Santinelli. "What is it?"

Khull just moaned something unintelligible.

"Get the lights!"

"Where are they?"

Cursings, fumblings in the dark, tripping, stumbling, Khull growling, cursing, bumping into things, the wooden chair toppling.

"What was that?" said the man upstairs.

"Out!" said Goring. "Get out of this house!"

Steele found the lights.

"Khull!" said one of Khull's men.

Khull was holding his chest; his shirt was slashed, red with blood. He'd carved a wound across his own ribcage.

"Where's the woman?" he cried, his eyes wild with rage.

The Strongman and Destroyer were blinded for an instant. Something had struck them. They blinked and squinted, trying to recover.

"Where's the woman?" the Strongman howled.

Destroyer stared in horror at the spirits of Broken Birch—they were strewn about the room as if by a bomb blast, dazed, disoriented. The Strongman's aides looked this way and that, but saw nothing.

"There!" a spirit shouted.

The light of day hurt Sally's eyes. She was out in the morning air. She could see the herb garden and people gathered there.

A huge man held her, his face like bronze, his hair like gold. He set her down and pointed toward the mountains.

"Run, Sally! RUN!"

New strength coursed through her legs, and she ran.

The demons hurled themselves at Tal with suicidal abandon, their eyes crazed with bloodthirst. He darted, dodged, feinted, meeting their swords with his own, kicking whom he could, swirling, dashing, jabbing, keeping them back.

"YAHAAA!" came Guilo's voice behind him. Now Tal had some help. Struck demons began to fly across his vision, limp and dissolving.

He could see Sally Roe, still in the clear, still running. *Run, girl! RUN!*

43

Sally ran like a frightened gazelle, her thoughts set on that front gate, her stride never breaking. She bounded into the herb garden and whisked right past the blond singer and his little group.

"Hey, who's that?" someone asked.

Then came Sybil Denning's voice. "Well . . . ! Sally! Sally Roe! Sally, is that you?"

Sally didn't look back, she didn't slow down; she just kept running, her long hair blowing in the wind behind her, her arms pumping, her legs grabbing up distance. She dashed out of the herb garden, across a lawn, down a pebbled path, and into the main parking lot. She could see the main gate.

Goring was just herding the two psychics out the front door against their protests when someone else ran up full of questions.

"Hey, who was that we saw running? What's going on around here?"

Goring asked directly, "Was it a woman?"

"Yeah. Man, she looked scared—"

"Which way did she go?"

"We're *all* scared! What's happening?"

"*Which way did she go?*"

"Well, toward the front gate. She was splitting the place!"

"I'll look into it."

Goring closed the door right in their faces and called to Khull's men. "She's outside, heading for the front gate!"

Khull's four hooligans were just bringing Khull upstairs.

Goring was indignant. "Don't bring him up here! You'll drip blood on my carpet!"

"Get the woman!" said the Strongman.

Destroyer shoved and swatted the Broken Birch spirits into action. "You heard him! Get the woman!"

Khull ordered his men, "Get her! Bring me the pieces!"

They bolted for the back door.

Amethyst was only one of a mob of hysterical demons who converged on the Bacon's Corner Elementary School, but there was no rescue here either. The Host of Heaven had already struck the place, and demons were scattering from the roof, from the playfield, from all around the school, like hornets from a burning hive.

Ango, the boastful lord of the school, was fluttering about the sky with half a wing gone, wailing, cursing, spitting his hatred and screaming for help; but all his hordes had forsaken him and fled. Out of control, he careened crazily into a cluster of brilliant warriors, met their swords, and exploded in several directions, vanishing in trails of red smoke.

In the school office, Miss Brewer was having a face-to-face confrontation with Mr. Woodard, the school principal.

"No way!" she said in a voice just below a scream. "I'm not responsible for selecting that curriculum, no matter what anybody says! You told me to teach it! You and that LifeCircle bunch were behind this whole thing, and I'll tell that to anyone who wants to know! I'm not going to take the rap for this, not for anyone! *You're* the principal! *You're* the one responsible! You can fire me if you want, but I won't be your patsy. Is that clear?"

"I'll look into it," said Mr. Woodard, looking pale.

Miss Brewer went back to her classroom. Mr. Woodard picked up the phone and dialed Betty Hanover, the Number One power-holder on the school board. "Betty? Bruce Woodard. Listen, I don't know what's going on here, but I want you and the rest of the school board to be clear on where I stand in these matters. I will *not* be left holding this thing, understand? I can be heavy-handed if I have to be . . ."

The demons from LifeCircle and now the survivors from the elementary school turned and fled before the pursuing angels. Terga, the Prince of Bacon's Corner! He controlled the school board! Surely *he* could stem this tide and stand against this attack!

Amethyst was not quick to flee, but indecisive. Where was Ango?

The demons rushed away, leaving her behind. She searched for Ango. Was he here?

STUNG! An angelic sword caught her under the arm and she went spinning, plummeting down toward the school. She reached toward that black tar roof, even pushed toward it with the power of her wings. It was a safe place. She'd flourished in those rooms before. Maybe someone below could help her, hide her . . .

The black roof slapped by her, then the rafters, the insulation, the ceiling, a classroom full of children—

SWIPE! A warrior finished her, and she fell dissolving to the floor, a smoldering heap just behind Miss Brewer, just below a crayon drawing on the wall, a marvelous picture of a purple, winged pony under a rainbow.

Sally ran toward the big stone gate. Right now that gate seemed like the gateway to Hell itself, but she was getting *out*, she was escaping, she was breaking free! *Come on, girl, get through that thing!*

Khull's men raced through the hedges and down an obscure pathway toward the highway to head her off. So far they hadn't been seen by any conferees, but that was due more to luck than caution.

"The woman!" cried the spirits, their attention diverted from the battle overhead to the fleeing figure on the ground. That diversion cost many of them their presence in this world. The angels were there, swords flashing, and no one could stop Sally Roe.

She reached the gate. There was no invisible barrier, no burly thug to stop her, no dirty hands grabbing. She passed through it like a bird out of a cage, her heart soaring. *O Lord God, my Savior Jesus, will You save me? Are You running with me now?*

She crossed the highway and ducked into the forest on the other side. First she would get some distance behind her, then perhaps double back to the village, get a ride, hike out, whatever. *Just stay alive, Sally, just stay alive! Hang on!*

Khull's men saw her cross the highway. They fanned out. The demons of Broken Birch stayed close to the ground and followed them, goading them on, filling their blackened minds with thoughts of blood and murder.

The cloud of spirits began to change shape. The base began to shift sideways, crawling up the mountainside, spreading a mantle over the path of that solitary, fleeing figure.

Tal shouted to his commanders, "Keep her covered, but let them follow!"

They understood, and backed away before the advancing demonic hordes.

The thick mantle over the Summit Institute began to pull away, leaving it open and vulnerable.

Demonically speaking, LifeCircle was a desolate ruin, the elementary school had fallen to the enemy, and now as the wilting, bleeding leftovers from those two defeats fled to the homes and businesses of the Bacon's Corner school board, they discovered Terga, their mighty prince, all by himself, flying in crazy circles over the town, screaming in rage.

"Cowards!" he shrieked. "Deserters! Come back and stand!"

The demon lords under his command were nowhere to be seen, but had fled before the advancing flood of heavenly armies. The Oriental, Signa, was right at Terga's heels. Terga was as good as finished and presently out of his mind.

Mota had already led a powerful contingent of warriors on a bold sweep through the home of board chairwoman Betty Hanover, routing the ruling demons of that household and leaving Mrs.

Hanover feeling unsure of herself—especially now, when a federal postal agent was on the phone.

"Just trying to track down some information," he said. "We understand your elementary school was using a curriculum written by the woman in question, a Sally Beth Roe."

"Uh . . . well, I don't know anything about that."

"We understand that Sally Roe lived right in your area."

"Really?" Betty tried to sound surprised, but never was much of an actor.

"Well, we're just trying to find her. We have to follow up on a complaint."

"Complaint?"

"Mail tampering, for one thing."

"Well . . . you might try talking to Claire Johanson . . ."

"Already did. She said to call you."

"She—" Betty buttoned her lip, but cursed Claire up one side and down the other in her mind.

"Hold on," said the agent. "I've got the name of the curriculum right here . . . Yeah . . . *Finding the Real Me.* Ring any bells?"

"The Omega Center!"

"Beg your pardon?"

"The Omega Center for Educational Studies in Fairwood, Massachusetts! They're the publishers of that curriculum! They'd know the author, I'm sure. We don't know anything about the author. All we did was buy the curriculum from Omega. They're the ones you should talk to. We don't know anything."

"All right. Do you have their number, address, all that good stuff?"

"Just hold on."

She gave him the information and hung up the phone, unable to stop shaking.

The phone rang again. It was school board member John Kendall. "Betty, I'm calling to warn you—"

"You're too late," she told him.

School board member Jerry Mason called right after she hung up on John Kendall. He wanted to know what she knew about this Sally Roe/mail tampering/lawsuit/curriculum thing, and didn't Sally Roe commit suicide a while back? She wanted to know what he knew, they both wanted to know what Claire Johanson knew, and both agreed that none of them knew a lot and that all of them wanted to know a lot more, especially what the *feds* knew.

The demonic powers and authorities of Bacon's Corner were scattered. Terga's best warriors fled elsewhere to find a new home for their mischief; Terga, alone except for the deserters who joined him on the way, set out for the Omega Center. Perhaps there was time to warn Barquit, Omega's prince. Maybe Barquit would have the strength to save them and stop this onslaught.

Far away from it all, in the city of Westhaven, the Circuit Court of Appeals, with all parties oblivious to the spiritual racket steadily growing and spreading out of Bacon's Corner, convened at two o'clock in the afternoon. Wayne Corrigan and Tom Harris took their places at the defendant's table on the right side of the courtroom, while attorneys Ames and Jefferson took their seats on the left.

"All rise," said the bailiff, and they all rose, and in strode the three appellate judges, one younger man, one older man, and one sagging woman. They sat down, the three lawyers sat down, the clerk and bailiff sat down, and the court stenographer poised her fingers over the little keys.

Tom looked around the courtroom. Apart from one reporter that had shown up looking a little bored with his assignment, the gallery was empty. Of course. The public was waiting for the real show, the trial.

"Ah well," Corrigan whispered, "it's going to be a short day anyway."

"No earthshaking surprises?" asked Tom.

"To be honest, I'm not expecting any."

The older judge put on his reading glasses and referred to his papers. "This is the case of *Brandon v. the Good Shepherd Academy*, the defendant appealing the lower court's ruling as to compelling a child witness to be examined by defense's experts and to testify in this case . . ."

Corrigan sneaked a glance at Ames and Jefferson. They looked bored. Boy, now there was confidence!

In Fairwood, Massachusetts, the Omega Center was in full swing, with classes in progress, fair weather on the campus, and—by their standards—nothing weird or unusual happening. A gang of young adults continued their good-hearted game of touch football on the playfield; on the Tai Chi plaza, two dozen practitioners moved in slow motion through time, space, and spirit; in the classrooms, high school kids, adults, and even senior citizens learned the latest westernized twist on Hindu mysticism; and in the quiet, cushioned meditation rooms, young transcendentalists watched with eyes closed as demons played cosmic movies in their brains.

Cree and Si, their armies in position, were ready and waiting. Any moment now . . .

Barquit, Prince of Omega, was troubled when he first heard the humming and whistling of frayed wings and then the anguished wails and laments of spirits far away. He took wing and hovered above the Omega Administration Building, peering westward until he saw the spirits from Bacon's Corner approaching, screaming with alarm.

Something was up. "Forces!"

FWOOOM! He covered his head, blinded by brilliant light exploding on every side, obliterating the forests and hills, washing out the blue of the sky, bleaching out the colors of the Center. Spinning about in panic, he drew his sword, but it was struck away before he even saw his attacker.

He fled into the sky, feeling the burning light of Heaven at his heels.

Telephones began to ring in every room on the campus, and every teacher, group leader, and facilitator got the word: the football game was over, classes were canceled, and anyone out in astral travel would have to come in for a landing. Mr. Tisen, the head of the Omega faculty, had gotten an angry call from Betty Hanover, a threatening call from Claire Johanson, and last but not least a nosy and intimidating call from the FBI. He was clearing the campus, and that meant everyone.

Cree and Si led their forces through the campus like a flash flood, whipping through and around the buildings, flushing demons out of the rooms, chasing them through the surrounding woods, cutting them down out of the sky. The demonic deceivers were swamped and confounded. They called for Barquit, their crafty leader, but he was long gone. They had little time to lament about it before they were gone as well.

Barquit looked back only once, just long enough to know that Omega, his empire, had fallen.

The Strongman! This is his blunder!

"Classes are canceled," said Tisen over the loudspeakers. "Everyone to your dorms. Get your belongings loaded on the buses and be ready to roll!"

The classes ended so abruptly and the students were sent out so quickly that many thought it was a fire drill, or even an air raid. Some were still slipping on their coats as they hurried outside; others, still half-entranced, had to be led by the hand. The teachers were gathering up their coats, grabbing their briefcases, handouts, and curricula, shutting off the lights, locking up the rooms.

The football game broke up, and the players jogged back toward their dormitories full of questions.

Within an hour, the buses began to roll down the drive to the main road, carrying away faculty, students, even maintenance personnel, all chattering and wondering together just what in the world was going on.

Only a few noticed the plain olive sedan parked in front of the Administration Building. It hadn't been there long.

"I'm sorry," Tisen told the two federal agents now standing in his office. "You've come at a hectic time. We're just closing down for our midspring break. Hardly anyone is here now."

The two men exchanged glances.

"*Midspring* break?" asked one.

Tisen smiled. "We follow a rather unique calendar here, gentlemen."

"We'll have a look at it."

The other agent noted, "We saw the buses pulling out. It looked like an evacuation."

Tisen grinned sheepishly. "Well, most of them have planes to catch . . ."

The agents didn't waste time. "Like I asked you over the phone, this is the same Omega Center that published the *Finding the Real Me* curriculum?"

"Well . . . yes, it is."

"Then you must be familiar with the author, Sally Beth Roe?"

"You mean me personally?"

"I mean you personally or any other way."

"Well, of course I'm familiar with the name . . ."

"Where can we contact her?"

"Um . . . Well, I'm afraid she's deceased."

"How do you know that?"

"Well, I—"

One agent consulted some notes. "What about an instructor here, a lady named Sybil Denning? Is she still on the campus?"

Tisen shook his head with just a little too much sadness. "No, I'm afraid she's gone."

"Do you see much of Owen Bennett anymore?"

Tisen looked shocked at that question. "*Owen Bennett?*"

"He used to be on the Omega advisory board, right?"

"That was a long time ago."

"How about the director of this place . . . uh . . . Steele?"

"He's gone."

"The *director's* gone?"

"He's away at a conference."

"What conference and where?"

"Well, um . . . Do I really have to answer all these questions?"

"Maybe now, for sure later. Suit yourself."

These guys were intimidating. "He's . . . he and some other people on our faculty are at the Summit Institute."

The two men nodded to each other. Apparently they already knew about that place.

Goring, Steele, and Santinelli stood in a close cluster near the big fireplace, trying to lay a contingency plan. They paid little attention to Khull, who still sat at the top of the basement stairs trying to tape up his wound with gauze, cotton, and anything else he could find in Goring's first aid kit. So far he was only making a mess.

"You know what she said in those letters!" said Goring. "She didn't leave out one thing!"

Steele asked Santinelli, "How would our chances be in court?"

Santinelli was grim but determined, and spoke in a low mutter. "There are many variables and contingencies. We should immediately inventory and eliminate any liabilities." Goring and Steele couldn't help a quick, sideways glance at Khull. Santinelli cleared his throat to correct them. "Any connections at all with the Bacon's Corner case must be eradicated. I can call my office on that. As for material evidence . . ." He shot a glance at the coffee table. "I strongly suggest we burn these letters!"

Khull pretended he didn't hear anything.

The telephone rang. Goring cursed, but decided to pick it up in the kitchen. He stepped out of the room.

"Power in the right places will also be a crucial factor," said Santinelli. "This will be a test of how much we really have."

"Mr. Steele!" Goring called. "It's your faculty head, Mr. Tisen!"

Steele motioned for Santinelli to follow him, and they joined Goring in the kitchen.

"It sounds urgent," Goring whispered.

Khull saw his chance, and struggled to his feet.

A sleek, blue sedan pulled into the parking lot, and three men in business suits got out, getting a good look at the place and acting just a little bewildered.

"They're going to think we're crazy," said one.

"Let's make this quick," said another. "I want to get back in time to see the Broncos game."

They encountered a beautiful blonde woman just getting out of her Mercedes.

"Pardon me, ma'am," said the group's leader. "We're looking for . . . uh . . ." He lost his train of thought.

The second man stepped in. "We need to talk to the people in charge of this place."

"Oh," said the woman. "Why don't you try Mr. Goring? His chalet is right over that way, beyond the herb garden, see?"

She gave them just a few more pointers and then went her way. One man was ready to head for the chalet, but the other two just kept staring after the woman.

"C'mon," said the one, "let's go."

"You know who that was?"

"C'mon!"

"That was . . . you know, What's-her-name, from that TV show . . ."

Tal's brushfire continued to rage.

Far away, on the Bentmore University campus, there was quite a buzz about the School of Education closing down so suddenly. Information was scarce. There were isolated conversations here and there about the sudden death of Professor Samuel W. Lynch. No one seemed to know how he died, or at least no one was willing to talk about it. The only news being consistently repeated among the faculty and students was that he'd been found dead in his office and that the School of Education was suspending classes indefinitely. There were rumors, of course: Lynch may have been murdered, and there might be some kind of scandal afoot. There might be an investigation. Student reporters for the *Bentmore Register* were hoping for an exposé.

Corrupter, the bloated demon Prince of Bentmore University, was dethroned at last, and it was Chimon the European and his British friend Scion who batted him out of his position like a beach ball over a fence. The angelic forces had done their job quickly, and now homeless demons were aloft and wailing, most of them heading for Summit. Soon they would descend upon the Strongman along with all the other evicted and dethroned spirits, demanding rescue, answers, relief.

Immediately, with the slamming down of the phone, Goring, Santinelli, and Steele came dashing around the corner and back into the living room with one goal in mind.

And one huge shock waiting for them—an empty coffee table, and no Mr. Khull.

"The letters!" cried Goring.

"Khull!" said Steele.

"That devil!" said Santinelli, dashing out the door.

44

Sally's heart pounded and ached in her chest as she scurried and stumbled over damp pine needles and patches of crusted snow, grappled and groped through prickly, dead branches, and tried with all her rapidly ebbing strength to stay ahead of the snappings, huffings, rustlings, and footfalls of the devils pursuing her.

Two were directly below, but invisible behind limbs and thickets; a third was to her left, and she'd seen him twice, so close she could read the demons in his eyes. The fourth was silent and invisible except for his eerie, intermittent whistling to let the others know where he was.

They were getting closer. *O Lord Jesus, help me run!*

"Hey," said one of the three visitors, "now who's that?"

His friends expected to see another celebrity. What they saw was a silver-haired man in a business suit running like a wild man across the herb garden.

"Guys, I just have this feeling . . ."

Khull, his chest still reddened from his wound, had Goring's briefcase full of Sally's letters in one hand and the keys to the van in the other. He stood by the van, unable to find the right key to open it. He could see the key to the door, but it kept falling out of his fingers and dangling from the key ring.

Guilo stood by him, flicking at the keys with the tip of his finger, making them dance, slip, flip, and turn every which way but where Khull wanted them.

Tal swooped low over the parking lot with a message: "They're on the way!"

"Splendid!" said Guilo.

Santinelli was gasping for breath and about to collapse when he reached the parking lot, but the sight of Khull holding Goring's briefcase fed his rage and his rage kept him going. He got to the van in mere seconds, pointing his shaking finger.

"I'll . . . take . . . those!" he gasped.

Khull smiled mockingly. "Huh? You mean *these*?" It was a great joke to him.

Santinelli was losing all semblance of dignity. "You devil! How dare you betray us!"

Khull held up his hand. "Hey, just who was going to betray who? We're all devils, right? You said so yourself. I'm taking these for insurance: number one, to make sure I get paid, and number two, to make sure you and I always remain close, trusting friends!"

Santinelli had more rage than sense, and grabbed at the briefcase. Khull wasn't about to let go of it.

Guilo let them go ahead and tangle. He was waiting for the right moment.

All right. Good enough.

With his huge hand, he batted the briefcase free. It struck the pavement, flipped twice, then flew open, throwing the letters everywhere.

Santinelli—dignified, honorable, distinguished, high-powered attorney Santinelli—stooped to grab up the letters, but so did bloodthirsty, demonized, Satanist murderer Khull. They went to their knees, playing one on one, grabbing faster, grabbing more, shoving, jostling, grappling, ripping . . .

Until they came to the feet. Three sets of feet. Nice shoes. Nice suits. Three men.

One man held out his badge. FBI.

Destroyer braced himself, but the Strongman didn't roar this time. He didn't even slap Destroyer around the room. Instead, with defeat in his eyes, he looked above and all around, just watching his empire crumble.

The cloud of demons was so hacked apart by this time that the light of Heaven was shining down on the Summit Institute in alarmingly large patches, turning the Global Consciousness Conference into a shambles. The psychics were unable to get any readings, the channelers' spirit entities weren't speaking, the tarot readers couldn't remember what their cards were saying, and every "higher self" on campus was out to lunch and not answering.

In the meantime, word was getting around the campus that three federal agents had just arrested someone and were still checking around. Something big was going down, and few conferees had their minds on their own hidden potential and godhood, a shot in the arm the demons could have used.

All this was distressing enough, but then the other spirits began to arrive from Bacon's Corner, the Omega Center, Bentmore University, and other centers of demonic power disrupted by the spiritual shock waves. One by one, in various stages of dismemberment and injury, they tumbled into the basement of the chalet, screaming, scratching, clawing for rescue, for answers, for someone to blame.

Terga, the Prince of Bacon's Corner, was slowly withering, and pointed at the Strongman with his one good hand. "You brought this upon us! You and your ridiculous Plan!"

Corrupter, only half his original size, rolled across the floor like a lame rat and spit out his accusation. "Have we built our empire at Bentmore only to feed it to Heaven's Host?"

Barquit kept his wings tightly wrapped around him, humiliated by his defeat and now swordless. "Your Plan! Always *your* Plan! Is this why I was never warned of the woman's coming, *or* of this ambush laid against my principality?"

Then from all around, from every fanged, drooling, spitting

mouth, came the big question: "What have you done about the woman?"

The Strongman had one simple answer for all the questions. He pointed to Destroyer. "*There* is your betrayer! If he had killed her when he should have, we would not be in this state today! It was *his* idea to capture her letters, and now her testimony is *in writing* and defeats us! He is the one whose harassments did not destroy her, but drove her to the Cross!"

The Cross! That was all the spirits needed to hear. Swords appeared. "You will pay for this!"

Destroyer met their murderous eyes with his own, drew his blazing sword, and sliced the air with ribbons of red light. "So you are better than I? Then show it now!"

They stood in their places, spitting and cursing at him from a safe distance.

He huffed at them in anger. "To the Abyss with all of you! I will finish what I have started!"

The Strongman shook his head. "You won't, Destroyer. She belongs to the Lamb. He has redeemed her from our grasp!"

Destroyer clenched his teeth and growled, "I *will* finish!"

The Strongman spread his wings in Destroyer's path. "We are withdrawing, Destroyer, and Khull's henchmen will not go with you. Without men to do your killing, the *woman* will have power over *you*!"

"She doesn't know that!" Destroyer pointed his sword right at the Strongman's belly. "I will finish what I have started!"

The Strongman studied Destroyer with probing eyes, and then stepped aside. The hate-crazed demon shot out of the chalet.

"We will not see him again," said the Strongman. He turned to the battered, tattered assemblage. "Princes, we are restrained! We will wait for a better time."

In a burst of black wings, chugging sulfur, and trails of red smoke, the Strongman and his princes scattered in all directions from the Summit Institute, abandoning it like a sinking ship, letting the clamor and smoke shrink into the distance behind them.

Follow the woman, follow the woman, get her! The spirits of Broken Birch thought only of the woman and stayed close to the ground in hot pursuit, guiding and empowering the four killers who now thrashed and clawed their way through the forest looking for their fleeing prey.

There! The killers spotted her, struggling up a steep bank, losing strength, stumbling, falling.

Tears streamed down Sally's face; her shirt clung to her back, soaked with sweat. She clambered over some stones and then flopped to the ground, her lungs heaving. Every muscle in her body trembled and quivered; her legs and arms would no longer move. She couldn't see, she couldn't think; she felt she was dreaming.

The demons jumped on the backs of the killers. *Kill her! Kill her! Chop her into little pieces!*

There was a roaring sound behind them. The forest was flooded with light.

Behind them?

Some looked back. They screamed, and others looked back also.

They could no longer see the Summit Institute, their haven, their fortress—all they could see was the Host of Heaven!

Cut off! Ambushed!

"Take them!" said Tal.

Red smoke.

Killer Number One collapsed to the ground, gasping for air. He'd had enough of this mountainside.

Killer Number Two, further up the slope, turned when he heard Number One hit the ground. "Hey, c'mon!"

Number One didn't answer. He just wanted to breathe.

Number Three had just broken into a clearing and could see the Institute. He whistled at them. "Hey! Looks like feds down there! They've got Khull!"

Number Four saw the woman tumble behind some rocks. He took his knife in his hand. He was almost there. He paused just momentarily to look back, then cursed. "It *is* Khull!"

The Summit Institute looked like a model of itself from up here, with neat rows of toy cars lined up in the blacktop parking lot and rough shake rooftops nestled among the trees. Khull wasn't hard to recognize, staggering along between two men in suits with the front of his shirt all red and his hands behind his back. That guy behind him had to be Santinelli, being led along by a third man. There was no sign of Goring, but just seeing this was enough.

"Good-bye," said Number Three, heading back down the mountain.

Number One followed him. "Let's get into town. I'll hot-wire a car."

There was an immediate consensus.

Sally did not hear them go. She lay among the rocks in a dead faint. The Satanists had come within four feet of her hiding-place before turning back.

In Claytonville, former Police Sergeant Harold Mulligan locked the front door of coroner Joey Parnell's home and put Parnell's house keys in his pocket. He'd just dropped by the Parnell residence on a business call—but it wasn't police business. Mulligan was in civilian clothes, and was driving his own private vehicle, an older Ford. He did not linger, but got into that Ford, backed down the driveway, and drove out of that neighborhood, out of that town, and, for all practical purposes, out of existence. He would never be seen again.

Within a few days, the papers would report the mysterious gunshot deaths of Parnell and his wife, both found dead together in the Parnell home, apparently from a mutual suicide pact. Satanic literature would be found in the home, along with evidence linking Parnell to several unsolved murders in that part of the state.

Sally awoke with a start and stiffened. Don't move! They might be near you! She stifled her breathing and remained still, listening.

There was no sound except the cold breeze. The shadows were longer. It was the only way she could tell that any time had passed. She lay among some large stones, flat on her back. She raised her head slightly. She felt cold.

Then she felt fear. Steady. Pounding. Growing. Like footsteps behind her in the dark, like some . . . some *thing* lurking around the next blind corner, like a crawling, unstoppable monster approaching while she was unable to move.

She whispered so quietly she only mouthed the words, "Who's there?"

EYES! Scales! Blackness, power, sulfur, *hatred*!

It stood tall before her, a waking nightmare, a black, towering silhouette against a surreal, blood-red sky, the bulging yellow eyes leering at her, never blinking, never wavering.

She knew it was there. It was not material, and physical eyes could not see it, but she'd had such visitations before, and she knew it was real. She tensed, rose to her elbows, looking up at it while it looked down at her, the sulfur blowing in silken wisps from its nostrils, its fangs bared as it grinned with fiendish delight.

It spoke to her in her mind. *You know me.*

She did, and now she had good reason to be terrified. She pushed herself away, wriggling backwards on her hands and elbows, speechless, shaking.

The thing's words throbbed in her head. *You know me, Sally Roe, and you won't get away!*

The huge red sword came down like a meat cleaver.

Tal heard Sally's scream above the battle and shouted, "Guilo!"

"YAHHH!" came Guilo's answer as he shot up from the center of the ebbing cloud. He'd heard it too.

Side by side, with wings spread full and trailing fire, they dove like meteors for the mountain, rolled sharply to the right, then dropped into the forest, lighting up the treetops.

Sally tumbled over the rocks and rolled down the steep incline, arms thrashing, kicking up pine needles, dirt, and pebbles. The ground was washed red with the light of that huge sword as the thing glided down the slope after her, wings spread like a canopy. She could hear its huffing breath, the rippling of its leathery wings.

She came to a stop against a tree.

WHOOSH! The sword split the air once more. Sally ducked, scrambled down the hill, fell, and rolled again.

Tal banked to the left, Guilo to the right; they would strike from opposite sides. Tal shot up the mountainside, chest just above the rocks and brush, then cupped his wings, swung his feet out before him, and doubled back.

He could see Sally tumbling down the slope with the black spirit pouncing on her like a murderous vulture, red sword flashing again and again. Beyond the spirit, he saw Guilo as a fast-closing ball of light. Tal hauled back his sword, ready to strike.

The loathsome spirit saw them coming and stood his ground, ready to meet them. They came at him like two colliding trains. With incredible power, he batted them both aside. Guilo went tumbling uphill, trying to come out of a spin, while Tal cannonballed downhill, passing through and between the pines, disappearing into the thick forest below.

You are mine, said the spirit, *and I will finish what I have started!*

"No!" Sally pleaded. It was the only word that would come to her mind.

ZING! The sword caught her in the leg. She fell against a tree, then to the ground. The sword came down again, just missing her shoulder.

Brilliant light! Two comets! Guilo from above, Tal from below, closing again!

Guilo struck first. The spirit batted him aside, but caught a stunning blow in the back from Tal's sword and teetered forward before spinning and meeting Tal's sword with a jolting parry that sent Tal fluttering into the forest again.

Guilo dove and struck the thing's neck. It elbowed him several miles out of the way.

Tal righted himself, gripped his sword tightly, and shouted, *Sally Roe! Stand against him! Turn him away!*

Sally didn't seem to hear. She was crying out, trying to get on her feet. The thing leaped upon her, digging its talons into her. She could feel them searing her flesh. She was choking on the foul breath. It raised the sword again.

OOF! A streak of light passed overhead, and the thing pitched forward. Guilo looped in a tight circle and came in for another pass, and there came Tal, straight down from above.

The spirit rose to its feet and faced them head-on, wild-eyed, sword ready. Guilo came in low; it kicked him aside. Tal dropped from above; it batted him into the treetops.

Speak up, Sally! said Tal.

"Stand aside," the thing roared. "The woman belongs to *me!*"

With that, it stomped its black, scaled foot down on the fleeing woman's leg, knocking her down, holding her there.

Tal shouted, "She is *ours*," and dove for the demon again, at least to keep it diverted.

This time their swords met in a shower of sparks. The blow sent Tal reeling.

Take authority! said Tal.

You are mine, Sally Roe! said the demon.

"No!" said Sally. She'd found some words. "I belong to Jesus, the Son of God!"

That's it, that's it, that's it! Guilo roared, rushing through the trees with incredible fury.

His blow knocked the demon backward. The thing whipped his sword around, but Guilo pulled his feet in just in time and got away.

You do not belong to Jesus! the monster screamed. *He could never love you!*

Sally was distraught, groping for words. "Jesus loves me! The Bible tells me so!" A child's Sunday school song. It was all she knew.

Tal scored a hit and sent the demon tumbling into the trees.

Sally went running for her life, crying out, "Jesus, help me! Help me!"

The demon recovered and roared after her, wings thundering. *You will burn in Hell with me! I will drag you there myself!* He swung his sword at her, but his reach was short.

She fell, twisted, looked up at those yellow eyes.

He landed on her, knocking her flat with his knees, clamping her down.

Their eyes met.

"Jonas!" she screamed.

He broke into a wide, hideous grin, the fangs dripping, the brow furrowed with wicked laughter. The sword went high over his head.

"Jonas," she said, extending her open hand toward the gnarled face, "STOP!"

The sword remained above his head. The eyes narrowed. *You are mine!*

She rose up on one elbow. She was gaining new courage. "I am *not* yours! I belong to Jesus!"

No . . . no, Sally Roe!

She was amazed. The sword teetered above the demon's head. He could not lower it. She spoke again. "I belong to Jesus now; He paid for my sins with His blood, and you can't torment me anymore!"

I will do what I wish! I am going to kill you! Suddenly the demon didn't sound too convincing.

"My Lord has defeated you!"

Destroyer stumbled to his feet, holding his sword limply, his eyes losing their fire.

"Get out of my life, Jonas! Forever! Do you hear?"

THUD! Tal came in with a blow that sent Destroyer spinning. The black demon righted himself and held his sword ready. Guilo came in from the side and assailed him again with a clash of blades and bursts of light.

"The woman belongs to *me!*" Destroyer roared.

"She is *ours!*" said Tal.

Sally's desperate, screaming voice came across the distance: "I belong to Jesus! Jonas, I *renounce* you! You have no claim to me! Get out of my life!"

The words hit Destroyer like poisonous darts. Then a revelation hit like a salvo, and Destroyer stood still, facing his archrival, the Captain of the Host.

"You *knew*, Captain of the Host! You knew she would do this to me, to *us*!"

Tal held his sword ready, but answered, "I knew what you would do to *her*—that you were commissioned to destroy her."

Destroyer's mouth spread open, and the fangs went dry. "*You* placed her there, in Bacon's Corner!"

"And you tried to kill her, as always!"

Destroyer began to wilt. "She . . . was *mine*, from her youth!"

"Ours—our Lord's," said Tal, "from her mother's womb."

"Get out of my life, Jonas!" Sally cried. "Jesus has conquered you—so get out!"

The sword quivered in Destroyer's hand. "She has taken away my name!"

With an agonized roar and a final burst of fury, the weakened demon dove at Tal, bringing his blade down in a fiery arc. Tal parried, jabbed, let him keep coming. The red sword swung from the side, came back again, cut through the air. Tal sidestepped it, struck it aside with enough force to throw the demon off-balance. He delivered a stunning kick to the demon's flank, jolting him, toppling him. The demon twisted about, swung at him; Tal met that clumsy attack easily, then brought his own blade down in a shining arc.

The air filled with red smoke. Destroyer wailed like an eerie siren, clutching his opened side, floating, withering, fading. He pushed himself backward with one foot, hovering on erratic wings. Tal hauled back for one more blow, but it wouldn't be necessary. As the demon's eyes remained fixed on him, ruby-red, bulging in hate, the wings fell silent.

With the dying, groping lips forming a silent curse, the thing pitched forward, sighing out sulfur, and slipped into oblivion.

The forest was suddenly quiet. Now Tal could hear the muffled weeping of Sally Roe. He sheathed his sword.

She lay nearby, facedown in the dirt, weeping, physically exhausted and emotionally spent. Guilo sat beside her, his wings spread over her, stroking her head and speaking soothing words to her soul. Tal approached quietly, knelt beside them, and spread his wings high and wide, joining Guilo's wings to form a canopy to keep out the world for a while.

"One more season of restraint," he said. "She has gained it for all of us." He touched her head, now scratched and dirty, and said softly, *It's over, Sally. You've won.*

In the valley below, the sounds of battle continued—rumblings, shrieks, clashings, flashes of light like distant lightning. But it would settle eventually. The outcome was certain and only a matter of time. For now, they remained with her.

45

In Westhaven, in the quiet, dull courtroom, Wayne Corrigan was just finishing his rebuttal to Gordon Jefferson's arguments.

"And so, we hope that the court will be careful to protect Mr. Harris's constitutional right to due process and his right to confront his accuser. We confirm once again that we have no intention of harming Amber Brandon or causing any further trauma. We only desire to get to the truth, and that, we believe, is the least our judicial system must allow any defendant. Thank you."

He took his place next to Tom Harris. Tom had been watching the clock. It was just about 4 in the afternoon.

The three judges had been watching the clock as well. The one in the middle, the older man, shuffled his papers together.

"Thank you, Mr. Corrigan, and thank you, Mr. Jefferson and Mr. Ames. Arguments were thorough and well-presented. Court will recess for the day. We'll have a ruling for you by Thursday, the day after tomorrow."

WHAM! The bailiff rapped the gavel and ordered, "All rise!" and they all rose, and the judges went out.

Ames and Jefferson seemed just a little somber, even angry, as they rose, gave Corrigan and Tom a carefully sculpted dirty look, and left the courtroom.

"Hm," said Corrigan. "I didn't think I did that well."

"I thought you did great," said Tom.

Corrigan shrugged. "Well . . . we've been praying. It's in the Lord's hands." He gave a weak smile, looked at the floor, and admitted, "But I don't know, Tom. Sometimes I wonder if I'm just a rotten lawyer or if God chooses to stay out of courtrooms. I haven't had much to feel good about lately."

Tom's smile came from deep inside. "Oh, whatever happens, God isn't mocked. He's Lord, Wayne. However He wants this to turn out, I'll accept it." He slapped Corrigan on the back. "Let's get some dinner."

Corrigan fumbled a bit. "I hope you have some money on you."

"Uh . . . I have three dollars, I think."

"Okay. I think I can match that."

"We'll make it McDonald's!"

The lake was calm, like a mirror, reflecting the trees on the shoreline with clear, unbroken lines and deep spring colors while just above the water's surface myriads of bugs danced in the sun like tiny golden sparklers. The lone fisherman sat in his aluminum boat, glad for the quiet, glad to be alone. He was somewhere in his fifties, with salt-and-pepper hair and a youthful face, dressed in jeans, flannel shirt, and a drooping fishing hat that had to have been his favorite for years. The fish weren't biting much, but he was getting the peace he'd come for, and he was satisfied. For now, he reclined lazily against a boat cushion, just floating, relaxing, and not thinking much.

Somewhere in the middle of the day, he heard the rumble and gentle splashing of boat oars, and looked out from under his hat brim. Yes, someone was coming toward him in a small wooden dinghy.

When the visitor drew nearer, the fisherman sat up. He knew that slightly rotund, bespectacled man in the straw hat. They weren't exactly friends, but they'd bumped shoulders on many occasions. What was he doing here? This was supposed to be the fisherman's hideaway.

The visitor looked over his shoulder, smiled, and kept rowing closer, not saying a word.

The fisherman had an eerie feeling about this encounter. If the visitor wasn't going to speak, then *he* would. "Jim?"

Jim looked over his shoulder. "Hey, Owen." With a few last oar strokes, he brought the little dinghy alongside. Owen used a short piece of tether to join the two boats together. "Ah, thank you much."

"To what do I owe this visit?" asked Owen Bennett. "I hope it isn't business. I'm out of the office right now."

"Oh, I figured this would be a great place to have a chat, just you and me." Jim looked back toward the resort. Some families were picnicking near the lakeshore. "But I'd talk quietly, Owen. The sound is really carrying today."

Owen lowered his voice and asked, "So state your business. I'm very busy doing nothing today and I'd like to get back to it."

Jim heaved a deep sigh, rested his forearms on his knees, and just looked at Owen for a moment. "I'll come right to it, but even that'll take a while. I suppose you've been keeping up on that case out of Bacon's Corner?"

Owen stared at him blankly, then shook his head.

"Never heard of the place?"

"No, afraid not."

"Well . . . I never heard of it either. Never cared to, except that the ACFA started a lawsuit there, and I know they were coming your way with it. They were going after a Christian school again, and thought they had all their ducks in a row, including you."

"Well, if it's a pending case, obviously I can't discuss it . . ."

Jim held up his hand. "Oh no, no . . . don't worry about that. We don't need to discuss the case, no sir. We can talk about other things."

"All right."

Jim looked across the lake, gathering his thoughts. "We can talk about a few personal items, I suppose . . . like a particular secret society, the Royal and Sacred Order of the Nation?"

Owen smiled. "Well now, if I talked about that, it wouldn't stay a secret, would it?"

Jim nodded. "So I've gathered. You know, I'm amazed at how many supposed friends of mine know everything else but what I want to find out about that bunch."

"It's just a lodge, Jim. It's nothing to worry about."

Jim wasn't that willing to brush the matter off. "Ehhhh . . . you have to understand, a man in my position gets a little spooked when men in your position start protecting each other and keeping little secrets among yourselves. Well, I said *little* secrets, but I don't know *what* size they are, do I?"

Owen remained tight-lipped. This was Jim's meeting; let him carry the conversation.

Jim did. "I hear that Carl Santinelli's a member, and *that* would concern me, as much as his name gets around Washington. To think the two of you are bosom buddies in the same secret society curls my hair just a little."

Owen got a little tense, and his voice had an edge. "That raises an obvious question for me, though I doubt I'll get an answer: How did you find out?"

"I've been reading some mail, Owen. A lot of mail." Jim looked directly at him. "Letters written by Sally Beth Roe."

Paydirt. Jim could see a definite reaction all over Owen's face. Owen lowered his head and muttered, "Oh, boy."

"Aw, we've all got a few skeletons in the closet, Owen. You know that about me, and I know that about you."

Owen couldn't contain his curiosity. "What . . . Did she write to *you*?"

"Oh, no. She wrote to the headmaster of that Christian school —I guess to give him some inside information and help him out."

"Well . . . I hope you can recognize truth from vindictive lies."

"Mmmm . . . one of the first things she wrote was that she wasn't dead, and I was impressed by her truthfulness."

"Jim, I think you're talking in riddles!"

"Well, okay, stop me if you've heard this one: Sally Roe wrote a whole stack of letters to the headmaster of that school, I guess to help him out. The only problem was, he never got the letters because somebody tampered with United States mail and snatched them all. Turned out it was the local postmaster, also the plaintiff in the suit, but she agreed to cooperate and told us where she sent them all. You'll never guess where: the Summit Institute! Some FBI agents went there and found every one of them in the possession of—are you ready for this?—Carl Santinelli, Mr. ACFA himself. He's in real hot water right now."

"That has nothing to do with me."

Jim was a little shocked. "What happened to the old team spirit, Owen? I thought you guys were lodge brothers."

"That means nothing."

"All right, all right, we'll try not to place guilt by association."

"I would greatly appreciate that."

"But just for my own information, don't all you Nation guys have some kind of membership ring, some funny gold ring with an ugly face on it, and your secret code name on the inside?"

"I don't have any such ring."

"Well, I know you don't have yours. Sally Roe has it. Well, she *did* have it. Now we have it."

Owen just stared.

"Yeah, it's yours, all right. We checked your secret lodge name against the Nation's official membership rosters. 'Gawaine,' wasn't it?"

Owen's face was like cold stone. "What game are you playing here?"

"The game we all play, Owen. Sally says she learned it from you. That's why she saved your ring all these years. It's a nice ace for her to play, and it makes her story credible, especially since she happened upon another ring, this one belonging to some kid brother of yours in the Nation, James Bardine, a hotshot punk lawyer with Santinelli's firm. Bardine's ring turned up on the finger of a Satanist." Jim added with an appropriate, sinister touch, "A woman who was hired to kill Sally Roe." He quickly added, "The assassin blew it. She got killed herself, and now we have that ring too.

"So that sort of ties all four of you together in this thing: you, Carl Santinelli, James Bardine, and that Satanist lady—uh, make that woman, or something derogatory if you like."

Jim removed his straw hat and wiped his brow. "Owen, I'm ready to lay odds you already know the rest, the whole lawsuit over that little girl having some kind of psychotic, personality blowout of some kind, and the ACFA blaming the Christian school just to get the government through their door, and . . . Well, it was quite a plan, yes sir." Jim looked directly at Owen for his next comment. "A plan worth killing Sally Roe to protect—a plan worth covering up the fact that someone tried to kill Sally Roe to protect. A plan worth tampering with the mails and hunting down Sally Roe to protect."

Owen occupied himself with his rod and reel, and didn't look up. "Jim, I believe I'm growing tired of your company."

"That was your baby, wasn't it?"

Owen froze for a moment. If Jim was attempting to shock him, the attempt succeeded. He reached down and began to untie the tether between the two boats. "I think you'd better leave."

Jim placed his hand on Owen's to stop him. "You were on the advisory board at the Omega Center, and you got her that position at the Center after she graduated from Bentmore. You spent a lot of time with her, didn't you, every time you flew out for meetings with Steele and the others?

"Until she had that baby instead of aborting it. Now there was a wrench thrown into your career! She could have sued you for child support, laid the whole thing open in public, right? What better way to solve that problem than to remove the only tangible link between the two of you—and destroy the woman in the process?"

Owen straightened up defiantly. "Do you actually intend to argue that *I'm* to blame for Sally Roe's incredible delusions?"

"*You* believe in that spirit stuff, don't you?"

"That's my personal business."

"And at the time, *she* believed in it—with a lot of help from you and that Omega bunch."

"That establishes nothing."

"Who says the newspapers and networks ever have to establish something as juicy as this? They'll print it now and prove it later. You've slipped them some goodies yourself from time to time, you know that."

"And we could slip them some more—*you* should know *that*!"

Jim nodded. "Yeah, that's right. We could make life pretty difficult for each other, no question." Then he chuckled. "But I sure enjoy the picture I get in my mind of you hearing a case brought by some of your lodge brothers in the ACFA, knowing they tried to protect their case by killing a woman you once had an affair with. Top that, Owen!"

Owen Bennett looked across the lake and thought for a moment. "So what do you want?"

Jim smiled. "Have I done it, Owen? Do I really have a lever on you?"

Owen snapped, "What do you want?"

"The sound carries, remember." Jim stopped to think for a moment. "Owen, I think I've been a pretty good attorney general, and I think I could do an even better job if certain parties would take all their weight and push it around elsewhere. I want this leash off my neck."

Owen looked grim. "I didn't put it there."

"But you have pull with the people who did. You're one of their star players."

"I can't cross them, Jim. You know that."

Jim shrugged. "Well, you could always step down, I suppose."

"I can't do that either."

Jim was resolute. "I'm giving you a choice, Owen."

Tom Harris grabbed the *Hampton County Star* from his front porch and stepped inside to the smell of hot biscuits, eggs, hash browns, bacon, the works.

"What's new?" asked Marshall.

"Oh, quite a bit," said Tom, perusing the front page.

It was Friday morning, it had been a week like no other week, and the core group, the central players, were gathered in Tom's house for a big breakfast, just to be together: Ben and Bev Cole, Mark and Cathy Howard, Marshall and Kate Hogan, and Tom. Just Tom. If social worker Irene Bledsoe had heard of all the shake-up, she wasn't saying, and so far she wasn't returning Tom's calls.

Ben asked, "Any speeches from the ACFA boys about the court's decision?"

"Kind of a moot point now anyway," said Mark. "The lawsuit's been dropped. It's all over."

"Too bad," Tom quipped. "I was scheduled to give a deposition next week. Now I'll miss out on the wonderful experience."

"But it ain't over, not yet," said Bev. "I mean, we're talking 'bout a big investigation here. We're talking 'bout some arrests!"

Marshall smiled a weak smile and shook his head. "Probably not."

"Are you crazy?"

"Sometimes I wonder . . ."

Mark asked, "Well, the authorities *are* going to look into this?"

"My FBI friend John Harrigan doesn't think so. There are cases and there are cases. Some you go after, some you don't. A thing like this is . . . well, such a big can of worms; there's so much of it going on in so many places, and you can't arrest *everybody*."

"Hey, listen to this," said Tom. "Here's a quote from Gordon Jefferson. There's even a picture of him here, standing outside the courtroom . . ."

"Wait," said Ben. "I want to sit down."

Tom read the quote from the ACFA lawyer. "'We sincerely regret this monumental breach of justice and of the rights of children everywhere. The clock of progress has been set back severely by this ruling. Had the court ruled in favor of the child, this lawsuit could have continued, and we could have fought against the scourge of religious bigotry and intolerance against our children. Mrs. Brandon wishes me to share her deep regrets and her thanks with all her supporters everywhere, and to express her heartfelt dream that the fight for our children will continue. For now, she has asked, and we have agreed, to drop the suit, pick up the pieces, and go on with our lives as best we can.'"

Kate was appalled. "What a pile of *lies*!"

"But what great PR!" said Marshall. "Official ACFA policy: No matter what happens, come out the hero!"

"Let me see that," came a voice from the kitchen. Tom handed the paper to Lucy Brandon herself as she came into the room. She perused the story and just shook her head. "I dropped that suit on Tuesday, *before* that hearing!" She passed the paper on to Ben and said angrily, "But they'll never tell, will they?"

Tom remarked, "Wayne Corrigan and I were wondering why Ames and Jefferson gave us such dirty looks. They *knew* the suit was dropped!"

"But they still wanted that ruling," said Marshall. "Every little step helps."

"Well to be honest," said Mark, "I think they did just fine. The judges handed down some pretty strict guidelines."

Ben searched through the paper glumly. "Nothing more about Joey and Carol Parnell."

Bev put her hand on Ben's shoulder. "Ben, you just got your job back. Don't go chasing another phony suicide. Leave that for the Claytonville cops."

But Ben was obviously frustrated. "I'm having a hard time being patient with all the inaction I'm seeing!"

"I should have warned you about this part," said Marshall. "It's tough to get action out of the authorities when the case is so vague and untraceable . . . and when the authorities are part of the problem."

Ben passed the paper to Marshall, still fuming. "Well, this is one authority who's going to earn his pay. There has to be a way to stop them!"

Marshall skimmed the first few pages and then smiled. "I think we did."

"No, we didn't! There's been no investigation, no arrests, not even truthful reporting in the papers about what really happened. We all know the kinds of things these people are getting away with!"

"Oh . . . we hurt them, Ben. We hurt them. We won this round." Marshall passed the paper to Kate. "And . . . well, I think we stand a good chance of recovering our POW's too."

"Josiah and Ruth?" asked Tom.

Marshall nodded. "Stomp a mole in your yard, you've killed your neighbor's mole too. We'll see."

"What about our MIA?" asked Kate.

"Sally . . ." said Marshall. The thought was painful.

"What did Harrigan say?"

Marshall hesitated a little on that one. "That's a tough situation. Khull and his people were apparently in the middle of some Satanic ritual in Goring's basement when the feds got there. They had to have had a victim, but there was no sign of Sally, and Khull isn't talking. The only thing they found was Sally's letters. She could have escaped, or maybe the Satanists—Khull and his bunch—killed her and disposed of the body before the feds got there. We just don't know."

Tom grew very somber. "We owe her everything. She's just got to be alive somewhere."

"We're gonna be prayin' for that gal, that's for sure," said Bev.

"And I want to meet her," said Tom. "After reading all her letters, I feel like I know her. No. I *do* know her."

"An incredible woman," said Kate.

"That she was," said Marshall.

Just outside Claytonville, a housepainter pulled his battered, laddered van to the side of the highway and let off a hitchhiker. "Sure I can't drive you further? You're out in the middle of nowhere."

"Thank you, no," said Sally Roe.

She remained there on the highway shoulder, a very tired, dirty, bedraggled vagabond in jeans, soiled blue jacket, and checkered scarf, watching the old van pull away, its rocker arms clacking, its exhaust pipe blowing smoke, its springs sagging under all the ladders and paint cans.

She felt just like that van. Her face was etched with the miles, her soul was weary from the pain, her body was bruised and dented from the abuse. But . . . she was still rolling, still chugging along, and at least now she had a good reason.

She crossed the highway as soon as she got the chance and ducked into the woods, following an old, rutted, surveying road she'd visited in the darkness of night . . . When was that? It seemed like years ago. She almost wondered if it was the same road, it looked so different in the daylight—inviting, peaceful, canopied in the fresh, new-growth green of spring, and not at all the horrifying, demon-infested hell it was the last time she was here.

She walked for some distance, following the meandering, rising, and dipping road through thick forest, tangled brush, and low-hanging limbs. She didn't remember it being this far. Perhaps she'd missed a turn somewhere. Maybe she'd hidden that truck a little too well.

Oh! There, through the limbs and leaves, she caught a familiar blue tint. Well! Still there!

Mota and Signa stood next to the old Chevy pickup, hands on swords, eyes alert, waiting for her arrival. Their warriors had closely guarded that machine since Sally left it there. The kids on dirt bikes, the hikers, the equestrians, and any would-be vandals had all passed it by, so it remained untouched, slightly overgrown with brush, but ready to roll.

Sally pushed through the new growth, pulling the keys from her jacket pocket. The door opened with its familiar groan; the smell of the cab was the same; she still remembered to avoid that small rip in the seat lest it grow longer. Her heart danced a little. This old truck was a blessing because it was familiar, it was hers, it was a piece of home.

It moaned a bit, hesitated, cranked over a few times, and then, with Sally's well-practiced pumping of the gas pedal—something that had to be done just right—it lurched to life!

Mota and Signa gave her a push, and with little difficulty she got the truck turned around. The two warriors hopped into the back, and they were all on their way back to Bacon's Corner.

46

"I would like to know the real reason why I'm being fired," Irene Bledsoe demanded.

Her supervisor was an older woman with white hair pulled tightly to the back of her head and held there with innumerable pins; her hair was tight, her expression was tight, and due to her obesity, her clothes were tight. Everything about the woman was tight, especially her patience.

"You know your driving record better than I do," she snapped, hardly looking up from the work on her desk. "Such irresponsibility on the road, especially while transporting children, is a liability to this organization and cannot be tolerated."

Bledsoe tried to maintain her professional dignity, but she was definitely indignant. "Ms. Blaire, I have here in my hand the driving records of no less than a dozen other Child Protection Department employees; I even have some aptitude test scores—"

"I have seen them all, and do not wish to see them again."

"Ms. Blaire, you are tangling with the wrong person!"

SLAM! Ms. Blaire slapped her papers and pencil down on her desk and bored into Bledsoe with eyes of cold steel. "You just *said* that to the wrong person. Ms. Bledsoe, you are addressing, in essence, the state. We don't 'tangle' with anyone; we set our agenda and judge our employees by how efficiently they carry out that agenda. The fact is, you have been judged to be a liability to this department, and as such, you have been terminated."

"It's because of the Harris case, isn't it? That *is* the real reason?"

Ms. Blaire answered coldly and mechanically, "It is because of your driving record, Ms. Bledsoe. You—"

"I was only fulfilling the orders I received!"

"You simply can't be trusted to transport children safely, and that is my final word on the subject. Now finish out your duties properly, or I'll see to it that you forfeit your severance pay!"

"You . . . you can't do that!"

Ms. Blaire only smiled her cold, calculating smile. Oh yes she could, and Bledsoe knew it.

"All right. All right. I've cleaned out my desk and handed over my caseload to Julie and Betty. So what's left?"

"Drive the Harris children back to Bacon's Corner."

Ed and Mose were still sitting at their post in front of Max's Barber Shop, just taking in whatever passed before them on the Toe Springs–Claytonville Road.

Ed was looking through the latest *Hampton County Star* and making sure Mose was kept up to date on everything whether Mose was interested or not.

"The Big White House is for sale," he said.

Mose was watching a mud puddle across the street and wondering if maybe the Mercantile needed new gutters. "Heh?"

"I said the Big White House is for sale. That couple living in sin finally decided to move on."

"What? They splitting up?"

"It's just an ad for the house, Mose. It doesn't say anything about that."

Mose took a moment to spit into the street. "Yeah, probably doesn't say anything about Sergeant Mulligan either. He was living in sin too, I hear, him and that superviser from the door company."

"You mean with each other?" Ed wondered.

"They're both gone, aren't they? Both took off at the same time. Somebody saw them together. I wasn't born yesterday, Ed."

Ed thought for a moment. "Eh . . . I don't mind them leaving. They were a strange bunch, them and their friends."

"Not a very good cop either."

"Jon Schmidt was a cop?"

Mose was astounded at Ed's dullness today. "No, friend, *Mulligan!*"

"Well, I'm glad to see him go too."

"Yeah, and that bunch at the Big White House, I'm glad to see them go."

"*Everybody's* going. Looks like the whole town's quitting."

"Who's quitting?"

Ed turned the paper toward Mose, and Mose adjusted his glasses. "See here? You've got . . . uh . . . these three folks on the school board, uh, Mrs. Hanover, and John Kendall . . ."

"John Kendall? That stubborn—! Who finally talked him into it?"

"And look here: Jerry Mason. That's three."

Mose was amazed. "Well . . . wasn't it just yesterday Elvira was telling me that the grade school lost the fourth grade teacher, Miss Beer?"

"Brewer."

"The same. She and that Woodard got into a fracas."

"Woodard's getting old, that's his problem. He's retiring."

"Say what?"

"He's retiring end of this month."

"He didn't seem that old."

"You been looking in the mirror too much, Mose."

Mose tilted his hat back. "Well I'll be. You're right. Everybody's quitting! Maybe they know something we don't! Hey! Hey, wait a minute there!"

"What?"

"Well, flip back to the second page there. Look there."

"Well, give me wings and call me an angel . . ."

"There's something going around, Ed. Something going around."

They were looking at a news item: SUPREME COURT JUSTICE STEPS DOWN.

Ed tilted his head back so he could read through his bifocals. "Who's this Owen Bennett?"

"Newest man on the Supreme Court. Hasn't been there long."

"'Bennett attributes his resignation to ill health and personal reasons.' But he looks kind of young, don't you think?"

"You been looking in the mirror too much yourself, Ed."

"Well now, that could be . . ."

Mose broke out laughing. "Hey, you know what, Ed? Maybe we oughta quit too."

Ed thought about that a moment and replied with great seriousness, "Mose, where would the world be without us keeping an eye on it?"

Then they both laughed, hitting and poking each other and having a great time; you could hear them for blocks.

Sally drove on toward Bacon's Corner, turning over and over in her mind just how she was going to present herself to Mrs. Potter, back from the dead as it were, and ask to continue renting the old farmhouse. Of course, that would be contingent on getting her job back at the door factory, and that was probably contingent on whether they would accept her excuse for being away so long without saying anything, and that raised the whole question of what she was going to tell them, and that was going to depend on what she could and couldn't talk about in public during the course of the investigation, and then again, she didn't know yet if there would even be an investigation.

She slowed as she approached an intersection out in the middle of the cornfields. She felt a slight tension in her stomach. This was the same intersection where that Bledsoe woman just about rammed her with Tom Harris's kids in the car.

Anyway, the first thing was to find out what was happening in Bacon's Corner, and how that lawsuit was progressing, or if it was still progressing at all. Bernice Krueger should have gotten that last letter by now, and she must have sent all that material to Tom Harris, so *something* should be brewing. She hadn't seen any newspapers in the last several days . . .

Well! What was this, a flashback of some kind? She had to be seeing things!

There was that same green Plymouth!

Irene Bledsoe made sure to stop carefully and safely at the notorious intersection that had cost her her job. Josiah and Ruth were buckled in snugly this time. The intersection looked the same except that the corn was taller. It was almost like *deja vu*, sitting here waiting for that . . . that blue pickup truck . . . being driven by the lady with the checkered scarf . . . !

Sally stared transfixed. She couldn't help it. This was Irene Bledsoe again! And there were the two Harris children!

From the back of Sally's pickup, Mota and Signa waved to their two comrades, Chimon and Scion, who rode atop the Plymouth. This encounter had timed out nicely!

Irene hesitated. She was the vehicle on the right, so she was supposed to go through the intersection first, but she just couldn't move. This couldn't be!

Josiah saw the woman too, and marveled. "Hey, look! There's that lady in the blue truck!"

"Yeah," said Ruth. "I remember her!"

So it wasn't a hallucination! Irene pressed the gas pedal gently and began to creep across the intersection, just staring at the woman.

"Hey," said Josiah, staring as well, "she's crying."

Sally watched the Plymouth pass in front of her and speed away, and then she wiped her eyes.

Lord, this was from You! You've used this to tell me!

Now she knew. This encounter, this scene before her, said it all: Somewhere, somehow, the darkness had been pierced; it was broken, fallen, its power was gone.

The children were going home!

From high above, Bacon's Corner looked downright cheery, warm, and inviting, like a little town from a model railroad, its brown, red, and black roofs bold against the surrounding patchwork green of the fields, and its silver elevators stretching toward the sky, flashing in the sun.

The skies were clear, both of clouds and of spiritual filth, washed with Heaven's light, freshened with prayer and praise to the Maker of it all. It was good to be back, good to see the place so clean. This was victory's reward.

Tal and Guilo began a gentle descent, their wings spread wide and motionless to carry them lazily over the town, high over Front Street with its cars and pickups jostling through the one intersection, over the Mercantile with its chimney smoking and red rototillers out on the sidewalk, over the small cluster of houses and garages on the Strawberry Loop, just over the top of the big silver water tower with the red light on top, steadily lower over some small farms—from up here the chickens looked like little white, black, and red triangles—and finally, at rooftop level, across the Pond Road and to the roof of Tom Harris's house.

They came in over Tom's front yard, pulled up, and stalled just above the peak of his roof, alighting upon it. They could hear breakfast in progress below; much chatter, sharing, rejoicing. Good enough. The others would be arriving any moment, and then that almost happy gathering below would be completed.

Guilo pointed to the northwest. Two streaks of light were descending rapidly out of the sky. Nathan and Armoth, just returning from Ashton!

Two more trails of light appeared in the eastern sky; Cree and Si were returning from the rout at the Omega Center.

Within moments, Nathan and Armoth passed over the house like two shining eagles, waving their swords in greeting. Tal pulled his glimmering sword and directed them to land on the left side of the front yard.

Cree and Si dropped steeply from above and cupped their wings to break their dive, settling like paratroopers to the right side of the front yard as Tal directed them.

Then they waited, every warrior in his place.

"Ah, here they come," said Tal, looking up the Pond Road toward town.

It was the green Plymouth, with Chimon and Scion still riding on top, their wings trailing like flashing, flickering banners. They waved their swords at their fellows, who waved back.

Irene Bledsoe eased the Plymouth to a stop out on the road in front of the house. She was about to reach back to help the children unbuckle and get their things, but there was no need; Josiah and Ruth burst out of that car like kids out of school and raced down the front walk without looking back.

Bledsoe turned her sharp nose forward, hit the gas, and got out of there. Chimon and Scion spread their wings, lifted from the roof, and let the car shoot out from under them. Then they settled to the ground on either side of the front gate.

The kids didn't knock or announce their arrival at all, but simply yanked the front door open and burst into the house, raising such a reaction from the people inside that Tal and Guilo could feel the noise through their feet.

In Heaven, reunions like this happened all the time, and the angels always found it absolutely riveting. Only human souls made in the image of God could fully know the soaring joy, the tear-stained ecstasy of losing a loved one and then, after a stretch of time that is always too long, feeling their warm embrace again, hearing their voice, sharing all their news. But moments like this were what the angels worked and fought for, and it was their fathomless joy, their greatest reward, to behold it once again.

The warriors in the yard could see through the front door. Tom was on his knees, clutching his children, weeping with joy. His friends were gathered all around, touching him, touching the children, murmuring prayers of thanksgiving and praise, asking questions, but getting no answers in all the confusion, and not minding at all.

The wings of the angels rose with their emotions, reaching high, spreading wide, shining like the sparkling joy that filled the house this day. They began to worship.

"Can we stay home now, Daddy?" Ruth asked through her tears.

Tom hesitated. He was afraid to answer.

Marshall touched him. "You can tell her yes."

Tom's eyes shone with deep joy and assurance. "We *did* win, didn't we?"

Marshall indicated the kids with his eyes. What more proof did they need?

Tom said, "You'd better believe it! We're never going to be apart again!"

More hugs. More tears.

A quiet squeak of brakes. Tires on gravel. A glint of blue.

Tom didn't notice, for obvious reasons, but Marshall did. He looked out the open front door.

He couldn't be sure. He couldn't believe it. He moved toward the door while the others stayed in their little rejoicing huddle.

There was a woman out there, parked across the street in a blue pickup truck.

Sally tried to keep low, tried not to be obvious as she examined Tom's house. She listened, and could hear the rejoicing through the open front door. She'd seen Irene Bledsoe driving off, and she'd seen the children run inside. They were all having such a wonderful reunion in there. She didn't feel she belonged. She didn't know what to do.

Mota and Signa hopped out of the back and stood by the cab, speaking gently to her. *They aren't going to hurt you, Sally.*

Hey, they won't mind the way you look.

I look awful, she thought. *I smell bad. What if they don't know who I am? What if this is the wrong house?*

C'mon. They'll be glad to see you!

She turned off the engine and sat there for a few more moments, just staring ahead and thinking. Her hands were shaking; she was so nervous her stomach ached.

They sound happy in there. They seem like a friendly bunch. I've just got to know how things turned out. They can reject me, I suppose, but I've got to know.

She opened the truck door and stepped out onto the shoulder. She walked toward the back of her truck—from this angle she could peer through the front door and see what was going on in there.

Oh, brother! They'll be able to see me too! I think that big guy did!

At that one, fleeting glimpse, Marshall thought he would soar through the roof and straight to Heaven! This was the Lord's work, all right! Oh, He does all things so well!

He moved carefully to the front porch as if approaching a timid deer, afraid of scaring it off.

Tal dropped to the porch and stood beside him. *That's her, Marshall. Don't let her get away.*

Sally hurried back to the cab of the truck and started to climb inside. She was going to bag this idea. Maybe she could write Tom another letter; this was just too awkward!

"Sally!"

She froze, her hand on the door handle, her right foot on the truck's running board. She didn't know if she should be Sally Roe or not. Who was this guy?

"Sally Roe?"

She remained still, just staring ahead. *If I turn my head, he'll know. Who is he?*

From inside the house she heard the children laughing. "Wow," said the little boy, "my own bed again!"

Am I safe? Is the running over?

"Thank You, Jesus," came a black woman's voice. "Oh, thank You, Jesus!"

You're safe, Sally.

She turned her head and looked at the big, red-haired man standing on the front porch. His eyes were gentle.

"Yes," she said, not loudly. Having said it once, she said it loud enough for him to hear. "Yes! That's me!"

Suddenly there was a crowd of people on that front porch, all looking her way—a lovely red-haired woman, a good-looking black couple, a kind-looking gray-haired man and his blonde wife, and . . .

Sally stared at that man as much as he stared at her. She'd seen his picture.

Tom had seen her pictures too.

You could cut the silence with a knife.

Marshall broke the silence with an invitation. "Sally, Tom Harris—and all of us—would like very much to meet you. Would you like to come in?"

She relaxed just a little, but tried to hide behind the open truck door. "I'm . . . I'm hardly presentable . . ."

Tom replied, "You're among friends!"

Tal had to laugh. Hardly presentable! Wasn't it strange, the way humans looked at themselves with eyes of flesh and not of the Spirit? Certainly that dear woman had been through mire and filth of every degree; she was scarred, exhausted, ragged, and dirty.

But to the angels, she appeared as God Himself saw her, just as any other redeemed saint of the living God: pure, shining, clean, dressed in garments as white as snow.

With a little loving prod from Mota and Signa, Sally crossed the road, a tired, blue-jeaned vagabond coming home. She passed through the front gate, approached the front porch, and then, as angels and saints alike watched in tremendous awe, she extended her hand to the lone man standing between his two bubbly children.

"Tom Harris?"

"Yes."

"I'm Sally Beth Roe."

Tal clapped his wings just enough to return to the roof, then settled there in a comfortable sitting position, his sword at rest by his side.

Guilo asked the question for all of them. "What now, captain?"

Tal looked down at the laughing, praising group below. "I think we'll stay a while."

The warriors were glad to hear that, and moved in closer to listen to all that marvelous conversation, all that sharing and catching up.

Tal smiled and shook his head in wonder. "Redemption. It will never cease to thrill me."